G000124262

STRIPPED FOR ACTION

An omnibus edition
LOVE ALL
UP TIGHT
FULL UP

By the same author

WRITE UP
GOOD GOLLY MS MOLLY
SWITCHBACK
FAST AND LOOSE
PURPLE PASSAGES
UP AND COMING
A BITE OF THE APPLE
LOVE BITES
BREAST STROKE

STRIPPED FOR ACTION

An omnibus edition
LOVE ALL
UP TIGHT
FULL UP

W.H. ALLEN · LONDON
A Howard & Wyndham Company
1983

Copyright © 1974, 1975, 1976 by Molly Parkin
Omnibus edition, copyright © 1983 by W.H. Allen & Co. Ltd

Printed and bound in Great Britain by
Biddles Ltd, Guildford & King's Lynn
for the Publishers, W.H. Allen & Co. Ltd,
44 Hill Street, London W1X 8LB

ISBN 0 491 03331 1

This book is sold subject to the condition that
it shall not, by way of trade or otherwise,
be lent, re-sold, hired out or otherwise circulated
without the publisher's prior consent in any
form of binding or cover other than that
in which it is published and without a similar
condition including this condition being imposed
upon the subsequent purchaser.

LOVE ALL

Love All
especially Patrick

'Lick it,' he said. That's the first thing he said. Not even hello when he'd opened the door. Just stood there with nothing on, lay down on the cold lino, legs apart, and said 'Lick it.' I was holding my handbag, but he looked so strained that I didn't wait to put it down first.

Afterwards everything was all right.

'Cup of tea?'

'Would I!' I said. 'Nearly caught my death at the station. Twenty minutes' delay.'

'I thought you were never coming. Toast? See you've brought a new pot of jam.'

I patted my hips. 'Not for me, thanks. Got to keep an eye on it.'

He took his teeth from the mantelpiece, put them in his mouth, and started eating on his own.

When I'd crossed the street I turned round and waved goodbye. He parted his net curtains, but other than that made no sign. Round the corner I took the first taxi I saw. It dropped me at Brighton Station. I was lucky—a London train was just about due. When I was on I went straight to the buffet car. I really had meant to ask for tea.

'Brandy, right?' asked the man behind the bar.

'Do I look that bad?'

He gave me the miniature and a plastic glass. 'No better cure!'

It was a good suggestion. I sat in the deserted carriage at a corner table and twirled the brandy, taking small sips and staring out of the window. I knew the landscape by heart, could tell at which point telegraph poles gave way to trees, ordered streets turned into fields. I'd seen it through all seasons—every Monday.

'She's dead,' he'd said. That had been the start. No tears. Helpless.

'But I'll come.'

'She's dead.'

'Yes.' After that impossible to say no. Anything he'd have asked. Anything to melt the numbness of his face, to kindle up a spot of life. To make him as he'd been before.

7

The train drew into Victoria where I took my clothes from the locker and changed in the ladies' lavatory. Then I went to collect my car. The shops were still open so on the way home I stopped off to buy a new lipstick. There was nowhere to park, so I left the car right outside on the double yellow. The store was very hot and highly perfumed and the assistant who served me was sexy and young with lots of false eyelashes. 'I'm not wearing mine today, but I do usually.'

She didn't answer. So I bought three lipsticks instead of one, but I needn't have bothered. I went through to Lingerie. Hard to resist a new bra. Uplift is right, in every way. All the display stands were stacked with breasts. Cups A to D in black, white and flesh.

'Anything scarlet?' I asked.

The saleswoman shook her head. 'No call.'

'Violet?'

'Never. Flesh. Flesh is what they like now. These, not a seam in sight. For under see-throughs. Many of my older ladies buy them for bed. Swear that under a nylon nightie not even their husbands would know.'

'I think I'll try black. I'd never wear a bra in bed anyway.'

'As you say. For those who can get away with it.'

'But they do look very good so I'll try a flesh as well. Sure to come in handy.'

She followed me to the fitting room.

'Thank you,' I said quickly, and tried to shut the door.

'Nothing like the advice of a trained corsetière. I received my first certificate in 1932. Now I am the most highly qualified in the whole department.'

I took off my coat and prayed God my deodorant hadn't given way as I pulled my sweater over my head. She undid the bra I had on.

'This has seen good service.'

'An old favourite.'

'Now then.' She stepped back to get a good look. 'Children?'

'Yes.'

'You're very lucky. They've held up well!'

She caught hold of a handful. 'Bend over. Best way is always to drop them in. That's it. Perfect. Just a minute.' She lightly squeezed one straying nipple into place. 'This little piggy went to market. Tut, tut. Should always be perfectly central.'

'Thank you very much,' I said. 'Perhaps I won't bother trying the others on. This seems fine.'

By the time I'd got out my car had gone. A window dresser tapped on his side of the glass. 'Towed away,' he mouthed. 'Thank you,' I mouthed back. And smiled as if it didn't matter.

It was two hours later than I'd thought by the time I got home, but it made no odds—there were no calls anyway. The children were already in bed and asleep. Their father had been and gone and the au pair, Françoise, was preparing to entertain up in her room. She was loading a tray with ice and tonics and the last of the gin.

'May I?'

My heart sank, a very big gin and tonic was just what I could do with. 'Of course, have a nice time.'

She winked and went upstairs. As she passed I smelt my favourite perfume. For the next half-hour the doorbell rang at regular intervals. High-pitched excitable French voices drifted down from the hallway. All girls. Then silence. God knows what they got up to in that room. In the morning I'd pass one on the stairs again and both of us would be embarrassed and look the other way.

There was hardly anything in the fridge. The children must have had cornflakes for supper again because all the bottles of milk had been opened, with the creamy tops gone. But there was one bottle of champagne. I looked at it, wondering whether to or not. Other than that, all the drink shelf offered was a bottle of Wincarnis which someone had brought me at the time of my abortion, the remains of some extremely sour Algerian wine and a miniature coffee liqueur. Tomorrow I'd stock up again. The cork popped out and hit the low ceiling, adding to the other cork marks already there. Time soon to have this room repainted, and most of the others, come to that. I unplugged the portable television and carried it and the champagne to the bathroom, turned on the hot, undressed and settled down in steamy luxury to drinking.

I was still in there when the phone rang. I didn't hear it because I'd fallen asleep but woke when Françoise banged on the door. 'Coming,' I said. The water had gone cold, the champagne bottle was empty. A clergyman was talking to himself on the television. I'd lost all sense of time.

The voice at the other end of the line was thick and blurred. At first I didn't recognise it, then I did.

'How are you after all this time? Just passing through London, been to a ghastly business dinner. Tried to ring you earlier. Did you get my message?'

'No,' I said, still sleepy.

'I say. Well, what about it? Me popping round just to say hello. Quick night cap, that's all.'

'How awful of me. I'm afraid I've run right out of drink.'

'Leave that to me, little lady. Now jog my memory, what's the address again?'

When I'd put down the phone I looked at the bedside clock. It was half past twelve.

I thought I oughtn't to be in a nightie when he arrived, so I put on a clean pair of black tights, my black suede high-heeled boots and my new black bra. Looking in the full-length mirror I thought what a shame it was that I had to put anything over the top at all. The champagne I'd drunk made me feel incredibly sexy. I smelt my shoulders and ran a hand over each breast, adjusting the nipples the way the shop assistant had done. I smoothed my bare midriff and watched in the mirror one hand straying between my legs. 'Not yet,' I thought and turned away, deciding what to wear. I chose a pair of silky trousers, full in the leg but very tight around the hips. On top I wore a skimpy long-sleeved shirt with three buttons from the neck. I left them all undone. I did my face, lots of gloss on the mouth, lower lashes, perfume splashed—nothing left to do except lower the lights and put on a record. Then I sat and waited.

At half past one I remembered glasses, so I went and got two from the kitchen and filled a container with ice, in case he was bringing whisky, and took them back to my room. It had originally been two rooms but, when we'd bought the house, my husband had knocked the dividing wall down and made it one. At one end was my double bed—it had been ours—at the other was a large low table and an arrangement of easy chairs. Sitting-room style. The colour television was in the middle and could be swung in both directions, but I usually looked at it in bed. At two o'clock he still hadn't come, so I fetched the miniature coffee liqueur and drank it in one go. Then I undressed and went to bed. I left all my make-up on and one light, just in case.

When I opened my eyes I felt something falling on my cheek. The lashes from my left eye. He was standing by the side of the bed, undressing. There was a brandy bottle, black and opaque, Napoleon I supposed, on the bedside cabinet and two full glasses. He was very drunk. I put my lashes carefully in an ashtray and sat up to say hello.

'How did you get in?' I whispered, surprised.

'A couple of Froggies were leaving as I arrived, and how's the little lady, got waylaid, sorry, so sorry.'

Still wearing his shirt and tie, but nothing else, he fell on the bed and went straight to sleep. I got up and went to the lavatory. When I came back I took the lashes from my right eye, put them with the others in the ashtray, got in my side and started drinking one of the brandies.

He was flat out, snoring, so I lifted his shirt to look at his genitals. It was a particularly slack set. The penis lolled unhappily, like a stranded fish, slightly to one side. I fingered the balls, their bag was far too big for them. Never mind, he had nice legs. So, concentrating on those I rubbed myself off, then covered him with a spare blanket and set the alarm clock. I put it at extra early to get him up and out before the children came down. That was always what I did. Mornings and me was for them, nice cuddles and breakfast in bed for the three of us. But by the morning he'd gone anyway. Apart from the brandy bottle and two empty glasses—he must have drunk his when he'd got up, something I couldn't ever quite face myself— there was nothing to show that he'd been there at all. An hour later a dozen red roses arrived. The note said, 'Apologies, little lady. Better performance next time. Promise. J.'

I don't know why, but I felt particularly wonderful. Not that these days I ever really felt anything but. Divorce over and done with. Money now paid neatly, banker's order, every month. At first, before everything had been finalised, we used to have a different arrangement. Paul gave me housekeeping every Saturday, just as if we'd still been together. He'd ring in the morning. 'Meet me for lunch. I'll give you your money.' 'Thank you, Paul,' I'd say gratefully. As if I were the guilty party. In the restaurant, with the children looking on and both tables either side, he'd count it out in one-pound notes, holding each to the light to make sure they weren't forged. Always a couple short. 'Just missed the bank.'

My lawyer was appalled. 'Calculated humiliation' was how he put it and told me off for lack of dignity. I privately felt pleased to get anything, whichever way it came, but I agreed it did seem rather weak. It was much better now this way. More civilised to have things cut and dried. But it didn't have any closeness.

The children snuggled up, one each side of me. Two small girls, their bodies slippery and simple. Un-complicated by breasts or hair growing other than on their heads. Impossible to remember when I had been like that. I held them tight and tickled them and we were all still laughing when Françoise came in with the breakfast tray. She looked slyly at the brandy and two glasses so I got it in first.

'Nice party last night?'

She shrugged. 'My best friend, she did not come.'

Oh Christ, she'd be moody for days. 'Oh dear, what a shame.'

'But I ring 'er and she say tomorrow.'

'We must remember to buy some more drink then.'

At that she brightened. 'Scotch whisky, very good.' 'Yes, it's a nice drink,' I said, and made a mental note to buy wine. Not mental enough.

'Scotch whisky and gin tonics and Bloody Maries. But wine in this country, not so good I think.'

'I'll make a list today,' I promised, defeated.

She'd warmed to her subject. 'But more I like champagne—'

I interrupted briskly. 'So do we all. Don't be late for your classes now.' But I smiled to soften it.

'Here I go.' She blew kisses to the girls, who blew kisses back, covering the bed with crumbs.

They were very fond of her. She was sweet really. It had taken a lot of doing, the final deciding to have a stranger share the house. But more than that, to have one share the children. We'd never had anyone when Paul was still here. I don't know why quite, except that I may have been put off by stories of other husbands ending up in the au pair's bed. But I wouldn't have admitted to those thoughts then. Nor to any thoughts of infidelity on his part. Looking back I see I was half-baked. Later I knew differently.

Now, looking at his daughters, I saw how much like Paul they were. Strong straight hair, very fair, green eyes—

12

pale like gooseberries. Long lashes. Later on I'd teach them how to darken those with dyes, and apply thick coats of mascara. Look much better. Like him, they were beautiful.

Breakfast over, I drove them to school. On the way the youngest, Fanny, said, 'Daddy said on Saturday he'll take us to the zoo.'

'You'll like that, you'll be able to ride on the elephant.'

They squealed excitedly. Harriet was named after Paul's mother, always a sore subject. After all, my mother was dead, if we had to go in for family names why not hers. 'What, Violet?' 'Well, why not?' 'Too common!' And that had been that. Harriet said, 'You didn't say good night to us. Daddy did.'

She pulled her mouth down and stared accusingly and by doing so managed to look incredibly hostile. Fanny copied her immediately. It occurred to me that when they were grown-ups they might not like me at all, well, or me them for that matter. We'd look at each other all the time then with that same hostility.

We'd reached their school, I turned the engine off. 'You know on Mondays I'm very often not back in time,' I started to explain. But they weren't listening any longer. They'd spotted friends and were already shouting at them and clambering out of the car. 'Have a nice day,' I called. They both turned shining faces full of love. And mine shone back. Years away from any worry.

I drove home, past other mothers just like me dropping their children off at equally expensive so-called progressive private schools. Masses of them in that area. All more or less the same waste of money. My view, not Paul's. State schools later on. If I could fight it out. I turned into my street. It was a marvellous morning. Spring in the air. A still cold sun shone on immaculately clear windows and novelty brass door knockers. Budding daffodils in window boxes matched the colour of front doors. Mine included.

''Morning, miss! Lovely day. Like the front sweeping?' Same question every week. Same street sweeper for the past five years. He'd already got his broom in the tiny paved front garden, and was bearing down ferociously on a small piece of torn newspaper which had blown in. 'If you could, thank you very much,' I smiled as I dropped a coin into his waiting hand. But inside me I went all hot. Playing the gracious lady. Paul would have been proud.

It was Tuesday, the week was beginning, the hours stretched ahead like an empty harbour. I loved it like that, no one in the house till late afternoon when Mrs Bowen would arrive to clean and before the children were collected by Françoise on the way home from her classes. Well organised, considering how chaotic the household arrangements had once been.

The phone rang. 'My darling.' Charles. The lowered, hurried voice. Phoning from home, wife out of the room? Phoning from the office, secretary in the outer one? 'Can we possibly switch tomorrow to today?'

'Of course.'

'One o'clock then. Ah, documents here, Miss Dean.'

I smiled as I replaced the receiver. The office!

I opened the windows and looked to see if I should change the pillow-cases. He was very particular. Mine seemed fine. As I was putting a clean one on the other, the phone went again.

'Good morning, gorgeous.'

'Sam,' I said.

'Got tickets for tonight. Great play. Think you're going to like it.'

'How lovely.'

'Right, I'll pick you up at seven, we'll have a drink there and eat afterwards. What are you wearing, honey?'

'I may wear long or perhaps trousers.'

'Now, I mean.'

I laughed. 'Not wearing any, only tights.'

'Whore!' he said. 'Mad about you. How was yesterday?'

'Fine,' I said. 'Much as always.'

'You and your social work. See you tonight. Be ready, slut.'

By five to one I was in my dressing-gown, the bedroom looked beautiful, curtains closed. Phone off the hook, hidden in the cupboard. All chaste and warm and welcoming. At the last minute I remembered the vase of roses but it was too late. Charles was at the front door already. He stepped in quickly, nervously glancing towards the street as he did so. He double-bolted top and bottom.

I put my arms around his neck. 'It's quite safe,' I soothed. 'No one can possibly come.'

We went into my darkened room. A shaft of sunlight gleamed through where the curtains weren't quite

14

together. He took off his glasses. 'Now let me look at you.'
We laughed, it was an old joke that we both felt safe with.

'Nice day for a picnic,' I said and we laughed again.
Another old one.

He put down his carrier bag, Fortnum's. 'An exceptionally fine claret and duck pâté with garlic to your liking, madam?'

I moved forward to kiss him on the mouth, but he was already looking around for his coat-hanger. He never was one for kissing much. I still couldn't get used to it. And he was shy about undressing too. But that I understood more, so looking the other way I quickly took off my dressing-gown and waited for him in bed.

The first was always far too quick, no sooner in than over, and the second which began almost immediately was only marginally longer.

He lay back. 'How was that for starters, madam?'

'Perfect,' I said, though as usual I was feeling stranded and up in the air. But the wine soon sorted things out, and the pâté, so that by the third time it was just about as good as it ever could be.

Afterwards I was desperate for a cigarette. I'd known I would be. That's the effect our loving had on me. 'I wish you wouldn't.' He watched me lighting up.

'Sorry, Charles, I have cut right down. I'm giving it up soon.'

'A filthy habit. Besides which I worry about your health. Don't you ever? Don't you see how irresponsible it is? What would happen to the children? You seem to forget you're a mother.'

I changed the subject. 'How's Dierdre?'

He sighed and began tidying the remains of the picnic back into the Fortnum's carrier bag. 'Napkin? Here, give it to me. Is that the cork there? Would you like me to wash these glasses out? Pass me the bottle, done in, isn't it? Right, I'll get rid of it all on the way back. Wouldn't do to leave traces.'

'How is she?'

He sighed again. It was his favourite topic but even so he liked several prompts. 'Oh, my darling. Why do we ever mention her name? When just to be with you is such perfection. Why spoil this heaven—how is she? She's unbearable. She's everything that you're not. She's insensitive, selfish, extravagant, stupid, vain. We're

15

neither of us happy. We hate our life together. But will she admit it? No! And there are the children. She knows I can't leave whilst there are the children to consider. Do you know what she said to me this weekend?'

'No, what?'

'She said, she actually said, "Charles, if you left me I'd see to it that you'd never ever have access to the children for as long as you live." How could a man in my position leave anyway?'

'She's no right to say that.'

'No right! She said it, my dear. Oh yes, she said it.'

'Legally, I mean. She couldn't enforce it.'

'But it shows the thinking, you understand. It illustrates so clearly the vicious character of the woman. Doesn't it just! She knows perfectly well that there isn't anything I wouldn't do for those children. Why, that boy of mine—as bright as two pins. Almost walking now, you know. Not bad for eighteen months, eh? Clever as a cartload of monkeys. Be sitting on a horse in next to no time. You should see his sisters, both of them show-jumping standard. Dierdre takes them for a canter before breakfast every day now. Oh yes! I've got to hand it to her, fine woman in the saddle. Pity she isn't the same on the ground, or bed for that matter. You know the latest development, don't you?'

'No, which one is that?'

'This sleeping apart malarky, separate rooms now. That's grounds alone, isn't it?'

'Restitution of conjugal rights, I think.'

'Something like that. I tell you if it weren't for those children and my constituents—'

'What would you do, Charles?'

He'd heard his name, the conversation changed course again. 'Good Lord.' He glanced at his watch. 'This won't do. Tempus fugit. Got to give an address tonight. Have the speech to write. And a hundred other pressing appointments. Cocktails at the House.'

Still talking, he got out of bed and started dressing. In the darkest corner of the room. With his back to me. When he'd finished, he put on his glasses and carefully combed his hair. Then the vase of roses caught his attention. 'Particularly fine blooms.' He frowned. 'Not another admirer, I trust.' And he laughed at the idea.

'I was thinking of your buttonhole, but I bought a

16

bunch to give you a choice,' I said.

He sat down on the bed and held my face in his hands. 'That's the most wonderful thing I've ever heard, my darling girl.' He even kissed me.

When he'd gone I took the phone out of the cupboard and replaced the receiver. I rang the off licence, the grocer and the greengrocer to order stuff. At each they reminded nicely that my bill was overdue. 'Tell me the amount and I'll give a cheque to the delivery boy,' I promised and apologised profusely. It wasn't even as if I hadn't the money. All that was lacking was organisation. I was appalling at accounts—anything of a financial nature. Bills came, like letters, and lay unanswered, just hanging around till they got lost. I liked the phone much better than the post—more immediate, talking to people, more involving altogether.

The three deliveries came all within ten minutes of each other. The first time I answered with just my silk dressing-gown on, but as I was writing out the cheque I saw the grocer's boy staring at my nipples. He was very young, he couldn't have seen many. I don't know who was more embarrassed. I was meaning to have a bath, there was no point getting dressed but even so, when he'd reluctantly gone, I went and put on my bra and knickers under the dressing-gown to write cheques for the other two. Funny that, shy at my age.

In the bathroom, running the water, I put a face pack on. Honeymask, it had a marvellous smell, meant to be on for fifteen minutes. 'Follow instructions carefully for maximum satisfaction.' Best to obey instructions. I'd only taken to going in for skin care and all that quite recently really, but from the look of me it was paying dividends. I hadn't bothered so much when I was married but that was because Paul had been so adamant. Though he'd seemed to approve of women when we were out who I thought were dreadfully done up. 'But you're different,' he'd say. 'It's not your style. There'd be no point!' By the end, of course, there hadn't been. But now I'd come to love it, the pampering, applying oils and creams and perfumes. The private swooning at the secret smells of me.

I poured lots of costly bubble from a bottle into the full bath, then got in carefully so as not to splash my setting mask. Near me on the shelf was Paul's expensive badger shaving-brush and the old-fashioned razor he'd left

17

behind, anyway he'd switched to electric. But I liked shaving with them on my legs and under my arms. I loved to work up a good lather. The soap I used was household and smelled slightly of carbolic but you could get the best lather of all with it, bar proper shaving sticks of course. It reminded me of my father, and of the first boy who I'd ever let touch me down below. He'd washed his hands with it after. I hadn't much growth to shave off anyway but I liked to catch it before it got to the bristly stage. I'd once known a man who claimed to have had an orgasm on the train to Edinburgh from sitting opposite a woman with hairy legs, and the story had so impressed me that I'd gone all summer not shaving. He was a vegetarian. The bubbles in the bath had almost disappeared, I still hadn't managed to find a make which lasted through to the very end. The water was very silky though—I could feel it doing my skin good—and the surface when I lay perfectly still was shinily unbroken like summer seas abroad. I started at the tap end, left to right, sometimes I did it the other way around. Searching with my eyes, otherwise not moving a muscle, for those infinitesimal dark brown dots floating on the surface. A childhood habit. My mother would catch me scratching—'She's got fleas again. That means the last of the hot water.' Only way to catch them was to drown them. Me in the zinc bath in front of the fire. Everyone crowding round. Whoever happened to be there—usually a neighbour, always my father, an auntie good on gossip, my sister. All joining in. 'There it is!' 'No, that's dirt!' 'A tealeaf!' 'See if it cracks between your nails!' 'Stay still!' 'Got it!' The satisfaction of seeing it squashed, pinprick of blood, my blood, staining the nail. Its belly full, emptied. Dead legs coming out at all angles.

Thirty years on and I'm still looking. No chance of a killing these days. Life was far too sanitary, except at Brighton. The fifteen minutes was up. Time to rinse my mask off. Tingle, tingle. Tight-pored. Perfect. On sheer impulse, I started washing my hair still sitting in the womb-like water. All the wrong way round, of course, because now the dripping shampoo and the steamy hot from the shower attachment was opening up all the pores which I'd just taken such trouble to close. Oh well. Drying myself, I thought I heard the front door click. Much too early for Mrs Bowen. I called out quickly but there was no answer. Nobody. It was irrational I knew to be so resentful

18

of unexpected intrusions when for so much of my life home had been an open house. Perhaps that's why—why I took such childish delight in my separate existences. No area overlapping any of the others. Only me knowing exactly what was going on with whom, where and at any one time. None of it was by chance.

As soon as Paul and I had broken up I'd started thinking about how my life should be. The very day the divorce came through I gave a party for as many people as I could think of. A form of farewell really, because the next evening, when the sourness of my hangover had subsided sufficiently for me to be sure of my judgement, I sat down on my own with the guest list and a pencil. And started striking off all the people that I knew I never wanted to see again. Lots of them were married friends who'd only come to the party as a nice gesture, but with divided loyalties. They were no good. For them to feel comfortable I had to be married too. They were people Paul and I had gone to the theatre with or stayed with for weekends, all of us together with our children. Others were single girls, old enough to think themselves on the shelf, defeated creatures, ones I'd tried to pair off hundreds of times. I put a line through those too. It depressed me to think that now they might consider me one of them. The last thing in my mind was to turn into a loser. I'd seen too many women sitting together in restaurants, hair set specially, selecting out of season strawberries, flirting decorously enough with the waiters, but inside manic for a man. That brought me to the bachelors. There were a lot of those. Some I knew I'd never see anyway whether I struck them off or not, where Paul had been the appeal.

By the time I'd gone through everyone I was surprised to see how few were left. A small kernel of friends, close, but not to be thought of as confidants. So that was it. Time to start again. It was much easier than I'd expected.

Who had I met first? Charles, I think. But then again perhaps not. His face by the time I met him was so familiar to me from television anyway. Tortoiseshell glasses, carefully combed hair, beautifully cut suit—tailor's dummy. 'This vigorous young politician.' Later on in line for who knows what. Party Leader? Tory, of course. Not my type, not one bit, too much of the schoolmaster. And I'd had enough of Tories. But obviously I hadn't. We met at the dentist's of all places. In my time I'd spent a small fortune on my teeth, most of them capped now. They started going, two, three at a time, when I was about thirteen. All those sweets. Paul had ordered me to Harley Street. The first time I'd opened wide the dentist had called his partner to come and look. 'Ye gods,' is what he said. Since then it had been regular visits.

I was done up to the nines the day I met Charles. The receptionist showed me into the waiting room and there he was. I'd been shopping in Knightsbridge, had bought, just like that, a lovely dress I'd seen in the window of an expensive little Madam-type shop. Normally I wouldn't go near those places—I don't like their sales pressure—but I'd fallen in love with the dress. They'd only just put it into the window, so they said, and tried to palm me off with other things. But I insisted, funny for me. They took it out so that I could try it on. It fitted perfectly, wasn't tight but clung discreetly and made me look very curved and enticing. It had long sleeves, full ones which buttoned tightly at the wrists with tiny buttons, four or five of them. They were grey, sort of gunmetal like the dress, but the material was a jersey silk which changed colour in the light, sometimes pale like a pigeon's chest, in other places sharp and silvery. It ended just below the knee and was the most expensive thing I'd ever bought. But then I was due for a change. 'Perfect for cocktails, the theatre, dinner,' they said in the shop and purred approval as they took the price tag off. It was ten o'clock in the morning. 'I'll keep it on, thank you,' I said and walked out feeling fabulous. I went straight down the road to Harrods. An hour and a half later I stepped out grey from top to toe. Huge silver-fox hat, soft suede gunmetal handbag, gloves, stockings and suede high-heeled boots. Loaded with carriers containing what I'd originally been wearing. I didn't like to think what it had all cost but at that time I still hadn't got used to having money in the bank. 'Do you mean to tell me you actually have no idea at all of your husband's income?' the lawyer had said irritably. 'It didn't seem important somehow.' 'It does now, however.' When he told me what I would be entitled to I was flabbergasted. I could see my stupidity got on his nerves.

The commissionaire sprang forward to hail a taxi. 'Harley Street,' I said. I could have said Buckingham Palace and he wouldn't have batted an eyelid. Clothes maketh the man. Me too. The dental receptionist gave a gasp when she saw me. Normally she was a miserable old trout troubled badly with arthritis. She'd wave towards the waiting room with her stick and let me open the door myself. But today she actually straightened up and pulled her shoulders back as if we were in some sort of competition. 'Mr Bruce isn't quite ready for you yet. His last appointment arrived a little late, I'm afraid.' Charles looked up from his *Country Life* as I walked in. I recognised him right away. 'Good morning,' I said and gave a charming smile full of enchantment and subtle promise. I'm good at those when I try. Looking as I knew I did I could have taken anything on. 'Love at first sight'— that's what he'd said afterwards. Oh yes, he had his romantic side. My own feelings were far more comp-licated. The second I set eyes on him he became a challenge. To be seen out with someone so well known for a start. But it never had worked out to be that. 'Far too risky, darling.' Since then all he'd seen me in was a dressing-gown, twice a week, whenever he could manage, but not evenings and never weekends. Served me right really.

The second had been Sam. Well, not the second, there had been others in between but not ones that were suitable for my stable. I'd been playing with the kids, it was their bedtime but we were pretending we were all three going to a party. They were wearing my shoes and old mini dresses which on them came down to the floor. Fanny had on a pair of elbow-length evening gloves which reached her shoulders and a long cigarette holder with a sweet cigarette in it. Harriet had found a wig which I once used to wear. I made up each of our faces. I put crimson polish on all our nails. Lots of black and violet eyeshadow. We'd sprayed behind our ears and were just dabbing extra down our cleavages, which they found very funny, when Paul rang. 'What are you doing?' he asked in his abrupt way.

'Putting the children to bed.'

'Rather late isn't it?'

'Only seven-thirty.'

'It's ten past eight, they should both be asleep by now.'

'Oh dear,' I said, 'well, they're just dropping off anyway.'

'I've got a do on tonight. Advertising Executives' Guild. Dinner-dance thing. Would you care to go? Means being ready in half an hour.'

I knew what it meant all right. Whoever it was had let him down at the last minute, too late now to find another fill-in. I looked at myself in the mirror, well I certainly was dressed for a party and what was the alternative—washing my hair and an early night to be fresh for Charles in the morning. I hated those advertising do's—smooth-tongued Hooray Henrys, corpulent balding chairmen, dieting bitchy wives.

'Why not?' I said. I was just in the mood to get drunk.

I tore Françoise away from the television to put the girls to bed. I promised they could wear their nail polish to school if they pretended to be asleep when their father arrived. Then I kissed and hugged them good night.

I looked pretty startling, even I could see that. Hell, I thought, and why not. I'd been too many times before, with Paul, discreetly playing the dutiful wife, drab as a shadow. I'll leave my eyes as they are. They looked enormous already, violet shadowed and mascara'ed, but for extras I put some lashes on as well, heavy black ones top and bottom. I powdered my entire face almost white including the lips. Then I gave them a coat of gloss to make them very shiny. I wound round my head a long black silk scarf till it looked like a turban and hid every bit of my unwashed hair and I pulled it right down to my eyes over my whole forehead. It looked like some religious order. I had two long black dresses, one was very bare about the shoulders with tiny shoestring straps, the other had tight sleeves at the wrist, a narrow skirt and high neck with a tightly fitting bodice except that it was slit in the back from the neck to the waist which meant you couldn't wear a bra with it. Out of curiosity I tried it on back to front. It looked incredible, a startling strip of creamy skin and cleavage, everything self-supporting and in its place. But did I dare? It seemed to be asking for trouble. But then that was what I was looking for after all. I could hear Paul's car outside and in last-minute panic loosely tied a floor-length black feathery boa round my neck so that it hung centrally and hid the possibly offending breasts. Then I went to open the door.

He looked at me critically in the dim hall light. 'Anybody I know? Put my name on the wreath if so.'

'Everything else is at the cleaners,' I said. 'The girls are asleep, I'll get my bag!'

'Won't people think it funny me coming with you?' I asked in the car.

He turned on the car radio and started swivelling the programme dial. Ear-splitting snatches of husky continental crooners, American country-style music, pontificating pundits and highly charged dramatic dialogue ripped my ears off. I knew it would annoy him so I said it again, this time yelling at the top of my voice. 'Well, won't they?' I hand it to him—he has the most delicate wince in the world.

'Not if they're civilised,' he said quietly in a momentary hush. Then he found Wagner and for the rest of the way steered with just one hand and with the other conducted an imaginary orchestra in the loudest performance of their life. I was glad when we got there—it had been just like being married.

Our table was worse than I'd feared. My place name put me off for a start: Miss G E M Shottie-Green. The man on my left must have got there first and memorised all the names. 'Daughter of General Shottie-Green, by any chance?'

'I'm actually Charles's ex-wife!' For the rest of the evening he introduced me as 'General Shottie-Green's first wife. Have you met?' The man on my other side turned his back after the first five minutes. 'Which branch of the business are you involved with?' he asked. 'I'm a Media Director myself.'

'Oh, I'm more a housewife.' The electric light switched off immediately. 'Which automatically puts me at the consumer end.' I knew the jargon by heart.

'Quite.'

I'd managed on the way in to down three gin and tonics in a very short time. I was actually hoping to get a fourth in but I hadn't moved quite quickly enough. Charles had his eye on me.

'Go easy.'

'That was only my first,' I protested.

'Untrue.'

It was easier at the table, I think the wine waiter had got my number. Charles was seated far enough away for his frowns to seem a bit of a fake. By the fruit salad I was just beginning to glow. But I had no one to talk to. I looked across the dance floor and all around the banquet room, the band was assembling, plucking, strumming, tuning up. In a minute I'd have no one to dance with either. Everyone else was still seated so I stood up to make sure of being seen and made my way to the Ladies' Room. As I reached it there came a sudden silence preceded by the banging of a gavel and a pompous voice announcing 'Ladies and Gentlemen, our President.' Hell, fancy missing the President. When I came out he was still speaking. I could see between the ornate pillars which separated the banquet room from the long bar where I was that everyone was entranced, hanging on his every word.

'Jesus Christ! What a crap bag! I tell you, kid, you've got beautiful bowels, they moved you at the right moment. I'll tell you something else, you're no chicken but you're the best-looking broad I've seen tonight.'

He caught my hand, walked me to the deserted bar, took two brandies from one of the loaded trays and held them up. 'To both of us.'

'To both of us. And to my bowels,' I supplied.

That was Sam.

We stuck together from then on. We drank and danced and danced and drank until in the end we could hardly stand up. Everyone was staring, not just at my scandalously spilling breasts but at the splendour of Sam himself. He was a huge man, built on the lines of Orson Welles, and he was wearing a white dinner jacket and black and white check trousers which straight away set him apart from the formal suits of all the other men. Paul approached us at one point, mortified and mad at me for making an exhibition of myself, I could tell, but towards Sam he was as smooth as silk.

'Departure time I believe.'

All I did was giggle. Sam slipped his massive arm around my waist and kissed my ear.

'Departure time is my department, right?'

'Right,' I said.

Paul turned on his heel in time to hear Sam growl, 'Who the hell was that prick?'

'Only my first husband.'

'Who's in line for your second, kid?'

'Who knows?' I said and kissed him in the middle of the crowded floor.

We left in the end because we were asked to. That became the pattern of all our outings—spectacular exits. Always the centre of attention. There's no doubt about it he was a drinking man, and an eating one too. Meals with him lasted three times longer than with anyone else,

24

so did other things. 'Climb aboard,' he'd command, 'and work me over.' Lying back on a double bed he all but covered it. There was no question of him on top. 'Cause of death—smotheration.' He rarely if ever got an erection, but we had a lot of nice times trying. If he was troubled, he never showed it. We put together a whole library of tantalising pictures to see if that could get him going. He'd prop himself up with a pillow and study them carefully while I stroked and kissed and licked his huge erogenous zones. A few times there was a flicker, but no more than as if a tadpole had swum through the sea. I was always the first to fall asleep—after two or three hours I found it pretty tiring work. I couldn't have kept it up every night as he would have liked. And I couldn't have kept up with the drinking either, I would have minded too much being an alcoholic as compared to just liking to drink. What he got up to when he wasn't with me I never asked. I knew there were ex-wives somewhere, still in America I supposed. Neither had children. And I knew that he lived alone now, though I hadn't been to his home.

'What the hell a man like me is doing out with an old woman like you, Christ knows,' he'd keep grumbling. 'Jesus, people are going to think I can't get it up any more. Nubile nineteen-year-olds is what I'm used to, not a rat bag with two brats in tow. C'mon now, open my pants and take a peek, at your age you've gotta be grateful.' Then he'd bellow with laughter and give me a bear hug. We understood each other.

By the time Mrs Bowen arrived to clean I was down in the kitchen making tea for the girls. Cauliflower cheese, one of their favourites. She came straight in and sniffed.

'Nasty smell of them old caulis. Goes right through the house. I never have them myself.'

My stomach tightened, I'd dealt with Mrs Bowen's dark Welsh gloom for five years. Today I could tell she needed more than normal cajoling. 'I'll open these windows, that will clear the air.' She took off her coat and shivered. 'Very cold today, I should have worn my cardi.'

'Have a cup of tea, that will warm you up,' I said and plugged the electric kettle in. 'I'll have one with you.'

'Oh no, not for me. Too much hoovering today! No time for sitting with tea in my hand.'

Piss off then. 'Later perhaps.'

25

She didn't answer, just went 'Phew,' stared accusingly at the cauliflower and waved the air in front of her nose. Minutes later I heard the hoover droning on the floor above. As a souind it depressed me more than any other. That and ballet music. I gritted my teeth and grated a crumbly lump of pale orange Cheddar on to a yellow plate. Lovely colours together. The sound came closer as Mrs Bowen started on the stairs. I slowly stirred the grated cheese into the smooth creaminess of the sauce and watched it melt. My mother had gone out cleaning. When I was very small she'd taken me with her. 'Sit on that chair and don't move till I tell you.' Hours of staring at mantelpieces crammed with family photos and china dogs and brass candlesticks, all being carefully spat on and polished by my mother. Trapped on an island, scrubbed and dusted and swept around. Then back home where nothing of that sort went on at all. To my father sitting by the fire with his cup of tea and bad chest. Pensioned off at thirty-three.

I strained the boiling water from the cauliflower taking care to keep it intact, and removed it to an orange ovenproof dish. Then I poured the thick sauce over it, dotted the surface with butter and a fine layer of cheese crumbs and popped it under the grill. Seconds later the girls arrived and the house came to life.

After I'd given them tea we looked at television together. Françoise had a drink. She was lit up before it touched her lips, just from seeing so much of it on the shelf.

'This is to see us through the month,' I said warningly.

'Un mois.' She pursed her lips and lifted her eyebrows. I could tell she was trying to translate it from French to English in terms of evenings in her room. Mrs Bowen came in to say she'd see me tomorrow and caught Françoise with a glass in her hand.

'Would you care for one?' I said quickly.

'Me? Me, I never touch the stuff. You know that. The sherry you gave me last Christmas made me bad in the night. I was up all hours. No. I'll be off now for my bus. Let's hope the queue's not like it was last night.'

'Say good night to Mrs Bowen, girls,' I said.

'Good night,' they chorused, but neither took their eyes off the screen. So I stood up and saw her to the front door to make up for it. Halfway down the path she turned round frowning.

'Those children are getting to be real madams.' I thought she wouldn't let it pass.

As I was shutting the door I saw Paul's car draw up. There was a girl sitting beside him in the front seat. I saw him switch the engine off and bend towards her in conversation. Before they could see me I closed the door and went quickly into my room. When the bell rang, the children, expecting him always at this time, ran to answer it.

'My poppets,' I heard him say. I peeped through my curtains at the girl in the car. She was about seventeen, eighteen at the most. Blonde, very pretty, groomed like a poodle. Money.

'Is your mother here?' I heard Paul ask.

Fanny fumbled at the door handle. 'Mummy, Mummy.'

It swung open wide. Without knocking Paul walked in, snapping on the light. 'What on earth are you skulking in the dark for?'

Now I felt caught out.

'Don't tell me you're attempting to economise on electricity for a change.'

Once I would have turned to tears at that. The critical stare, the curt voice—now I just laughed, which made him worse. He frowned.

'Yesterday,' he said coldly, 'I made a promise to the children. I mentioned Regent's Park Zoo. However, circumstances have altered. This weekend I shall not be in town. I have to fly to Munich on business.'

Blonde?

'That's all right,' I said, 'I'll take them to the pictures instead.'

'The cinema isn't the only alternative.'

'No, but it's the nicest.'

'Yes, yes, yes,' squeaked the girls.

'I'll try smuggling them into an X film. They could go in as middle-aged dwarfs.'

'Could I have a moustache?' shouted Fanny.

'And me a hunchback?' said Harriet.

'Perhaps,' said Paul, the light of battle in his eye, 'Mummy could take you to the ballet. You'd love that wouldn't you? Harriet? Eh, Fanny? I'll arrange the tickets tomorrow.'

'Ooh,' they both sighed, silenced.

The bastard.

27

'How wonderful,' I said sweetly. 'Three tickets for the ballet. Say thank you, Daddy.'

'Oh, Daddy, Daddy, thank you. You're a lovely daddy.'

'That's settled then,' I said brightly. 'Saturday the ballet.'

I stepped past his satisfied smile and shouted, 'Françoise, ballet tickets for Saturday—you and the girls, isn't it exciting? Thank you, Paul, good night.'

An hour before Sam. Time to try a dozen things on. Whatever I wore he always noticed. 'Shock 'em, honey,' was his way. On one occasion when I'd met him at a restaurant, I came wearing black stockings, a black dress with tiny white cuffs and collar. 'Christ,' he'd thundered when I took my coat off. 'People'll think I'm eating with the waitress.' And he'd sent me home to change. When I came back I was wearing just the same but with a frilly white apron tied round my waist. This time the rest of the diners took a dislike but from Sam I got ten out of ten. 'That's my gal. Why how you're learning!'

By ten to seven I was ready and went to kiss the girls goodbye. Françoise whistled appreciatively and gave me one of her winks.

'You look like a man,' Fanny said and rolled on the floor in a giggling fit.

'Are you going out like that?' said Harriet doubtfully.

'Why not?' I said and looked in the mirror.

'Won't people stare?'

I had on a crimson satin trouser suit, very tailored, and under it a bright red satin shirt with a red and white spotted tie. On one lapel I'd pinned a scarlet artificial poppy. I combed my fringe to reach my eyes, the rest of my hair I'd pinned into a tight little knot at the back. 'Stare? I hope so,' I said. 'What's the point of dressing up if people don't stare?'

'Your mummy,' said Françoise, 'she have very good taste. She know which goes with what. Me I stay safer.'

'So did I at your age—now, girls, bath time. Can you see them up, Françoise, please?' They all three pulled a face. 'You can use my best bubble stuff if you go this minute.' They got up right away, Fanny chasing Harriet.

Françoise lingered. 'And for my bath too yes? I have a new friend, she come later.'

I sighed inwardly. 'Don't use it all. You only need a drop to do the trick.'

She smiled and nodded and wrapped her arms around herself. 'It make me feel so sexy, so silky, smelling sweet in the bath. All the time I am thinking naughty things. I am—'

'I'd see how the girls are getting on—they could be drowning by now.'

She gave herself a final reflective squeeze, grinned conspiratorially and went upstairs.

Sam arrived in a taxi which he kept waiting. He pressed the bell with one finger and kept it there till I'd opened the door. 'Where the hell were you? In the middle of a shit? Been standing here hours—' He broke off in mid growl. 'Jesus, you look great—what are you trying to do, you cunt, outshine me?'

In the back of the taxi he slid his arm around my shoulders. 'Missed me? It's been two days you know.'

'Not at all.'

'Bitch, don't expect anything from me tonight. I been balling all day with a Bavarian sex bomb. Thighs like a giraffe, tight little titties like golf balls. No nipples on 'em, though. Cul-de-sacs. Two blind alleys.' He slid his other hand under my jacket and squeezed. 'Not like these.' I caught the taxi driver's eyes. So did Sam. He leant forward. 'The wettest little pussy in the world. Aren't you proud to have that as a passenger?' And he slammed the partition up and lay back roaring.

When we got out I made a point of saying good night to the driver as Sam was paying him. He didn't look up but as he steered away from the kerb he yelled back, 'What do you feed it on—fish fingers?'

'Great guy,' said Sam. 'Great sense of humour.'

'Where are we?' I asked.

'We're behind the Hilton, Park Lane, London, my little flower, about to refresh our souls with several stiff martinis and endanger our minds and moral fibre in social intercourse with several of my accursed compatriots,' he said in his W C Fields voice.

We stepped through smoked-glass doors into a discreetly lit, carpeted hallway, complete with porter. As the tiny lift slid smoothly up, Sam cupped my chin with his hand.

'Don't leave my side, you faithless girl. These men are movie moguls. If one of the fuckers offers you a contract I wanna be there for the percentage. They're looking all over for someone to replace Rin Tin Tin.' He patted his pockets. 'Theatre tickets—'

'Are we still going?'

'Nag, nag, Jesus. Play it as it comes—see how we work out, kid.'

We stopped opposite a stainless-steel door with a shiny microscopic eye in it. Sam pressed a large black bell on the wall, a second passed while someone the other side was obviously scrutinising us. Then, soundlessly the door slid sideways, and we stepped in. Everything was black and white. Ceramic tiles, set alternately on the entrance floor, shiny black patent leather walls. All-white paintings hanging at regular intervals. A white marble gravestone angel, wings outspread, holding in her praying hands a big black city umbrella. Open above her head.

'That's bad luck,' I said, 'to open a brolly indoors.'

'Bad luck, design, taste, idea, a crap film set—mindless,' Sam rumbled.

He moved into a long low-ceilinged room, still all black and white, another film set, this time with full cast assembled. A black man in a white suit sat at the white grand piano playing Cole Porter, while a white man in a black suit, shirt and tie rushed towards us shouting out, 'Sam's here.' Suddenly we were surrounded. Someone thrust a martini in my hand, I took a gulp and within minutes felt the first kick, starting first in my stomach, then at the back of my knees. I remembered that apart from Charles' pâté I hadn't eaten all day and decided to pace things a bit otherwise I'd be flat on my face within the hour. It had happened before. I looked at Sam, he was already taking his second. We'd be lucky to reach the theatre, that was for sure. Most people's faces seemed familiar to me, but I didn't know a soul. Sam was too busy talking to introduce me. Like all parties, the first ten minutes was the worst. Gradually from being the centre of the group I found myself at the edge. Time to flick through the gramophone records or examine the books on the shelves, pick up small assorted objects as if I was interested in where they came from. Ivory carvings, jet-black geometric puzzles. Clear perspex boxes, crammed with cigarettes. I took one out and looked round for a light.

'Allow me,' said a woman's voice, while a hand weighed down with jewelled rings flicked a flame towards me.

'Thank you very much.' It was the first time I'd heard my voice since I'd arrived. It sounded forced and artificial, over-careful.

'Enjoying the party?'

'Not yet,' I answered, 'but I expect I will.'

She laughed, 'Happy optimist,' then drifted away. I watched her go. She must have been about fifty-five, I could tell by her neck, but her face was smooth and unlined like a teenager's and her body was slim and straight with extraordinarily high breasts. I wondered when she undressed how many seams and tucks there'd be. None, if she was clever with her lighting, that anyone would see. Except with their fingertips.

I caught sight of myself in one of the many mirrors and saw with surprise how very much at home I looked. Sophisticated, slightly bored, suitably beautiful. It didn't please me, not one bit. Too unfriendly. My glass was empty, time for another and to join the attack. I drank it in one go. A handsome young man at my elbow watched in amazement. 'Darling, was that wise?'

'Terribly unwise,' I said and, because he was still looking, reached for another.

'Well, if it's that sort of night, I'll join you,' he said and did the same.

I clinked my glass with his. 'Why not?'

From then on it was plain sailing.

'You're divine,' he said. 'Where did you get your suit?'

'Yves St Laurent.'

'Where else?'

'And yours?'

'The same.'

'Of course!'

'Who does your hair, darling?'

'I do.'

'Why not try Vidal?'

'I have had it cut there but now I'm growing it, so I wash it myself.'

'But that's madness. Why grow it? Go to Roger, get him to cut it all off, except the fringe. And have that dyed red or better still green. Be divine!'

'Do you think so?'

'Of course! Everyone's having it. I'm going to tomorrow.'

'You're not!'

'Come with me. They can do us together. Be fabulous, darling.'

'Well, I might have it cut but I don't know about the colour.' I was thinking of Charles. 'My children mightn't like it.'

'You can't have children. But you're so young.'

'Child bride,' I said.

'How chic.'

'Divorced now, of course.'

'Who isn't? Where do you live?'

'Chelsea. Where you'd expect.' And I told him the street.

'How grand. Flat or house?'

'Whole house, but it's very small.'

'Bijou,' he corrected.

'Whole house, but it's very bijou.'

'Oh, you are funny, darling. Do you know everybody here?'

'No, do you?'

'Intimately. Alas. At one time or other!'

'And where do you live?'

'With whoever I'm with. Currently I'm between engagements. Last summer I was in Rome. I spent Christmas in Tunisia. I was hoping for this spring in the Seychelles but instead I'm staying with my mother.'

'Oh, where's that?'

He lowered his voice and looked around. 'Can you keep a secret?'

'Of course.'

'Streatham Hill!' He held up his hand. 'Now I know what you're going to say—parts of that are very nice— don't bother. We both know it's appalling.' And he gave a beautiful shudder.

He was amazingly handsome, too much so by half, with a long lean body and the sort of teeth you read about, very white and even. And very thick brown hair with sunburnt streaks. But his mouth was too full and sort of babyish, it made him look as if he'd cry easily. I liked him already. I wanted him to feel that everything was fine and that he didn't have to try so hard. Something of it must have crossed my face. He leaned forward.

'I'm glad we got together. To tell you the truth I was feeling a bit low when I arrived. I'm Rupert.'

'Rupert Bear,' I said.

'Adore him too. What's yours? No, don't tell me! Let me

guess. Rowena? Rebecca?'

I shook my head. 'How about Myopia?'

He gave a scream of delight. 'What a marvellous name. That, darling, is what I shall call you. Myopia. You're not sensitive about your sight? I mean, you don't wear lenses or anything?'

'Perfect eyesight. Can see for miles.'

'That's it then, Myopia. Come on, let's try it out on someone.'

He looked around excitedly then stopped and put his hand on my arm. 'Before we lose each other, what are you doing tomorrow? Because, apart from having my hair done, I've promised to go to Joe Garibaldi's fashion show. You'd adore his clothes—would you like to come? Do say yes.'

'What time?'

'Lunchtime at Animals. It's divine. Haven't you been there? Oh you must have. Everything leopardskin. Even the plates.'

'How horrible. Does the fur get in your mouth?'

'Printed plastic, silly. Joe's taking over the whole place. Champagne and smoked salmon.'

'How lovely. I think I'd love to come. I've seen his clothes but only in magazines.'

'Dauntingly expensive, my dear, but such panache! You'd look a dream in them.'

'I think I'd feel uneasy spending that much.'

He laughed and flicked my fringe. 'What a sweet child you are, get a boy friend to foot the bill. That's what they're for, darling.' He lightly fingered his superbly cut lapels. 'My dear, you don't imagine I paid for these?'

I gazed at him for a second and then looked across the crowded room at Sam. 'I don't seem to be very good at that,' I said. His eyes followed mine and seeing Sam he sighed.

'Now that's the sort of money we all need.'

'Sam? He's who I've come with. But I think you're wrong. He's not very rich.'

He let his jaw drop. 'You're joking!'

'No I'm not. I've been seeing him for ages.'

He leant forward eagerly. 'He bought you the house.'

'Don't be silly. He hasn't bought me anything, except dinners and things. Honestly.'

He drained his glass and groaned. 'Darling innocent,

you're sitting on a goldmine picking daisies. I can't bear it!'

'What do you mean?'

'What I mean is that Samuel Gregory Jr. is Contemporary Films Incorporated. He owns it all now. His father died last year.'

'Oh, he said his father was dead, and his mother. My men are usually orphans.'

He groaned again. 'Don't tell me they're all millionaires too. You probably wouldn't know. Darling, I can see you need taking in hand. My God, Myopia is nearer the mark than we'd imagined.'

'I've gone all dizzy,' I said. And I had too.

'Quite understandable, darling. So should I have in the circumstances.'

'I think it's the drink. They're very strong these martinis. I'd have been safer on gin and tonic.'

He took a glass from my hand and shepherded me to the door. 'Squat a while in the loo, darling. Much the chicest place to collapse! I'll see you when you come out. The party will still be here.'

I sat for what seemed like a month on the open oval lavatory seat. From time to time people discreetly rattled the door handle, but I couldn't move. I tried to focus on my feet. There were four of them. My satin trousers flopped in concertina folds around them all on the floor. When at last I stood up I saw in the mirror, by twisting round, that the seat had bitten into my buttocks and left a ludicrous red frame around my hole. All it needed was the artist's signature. I pulled my tights and trousers up—and fished around in my pocket for a lipstick. After that my flat slim compact. A spot of powder and I felt fit to face the world. I didn't have any money on me at all. If Sam had gone, Christ knows how I'd get home.

He hadn't and nor had anyone else, come to that. If anything, it was even fuller. Perhaps I'd only been in there minutes, after all. It does that, drink. Robs you of all sense of time. So does pot, of course, but much more so, floating for centuries when in fact it's only half an hour. Both at the time seem a way of getting through life more quickly, what they do instead is slow it up.

Swaying slightly, I looked around. I couldn't see Rupert anywhere. I liked the idea of the dress show. I hoped I hadn't lost him for good. Sam was still surrounded, he was astonishingly popular but thinking about it, if what Rupert had said was true it was hardly surprising. At that moment he looked up, towering above everyone else, and caught my eye. His face broke into an enormous grin and he beckoned. I didn't attempt to go towards him, just grinned back and waved. His smile froze and turned into a frown. He beckoned again, but this time angrily. He was drunk.

'You'd better go to him, darling,' said a voice behind me. Rupert's. I turned round with a dazzling smile.

'Why?' I was drunk too. 'Kiss me.'

Rupert's startled eyes and anxious mouth were the last things I saw. What I heard was the smashing of fine glass, the rip of expensive satin, and an animal roar from Sam as my head whammed against the wall. It took the full strength of five men to hold him off. Numbed as I was, with bells jingling in my ears and soaring specks of light looking uncommonly like stars before my eyes, I still was all for hitting Sam back. But restraining hands kept me where I was, on the floor. I slowly lifted one foolish finger and touched the egg which was swelling on my head. My shoulder was completely bare. I looked down at it with surprise, at the fringed edges of the torn beautiful jacket and the shredded shirt beneath. Then I looked at Sam. His neck was dark red, his eyes glaring down at me were wild and bloodshot. Sweat was pouring down his face. It was a terrible tantrum!

'Sam,' I said weakly. 'That was very silly. Serve you right if you have a seizure.'

There wasn't a sound in the whole room except from the pianist who had switched from Cole Porter to Noël Coward *Mad About the Boy*, that's what he was playing.

People helped me to my feet. I shook their hands away and walked the few unsteady steps to Sam. The five men tightened their grips and Sam, blinking hard, flinched as my hand came up to his face. But all I did was lightly touch his mouth. Very slowly I undid his tie, unbuttoned his collar and with two hands tore as hard as I could till there was no shirt left at all. Then I kissed him. The laugh started in his stomach just as it did in mine. He looked me up and down, saw that half my jacket was still intact, took hold of that sleeve and ripped it from its socket. We were convulsed. The astonished rest of the room began to giggle from nervousness. Sam undid his flies. 'Dare you, cunty.' I grasped a handful of trouser either side and pulled as hard as I could in all directions. Every seam went. What was left slithered down his legs to the floor. Tears of appreciation ran down his face. With one swoop, wearing now only his jacket, tie and underpants, he picked me up and slung me over his shoulder.

'Great party,' he boomed between laughs. 'Sorry to leave, folks, but we gotta go.'

As the lift went down I caught sight of Rupert's face white and excited. 'Animals at one. Bring Sam, he can buy you a new suit!'

When I woke in the morning my head ached hellishly. The egg was still there but the whole of the left side of my face was now puffy and painful. More than anything I was terribly hungry—we never had got round to eating the night before. It was raining by the time we'd left the party and Sam was all for walking round to the Hilton for dinner just as we were. The hall porter wouldn't hear of us walking anywhere. Said we'd be sure to be picked up for indecent exposure. He insisted on ringing for a taxi and made us wait in his little office whilst he did so. As it was, when the taxi arrived, several residents passed us in the hall and all made a point of looking the other way at Sam's 'Mind now, darlings, enjoy yourselves' said in a silly English accent. Sam held on to me very tightly, as much I suspected to support himself as anything else.

'You've not to come in tonight,' I said. 'You're to go straight home when you've dropped me.'

'You're mad at me, you bitch.'

'I'm not at all.'

'You're mad at me because I whammed you, and I only did that because you were out petting with some guy half the party.'

'I wasn't. I was in the lavatory.'

'With some guy. Honey, I saw you go. What are you trying to say—I'm blind, for Jesus' sake!'

'What, Rupert? Don't be silly. He's not like that.'

'You mean he's a fuckin' faggot? That doesn't fool me, not for one minute. I know faggots, I know one faggot who's a grandfather, for Christ's sake. What do you make of that? He's got more in his trousers than a chocolate éclair.'

'Sh, sh, calm down, Sam. You're marvellous. You know I think you are. I'm not mad, not a bit, but now I'd like to go home and to bed. My head is hurting, that's all. Please.' I took his hand and held it tightly to my mouth.

He stroked my hair. 'Shall I see you tomorrow, honey?'

'Ring me in the morning.'

He looked anxiously in my eyes. I started to laugh. So did he then.

'Hey, what do you suppose they thought, that set of wankers?'

'Disgracefully bad behaviour?'

'Livened the evening, though. What do you suppose they're doing now, talking about us?'

'Tearing each other's clothes off?'

He stopped chuckling and touched my shreds. 'You looked so gorgeous tonight. You know that. Tomorrow I'm going to buy you another of these. Not just one—ten, twenty—anything you like. You're not much of a screw but you're a bold little bugger.'

I got up well before the girls and Françoise. I made some tea for myself and took a couple of aspirins for the pain. Then I splashed the puffiness with iced water and skin tonic which seemed to make it go down a bit. My hair was agonising to brush, each stroke set my scalp going, so I gave it up and instead pulled on a little purple silky cap which covered the whole lot. The hairdresser's, having it cut or coloured, was out of the question today. I found a pair of purple sunglasses and a favourite old dressing-gown, striped pink and purple, and went down to the kitchen to make breakfast. By the time Françoise came down everything was ready. Freshly pressed orange juice, ice in each glass. Boiled brown eggs with everyone's name written on in red biro and a whole dishful of golden buttered toast cut into narrow strips for dipping in. I heard the girls shouting to find my bed empty. 'Mummy, Mummy.' 'She's not here.' 'She's gone.' 'Where is she?' I turned the radio on extra loud to give them a clue and they came running down and tried to climb up me, one on each side. Françoise was delighted to see everything done.

'Special treat,' I said in case she thought it was the start of a new régime.

'Why, Mummy, why?'

37

'Just because.'

'I like just because,' said Fanny banging her egg with a spoon.

'I like just because too,' said Harriet carefully slicing hers with a knife. 'I like it because the breakfast is nicer.'

'That's not true,' I protested. 'Françoise makes lovely ones.' I could see her face.

'I try to do good for you, Harriet.'

'Yes, but you burn the toast and then you scrape it but I can still tell by the taste. Mummy's is much better.'

'Ah,' I said, 'but I can't make coffee and Françoise is very good at that.'

'You always drink tea, though, Mummy.'

'That's because I can't make coffee as well as Françoise. Eat up before it gets cold.' My head was beginning to thud again. 'I'm going to a dress show today,' I said brightly. 'Beautiful clothes being shown off by beautiful girls.'

'Little ones? Will there be anything for us there?'

'Models. Grown-up ones.'

'Mannequins,' corrected Françoise. 'My friend in Paris she is a mannequin for Dior. I know her all my life. She have very bad hacnee—acknay? Many plackheads and pimpoles. Open paws. It's horrible! Ugh!'

'How did she get the job at Dior?'

'She get it because she have very thin elbows and no front and back and she have a tall neck like a chimney—'

'Does she smoke?' Harriet asked, and spluttered egg all over her orange juice.

'Don't be silly, Harriet,' I said. 'That's rude. Françoise was still telling us about her friend. Go on, I love hearing it.'

Fanny was all eyes, she'd put down her spoon and was examining her elbows and feeling her front with both hands. 'I've got one, haven't I, Mummy? And a botty too,' she added sadly.

Françoise went on as if there had been no interruption at all. 'She show me many photographs of herself. Because of her tall neck she is modelling the beautiful hats of Dior, but always from the back.'

'Oh dear, but perhaps that's the best angle for hats. Lots of them have bows and things there.'

'Not so at all,' said Françoise triumphantly. 'If she face the camera she would break it. I count once how many plackheads she have and it take me—'

'Poor thing.' I stood up. 'That's a lesson to wash your faces, girls, isn't it? Up you go. You too, Françoise! I'll clear these.'

I piled everything on a tray. Going up the stairs Harriet shouted down, 'Thank you for breakfast, Mummy,' and then to Françoise, 'How long did it take you?'

The answer drifted down. 'It take me the all of a week—'

I'd driven the girls to school.

'What are we having for tea?'

'You only just had breakfast.'

'I'm hungry.'

'You can't be.'

'She is. And so am I.'

'Perhaps you'll have nothing then, if eating makes you hungry.'

'We're not a bit hungry. It's a joke.'

'Very funny.'

'Can we have cake and buns and chocolate biscuits like other people?'

'What, all at once? Which people?'

'Chubby. She brings buns for playtime.'

'So does Podgy Olive, she eats them on the lavatory.'

'If you want to be called Chubby and Podgy, I'll stop off now and buy you some buns.'

'Podgy Olive has got lots of dimples,' Fanny said wistfully. 'I haven't got any.'

'Later in life you'll thank me.' I kissed them goodbye. 'But I know it's hard to see now. When I was your age I was called Fatso and Jumbo and Piggy, you couldn't see my face for dimples. But it wasn't anything as nice as you think.'

When I got back the phone was ringing, but as I reached it, it stopped. Hell! I went up to run my bath, I had the first foot in when it rang again. One wet footprint all down the carpeted stairs. Man Friday.

'Hullo.'

'Darling, it's me!'

'Charles. How lovely.'

'Must be brief. Friday. Friday evening. Paris. Back Saturday. What do you say?'

'For the night? But, Charles, how can you? You never can in the evenings, let alone a night.'

'I'll explain later. Now, yes or no, darling?'

39

'Let me think. Well I suppose so. Françoise will be here but Saturday is her day off.'

'We'd be back before breakfast, darling. I've got to be.'

'That's all right then—oh how lovely. I love Paris. What a wonderful surprise, Charles.'

'Settled then. I'll telephone you in the morning with further details. If time allows I'll drop in later in the day. Good morning to you.' His office voice all of a sudden. He replaced his receiver briskly. Click.

'Good morning to you too, sir,' I said and replaced mine.

I ran up the stairs two at a time but slowed down when I felt it doing my head no good. Friday. I'd be better by then. Well, I felt better all ready. I loved a journey. That's what I liked about Mondays as much as anything. Getting on the train. Being on the move. Paris in the Spring . . .

'Let's save up and go, it'll be smashing. All those sexy French men. They love English girls. They'd go mad about us!'

'Don't be so daft, Jean. I'd never save that much.'

'You would. You could work all Easter holidays on the Palace Pier and then we could go just for a week before term starts. Anyway you've got your grant.'

I laughed at that. She had no idea, Jean, of what grants were. She thought they were some sort of personal allowance like the one she had from her father. She was by far the richest girl in my lot at college, but for all that never looked very much. 'It's these glasses. When you're saddled with glasses there's no point in trying. Do you know, I've never been out with a boy! No one has ever asked me.' From then on we were friends. Well, I thought it was such a shame, because she was lots of fun and her figure wasn't at all bad. And it wasn't as though she wasn't keen. Keen as mustard. Much more than me. But then at that time I was recovering from a broken heart. It was because of my broken heart that my mother said, 'Go. Paris is just what you could do with, love. If you can get the money together.' I think she was sick of me mooning about the place. Later, I heard next door telling her, 'Ooh Vi, them frogs. 'Ope she don't come back wiv no big belly.' 'She's a sensible girl,' was my mother's reply.

I got a job on the Palace Pier, well more under it really, in the arcade beneath the prom. About ten strides from the

40

Gents; it wasn't too pleasant for the first day because the wind was blowing my way. But in the end it proved all to the good. It was a wonderful Easter weekend financially. It rained from morning to night which brought everybody, all the trippers, down into the arcade for shelter. They were so drunk most of them that they didn't know what they were spending on. Mr Pilsky, who owned the cafe where I worked, said he'd never known such bumper takings. It was his wife, Ruthie, who'd taken me on.

'Experienced waitress?'

'No, but it won't take me long to learn.'

'You don't learn on my time, dear. Out of season different. With the Easter crowd I need speed. Right then, washer-up?'

'Thank you,' I said. I was in the windowless passage they called the kitchen for about five minutes, I'd already slipped once on the greasy floor. Chef, he introduced himself as that, had dropped a whole pan of boiling fat by forgetting to hold it with a cloth. Already it had formed a fine white coagulating skin. He was a frightening-looking man, covered in sores all up his arms and over his face. His collar where it met his neck was stained with old pus and fresh blood.

'Wouldn't get too close if I was you. Best fish fryer in the business but riddled with pox. We don't touch his food here, kid, I bring me own sandwiches. If you're cute you'll do the same,' whispered the friendly counterhand.

After the five minutes Mr Pilsky had come in. He looked me up and down, turned me round and pinched my bottom.

'Who are you?'

'The new washer-up.'

'Madness! Ruthie, who put this kid in the kitchen?'

'I did, David. Did I do wrong?'

'Wrong? Where's your business sense, girl? What, this kid? Knockers like hers, that face? Should be out front for the customers to see. Pull the fellas, you fool!'

'She got no experience, David. She don't—'

'Experience! Experience! Showmanship, Ruthie! We set up a counter outside—soft drinks, ice-cream, chocolate, anything! Get it?' He put his arm round my shoulders, right round so that his fleshly hand pressed hard against one bosom. 'What have we got for the little darling to wear?'

'The overalls are in the cupboard, David. Take your pick,' said Ruthie, but the way she looked at me!

'I'll see to it, all under control. Now you get it set up outside. We're here to make money, girl,' and to me, 'Student are you?'

'Yes.'

'Thought so. Can always tell a student. Flat shoes and no make-up! Right! But you're a good-looking kid. Should make more of yourself. Don't you wear no jewellery—earrings, I mean, and suchlike?'

'No, but I could get some at the end of the week when I have my wages.'

He opened his wallet and peeled off a note. 'Get yourself some on the way in tomorrow and while you're at it a bit of lipstick at the same time.'

I looked at the note and said innocently, 'Will this be enough?'

A strange look passed over his face. He came closer and cupped one of my breasts, his other hand he put between my legs. 'Don't come that line till you've done something to earn it, kid. Please me and I'll please you.' Then he turned round and started sorting through the clean overalls in the cupboard. 'Ahhah, this one will do a treat. We had to have it made special for a girl last year. Very small she was, like a child you might say. Get it on.'

I held on to the sleeve of my jumper and pushed it through the short arm of the stiff white overall, then tried to do the same with the other arm. 'It's too small,' I said.

'Rubbish.'

'It is. I'll never do it up.'

'Get your jumper off then. Go on.'

'Is there anywhere to change?'

'Here's all right by me. And get your skirt off too. You need a nice tight fit on an overall.'

I felt like crying, which was silly. I put my mind to Paris which was the only reason I was with this horrible man. What a time we'd have there Jean and me. I thought of good-looking French boys with black hair and nice brown hands. I thought of dancing and afterwards kissing by the Seine. I kept on thinking all that and then I turned my back on his disgusting face and slowly took my jumper off. His voice rasped through what I was thinking.

'You walk around half naked—where's your brassière?'

He spun me round to face him—my arms involuntarily

came up to hide myself. He pinned them to my sides and took one step back. 'Bloody hell, they're the best titties I've ever seen. Why wear a brassière with that lot? You got some sense, girl. Ruthie, come 'ere, Ruthie. What do you say to this pair? Long time since you saw some like these, eh?'

Ruthie came through and stood there speechless, so did the counterhand and the two waitresses and last of all Chef, skidding on his greasy soles. 'Phew.' 'Blimey.' 'I could pay more than me rent with them.' 'She'd make a fortune on the game.' 'Worth spending a bit to set her up.' The counterhand caught my eye but I could only just see her. Jean and I were strolling down the Boulevard St. Germain. We were approaching Les Deux Magots. We sat down at one of the tiny pavement tables and ordered two Pernods. 'Scott Fitzgerald might have sat on this chair.' 'Or Hemingway.' But it must have been raining because everything was blurred and shiny. My face was wet and there was a salty taste in my mouth.

'There you are, you coarse buggers. You made the poor little sod cry.' The counterhand came forward. 'Don't take no notice, love. It's all in fun. It's just you're not used to it.'

'Ooh, listen to Nelly.'

'Yeah, listen to 'er—she'd be the first to get your drawers down, kid. You like a pretty girl don't you, Nell?'

Lots of laughter and cat-calls.

'Shut up, you lot,' Nelly said fiercely.

Ruthie stepped forward and put her hands on her big hips. 'David, am I wrong? Is this a café due to open in five bloody minutes or is it a fuckin' striptease?' and to me, 'Decent people, girl, do not go round without undies on— or don't they teach you that in college?' She spat it out. Mr Pilsky let go of my arms. I snatched my jumper up and held it across my front. I stopped crying but my face and chest were still splashed with the tears that had just been.

My turn to spit, I spun round on Mr Pilsky: 'And decent people don't go round undressing other people just for a chance to see their body. Not that is unless they're dirty old men. If you want to know, my brassière is in the wash!' But I ended childishly 'So there!' And I stuck my tongue out. Nobody said anything. The waitresses looked uneasily at each other. Chef became interested in how his greasy soles were sticking to the dirty lino. Nelly muttered, 'Good kid, tell them.' Ruthie was glaring at her husband. I'd gained

43

ground. They were all pathetic.

'Well,' I said gaily, 'would you like one last look before I get ready for work?' I dropped my jumper, quickly unzipped my skirt, stepped out of it and did a twirl around. I twanged my knicker elastic towards Ruthie. 'Undies, see?' Then I picked up the ridiculously small overall, buttoned it up and pulled the belt as tight as it would go. 'Should get in a bit of business, Mr Pilsky?'

I didn't tell my mother, she'd have had me out of there in no time. Paris or no Paris. But days later I told Jean.

'I'd have walked out.'

'Where to?'

'There must be other jobs.'

'Not this late, everything had gone on the Palace Pier and the West Pier. I tried.'

'But aren't there jobs in the hotels on the front? What about the Metropole or the Grand?'

'Not for three weeks, you fool. They want you for the whole season. Anyway, all there was was chambermaid and my mother said no.'

'Why?'

'Because she said my father had said I wasn't to. He told her that these hotels are full of dirty old men who get the chambermaids into bed when they bring the tea in the morning. And then don't even leave a tip!'

'He'd go mad if he knew about old Pilsky.'

'Pilsky is no trouble now. Anyway Ruthie is there keeping an eye on him. She doesn't let him out of her sight. To tell you the truth I play up a bit now, you know, bending over a lot and leaving a button undone. He goes all hot and bothered. It makes her really mad.'

'Aren't you awful,' Jean said, but I could see she was impressed.

'Yes, I could turn into a terrible flirt, just like that.'

It was true. There was something infectious about the arcade. Everyone on holiday, paper hats, pop bottles, candy floss, beer. And I'd got used to the revealing tightness of my overall. It was filthy after the first day from heaving cases of fizzy drinks and bending over the dusty fridge fishing out ice-creams. But all the grey patches did was emphasise on the white starched cotton what curves lay underneath. The Hourglass. That's what they called me.

'You should get entering for the Bathing Belle contest.

They're running heats this week on the end of the pier,' said Lottie, one of the waitresses. 'Shouldn't she, Mave?' she said to the other.

'Yeah, you'd win hands down.'

'Oh, I wouldn't. I know I wouldn't. My legs aren't long enough. You have to have very long legs for that.'

'Well, love, you want to get out of them ballet slippers for a start. What do they call them? Pumps. They don't do nothing for you. Do they, Mave?'

'Hopeless. Get up the road to Tip Toes. They got smashing high heels. Ever so cheap. Nice pair of white ones. Really smart. Only ten bob. Make your legs look like Rita Hayworth's.'

'That's all you need, love,' said Lottie, looking at my legs.

'And a nice perm,' supplied Mavis.

I thought seriously about the shoes but not about the rest of it. I'd rather have died than parade about in a swimsuit. Anyway my father would have put his foot down. He didn't approve of beauty queens any more than chambermaiding. Besides, how would I have time off? Only ten bob. I had ten bob. The change from old Pilsky's pound. I'd bought the earrings, huge brass gypsy rings from a shop near the station. They'd cost five bob. Another five bob had gone on a lipstick, Sun Kissed Orange (refill: half-price), and a thick soft black eyebrow pencil which I rubbed on my eyelids with Vaseline to make them dark and shiny. I always washed it off before I went home and I didn't show them the earrings either. 'Tarty.' I had half an hour's dinner break each day when Ruthie relieved me at my little kiosk. I was always pleased to see that at those times the till showed hardly any sales at all. 'Oh,' I'd say glancing at it, 'a quiet spell.' She never bothered to answer.

This day I skipped my sandwiches and ran as fast as I could to Tip Toes. Half an hour later I was back in my first ever high heels. I'd walked in them all the way down the prom. Shoulders back, head high, careful steps, only way to keep balance. Twice I turned my ankle and nearly fell. Some silly boys started marching alongside. 'New shoes?' Lots of titters. But I took no notice. Nothing since, no dress, or fur or piece of jewellery, has made me feel as glamorous as I did that day. I wore them home when I'd finished work.

'Now you're talking,' Lottie had said approvingly.

45

'That's more like it, kid,' said Mavis. 'What did I tell you? Rita Hayworth.'

Even Ruthie sniffed. 'Nice to see you smartening up, about time.'

'Haven't we got a high stool for her to sit on, Ruthie? Show the legs off a bit?'

'No, David. We haven't.'

But my mother wasn't too impressed. 'Shoddy, made of cardboard. You'll be lucky if they last a week. What do you think, Dad?'

'Make her legs look funny, too long or something. All out of proportion. Take them off.'

I took them off but in my bedroom I practised walking for hours with them until in the end I'd perfected a wonderful hip-swinging cross between a slink and a wobble. Jean was terribly jealous, she went straight to Tip Toes and got herself exactly the same ones. White, slingback, peep toe, high stiletto heel. I didn't mind at all but I said to her, 'Jean, that's silly. You've got the money. You could have got real leather ones. Much nicer.'

'But not so sexy. Come on, show me how to walk.'

She kept her shoes at our house; if she'd taken them home her father would have burnt them right away.

Time was drawing on. Already I'd been at work ten days. About ten more to go. The first week had been frantic. Sometimes we hadn't shut till twelve o'clock at night but that had been Easter week. It meant a long walk home for me because by the time we'd cleared up my last bus had gone. But it was worth it, for the extra I earned. Then it fell off altogether, the weather had changed for the worse. Brilliant sunshine. The beach was packed, but people were bringing their own picnics. We did quite a turn-over with beach tea trays and my lukewarm ice-cold drinks, the lollies and ice-creams, but the café was half-empty. People didn't fancy heavy fries in that heat. Takings were down by a third. Mr Pilsky was sunk in gloom, he didn't even have the spirit to ogle me any more. By eight at night there was no point in staying open—sometimes we even shut at six.

'At this rate I'll never have enough saved,' I moaned to Jean.

'Perhaps the weather will break.'

'Pray.'

She must have, because two days later when Paris was

beginning to appear as unlikely as Paradise, it poured all day. I shortened my bra straps to give a bit more cleavage, got round the front of my kiosk, pretending to clean it as often as I could, to show off my legs. And by midday had sold out of ices. At one point Nelly came out for a smoke.

'Hope you're making up your money, love.'

'Oh yes, I've been non-stop. Sold out on ices.'

'That makes no odds. Ices they check on.' She looked over her shoulder and jerked a thumb at Pilsky who now was on top of the world. 'That's what you fiddle, love.' She nodded at the ice-cold orange, a circular glass tank full of acid-looking orangeade with a plastic orange floating on the surface. 'You keep the colour going but dilute it right down with water. Fifty per cent you forget to ring on the till.' She winked. 'Use your loaf, love. Believe me, we're all at it.'

Two hours later I'd made ten shillings and felt as guilty as hell. My pocket bulged with coppers and sixpences. Nelly caught sight of me and darted out. 'Shove it in the till and take it in notes, you little fool.' Then she winked again. 'Atta girl.'

I was at it every day after that.

'Four fizzy lemons, miss.'

'Why not try the ice-cold orange? Really sharp and tasty.'

'Try anything once—'

Lots of them spat it out on the spot, leaving the remains in their waxed cups still sitting on the counter. Pouring it back? Lightning wasn't half as quick. By each night I was making at least two pounds extra. 'That's what you call private enterprise,' Nelly said. But the day after she said it, old Pilsky caught her in the act. She was sacked on the spot.

'Don't go giving up,' she whispered on her way out. 'Just go careful. Got it?' A final wink and she'd gone.

I couldn't have given up anyway, it was like a drug. I came to understand what excitement a real burglar must feel. Five days before I finished I sold my first pair of earrings. Just like that, off my ears.

'Smashin' earrings, darlin'. 'Ow much?'

'Oh, I wouldn't sell them.'

''Ow much?'

(Quick sums, hundred per cent profit.) 'Well, I paid ten shillings for them.'

'I'll give yer fifteen. Do lovely for the missus.'

'But I don't want to sell them.'

'Pound?'

'Right!'

On the way in next morning I spent the whole pound on four more pairs. That's where being so near the Gents' came in handy. They used to spill in there straight off the charabancs, come out and then catch sight of me. And my earrings. Twenty-five pairs I sold by the end, with me paying less than five shillings for them. I got my own price knocked down for buying in bulk, but I still charged the full pound.

They were sweet on my last day. Lottie got quite tearful.

'Ooh, we will miss you. Won't we miss her, Mave?'

'Don't be so soppy, the kid's going to Paris. You should be saying bon voyage. It's very romantic. *Paris in the Spring*—'

'Toujours l'amour,' Lottie sang out.

'Up against the back door,' sang Mavis back, and went into peals of laughter. Then she was serious. 'Have you done it yet, kid?'

'What?'

'Give it away, I mean. You're not a virgin, are you?'

'Sort of.'

'Blimey, what's sort of?'

'Well, I had a boy friend. But he couldn't find the hole.'

'Bloody hell. Was he blind?'

'Actually, yes. Yes, he was born blind. But he doesn't see me any more. I'm just getting over it.'

'Cripes, you don't want to hitch up with no blind bastard. Not at your age. I wouldn't let no daughter of mine. Play the field and then pick the best. Somebody who's going to make a bit. But if you're going to come up with the goods, for God's sake see they got a french letter on! If you're caught short and they haven't, mind to have a wipe round with a soap and flannel after!'

'My sister had it off with a French sailor once,' Lottie sighed. 'At the back of a pub in Portsmouth. Said she'd never known anything like it. The different things he did.'

'That's right, kid. A bloke who knows what he's doing, believe you me, can get goosepimples growing on your eyeballs!'

Ruthie was relieving Chef when I said my goodbyes. I was quite glad he wasn't anywhere around. I was afraid

48

he'd want to shake my hand with his sores or, worse still, kiss me. How shocking to go to Paris with the pox! She stood at the chip machine, sweating in a cloud of blue smoke. Half of them were burning as usual. 'You're off then,' a wave of the fish slice, and a turned back. Good riddance to you too!

Old Pilsky paid me off taking as long about it as he could. Finally he handed me the full amount and pressing it tightly in the palm of my hand said thickly. 'You're a very silly little girl. You could have made ten times this if you'd used that,' and he pushed a podgy knee between my two. Afterwards I thought of all the witty things I could have said back. Some came at the time but I let the moment pass, I don't know why but I didn't even pull away.

He came terribly close, was getting very excited, pressing up against me. I could feel it in his trousers, thick and bulging down the side of one leg. We were in what he called his office, a partitioned-off space no larger than a cupboard. It was the end of the evening but I was going off an hour early to pack and get ready for tomorrow. The day's takings were in a tin box on his small table. In my high heels I was taller than him. His bald head was about level with my breasts. The rancid smell of his greasy scalp whiffed into my nose. He'd taken his jacket off and just above where he'd rolled his sleeves up I could see the week's sweat stains on his shirt. He was sweating again now, his face was wet with it, dripping on to me. I was still in my overall, thank goodness. Both arms around me now, knee working furiously prising mine apart, he whispered hoarsely, 'Come on, girl. What are you saving it for? We got time now. Come on quick. I'm crazy about you.' I made no reply. Suddenly he broke off, reached towards the tin box and took out a five-pound note. I still stood there not moving but my heart was going like mad. He stuffed the note down into my brassière and keeping that hand there forced his fingers in towards my nipple. With his other hand he drew one of mine between his legs. I half-heartedly tried to pull it away. Why so half-heartedly? Was it the money? It wasn't really, because with all my fiddling and earnings on the side, not to mention my overtime, I now had much more than enough. But I'd got greedy. I wanted the fiver as well. I felt it stiff and scratchy against my skin. I'd put that aside for presents. Jean and me on the last afternoon, into Galeries Lafayette. Scent for my

49

mother or a string of beads or a square silk scarf, views of
Paris printed on it. Socks for my father, red, or braces,
canary yellow, to show off and lots of those miniature
liqueurs—he'd like that. Initialled handkerchiefs, French
cigarettes, belts and shiny handbags. A tiny baby's dress,
white, edged with broderie anglaise for my sister,
expecting next month. He was undoing his flies, forcing
in my unprotesting, lifeless, fingers. Jamming them
round his swollen clammy thing, squeezing and rubbing
up and down. I could tell by the feel what colour it was,
putty and slugs, underdone pork. On my very first day I'd
buy some new shoes, very high, suede perhaps, toffee-
coloured. Pack a tin of elastoplasts in case they made
blisters. The smell of him had got right down into my
stomach. I kept swallowing hard and trying to breathe
through my open mouth. Why was I letting him? Why on
earth? Because of the danger that someone, Ruthie, any of
the others, could come in at any moment; because he was
pathetic and I could make him do anything and I felt sorry
for him; because he'd given me the money; but most of all
now, because his excitement was becoming so unbearable
to him, so highly charged and quivering that it was
exciting me too. There was no doubt about that, I actually
liked his fingers clawing in my brassière. My nipples were
stiff and sticking out like anything. And between my legs I
felt all sticky and sort of tingly. Throbbing. If a doctor
were here he could place a cool finger in and take my pulse
from it. 'My God, my God, my God,' moaned old Pilsky,
and letting go of my hand he quickly pulled a dirty hanky
from his pocket and plunged it into his flies. 'See what
you've done, you bitch! Get out! Go on! Go.' He shut his
eyes and sat down heavily on the small table, still holding
his hanky in, moaning softly to himself. Was it hurting or
what? He seemed in pain.

'Do you think he was then?' We were sitting on the boat
train. The carriage was empty.
   'I didn't wait to enquire, Jean! What on earth have you
done to your hair?'
   'Isn't it awful? Mummy took me to her hairdresser
yesterday and made me have the ends permed. I look a
sight, I know.'
   'I've got a pair of nail scissors. Would you like me to cut
them off?'

'What, now?'

'When we get there. This train is too jerky.'

'Yours looks nice. Lovely and shiny.'

'I ironed it, that's why. It makes it very shiny. And straight. I hate my hair curling. Do you know, I was up at five ironing everything. I had to wash all my clothes last night to get rid of the stink from the café, I swear it's even got into my shoes. I put a bit of blanco on them to hide the scuffs. My mother was right, they haven't lasted very well.'

'You've brought mine?'

'Do you want them now?'

'Yes let's, come on—put yours on too.'

They looked awful away from the arcade, very cheap, terribly tarty, but it got us in the mood.

'Have you done what I told you, Jean? The glasses.'

'Shut your eyes, I'll put them on.' She scuffed in her handbag. 'All right, open! What do you think?' she said anxiously. She sat on the edge of her seat, frizzy-haired, pigeon-toed like a child, wearing on her face an enormous pair of sophisticated dark glasses. I started laughing, I couldn't help it. They looked so out of place. Her mouth went down at the edges. 'Well, you said to get them.' There was a small break in her voice. I went on laughing.

'Oh Jeannie. They're lovely. They really are. That's why I'm laughing. You look like a film star.'

She stood on tiptoes, the slingbacks slipping off her ankles, and looked in the mirror above her seat. 'Do I? Do I really? You're not making fun?'

'Well,' I said. 'Stand here. Let me see. The glasses are film star but now we've got to fit you round them. Perhaps I better cut your hair after all now. What about having it really short? Will your mother mind?'

'She'd have a fit, but it's got a week to grow a bit. Go on, do what you like.'

I left about three inches all over, it was almost a crew cut.

'You'll have a shock when you see it,' I warned. 'But before you look, let me put some lipstick on you.' It was a pleasure painting her mouth. It was a very big one, full, wide, and went up at the ends. I felt like kissing it when I'd finished, coloured bright orange it looked such a happy thing. Before I let her look, I replaced the dark glasses. Without the silly frizz around her shoulders her head was a beautiful shape. It narrowed into a vulnerably child-like sweet little neck, her ears were tiny and close to the scalp.

51

Completely exposed, her jawline was sharp and perfect. 'Now look.' I'd made her beautiful!

We stood together at the mirror. She couldn't say anything at first. 'Is it me?'

'Can't you see in those glasses then? They've got your prescription lenses, haven't they?'

'I can see perfectly, it's a bit dark that's all, but I can see as well as with my others.'

'That's all right then.'

'What do you think?'

'Smashing!' I said. 'You look like a bird, like one of those bush babies with the big eyes, or an owl. A sort of sexy owl—I can't describe it really.'

'But sexy?'

'Oh yes, with that lipstick. It draws attention to your mouth. I should think the whole of Paris will be trying to kiss it.'

She kept on looking in the mirror, turning her head slightly this way and that and running her tongue lightly over her upper lip.

'Don't do that, you'll lick it all off.'

'It's got a funny taste, like peardrops.'

'It's only a cheap one. We'll buy nice ones when we get there, ones with more oil in which makes them shinier, more expensive of course.'

'What would your father say if he knew you wore lipstick?'

'Kill me, what would yours?'

'Kill me too.'

'It's a wonder they let us come you know.'

'But then they can't guess what we're going to get up to, can they?'

I didn't answer, just looked out of the window thinking, then, 'Jean, what are we going to get up to?'

'Wait and see,' she said. In many ways she was much bolder than me.

We arrived at the Gare du Nord at five to four. Everyone was talking in French.

'They're all talking in French.'

'I know, isn't it funny?' We stood on the grey platform with our cases in our hand, cocooned in our own Englishness. Completely lost. My mother'd be putting the kettle on now. 'Jam or Marmite?' to my father.

Jean cleared her throat and took control. 'We'd best

change your money first.' She'd got her francs already, her father had arranged it all through his bank. 'Go and ask in the post office, see if they'll do it!' mine had said.

A young porter seeing us standing there rushed up and seized at our cases. 'Non, non,' Jean said and added, 'merci beaucoup.' He shrugged. 'Okay, pretty girls. You no want I help,' and putting his bunched fingertips to his puckered lips gave a big kissing noise. We started walking towards a sign which said Bureau de Change but we had to go quite slowly because of our shoes.

'We should have practised walking with the cases,' Jean said.

'Just go carefully and try to relax. Keep your shoulders back like me.' My hips swung easily left to right.

'I am,' then after a minute, 'What are they all staring for?'

I had to admit people were staring, or so it seemed. Men. Men walking towards us, gazes directed first at our feet, travelling swiftly up the legs, hovering at suspender level, taking in the waistlines and particularly above, fastening on the mouth, fixing finally on the eyes. Bold looks. To make you blush.

'Assessing,' I said.

'Undressing more like.' I could hear the excitement in her voice.

'Go easy, Jean. We're not even out of the station yet.'

'No, but it makes you see what it's going to be like. Come-to-bed eyes everywhere!'

We had no idea where our hotel was in relation to us. However close, our cases were too heavy to walk. The metro seemed too confusing by far so we took a taxi.

'We won't do too much of this,' Jean said as soon as we were in. 'We'll find men with cars and they can drive us round,' and she added, 'We won't spend on food either, because we'll get taken out for that.'

I looked at her, she was bubbling over. Back home she always was on the boil but it was a bit too tomboyish, had too much of the giggly schoolgirl to fascinate. Here her high spirits had altered mysteriously to a sort of radiance. She still looked mischievous; but ripe. That was it. Ripe for the plucking. Beside her I felt tired. The last three weeks had been a harder slog perhaps than I'd thought at the time. 'We'll have an early night, I've just worked it out, I've been up twelve hours!'

53

She lifted her dark glasses and peered at me in short-sighted horror. 'On our first night?'

'Well, if we have a good rest tonight we can get going tomorrow.' It was Mother talking!

'Don't be silly. Tonight we're on the town.' She looked through her glasses at me and frowned for a second. 'You look a bit tired I admit.' Then she brightened. 'But after a bath you'll feel much better.'

'But—' I was going to say I had my bath last night. In Jean's house they had one every day. Her father had chosen the hotel, arranged the bookings, or rather his secretary had. 'What will it be like, the hotel?'

'If Daddy's had anything to do with it, safe and respectable. Suitable for two nice girls. I thought perhaps tomorrow we could move.'

I lay back and laughed, from sheer weakness.

'The first thing I'm going to do is treat you to a Pernod. How about that?' Her grin stretched from ear to ear. Like a cat about to lick the cream.

'Whatever a Pernod is I'll love it, in fact for all of tonight I put myself completely in your hands.' I leaned forward to see more out of the window. There was a slight drizzle and the dampness shone in patches on the peeling buildings. Everything was grey, a dull pink, a depressing shade of dung. Thronged with people who looked much the same. The whole thing matching. It had a strange look to it, the colour of a pigeon, I thought. But something about it affected me strongly. The atmosphere, the shuttered windows and unexpected alleyways, small streets, balconies, signs and fading notices, cafés, bars, bright lights. It made me think of holding hands, forbidden fruits, darkened doorways, getting in at all hours. Romantic. That was right. A fine thread of excitement circled slowly in my stomach, increasing in speed until it formed a tight and unbearable coil. I sat back and looked at Jean. 'I hope we're nearly there,' I said, 'I think I'm getting diarrhoea!'

I didn't know where Animals was so I took a taxi. 'Animals? New place, isn't it? Behind Covent Garden. Lots of weirdos.' His eyes flickered from my pale face and parma violet lips to my matching long false fingernails. 'Yes. That'll be it.'

'I expect so,' I said and got in. We moved off, heading towards Hyde Park.

'Mind you, by my recollections they only open at night time.'

'I think you're right,' I shouted back. 'But today they're putting on a fashion show.' We slowed down for red lights and he twisted round to look at me.

'You a model then?'

'Oh, no, nothing like that.'

'In films?'

I laughed. 'No.'

'You should be. I could swear I seen you on the telly.'

Must be my day, I thought. Sam had rung.

'How're you doin'?'

'I've got a head the size of a house, and one side of my face is completely paralysed.'

'Hypochondriac! Have you sewn that suit up yet?'

'It's in the dustbin.'

'What! What in hell's name sort of woman are you? A little tear, you throw a good suit away. Move that sexy rump and go get a needle and cotton or I'll come round with a horse whip. Come to think of it, that's one we haven't ...'

'I'm just going out.'

'That's right, you're going out,' he imitated. 'With me,' he added.

'Well, in fact, I'm going to a fashion show at a place called Animals. But I ...'

'Meet you there. What time?'

'At one, but Sam ...'

'What now, for Christ's sake? I'm a busy man, get off this fuckin' line, can't you?'

All I hoped was he wouldn't be rude to Rupert.

I needn't have worried. In the end Sam didn't come. We saved a seat for him, Rupert and me, but as the show was about to start he telephoned. The receiver was handed to me in some awe.

'Honey, I can't make it.'

'What a shame. I've kept you a seat.'

'Worse than that, I'm flying back to Rome right now. Back tomorrow night. Save it for me, huh? And try to be good.'

'Of course. I'll see you then.'

'Whose clothes are you gawping at? Do you like 'em?'

'Joe Garibaldi's. Oh yes, they're beautiful.'

'Right, put him on the line.'

'But ...'

'Sweetheart, I'm just paying that pimp a fortune to design what amounts to five pinafores for one of my movies. Is it too much to ask him to come to the telephone?'

I handed the phone over and escaped back to my seat.

Rupert was all excited. 'Darling, what did he say?'

'He can't come, he's flying back to Rome, he'll be back tomorrow and he wanted to speak to Joe Garibaldi,' I whispered.

'Here he comes now,' he whispered back.

'Who?'

'Joe.'

'Oh, is that him?'

A tiny, smiley boy walked carefully towards us. Lots of people started clapping and he acknowledged it by lifting his narrow hands and extending the fingers just like Royalty. He slipped into the empty seat we'd saved for Sam. Close to, I could see he wasn't half as young as I thought. Fortyish, I'd have said. He was wearing tight black jeans and a black polo-neck cashmere sweater, with plimsolls. Like a dancer, there wasn't an ounce of surplus anywhere. He looked at Rupert through his black lashes. 'Rupert!' And Rupert looked steadily back. 'Joe!' They obviously knew each other very well, or had done at one time.

'Well,' he said, turning to me. 'And who's the lucky girl today? Mr Gregory, patron saint and bless his drip-dry soul, had ordered a la carte for you, my dear. The whole collection if madam so desires. His very words.'

'Sam's? For me?' I gasped.

'Well, not exactly his very words. You no doubt are as familiar with the gentleman's vocabulary as the rest of us but that was what we took it to mean.'

Rupert was beside himself. Well, so was I, but inside me I heard my mother's voice. 'There's nothing for nothing, remember!'

'Do you think I should?' I said out loud.

Rupert gave a low moan of anguish, and did his jaw-dropping act. Joe didn't bat an eyelid.

'Look upon it as payment for services rendered, my sweet.'

I permitted myself a worldly smile. 'Well, put like that I'm delighted to accept.'

'Don't do that, Myopia. You made me quite ill for a moment there.'

I patted Rupert's hand, the show had started.

I couldn't see a thing. It was pitch black. There was a funny noise going on. A sort of faint hissing like escaping gas. I sniffed. A crowd like that, we could have been dead in minutes. Who'd look after the children? It got louder as if a lot of people were blowing softly into tin whistles, which they must have been because from being very soft it gradually got unbearably shrill and finished off all hell let loose with bloodcurdling screams and bongo drums and fierce trumpet blasts and God knows what else. Spotlights, dozens of them, snapped on out of nowhere, playing round and round on an exquisitely sequinned human artichoke unfolding on the floor. I hoped they'd dusted. Every segment was a different dazzling colour. With each fresh blast of brass one broke away—emerald from top to toe, or purple, deep turquoise, a delicate glinting pink— and danced a solo round the whole. The audience was in raptures. I looked at Joe, expecting satisfaction, but instead he sat tensely on the edge of his seat staring into the heart of the artichoke. A look of horror on his face. As the final girl unfurled, he covered his eyes with his hands. 'My God, I can't bear it. The whole effect ruined. She's wearing the wrong tights. Petunia! They should be petunia, petunia. Not, not PUCE!' Unable to bear it any longer, he sprang up and darted away.

'Oh darling, there'll be hell to pay for that,' Rupert whispered to me.

'He seems highly strung, I must say.'

'We're better off without him if you're choosing what you want. Otherwise he could take awful umbrage over the ones you don't tick. You've got your programme, darling. Here's a pen. Oh, isn't it a thrill!'

'You must help choose, Rupert.'

'Thought you'd never ask.'

We were both over-excited by the end, pointing and nudging, deciding and ticking. There were about fifty-five outfits, but each came in at least three colourways.

'Oh, it's so you,' Rupert kept saying, or 'No, rather too,' or 'You'll die if you don't have that.' We agreed on everything except two all-white things.

'I'm not very good with white. It shows the dirt.'

'Darling, you must have *some*thing white. Don't be ridiculous.'

'But it would only do for the summer.'

'Why?'

'Well, I'd have to be brown to look right.'

'I'm ticking them for you. Give me your programme. Where are they? "Snow Siren"—Ivory crêpe de chine lounging pyjamas, batwing sleeves, stiffened face-framing collar. Crystal beaded loose tie belt and matching skull cap. Perfection! Where's the other? "Ice Maiden"—White glacé kid ankle-length trench coat, with tailored, matching kid trouser suit, gauntlet gloves, and shallow-brimmed pull-on hat. Divine, darling!'

'Oh dear, I've no notion how to clean white leather. It's dreadfully impractical, Rupert.'

'What are you planning to wear it for—washing the car? Do stop being so *hum*drum. It doesn't suit you one bit.'

'It's my mother coming out again.'

'She,' he sighed, 'has a lot to answer for.'

'Let's do a count-up. How many ticks? Two, four, six— help! Fourteen, I make it.'

'Fifteen, you're forgetting the suede dinner dress. Cherry Ripe. You've got to have that, it's the only halter neck.'

'Rupert, it's much too many. It looks so greedy.'

'I lose all patience! I really do! The whole collection if madam so desires, that's what Sam said.'

'Yes, but half the stuff I haven't got anywhere to wear them.'

'First rule of life. Never underdress, otherwise you end up sitting at home. Two, look as though you ought to be *somewhere* grand and soon you'll find you are.'

'Sounds pretty trite to me.'

'Trite but true, dear heart.'

'Anyway . . .'

'Anyway. Grab it whilst the going's good. It isn't always there. Well, look at poor me—stranded at Streatham Hill. At my age!'

'Rupert.'

He turned a tragic face. 'Myopia?'

'Here comes the champagne. Let's drink to an early release.'

'And then we'll pin down Joe and present him with our choices.' He'd snapped out of it already.

'When do you think I can have them?'

'Depends.'

'On what?'

'Well, on whether the glossies have photographed them yet or not. Whether there's another show for clients or another for overseas buyers, lots of things. You can't take them off the models' backs just like that, darling.'

'How disappointing. I'm going to Paris on Friday. I was hoping to have something new for that.'

'Paris, how divine. For long? Oh, I *shall* miss you.'

'Just for the night.'

'Oh naughty! With Sam or am I being indiscreet?'

'Yes.'

'Which?'

'Indiscreet.'

'With another! Oh, my dear. You must tell me who.'

'Perhaps I won't.'

'Spoilsport! Is he rich too? Oh, what a silly billy question! You don't know.'

'Actually I don't. But as far as I know, not.'

'In that case, he's rolling. Or famous?'

'No, honestly, Rupert.'

'Sure to be!' He held up a hand to silence me. 'Let's find Joe.'

We found him but he was surrounded.

'Aren't they ghastly, these sycophants?' Rupert murmured.

'Well, at least we're here on business,' I replied smugly.

Joe caught sight of us. 'Ah, here she comes.' He waved us in, people turned to look and make way.

'Well, my sweet, did anything at all catch your imagination? Tell me, which shred would you consider shrugging over your shapely shoulders?'

It was a tricky moment. Rupert came to the rescue.

'There wasn't one that she doesn't simply die to wear. We managed to whittle it down to a mere fifteen—but is it possible, do you suppose, Joe, to go further and duplicate all those in black as well?'

There wasn't a moment's hesitation.

'Black. Black sequins, satin, feathers, silk, black chiffon, cotton, leather, lace—magical, my angel.' He snaked a sinewy arm around my waist. 'What an utterly awful scamp, she glances at my collection and already predicts what my next will be.' Then he shrugged and laughed.

59

'No secret any longer. Let me see what you have chosen.'

He cast a practised eye down the list and gave a gurgle of pleasure. 'All my favourites. Oh, I couldn't be more pleased. Each a statement. Pure drama on you—what more could I have hoped for?'

He turned to an astonishingly well-groomed skeleton at his side, whose face, despite its glossy henna'ed hair and bright red mouth, brought 'beasts of the field' to my mind. Something about the fierce, wet, rolling eyes and long upper lip.

'Moo, my pet. Here's your answer. A superlative stroke. What could be more appropriate than to photograph my collection on this gorgeous girl. After all, the clothes will be hers. My latest client. "Personal Choice"—how about that for the heading?'

Rupert gave me a small shove. 'Myopia, this is Moo Moffat-Paw, the editor of *Chic*.'

She held out an icy claw, covered in sparkling rings, and drawled, 'Myopia! What a charming name! An invention?'

'Well, I'm actually called ...'

'I'm certain I'd prefer Myopia! It's a frantically bright idea, Joe. No need to look further. Impossible these days to get Dietrich. Elizabeth Taylor's far too fat. I myself am bored to distraction with black girls, however beautiful. It's about time we launched a new look. Gilbert shall do the face. You have beautiful bones, my dear. Are you Russian?'

'Willesden Welsh,' I said quickly. 'But I do know about photos.' I could feel nervous perspiration exploding out of every pore. 'I always look dreadful in photos. Everybody says so.'

Everyone stared at me appraisingly. I sucked my stomach in as much as I could.

'Ideal,' said the awful Moo. 'Not too young, not too old. An age for our readers to identify with.'

'Well, Moo, and which photographer?' said Joe.

Rupert pinched me. 'Myopia's off to Paris in a day or two, so you'll have to fit around that!'

He was pushy! As if I spent my whole time flying around the world!

'Lopasto's in London. He was working for *Vogue* yesterday. We could try him.'

'Or Pustansky?'

'Oh, I don't get on with Germans, not at all,' I said. 'And they never . . .'

Joe snapped his fingers. 'We need womanly warmth, the elusive aura, sensuality.'

Moo's liquid eyes began to leak. 'Mystery, Mother Earth, and her Modern Wardrobe, no—not Earth Mother—the Mood of the Moment. Garibaldi—clothes for the Gadabout Goddess. Oh, it writes itself, Joe.'

'A woman photographer, that's what it needs, Simpatico. Strength. Moo! How about Jan Crump?'

'Frightful creature. Far too butch. Makes everyone look like a lorry driver. Oh no! But you're right. A female.' She tapped her teeth with a crimson talon. 'Tammy Sprigg. A new girl but too pop. Lawn Adone—too fey, far too.'

Joe threw his hands in the air at exactly the same moment as Rupert. They looked at each other and burst out: 'Damson!' Moo looked at me dubiously. 'Ought we to?'

'Ideal,' they chorused. 'Exactly right!'

'Why did that awful woman say "Ought we to"?'

'Darling?'

'Rupert, you heard.'

'Who, Moo? That rhymes: Moo Who! Who Moo!'

'Why? What's she like, this Damson?'

'Divine. A fantastic photographer. Uses animals a lot. Myths and legends stuff. She'll probably pose you being ravaged by a pig or with bees swarming on bare breasts.'

'What—in my new clothes? I don't want them spoilt.'

'Or I'm not sure she's not passed on from animals.'

'To what?'

'Well, you'll soon know on Friday. They're frightfully lucky to get her. She works all over the world now. Must be fate that you're both going to be in Paris on the same day.'

'Yes, but I wasn't going till the evening. I'm not sure what who I'm going with will say to travelling separately. I mean, that's half the fun of it, the going together, isn't it?'

'Don't be silly, darling, you can meet him there. You mustn't start having second thoughts now. You'll be famous after Damson's photographed you. Everyone always is. Don't you remember the ones she did of Princess Margaret?'

'Why did Moo say "Ought we to" then? Because of the animals?'

'Just one dyke distrusting another, my darling. Nothing for you to worry your beautiful head about.'

When I got home there was a telegram waiting for me. Unsigned, but I knew who from. 'Paris cancelled. Deirdre dead.' It was in the early editions of the evening papers. 'Saddle Tragedy.' 'Political Hostess Dies Hunting.' 'Broken Neck for Earl's Daughter.' With snaps of Charles hurrying from the House of Commons looking grief-stricken, when, by what he'd said to me about her, he was probably overjoyed. Oh dear, what with one thing and another! I thought about going to bed with a cup of tea to think about things but there seemed too much of it to take in at one go. So instead I left a note for Françoise and walked up the road to the cinema where I wouldn't have to think at all. It didn't even matter much to me what film was on. It was the getting in there I liked most, the seedy glamour, the scented warm, the comfy seats, sitting in the middle of a crowd and getting lost. It never worried me either if I went in halfway. I always stayed to see it through again anyway. That's where going with other people spoilt it. Always, 'Come on, let's go, this is where we came in.'

I paid my money and went to the cheapest seats, right in the front row, between two teenagers and an old-age pensioner. Swallowed up by the screen, in the thick of things. A tear as wide as a river flowed from a bright blue eye, the soundtrack was very sweet, lots of strings with a sob in them. The teenagers were kissing like mad, and the old-age pensioner was snoring so I knew it must be a Romantic Love Story. Just my sort of thing, especially if it all went wrong. That's what pleased me most. One of them killed off. Like Deirdre. Except that now thinking about that, which was what I was trying not to do, I wasn't pleased a bit. It had a feel of crisis to it. Things to be decided upon. Resolved. Oh well.

When the interval came, I ignored the calories and bought an ice-cream but after the first mouthful my mind flew to Friday's photographs and to wondering whether I'd fit into the clothes or not. So I stopped eating and put the almost full tub carefully under my seat. The old-age pensioner had woken up and was watching. I stood up and headed for the ladies'. When I came back he was licking his fingers, the empty tub rolling by his feet. I nodded and smiled.

'Nice stuff, ice-cream.'

'What?'

'I say, it's very nice, isn't it?'

He stared at me as if I wasn't all there.

'Ice-cream, the taste. But unfortunately fattening.'

He was terribly thin. I was still blushing when the lights went down.

I walked home slowly, stopping now and then to look in shop windows. The delicatessen had trapped a fly for the night in a large cheesecake. The upholsterer's was full of nude sofas, calico coloured, waiting to be loose-covered in an assortment of fabrics, customer's own choice. The TV shop had all its tellys on with the sound switched off. Several people stood on the pavement in front of the flickering screens, lip-reading and laughing at the jokes.

I crossed the road. The nice old-fashioned chemist's had had a face-lift, all its frontage ripped out and replaced by sheet glass, top to bottom. Inside they had a fitted carpet. One half of the window was devoted to cosmetics, seductive photos of sullen girls with sly eyes. The other presented the alternatives. Hot-water bottles, laxatives, weighing scales and dietary aids.

Life in the launderette was in full swing. Oh, I would have given my eye teeth for such a meeting place in my bedsitter days! Taking your pick as you're packing in your undies, smouldering away all through the second wash, exchanging shy smiles at the dry-spinning stage. Afterwards a nice walk home, dropping in for a drink in the pub on the way. Not, I suppose, that I would really have found it so nice then. After all, my sights had been set on higher things—night clubs, sports cars, meeting men with cultivated tastes like that.

The chandelier shop was adrip with diamond lights. I'd been passing the place for years, identical arrangements, nothing ever changed. How the hell did they keep going without selling, unless it was just a front for shadier dealings? I had a soft spot for chandeliers, very big ones the size of a small room. Nothing in it but that—if you could spare the space. With electric fans to keep it on the tinkle. And a feather duster tied to a broom handle for reaching the top.

My toes were beginning to ache, well it was ages since I'd eaten. I could do with a drink, I thought, as I reached the top of my street. And a steak and two sliced tomatoes icy cold from the fridge, then getting into bed with a bottle of wine and a book. Three cigarettes left, I worked it out, from my ten-a-day discipline. Not bad going. I smiled at the comfortable hours ahead. A passing neighbour, whom I'd never spoken to, smiled back. I looked at my watch, eight o'clock, time to catch the girls before they fell asleep.

Paul was a marvel at precision parking. His car, just so, sat evenly cheek to kerb, mine in urgent need of a wash, one wheel on the pavement, sprawled wantonly behind it.

Françoise rushed to the door as I turned the key.

'Your 'usband he wait hours.' She rolled her eyes and pointed to my room. My heart lurched, but I said calmly, 'I'll say good night to the children first.'

The television was on in my room, swivelled round so that it faced my bed.

'You can go out if you like, Françoise. I'm staying in tonight,' I said.

'Oh yippee. I go right now.'

Paul's eyelids flickered as she slammed the front door behind her. He was lying fast asleep across my bed, hands folded neatly like a knife and fork on his long flat stomach. Upstairs, our daughters, also asleep, looked exactly the same. I'd kissed them both, but they hadn't stirred. I wouldn't risk it with him. It was three years since I'd kissed him last. And then, without any heart in it. More hate than heart. Which as far as the kissing went and what came after was all to the good. But it had made bed a violent greedy playground. Full of guilt on his side, and seething suspicion on mine, softened only by the pillows. Nowadays with sexual indifference set like cement between us it was all very hard to recall. But he had a big one. On that my memory served me well. A mighty sword! The size to confound King Arthur! John Thomas the Terrible. Perhaps that's why he'd needed others as well as me. To help empty the outsize tank. An unpaid team of pumpers.

I laughed out loud, mirth had replaced misery, and he woke immediately. Irritable like a child.

'What's there to grin about? I nodded off. You were out,' he added accusingly.

'Yes.' I was about to explain but why the hell? 'Yes, I was out. It's true.'

64

He lit a cigarette, coughed and ran his fingers through his hair.

'Ooh,' I said, 'it's starting to recede.'

'Don't be cruel.'

'It happens to everyone. I'm sure mine is too.'

He rubbed his eyes and yawned. 'God, I feel awful.'

'Go and have a wash. That will wake you up.'

'I'll have a drink instead. What have you got?'

'Everything.'

'Jack Daniel's?'

'No, I haven't got that.'

'Glenfiddich?'

'No.'

'Just whisky, any will do,' he said wearily. 'Lots of ice. I assume that's not asking the impossible.'

'It's foolish to assume anything with children in the house,' I said annoyingly, as I went out. Hell, I thought, it ought to be possible to be more pleasant than this.

I handed him the brimming glass, ice clinking invitingly, and managed to spill some on his trouser leg.

'There. Take a swig of that.' Perfectly pleasantly.

He mopped his wet leg with a pristine handkerchief.

'It's remarkable how accurately you combine the sailor's barmaid jargon with the expected degree of slap-happy service.'

All right then. Right. 'I think I'll light up,' I said. 'Now where are my fags?'

'Would you care for one of mine?' He leaned forward over-politely and snapped open his Asprey's gold case.

'What? Gauloises?' I said coarsely. 'Give shocking halitosis. Where I was last week a man emptied the whole bar with his bad breath. He was smoking Gauloises. No, I'll stick to my own. Less anti-social.'

We both of us stared somewhere over the other's head. He cleared his throat and coughed, again.

I looked at him. He swallowed hard.

'Is something wrong? You're clearly nervous.'

He sighed heavily and said sarcastically, 'Since when has the need to expectorate indicated neuritis?'

'Oh. Well, you can spit in the ashtray if you want to.'

Another silence. Then, 'Is it deliberately done to irritate?'

'What, Paul?'

'This assumed vulgarity. Is it for my benefit alone?'

I thought for a moment. 'You've twigged it. Yes, I think it is. And your offensive pomposity. Is that for mine?'

'Possibly so. I apologise.'

'That's all right. Don't apologise. Just say sorry. Your glass is empty. Would you like another?' Whenever was he going?

'Sorry. Please. I'd love a second.'

We both spoke as I was pouring.

'What ...'

'What ...'

'Sorry, you go.'

'No, you, mine's not important.'

Well, in that case, I was wondering what your plans for dinner were.'

'Who, mine?'

'There wouldn't, unless my eyes deceive me, appear to be another person present.'

'You're at it again.'

'So I am.'

'It's a bad habit. Is that how you speak to everyone now?'

'I need you to puncture me. I always have.'

Whatever was he working up to?

'No plans, really. Except an early night. Yes, you're better deflated.'

'I hadn't meant to make it late myself. I just have several matters to discuss. Best done over dinner. Where would you like to go?'

'Would have to be near. I've just given Françoise the night off.'

'Near or far, what difference does it make? It's highly improbable that you'll be able to perceive the house from your plate or for that matter hear piteous infant screams, should they occur above the chomping of surrounding Chelsea jaws.'

'Are you pleased with that?'

'Modesty prevails,' but he allowed himself a small smile.

I laughed. 'Come on then. But I'd still prefer nearer. If the house burns down, it'll look better if I can say I was out posting a letter.'

We were in bed by the time Françoise returned. I heard her switching the lights off as she went up the stairs, listened

66

to the gasping lavatory cistern, and in the silence that followed, looked at the illuminated hands of the alarm. Paul lay fast asleep in my arms. Half past twelve. We'd been there exactly an hour. He was still in me, slippery and warm, as soft now as the tongue in my mouth. Yes, he was still there. His cheek lay on my left breast, the happy damp nipple resting between his open lips. Like a baby, fallen asleep in mid-feed. I smiled in the dark. The sort of smile that model mothers do when they're selling washing powder on the television. Indulgent, understanding, ever-loving and very kind. Which was exactly how I felt. Oh, I wouldn't have at one time, even so much as up to a year ago. But now I had more than one egg in my basket. That's what made the difference. I stirred slightly and stroked his head. He clamped his lips together and started stucking, his hand on my other breast, slowly tightening, relaxing, then tightening again. No. I would have been cold and resentful at even the sign of an approach. Well, he'd tried before and I had been exactly that. I'd thought, 'Being made use of, after all that's happened, he still wants to make use of me.' But tonight it had happened quite naturally. Without any fuss. Truth was we'd made use of each other. Equals. He'd caught my eye, over the carré d'agneau, but in fact had been consciously courting me all through the avocados. He'd caught it and wouldn't let go.

'It says everything, that look,' I said at last.

'What does it say?'

'It says animal lust.'

'Oh, I'd put it more daintily than that.'

'There's no need. I can read.'

I still hadn't made up my mind by then.

'You're trying to seduce me.'

'Because you're so seductive.'

'Am I?' I said. 'I'm not trying a bit.'

But by the end of the crême brulée, I'd decided, as well he knew. I looked round the restaurant, everyone was at it, all couples holding hands, bending heads together, whispering. Thrumming with love. Very catching. Our legs lay lightly touching underneath the long tablecloth. Mine were stretched out and crossed at the ankles. His were either side of them, tightening all the time.

'Do you do it the same?' I said. 'Or have you learnt lots of new tricks?'

67

'Brandy, darling?'

'I've learnt some. You'll have to tell me after if you see a difference.'

'Hardly romantic.'

'Oh, I don't like that any more. Sighing and stuff. People only do that when they can't think of what to say. It's a question of age. It's normal to be inarticulate when you're young. But by our age you can get closer with words.'

'Though not necessarily comparisons.' He took my hand and kissed it. 'This feels the same.'

'There you are, that's a comparison.' I was hot and getting bothered down below, sipping my brandy. I sat on my chair, my insides lurching around impatiently. For two pins I'd have stripped everything off there and then. Stood up, stretched over and stuffed both breasts in his mouth at once. Pinned him down with a naked knee, unzipped him quick and yanked it out ...

'Oh dear,' I said in the end.

He squeezed my fingers. 'Anything up?'

'I've got a feeling I'm oozing. Preparatory lubrication. Quite beyond my control, my genitals are one jump ahead.'

'How extraordinary. So are mine. Slip your shoe off quickly, you can feel it with your foot.'

'That's all very well,' I said with some concern. 'But I just hope I haven't leaked through my dress. Don't laugh. They're very funny at the dry cleaner's. They won't take stains they don't understand.'

Paul. I lay there cuddling him, thinking fondly of Sam and Charles. It's easy to love men, all of them, when one is asleep in your arms. It's when you haven't got any that you hate them. I'm like a pond, I thought, with sun shining or rain falling, grey mists or just dark blackness and these are things which happen to change my surface. But at the bottom, it's solid, solid earth which is never affected at all. A fish pond. These men, my children, they were fish who happened to be swimming through me. One day I'd be empty, but not until I dried up altogether.

He woke suddenly, bathed in an unexpected fine sweat. I put a low light on at the side of the bed and he buried his face in my shoulder.

'Paul.'

'I'm boiling. There's no air.'

I threw the bedclothes back and in the sudden movement I lost him. He'd slipped out leaving a purring, sticky space. His long body glistened palely all over.

'You're all of a sweat. It's pouring off.'

I slipped a finger underneath his arm, then sniffed it.

'It's got a lovely smell. Very fresh. Like young cats.'

He squeezed me. 'How do you feel?'

'Rather philosophical. And fanciful. I think I've gone a bit funny.'

'A cup of coffee?'

'That might pull me round.'

'I'll do it, shall I?'

'Everything's in the same place. Can you remember?'

I sat up and lit a cigarette. How friendly it was! Friendlier than for years. Just because I'd given in—gracefully—or rather, grabbed what I'd wanted. But when he came back he said, 'We haven't talked yet.'

'So we haven't.'

He didn't look at me. 'I'm thinking of getting married again.'

The coffee slid smoothly down my throat, just the right amount of milk in it. 'When?'

'Next Monday morning. Will you be free? I thought it would be nice if you brought the girls.'

Now he did look at me, anxiously, like a child who's not quite certain how the adult will react.

'Is she expecting?'

'Good Lord, no. Nothing like that. I've made it quite clear I don't want any more!'

'Have you known her long?' All the time I was asking I was trying to think how I felt. Wise like a Mother Superior. Being begged for a blessing. Very heady, ego-boosting. They had some perks in their business, those nuns.

'Long enough.'

'And how long is that?' I was in fear of overdoing it. Too much concern and knowingness.

'About three weeks.'

'Ah,' I said, all understanding. 'Love at first sight.'

He kissed my lips, took the coffee cup from my hands, put it on the floor and held me tightly. 'Will you come?'

'Well now,' I said in a businesslike way. 'Monday, I can't because of Brighton.'

'How is the old bastard?'

'Getting older,' briefly, 'but the girls could. I can get them ready before I go. They will have broken up for Easter.'

'That's the other thing. I'd thought of flying off somewhere and taking them too.'

'What? On your honeymoon?'

'It'll kill two birds with one stone. I've been promising them a holiday for ages. I'd thought of Greece.'

'What does she say?'

'Oh, she's not politically minded.'

'About the girls coming.'

'She'll love the idea. She's seen them from a distance and adores them already. She's mad about the house too,' he added.

'Is she? Are you thinking of moving in?'

'Why? Do you feel like a change?'

'I hadn't. But you never know. Anything could happen, couldn't it?'

He kissed me again. 'That's what I admire about you. Your attitude to life.'

Next morning with the sun streaming through every window and the house inside humming with hilarious excitement, I wondered exactly what my attitude to life was. That was the trouble. I didn't have one. Just an awful eagerness to please.

Françoise was on the phone to France. I was paying her fare and she was going home for a fortnight. On Monday. Everything will happen on Monday.

'Will we be bridesmaids? Shall we have special dresses? And carry flowers? Is she pretty, Daddy's wife? I'm going to call her Mummy.'

We got to the school just as Harriet's teacher was walking in.

'Good morning, Harriet,' I heard her say stiffly.

'My daddy is getting married on Monday. I'm going to be his bridesmaid.'

'Are you indeed? And where is your Good morning?' Old misery!

I bought all the papers on the way back to read about Charles. Now an eligible widower, of course. I was just settling down to it when he rang. I couldn't think what to say.

'I was just reading your name. Isn't that funny?'

'You got my telegram.'

'I did. How are you feeling?'

'I must see you.'

'Of course. I'm here.'

'This evening?'

Sam was back by then. 'No, I'm afraid not tonight.'

'Surely you can.' He was cross.

'No, I don't see how. It's a bit short notice. Sorry.'

'Tomorrow then.'

'Oh dear, I shall probably be in Paris after all, tomorrow. You see, I'm doing sort of fashion shots ...'

'Fashion shots?'

'Yes, for *Chic* magazine.'

'Really, darling. I'd rather you didn't. The whole situation has changed now, don't you see? You'll have to start being a little more responsible for your actions. You must remember I'm in the public eye.'

Everything was on roller skates, flashing by, going far fast.

'They'll be very respectable, honestly. Not in the nude or anything like that. She's a marvellous photographer.' I thought of the animals and stuff. 'She's done Princess Margaret.'

'What time will you be back?'

'It depends how long it all takes.'

'Here's a number to ring. I'll expect to hear from you at about five o'clock tomorrow to say which plane you're catching.'

'All right. But Charles, how are you feeling?'

'I'll talk to you tomorrow. But ...'

'Yes?'

'I'll tell you something. I need you very much.'

Oh dear. Would I let him down? I walked round the house, opening the windows. I felt suffocated. In the children's room, I started sorting through their clothes. 'Go to Harrods,' Paul had said, 'for anything they'll need. Put it on my account.' Kneeling on the floor I began a list. Sandals, swimsuits, knickers, vests. No, not vests, not in Greece. I crossed vests out. Summer nighties, sleeveless towelling beach robes. Do as dressing-gowns when they got back. New toothbrushes. Who would see to it they cleaned their teeth? Will they be all right? Will you be? you mean. Two weeks alone. I lay flat on the floor and looked at the ceiling. It had looked wonderful when it was done.

Bright red. Fiesta, that's what they called it on the colour chart. I'd have liked it all through the house. Now it looked tired and old as if all the life blood had been drained away. The fiesta had flopped. It needed doing up, the house, needed licking with soft brushes and coaxing with hot coats of colour. That's what I could do, get the decorators in. I sat up, then slid back again. But not if I wasn't going to stay. I wouldn't mind a move, the more I thought about it the more I could see that I wouldn't mind. And this time wherever I went I could have whatever colours I wanted. All black or gold or silver. An emerald green from top to bottom. Like my sequinned dress from Garibaldi. God, I promised to ring Moo Moffat-Paw.

I made a cup of tea and took it to the phone. '*Chic*? Miss Moffat-Paw, please. Oh sorry, Mrs.' How could she be Mrs if Rupert said she was a lesbian?

'Myopia? Well, all set for the morning, my dear?'

'There's been a slight alteration. In actual fact, I won't now be going to Paris.'

She screamed so loudly that I had to hold the telephone right away from my ear. When I put it back she was still gurgling. It sounded like a death rattle. What an hysterical creature she was!

'Just a minute, I haven't finished.' I spoke calmly as if to one of the children. 'I mean to say that I am still free to go but I'd like to have it clarified as to who will be making all arrangements and meeting the expenses.' I enjoyed saying it. Very hard and businesslike.

She screamed again. A ghoulish attempt at girlishness. What a difficult woman to live with!

'My dear. These are minor matters. My minions will deal with those. The important thing is that you're free, to go to Paris of course, I mean. We have four glorious colour pages depending on you. Now, what time today will you be coming in? I'd like to try everything on and choose which outfits we'll take.'

I hadn't thought of it, but of course she'd be coming too. 'This afternoon?'

'Around three. You know where we are, off Berkeley Square. By the way, what shoe size are you? Not that necessarily we'll be going down that far, knowing Damson, she's rather keen on close-ups, but it's best to play safe.'

'I'm size four.'

'What a tiny toes! This afternoon then. Don't forget your passport. We need that to arrange francs. Apart from that, you may take your choice. Either be paid a normal modelling fee or, if we use your name and do it as a personality piece as we've discussed, be paid nothing at all.'

'I'll think about it, can I?'

'Of course, though if you're wise, you'll choose the latter. Such a lovely name to see in print "Myopia".'

We sat in the garden discussing it, Rupert and me. He'd rung the doorbell as I'd put down the phone.

'Oh, how nice. Just who I was hoping to see.'

'You don't mind me dropping in? A terrible cheek, I know, without phoning first. But I just happened to be passing in a taxi!'

We both knew that he'd taken the tube specially from Streatham on the off-chance that I'd be in, but it made no odds.

'I'm at such a loose end, Myopia. It's awful.'

'Oh dear, let's go outside and sit down, you can tell me all about it.'

He plopped into a blue and white striped deckchair. He was wearing white trousers and an open-necked white shirt, and around his neck he'd knotted the sleeves of his sweater, the colour of forget-me-nots. I smiled because he looked so perfect, like an illustration in a women's magazine. The handsome hero. Or one of those men in knitting pattern books.

'Smile, Rupert.'

He tried. He opened his sculptured mouth, and pulled his lips back to show the stunning teeth. 'You should be a model, you'd be very good at that.'

He let his mouth relax, back into its about-to-cry look, and shook his head so that one blond lock fell over his eyes.

'I've tried. I've been with Boy's Agency for nearly two years, but they never get me anything. Now I'm getting too old, that's the trouble; when they took me on I still looked about seventeen.'

'How old are you?'

'Twenty-six. Isn't it appalling? There seems to be nothing left now. Nothing to look forward to.'

73

'What? At twenty-six? Don't be silly. Looking like you do?'

'That's all I've got though. I've never had anything else. I used to want to be an actor. I did a year at drama school, but in the end they told me it was a waste of their time and mine.'

'But people can be late developers. Anyway, there are lots of jobs you could do. Where it wouldn't depend on your looks, Rupert.'

'What? Like what?'

'Well, I always think if the worst came to the worst I'd be a lavatory attendant. They take anyone for that. You don't need qualifications. But I think you have to be over eighteen. Perhaps it's twenty-one. It could be very nice because you have a little room for making tea and there'd be a regular clientele and all you'd have to do is train yourself to breathe through your mouth. So as not to be able to smell anything. I've trained myself already from changing babies' nappies. It's the first thing all mothers learn. You could say you were a civil servant, if people asked.'

'Oh, you are funny, Myopia. It's a tonic just to be with you.'

'You think I'm joking, but I'm not at all.'

He stretched his legs, lay back and closed his eyes.

'This sun. Oh, it makes me die to be on a beach. Doesn't it you?'

I stared up through the branches of a tree. New spring leaves patterned the sky like a paper doily. 'It would be nice.' I imagined a smooth sea, crinkled at the edges like a lettuce leaf, sucking on fine bleached sand. Shining like a strip of sheet metal, disappearing into a distant sun-bright silver sky. And everywhere the smell of bronzing oils and melting ice-cream. Transistors crooning Latin love songs. Lots of bouncing going on, beach balls, babies, big-breasted women and boys with barely covered buttocks. 'I like lively beaches best,' I said, 'with everyone sandwiched in like sardines.'

'Oh, so do I.'

'Do you? I somehow thought you'd prefer secluded spots. A private beach with a motor launch and a waiter in a white coat serving chilled champagne.'

'I've done all that. But if you don't like who you're with it's no fun at all.'

No. That's what I kept telling Jean but she wouldn't have it. 'I don't want a repeat of Paris, Jean,' I'd said.

'What do you mean? We had a super time!'

'Me saddled with the sugar daddies and you getting off with good-looking gigolos.'

She sighed. 'They were marvellous at making love.'

'Of course they were. The tools of the trade.'

'We ended up staying at the Georges Cinq.'

'With me as bait. Me paying the price. That old man there was disgusting, what's more what he did was very dangerous. Sticking that strip lighting in. He could have killed me.'

'It didn't sound very nice when you said.'

'It's not how I'd thought of losing my virginity, not by neon.'

'Mine was by moonlight. We left the window wide open. I could see the stars over his shoulder.'

'Yes, and that's another thing. On my new red towel, why couldn't you have used your own?'

'What, my white one? I wouldn't have dared. Mummy would have guessed the worst if I'd brought it home all bloody.'

'Well, now we're experienced women we must learn to pick and choose this holiday.'

We were on the plane to Italy. I'd saved for the student trip by working the summer at the local Odeon. Usherette and ice-cream girl. Spot-lit at every interval. I'd sold 420 choc bars, 310 vanilla tubs, smuggled my parents in twice without paying and seen Walt Disney's *The Living Desert* eighteen times from start to finish. My neck was still aching from carrying the tray. While Jean had been fishing in Scotland with her father.

We sucked on the barley sugar we'd been given for take-off. 'Was it nice in Scotland?' I thought of husky young lairds in shooting brakes, wearing hacking jackets and checked Viyella shirts. Strong like Heathcliff, striding over the heather in stone-coloured cavalry twills, and canary yellow socks.

'Not a sausage. Nothing in sight. I could have done with a couple of kilts and a strong wind I can tell you.'

'What, no men at all?'

'Only Daddy's unutterably dreary friends. Chartered accountants and quantity surveyors. That sort of thing. With their wives. They used to send me to bed after dinner, can you imagine! I'd have died of boredom but I found this book. I've brought it. It's filthy. *The Life and Loves of Frank Harris*. Just our cup of tea.'

We spent the rest of the journey sussing out the others and came to the same conclusion. No competition amongst the girls and nothing to write home about in the boys. Really nothing, but we let them carry our cases. Two Japanese students from Oxford were the most attentive. They both wore grey flannels, white stiff-collared shirts and serge blazers with badges on the breast pockets, which looked exactly the same as our Co-op Darts Team. My father had one.

'I didn't know they let Chinks into Oxford,' I whispered to Jean. 'Is it a new thing?'

'They're Japs, not Chinks. Look at what their cameras cost. Made of money.'

Hers was short and fat with slicked back shiny hair which smelt of Lily of the Valley. Mine was short too, but made from pipe cleaners, his wrists were the width of my thumb. I wondered what he had in his trousers. Something the size of a cotton thread I supposed. 'I wish they'd stop smiling. We haven't seen their eyes yet. Not once.' But she would keep encouraging them, Jean.

'It's not as if our cases were even heavy.' We were in our hotel room, unpacking.

'Honestly, you can't see further than your own nose.'

She unzipped her skirt and put on a pair of dangerously short pink cotton shorts.

'Jean!' I said horrified. 'You're not wearing those.'

'Why not?'

'They're shorter than your knickers! I can see them at the back.'

'Can you? I'll take my knickers off then. There, how's that?'

'All right. If you don't bend over.' But I still had my doubts. 'It's a good job your pubic hair isn't any longer. Otherwise wearing those you'd have to plait it up and sellotape it to your stomach or something.'

'I could just shave it off.'

'You have to be careful. You can get a nasty rash with a razor. I've tried it.'

'What's it look like?'

'Very naked. Like a big baby with a nappy rash.'

76

'Better with a bit of fur.'

'The point is they could come in useful if we wanted to go somewhere ritzy. That's what I'm thinking of.'

'Those shorts?'

'The Japs. Places where they won't serve girls on their own. Where we couldn't afford to go anyway. They're loaded those two.'

'But I'd like someone to fall in love with this time.'

'Yes, but not stuck on the beach with this lot all the time. You'd like to go in a speedboat, wouldn't you? Laze about on a yacht? Sit on the sun terrace of a grand hotel? Swim in their pool and get dressed up for a night club?'

'Well ...'

'Well, all that means men with money. Leave it all to me. I understand how these things work.'

'You do,' I said. 'It's easy to see your father's an accountant, I must say.'

She came over and gave me a squeeze.

'Look, this is our holiday. Don't let's quarrel. We've got ten days. Long enough to do it all. Have a fling and fall in love. Both of us, I promise.'

'What about going then? The two of us, Rupert? Next week?'

He lay in his deckchair, eyes shut, lashes as long as bootlaces. Like a beautiful corpse. 'Are you dead?' I asked after a while. 'Did you hear me?'

The tears slid out like tadpoles, separately formed yet still joined together. Leaving a shiny transparent path, they travelled his cheeks and melted into his mouth. I just sat forward and stared. I was fascinated to see if his nose would start running and spoil things. It wasn't till I looked at his hands, knotted together, nails digging in, that I knew he must be making a big effort to control himself. I went indoors and came back with a brandy.

'Nice big brandy,' I said. 'And a tea towel to mop up with. You can blow in it, I shan't mind. I haven't got a hanky.'

That did it. He started to laugh and within seconds was sobbing, shaking all over and shuddering to catch his breath. It's best to let go when things get beyond you, the only way in the end to keep your balance. I lit a cigarette and wandered a few steps to see how my daffodils were doing. When the worst was over, I came back. He cleared his throat, a congested sound like the gear box of a car in need of a service.

'I feel so bad ...'

'No, you don't. You feel much better now.'

'In front of you ...'

'Oh me! Oh, I'd far rather see a scar than a stiff upper lip. Go on, have a sip of brandy.'

He blew his nose in the tea towel, one I'd bought with the children in Carnaby Street. It was printed with a map of London Underground. 'At a rough guess, I'd say you've just blown your nose in Leicester Square Station.'

He didn't look, just kept his finger and thumb squeezed on the spot.

'I'd say more like Baker Street, myself.' He spread it out. 'Too late to change your mind. Both wrong. Chancery Lane!'

'Well, what about it? Don't start looking sad again.'

'What would it cost? I can't ...'

'Cost? Who cares? I've got some money. We can go on that. No need to do it in high style. All we want is a bit of brown on our bodies, isn't it? Just what you need, it'll buck you up no end.'

'But it isn't right, you paying.'

'Why not? It's only luck that at this moment I have something in the bank and you haven't. Next year or even next month, it could be the other way around, couldn't it? And then I can come and lean on you. If you'll let me. I never worry too much about money—there's always some way out.'

'I never used to either, but now I've begun to worry about everything. I've developed into a manic depressive.'

'Has the doctor given you pills?'

'Yes, but I've run out. I should go back for more.'

'Don't do that. See how you feel after our holiday.'

'All right then. You've talked me into it. We can sit on a beach and sort out my future.'

'That's it! And while we're at it, we can sort out mine too.'

I persuaded Rupert, since he seemed so persuadable, to come with me to Chic House. He could see I was having second thoughts without me saying. That's what he said. I wasn't at all, in fact. I was quite looking forward to it, but

78

it was still nice to have his moral support. I only had one big nagging worry. One that Rupert might have found it hard to understand. The stretch marks on my stomach. They'd come with Harriet and had got even worse after Fanny. We used to compare, other mothers and me, in the post-natal clinic. Mine were always the worst. 'Can't be helped,' the sister had said briskly, 'mere battle scars, with baby as bonus. Count yourself lucky they're not all over your breasts too.' But I was obsessive about them then. Until Sam. 'Christ almighty,' he'd thundered. 'What the hell are those? Lace curtains or a shoal of fish?' Then he'd seen my face. 'C'mon, honey. We can get round it. Tomorrow you go buy a corset and wear it in bed.' That relaxed me.

Not that they'd show in Joe's clothes, it was just that walking into *Chic*, that temple of perfection, I felt a fraud knowing they were there! The foyer was covered with big blow-ups of past copies. Centre spreads of beautiful girls in bikinis posing amongst bewildered peasants, nocturnal shots of flimsy nighties, floating through moonlit forests, a detailed study of fine-pored skin with a butterfly about to settle. The close-up of satin high-heeled shoes, arranged carefully amongst a pile of cripples' crutches.

'That's not in the best of taste is it?' I pointed.

Rupert glanced briefly. 'Herman Bosch. He always does things like that. Goldfish bowls full of glass eyes to show off false eyelashes. Frilly bridal suspenders on skeletons. He's said he won't work for *Chic* again, though.'

'Why not?'

'They refused to print his last lot of photos. The latest handbag by Dior. He'd shot it half-open but he'd filled it full of dentures!'

The commissionaire stared frostily as I started to laugh. Rupert pressed the lift button, it arrived immediately and we went up to the fourth floor. We were exactly on time.

The first thing that hit me was the smell. You could drown in it, like the perfume counter of an expensive store, like a room full of wealthy women, like a very high-class hairdresser's. Seducing you. A devastating bank of flowers faced us as we left the lift. I squeezed a petal as we passed to see if they were real. The carpet was as thick as double cream, peach. The walls were a sweet warm apricot. Giant free-standing lamps cast the sort of amber glow you get when children put a lighted torch in their mouth and shine it through their cheek. Seated against the wall were six or seven ravishing models, their specimen books by their side, each a perfect example of their type. One in sawn-off jeans and faded tee-shirt, a carefully painted spattering of freckles on her sunburnt face. Another aloof and olive-skinned. Two talking together in pillbox hats and platform soles. And next to them a milky blonde with mile-long legs and waist-length hair. All of them waiting, cross-fingered, for work. How horrible to be hanging on the whim of the Moo Moffat-Paws of the world. A receptionist, with the best ironed blouse I'd ever seen, looked up and smiled. When she spoke it sounded as if she'd just eaten a plate of hot buttered mushrooms and enjoyed them very much.

'Can I help you?'

I scooped up all the charm I could summon from my bloodstream and smiled back. Rupert answered and we were directed on our way. 'Here we are, darling.' He knocked on the door. 'The inner sanctum.'

'Step inside,' called a voice from within.

'Said the spider to the fly,' Rupert whispered to me.

It was just like walking into a flock of sheep. There was so much mirror set at adjacent angles, with Moo standing in them all. She had on a particularly unfortunate curly woollen thing, a cross between cream and fleecy grey. From its high-collared neck, her mournful head emerged as if all set for the slaughter. The upper lip looked even longer than I remembered; when it began to quiver I half expected a bleat.

'My God,' she moaned, 'it's been an absolute bitch of a morning! Myopia, my dear, you look exquisite, do sit down. Rupert! Just the boy! I've had such trouble with Damson. Tell me, how well do you know her?'

I took the cigarette she offered, allowed her to light it and looked around the room. A portion of it was partitioned off into a large walk-in wardrobe; through the open door I could see piles of shoes, handbags, hats. On a shelf, a glamorous paraphernalia of bracelets, beaded necklaces, space-age sunglasses, bottles of perfume and a huge conglomeration of cosmetics. And, hanging amongst masses of others, my clothes from Garibaldi. It was like looking in a sweet-shop window when you've already decided what to choose. You can taste it before it even touches your tongue. I could feel on my skin the peach bloom of soft suede, silk slithering like cold jelly, the fine imprint of hand-made lace. I sat there, glowing greedily, sheer self-indulgence like the sumptuous houri of a Turkish potentate. Or for that matter some curious clothes fetishist. The thought had not occurred before.

'Very well. I got to know her when I lived with Joe.'

So he had lived with Joe!

'Of course. And do you get on together?'

'Perfectly I'd say. Once you understand her there's no problem.'

'This morning I was tempted to cancel the whole operation. I spoke to her on the telephone, agreed to pay the fortune she's demanding, received her assurance that the photographs would be within reason. I mean, I can't print all that animal stuff. She said she quite understood but she'd prefer not to have me on the session! I'd send an assistant but unless she knows them it's quite on the cards she'd bar them entry too. It's ludicrous. Someone must take care of the clothes. Be responsible for the accessories. Organise everything.'

'What about Gilbert? Isn't he going to do Myopia's face?'

'That's another thing. She says his work is too hard. She's discovered a superb theatrical make-up man who's worked for years in the ballet and demands to use him. But it occurs to me, Rupert dear, that you might be the ideal person. Would you be free to go with Myopia tomorrow?'

'All expenses and a stylist's fee?'

'Naturally.'

'I couldn't think of anything nicer.'

'Oh, nor could I,' I said.

For the first time since our arrival Moo smiled, a frightening affair involving yards and yards of pale pink satin gum. I never thought to describe anyone as plain but with her it was the only adjective to use, coupled with the terrifying intensity, it made my eyes water just watching her. She stabbed a finger in my direction.

'Well, Myopia, dear, shall we start? I can't tell you, my dears, now everything's settled I'm quite limp with relief.'

We were there over two hours. Rupert was amazing.

'Invaluable,' Moo kept crying. 'Absolutely inspired.'

Joe Garibaldi would have gone mad as white was spiced with ginger, dove grey with petrol blue, pale lemon put with brilliant pink. All done by adding, switching, subtracting tiny handbags, outsize earrings, strings of beads, a well-placed brooch, a different hat.

'Won't Joe mind?' I said.

'Mind what, darling?'

'Well, that his outfits won't be photographed strictly as he presented them himself?'

'Good heavens no. Fashion photographs, especially in colour, are never meant to look like life. Larger than life, yes. They should be fantasy. That's why we're asking Damson to do these. To create a mood.'

'Oh dear,' I said. 'Am I the best person to use? I can look awfully ordinary.'

'You, never, and certainly not with the make-up her man will do. If we know Damson that will be the exact opposite of ordinary.'

'You'll keep an eye on that though, Rupert,' Moo said anxiously.

'We'll shoot it lots of ways,' he assured her.

'How about my hair? Should I wash it tonight or in the morning? It can go very frizzy if I leave it till the last minute.'

They both laughed and looked at each other.

'There'll be a hairdresser,' Rupert soothed. 'And at least a dozen divine wigs in every colour, I shouldn't be surprised.'

'I shan't know myself by the end.'

'Myopia,' Moo took my hand and set my flesh goose-pimpling. 'It will be the new you. Damson will do her damnedest to see to that.'

By the time I got home my period had started. Bloody blood! It hadn't been due for another two days. Brought on by excitement I shouldn't wonder.

Sam hadn't been able to believe it. He'd pulled me on to his knee and put a friendly hand between my thighs.

'Jumpin' Jesus! What the hell have you got in there? A loaf of bread or a leg of lamb?'

'That's my sanitary towel,' I'd said with as much dignity as I could. And primly put his hand away. I'd only known him a few weeks then.

'But it's as big as a fuckin' bolster! You mean to tell me that every month you're walking round with that in your pants! Christ!'

82

'I like them large. I find it a comfort.'

'But honey, those went out with the ark. Haven't you heard of internals?'

'I've tried Tampax, but I don't get on with them at all. It's like putting a white mouse in with his tail hanging out. A girl I knew mislaid one once. She forgot it was there, and went to bed with somebody and it got pushed up further and then went completely astray. She had to go to hospital in the end to have it surgically removed. They kept her there a week with complications.'

'Didn't she try blowing her nose or was she too stupid?'

'Anyway,' I went on, 'since I've had the coil fitted it seems like overloading to use Tampax too. They give me backache, with the congestion.'

'Aw, my baby! I love you and your little jam rags! You wear 'em all you want. Come on here to Daddy. I'm going to give my sugar an extra squeeze 'cos she's on the blob.'

He took a special delight in my periods, Sam. More than any man I'd met and certainly much more than me. It didn't put him off at all.

'Come quick,' I'd shouted to my mother.

She'd run up the stairs two at a time.

'I'm bleeding,' I said and started to cry. Ten I was. The first in my class.

'You're menstruating,' my mother had said matter of factly. 'Only two things to avoid. Head colds and hot baths. Remember that and you'll be all right. Now shush, you don't want your father to find out, do you?'

'This is something my mother always warned me against. She said on no account to do it.'

Sam lay back in the bath drinking pink champagne. He wasn't listening. 'Run some more hot, honey.'

'We can't have any more, it'll slop all over the sides.'

'Cuddle me. I'm getting cold. But don't for Christ's sake lose my cock.'

I was sitting on it, facing him, knees squashed in each side of his thighs.

'It's a terrible squeeze, Sam, in here.'

'Love it.'

'It's not as if you're a normal size man, they should build special ones.'

'C'mon, quit talking. I'm shrinking.'

He let his glass roll into the water and placed two huge hands on my bottom lifting it slightly then pressing down hard. Although we were under water my inside skin squeaked dryly against his.

'It doesn't make for as smooth a run as natural juices,' I said, then lay my head on his wet chest and just kept going.

I was freezing by the time we finished.

'Do you mind, Sam? I'm freezing.'

'Aw, honey, have a heart.'

'I have but it's gone cold.'

'Just a little longer, that's all I need.'

'It never is, though, Sam.'

'Five minutes,' he pleaded.

'Two then.' I looked at the clock above his head. 'But I'm timing it.'

'You frigid little cunt—who the hell could come with you anyway?'

He pulled me roughly towards him, stuck his tongue in my mouth, and continued heaving with renewed energy. Cold water slurped from side to side.

'You sound like a whale in a washbasin,' I laughed. 'Two minutes up—I'm pulling the plug out.' Then I sneezed.

He gave a roar of pleasure.

'Serve you right, you miserable girl. You should have listened to your mommy. I hope you've caught a fuckin' head cold.'

We towelled each other dry.

'Do you love me?'

'Ever so much, Sam.'

'What—an impotent, old, no-good screw like me?'

'I must be cracked.'

'Here, let me put your little nappy in place.'

'No, I'm trying a Tampax this evening. Just to get used to it for tomorrow.'

'What is all this "tomorrow" business?'

'I told you, Sam, I'm being photographed for a magazine.'

'What magazine again?'

'*Chic.*'

'Shit!'

'Why?'

'An unholy waste of time, honey.'

'Oh dear, I've said I'll do it now.'

'In hell's name, why?'

'Well, I suppose because they asked as much as anything.'

He sighed. 'You're a nice girl but it's time you grew up and learnt to say no to things you don't need.'

I sneezed again. Twice. 'I didn't need that bath.'

In the morning I woke up flooding, just in time to stop it soaking through to the mattress. So much for internal security!

I bundled the sheets up, put them in the laundry basket, made the bed up with clean ones and went to put the kettle on. Then I got back in with a cup of tea and thought about what Sam had said.

'It's about time to think ahead, kid.'

'Yes, where are we going tonight?'

'To the future.'

'I'm not taking LSD.'

'I'm too ancient a dog for all this crap.'

'What crap's that?'

'This getting out at ungodly hours for the sake of your fuckin' brats. Like some college kid creeping off with the dawn. Jesus, at fifty where's the dignity?'

'Jesus never was fifty.'

'Jesus was never dignified, for Christ's sake.'

'Fifty! In fifteen years' time you'll be an old-age pensioner, Sam.' I started to laugh.

'Yeah, and you'll be looking like my great grandmother. People will be saying "How come such a fine handsome guy gets stuck with such a lousy old crap bag for a wife?'

I stopped laughing.

In films the heroine always goes on. So does the young husband when he's told a little one's on the way. It doesn't sink in till six sentences later. Then it's 'Darling' and 'You mean' and a dawning comprehension in the eyes before the big melt.

But 'wife', it hit me right away. Wham. In both ears.

'I heard that,' I said.

'Then what did you say?' Rupert sat forward eagerly. We were on our way to Heathrow in the back of a car hired by *Chic*. It could have collected him first from Streatham but he hadn't wanted Moo to know that's where he was staying. So he'd come over to me in a taxi. When we left the girls were still asleep but I'd arranged for the same taxi to call back and take them to school later. Rupert had followed me as I tiptoed in to kiss them goodbye. It was the first time he'd seen them.

'What did I say? I didn't say anything much.'

'Except "yes", I hope.'

I looked out of the window. 'No, not even "yes".'

I could feel Rupert staring at me, sense his puzzled disbelief. Just how Sam had been. Thinking now of Sam's face a raw lump started aching in my throat. They have a wicked way of pleading, men. Even when they're not saying anything. It makes you do things you never dreamed you'd do and say reassuring, loving things which afterwards you're sorry you've said. Because you didn't mean them after all. This time I'd managed to keep my mouth shut. Imprisoned words which would have lit him up. Instead I'd enslaved him with unexpected doubts. And Charles would be the same. Why couldn't things just stay the way they were?

'Myopia! What are you thinking about now?' Rupert peered anxiously round.

I swallowed hard and cleared my throat. 'I was just thinking what a lovely friend you are. How uncomplicated things are between us. Is it because there's no sex involved?'

'There could be sex.'

'Could there?'

'There could be.'

'Oh. Have you ever been to bed with girls?'

'One. One girl.'

'What was it like?'

He raised his eyes and searched around. I prodded him with my handbag.

'What was it like? Rupert?'

'I'm looking for the word. Shush. I've got it. Ah! Obscene! Yes. It was obscene.'

We both laughed.

'Ooh darling,' he said shuddering. 'I've got goose pimples remembering.'

'There you are then, that's what I mean. Something like that wouldn't happen with us. The urge isn't there.'

'It might be different with you. For a start, you're much more mummyish.'

'Mummyish? Am I?'

'Not to look at, but you are inside. To look at you're quite the opposite. That's what's so attractive. The combination. I noticed you at that party long before we spoke.'

'Oh, did you? With all those people there?'

'But Myopia, you're gorgeous. Lots of people must have told you that.'

I lit a cigarette and thought back. Had they? 'Oh look, Chiswick,' I said suddenly. 'I love going on this flyover. You can see right into people's back gardens. Rupert, look. This side.'

'Ugh,' he said and shut his eyes.

'Don't you like it?'

'Loathe it. Depressing. Reminds me of Streatham. Cleaning the car, mowing the lawn and minding everybody else's business. Suburbia, darling.'

'Oh, I like looking at it. It's solid and safe. All the pieces fit, like a jigsaw.'

'Looking isn't living.'

'I didn't say living, did I?' Though on the other hand, I thought to myself, the mummyish side of me might find it very nice indeed. I smiled and stretched, then I yawned. 'Will you wake me up when we get there? I'm going to have five minutes.'

The clothes were packed in two large expandable suitcases. It worried me to see them whisked away after weigh-in. There were two young airline officials at the desk. One gazed steadily at me, the other at Rupert. Divide down the middle, just like with Jean. 'Are you sure,' I said to mine, 'that we can't take those as hand luggage, under the seat or something? I'd feel safer keeping an eye on them.'

They all laughed, Rupert too.

'Well,' I said to him. 'It will put the tin lid on things if they get lost. You won't laugh then.'

He took my arm. 'You're getting in a state. There's loads of time but let's go straight through. Have you got your passport? I'll buy you a drink.'

'I'm not in a state. Why should I be in a state?' I shook my arm free.

We didn't speak till we reached the departure lounge, where he steered me to the bar.

'What, at half past eight in the morning?'

'Decadent. Deliciously decadent. What will you have?'

'Pernod for Paris, I think. I hope I don't puke up on the plane.'

'I'll hold your paper bag if you do. You didn't say you were frightened of flying.'

'I'm not,' I said, drinking. 'Not at all. If it crashes, it crashes. That's what I keep thinking.'

'What, all the time you're in the air?'

'From the second I step on. I keep thinking of everything I should have done. Like making a will or saying what sort of funeral I'd like, all that sort of thing. Short flights are worse than long ones. On those you can at least sleep most of the way. Isn't it silly? I've never confessed it to anyone before.'

'Poor Myopia. We can come back by train if you like.'

'I'll be all right,' I said. 'Here, let me buy you another.'

'Gladly, if you find it a help.'

We boarded the plane in a cloudy yellow glow, completely reckless. I fastened my seat belt and watched the hostess mincing in the aisle, while another read out the life-saving instructions. I couldn't care less.

'Would people remember all that at the last minute?' Rupert turned to me.

'I wouldn't,' I said, 'I can never make head or tail of it. I can't now.'

A head of frizzy grey waves in front of me swivelled round, put her finger to her lips and frowned. I nudged Rupert and started giggling.

'Fusspot! First time up I shouldn't wonder,' he said loudly.

We were off the ground at last. I'd sung *You're the Tops* in my head twice all through take-off. Word perfect, start to finish. Easy peasy!

'I wonder what plane we'll be catching back, Rupert?'

'When?'

'Well, today of course,' I said, surprised.

'I wouldn't bank on that, darling.'

'But I've promised ...'

'Well you never know with Damson how long things will take. It will probably go into tomorrow. We've got enough money to stay the night. You can easily phone Sam.'

'Oh dear, I didn't bring my toothbrush. I shall have to buy one. It wasn't Sam I was thinking of.'

'The children then.'

'Oh the children, yes. Tomorrow I've got to buy them things for their father's honeymoon. And something to wear at his wedding.'

He raised his eyebrows.

'He's getting married on Monday. He asked me but I can't.'

'Marry him?'

'No, go. I have to go to Brighton on Mondays.'

'We'll be back by then. Can't he buy them himself?'

I thought about it. 'Don't see why not. He can take Françoise with them and do it together. Oh, aren't you clever? That was my chief worry.' I had Charles's number in my purse. 'The other I can sort out easily—I suppose.'

Unreliable, that's what he'd say. Irresponsible, that's what Paul would call me. Turning well-planned arrangements upside down at the last minute. Typical. I blew a raspberry which came out much louder than I'd intended. The man to the right of me looked up, astonished. I smiled at him alluringly so that he coloured up and quickly returned to the newspaper he'd been reading. Shy. A shy businessman. With two boys at prep school and a wife who played golf. I could have had a bit of fun with him, teasing till he wouldn't know where he was—but I couldn't be bothered. I snuggled down into my seat, pressed the button which shot it back to its lowest level and hit the head of the person behind, who'd been leaning forward.

'I say! Go easy!'

I shut my eyes. 'Good night, Rupert. See you in Paris.'

I shut my eyes. 'Good night, Rupert. See you in Paris.'

I dreamed I was flying. Running first, faster and faster, then leaping up, legs and arms doing the breast-stroke, like swimming. All along Oxford Street. High above Selfridge's and C&A, past John Lewis, right on to Oxford Circus, where I took a graceful curve, right into Regent Street. I glanced down when I got to Piccadilly. A crowd had gathered and was looking up. At me. I was naked from the navel down. I had a hat on, my Auntie Doreen's turquoise tulle and a home-made knitted jumper which didn't go at all. I pulled my knees up tightly over my stomach to try and hide my stretch marks and I tried to spread my toes to cover my crack, but they wouldn't go. They weren't long enough. Which only left my arms for

89

flying. I was breathless and beginning to cry as I felt myself falling.

'Fasten your seat belt, Myopia. We're nearly there.' Rupert shook me gently.

'My God,' I groaned, 'I dreamed I was flying.'

He raised one eyebrow. 'Hardly inventive.' Very dryly.

'You weren't there though. I had no knickers on. With a lot of people watching!'

He raised the other. 'Hardly the first time.'

'Oh shut up, you,' I said and started powdering my nose.

Our cases were the last to come out of the chute. We stood for ages watching everyone else's rotating around.

'About time,' Rupert said. He'd looked as anxious as me for a minute there.

'They did it on purpose, I expect,' I said. Airports make you like that, hostile.

We took a taxi from Orly. All the way in to Paris I kept saying, 'Gosh, this has changed.' In the end, Rupert was forced to ask, 'All right, you've been before. When?'

'When I was eighteen,' I answered promptly. 'You can work out for yourself how many years ago that was. I lost my virginity, as it happened, that time.'

'Nice?'

'Nasty. Very nasty. More obscene, I shouldn't wonder, than you and that girl. Really bad.'

'No fear of losing it this time.'

'Will we have any adventures do you think?'

'Sexual ones?'

'It seems a waste to be in Paris and not have anything happen.'

'Something always happens when Damson's around. You'll see.'

'I keep trying not to think about Damson. I can imagine what she's like, very bossy and tough, built like Southend Pier. German or something. About the same age as Moo. Fiftyish.'

'Moo's not fifty. She'd faint if she heard you.'

'What is she then?'

'Forty-five.'

'She doesn't look it.'

'No, she doesn't. It's her illness. I remember her when she looked wonderful. About five years ago. People say she's dying now.'

'Wonderful? Really? Dying? How dreadful.'

'She was still with her husband then. He was divine.'

'How can she be married if she's a lesbian then? That's what I want to know.'

Rupert laughed. 'She's got children. Two of them, grown-up. Why not?'

'Well, it doesn't seem right to me.'

He laughed again. 'You are funny, Myopia. You must go round with your eyes closed. People aren't half as cut and dried as you think. It's possible to be all sorts of things at the same time. Haven't you found that out yet?'

We lay on the bed, Jean and me, naked, covered in boys. There must have been seven of them, three on her, three on me, and Sergio, that was his name I remember, he was odd man out. Scrabbling around for any bit of bare flesh he could find. My left breast, Jean's right buttock, now and again a mouth. Siesta time, the rest of the hotel asleep. What a holiday we were having. Better than Paris, much better, heaps. We'd ditched the Japs on the second day. I'd got Jean to agree to that.

'It's a great pity,' she'd sighed. 'We're saying adios to molto lire there.'

'Oh, come off it. If that's what you're after we can do better on our own. I've never been so self-conscious as last night. A grand place like that, all dressed up and me dancing with a grasshopper. He opened his flies on the way back. It was pathetic. Like an eyelash dipped in gelatine. I haven't come all the way to Italy for that.'

But what we'd got! Help! We'd never bargained for that. They'd arrived at our hotel on the fifth day, the boys. Students too. All Italian. Smashing age, twenty-oneish. Medical students, not much English, but that made no odds.

'They're used to working with bodies. It will be all right,' Jean assured me. 'They'll know their way around without dialogue.'

We looked at them, they looked at us.

'That one there, green eyes, black hair, yellow shirt. Bagsy me,' I said.

'Welcome. Looks like a hairdresser. I've seen mine.'

'Which one?' I felt a bit miffed.

'The one next to him, very blond.'

'Right. I'll have him then too.'

That's how it came about. We had them all.

91

Tomorrow we'd be going home. I turned my head on the pillow to talk to Jean. We often did that, had a chat in the middle of things—they couldn't understand what we were saying. One of them, I can't possibly remember which it would have been, took my movement to mean I wanted my neck love-kissed. I already had a neat string of passion bruises all the way round, which meant I'd have to go home in a scarf.

'Dracula's at it again,' I said.

'I see he is.'

'Me in polo-necks for a month.'

'We're going to miss this when we get back.'

Someone came inside me. 'Mmm.'

Our heads lay close together, so close that I could smell her breath.

'I can smell your breath,' I laughed.

'Ooh. Is it bad?'

'It's beautiful. A soupçon of garlic overlaid with grape.'

With difficulty she disengaged one arm, cupped my chin with her hand and put her nose against my mouth. 'Open up.'

I'll never forget that first kiss. I swear her tongue got as far as my tonsils. There was no getting away, her hand held me firmly in place but after a bit there was no need, anyway by then she was putting it to better use.

Neither of us noticed the boys leave, at least so we said after. I did see their faces though. All of them registered the same emotion. Horror, I would have put it at. They didn't come in to dinner that night and we didn't get a chance in the morning to say goodbye because the coach left before the hotel breakfast time. That was a shame, I should have liked to at least exchange addresses.

'We must have really upset them, Jean.'

'Their egos,' she tossed her head. 'Their miniscule mannish pride. We made them feel superfluous that's all.'

'I liked them though. I thought they were lovely.'

'Well,' she said triumphantly. 'It all came true, didn't it then?'

'What?'

'What I said. My promise. I promised we'd both have a fling.'

'And fall in love you said.'

She looked at me for a long time, her eyes suddenly shiny and very bright, like someone hugging a secret.

'Well,' she said at last. 'We have, haven't we?'

'Look, Rupert. Galeries Lafayette. I'd love to pop in there.'

He looked at his watch. 'No time for popping anywhere. This driver's taking us a funny way, I must say.'

'Is he? Do you know Paris that well?'

'I lived here for two years.'

'Oh Rupert. I keep forgetting you're the international set.'

'Piss off.'

'How coarse.'

'Shh, I'm concentrating,' He tapped the driver. 'Monsieur!' And they went into a long discussion about the address.

I couldn't understand a word. My French by now must be non-existent, I thought. But Rupert was doing marvellously.

'What a wonderful accent you've got,' I said when he stopped.

'Quite good in all modesty.'

'Very good! Very good on the R's, all in the back of the throat. I couldn't ever get the hang of that bit. I'm hopeless at languages.'

'They're easier to pick up if you live in the place.'

'How many do you speak then?'

He counted on his fingers. 'French, German, Italian, Spanish and a smattering of Arabic.'

'Good Lord! You've lived in some places.'

He looked all around. 'We're here. I'll pay. My francs are handy.'

'I can do it.' I opened my bag. 'Well, all right. It makes no odds. We're sharing everything.' I watched him counting out the fare. 'Isn't it funny, seeing you doing that makes me feel for the first time that we're abroad. It takes spending different money, it wouldn't be half as much fun if all countries had the same currency. This way it's more like playing Monopoly.'

I got out of the taxi and stood holding one of the cases. Rupert picked up the other as the driver drove away. 'What a miserable sod he was. Do you ever win?'

'With taxi drivers?'

'At Monopoly. I never do.'

'Always, at the end. I come out owning everything. After

93

crippling financial setbacks I effect a startling come-back, as they say in stockbroking circles.'

'You'd go a bomb in the city. Come on, this is us.'

He pushed at a peeling brown door, it opened on to a small courtyard around which sagged a high building with masses of mostly broken shutters—the ones which weren't tightly shut. There wasn't a soul or sound anywhere.

'Ooh, Rupert. It's rather sinister. I don't like it. Can we go back?'

He took a piece of paper out of his pocket and read aloud. 'Cross courtyard. Take right-hand corner door, up stairs, top floor. Apartment 20.'

'Top floor,' I echoed. We looked at each other and burst out laughing. 'Your face!'

'Yours!'

'There won't be a lift.'

'I've got it. There will be a lift—but ...'

'—Broken!'

We walked past the broken lift and started up the stairs. 'They usually have little old ladies in that bottom room who come out to see what you want.'

'Concierges,' Rupert gasped. 'Now stop talking for Christ's sake.'

On the fourth landing I sat down for a rest. 'This separates smokers and non-smokers. There was a time I would have run up these,' I said and lit a cigarette. But Rupert soldiered on.

'These bloody cases,' his voice drifted down.

I must be daft doing this, I thought, all this way to get doshed up for some photographer to live out her inner fantasies. Involving a tender plant like Rupert, getting him lugging a caseful of fancy clothes heavy enough to break the strongest stem.

'Mind you don't get a hernia,' I shouted up.

'Hernia-hernia-hernia,' the building shouted back. What if she wouldn't use me, didn't like my face, caught sight of my stretch marks? I'd have to go back to Moo Moffat-Paw and say, 'I'm sorry but I simply wouldn't do.' My powder compact had a mirror in it. I took it out to have a look.

It wasn't a face I would have made so much of a fuss about myself. Everything was in the right place. Exquisitely so, perfectly proportioned—neat nose, narrow chin, wide cheekbones. A perfect oval—which is what true beauty is all about. I'm always reading that. They usually give diagrams and exact measurements so that you have to take a ruler to your face and find out what you are. Round, square, long or heart-shaped. Or oval like me. They never put hatchet in, though there are plenty of hatchet faces around. Or lantern jaws. Beauty writers won't allow their readers lantern jaws. Or jowls or piggy eyes or prissy mouths or stumpy necks, so I was all right because I certainly don't have any of those. In fact, looking at my face now I could see that if everyone believed what they read they would consider me to be devastating. As Rupert had said, 'simply gorgeous'. Jean used to grumble about it in the beginning. 'I must be crackers going around with you. What chance will I stand—except with your leftovers?' But as it turned out we ended up equals.

'You've got the gift of the gab, you see, Jean. They soon get tired of staring at me. I would too if I was them.' Though now that I was older there was somehow strangely more that you would stare at. There was artifice for a start. Clever highlighting which modelled the bones and made them even more dramatic. And luscious heavy eyelids which experience had taught the grown-up trick of drooping, just a little. The lips had lost that apprehensive tight-together touch, they'd turned into a loose and lovely kissy pair. I parted them into a different shape, blew cigarette smoke straight at the small mirror and watched my image slowly blur.

'What on earth are you up to now?' Rupert's flushed faraway face peered down over the banisters high above.

'Are you at the top?' I stubbed out my cigarette. 'I'm just coming.'

'I've rung the bell already,' he shouted.

He'd gone by the time I got there. The open door faced me. I heard his voice, inside. He was laughing excitedly, chattering nineteen to the dozen like a child. From time to time he'd say her name, Damson this or Damson that. She couldn't get a word in edgeways. When she did I had no doubts at all. The accent had changed but there was no mistaking the voice. I knew at once who Damson was.

'Jean!'

'Mother of Jesus!'

'You've met before.' Rupert looked amazed. He watched us hugging. 'You know each other!'

'Intimately.' Jean stood back to look at me and chuckled appreciatively. 'But bye-bye and hello again I'd forgotten what I'd been missing.'

I'd only just have recognised her. I totted up—twelve years. She spun round and waggled her bottom. 'What do you see, love?'

'A change,' I said uncertainly.

She gave a fruity laugh, full of freshly baked bread, plates of pasta, chocolate gateaux, whipped cream, laced coffee, sweet liqueurs.

'You've put on a bit, Jean.'

She dimpled delightedly. 'Five stone. Brings me up to thirteen. Lucky number. Do you like it?'

'You look amazing. I must say that.'

Like a lampshade with a high watt bulb burning inside. The sort of lampshade you'd see in an eastern brothel, all fringed and beaded and tasselled. As wide as it's high. Brightly coloured from top to bottom, that's what she was. Her hair was very long, about to the middle of her back, a dark rich cherry red, it hung like corrugated cardboard. Horizontally. She saw me looking and held a glowing strand in her hand.

'I try to make it look as creased as possible, as opposed to curled. I used to have it permed but it came out too frizzy. Now I get someone to iron it, the woman who does my laundry. She fits it in after the sheets. Folded in just the same way.'

She held it to her eyes and squinted. 'Mm, needs more crimson. This Paris air is shocking. Fades everything. Good colour though, isn't it? That's how they came to call me Damson.'

'It's a far cry from Jean.' Rupert pulled a face. 'My sister's called Jean. I'm glad I didn't know you then.'

'Well,' I ventured. 'She was quite different. You probably wouldn't have bothered.'

'Oh, I don't know.' Jean tossed her hair back, soft flesh shook gently all over her face and rippled down her neck. Fascinating. 'He'd have liked my bum. It was smaller than a sparrow's fart. Tighter than a spy's tongue. You'd have liked that wouldn't you, Rupe?'

'Impossible to imagine, with all due respect, darling Damson. I adore you as you are now. How about Myopia? Has she changed?'

They both looked at me. Damson critically, I thought.

'No,' I said for her. 'I feel at a dreadful disadvantage. Static. I haven't changed one bit, have I, Jean? Go on, say it.'

Her brown eyes, smaller now in so much extra skin, but still bright like a naughty bird, danced mischievously all over my body. Then returned to my face. She smiled with the same wide happy mouth she'd always had and the eyes took on a warm and different glow. 'No.'

That's all she said, 'No', but in such a soft, insinuating, seductive way that I began to blush self-consciously and feel as shy as if I was with a stranger. Which made me mad and more defensive. 'Better clothes, though, surely now?'

She put her head on one side, considering, but her expression didn't change. 'A veneer of sophistication, but basics unaltered, I'd say.' She ran a small plump hand over my breast into my waist and let it rest lightly on one lean hipbone. 'Structurally superior, in fact. Have you had children?'

'Two.'

'Improved you. Tightened you up. Does that to a lot of women.'

She took her hand away and with the other touched my chin and swung it round so that my head was in profile against the light.

'Face leaner, eyes larger, mouth more relaxed, skin marvellous. Time has treated you well.' She spoke briskly like a professional, which, of course, was what she was but I'd forgotten that. 'I'm more interested in the mind for my photographs.' She tapped my forehead. 'And what has altered up there.'

Rupert looked on silently as if now he was in awe of her. Which, most irritatingly, was a bit of how I felt myself. She spun round to him and laughed. 'Believe it or not, Rupert, this beautiful beast, this femme fatale, was my best friend. We were students at this crappy college until my family left for the States, then we lost touch altogether. For one whole term I used to just stare at her. Everyone did. All the men were mad about her, staff included. And guess what she was going out with?'

'Don't be awful,' I said.

'This blind bugger. This music student who couldn't see what he'd got hold of and in the end chucked her and turns out to be queer anyway. Went off with an organist.'

'Sounds sweet,' Rupert murmured.

'Anyway when we eventually got chummy I see that inside she's like a child. As daft as you make them. No idea of what she looks like, obsessed with ideas of social inferiority. Brought up by a family on the edge of being certifiably insane.'

'Jean!'

'They were, love. Crackers! The whole lot of them. Your father was mentally defective, I swear it. He used to sit there. Rupert—'

I opened my handbag. 'Where's the bog?'

'He used to sit there picking his nose and ...'

'I said, is there a lavatory here?' I moved towards the door.

'Oh, don't go. Isn't it true? Tell Rupert.' She turned to him. 'They lived in this place, honestly, there was no bathroom and her mother used to ...'

'Jean!'

'No, let me just say. Her mother, when they ...'

I slapped her right cheek so hard it hurt my hand and then, with the back of it, I slapped her left so swiftly I didn't know I'd done it. Inside I felt cold and completely detached as if my limbs were working of their own accord. She thinks she's riled me, I thought, driven me to such anger that I have to strike out. But, in fact, it isn't so at all. She's a fat unhappy girl for reasons of her own and likes to play a childish spiteful game. And to please I've gone along with it. What she'd like now is for both of us to cry, become emotional and make up. I felt the tears spring to my eyes and the next moment her arms were around me.

'Girls, girls,' Rupert said anxiously.

Jean hugged me tightly and raised a tear-stained radiant face. Each cheek was scarlet from my blows. 'That's what I wanted to find out,' she choked between sobs, 'what's happened in your mind. Had you learnt to be less passive, always out to please ...'

I took a hanky from my bag. 'What's happened to your glasses, don't you wear them any more?' And wiped her nose as kindly as I could.

'Gave up glasses, gave up girls, grew my hair and took to gourmandising all in the same year!' Jean skewered a steaming snail with a two-pronged silver fork and sucked between her teeth. Then she tore a piece of bread from her roll, soaked up garlic butter and swilled the whole lot down with red wine. Rupert and I sat in the crowded café watching her. Two dozen snails she'd polished off. Just like that!

'Oh yes,' I said politely. 'And which year was that?' Like an historical researcher making certain of his dates. She glanced at our two empty glasses but poured the remaining wine into her own. 'Thank you, darling,' Rupert said pointedly.

'Lowest form of wit.' She took a swig and smacked her lips, then burped so loudly at a passing waiter that he spilt the entire contents of his tray. Two Pernods, three Perriers, and one small cognac. He swore and scowled in her direction. In answer, she held our empty bottle up. 'Un autre, s'il vous plait.' Then turned to us and laughed. 'The only way to get attention in this place! Now, what were we saying? Oh, yes. Well, let me see when. One, two, three, must have been five years ago because Freddie's been dead two. It's terrible, you know, I still miss him. I wake up in the night and swear he's sitting on my bed. I still can't see steak mignon on a menu without thinking of Freddie. He was mad about good food. The more I ate the more he loved it. After a particularly fine meal we'd go home and he'd lick me all over. It was as much as I could do to stop him biting! He would have eaten me if I'd let him.' Her voice shook. 'Strangely enough, this place was one of his favourites. We used to come here all the time. He was great friends with the owner—' She broke off abruptly and stared across the room, then she started waving and stood up. 'Oh, excuse me, I've just seen Babette. I must go and have a word.'

She moved nimbly, no mean feat, between the closely packed tables. As she went, I felt my energy ebb away as if without her igniting presence my life supply was lowered. It was extraordinary.

'Phew.' I let out a long and gasping breath, then turning to Rupert asked, 'And who on earth was Freddie then?'

'Freddie?' he said simply. 'Freddie was her dog.'

I timed it. She was away from us for twenty minutes. The centre of attention, the other side of the room, laughing loudly, greeting new people, kissing everybody. I watched her. Rupert looked at me.

'You're thinking she's on something, aren't you?' he said.

'What do you mean?'

'You're wondering if she's on pills or something stronger. She's not you know—'

'No, I wasn't—'

'She's just on life.'

'Yes,' I said. 'She always was.'

What I was actually wondering was when we were going to get down to work. I looked at my watch. It was half past two. In just over two hours' time I'd be ringing Charles. 'I'm sorry, Charles. We don't seem to have quite finished. It looks very much as if I won't be back till tomorrow. By the way, have you buried Deirdre yet?' I wasn't exactly understanding mistress material.

Rupert stood up. 'She's beckoning. Come on, we'd better go over. Take a tip from me and forget about time. Damson starts work when she wants to. It could be when everyone else is half dead on their feet, so don't squander any stamina you've got. Not at this early stage.'

I stood up too. 'You mean grin and bear it?'

He shook his head and looked vaguely worried. I laughed and touched him reassuringly. 'Ah, it's all right. I'm getting it now. "Hang loose!" Is that better?'

He looked at me quickly but I smiled innocently back and by the time we'd reached Jean, or rather Damson as I'd now decided to call her, I was hanging looser than I'd ever done in my life. So loose in fact that when five o'clock came I did nothing about calling Charles and couldn't have cared less if Deirdre was six foot under or still receiving callers in her coffin.

Over the hours our group enlarged, sometimes to over twenty, even more, but through it all a solid core remained, with Damson at centre, holding court, and me at her side. The new consort. That's how it felt.

'I'm not calling you Jean any more,' I said to her early on. 'It's Damson from today.' Her eyes flickered for a second. 'And you might as well call me Myopia to stay in the mood of things.'

'Mercy me,' she'd blinked. 'We've just murdered each other.'

The girl called Babette sat on Damson's other side staring at us. A strange expression on her face, watchful. She hardly spoke at all. She had an extraordinarily long neck, like a Modigliani. Or, nearer the mark, a young giraffe because when she stood up, which she did quite often for no apparent reason, her arms and legs went on for ever too. She was dressed from neck to toe in yellow, slightly shiny so that she put me in mind of an old-fashioned fly catcher. Those thin long sticky strips that used to hang from people's ceilings. My mother always had one in our kitchen. Dotted with dead flies, like the flag of death waving above your dinner. Yellow.

'Babette is a model,' Damson had introduced us. 'She works for Dior.'

Something clicked, I studied her complexion.

'What beautiful skin you have. Flawless.'

'Christ, yes!' Damson shrieked. 'But you should have seen it before! Craters of the moon. Covered! Acne Virulus. Pimples, spots, boils, scars—'

'Oh, I believe we have a friend in common—'

'Seven layers of the stuff they sheared off. She had the operation last summer. For a beauty article. I did the before and after snaps. Miraculous success. A perfect peel.'

'Yes, she's living in London. Her name's Françoise.'

Babette spoke for the first time. 'Ah oui,' her eyes lit up. 'Françoise.'

'She actually lives in my house.'

She frowned suddenly. 'Francoise? She live with you?' And glancing quickly at Damson, began a low-pitched, highly charged conversation. From time to time Damson snorted or turned her back deliberately. I sat watching now; they were obviously having a quarrel.

Rupert sat opposite. I leaned towards him. 'I think those two are quarrelling.' He didn't move his eyes. 'It's Babette,' he whispered. 'She's impossibly jealous. I'd go easy if I were you.'

Me? What had I done? There was a sudden commotion to my left. Babette stood up, glass in hand, while Damson remained seated, drenched in wine. It ran slowly down her dimpled face, glistened in the glorious hair. She looked up, laughed and licked her upper lip. Babette gave a strangled sob and pushing past the people next to her disappeared through a door labelled Dames. Everyone went on as if nothing had happened.

I picked up a napkin from the table and started mopping. 'That's the second time today,' I said crossly as if to a child. 'Whatever has come over you? Do you like these emotional scenes? Is that how you go on all the time?'

She twinkled wickedly. 'I thrive on disturbance. I like to scratch away the surface—'

'Like a rat—'

'What's underneath is so much more inviting—'

'An avaricious rat.'

'A conjurer with a pack of cards.'

'You'll drop them all one day.'

'When I'm dead.'

She always liked the last word. 'You're still the same, Damson. A blockbuster.'

She patted her hips and plaited ten small fat fingers over her swollen stomach. 'What do you think of this belly?'

The thought struck me. 'Are you pregnant?'

She laughed and laughed till the tears came to her eyes.

'It looks like it,' I said nastily to make her stop.

That brought on another burst. 'Oh dear, oh dear!' She gasped at the end and weakly wiped her eyes. I stared coldly with what I hoped was open dislike. 'What's so funny?'

She gave one last happy giggle. 'You are, my love.' She leant forward and tickled me under the chin. 'I can tell you've been wasting too much time with pompous asses.' She wagged her finger. 'You have to be careful, certain qualities can be very catching.'

I took a deep breath, she was doing it again, deliberately provoking.

'You're a monster,' I said, 'let's leave it at that.'

She looked just slightly put out. 'But we haven't started yet—'

'I realise that,' I cut across, 'however, we're postponing further action for the moment.'

'Why?' she persisted.

'Why?' I sat back and faced her squarely. She looked sumptuous, like over-ripe fruit, insistent, disturbing, self-confident, exciting. 'Why? Because you're beginning to bore, that's why.'

I caught a glimpse of Jean, just for one split second, standing pigeon-toed in tarty shoes with film star glasses on her nose and a mouth which trembled very slightly. Rupert leaned towards us.

'Going over old times, you two?'

Damson didn't answer. I lifted my glass and clinked the one in front of her.

'Preparing for new, more like.' And started hanging loose again.

'How I'll miss you when I go.' It had been like a bombshell. America.

'How I'll miss you, Jeannie, too.'

The evening before she left we bought two bottles of strong cider and locked ourselves in her room. Her mother had looked in on her way out. 'We won't be back till very late, darling. Make sure you're all packed.' And to me, 'Goodbye, my dear. I do hope you'll write to Jean. You've been such good friends. She'll be fortunate if she meets someone like you over there.' Then almost absent-mindedly, 'Such a beautiful girl.'

Jean winked slyly behind her mother's back. 'Good night, Mummy, have a nice party. I'll be asleep when you get back, I expect. Don't bother to look in.'

I watched them briefly embrace. What niceties they knew. A car horn hooted impatiently outside, a rich imperious signal.

'Oh dear,' the mother became prettily confused. 'Daddy is anxious to be away. He's started fretting. Blow him a kiss, darling.' She left the room as Jean ran to the window.

'Coo-ee, Daddy, kiss kiss.' She spread her fingers wide and brought them to her lips, then threw these parcels of daughterly affection over the front lawns, down the drive, past the clipped privet, to her father in the waiting car.

We listened to them drive away.

'That's that.' Jean began a slow grin and opened the first cider. 'Now what about this?'

We drank a full glass each, slowly, non-stop, staring at each other over the rims. We were sitting on the floor and I wiped the bottom of my glass carefully before setting it down in case it should stain the carpet.

'Your mother and father are mad about you, aren' they?'

She looked surprised. 'What a funny thing to say.'

'No, but I mean they show it so much.'

'In no more than a normal way. All parents are like that.'

'Mine aren't.'

'No, well, yours—' She broke off and looked embarrassed. 'I mean I think you'd find most normal middle-class families behave like mine. Boring, isn't it?'

'I think it's nice.'

'What, sitting on Daddy's knee and arranging his hair in little curls—'

'I wouldn't dare do that to mine.'

'I've always done it. It's his favourite thing.'

'Yes, but don't you think it's funny? Now? At your age?'

'What do you mean? You think it might get him going? If it did he certainly wouldn't let on. He sticks too closely to the code.'

She imitated her father's Scotch-on-the-rocks-just-a-spot-of-water voice. 'Oh, my goodness, yes!'

I let the cider slip along my skin until it reached my wrists. I held them both up and watched my hands dangle loose. Then I dropped my head heavily on my chest and thought about sitting on my father's lap, running my fingers lightly through his hair, shifting slightly to redistribute my weight, feeling his shoulder press against my breast.

'Oh, no, I wouldn't dare do that to mine.' I swear it's the last thing on earth that I'd dare to do.

Jean poured a second glass for us and we drank it as we had the first. I felt the pressure mounting in my bladder. 'I'm bursting for a pee,' Jean said, 'but I'm not going.'

I stared at her, my own need suddenly receding. 'Why not?'

'Haven't you ever tried it? Holding out till the last minute. It makes you really randy. I discovered that years ago.' She laughed and started rocking on her heels. 'An exquisite pain. Ooh. I've even had a few accidents, leaving it too late.'

'What do you mean?' I was secretly appalled, and unexpectedly excited.

'Pissed my pants. Wet my knickers. It makes you feel wonderfully naughty.'

'Jean!'

'Try it now. Holding on. We both will.'

I stood up, needing now urgently to go. 'I'll have to keep on the move.' I crossed my legs. 'And cross fingers.'

She stood up too, hopping from leg to leg. 'I'll put a record on, we can dance. That will help.'

The music was very loud, good for dancing but with a steady, insistent beat which only served to heighten my discomfort. We pranced about the room, going redder and redder. The record came to an end, I put on another. When

I turned round, Jean was wriggling furiously behind, one hand between her legs. We both wore skirts, hers was all hoicked up at the front so that I could see where her fingers pressed against the gusset of her knickers. My eyes started watering; what she'd said was true. I did, despite my agony, feel unbearably aroused.

'I can't hold on much longer, Jean.' I bit my lip and crossed my legs tightly.

'I know.' She came towards me, scarlet-faced. 'I'll hold yours and you can hold mine.' She caught my hand and pulled it to where hers was.

'No.'

'Harder than that. Press harder or I'll do it.'

'Jean!'

I felt the warmth seeping through the thin material, felt at the same time her fingers on mine. We both, standing closely, our hands on each other, let our insides stream out together.

'All over the carpet,' I remember thinking anxiously, but then I surrendered to the unbelievable joy of the moment, releasing tension like air from a child's balloon. Warmth, wetness, dribbling down our legs over all four feet into toes, until at last there was nothing left. Except the hammering of her heart against my own, her arm held loosely round my waist and her happy mouth kissing busily in mine.

'Well,' I said, as soon as she'd let me, 'that's the rudest thing I've ever done.'

She laughed slyly. 'There's ruder things than that to do. There must be, otherwise there'd be nothing to look forward to, would there? That's why people live as long as possible, to get it all in.'

The pleasant warmth was beginning to fade, replaced by an uncomfortably soggy coldness. I looked down, our two separate pools were puddling into one. Anxiety and guilt flooded through the elation I still felt.

'Ooh,' I said, 'I feel awful now. It's just come over me. As if I could cry.'

Right away she started bossing. 'Down with your drawers. I'll wash them out with mine. I'll put them on the radiator. Be ready in no time! Here, hand me that hair drier, it will do for the carpet. Now you, you take your skirt off, dry yourself with this towel and when you've done that, get into bed and wait for me.'

I stood there numbly. She clucked impatiently, stepping out of her dripping clothes and, giving me a small shove, she added softly, 'Go on, dopey. Do as I say. Don't I always know best?'

A whole year, it had taken, to get going again. After she'd gone. Six or seven letters I wrote to her, but I never heard a word back. 'Any news of Jean?' people were always asking. I'd shake my head. 'Nice friend,' my mother would say meaningfully. She'd never liked her much. But I felt as if one half of me had died. The lower half.

Half past seven. We hadn't stirred. Even Rupert looked concerned. I stood up. Damson put a cheerful hand on my arm.

'Where are you going?'

Back to London, you self-opinionated, fleshy lump! You mad, mindless, middle-aged ... hippie!

'I'm going to use the telephone,' I said.

She smiled with a sudden rush of enthusiastic energy. 'Don't take too long. Here are some jetons, you'll need them for the phone box. I'm waiting to talk about work.'

I fumed all the way to the phone, frowning at a handsome sullen face ahead which seemed to be approaching until I reached the wall mirror and saw it was my own. With the sulks? Why?

A thick-set, swarthy Frenchman was talking on the only telephone, shouting into the mouthpiece, shrugging his shoulders and stressing conversational points with his free fist. An empty packet of Gauloises lay at his feet. I thought of Paul. Posh voice, fast car. That had been enough for me then. And a way with him in bed that had put me in mind of Jean. Pushy, forceful. Both products of the middle classes. The man kicked savagely at the paper packet, gave a gutteral grunt and then suddenly noticed me waiting behind him and turned to face me. He gave a dazzling grin, showing two gleaming gold teeth in the front. Quite nice, gold teeth. Funny things to think of having. I smiled back, rather wanly, and sagged wearily inside as I saw his eyes begin to wander. I turned my back deliberately, lit a cigarette and leaned against the open door, looking into the length of the cafe. We'd been there eight hours. Incredible. You couldn't do that in London. All over the world, just about; talking, drinking, eating for hours on end. But not in London. Not unless it's a club. Where people have to be passed before they can be members. Then it's pointless because you're always meeting everyone that you'd expect to meet. No element of surprise!

I jumped at the pinch and turned round quickly. The man had finished with the phone but kept his hand on my bottom. I brushed it away, remembered 'Merci beaucoup' and began dialling London.

Françoise answered. I could hear the children in the background.

'First of all,' I said, 'is their father there? Oh Paul, hello,' and I began to explain. It was only when I'd said good night to the girls, got Paul to agree to the new arrangements, that now I'd probably be back on Sunday night, and replaced the receiver that I remembered I'd forgotten to tell Françoise I'd just met her friend Babette. Closing my purse I caught sight of Charles's number on a piece of paper. He won't be there now but I can at least in all honesty say I tried. Two and a half hours late.

He answered immediately. I heard the ringing tone, it went twice. He sounded awful, no sign of anger, just strained and very sad. 'I've been waiting. I knew you'd ring if you possibly could.'

'It's the first chance I've had, Charles.' I crossed two fingers to cancel out the lie, one polished nail was chipping I noticed.

'My darling, when am I to expect you?'

For one surprising second the pleading stirred up a fierce and cruel streak. Before I could stop I'd said it. 'Have you buried Deirdre yet?'

The coarseness horrified me more than him. 'What? Oh! Funeral tomorrow. Now which plane will you be on tonight? I'll meet it.'

'Charles.' I seemed like someone else, not me at all. 'What are your plans exactly now?'

'My plans?' He sounded surprised. 'Well, I thought I'd meet you, then chance dining in a little place I know. No fear of bumping into anyone ...'

'No, I mean not now tonight, but from now on.' Why in God's name was I asking that?

There was a silence at the other end. When he spoke he sounded very quiet, but confident. 'Ah, well, that. That is something we have to discuss. The telephone is hardly the

107

way in which I would have liked to . . .'

'To what, Charles?'

'To—well—ask . . .'

'What? Ask what?' Like a rat myself! Avaricious!

'Very well,' he blustered irritably, coughed, cleared his throat—I knew he had one hand on his spectacles. 'Ask a lady for her hand,' then he said it again, but with better delivery. His public speaking was standing him in good stead.

'My hand?' I said into the phone. 'Charles.'

'Don't be deliberately obtuse,' he said suddenly, shouting. 'Darling, did you hear me?' His voice rose to its fullest pitch. 'Goddammit, girl, I'm asking you to marry me. Wasn't that always the idea, once the obstacle was removed . . .'

'Your wife.' I said it softly, giving him a lead.

'The damn woman's dead,' he was still shouting. 'And jolly good riddance too. A fool's trick that jump. And she knew it. Been warned time and time again! Died in triumph, actually laughing. The expression on her face—challenging! The poor undertaker had the devil of a job to reset it into some semblance of dignity . . .'

I held the receiver away from my ear, his voice went on and on, Deirdre as powerful in death . . .

'Charles,' I interrupted. 'About my plane.'

He was still excited. 'Yes, darling?'

'I shan't be home till Sunday, I'm afraid.'

When I turned round I found Damson talking to gold-teeth. She had her arm round his neck and they were laughing together, like very old friends.

'Come here,' she said, 'André wishes to be introduced.'

He clicked his heels and bowed from the waist, then he held out one hand. It had a gold ring on the third finger. I pointed at it and said foolishly, 'To go with your teeth.'

He laughed and said in French-American-English, 'Aw no, to go with the woman.'

They both looked at me, Damson and him, expecting something witty back but I'd given up the ghost. I looked down at my hands, one of which Charles had just asked for. A fact which only now was beginning to sink in.

'Is your wife dead?' I asked.

André looked surprised and burst out laughing. Damson took my hand and led me gently back to our table.

André followed. 'I can see you're tired,' she said. 'André owns this place. He's the proprietor.' As if that simple fact explained everything.

I lost the evening. It approached like an ocean, each hour a large and powerful wave which broke above my head and swept me further out to sea. Several times I was sick, but in between these bouts I floated, staring at the sky. At times it was completely black, at others full of blinding lights— and faces that I knew. Rupert's smiling encouragingly; Damson's. But an unfamiliar Damson, gazing up from down below, her mouth concealed by a crinkly dark moustache which I knew to be my pubic hair. A man I'd seen before, but only once, with a mouth of gold pressed close to mine. And another that I didn't know at all who came repeatedly with coloured crayons in his hand. Often I was tossed and turned and felt upon my limp skin the slithering touch of rich and varying sensations, some smooth like water, others soft as smoke ...

Once, as a child, I'd had a long and dangerous illness. Death's door was where they said I'd been but I could only remember the hospital. And sleeping out of doors at night on a high veranda inches from the stars. Towards morning clouds would form, shepherded like sheep, into some sort of formation by a bigger, billowing shape that I took to be an organising angel. I knew it even then, I saw it, since angels come neutered like cats from the vet, it hung each day throughout that bandaged summer directly above my bed. While the clouds drifted slowly about their business this angel didn't budge. Its wings were as wide as the hospital grounds, beautiful, and beckoning—but it had a grotesque and dreadful double chin. Like a well-filled shopping bag which hung from each ear and billowed about in the middle of its chest. A strange woman would come each day and sit silently by my bed. We'd stare without speaking at each other until eventually her eyes would fill with tears and I'd shut my own and hope that when I opened them again she'd be gone. One day when the angel was closer than it had ever been before I lifted my finger and pointed. 'Do you see?' I whispered to this woman. 'Up there, an angel with a double chin?' Two nurses took her away sobbing and another placed a cold thermometer in my mouth.

I was reminded of that angel now while white distorted

109

shapes floated haphazardly before my eyes and for an instant formed into a shining pair of wings—without the shopping bag. I smiled and laughed. Chin up! It's learnt to stretch its neck! Then I opened my eyes.

'At last Sleeping Beauty awakes!' It was Rupert's voice.

'Welcome to the land of the living. How're you feeling?' Damson's.

I sat up. 'Slightly sick. Seasick.'

They came over and stood above me, smiling down. 'You won't be. Nothing left in you now. We saw to that before we put the clothes on. Couldn't have you soiling the spoils.'

'Or spoiling the shots,' Damson added.

A dull ache prickled slowly over my scalp, my mouth felt as dry as a dead moth. I ran a swollen tongue over my upper lip and, surprisingly, tasted a perfumed film of lipstick. Rupert laughed. Two gold teeth twinkled beside him. André of course. It was André. He handed me a cup with black coffee in it. 'Drink up, honey.' A nice voice.

'And then come and see how you like yourself,' Damson said.

My head prickled painfully again. I put up a hand and felt a mass of tiny tight coils kept in place by hundreds of small hair pins. An anxious voice with a heavy French accent said, 'They are hurting you, no? The pins? I will remove them at once.'

A boy stepped towards me, very much like Rupert, amazingly so.

'Jean-Paul.' Damson held my hand up. 'This is Jean-Paul. He's been making you pretty! You must say thank you, Myopia.'

I sat there stupidly, staring at them all. 'Thank you, Jean-Paul.' And drained my cup.

'Another?' I nodded.

'Oh, come on,' Rupert put an arm around my shoulders. 'She looks so amazing, let's show.'

I'd been lying on a chaise longue, velvet, the colour of violets.

'We should bring that with her. Honestly, darling, if you could have seen yourself! The colour—' He kissed his finger tips and closed his eyes. 'Mm, mm, deevine.'

I allowed myself to be guided to the mirror—was I drunk or drugged or what? 'I'm hallucinating,' I said and gave a ghastly grin. The technicoloured film star smiled

110

gravely back. I watched the glossy lips move. 'That's not me, is it? My God, my own mother wouldn't know me!'

'Oh her, she wouldn't—' I heard Damson's voice begin, but I'd stopped listening.

'Perfection,' I sighed and allowed a soft and pleasurable gasp to escape under my long skirt.

'She's farted,' Damson said. 'Well, I'll be buggered. We've all worked our balls off.' She spun me round. 'Ten outfits we've fitted you into—photographed them all with you snoring like a pig and your first reaction is to fart.'

I stared at her wide-eyed, suddenly awake. 'You've done all that?'

Rupert answered. 'Don't you remember? It was your idea! Just before you conked out you told us about your dream, so Damson's done the first part already—"Beautiful Girl Dreaming"—'

Damson interrupted eagerly. 'We run those pictures along the top of each page, shows the whole thing. Hair, shoes, outfits, the lot, and then printed large we show the dreams, close-ups of you in different situations. Like your dream—only with variations—'

'I can't remember anything. Was I very drunk?'

'It was the hash. You foolishly ate hash fudge. Hussein gave you it. He's always doing that. His idea of a joke. Really strong stuff. He'll kill someone one day. It doesn't mix with booze. You'll be okay, now, with a good few hours' more sleep. We've all been waiting to go to bed but we were waiting just to see you were all right.'

'How awful. I am sorry. Whatever is the time?'

Rupert yawned and looked at his watch. 'Six a.m.!' He and Jean-Paul glanced at each other. 'Are you sure you're better, Myopia, because if so we'll be getting along.'

'We? Who?' I said, stupid again.

He kissed me on the cheek. 'I'm camping round at Jean-Paul's. Damson's only got room for you here. We'll report for work later in the morning. Goodnighty, darling! You were wonderful!'

'Wonderful,' echoed André and hugged me. 'I too shall see you, yes? Today,' he whispered in my ear, 'my sweet darling.'

Before I'd known it, they'd gone. Damson saw them all out. When she came back I was still at the mirror. How much had I imagined? One thing I suddenly remembered, one physical fact that must have been obvious to all of

111

them over the hours. The thought turned me scarlet. I heard her cross the room, then stand behind me, gazing in the glass at our two reflections. I didn't turn but said slowly and with considerable embarrassment, 'What on earth did you do about my period and all those clothes?'

She flung a plump and friendly arm through mine, squeezed it and laughed. 'I threw away your old towel and put a Tampax in!' Then she lifted my chin. 'Was that in order, madam?'

I gave a mortified nod.

She laughed again. 'Right then. Now do as I say and get to bed.'

But I couldn't sleep. I lay on my side of her large bed and she lay on the other, nowhere did our bodies touch. A small amount of early morning light filtered through the wooden shutters, enough for me to dimly see her face. She'd fallen asleep almost at once. Without so much as a goodnight peck. But, was I pleased or piqued? I couldn't tell, myself. I flicked my lighter, lit a cigarette and holding up the flame looked with interest around the room.

Everything went on in it, a cooker and sink in one corner, the chaise longue I'd been lying on, a huge workbench table running down the centre and along one wall a battery of lighting equipment and cameras. There were photographs everywhere, covering the table, on the floor, pinned to the walls. Hundreds of her dog. Freddie, that was it. A Saluki, with a fine aristocratic face and graceful, greased lightning frame. Not what I would have chosen for a pet, but then I liked cuddly little animals, guinea pigs or pekineses, or fluffy things like day-old chicks and Persian cats. Or even bright pink squealing things like pigs. Not that you could keep a pig in Paris. Not in this apartment at any rate. The stairs for a start. The poor thing couldn't cope with those each time it went for a walk.

I studied Damson whilst she slept. She looked not unlike a pig, I thought, a pretty one with a little nose and deep-set eyes and curly laughing lips. But mostly it was her skin, so pink and soft and squelchy. I felt an irresistible urge to prod her, push a finger in and see how far it sank. To the knuckle or nearabouts, I would have said. On really fleshy bits—her thighs, her breasts, her bottom—right up

112

to the wrist! I shut my eyes, and turned over. I'll tell her that in the morning, I thought. I'll tell her that—and try it out.

But in the morning she was nowhere to be seen. There was a note on her pillow—'Sleep on, see you soon.' I got up when I read it, put the kettle on and looked around for a clean cup. Everything was fouled and filthy. Mrs Bowen would have gone clean out of her mind, that or asked for her cards. Half a ham roll, dead, stuck out of the sugar bowl. Stale ground coffee stood in all the jugs, one with furry green verdigris growing on its surface. A broken egg lay on the floor, with a bloated fly inside. I found my cup from last night, recognising it by the lipstick stain, washed it out and drank my coffee black. There seemed to be no milk. My heart began pounding, pumping nineteen to the dozen. I spat the rest away, then started cleaning up. I knew what she'd say when she came in. 'Proper little pit wife.' Well? And so what? But by ten to ten, when I'd turned it into a presentable palace, there was still no sign of her. So I ran a bath and got in and while I was at it, I washed my hair. As I was rinsing it, a slow job done by filling a jug from both taps to get the right temperature, she came in. I stopped in mid-pour, and squinted through the dripping strands, on my knees, my bottom high in the air, nipples hard and pointing down.

'Good morning, my love,' I heard her sing out. 'Myopia?'

'Here,' I shouted back. The bathroom door opened in a rush.

'Do you mind? I've got this turd up my ass! It's bigger than a battleship.'

She sat down on the lavatory and grinned cheerfully. 'Only hope it doesn't break the bowl. I've carried it over from the other side of Paris.'

I heard the splash.

'Ah, that's better.' She stared at the ceiling, concentrating. 'To be followed by several smaller vessels.' Then she wiped herself with paper, half a roll it looked like, pulled the chain and sniffed. 'Not too bad! Now, how are you today?'

It had happened so quickly I hardly took it in. I noticed that she didn't wash her hands. 'Can I make you something to eat? I've got fresh bread, milk, eggs ...'

'I'm just washing my hair,' I said quickly. 'I'll do my

113

own in a minute,' and started on the taps again.

'Hey,' she said slowly. 'Look at me.'

I lifted a wet and sudsy face.

'Don't move,' she pointed imperiously. 'Just stay like that, I'll get my camera,' and darted away.

When she returned I was in the same position, bubbles sliding down my skin, streaming over each breast.

'Good girl.' She put the lavatory lid down and stood up on it. 'Now to me, your chin. That's it.'

Soap ran into my eyes.

'Don't do that!' she shouted when I shut them.

'It's stinging though, the soap.'

'Keep your mouth still! Now laugh! Not like that, really laugh. Teeth, teeth! Yes!'

She clicked through a whole roll of film then put another in and kneeled on the floor beside the bath. 'Now sit on your feet, go on, just sink back on the heels. Straighter back. Titties out. Point them! Point, I said, not pout. Now fill that jug and pour cold water over your head.'

'Cold? I'm not pouring cold.' I turned the hot on. She turned it off impatiently, filled the jug to the brim with icy water and tipped the whole lot over me. I swear my heart stopped with the shock—my arms involuntarily lifted to shield my breasts.

She clicked unmercifully. 'Get those arms down,' she said so fiercely I did so right away.

Wet hair hung like a thick straight curtain all over my face. I pushed it to one side and glared at her. 'You cow, you bloody cow.'

'Beautiful,' she cooed, 'keep that look.'

'Keep it yourself,' I snarled and stood up, goose-pimpling all over. My teeth started chattering uncontrollably and I reached for a towel.

She didn't stop, quickly reloaded the camera and just went on snapping. In the end I took no notice, dried myself all over, wrapped the towel round me and with another started rubbing at my hair.

'That's enough. I think we've got it. Okay. There'll be some beauties in those, unless you're totally, irredeemably unphotogenic.'

'I am,' I said sourly.

She laughed. 'We'll only know that later today. They're rushing through the stuff I shot last night. That's where I've been, to my printers. We'll have them by six. Isn't it exciting?' She tapped her camera. 'But these, I'll develop myself. Now, I think.'

Curiosity overcame me. 'Yourself, where?'

She pointed to a door in the large living-room. 'My dark room. I always do my own black and white. You can experiment so much in the printing. That's the best part.'

'Why not do last night's then?'

The question bored her but she answered patiently. 'That was colour. It's a different process. Has to go to a colour lab. What we'll get back this afternoon are transparencies. You experiment with those in a different way, like laying one or even two on top of the other, but all that will be done in the art department at *Chic*. I shall come over with them and have a say in the laying out. There's not an art director in the world that I'd trust with my work.'

I stared at her, it was a different Damson today.

'Can I stay with you?'

'What? I was just thinking!'

'Can I stay with you—in London?'

'Yes! Yes, of course you can. I've got plenty of room.'

She laughed. 'I thought you would. I can imagine your house. It is a house, isn't it?'

'Yes.' I felt almost defensive. 'A nice house. In need of decoration though,' I added.

'And does that worry you?' She looked at me very seriously.

I thought carefully. 'Well,'—well, did it? 'Well,' I said again. 'Well, if it did I would hardly have let it get like that, would I?' And right away felt better.

She nodded encouragingly.

'In actual fact, I don't know why I've stayed there. It's a family house meant for a husband and wife with children. Like living in the past.'

'You've got children—'

'I haven't got a husband, though—'

Her eyes widened.

'I mean, I had one, but we're divorced,' I said quickly.

She laughed easily. 'Yes, I'm divorced too.'

The shock had as much impact as that cold water. I don't know why. I stared at her in disbelief. She laughed again.

'We've got a lot of ground to go over,' and taking the towel from my hand, started rubbing at my damp hair.

'Don't worry, we'll do it. But there's plenty of time ahead.'
She stopped rubbing for a moment and said reflectively,
'It will be strange to be in London again. Funny to see
Moo.' There seemed no answer. I remained silent. 'Five
years,' she went on, 'that's when I saw her last—that's how
long it's been since I was there.' Her hands towelled
briskly over my head. I relaxed, soothed by the firm but
gentle pressure. She had a fine, experienced touch. I
wondered how often she'd shampooed Freddie.

'She's changed, so Rupert says. Looks completely
different now. Isn't she meant to be dying?'

Her hands rubbed more fiercely, I imagined, for a
moment.

'Dying? Yes, so I've heard. But we're all doing that,
aren't we, dying?'

'Well,' I said, 'then she's doing it faster.'

'My goodness,' Damson said heartlessly, 'she'd better
watch out. She'll lose her licence for speeding.'

'Her life anyway.'

We both laughed.

'Spot on, old girl.' She sounded like her mother. 'You're
dry now, I'd say.'

'Thanks.' I took the towel. 'Shall I wash this out?'

'Don't be boring. I'd leave it on the floor. Let's go and
have a bit of grub. The boys will be here before we know
it.'

I followed her, the towel tucked around me, my hair
now haloed round my head like a curling cloud of sooty
smoke. She glanced back, her expression changing. Click,
click.

'Oh, don't do any more!' I protested.

She took no notice. 'Just finish the reel. I've got a good
idea here. If it works out we can both make ourselves a lot
of money.'

I gave up, obeyed each curt command, tossing my head,
when she said to, smouldering straight at the camera,
staring stonily through my long fringe. It got so that I
gradually began to enjoy it all. Like flirting with the lens,
having a private love affair. But I didn't laugh once. That
would have felt too false. She stopped at last.

'That was really great. You're getting the hang of it
now. Much better than the last lot.'

'It felt better.' Adrenalin was high. I could have done it
all over again for two pins.

'You could well become a real pro. You should practise expressions in front of a mirror and play around with your body. Make it fall into your own sort of angles, really get it working for you.'

'I don't feel right laughing.'

'Don't do it then. That's what I mean. Get your own special look going. Savage or sulky, whatever feels right.'

'I'd like to look soft and friendly most of all, that's how I feel inside, but it's not somehow how my face falls. It's funny that, don't you think?'

She turned away. 'Bollocks!' she said shortly. I had been about to enlarge, clumsily, granted, but still prepared to go on. Giving her the benefit of . . .

'What?'

'Bollocks!'

I stood still to let it sink in. 'Right,' I said eventually. 'Bollocks back.'

'That's better,' she said. 'Now lay the table.'

She cooked like an artist, the sort of arty artists they show in films, flinging colour at the canvas and stepping back appreciatively. Slap dash. On it went. Egg shells thrown to the floor and four winds. Butter browning to burning point. Cheese flaked furiously everywhere. I watched my recent houseproud efforts reduced once more to havoc.

'Omelette,' she said and banged it on the table. I took a mouthful dubiously.

'Delicious,' I said as it melted away.

She smacked her lips juicily, grease glistened on her chin. 'You should taste my soufflé—sublime, though I say it myself. Not that I cook that much any more. Usually eat out. At André's or other places. Creates too much chaos here.' She waved a fork. 'As you can see.'

I looked around. 'What would your mother say?'

'My mother? Who's she? I'm a grown-up now, I've got no mother.' She leant forward. 'And nor should you. At our age we've learnt to cut family connections, surely. That dependence, and not daring to do—'

'But you were very close to yours,' I protested. 'You all liked each other.'

'They liked me.' She gave a short laugh. 'They probably still do—if they're alive—'

'You mean you haven't kept in touch at all?'

'Listen, I got married at twenty. Six months later I was a

117

mother myself and divorced to boot.'

'I didn't know you had a child.'

'I haven't any more.'

'Oh dear, did it die? I am sorry.' I touched her hand timidly and pulled a tender, sympathetic face.

She laughed cheerfully. What courage she had. 'It might have died for all I know. No, I gave it away.'

I froze. 'Gave your child away?'

'Yes.' She laughed again. 'Your face, it's a sight. Yes, I didn't like it, so I gave it away. What's wrong with that?'

'It's honest,' I said stiffly. 'But I couldn't do it.' I bent my head to light a cigarette and saw Harriet and Fanny in the flame. Each side of Paul. 'Going up' in Harrods' lift. Turning left to Children's Clothes, with Françoise trailing moodily behind. Paul fighting it out, oh so subtly, with some assistant as to who should show the snootiest front. Harriet cleverly sensing it, exulting in her father's victory. Fanny missing me. And me, instead of being where I should, with them, me smoking in a Paris studio, listening to Damson telling me how she'd calmly given away her child.

'No, well,' she was saying, 'I expect you see your children as your life.'

'Not all of it,' I said, on guard.

'Them and a selection of lovers,' she said shrewdly. 'Is that right?'

'On the nail!' What else was there to say? I suddenly felt completely pointless. My life laid there amongst the dirty dishes. Appropriate placing. Like yesterday's left-overs. To my horror, my eyes went wet. I swallowed hard. 'It's not enough, is it?' I said dejectedly.

She stood up, smiling like a satisfied sphinx. 'Oh, I wouldn't say that, not by any means. After all, I expect you spread a lot of love around and that's good stuff, isn't it? Now,' she said briskly, 'don't for Christ's sake start indulging in self-pity, there's a good girl. I've got to get started.' She moved across the room and left me sitting all at sea. 'When the boys come, bang on this door. I'm in the dark room, okay?' I nodded miserably. She laughed wickedly. 'Cheer up! It does everyone good to get it in perspective.'

She banged the door behind her. I got up suddenly, strode across and, standing close to, I shouted through, 'So

118

sayeth the bloody prophet!' But all I heard was her answering laugh from the other side.

They'd been at it. I could tell the minute they came in. Rupert and Jean-Paul. But now things were going badly. It's ugly when it ends like that. Enchanted evenings, laced in heady anticipation—undressing, a bit embarrassed, cleaning teeth, closing the lavatory door, aiming urine carefully so the sound won't carry. Lights out, let's make love. But then the rhythm's wrong, or the smell close-to, or something in the skin. My ideal is smooth skin like my own which people think in men is nancyish. Not me though. I like it fine-grained, rather soft, no hair, with a body temperature similar to mine. Like—I tried hard thinking just who like. Well, like no one that I knew. Not now at any rate. Charles had a hairy body, hairy from top to toe, like coconut matting on his chest. When he sweated, wet strands clung together, went shiny, looked not unlike a river rat. Felt slimy to the touch. Sam? Sam never sweated which for such a large and heavy man was something I found very strange. Well, never sweated much that is. And yet was hot. Hot and dry like the desert, with skin as coarse as sand. You could have cut it up in squares and sold it at a hardware shop. Sixpence a sheet, no trouble. Physical facts, not serious, but if encountered just by chance and added on to other things, enough to put you off. Like buttocks pocked with pimples and roughly peeling nails. And chins that need a shave. And breath turned bad by dawn.

Looking at poor Jean-Paul and Rupert now, each so conscious of the other but communication temporarily abandoned, I wondered idly 'what had been the cause. They greeted me separately, both with a kiss. Jean-Paul gave two, being French. One on each cheek, but I'd turned away before the second came so that it landed in my ear. We both laughed.

'Where's Damson?' Rupert said abruptly as if now he was at odds with me too.

'In there.' I pointed. 'In the dark room. She said to bang on the door when you arrived.' I looked around trying to locate my own clothes. 'I'd better get something on I suppose. Oh don't worry, I can dress in the bathroom. That is when I see my stuff. Do you know where it is, Rupert?'

119

He shrugged irritably and shook his head. Jean-Paul put up a soothing hand.

'No, Myopia, for me to do your make-up you are perfect as you are. This first shot I think you are wearing only the hat and skirt so that I shall also be applying foundation on your upper half.'

I stared at him and then at Rupert. 'What?'

What. I could hear them all saying it. Back in London, buying *Chic* from Smith's counters. Charles frowning, 'What the devil!' Sam smiling, 'What the hell!' Paul perplexed, 'What on earth?' And the children giggling, 'What are you meant to be doing, Mummy? What—'

'What?' I said again.

'Oh, just a little painting on the bosoms. Such as one would apply to the cheeks—'

'Cheeks?' I sat down on them quickly.

Jean-Paul touched his face delicately. 'I polish and shine your oh-so-pretty breasts and on those charming nipples apply a little rouge.'

When had he seen them then? Last night? 'Well,' I said uncertainly.

Jean-Paul twinkled flirtatiously. 'It will be a labour of love for me, Myopia.'

Rupert snorted and began banging. 'Damson!'

There was a short silence the other side of the door then it opened slowly and Damson came out.

'Contacts,' she said triumphantly and waved two long strips of shiny paper along which were printed small grey photographs, about the size of postage stamps. 'Mind, they're still wet, but it gives you an idea of yourself.' To me, 'Here, look at them through this,' and she put a square heavy slab of magnifying glass in my hand. I don't know what I was expecting but it wasn't what I saw.

We'd come across the place unexpectedly. One Saturday in a narrow street somewhere behind Tottenham Court Road. 'The Doll Museum.' 'Shall we go in?' I'd said to the girls. 'Oh yes,' answered Harriet right away. But Fanny had hung back. I took her gently by the hand, a tiny bell tinkled as we stepped inside and an old woman with a crumpled face like a Christmas cracker took our money and directed us upstairs. It was a narrow dark building on three floors, formerly a house, late eighteenth-century or thereabouts. There were dolls everywhere—over the walls, all the way lining the stairs, each with neat detailed labels giving dates and origin. Harriet was ecstatic. I looked with interest at them on the slow voyage up. Fanny said nothing but held on tightly. But by the time we'd reached the top her uneasiness had communicated itself not just to me but Harriet too. 'Oh look,' my voice sounded unnaturally loud. 'Oh look,' I continued in a whisper. 'This one's made of wax.' We all three of us studied it in silence, a hundred eyes stared back in that one small room alone. Unblinking, blind in delicately modelled perfect frozen features. Faces which had in the past given untold pleasures to their child owners and yet known none themselves.

That's how I looked, like one of those. Damson watched closely for my reaction. 'What do you think then, soppy?'

I shivered, the suddenness of the question and the sight of the cold pale face had set off a strange creeping sensation over my skin. That and the barely suppressed excitement in her voice. I cleared my throat, but kept on looking, moving the enlarging glass slowly up and down the strips of images. These were the last of the lot she'd taken. About ten towards the end of it, even to my inexperienced eye, seemed far superior to the rest. But by then I could remember I'd fallen more into the swing of things. She made a sudden movement of impatience as I continued to say nothing.

'Here, let the boys have a look. Go on, Rupert, you go first.'

I stood up, suddenly self-conscious. 'Anyone seen my cigarettes?'

No one answered. I hadn't expected that they would. The packet lay on the table, close at hand. I saw with surprise that my fingers shook slightly as I lit it. I wished they'd hurry up looking so that I could have another go. That was the bare bones of the matter.

Jean-Paul spoke first. He looked at me and said very slowly, 'Last night I make a big mistake. I make Myopia like a beauty queen. I make applications of colour that are crude and far too obvious. Damson, I wish to make a fresh start today!' He stood up.

'Oh sit down,' she said. 'Everything's perfect, don't you

121

see? Those, if they turn out as I expect—those will be just right for ordinary, well not ordinary, but conventionally beautiful, how-every-woman-longs-to-look, sort of stuff and that means that the dream ones can be much stranger, more like—nightmares.' She tapped the strip in her hand. 'This face denuded, raw, has much more impact, I agree, but let's make it even paler, emptier, more alienated ...'

'I do that,' Jean-Paul said eagerly. 'I use greys and amethyst so that she look like a ghost. Like someone dead who walks in the sleep.'

'Now you see,' Damson looked reflectively at me. 'I'm not so certain how I should do it. That first idea seems a little crass. What do you think, Myopia?'

'Who, me? About what?' I'd lost track.

She tutted and raised her eyes to the ceiling. 'Wake up!'

'Well,' I said defiantly, 'nobody has told me yet what the first idea was, have they?'

Rupert softened. His bad mood was beginning to fade. 'That's right. We hadn't properly explained.' To the others, 'Well, Damson had decided to do you as you were in your dream. That is flying over not London of course, but different parts of Paris. And not even flying necessarily but appearing in crowded places but always with some particle of clothing missing. So that for instance in this first shot that Jean-Paul mentioned you'd be nude from the waist up. The rest of you beautifully dressed of course—hat, gloves, skirt, shoes, but with your breasts bare, or in another—'

'Ah, you see,' I saw him floundering. 'That's where you run out of erogenous zones. There wouldn't be enough for six pages—'

Damson cut in. 'Don't be silly. It's not a question of that at all. I'd shoot profile, front, back, from above, below. It's not the content that's important but what the camera does with it.'

'Thanks,' I said, but cheerful.

Everyone laughed. 'Well,' Damson put up her hand, 'since then we've seen these, so what do we think? It introduces a new element, wouldn't you say?'

'I would,' I said, 'me.'

'Go and say goodbye to your granny,' my aunties clucked. Maiden aunts, all of them, which meant they weren't allowed to wear finger rings or go without their pinafores.

122

Or put curlers in their hair. Or stuff on the pale, slab-pastry faces. In case there was a chance their maidenhood or something should be snatched away from them when they weren't looking. 'Go on,' they pushed me towards the parlour door. 'Go and say goodbye to Granny.'

I'd shrunk back. 'No.'

Coarse, capable hands caught me by the shoulder. I struggled, but it was not an equal fight. The door was opened, shut, the key clicked in the lock and I was inside alone.

Alone with Granny who lay in a long wooden box, its top leaning against the small piano. The blinds were drawn and it was very black, as black as the armband they'd sewn on my cardigan. I'd been the centre of attention in school, all week, because of the armband. Asked to join in all sorts of games in the playground. Accorded a new respect. Next week they'd said they'd take it off. Two candles burnt by Granny's head, on each end of the mantelpiece. I went right up to the box to get a better look. She was wearing her new nightie, the one she'd sent me to get from the shop, the day she'd been taken bad. It hadn't been paid for yet, I knew that, since she'd asked me to get it on tick. I'd taken a bit of time choosing, made old Miss Tidy show me all there was. By the time I'd got back she was dead. But I'd got her a nice nightie. I picked it up to see if they'd left her knickers on. But there was nothing there except a matted, mossy grey triangle which looked to me as if it could have done with a comb. Her hands, knobbly things, normally with cuts and countless chilblains, were folded smoothly like a pair of gloves. And her face was very smooth too, as if someone had taken a scalding iron to it. It looked like Sunday best. Her eyes were shut, not tightly like they used to be when she was crying, but easily, just right. The lids sat on the eyes like a shell covers an egg. I poked at one with my finger but jumped back at the cold. It was colder than the toad my teacher had at school. And very white. Very sickly white. Like the maggots and lice you find under a stone. Sort of 'see through' white.

Jean-Paul stood back proudly to survey his one and a half hours' steady work on my face. I stood up slowly and looked at it too.

'I won't sit you before the mirror as I do it—'

'Oh please,' I'd begged, 'I'd love to see how you start and go on.'

'No,' firmly, 'you must wait till is all complete.'

'My God,' I gasped, 'I look just like my granny.'

His face went strained and disappointed.

'Oh no,' I said quickly. 'Not meaning rudely. Really! But the colour. It's the colour of a corpse—'

He gave a brilliant smile and a little bow, almost a curtsey. 'Then I have achieved the effect I was after.'

Damson was in the dark room, printing blow-ups from her morning's contacts. Rupert was with her, helping. Jean-Paul hugged me, carefully keeping well away from my head.

'I call them now, yes?'

I nodded and laughed. 'I won't turn round till they're in the room. Wait a minute. Take that white sheet off the bed. That's it. Drape it round my shoulders. I'll stand by the window. Looking out.'

We giggled like schoolchildren. He suddenly stopped, frowning. 'Not too much, the laughing. You might crack your maquillage.'

I nodded solemnly and stared at him with cold and distant eyes. He seemed mesmerised momentarily, then gave a little shake like a puppy faced with something deeply disturbing. 'You are, Myopia, far too lifelike,' he said in a funny voice.

I continued to stare and murmured softly, 'Life*less*.' Then, at his silly expression I winked one eye, remembering to keep my face as straight as possible.

They came in excitedly. 'Look at this blow-up. Look, it's sensational,' but I didn't turn round, not immediately anyway. I wanted to savour the moment.

'Let's have a look, then,' Damson said.

I swung round in my sheet, quietly, like a film in slow motion and held my arms out straight on either side. Since I'd chosen to look, eyes wide, at a distant point above their heads I'd done myself out of the satisfying sight of their faces in first impact. By the time I focused on them fully they must have had time to collect their senses and gather up their dropped jaws.

'Jesus wept!' Rupert whispered. Jean-Paul looked delighted. He turned to Damson enquiringly.

She swallowed, then croaked, 'Fucking fantastic, boy.'

I started to glide towards them. Each involuntarily took

a step back. 'Now look here, get off all that,' Damson said, but I was beginning to really enjoy myself. 'Bloody death's head,' she said again. I went over to her and softly laid my fingers on her cheek. She jerked away. 'Feel her hands, they're freezing.' She sounded really angry.

I stopped. 'Does it give you the willies?' I said in a normal voice, and looked at them with a friendlier face. Rupert took a deep breath.

'It's pretty strong stuff. Do you feel all right inside? You look—I don't know—drained.' He stared closely into my eyes. 'There's no blood in there at all, no blood vessels or veins or anything.'

'Eye drops that I have put in.' Jean-Paul spoke. The first dealings of the day with Rupert, I noted. 'That makes the whites of the eyes very clear so the pupil and iris become more dramatic.' He shrugged. 'An old trick, of course, but this, this is a new Italian make. Is excellent, no?'

I looked in the mirror and paused. 'I'm doing more of this looking in the mirror since I've been in Paris than I have for the whole of the last half of my life.'

Jean-Paul looked surprised. 'But of course. You are doing a professional job. How else can you become able to know your face?'

'You're muddling it up with vanity, Myopia,' Damson agreed. 'Quite a different thing.'

I looked at their three faces glowing with life and good health and then back at my own. My grey eyes, always grey, grey as cigarette ash, grew lighter as I looked. I found by concentrating, lasting as long as I could without blinking, that I was able even to control the colour. That by turning my head whilst keeping my eyes on the same spot they reflected and echoed the waxy subtleties in my skin. 'Perhaps it does help to practise.' But it was as if I were talking to myself. 'Wouldn't it be strange if you, knowing what you looked like, glanced in passing at a mirror and saw yourself like this. The same but as if you were dead.'

I stopped. Damson listened carefully.

'Well, of course,' I continued, 'and also the other way round. As if a ghost or someone looking dead like me now were to see in a mirror herself but alive.'

'Yes,' Damson dragged the word out slowly. 'Yes, the mirror image ...'

I took from her hand the large print that she'd come

running in with. Apparently now forgotten. Black and white, just of my face.

'This is beautiful.' Rupert and Jean-Paul clustered round. 'Isn't it?'

'What do you think of yourself then now, Myopia?' Rupert said teasingly.

I considered seriously. 'Well, I think there's a lot there that you can do things with.' He laughed. 'No, I mean it's got me thinking myself ...'

Damson snapped her fingers. 'It bloody has. Could be great that idea of hers. I could do it, you know, the mirror thing.'

We stared at her, she'd gone bright red with excitement.

'I've thought of something else,' I started.

'I mean,' she interrrupted, 'the semi-nude dream thing. You see tit and bum everywhere now, nothing new ...'

'Anyway,' Rupert added, 'you never know, Moo might not think it "quaite naice" enough for *Chic* and just run the normal sleeping ones we've done. She's always an unknown quantity. Lots of snaps get chucked out last minute if she doesn't quite "see" them ...'

'I've thought of something else,' I tried again.

Damson gripped my hand so tightly I flinched. 'You've thought of enough, my beaut.'

'No, listen. What about if it's the dead image in the mirror doing that in black and white ...'

She opened her eyes wide.

'Well,' I said uncertainly and held up the big print. 'It just seems to look so much stronger without colour and ...'

'And,' she nodded, 'we'll have the rest of the photograph, the real you in colour, which means the clothes ... Yippee, God almighty, it's going to be tricky. But let's get going. We'll start with a head shot first. If that comes off a treat I can see it ending up on the cover.'

We all us of beamed, carried by her enthusiasm.

'What excitement,' Rupert cried.

I laughed out loud till I caught sight of Jean-Paul. He shook his head mournfully. I put a quick finger to my face.

'No!'

'But yes,' he replied sadly. 'You have cracked your beautiful maquillage. Now I, I must set about repairing it.'

126

At six o'clock Damson sent Rupert to collect the previous night's colour transparencies. He was back with them by half past. Damson took them carefully out of their small plastic boxes and switched on a square light box in the corner. She placed them on top of it so that they looked like brilliant gems on a jeweller's cloth.

'Now,' she took a deep breath, 'the moment of truth.'

They had me arranged beautifully, conscious or not, head resting on one limp arm, hand hanging gracefully weighed down with jewelled rings. Each frame contained a clearly consistent colour theme with only the violet chaise longue to link them. In every one the hair was arranged differently and looking closely I could see that in all not only had the face been repainted but so had even the finger nails to match whatever I was wearing. Like a bird of paradise, a peacock, the pure stuff of dreams.

Rupert sighed. 'Jesus, I've got a job on now.' I looked at him. 'I'll have to go all through that lot and list every bloody thing—lipstick, Thunder Pink by Elizabeth Arden, Rose Soufflé nail lacquer by Helena Rubinstein, eye shadow, Azure Haze by ...'

'Oh,' I said, 'did you use all those different makes, Jean-Paul?'

They all laughed. He shrugged. 'But of course not. I use everything that I have collected over the years. It's mostly theatrical but I have done many jobs like this for magazines. I know that always they must be labelled untruthfully.'

'To do with advertising, love,' Damson said cheerfully. 'Whichever beauty house has bought most space, that is placed most ads that month, they get the most editorial mention. Only practical, eh?'

'Well,' I said, 'I've been caught by that then. Liked the look of a lipstick somewhere in a beauty article, read what it was, bought it and found it's not the same at all.'

'That's it. You shouldn't believe all you read then, should you, soppy?'

'Stop calling me soppy, Damson.'

'Dopey, then, is that better? Now, let's choose the best of these and get on with it.'

'Oh,' I said, 'can you still use those? With no mirror in?'

'Let me worry about that. Tricks of the trade. As it happens everything's perfect—better than we could have bargained for. In these your eyes are shut, so we're giving a good show to eye shadow that'll please old Moo. She likes keeping in with the cosmetic queens. And then as the ghost or as death your eyes are open. Makes it stronger you see. You're now not looking into the mirror, merely sleeping in front of it, and lurking death is looking at you. Whew.' She looked triumphantly at all of us. 'What do you think of that?'

'Should she be wearing the same outfits exactly though, Damson?' Rupert pondered. 'I mean we've given enough coverage to Joe's clothes in these colour ones and I'm worried that in the black and white mirror one they won't register so well because I put everything together in terms of colour and not tonally.'

'Well,' Damson puckered her eyes. I looked carefully amongst the glowing squares. Redcurrant reds, piercing pinks, plum, blood, purple, dusk blue, sweet strong leaf green, lemon, canary, and melon yellow, brown, brown sugar brown, bitter chocolate, dark rich treacle. Something missing.

'There's something missing,' I frowned. 'White! Rupert, what about, what's it called, "Snow Siren"? Did we bring that? I'm sure we did.'

'We did, yes. But then I decided not to use it after all. It didn't seem to fit in with these.'

'But it would in the mirror.'

'In black and white.'

'Perfect! Get it!'

Damson sat down. 'Christ! What a team. Well, kids, we're inching forward. Let's have a look at this "Snow Siren" then.'

Rupert brought it from the wardrobe. It had travelled well. Crêpe de chine, not a crease in sight. He held it in front of me. I moved to the mirror and drew the batwing sleeves to their full width. The silky pyjamas rippled around my bare feet. Jean-Paul placed the crystal skull cap loosely on my head. White from top to toe. Immaculate. Pure. An angel. A moonlit creature. Someone from the other side.

Damson stepped back and placed her fingers to her eyes, making a small square of them through which she looked, as if through the eye of a camera.

'Sensational,' breathed Jean-Paul. 'Ca c'est sensational.'

Damson glowed happily and nodded. 'It'll do,' she

said grudgingly but her eyes held that special look again.

'There you are, darling, didn't I say you should have this?' Rupert said smugly. 'Now just look how useful it is after all.'

I looked at myself and saw two wax candles flickering on a shabby mantelpiece casting shadows along smooth and waxy flesh. Picking out impoverished rayon lace, more suitable for a bottom drawer than a going away dress on the dead. Old Miss Tidy's best.

'Yes,' I said slowly. 'It has come in useful. Nearly as nice as my granny's nightie.'

Jean-Paul painted my nails white, they looked like pearls by the time he'd finished. And over my hands he smoothed the same foundation that he'd used on my face. But he was disturbed by my hair.

'This,' he said, lifting it and looking at Damson. 'This I think is too dark.'

She agreed. 'Do what you think.'

He tried pinning it flat and pushing it into the skull cap. 'You agree?' he said to me. 'We should have no hair.'

I nodded. I knew perfectly what he meant. It was no good, strands kept falling out, there was just too much of it.

'Well,' I said in the end. 'Cut it off then. Go on, all of it, I shan't mind.'

They looked at me approvingly.

'Really short,' I went on, encouraged. 'And what about while you're at it plucking my eyebrows? They're surely too dark aren't they?'

Damson nodded. 'Be better with none at all.'

'Yes,' I said recklessly. 'I can always draw them on till they grow again.'

'What the devil have you done to yourself?'

'I've cut all my hair off and shaved my eyebrows, Charles. Do you mind? It looks a little bald I know, but it will soon grow back.'

'Am I to understand that alopecia is now all the rage?'

'Something like that, yes.'

'Perhaps,' I said a little fearfully to Jean-Paul, 'you could at least leave me my fringe.'

We worked until past midnight. Damson drank steadily all the way through. Red wine.

129

'I could do with some of that,' I said at one point.

Jean-Paul frowned. 'Oh no, it will spoil your white lips.'

'She can have it through a straw.' Rupert fitted one carefully in but removed it too quickly while I was still drinking. I felt a thin trickle run from the corner of my mouth and heard Jean-Paul curse.

'No, wait! It looks good, like a vampire,' Damson shouted from behind her camera. 'Let me do some before you clean it up.'

I'd got the no-blinking off to a T by then. In fact I'd slowly turned into this other self completely. I made my mind an empty room and allowed its walls to ripple with imagined horrors. Harmless particles of dust drifted together, turning into nests of insects' eggs which, feeding on each other's warmth, metamorphosed behind my eyes. Until the surface of the room became a heaving shuddering mass of minute beating wings and threadlike sawing legs. Entering this space, at first confidently, drawn to my full height, erect, I was stricken by the inability to breathe. My flesh hung pouched and withered like an old balloon, with nothing left inside. My bones shrank and grew soft, took on the consistency of the toothless gums in the aged and infirm. My tongue quivered, forked inside my mouth, darting helplessly towards the throbbing life surrounding it. And they, the insects, gradually grew in size and with it, altered in their shape, exuded monstrous rotting fumes. Began to fly. But being now swollen and inexplicably without their wings they drifted down on unseen winds and settled on the slimy floor and me. Into my still moist eyes they came, so that when, with gigantic effort, calling on my last reserve of strength, I closed my lids I found with mounting panic that I had unwittingly trapped them there inside. And that now they were doing exactly what they wished to do. Devouring me internally. But still I stayed alive, though not in any physical sense at all since my body had long been sucked apart by those who surrounded it.

'Right, that's it then! Done!' Damson's voice reached me out of another world. The one to do with morning tea and putting on of radios. And blowing noses and buttering toast. All the ordinary actions that let you know there is no other world at all beside this one where these things exist. And that if you think there is you certainly are a very

130

foolish person indeed. And serve yourself right for going off like that alone.

'You must stop this screaming in your sleep. Your poor father and I couldn't get a wink last night. Do it once more and we'll get the doctor to you. I won't warn you again. Now hurry your food down and be a little more sensible. You look awful. People will be wondering what I'm feeding you on.'

Damson snapped her fingers. 'You in a trance or what? Come on! I'm dying to eat. We'll have a blow-out at André's, eh? He'll be open still.'

I blinked for what seemed like the first time all day. 'I went all funny then. It was awful. Was I all right? Did I do it well?'

'Superb! You want to be careful though, Myopia, not to get too fanciful. It runs in families they say.'

'Don't be silly. Jean-Paul, can we take this face off now? I feel it's eating me away somehow.'

He laughed. 'Well, it isn't wise to keep it on too long. The pores can't breathe, you know. It has in it a certain substance, like lead white, that if I had put it all over the body in two hours you would indeed be dead.'

'Good God,' I said, alarmed. 'Now is a nice time to tell me.'

'Could have made good pictures though,' Damson said cheerfully. 'Now, Myopia, what's it to be when we get there?'

Rupert's tired voice said plaintively, 'Champagne surely is called for. I don't know about anybody else but I'm completely buggered.'

Damson laughed. 'Uncross your legs, Rupe, and tonight you might get lucky.'

I glanced at Jean-Paul but he was bent over his tin of cleansing cream, lifting out a scoopful on his fingers like delicious cold ice-cream. I wondered what would happen tonight. Rupert went to the bathroom.

'You oughtn't to have said that, Damson,' I said to her reproachfully, quietly, so that Jean-Paul shouldn't hear. 'You go trampling in until before you know it you could kill something beautiful.'

She pulled a face and said mockingly, 'Oh dearie me. I must mind my Ps and Qs, must I, madam?'

It came right out of the blue. 'Why didn't you ever write back to me?'

131

'What?' She looked taken aback.

'You heard! I wrote and wrote and never had a word from you. I was terribly unhappy, you pig.'

She glanced over at Jean-Paul. 'I wasn't entirely unmoved myself.' Rupert came back into the room looking sulky and withdrawn. 'We'll go into it later.' Hurriedly, 'Now get a move on, Jean-Paul. Tell you what, Rupert and I will go ahead and warn of our arrival. What about that?'

I nodded, I felt like a spot of peace and quiet. As if it would take time before my feet could realise they were actually touching ground. Jean-Paul took my skull cap off and carefully helped me step out of 'Snow Siren'. I put a towel around my body as I had that morning before it had all begun and closed my eyes whilst his firm fingers lathered the comforting cream all over my face. It smelt like Harriet and Fanny had when they were very small. Sane and sweet. Dimpled and damp and everydayish. Tomorrow I'd be back and Paris would be in the past. Except, of course, before then there'd be tonight to get through.

I'd had my fill of fine clothes for a bit. 'I can't be bothered to dress up now, Jean-Paul. This is all right, isn't it? I'm not in the mood to be looked at any more.' I stood in black trousers and polo-neck sweater, cropped head like a boy, thin long fringe almost in my eyes.

'The urchin, but why not?' he said.

We smiled at each other. 'The end of a long day.' I felt aglow all over, deeply satisfied, like after a strenuous ocean swim or when you've done the week's wash and you're piling it clean and pressed into the airing cupboard.

'You're a very, very clever boy, Jean-Paul.' I put my arms around him. 'And I love you dearly.'

I was thinking of food as I said it, with all four of us sitting down and tucking in. And André in charge and taking care. And I was hoping in a generous flooding tender way that things would work out nicely for Rupert and the boy in my arms. I dropped them lightly to my sides.

'Time to go,' I said brightly.

But he didn't move, just stayed glued to my front all the way down, his cheek hard against mine. I felt him trembling slightly, and turn a searching mouth towards my own.

'That's torn it,' I thought. I made my body go as hard and sexless as I could, stiffening the spine and trying to squash back my breasts to be as small as they'd go by taking little shallow gasps of air. I don't know why I bothered, it had never worked before. And it certainly wasn't now. You could try anything when a man's in full flow. You could cross your eyes, put snot on him, cut orange peel teeth and place them on your own, begin to sing in high soprano, but nothing of it puts him off. Not with that sticky, stuffy goal in sight. I tried a kind, long-suffering sigh and a dose of solid British good sense.

'Look here,' I said. 'Jean-Paul. This just isn't good enough you know. Now pull yourself together, there are people waiting after all.'

Quick as lightning he frogmarched me to the bed, yanked my trousers to my knees, threw me on to it and pulled his own pants down. A sweet pork sword, a tender chipolata. Much earlier on that day my troublesome period had disappeared. They do that some months, put in a quick and painful appearance then leave a spotless sanitary towel as a visiting card. 'Just as well,' I thought. 'Not today, tomato sauce, merci beaucoup, maître d'hôtel. We don't take it with all our meals you know.'

Twelve thrusts and a sharp sly twist at the end, to make the cake perfect. Then out of the oppressive heat of the oven and back into the open air. Into the cold to shrink the thing into a reasonable shape again. He did his trousers up with difficulty and, shrugging, looked down at me and laughed.

'It is not ready yet for sleep, my friend.' He reached down for my hand and placed it on the bulge. 'You excite too much, Myopia! Now I once again prepare you for your next appearance.'

I lay there pulsing like a stranded fish, my knickers round my knee, one breast still lower than the other, when eager hands had snatched it from its brassière cup. I looked beyond his head and saw the door, then froze. It was open. Just half an inch, no light on the landing but enough in the room to catch and hold a strip of colour. The width of a fly catcher. Shiny yellow. Jean-Paul saw my expression change and swiftly looked around. Not swift enough. In that infinitesimal instant it had gone. I stood

133

up, pulled myself together, literally in all ways, and walked across the room. The door swung back easily and I stepped outside. There was no one there, but there had been, the perfume lingered on. Musky, cloying, unmistakable. 'Babette!' I called. 'Babette!'

Jean-Paul joined me. 'You imagine, Myopia. There is no one here.'

'Well, smell,' I said. 'What's that?'

He laughed easily. 'That is Damson's perfume. I know it is a special one which only she must wear. It has a musk base.'

'It's the same as Babette's,' I said, 'because I smelt it on her yesterday.'

'Ah well,' he said, 'Babette. Yes, maybe she has stolen some at one time to remind of her beloved Damson. Or maybe Damson foolishly has dangled it before her eyes to take yet more delight in her distress. But come, we must go. There is nothing for you to worry about.'

So that was to be that. We walked along to André's, passed similar but smaller cafés, all still full. Passed dress shops labelled 'Chypre' and 'Chère'. Crossed cobbled streets and traffic lights with Jean-Paul's hand held companionably around my waist with not so much as a glance from anyone. 'He's fifteen years my junior, doesn't that seem funny to you?' I wanted to shout. But, of course, in Paris what was that? And in any case I was deceiving myself if that was what I claimed to be disturbing me. I thought of Rupert crying in my garden, how stranded he'd looked this morning coming in with Jean-Paul. And how pleased and hopeful he'd been last night. I saw Babette's shut and watchful face, and the long yellow line of her dress at the door. And then I thought of Damson. 'Well, anyway. So what. She didn't write back.'

As we came to André's door I broke away from Jean-Paul's hand and entered separately, alone. They were sitting on the far side, Rupert, Damson, Babette I saw, and André. He rose to greet me, as I approached, his gold teeth glinting in the lowered lights. The others stared as I held out my hand. He bent to kiss it but kept his dark brown eyes on my face. 'Myopia,' he murmured.

'André,' I answered softly, and thought as I said it, 'Oh well, in for a penny, in for a pound.'

Midnight. A corner table in a French café, criss-crossed

134

with fierce undercurrents of emotion. Cutlery in hand. 'You could cut it with a knife,' I thought. 'This atmosphere, scoop it up with a spoon and swallow it, except for fear of indigestion.' Damson was tucking in to second helpings, so she'd be getting it anyway. Indigestion. Unless the gods and her innards were looking the other way. Enchaud de Porc à la Perigourdine, that's what she was on, which translated comes out to be Loin of Pork stuffed with Truffles. I knew that because André told me. 'You run a very good restaurant.' That's all I could think of to say back, but it pleased him. In fact everything I did seemed to please him, even when at one point my food went down the wrong way, bubbling up in the back of my throat. 'Ugh, ugh,' I coughed. 'Ugh.' Everyone laughed but then I felt André's hand rubbing my back, putting things to rights. Underneath my jumper! 'Ugh.' Final cough, last little splutter. 'That's better,' I said. 'All gone. Thank you.' But he kept his hand where it was and I sort of had to let him really. It would have seemed too churlish to do otherwise at that point in the evening.

We did a lot of talking about what we'd done. Damson reckoned they were the best photos she'd taken. Except for one very secret session she'd had with Freddie. That's how she put it—'one very secret session'—and I bent over my plate blushing a bit at the terrible thoughts of what she could have been getting up to.

Whenever I looked up one or other of them was watching me, as if somehow I was to be the deciding factor for the events of the night. The other tables were emptying until by half past one we were the only ones left. André told one of the waiters to lock up, then he sent him and the rest of them home. A bottle of cognac was passed around between us and came quite naturally to rest in front of Damson. I wondered briefly who was paying. Rupert and I had plenty of francs—we hadn't spent anything yet, only on the taxi from the airport. He was sitting next to me.

'Rupert,' I whispered, 'we should pay for this dinner surely.'

But his face when he turned it to me was so dreadfully miserable that I said quickly, 'What I mean is that *I* should, don't you think?'

He nodded dejectedly. Jean-Paul was talking excitedly to Damson and had paid no attention to Rupert for the

whole of the meal. 'Perhaps I should think of keeping my
money for a hotel tonight.'

I was appalled. Oh dear. Dearie me. I took his limp
hand.

'Is it all over then?' And cast a glance towards Jean-Paul
to show what I was talking about. Well, I thought, I've
surely got some influence in that direction now! 'Would
you like me to have a word with him, Rupert? I can't bear
seeing you like this again.'

That set him off. He stood up quickly, scraping his
chair, and went off to Messieurs.

I looked at André. He shrugged and laughed, though I
don't think he'd heard what we'd been saying. I leaned
forward a long way towards Jean-Paul so that André's
hand fell out of my jumper on to my bottom, right under
it, fingers spread.

'Jean-Paul.' I said it with great urgency, to get it over
with before Rupert returned. 'Jean-Paul, is Rupert staying
with you tonight?'

His smile faded. 'Rupert?'

'Yes. You haven't quarrelled or anything really, have
you? Not really seriously, I mean?'

He lifted his shoulders, shrugged just like André, but he
didn't laugh. 'I do not know what I have done to Rupert
but he doesn't speak to me all day so naturally I do not
speak to him. That is all.'

'Well.' I could see Rupert coming back towards us.
'Please try, Jean-Paul, he's very unhappy. It would be a
shame to lose a nice friendship, wouldn't it?' I looked hard
into his eyes and lowered my voice right down so the
others couldn't possibly hear. 'After all, I could have
turned nasty and said no, couldn't I?' He looked
astonished but I kept on staring until at last a slow smile
broke out. We both winked at precisely the same moment.
Rupert sat down, looking sulky. It crossed my mind that
he must bring these situations on himself. You can't
expect to always bring things off by being babyish. 'A
spoilt boy,' my mother would have said.

'Would you like a cigar, you two?' They looked at each
other and nodded back at me. André went to fetch some.
'And me,' Damson shouted.

'You say yes to anything going in your mouth don't
you?' I said.

Babette glowered at her end. She really put me off, that

136

girl. I wished she'd get up and go. Damson was taking no notice of her at all. But I seemed to have pulled something off for Rupert with Jean-Paul. They lit their cigars together and from there on remained engrossed in each other. I don't care what anyone says, that lighting-up lark is a sure winner for breaking the ice. With cigars more than anything because they take so much longer to get going. And when all at once Rupert said, 'André, could we have the bill? I'm paying for this meal,' I knew everything must be all right again.

André wouldn't hear of it, of course. He waved his hands and shook his head. 'It is my pleasure, please allow me that. Tonight no one pays, okay?' But he kept his eyes on mine while he said it. Except me, I thought. I'll be paying indirectly. Not that I minded, not at all. I thought he was nice, very nice, and that was always enough. Anyway, I'd never had a man with gold teeth before. I thought of the schoolgirl joke.

'Tell me, André,' I said, 'your two front teeth, are they like stars?'

He looked startled. 'Stars?'

'Yes. Do they come out at night or are they cemented in?'

He threw his head back and roared.

'I'm only asking. It's not that funny.'

But he went on laughing, shaking helplessly. 'You like them?' he spluttered. 'Yes?'

'Oh yes, I think they're beautiful.'

'Ah,' he stood up, 'one moment then.'

I took the opportunity to change seats. Sitting in the lavatory, I tried to sort things out quietly. If I was Prime Minister or occupied the throne, that's where I'd rule the country from. The privy. Privy Councillor. Was that what it meant? Anyway, nothing like a confined space for clearing the head, clarifying the situation, concentrating on the central issue. It wasn't quite so easy in this one, too much effort had to be wasted in seeing that my trousers didn't get splashed. A tiled hole in the floor with ridged foot-rests either side. I'd have a word with André afterwards to see if he hadn't considered interior modernisation. This undignified squatting would hardly suit a Head of State.

Damson was the fly in the ointment. I knew now that I didn't want to get tied up with her again. Not in the way it had once been. Too much something or other had flown

137

under the bridge. Working with her was great, but barging into my life and taking over, knowing everything that was going on, making my decisions for me—that was a different matter. I'd stay with André tonight, that should make things clear to her, spell it out so to speak. And tomorrow before leaving for London I'd say it wasn't convenient for her to stay with me there. Babette should be pleased, poor creature.

When I got out, there she was. At the mirror, making up. She watched me while I washed my hands. 'Hello,' I smiled. She didn't answer. Well, I thought, she's half mad. She really is. That's what Damson's done to her. Well, she'd done it to me too in a sort of way. The year she left. Lost, that's what I'd been. Shot through with self-doubt, irrational fear and a dreadful fierce possessiveness. Or is that just what love does to you anyway? Hadn't I been the same with Paul? Unequal love then. When one is giving more and getting less than the other. A better balance is what's needed, so that though on one side of the scales it's all sugar and on the other a steel weight, things can still work out even if the proportion's right. You can't say that to people though, like the onlooker you can only see the game. I took the bull by the horns. I love that expression— as if anybody in their right senses would! What, with big wide nostrils snorting at you like a steam kettle? And bulging eyes as red and ripe as wild strawberries? You'd have to be pretty wild yourself. But I did it.

'Babette,' I started. She'd finished her face and was now filing her nails. I'd noticed her nails before, they'd reminded me of Moo's, the same shape, long and narrow coming to a fine point at the tip. Lethal weapons. I took a step back.

'Babette.' She didn't look up. 'You have no reason to worry about me. Not at all. Not about Damson and me, I mean.' That was putting it badly, but I was thinking about her understanding of English first and foremost.

She held the nail file as you would a dart towards the board, except if she let fly now it would have landed in my throat. When she spoke it came out a cross between a hiss and a curse, with her upper lip curled back like an attacking animal. 'Françoise, she is your girl!'

I laughed but I felt a prickly uneasiness, a desire to escape. Why hadn't I left well alone? Whatever I said I could tell she couldn't be convinced. From the restaurant I could hear Damson's rich and fruity laugh, echoing the lighter sound of Rupert's. And André's strong and reassuring voice, binding the whole thing together. I wanted to be with them, back there in the warm. But Babette moved quickly. More swiftly than I would have believed possible, she slipped behind me, locked the door and stood with her back against it. Something jolted painfully against my ribs, if she'd been closer I would have said her nail file except that this was happening from the inside and hammering hard now, right up in my eardrums. It's always amazed me how terribly tiring fear is. Real fear.

Harriet had run across the road once, when very small. I'd turned round and there she was with people shouting and speeding cars screaming to a halt. A stranger picked her up in his arms on the other side. 'Where's the mother?' they were saying but I couldn't move; from sheer exhaustion I couldn't take a single step—only sink down and sit where I was right there on the cold pavement.

I could have done with a nice chair now or tear gas or a cold water hose. Anything to get her out of the way. But somewhere the voice of reason came to my rescue. She looked insane, that was for sure, on the point of eruption, losing her cool, blowing her top, consumed, crackers!

'What a very pretty girl you are, Babette,' I said. Her eyes flickered for a split second. 'Françoise is always telling my children that, and how you model for Dior. She is my au pair. Next week you will be able to see her, she's coming home here for a holiday. Tomorrow when I'm back in London I shall tell her that we met.'

Her hands dropped to her side, the nail file fell to the floor. I took a smooth step towards the door, but it wasn't over yet. I could tell by her tense face. She spoke slowly in a dangerously tight, over-controlled voice. 'I should like to kill you. You are a hateful person. Like an artichoke, you give a little of yourself to everyone. I have seen—'

'Oh yes, Babette, I saw you seeing at the door—'

She stopped suddenly. Then threw back her head like a pony, puckered her mouth together and spat in my face. I felt it sliding over my skin, lifted one arm and wiped it away with my sleeve. Then I reached behind her and unlocked the door. As I walked back to the table I could hear her crying hysterically. 'Your girl friend is upset, Damson. If you're at all kind you'll go and see to her,' I said as I sat down.

Good in bed, I'd had lots of those without a doubt. Good at it. And I'm all for technical knowledge, knowing your job and using your instruments well, but you can still feel at the end of it a certain flat. Hard to put your finger on quite why. Perhaps when all's said and done it still comes down to conversation and not taking it too seriously. Or else taking it very seriously indeed. Like André.

'A bloke who knows what he's doing, believe you me, can get goose pimples growing on your eyeballs!' Who said that? Not Shakespeare. Mavis. Mavis and Lottie at old Pilsky's café under the pier. But would they swallow it at the optician's? 'It would appear that quite suddenly I need spectacles. I've been to Paris and now have curious protuberances all over my corneas!'

Spot on it was, right from the start. 'A small gift,' he said. 'For you. It's what I went to fetch before your little scene with pauvre Babette.'

'Oh yes. How sweet. What is it?'

He handed me a small white plastic box. 'With my love, Myopia. So you will never forget me. You must wear it around your neck.'

'Oh, André. Jewellery. You shouldn't.'

His eyes twinkled wickedly. 'Open it.'

Inside lay two gold teeth attached to a fine mouth-shaped wire with metal loops at each end. I looked at them in astonishment. Then at him. He smiled. 'Oh no, those you have there are my spare set. You were quite right, you see. Yes, my teeth are indeed like the stars. Except that I don't necessarily remove them at night as you will see.' Then he kissed me, holding my head in his hands, gently as if it were a small bird and not part of my body at all. In the middle I burst out laughing, thinking about the false teeth and how they'd look hanging round my neck. Instead of being put out he joined in too and must have known what I was thinking because when we stopped he said, 'You will, of course, remove the wires first.' I liked that.

His apartment was above the restaurant. I sniffed when we went in to see if the smell of cooking floated up. He watched me. 'No, you see. You smell nothing.'

140

I nodded, he was quite right. It was a huge place on two floors, with art books everywhere and paintings all over the walls. 'What a lot of paintings.'

He shrugged. 'That is my enthusiasm. I have collected since I was fifteen. It is where all my money goes. Like a disease of the blood.'

'Your greatest enthusiasm?'

'That and beautiful women, of course.'

'Of course,' I said, but right away I felt cold. He knew. He pulled my head softly round again so I would look him in the eyes.

'Myopia,' he said, 'you are a child if you think at my age there could not have been others. And you? You are a virgin?'

I opened my eyes wide. 'Me? No, of course not. Goodness, I've got two children.'

'Ah,' he said gravely, 'ah, then you have done it twice.'

'Oh, André, that's a very old one.'

He nodded. 'Like me it has been around.'

'Well, I've been around too but if you're a woman you're not supposed to say that, are you? Though I've never understood quite why. People don't say of a man that he's promiscuous do they, and there's no such thing as male nymphomania, is there? They call it a Don Juan complex, which comes out to sound like a compliment more than a curse of the blood.'

I stopped. 'Am I going on too much?' Sam would have said so. 'Jesus Christ, when I wish to indulge in a diatribe on the sexual pyschology of the sexes I'll go to a fucking bookshop and buy one. Now shut up, woman, and start sucking.'

'I'll get undressed now if you like, André.'

But he took my hand and shrugged, smiling. 'My Myopia. There is no hurry, we have until morning.'

I looked at my watch. 'Well, it's that now, after all—'

He covered the face of it with his fingers. 'Ssh, ssh, there are many hours left. But first we must prepare.'

I must admit my heart sank at that a bit. My idea had been to get into bed, have a quick cuddle and a bit of a poke then drop off to sleep together. Not a big procedure such as he seemed to have in mind.

'Well,' I said, 'it's been a long day and I've got a bit of a headache.' Which, as I said it, sounded a shade too housewifely for even my liking. All it needed was 'Have you set the alarm, darling? I plan to start the spring cleaning bright and early.' 'I'm sorry,' I laughed out loud. 'Now I do sound like a professional virgin.'

But he didn't answer. Instead he went out of the room and came back carrying a small glass with some treacly liquid in it. Just about a teaspoonful. 'Drink this, darling.'

'What is it?'

'Just drink it.'

'Not till I know what it is. It could be anything.'

He sighed. 'You think I plan to drug you? And what use would you be then?'

'What use? What a horrible way to put it. I don't have to stay here, you know. I've got money. I can go to a hotel.' My voice rose steadily. I listened to it in a detached sort of way with some amusement. It was years since I'd pulled that stroke, it always put them in a tizzy. Fish pie floating through the port hole! Fare thee well. Plop!

André stood calmly staring down at me, totally unaffected. He held the glass up. 'This is part of our preparation. The other part is in the bedroom. Now drink it.'

'Why?'

'It's a simple but immediately effective laxative.'

'A laxative?'

'To relax you, cure your headache and prepare the way for our lovemaking. A necessary step as you will understand later.'

I drank it in one gulp. 'Now you come to mention it I am a little constipated. My bowels are never quite what they might be after a journey.' What love talk! Quelle sweet murmurings! We smiled at each other.

'Good girl! Now I run you a warm bath.'

I sat where I was, waiting for the desired results. 'Constipation in varying degrees of severity is generally brought about by incorrect habits of living, chiefly dietetic. We therefore suggest a dietary of foods with a "high residue", such as green vegetables, fresh and dried fruits, wholemeal products and nuts. Olive oil and nut oil will also be found beneficial. Correction of the diet will generally prevent constipation in time. *Herbalene* should be taken until adjustment of the diet has been satisfactorily effected.' I knew that off by heart. It comes on the back of the *Herbalene* box, a pleasant packaging, bright yellow with a blue band across the top. *Herbalene* made by

William E. Lusty. (None genuine without this signature).
A greyish powder smelling of aniseed balls with a large
warning printed amongst the directions, *Do Not Masticate*. Just that, *Do Not Masticate*.

The desired results came sooner than expected. Speedy
Gonzales. We used to dance to that song. Thank God the
lavatory was separate from the bathroom. Divided off with
the bidet next to it. I felt as if a snow-storm was raging in
my stomach. Like an enema. André knocked at the door. A
less sensitive man would have barged right in. I saw the
handle turn. 'Don't come in, I haven't finished yet.' But he
stepped inside, smiling, with a cup of coffee in his hand.

'Well,' I said weakly, 'there's not much privacy around
here, is there?'

He lifted my head and tilted the cup towards my lips.
'To give you a little strength.'

'It'll go straight through,' I warned.

'So much the better. It is only with a clear passage that
perfect pleasure is achieved. Later you will express your
gratitude.'

'Later maybe,' I groaned. 'But at the moment I'm a little
busy expressing something else.'

I'd never liked it much before, in fact it was stronger than
that, most of the time I'd downright refuse. I'd heard of it
first, oh ages ago, of course. From this girl I worked with.
We were talking together about sex. 'Well, I'm a virgin
still,' she'd said. I looked at her doubtfully. Twenty-four if
a day, with the phone ringing non-stop on her desk from
men trying to make dates. 'I'm saving it till I get married.
I've promised my father.'

'Oh yes,' I said. 'Each to his own. It seems to work
anyway. Chastity. You've got them buzzing like flies.
Good luck to you.'

'Around my bum.'

'Beg pardon?'

'Around my bum. That's where they're buzzing.'

'Oh dear.' I choked on my chocolate biscuit.

'Well, my father never mentioned anything about
behind. A public schoolboy suggested it first to me and
I've been at it ever since. It's nice, you should try it.'

'No thank you very much. I don't take to the idea at all.'

A few months later she got married, in white. And her
father died the next day. A happy man. It had always

surprised me how many men seemed keen on it that way.
Of course they don't have to look at your face which saves a
lot of embarrassment. How could they look at it, when it's
dumped like an empty bucket upside down in the middle
of a pillow? The most they get is a sideways view of your
snout as you're coming up for air. Which is hardly
romantic. Apart from that it hurts. Hurts like hell. Or so
I'd found before. Men's things, if they were meant for
there, should have a definite thread on them like
corkscrews so that they could fit the puckers better—go in
clockwise or anti, depending on your ridges. The normal
way of doing things round the front it's not necessary.
There are no ridges, only folds, like curtain folds, so it's
simply a matter of parting them to let a bit of light in.
That's what I'd always thought, anyway.

After my bath, André led me to the bed, a four-poster. 'This
is nice,' I said, 'I've never slept in a four-poster.'
    'It's been in my family for years.'
    'However did you get it up the stairs?'
    'Oh,' he laughed. 'We had to dismantle it and then put
all the pieces together again.'
    'Really?' I stretched myself out. 'Well, I expect it was
worth the effort.'
    'Not that way, Myopia.'
    'What?'
    'Turn over please.'
    Oh God, I thought, here we go again. 'I'm not very keen
on it that way, André. Do you mind?'
    'Say nothing.' His voice was stern. I sighed and turned
over on to my stomach. It was a high bed, surprisingly
hard, a good working surface, I supposed. My head, I saw
when I turned it to the side, was about level with his upper
thighs.
    'Goodness me,' I gasped. 'You're massive. I can never
take all that up there.' And I stretched out to touch it.
    He smacked my hand lightly away. 'Now get up on all
fours and see what you can find under the pillow.'
    I did as I was told and brought out a shiny plastic penis.
Slightly smaller than his own but still a pretty good
handful.
    'Is this part of your art collection?' I giggled stupidly.
    He took it from me and pressed a switch. It started right
away, trembling gently like a well-set jelly. Then he

144

pressed again, at which it shook so violently it nearly jumped out of his fingers.

'See?' he said, 'Battery operated.'

I nodded. 'Keeps the place neater. No flexes to fall over.'

But I felt as apprehensive as when I went once to have a wart removed. 'It won't hurt,' the doctor had said. 'And afterwards all you'll have is a clean open hole.' 'What, always? Open I mean? What do you suggest I use then, Doctor? A safety pin possibly?'

'That won't overstretch it, that thing, André? I don't want to be walking round with a big hole in the back.' I could end up incontinent, I thought, with a useless set of anal muscles. 'And exactly what have you been up to, young lady?' they'd ask at the hospital. 'I must have sat on something.'

'Do we have to?' I said. 'Honestly, André, I'd far rather—'

He took no notice. 'Now first we anoint the temple.'

I felt his fingers, firm, insistent, nice like a nurse's, massaging, probing, oiling with a warm, slippery jelly.

'That's nice,' I said, surprised. 'Have you heated it, that stuff? How considerate.' Perhaps this time it would be different. He'd made a good start.

'Relax,' he murmured. 'Relax, Myopia.'

I knew what he meant, despite what he was doing or possibly just because he was, I'd tightened everything. Even my mouth and fists knotted up like balls of string. Clamped together like a stamp on an envelope.

'Look at yourself,' he urged. 'Straight ahead, look.'

There was a canopy of heavy brocade above the bed and all around it curtains of the same material. Drawn back now with tasselled ropes. The head of the bed was against the wall and in that space hung a large mirror with an intricately carved wooden frame. It had been tilted slightly so that it didn't lie flat but instead reflected completely the entire surface I was lying on. I'd seen that already but hadn't liked to look. Now I lifted my head and gazed at us both. André smiled, his gold teeth shone rich and coppery in the lowered warmth of the shadowed lights. Like the Turkish Delight commercial. Full of eastern promise. If I'd had a box in front of me it would have been jelly, both ends. Then he started with his piece of plastic, the quivering tip at first, set on low speed. It wasn't unpleasant, if you concentrated on something else. I

145

thought about the girls' last school reports. 'Harriet is a child with a mind of her own.' Whose else would she have anyway—the next door neighbour's? 'Fanny must learn to conquer her left-handedness.' I looked in the mirror, André was left-handed. He obviously hadn't learnt to conquer it but he was doing all right. Perhaps by the time Fanny was his age and still left-handed she'd be using it to wield a plastic weapon too. André smiled at me, he seemed a long way away. I brought my elbows up and rested my head on my hands.

'Are you enjoying it?' I said pleasantly.

'Are you?' he answered.

I let myself go to think about it. All I could feel was a dull drilling like at the dentist's when you know he's on a nerve but because of the gum injection you can't feel a thing. By the end it becomes sort of soothing, you miss it when he stops.

I nodded. 'How much have you managed to get in?'

'About half.'

'No! I wouldn't have guessed that. Well, go on then.'

I said it cheerfully. I felt encouraged though. Not as yet carried away with any great desire.

'Hey look,' I said into the mirror. 'At least I've stopped gritting my teeth.'

The excitement started slowly. On tiptoes, tapping softly like a blind man's stick, sneaking stealthily through to the front of me. A small washing wave at first which took me by surprise and set me all a-tingle. I lay quite still, conscious of a loud thudding heart, a rushing of saliva in my mouth and an urgent need to touch. I shut my eyes and began to spin. André knew, he must have sensed the difference.

'Now you are ready for me, Myopia.'

'Yes,' I murmured. Anything. A cold cucumber! A stick of Brighton rock! Anything so long as he wouldn't leave me empty. The plastic throbbing had stopped, there wasn't a sound now except the muffled ticking of a clock and my own heavy breathing. He rolled me slowly on to my side, brought my knees up and gently opened them. Then he slid himself inside me. I couldn't have said where first. Front or back, they'd become indivisible. When he was in one place the other ached for attention which right away his hand supplied. I curled around him, foetus-like, kissing him on to climax whilst wanting it to carry

146

through till dawn. And so it did. Three times in all we did it, which wasn't breaking any record. Not in quantity that is. And each of the times he deposited in a different place. The last I swallowed, sitting up to gargle with it first. He pulled me back till, smiling in each other's arms, surrounded by the early morning sound of Paris streets, we fell asleep together.

I just about remembered the way back to Damson's place, although by day it looked quite different. 'I shall come with you,' André had said. 'I shall come with you and then I will drive you to the airport.'

'No, don't do that! Please. I'd much prefer to say goodbye to you here, without anyone else around.'

He didn't argue. 'You'll come to Paris again.' It wasn't a question and as such needed no answer. I held his teeth in my hand.

'Next time you see them they'll be round my neck.'

I bought a packet of Gauloises and walked along the street, smoking. Boulevard St Germain. How excited we'd been, Jean and me, when we'd seen that first. Would my life have been different if I'd met André on that trip? I rounded the corner of Les Deux Magots and then on impulse retraced my steps, sat down at a pavement table and ordered a Pernod. I smiled up at the sky. Sunday. Sunday in Spring. And me full to the brim with light and bursting life, enough just about to get up and do a tap dance over the tables. Treat everyone to whatever they wanted. Take the whole of Paris on my knees and hug them half to death. If this was a film I'd be singing by now, I thought, and the string section would be twanging fit to bust a gut. Fred Astaire or Gene Kelly would be popping up out of nowhere to whirl me into the middle of the road, dancing like mad, stopping the traffic. Everyone throwing open their windows and tossing flowers down, all joining in the chorus. 'I love Paris in the Springtime. I love Paris in the Fall. Chorus: I love Paris, why, oh why do I love Paris— because my—because my—'

'Myopia!' It came at just the right time. I couldn't for the life of me have finished. What was that damned last line?

I smiled up. 'Hello, Rupert.'

'What on earth are you doing?'

'I'm singing, but I just got stuck. What's the end of *I love*

Paris? "Why, oh why do I love Paris because my"—? What comes then? "Because my"?'

He sat down. 'What are you drinking?'

'A Pernod. What comes then? I'm going mad.' I sang it softly in case he couldn't remember the tune.

'All right.' He joined in. People started looking from the next table. Looking and smiling. Perhaps they knew. 'I've got it,' Rupert said. 'Because my love is there. Right?'

I looked at him. 'That's not right. It doesn't rhyme.'

'I know it doesn't, but that's how it ends.'

'Are you sure? I'm not at all myself. I shall look it up when I get home. I've got Maurice Chevalier singing it somewhere if I can find the record.'

We looked at each other and burst out laughing.

'Now,' I said, 'shall we start again? You come walking towards me. Go on, get up and come towards the table. I'll be sitting here sipping my drink and I promise I won't be singing this time.'

'You're mad this morning, I can tell. Pots for rags. Crackers.' But he got up, reapproached and we did indeed start all over again.

'Myopia!'

I smiled up. 'Hello, Rupert.'

'What on earth are you doing?'

'I'm sitting here sipping a Pernod, soaking up the sunshine and simply oozing goodwill and happiness. How's that?'

'We were worried. I've already been round to Damson. We rang André and he told us you'd left. I was afraid you'd got lost.'

'I just felt like a daydream, that's all. Have I put you out? Where is Jean-Paul? Did things go well last night?'

He sat back and ordered a Pernod. 'Will you have another?'

'Better not.'

He ordered another anyway. 'We'll drink it up half each. Now, where were we? Last night! Oh, Damson wasn't too pleased. You should have heard her. It was awful—'

I sat forward anxiously. 'Not too pleased with me? You mean for staying—'

He looked surprised. 'With you? For staying with André? I should think she was delighted.'

'Delighted?' Something slight ached inside me, like seeing a one-time love linking arms with somebody new.

'In the circumstances it was the best thing that could have happened. With Babette. She became uncontrollable. Damson had to call her doctor. At one point she was trying to jump out of the window.'

'On that top floor?'

'If you'd been there she would have dragged you with her.'

'I don't doubt.'

'Anyway, the doctor called an ambulance and they've taken her away.'

'Poor thing,' I said. Taken her away! Yes, my mother was always saying that. They've taken her away. In the end they came and took her away too. She pegged it before they'd even got to the traffic lights so they might just as well have left her where she was. 'Were you there, then, you and Jean-Paul?'

'We had to be. Damson couldn't have managed on her own. Where did you disappear to?'

'I'm sorry. André said to slip upstairs while Damson was in the lavatory with Babette, and I thought it was best for her not to set eyes on me again. I felt I was the one who'd started it all off.'

'You might have said good night.'

'I didn't want to make a big thing of it, that's all. Anyway, was it? A good night, apart from all the trouble? Afterwards?'

His face slowly split in two like a sliced melon. It was lovely to watch. A Cheshire cat who'd been at the cream. Pleased with himself. Like an obedient angel who's been given the night off and then abused it by extremely bad behaviour. My own smile spread in sympathy. 'So it's all been worth it, this trip to Paris?'

He sighed. 'What?'

I sighed too. 'I feel much the same myself.'

He sat back, tilting his chair, folding his hands across his stomach as if after a deeply satisfying meal. 'But I'm in love, Myopia.'

An apprehensive breeze blew over me. 'Oh lord! Are you? With Jean-Paul? Is he?'

'He is. I am. We both are. Isn't it wonderful?'

'Yes,' I said lamely.

He brought his chair forward quickly and opened his eyes wide. 'Oh, we owe it all to you. Really we do. Yes, Jean-Paul told me about,' he bent his fingers in a

149

dismissive gesture towards me, 'you know, you and him. That's what decided him. He'd never tried it with a really beautiful woman ever. And he said if it couldn't even work with someone like you, then—then he'd be better off following his natural inclinations.'

'So,' I started to laugh. 'So—' and couldn't go on. 'Oh dear, oh dear,' I gasped, then at last I caught my breath. 'So,' I gurgled, 'having me has put him off girls for good.' I took his hand. 'Oh, Rupert, I am glad for you.'

He looked bewildered. 'Well, it was meant as a compliment, Myopia. He thinks you're the tops.'

'I know. And I'm extremely proud to have been of service. Where is he anyway, Jean-Paul?'

His eyes grew luminous and faraway. His voice came low and sweet. 'I left him in bed. He was exhausted.'

Mm. That's where I'd left André. We both sat staring into space until I shifted uncomfortably in my chair. 'These seats are very hard, aren't they? How about going?'

We walked back arm in arm, looking in shop windows on the way. What could be more out and out pleasant than this? I matched his footsteps with my own. 'Oh Rupert,' I said, 'you're not looking. You trod on a crack then, the trick is to miss them, otherwise—'

'Otherwise it's bad luck, I know.'

'Well, don't tempt fate, not when things are going so well.' I stopped in my tracks. 'Do you know what I was thinking yesterday?'

'What?'

'I was thinking that if these photos are as successful as we think, Moo Moffat-Paw will be offering you a job.'

'Oh Myopia, didn't I say? Jean-Paul has asked me to do a job with him—next week—for French *Mode*.'

'No!'

'Yes. They're doing a feature on British fashion and have already asked him if he knows someone good in London to get the clothes together. Well, I know everybody who's designing anything worth while. I can do it standing on my head. Hey,' he stopped and stared at me excitedly. 'So could you, Myopia, couldn't you? Why not?'

'What? Stand on my head? Don't be daft.'

'Model. Model the clothes. I've only just thought of that. Let's ring him, Jean-Paul. Let's ring him now and see what he thinks.'

'Can't we do it from Damson's? She's there waiting for us, isn't she?'

'No. She's not. She's working. Developing the "Snow Siren" ones to see how they look. Anyway we daren't ring from there. I'm sure *Mode* haven't asked her to do the photographs. You'll probably be working with someone quite different. Whoever it is, you'll find it a dream after Damson's.'

'It wasn't that bad,' I protested. 'I'd far rather work with her than someone dead from the neck upwards.'

He squeezed my arm. 'Don't worry, I'm exactly the same. That's the thing about Damson—the loyalty her friends feel for her. But what you have to remember is,' he paused, 'that it isn't in any way reciprocated. She's a very much of the moment girl. Here today and gone tomorrow. You know what I mean?'

'Yes. Yes, I do.'

I waited outside the phone box and watched Rupert talking. He kept turning round, winking and nodding through the glass. I had to laugh. I hadn't seen him so happy. I crossed my fingers and said a silent prayer that everything could stay like that for him and Jean-Paul. At least there seemed a likelihood that he'd be waving farewell to Streatham Hill. He must have seen my hands because he lifted his own crossed fingers too. Crossed fingers, crossed purposes, I thought. I couldn't have cared less about the job next week if it came off or not for me. I'd done my stint of modelling but it did occur to me that it might be nice to have a shot at earning my own money again. This could be as good a way as any. Independent. Independent of Paul. Free of the need to marry. Free to make love or not to whoever I wanted. To live in a place of my own choosing. To bring up my children however I thought. That wasn't bad. 'By golly not,' I said out loud. A small child with plaited hair, sucking an outsize lollipop, stopped to look at me.

'By golly not,' I said to her. 'Qu'est-ce que vous dites, ma petite?'

'Oui, madame,' she nodded gravely and went steadily on her way.

Rupert joined me excitedly. 'It's in the bag, Myopia.'

'No!'

'It is honestly. A friend of his—Serge something or other—is the photographer and he'd already spoken to

151

him this morning. Jean-Paul said he'd found a super new face, you, and Serge said if she lives in London why not use her.'

'Oh Rupert.'

'So they're ringing us tomorrow and will probably come over on Thursday. What do you think of that?'

'Thursday. That's all right if you can get all the things together.'

'You can come with me, to all the places, so we can choose things on the spot.'

'This week. Hey,' I said slowly, 'wasn't this the week we were going to go away? Sit on a beach and work out our futures?'

He slid an arm through mine and slipped easily into step. 'Well,' he said creamily, 'there's no need for that now is there? Our futures have already been decided.'

Damson had decided not to come to London. She looked worn and very irritable when we arrived. 'I've been waiting,' she said accusingly. 'Where on earth have you been?' Then she turned away. 'The hospital rang. I've got to go there. Babette keeps asking for me. They say she's refusing to eat or drink.'

'Oh dear, poor thing.'

She snorted. 'Poor thing! Bloody nuisance! It's like having a dog around, a fucking bitch on heat! At least with a dog you can kick it or best have it put down.'

'Damson!'

'What? They should let people like that die. Put her out of her misery. Get her off my back anyway.'

'What you suggest seems a little drastic, after all you must have given her some encouragement in the first place.'

She turned to me viciously. 'Oh shut up and go to hell.'

Rupert and I packed in silence. Damson went into her dark room, banging the door noisily behind her. I clung for all I was worth to my memories of the night, to the sweetness of André, and all we'd done together. But it was no good, everything kept evaporating. I went to the window and looked down, hoping to catch again the lightheartedness of those earlier hours, but all I could see was the cold deserted courtyard below and the gloomy walls surrounding it. What a view! Sunlight struck the

152

opposite wall like a shabby overcoat—threadbare, thin and weak. A pale reflection of the sun that shone even at this moment on Boulevard St Germain. I shivered, my mood spiralling down, a hard miserable knot tightening in my chest. I hate rows, any heavy unpleasantness hanging in the air. I like things to be—well, to be—comfortable. Comfortable like warm water or clean sheets or smooth green lawns. Comfortable like high teas, soft centres, postcards in the post. Everyone friends and getting on a treat.

Rupert caught my eye and made a face. I made one back. He snapped the cases shut.

'Have we finished?' I whispered. He nodded. I tiptoed to the dark room door and knocked. There was no reply. I cleared my throat, and knocked again. 'Damson?'

It came fast and furious. 'Fuck off you!' Like a smack in the face. Even Rupert looked shocked. My knees went all trembly, for two pins I could have burst out crying. Ridiculous. Rupert came and put his arm round me.

'She's impossible when she's in this mood,' he whispered. 'Have you got all your things together? Yes? Right? Take them and wait for me downstairs. I'll get all the photographs and film from her, that's my responsibility, not yours. Leave everything to me. Now go on.'

He gave me a small shove. What? Without even saying goodbye? Surely not! With so much still unsaid? 'But, Rupert,' I whispered back. 'I must—'

He opened the landing door. 'Get going.'

I picked up my case uncertainly and took one slow step. 'Should I leave a note or something?'

He lifted a finger and pointed without answering. Then he knocked at her door. Even from the top of the stairs, right outside the apartment, I could still hear her cursing. Then all was quiet. He'd calmed her where I couldn't.

I lugged the heavy case down, step by step. It seemed worse going down than it had coming up. I stopped and sat down in exactly the same spot to smoke a cigarette. Well, at least this trip had laid a ghost at last. Whose ghost? Jean's. Damson had done that without any help from me. Just by being over-greedy—for everything. My cigarette had gone out. I felt in my pocket for another light and my fingers touched a fine metal wire. André's teeth. I took them out to look at them. Then very carefully put them in my open mouth over my own upper set. A door

153

banged high above me and the dragging sounds of a heavy case drifted down. I heard Rupert whistling though how he found the breath I don't know. As he came closer I adjusted my upper lip until only the two gold teeth hung down, then when he reached me I spun round smiling brilliantly. 'Hello, Rupert,' I said, 'well, what do you think? Do they suit?'

Our taxi driver understood English. He was a handsome wolfish creature in the manner of Yves Montand with a lot of the rogue about him. Insolent and very sexy. I looked at him as we got in, without a word. But as soon as Rupert in his immaculate French had finished speaking and sat back I said, 'Isn't he gorgeous? A rotter through and through, you can tell.' Rupert frowned and put a finger to his lips. 'Ssh.' I stared out of the window. It hadn't occurred to me that he could conceivably have understood.

We travelled at great speed, shooting over traffic lights just as they turned red, overtaking, cutting corners, as if for all the world we had a special plane to catch. Paris was empty and depressing, no one in sight now we'd left the centre. All was withdrawn and shuttered. Shops bolted and barred.

'That's the worst thing about Sundays, the shops being shut, isn't it?' I said to Rupert.

'Well, at least there's nowhere to spend our money. It's practically still intact, you know.'

'Will we have to give it back then?'

He laughed. 'No. André gave me lots of bills after you'd gone to bed. We'll put those in as our expenses.'

'How sweet of him.'

'Well, I had to ask.'

'You are clever. I would never have thought of that. I wish there was somewhere open though. I want to buy presents for the girls. I'll have to get something at the airport. I'd thought of a bottle of Chanel No. 5 each and cigarette lighters in different colours.'

'What, at their age, cigarette lighters? Myopia!'

'Well, they make a nice flame. Children like that, a little bit of magic.'

The taxi slowed down to normal speed and the driver swung round, braking to a halt. In very good English he said, 'You want to spend your money?' I stared at him, blood rushing to my face. His smile went up at one end.

154

Sardonic, that's what you'd call it. Rupert answered. 'Well, yes, we do. We would like to buy a few small presents if you know of a place.'

He shrugged. 'But of course. The flea market.'

'Oh,' I recovered enough to speak. 'Is that open on Sundays?'

'Sunday? That is when everyone goes there. It is their big day. I can take you, wait and then continue to the airport.'

I turned to Rupert. 'That sounds nice. I've never been to the flea market. What about it?'

'Well,' Rupert looked doubtful. 'We have a plane to catch at some point remember.'

'Yes, but we're not booked on to any one in particular, are we? And this will only make us an hour later at the most. Come on, let's go.'

'All right. You've talked me into it. But you mustn't go mad there. Just in and out.'

'I promise.'

The driver twisted back and we shot off again, badly scraping a parked Citroën on the side of the road. We'd be lucky to arrive intact either at the airport or up in heaven at this rate. 'How was Damson at the end?' I felt more confident keeping my eyes off other cars. Was he drunk, the driver?

Rupert sat with a bulky cardboard envelope on his lap. He patted it. 'Well, I managed to get everything. All the films and colour transparencies are in here. Oh, by the way, I've got some contacts you can look at—"Snow Siren"—they're superb. Do you want to see them?'

I shook my head. 'No, I don't think I do. Not now. We'll look at them on the plane. Would you like me to put that in my bag? It'll fit in.'

'Okay, okay. If it will go. But for Christ's sake don't lose them. Above everything they're the most precious.'

I fitted them into my red leather bag, more a briefcase than a bag. 'They'll be safe in here. I won't let it out of my sight. It's got all my money and passport in anyway. Was she all right then when you left? I'm sure I should have said goodbye.'

'She wasn't really, no. She was fairly scurrilous about you, I must say.'

'Me?'

Rupert looked the other way. I could guess what she'd

155

told him. 'She must have minded about André after all.'

'Well,' I said slowly, 'we used to be very close at one time—'

'So I gathered from what she said.'

'But you wouldn't have guessed otherwise would you?'

'Not in a million years that someone as sane as you would get mixed up with Damson.'

'Well, it's done with now. We'll put it down to the inexperience of youth. I knew it wouldn't be the same the minute I set eyes on her. Too much of her had changed, not just her shape and name—'

'She thinks you hurt her deliberately, to get your own back.'

'Hurt her? Does she?' I laughed. 'No, I don't think so and then on the other hand perhaps I did. In which case, yes, so I got my own back.' I yawned. 'Now I'm boring myself.' I yawned again, and set Rupert at it. 'Whew,' I said when we'd got our breaths back, 'it's easy to see we didn't get our full quota of sleep. I could nod off now for two pins, couldn't you?'

The taxi slowed down. 'Don't do that,' Rupert said. 'We're obviously here.'

It was never clear whose decision it was to leave the cases in the car but it was clear to both of us that they were far too heavy to cart around. 'I wait here on this corner,' the driver had said. A chilly streak of caution curled sluggishly round my head. I should have taken note. After all, I'd made enough fuss at the airport. I did say, 'Will they be safe?' to Rupert but not until we were walking away. That's true. 'Well, we're not going to be that long, are we? And I told him on no account to leave them. Not for a second, especially not round here.'

'It's a mixed bunch all right,' I agreed on that, but even as I said it I could still see a pair of treacherous teasing eyes and that sardonic slanting smile. I turned round quickly but the taxi driver sat where we'd left him, staring after us. He raised a mocking hand in acknowledgement. 'I wouldn't trust him with money—'

'Myopia!'

'Well, I wouldn't.'

He took my arm impatiently. 'Well, we haven't done have we? Look, let's get a move on. We haven't got all day.'

We could have done with all day, I said that after the first five minutes. All day and carte blanche at the Bank of

England. The market was marvellous—a cross between Portobello Road and Petticoat Lane, Petticoat Lane as it used to be before they boxed it all in. You can kill an atmosphere stone dead when you cover it with a roof. Here it was all open air with narrow lanes and passages created by the positioning of stalls. You could buy just about anything—suits of armour, silver spoons, spectacles from the 1920s, feather boas, brimmed felt hats, Chinese clogs, candied ants, plastic boats and bottled ships. 'My girls would go mad,' I said. 'Now what shall I get them?'

Rupert picked up a pale pink heart-shaped box filled with tiny lace-trimmed handkerchiefs each embroidered with a day of the week. 'These are adorable.'

'What? Hankies? How appalling. Rupert, you could be a little more constructive than that. Children don't have hankies any more, not since Kleenex came in. These days they just blow and throw.'

'All the more reason to buy them these. They probably haven't ever seen a real handkerchief in your house, have they?'

'No, now I come to think of it, but who's going to wash and iron them? Not me!'

Rupert held up two boxes, one pink, one blue.

'They will. They'll do it themselves. They'll love it, like playing Mummy. Here you are, my treat. Bet you they're a great success.'

After that I allowed myself to be guided by him.

'Lots of little things, that's the trick with children.'

'How do you know?'

'Because it's how I felt myself. And still do,' he added.

Half an hour, that's all we allowed ourselves. Half an hour is what we'd said to the driver anyway.

'These unspent francs are burning a hole in the bottom of my bag,' I said. 'I never like it until I've spent the lot.'

'You can change them to English when you get back and give them to the children for pocket money. Now, where's this cab?'

My red bag bulged with bits and pieces, the precious envelope still safely in the bottom. I struggled with the zip, head bent. 'This bloody thing won't do up now.'

'Myopia!' Something in Rupert's voice made me turn. Panic.

'What?'

'He's not here. The driver. Nor the taxi. They've gone.'

They had too. Nothing on the corner except a boy on a bicycle and an old woman selling hot chestnuts. 'This is the corner, isn't it?'

Rupert was frantic. 'For God's sake, of course it it.'

'Well,' I said calmly. 'Are we early? He might have been moved on. No parking. He's probably cruising round the block.' A bench lay under the nearby tree. 'We'll sit down and wait.'

'How can you be so cool?'

'Would you like some chestnuts?' I said. 'Or will they give you wind?'

He sighed, sweat sparkled on his upper lip. I could see his hands were shaking.

'Rupert, keep calm. They're only clothes. He'll turn up in a minute. He's probably popped off for a cup of coffee.'

But he was near to tears. 'Only clothes! Over a thousand pounds' worth and that's without all the accessories. Moo Moffat-Paw will go mad, not to mention Joe Garibaldi.'

'Why?' I said. 'Why should they? Everything's insured isn't it? That's assuming the worst and this chap doesn't turn up.'

He stared at me. 'What on earth are you saying?'

I drew him to the bench and sat him down. 'What I'm saying is, my little love, that your reaction is all out of proportion. If the stuff has been stolen it's not the tragedy you seem to think it is.'

He put his head in his hands. I gave up for the moment.

'I'm keeping my eyes peeled. He'll come back, I'm sure of it,'

I glanced at my watch—11.30. Ten minutes later—11.40. And still no sign. I concentrated on tiny figures in the far distance. By the time that person reaches the third lamp-post from this corner our car will have come. Nothing. Right, by the time that blue Volkswagen gets to that empty hoarding it will have been overtaken by our man. No good! If I stare at my watch face for five minutes non-stop, he'll be hooting at the kerb. Like hell. Poor Rupert couldn't raise his head. Once or twice I felt his shoulders shuddering against mine. Oh Jesus Christ, come off the cross and find the cab. Please God, go round the corner and tell him to get a bloody move on.

We sat there for a whole hour. At last I shook his shoulder. His muffled voice oozed hopefully out of his chest. 'What news?'

'None,' I said briskly. 'I think we'll have to accept, my darling, that the bastard's buggered off. Now!' I added brightly, 'it's really not so bad. We've both got our passports and enough money to get to the airport. You're carrying the tickets and the photos are still all safe and sound. Let's have a look at you—it could be a lot worse. Come on. It's just a spot of bad luck. Let's forget it and go back to London.'

'I'm not going, Myopia.'

'Don't be silly.'

'I can't move. I'm staying here.'

I shook him gently. His head fell like a broken flower on to my neck. People walking past were glancing back curiously.

'Everyone is staring—'

'I don't care.'

'Rupert.' Alarm was setting in. 'What's happening? Are you having a nervous breakdown or what?' We hadn't got enough money for luxuries like that, couldn't he wait and have it on the National Health?

He began moaning softly, talking to himself. 'My first job! I'm finished. My very first job. Outrageous irresponsibility. Finished.'

I sat there, cradling him helplessly. After all, they were my clothes. But they'd served their purpose now. That's how I looked at it. We had a record of them. Years later I'd be able to fish out that one copy of *Chic* and say 'That's me. Do you like what I'm wearing?' Which would in itself be infinitely more satisfying than turning heads in restaurants or making small theatrical entrances into taxis on the street. Taxis on the street. Taxis on the street!

'Rupert, where did we pick up that cab?'

'What?' he mumbled.

'Where exactly? I know it was outside Damson's, but you found it didn't you? Was it on a rank?'

He shook his head dazedly. 'No.'

'But there was a rank there, just further up the street. I remember there was—'

'Yes.' Rupert lifted his head a little. 'But this one drove straight past it to pick us up instead of waiting his turn. Didn't you notice, that's why all the parked taxis started honking?'

I thought quickly. 'They must know him. At least someone must know him.'

I stood up. 'Look after this bag—no, on second thoughts, just sit there, Rupert, don't move! Do not move, are you listening? I'm going to phone André. If anyone can help, he can.'

One of the waiters answered. 'Monsieur André? Un moment.' I could hear the clatter of the restaurant, they must be right in the thick of things now. Twenty to one. He took ages to come. What on earth was he doing?

'Oui. C'est moi, André.'

Relief flooded through me, right through, from top to bottom as though someone was filling my body with hot sustaining soup through a neatly drilled hole in my head. Tilt the jug a little more, there's still a small space in my toes!

'Oh André,' I said feebly.

'Myopia!' His voice leaped over the line with such strength and joy, such deep pleasure and genuine delight that for a swift dancing second I was transported right back. Back to his high, hard bed, back to my own first, blinding, breathlessness, to slyly stirring inert skin and new fresh slow awakenings. We exchanged some numbed, shy sentences of love, and then I told him of our trouble. He was silent for a moment. No sharp words at our stupidity, no charge of carelessness, not a single scolding reproach. What a friend I'd found. I could hear him thinking.

'Well,' I said, 'we don't have the number of the taxi but I can tell you what the driver looks like. Sly eyes' (I could have said sexy but this was hardly the moment for such insensitivity); 'a sort of foxy smile, sardonic. Tall, I would have said, though we didn't see him actually standing up—'

André interrupted. 'Myopia—'

I ignored it.

'Actually, André, who he looked like more than anyone else was Yves Montand.'

'Yves Montand?' I heard a sharp intake of breath. 'Ah, I have it.'

'Oh!' I said. 'Do you know him?'

He spoke quickly, with great authority. 'Myopia, where are you now? What precisely has he taken? Describe the cases exactly. And when, how long ago was this? An hour? You have done well to telephone me. You have money to take you to the airport? You are certain you must depart

160

today?' He said that very tenderly. 'Yes? Ah well! So I shall meet you at the airport—you travel BA? Very well, I shall meet you at the BA desk at, it is now quarter to one, at two o'clock. Until then, ma chérie—'

Quickly, before he hung up, I shouted desperately, 'But André, what about our cases?'

I heard his throaty chuckle, could imagine a fiery flash of gold. 'They will be with me.' And then the line went dead.

The next hour was the worst. Rupert was inconsolable. At the airport I ordered him an omelette. 'You have to eat,' I said, 'It will help settle your stomach.' He shredded a whole bread roll, waiting, and then when his omelette came he claimed he couldn't eat it. I tried scolding. 'Now look what you've done, covered the whole place with crumbs. Come on, eat up, you can't offend the cook as well as the waitress.'

I tried to jolly him up. 'Why don't you ring Jean-Paul? He'll think it's a joke. Anyway, André seemed to know right away who I was talking about. That driver was probably not a driver at all, just a con man. I thought his English was too good to be true. Anyone can get taken in by con men.'

His anguished face looked up from his fork. 'Ring Jean-Paul?' he said, horrified. 'He'd never work with me again. You only have to be unreliable once in this business and the word goes around right away.'

I sighed. 'This business, this business. It's just the same as any other. People allow for strokes of bad luck, surely to God.'

'But it was all my fault.' That's all he'd say. Again and again. In the end I gave up.

There were seats available on the three o'clock flight. I took Rupert's ticket from his nerveless fingers and booked for both of us. 'What if André can't get the cases by two?' he said.

'Then he'll come here anyway and at three o'clock we'll fly on after thanking him for trying. That's all.'

But by five to two the tension was beginning to tell on me too. I'd long since stopped talking. 'Any luggage?' they'd asked at the BA desk. 'That's just on its way,' I'd answered. 'Be here in no time at all.' God forgive me if I tell a lie. Bastard.

At dead on two I turned to Rupert. 'Sit up, love, and at

161

least look a little less hopeless.'

'Why?' He slumped even lower.

'Well, I don't know, but it shows such lack of faith if André comes in now and sees us both—' I hadn't time to finish. André was striding towards us, grinning wide, teeth flashing, arms flailing all over the place. He wore a fine pale camelhair overcoat like an affluent gangster. It shocked me to see how distinguished he looked. He lifted his arms as if inviting me into his embrace—empty arms. Rupert said it first. 'Where are the cases?' But I'd gone past caring. I wanted to touch something solid. I ran towards him and threw my arms round his neck. Over his shoulder in the second before shutting my eyes I spotted the porter staggering towards us, a heavy case in either hand. Of course André would get them! Whoever doubted? Who on earth?

Rupert cried. Really cried. Tears of pure relief. Straight into his champagne. André and I kissed, pretending not to see. And then we all toasted each other. Again.

André wouldn't explain. 'Do tell,' we begged. 'What happened? How did you find them?' But he'd only shrug and pour us yet another glass. I drank, adoring him. Power is a pretty potent aphrodisiac. I didn't want to go when they called our flight. He squeezed my hand very tightly. 'Now at the last minute I confess to you. I arranged everything. The cab to pick you up. The driver to take you to the flea market. His disappearance with both the cases—all in order that you would call me and I should have the chance to see you once again.'

I held him very close then looked him in the eyes. They twinkled back at me. 'And impress me with your cleverness,' I said.

'Of course.'

'But how did you know I'd call you?'

He gave me a last long hug and whispered softly in one ear. 'Because, Myopia, my Myopia, I am your first French lover. Real lover. And as such your lasting friend. When you are in trouble you will always call me, of that I hope I can be sure.'

'Yes, yes. Oh my God, I must tell them when I'm coming back. Here's my number; tell them I've caught the three o'clock plane.'

Oh dear, how can you wave a man farewell with mascara running right down into your mouth? I turned to try but saw that sensibly he'd gone. Rupert put his arm round me, fully recovered, he was now a pillar of strength.

'He's a marvel that man,' I blubbed. 'A bloody marvel, that André. Do you know, so far he hasn't put a finger wrong.'

Rupert wore a grave and soothing expression, like a clerk from the Citizens' Advice Bureau. 'No,' he nodded. I had an hysterical urge to laugh. 'Not one finger wrong,' and then I gave another sob.

London looked lovely, bathed in the dusty glow of late afternoon. The river looped like a satin ribbon round Maidenhead, patches of green dotted here and there like discarded billiard tables. We slanted over it then steadied up for touch-down. 'Are you glad to be back?' Rupert shouted. The plane shuddered to a grinding halt. I rolled my eyes slowly. 'Whew, I'm glad that's over anyway. Now, what did you say? Am I glad to be back? Well, since you come to mention it, no. No, I don't think I am at all. There are too many complications awaiting me back here.'

'Are there?'

'Yes, complications of the heart. You know the sort of thing.'

'I can only think of Jean-Paul and how to last till Thursday myself.'

I sighed. 'Well, when there's only one on the scene it's all much simpler.'

We hadn't talked much since Paris, most of the time we'd spent in a companionable silence, both preoccupied with our own thoughts. Mine leapfrogged from Sam to Charles then on to Paul getting married tomorrow. But underneath lay the hard solid core of André. I could have asked André what to do about the others, he wouldn't have minded I was sure. And I could have told him about my weekly trip to Brighton. Yes, I could have told him all about that, every detail, which was something I couldn't have started to explain to anyone else in the whole world. Paul had never known, not the ins and outs of it, and we'd been married after all. We'd been married a whole year when it first started. But then it's common knowledge that women have more secrets from husbands than they ever do from lovers, or even from the hairdresser if it comes to that.

Rupert unfastened his seat belt. 'Who exactly are the others, Myopia? You still haven't told me. Sam, I know.

But who is it you go to see in Brighton?'

'In Brighton?' I laughed. 'Oh, he's not the problem.'

'Well, who is he?'

'He's—' I hesitated. 'He's just a sad and lonely little old-age pensioner.'

'Myopia, you're breaking my heart.' He said it mockingly. I didn't answer. Yes, I thought, it breaks my heart too sometimes. 'Well, who else is there? The man you were meant to come to Paris with in the first place.'

I turned. 'Isn't it a good job I didn't? What! I would never have met André if I had.'

'Who is he then and why couldn't he come at the last minute?'

'His wife died,' I said briefly. 'Yes, a form of insane suicide really. She threw herself out of the saddle. At least that's what Charles claims.'

'Died riding? Earl's daughter! I read about it. Lady Deidre! Yes, I read that in the papers.'

'You would have done, just before we left.'

'Charles Glossop's wife. Is it him then?'

'Yes.'

'Oh Myopia.'

'He proposed on the phone to Paris. That's the trouble. It's been going on for ages, before Sam even, but I never thought it would come to this.'

'But, darling, he could end up Prime Minister, that would make you First Lady.'

'Would it? After the Queen? Yes, I suppose it would. Unless marrying a divorcée would wreck his chances. Though knowing Charles he will have sought advice on that already.'

'I could be coming along to Number Ten for tea.'

We laughed. 'Only if I accept, Rupert.'

He sighed dreamily. 'Decisions, decisions. What a choice! A brilliant politician on the one hand and a bloody millionaire on the other. Oh for the chance!'

I stood up, brushed myself down and smoothed my fringe. 'They're only men, Rupert. And neither of them much good in bed, come to that.' I smiled. 'Not like André. Or even for that matter like Paul.'

'You're not still sleeping with him?' Shocked!

I picked up my bag casually. 'I did the other night. It was very nice.'

He looked bewildered. 'Why on earth do you bother

164

with all these different men, Myopia? Doesn't it ever occur to you to say no?'

'No? Yes, of course it occurs but I can't do it.'

I stepped into the gangway and turned back smiling. 'I love them all, you see.'

The air hostess greeted us as we were going. 'Goodbye. I hope you enjoyed your flight.' Affable, that was the word. The only thing to be was affable back. 'Tremendously,' I assured her. A clutch of aircraft mechanics in white overalls stood waiting at the bottom of the steps, looking up all the ladies' legs. My trousers must have been a bit of a let-down. Shame.

Rupert and I walked down a long plastic corridor, then waited in the queue to show our passports. 'What are your plans now—straight off to Streatham Hill? Would you like to come and have tea in my house first? The girls will be there, we can give them their presents.'

He looked grateful. 'Yes,' he said, 'it's a bit of an anticlimax coming back to nothing.'

Fifteen minutes later I would have given my eye teeth for it—to come back to nothing. They were all there! It was unbelievable, but they were. All there, waiting for me. Paul and the girls at the front. Sam somewhere to the left, and at the back, standing on his own, Charles. I saw them as a big crowd of people before us pushed through the swing doors. So far, none had caught sight of me. I gave an agonised wail. 'Rupert, oh God,' and, case in hand, I turned and in panic ran back. he followed me. 'Myopia! What is it? What's the trouble? Tell me—'

I sat down on a seat against the wall. Unable to speak. Frozen. What could I do? Just stay there? Take up residence, permanent residence. Yes. 'Three meals a day, please, brought on a tray. Just leave it on the floor, that will be perfectly all right.' Go out? And ignore all, sweep past as if I didn't know any of them? But not the girls. What about the girls? Jesus wept!

'Jesus wept,' I groaned.

'What?'

I pointed with a shaking hand. 'They're all out there. The whole slam bang shoot of them.'

'Who?'

'What I've said. Charles, Sam, Paul with the girls.'

'Together? Do they know each other then?'

'Don't be daft.' I spoke viciously. 'All separate.'

165

His face tightened.

'Oh, I'm sorry, Rupert. But what can I do?' I gave an animal wail. 'Go and sit in the Ladies' all night? You could come and fetch me when it's all clear.'

He sat down beside me. 'How on earth did they know? That you'd be on this plane?'

'God only can tell. But what difference does it make? They're all there now.'

Rupert began to laugh.

'Don't be awful. Come on, do something—'

He went on laughing. 'What's there to do? You'll just have to walk out there. Greet them all like a great lady acknowledging your public. This could be your solution, darling. At least it will separate the lambs from the sheep.'

'What do you mean?'

'Well, grown men don't give up in the face of rivals. It spurs them on. Let them fight it all out together. Like dogs over a bone.'

'Thank you.'

'All you do is stand back and watch. But you need to dress the part. With all due respect, Myopia, at the moment you look a positive mess.'

'I feel worse inside—mincemeat, 5p a pound.'

'Go and put "Snow Siren" on. We know that won't be creased. Quick, into the Ladies'. It will be the first time you've worn it in public. They'll be so flabbergasted by how you look, it'll take their minds off each other. Go on, quick.'

I arrived like an international film star. Rupert as my personal valet, weighed down with all our luggage, stood at my side. People starting pointing, and staring, somewhere a flashbulb snapped and I smiled, posing for an instant on the threshold. The girls were the first to break the spell. They ran towards me. 'Mummy, Mummy!'

'My darlings,' I gushed and bent down to kiss them both. Harriet rubbed her mouth with the back of her hand. 'You've put all lipstick over me!' Fanny giggled and pointed at my legs. 'Why are you wearing your pyjamas?'

Paul stepped forward stiffly. Something had happened. I could see it in his face. The wedding was off! I offered my cheek for a kiss in a theatrical manner, then pretended for the first time to see Sam. And Charles.

'Sam!' I shrieked as if he was a long-lost chum that I hadn't set eyes on since school. 'Charles!' I gave it a low vibrancy, an intimate thrusting ring. The voice you reserve for the family doctor. How good of you to come.

I held tightly to the girls, one on each side, like small protective poodles. My chaperones. All three men stood their ground, staring at me, stunned in their separate ways. A curling, leaping flame of pure mischief unfolded inside me. I turned, not attempting to introduce them to each other. 'Oh, I don't believe you gentlemen know Rupert, do you? Well,' I looked at him, my eyes full of laughter, 'this is Rupert, my colleague. We've been working all weekend in Paris and now we're so exhausted we thought a nice quiet tea somewhere. Any suggestions?'

Afterwards, Rupert rang to say it had been absolutely unbearable. I didn't see why, in a wicked way I'd quite enjoyed myself. 'You should have stayed to see it through, Rupert, instead of rushing off like that. They all took to their heels, there was no tea! I had to come home on my own. I'm here now doing nothing at all.'

'Alone? Are you feeling awful? I'll come over if you like.'

'Awful? Why should I feel awful? I love it. I'm luxuriating in bed, looking at television. I've got a face mask on which, wait a minute, what does it say, which "contains a highly efficient counteractive agent—discourages unsightly blemishes, tightens pores and banishes blackheads". There, it's doing all that at this very moment. I'll hold the phone closer, perhaps you can hear it.'

'But, Myopia, where are the girls?'

'Gone! They've gone to Greece with their father. The wedding's off. He's jilted her. Isn't it cruel? Serve him right if she sues for breach of promise. That's what I said. He claims he couldn't go through with it because of me. I'd fanned the flame of his original passion by letting him make love to me the other evening. I wouldn't have done it if I'd known. I'm trying to cut down on suitors, not accumulate more. He asked me to go to Greece with them right there and then, on her ticket. Cheeky thing. "No," I said. "I'm a working girl now, I can't go gadding about the world when the spirit moves me. I have commitments for this week which can't possibly be broken." That was right, wasn't it, Rupert? He can't expect to just creep back into my life like that, can he?' I lit a cigarette. 'He must learn to stand in line like the rest of them.'

'What about the rest of them? How did they react, Sam and Charles?'

'Sam stormed off as you would expect. Said the last thing he had in mind was a teddy bears' picnic with my dithering brats, and that if after seeing his way through a bottle of brandy he was still capable of doing so, he would call me. He hasn't yet, so perhaps he's not.'

'And Charles?'

'Charles carried it off with great dignity, upholding the honour of the British nation. He said he'd moved for too many years in diplomatic circles not to recognise an insoluble solution when he saw one and would I do him the honour of dining with him on the morrow. Then he tactfully withdrew. So I gave the girls their handkerchiefs each, which were a huge success by the way, waited to see them on their plane and then came home! Françoise isn't here, Paul said she could go to Paris a day early. We must have crossed flights, isn't that funny? She will be there by now. I wonder if she'll bother to go and see Babette.'

'Babette. All that seems worlds away, doesn't it?'

'Doesn't it! I still can't believe I'm back. I've been walking round all the rooms, opening cupboards and peering in the back of drawers just to see that everything's the same. And I've counted all the knives and forks and broken an egg in the sink to check if it was real. Insanity! Anyway, how is Streatham Hill?'

'Still the whirling cosmopolitan centre of South London. My mother's not here, she's gone to stay with her sister in Eastbourne. So later on I thought I'd take a cruise round the Common. Sundays can be very lively. You get a lot of vicars about.'

'Rupert! You're not considering being unfaithful to poor Jean-Paul?'

'Only physically. That can do no harm.'

'Well, watch you don't catch anything, that's all. Except of course with clergymen the one thing you can be sure of, I suppose, is that they're thoroughly clean.'

'Cleansed. Cleansed with holy water.'

'In that way. Baptists would be the best bet. You ought to enquire first before you embark on these casual encounters as to their denomination.' I gave a sudden yawn. 'Oh dear, I'm sorry. I've started yawning. My bedtime.'

'Well, Myopia, you're off to Brighton tomorrow. Will

you be taking the old fellow a rattle or is he not quite in his second childhood yet?'

'Don't be cruel. I shall be taking him a pot of Marmite. He's very fond of that. Perhaps you should take some into Moo Moffat-Paw. Say it's the very latest thing in Paris.'

He laughed. 'Cross fingers that she likes the snaps.'

I woke up much later than usual—no children rushing in, that was the reason. I'd probably have gone on even longer but for the telephone. It was Sam.

'Are you fucking still asleep? I've been ringing hours, you slob.'

'Oh have you? I was in the bath. I couldn't hear. How is your head?'

'What head? I have no head. I have a cage full of ferrets wearing hobnailed boots but I have no head. I'm holding the phone at arm's length. Can you hear me?'

'Perfectly.'

'Then stop fucking shouting! Now explain to me exactly what that scene was about yesterday. You never told me you wanted to be a movie star. Is that what you're after? A little part, my precious. Because if so I tell you now you turned in a lousy performance—'

I started to laugh. 'Oh Sam, how sad. I thought I was rather professional. I shall have to approach another producer.'

'Like hell, shit face! I happen to own all options on whatever you decide. Let's get that straight for a start.'

I saw through the window that my daffodils were dying off, the first fierce yellow browning at the edges like burnt butter. What a surprisingly capable cook Damson had turned out to be. This summer I'd fill the window boxes with scarlet geraniums and buy a canary each for the girls, pale lemon, the colour of cowslips.

'Canaries can't talk, can they, Sam?'

'Cheap! Cheap!'

'Yes, that's what I thought. They just go cheep.'

He roared down the phone. 'What the hell are you talking about? I said cheap. A cheap trick to change the subject—'

'Oh, what were we saying. I've forgotten. Anyway, I can't stay talking all day. I've got to get off to Brighton. It's Monday, remember.'

His voice altered. Became almost pleading. 'Honey.

169

What are you trying to do? Play hard to get? Have me run round in circles? Chasing your tail?'

'Certainly not, Sam.' I said it kindly. 'But I've been thinking about what you mentioned, about getting married, and it's made me very panicky to tell you the truth. I've got two children, whether you like it or not, and to judge by the way in which you refer to them I take it—'

'Jesus Christ! What the hell have your brats to do with this?'

'Don't interrupt. It's crossed my mind that you wouldn't make the most suitable of stepfathers—'

'Stepfathers! Holy ghost! Couldn't they go off to an institution—school or something? You mean I'd actually have to see them?'

He sounded so appalled, I laughed. 'That's it, you would. So couldn't we leave things as they are? Surely that's the best, till they grow up at least?'

'But honey, I can't get enough of you this way. I want more, you rat bag. More and all to myself.'

'Well, Sam.' I looked at my watch. 'You'll just have to make do with what you've got for the time being anyway. Now, I must go.'

His voice changed again. 'Say, honey. Can you get away this weekend? Take a trip to wherever you like. Charter a little plane and fly off? Sit in the sun? Sail? What do you say?'

'Well, you see, now you're making sense. As it happens, I can. The girls are away and I'd love to. We can do lots of things like that together. Isn't that more fun than just being married?'

I'd just shut the front door when the phone rang again. I hovered on the step, half knowing who it would be. Charles. I took a deep breath and went back in to answer. May as well get both of them settled in the same morning. Surprisingly, he was even easier than Sam.

'My dear, I understand exactly your apprehensions about matrimony. It is a serious decision, not to be embarked upon lightly. We both of us have already made foolish errors of selection. Mistakes which neither would wish to repeat. However, as I regard the current situation, the likelihood of remarriage at this immediate point is rather remote. I have spoken, in the greatest confidence you understand, with a certain colleague and he is of the opinion that to remarry within certainly two years would

170

from my point of view be political suicide. Added to this the delicate fact that you yourself are a divorcée, albeit the innocent party—'

'Yes, you should think of that, Charles. It could lose you half the votes of your churchgoing constituents for a start.'

He droned on and on. In his dear, dead, boring voice. He'd have got my vote for certain if only to shut him up. I interrupted. 'I'm afraid I have to go now. I have a train to catch, Charles.'

He sounded taken aback. 'Nine o'clock tonight.'

'What? Oh sorry! Where?' Was he talking about our dinner?

'On BBC2. Look in. I think you'll find it interesting. We're discussing World Economy and the Individual. I deeply regret the postponement of our dinner together. However, could lunch on Tuesday be a possibility?'

'Yes,' I said quickly. 'What, just the usual arrangement? Here you mean? Oh, I'd love that, Charles.'

'A bottle of Dom Perignon, wouldn't you say? We can toast each other on our unofficial engagement, my darling. Two years is a long time to wait I know, added to which we will have to continue meeting in our usual clandestine manner. However—'

'I think it's perfect, Charles,' I said, 'perfect.' And added coyly, 'After all, it always has been in the past.'

I whistled all the way to the station. Found a parking place with no trouble at all, changed my clothes in the Ladies' lavatory and deposited what I'd taken off in the locker. I loved that part of it. No one at home had seen my Brighton clothes. Dull green beret, skirt and blouse like a school uniform. Solid stockings, flat shoes. Sensible raincoat for possible showers. Even a change of handbag. 'A mystery woman was seen boarding the 12.25 for Brighton!' I bought a paper and saw with horror that my nails were still white. Pale shiny pearls from Paris. Oh dear, he wouldn't like that. I'd have to get some varnish remover and cotton wool from the chemist's shop. I glanced at the clock, ten minutes, still time.

I got into the nearest carriage and started scrubbing at my nails. By the time we'd left Victoria they were back to nature and bare again. Peardrops, that's what the remover smelt of. Nice. All finished, I stood up and moved along the corridor to the buffet car. Now what should I have today? A cup of tea? Or something stronger? Going to

Paris had put me on drinking, that was for sure. I'd have to watch myself. My Auntie Doris was a big one for the booze. They were always saying that in our house. My mother was anyway. 'Bottles and boys! Boys and bottles! She can't get enough of them, Doris.' Perhaps I was taking after her.

'Gin and tonic please,' I said. On the other hand, he'd be able to smell that. 'No, wait. What's got no smell?'

There was a new man behind the bar. I knew all the usual ones. 'Oh,' I said, 'you're new, aren't you?'

He winked, cocky, young, about eighteen. When he answered it was with a marked Irish accent. Fresh from the Emerald Isle. 'First day, lady.'

I didn't like that. Lady. It held too well the distance of years and counter.

'You're very young for the job, aren't you?'

His eyebrows shot up in mock surprise. 'Young? Young, you say? And me twenty-five.'

'You never are. Not twenty-five. I know that. More like eighteen, I'd have said.'

He was built like a brick house, whatever his age. With wide wrists and a strong straight neck like a Corinthian column. His hair was the colour of caramel toffee, tight and curly to his head, but his eyebrows were black, black to match his curly lashes. And his eyes were a marvellous blue. Really marvellous, spectacular, smiley. 'When Irish eyes are smiling'. Those sort of ones. Paddy. A puckish Paddy. It would be pleasant travelling with him each Monday.

He laughed to see me looking at him for so long. Well, he must be used to that by now. And it wasn't as if he hadn't taken his fill of me too. Had your pennyworth?

'You haven't answered,' I said. 'What's got no smell?'

'Ah. Ah now.' He did everything with a great animal flourish. Gusto. Glad to be alive. How I felt too as a matter of fact. 'Rum. Rum and coke. No trace at all. You might have been at your mother's breast. No one could tell the difference.'

I was sorry when we arrived. I was really. I'd not enjoyed a train trip, not like that since—ever. We'd made a date. Oh yes. Seven o'clock at Hammersmith Palais. He wanted to show me his dancing paces, that and his extraordinary drinking abilities. I was looking forward to it. Why not?

I walked from the station humming. Breaking at one point into a neat paso doble. Six days non-stop of sun and

172

Brighton bustling with the heady excitement of a good season ahead. I took a deep breath. Ozone.

When I got close I stopped at the corner shop for Marmite. 'Large one please. And a packet of Osbornes while you're at it. Oh, and a nice malt loaf, and a tin of peaches with a small condensed milk.' Onnie connie. He couldn't get enough of that, straight from the tin sucking on a teaspoon.

'A regular feast,' the woman said. 'How is the old fellow anyway?'

'Fine. I'm just in to see him now.'

'I caught sight of him last week. He seems to be breaking.'

I pocketed the change and turned to go. 'Seventy-two next month and not getting any younger.'

But still keen on it. The old devil. We could be had up for what we did, surely we could. Comforting the aged, that's what I'd get my counsel to plead. 'For years, m'lord, this young woman has given freely of herself body and soul. Unstintingly complied to the strange requests of this venal old man. The raw truth, the bare bones, the actual fact that in this relationship he happens to be . . .'

I'd reached the door. He was at the window waiting. In a hurry again. I laughed, easily. What the hell? Where's the harm? Charity begins at home, my mother was always saying that. He opened the door and grabbed me in. Same as ever. Nothing changed in seven days. Teeth on the mantelpiece, trousers down. A terrible old trout, tortoise neck, knees like turnips. The oldest by far of all my men, but with a greater need than the whole lot put together. I looked at him, warmth, love, pity and a fierce protective-ness flooding through me.

'Hello, Dad,' I said cheerfully, 'have you had a good week?'

173

UP TIGHT

To Mama
who first thought of me

We sat in the crowded, chandeliered restaurant with his celebrated hand inside my Marks & Spencer knickers.

'Ooh! Ouch!' I said. 'You're hurting! What's happened, I think, is that my pubic hair has somehow got caught in your watchstrap. Half a mo' and I'll untangle it.'

It was just as well that we'd both ordered salmon for starters. I wouldn't have wished to taint the taste of, say, an artichoke or some other such dish of delicate flavour requiring fingers as forks. But by the time we'd reached the brandy stage he was back in there again. And what's more, now, was making heavy demands that I should similarly explore the ageing content of his own much more expensive underwear. But 'No,' I'd insisted. 'Not here.' Best that one of us at least should appear to have both hands above the table. I wouldn't have known how to walk out if the management had asked us to leave. 'In any case,' I'd added, 'what about the time? I can't be late for school again tomorrow. I'm having a hell of a do these days with the Head!'

In the morning he drove me to school. 'Oh, don't drop me right outside,' I pleaded. 'The girls will get the wrong idea.' But he had, of course, right up to the main entrance, in amongst the greatest mass of them, laughing loudly as he pulled the powerful engine to a halt. They gathered like ants, amazed in the first place to see anything other than an industrial lorry, a costermonger's barrow, or the rag-and-bone man in the drabness of that street. Let alone the scarlet splendour of his Aston Martin Sports. I cringed in the low-slung seat, expecting the worst when they recognised his face—and saw me with him. He leaned across, preparing to embrace before them all, but I escaped in time. 'Take care, little one,' he growled affectionately. 'You're a bastard,' I said as I slammed the door and braced myself for the storm. I could still hear the hum of his departing car as I reached the staff-room door.

The news travelled like greased lightning. Miss and a film-star! Yes! Was he my boyfriend? He couldn't be, that old! Did he know my dad then? Grandad? Who, and why

177

and where—and what was I doing in his car?

'If this stupidity doesn't cease this instant,' I said, 'you will all, the whole damn shoot of you, be sitting with your hands held on your heads for the entire lesson! No art class, none today, nothing—do you understand! Just sitting, looking straight ahead, not a word from anyone! Now what's it to be? Painting or a form of purgatory—I leave it to you to decide—'

'Oh, painting, miss! Yes, painting! Mmmmmm ...' They droned and mumbled like a swarm of bees. And though their actual questions ceased, their curious eyes and lifted brows maintained the tense excitement of suppressed enquiry until the morning ended.

I couldn't wait till dinner break to pour it out to Winnie. We were in luck; it happened to be her playground duty day, which meant a good long gossip without too much fear of being overheard. We met in the upper staff-room, where several other of my colleagues—conscious that I'd been hauled in by our headmistress yesterday after they'd left—were waiting with Winnie to hear the worst.My unpunctuality had now become almost legendary amongst these fond acquaintances, despite the fact that I hadn't been teaching there for all that long. Almost a term, the same as Winnie. The first teaching post for both of us. She spoke up first, still patently concerned on my behalf—despite the blinding wideness of my entering smile. 'Well?' She wavered anxiously. 'How did it go with old Pritchard?' So much had happened, of course, since then that I'd almost forgotten that bit. 'Oh yes,' I laughed and allowed myself a leap of triumph up and on to a chair.

'Well, congratulations are in order! I've managed to lose my class! The final disgrace! Stripped of the form mistress's responsibilities! No more morning register to call, or dinner money to collect—or daily squatters in my art room! All back to what it always should have been—a straightforward specialist post!'

'It gives you a leeway of half an hour on either side in the mornings anyway,' Winnie said as we walked around the playground. Two girls had evidently, from an over-excited, evergrowing group around the lavatories, locked themselves in together and were indulging in a rude and running commentary. 'Oh leave them, Winnie. Why bother? It'll be Doris Wellington and that daft Pauline playing boyfriends with their pencil boxes, I expect. He rang again anyway last night, Nathaniel—I slept in his hotel, the Cadogan Court, can you imagine! What are you doing after school tonight? We can have a cup of tea and I can give you all the details!'

She shivered slightly. From the cold? Or was it pure excitement?' 'Oh yes, I've nothing on at all, except—' She hesitated. 'I promised I'd help mummy in the shop. She's having trouble with the bacon slicer—'

'You're barmy, Winnie, living at home, especially in a shop! There's no hope in hell of you getting any sort of love life off the ground whilst you will stick on there. It's impossible! Blimey, look at how I used to be before I made the break ...'

'You should apply for a teaching job down here in Sussex, my girl. Be nice and near to give your mother a hand—she's not getting any younger. And business as it is, with everyone stocking sweets and bloody cigarettes—he's got them over in the greengrocer's now, you know—we're staying open that much longer to cope with the competition. We could do with a spot of help, come evenings. And teaching art, you won't have homework to mark. And there's your bedroom upstairs to do your paintings in—you want to think seriously what's best all round, now, girl!'

'Yes, dad,' I said, 'I am.' I lifted the lid of the deep double fridge to lower the lolly ices. He came closer and peered over my shoulder at the shimmering moulded tray, frowning down at each of the twenty-four circular sections—and rearranged the wooden sticks of one entire line.

'Go easy, if these sticks aren't put in at the appropriate angle, the entire lolly falls to pieces when you're trying to get it out. Your mother has calculated that it only has to happen to as little as five for the whole profit margin to be wiped out on us doing these home-made lollies—'

'Yes, dad,' I said. 'I know.'

'Anyway,' he continued, 'it beats me what it is you see in London. You'll find the cost of living vastly different. No chance to save your earnings, none at all. So no one will see the benefit, least of all your mother and me, for all the years of education that we've given you. I'm not sure now I see the point. I honestly think that, given the decision all over again, I ought to have stuck to my guns and put my foot down and had you out in a job. It was your mother's doing, not mine, sending you on to art school. But it's my belief that artists are born and not made, and all that's happened is that you're ending up as a teacher anyway, so if you had to go on you may just as well have gone to an ordinary teachers' training college. Which would have made it at least only two instead of the five years—where are you going now? Out? Mind to be back before long. We'll be getting busy then and your mother's having a lie down—'

'Right, dad. I will.'

'Where are you off to anyway?'

I hesitated before answering, but he pressed home irritably: 'Eh, where?'

'I'm going to say goodbye to Derek.'

His lip curled, he turned his back, but not before making sure I heard. 'Goodbye! Good riddance! Jewboy! Bloody yid.'

Derek was waiting for me at the entrance of the Palace Pier. My heart tilted over when I saw him. He was looking at another girl, appreciatively, appraisingly, from head to toe. And she was looking back, laughing over her shoulder as she passed. I could have slapped her on both cheeks. That wasn't unusual, not with Derek, I'd known it from the start, what a terrible flirt he was. I'd watched him flirting with everybody else whilst biding my time to catch him. And I had caught him too, at Christmastime. I hadn't known till then that he was my father's *bête noire*— Jewish, the thought hadn't occurred. He looked more French, more Continental in his clothes and with his well-cut beard. He seemed so much outside these things, more of the world, more cosmopolitan. Like all those London students in our final pedagogic year. He must have found the rest of us appallingly provincial. That spurred me on, of course, to catch him more, to prove that I was somehow just a cut above. And I was as well, as he so very soon had found out. The brightest student of my year, the most imaginative of the painters. The most original. Yes, I was just as much a catch. 'Only in this setting,' was what he said to me. I'd have had a bloody sight more of a job to shine in the metropolis. In a keener ambience, like a London art school, where the competition was more crucifying. 'And the atmosphere more creative,' I'd added. 'I might in fact have done much better—' 'No, you're not the sort to thrive in competition. There's too much that's misguidedly arty in you. A false fostering of sensitivity. That's the danger of these sort of places, out of the artistic swim. You're so conditioned, you, that you might find it rather better to remain a big fish in a small pond—'

They were challenging words, as well he knew, and I didn't believe them anyway. Even then, before I'd claimed him as my own, London was already my Mecca. And now, with everything in shreds between us, where else was there for me to go?

The turnstile to the Palace Pier was jammed; he helped me to jump over. 'Thank you, Derek,' I said, mock-formally, hoping he'd hold me longer. He couldn't meet my eye and, though he took my hand in his to walk along together, his fingers too felt cold and strained and even, now, unfriendly.

I'd wanted our last goodbyes to be back in his room. I'd wanted in fact to say goodbye in bed, but he'd said 'No, the thing would be too searing, too painful, too emotional for either of us to bear.'

'No more than it has ever been,' I'd said, trying to make a joke. He'd looked at me like a stranger. I'd laughed, knowing I was batting on a very silly wicket, but still unable to stop. 'Painful, I mean! It always has been that. Painful and impossible. But,' I sounded desperate even to myself. 'But,' and now my voice was breaking, 'it could be nice since it's going to be the last time, if we just got in and cuddled—couldn't it?'

'No. It couldn't.'

We passed the candy-floss machine and stepped around the children queueing for ice-creams. 'I made forty-eight ice lollies today,' I said. 'Twenty-four a day up on what we were doing this time last week. All orange, they go much better than the raspberry. Strange that, isn't it? You'd think it would be the other way around. I used to love dyeing my tongue dark red, the orange is much less lovely—it can look like catarrh.'

'Spare me the details, please.'

'Oh Christ!' I said. 'I'll shut up then.'

We'd reached the end. 'We've reached the end.' I took my hand from his and twisted round to face him. 'Symbolical. Shall we go under?' That sounded symbolical too, I thought. He answered as I had expected. 'No.' But I led the way, down the open iron stairs, past the line of anglers, right on until I'd arrived at the grid-like darkened structures underneath the pier. He didn't follow, and when he did, his face was sulky, like a little boy's. 'This is silly,' he said when I pulled him close. 'Pointless.'

We were alone, it was a lovers' place, secret and unseen by all those crowds above us. We'd been there many times before, in the early days, before I'd been brave enough to be persuaded back to his bed. Ironic that, that in those days he was the one who was so much keener. He'd said that's how it would be, that once he'd started me off, there'd be no stopping. It wouldn't be long now before I'd be looking at every man like that. Wondering, so he'd said, what they'd be like as well. The idea had intrigued me, but I hadn't let on then. Though possibly what he'd said might well come true.

I put my hand on his trousers pocket, he shrank nervously away, but I persisted in my quest. 'What are you expecting to prove by this?' My fingers closed around the stiffening shape. 'I've proved it!' He shut his eyes, threw back his head, so handsome, bearded—weak, and groaned. 'You look just like an El Greco. The crucifixion.' My hand began to work relentlessly and as rhythmically as the restricting pocket would allow. He made no sound at all. I cleared my throat. 'I'm playing the part of a philistine,' I said companionably, and waited for the smile to hover round his mouth.

It didn't happen, if anything the line became a little bleak. I stopped what I was doing. Suddenly and without a word of explanation. His eyes opened sharply in surprise, but I gazed steadily back. 'You're right.' I spoke flatly. 'It is pointless after all.' He was speechless, unable to formulate his feelings now in words. Between us, sheathed in flannel, grey—reared his great erection. I pointed to it. 'It looks like a broom handle under a blanket! Perhaps you'd better think of finishing it off yourself. I wouldn't like to walk along the pier, not with you and that. It could be construed as conspicuous!'

'He'd have made a shocking husband, Derek, anyway—everyone thinks that you're better off without him.'

'Yes,' I said dully, and concentrated on my tie-and-dye. It was going to be a brilliant emerald silky scarf, with a border of alternating white and lemon rings. A complicated process, involving lots of pebbles and pieces of string and various baths of brilliant colour. I wasn't very good at it, the discipline wasn't there.

'Am I doing this right?'

'Not really, the spacing's too irregular—anyway, you know you said he was catching the boat on Saturday, he couldn't have been because Fiona saw him standing at a bus stop in Portslade on Saturday—'

I swallowed. 'What time Saturday? In the morning?'

'No, very late at night—'

'Um, alone?'

'No,' she said brutally. 'With one of those French girls—those students who are up at the 'tech.'

'It's silly, this scarf. I've got nothing that goes with green—'

She came over and stood beside me. 'Don't give up when you've gone this far—it'll be something for your final show. Shall I try and retrieve something for you? In exchange for some help with my self-portrait?' I nodded, feeling slightly bruised inside. Why had he lied about leaving on Saturday? And if he'd had to sneakily see that French student, why couldn't he just stay inside instead of letting half the college see? Especially Fiona.

We were in the textile printing room, Pat and I, as we spoke, preparing for our end of course exhibitions. Derek was missing his, not bothering, bound by now on a big boat to South Africa. Summoned by his father, a good way to avoid his National Service. He'd been at home in here, the textile school, they'd liked his sense of colour and the intricacies of his small designs. Mine were too wild and swirling, so they said, chaotic and emotional. As one would expect from a Fine Arts, Painting student. Derek was aiming for the world of advertising, he was a crack hand at layout with ambitions of becoming an art director. Even from that fact of our opposite artistic standpoints, the affair could be seen to be doomed. Without everything else.

'Haven't you spoken to Fiona yourself, then?'

'No.' I shook my head. 'I haven't.'

Pat plunged my piece of now neatly tied silk scarf into a bowl of kingfisher blue, we both watched it soaking into its present brilliant yellow and gradually turn green. She prodded it to make quite sure it lay beneath the surface and then she ran cold water from the tap over her rubber gloved hands. 'I bumped into her by the bandstand—'

'The bandstand, the bandstand Hove?'
'No, Eastbourne.'
'I wonder what she was doing there—'
'Well, she wasn't sitting in a deckchair.'
'A sports car, probably.'
'With an appalling-looking chap—'
'No chin?'
'None! Lots of money by the look of him.'
'That was Humphrey,' I said. 'He's a Hussar.'

There had always been the three of us really. Pat and Fiona and me. But in the last two years we'd gone our different ways. Pat into textiles and fabric printing, an annexe of the art school, situated on the other side of the road so that physically it wasn't so easy to swap stories or pass the time of day on the stairs any more. Me into the rarefied regions of canvas and oils—and Fiona into the social whirl of her sub-deb world. We none of us had very much in common except that we were keen on boys, but each of us had come to art school for very different reasons. Sent by our parents: Fiona to while away the time in a socially acceptable pursuit and because her father had a weakness for water colours. On the walls of his prosperous lawyer's office. Pat to better herself by hopefully marrying one of the qualifying architects in the affiliated architectural school, instead of doing as her mother—now widowed—had done, that is, married a well-to-do master plumber. And me, well me to make good too, but in a different way. To excel. To be brilliant. To be a credit academically. 'Did you come top?' 'No, Dad. Second.' 'Who came top?' 'Someone else.' 'Next time then, see it's you, my girl!'

Not that I knew either of them that well. They spent a lot of time out on the town, hours which I preferred to spend on work. And they lived the sort of lives which meant a lot of coming and going into their various homes. I didn't have a home as such, not living above the shop—it was only in the last three years that we'd managed to make our outdoor lavatory in. And as well, compared to them, I was a late developer, filled out with under-the-counter chocolate, too fat to fit into the latest fashion, still wearing in fact my old school skirt for the first term. But even so, head bent and shoulders hunched, before I'd fined down to my present curves, both of them had sensed oncoming competition.

I came, strangely enough, into my own at the very point of separation. That is to say after the first two years of Intermediate had ended and everyone had decided in what to Specialise.

Fiona after deciding on Illustration, had suddenly switched to Painting, but at the end of her first disastrous term—which ended with her in tears and her father being advised to save his money—she was taken away. I saw her in the Christmas holidays. 'I've got four portraits on the go,' she boasted confidently.

'Have you? How impressive!'

'Yes, all friends of daddy's.'

'Men of good standing—'

'It's not at all difficult.' She leaned forward confidingly. 'I'm doing them all from photographs actually ...'

I tried not to show my distaste, and made an effort at sustained interest. 'That's nice—' So much so, in fact, that she insisted I join her for coffee, with her paying. I was flattered, it was the friendliest gesture she'd so far made.

She steered me into an exclusive olde worlde coffee shoppe, full of refined old ladies and rich retired gentility, and cheerfully sat down at the nearest table. A pinafored waitress swept across towards us. 'This way, madam, please,' she said. I'd already put my handbag down on the table, preparing to take a chair. But now I picked it up again. Fiona didn't move. 'This suits us fine,' she said and smiled, firmly. I shrank and picked a nail, I never liked a fuss. Fiona looked up and waved her arm at me and then said, simply but with a certain sharpness, as if commanding a rather dim domestic animal: 'Sit!' I did.

That was the start, I suppose, in fact. Her inexplicable loneliness and apparent need of an audience and my ridiculous pleasure at providing simply that, the someone to listen. She'd drop in on our Life Drawing Class or when we'd embarked on a long-term project involving Pictorial Composition encompassing Perspective, and she'd stand waiting wistfully till someone should enquire as to what she was up to now. It was always me. And then she'd gush in answer. 'Had lunch in London yesterday at the Chelsea Arts Club, and can you imagine—I was actually invited to become a member! As a Professional bona fide Artist!' And she'd take out a cigarette and place it in an amber holder. 'Lovely colour,' I'd say, and point at it to change the subject. But it wasn't until she invited me to her twenty-

185

first birthday party that we ever broached the subject of sex.

Pat had been invited to the party too, and so had her cousin, a medical student at Guy's Hospital up in London. Actually it was because of the cousin that Pat had been invited. 'He's the smart side of the family. My mother's sister, she married a dentist who did awfully well in Rottingdean. They've always had money. He's got his own car, Mark—shall I get him to pick you up?'

'Oh no, don't do that. I can get there on the bus.' I said it quickly.

She looked doubtful. 'I'm not sure that they have buses round Fiona's. It's what's called a very residential area.'

'I'll be all right. One of our neighbours can give me a lift.' Ted Grunt, the greengrocer's son, could drop me off in his van. On the corner, of course, not right up the drive to the actual front door! 'What are you wearing?' I asked a little fearfully.

She'd shrugged her thin and elegant shoulders. 'Oh, I never know till the night before. And then if nothing seems nice, I get old mum to fork out for something special on the day.'

That was one of the things I'd noticed about Pat right away, her incredibly narrow body which, but for the looseness, the athletic grace with which she held herself, would have been merely scraggy. She hadn't any breasts at all, but instead her legs reached up to her ears. She dressed in clashing, primary colours with calculated confidence and incredible style. The clothes themselves were rather cheap and badly finished—it was she who made them marvellous. Her mouth was always immaculately out-lined and carefully painted in to exactly match her nails. These days she favoured a stinging pink, with violet variations in whatever it was she wore. Apart from her legs and the magically achieved elegance, her crowning glory was her hair, side-parted very low down on her head so that the rest hung curtain-like across her face, below the level of her neck. 'What are you, anyway?'

'Black, I expect, as usual.'

'Smashing!'

It was in my first year of painting that I'd taken to black, in fact, after seeing a snap of Juliette Greco, and very soon after a French film about existentialists. My father nearly went mad, but I took no notice. 'You're not minding the shop with that muck on your eyes, my girl! You're not making a fool of your mother and me turned out like an undertaker—'

'Right then, I won't—'

'That's it, good girl.' He turned his back. 'Soap and water.'

'Mind the shop.'

'What!'

'That's it then,' I said. 'I said I won't mind the shop!' And I won, that time. If I'd shown the same gumption over Derek, I might have won there too.

But it worked a treat, my black, especially with my white face. And even with my brown, I found in summer. I'd done it overnight almost, everything I owned straight into the four-hour funeral service at Sketchleys. And less than five shillings spent on mascara, a soft black pencil and a box of magnolia pale powder from Woolworth's. It wasn't Pat's style, but it was just as strong. It wasn't Fiona's either. Hers showed a penchant for pastels and pearls, and fine tweed skirts and flat-heeled shoes, shone conker bright. And well-cut, glossy, county hair. And very clean teeth, and fresh complexioned cheeks. She smelt very good—always as if she'd just got out of the bath. But her legs weren't good. And as well as that she wore glasses.

'It'll be a good do! Posh. Plenty of nobs. Have you asked across the road? He'll drop you off, Ted, in the van—'

'Yes, dad, I've asked already.'

'That's settled then. I'll come up too. Just to see you in, girl.'

'Don't! There's no need! I'll be all right! Honestly!'

'Well,' he sniffed huffily. 'If what you're saying is you don't want me. You'd rather I didn't. You prefer to straggle in like some stray cat without a family, I quite understand, my high and mighty miss! You needn't think because—' But in the end he gave in. After I'd pleaded desperately for him to come.

Fiona's father opened the door. My own mistook him for the butler because of his evening suit, but I was the only one who blushed; both men appeared to take the situation in their stride. 'Well, sir,' my father spoke in a strangled, high, affected voice, quite unlike his own. 'I shall depart leaving my precious daughter in your undoubtedly capable hands. Should transport be required for her

187

return, you have only to ring our good neighbour, the greengrocer, Mr Grunt, and hey presto, her carriage will await!' He turned with a flourish of an arm towards Ted in the van on the kerb. Ted, taking it as some sort of signal, hooted back on his croaky horn.

'*A la* Cinderella!' uttered the charming host.

'Quite, sir,' answered my father.

I didn't stop sweating for an hour.

'Do you have a number, little one? I'd like to get in touch.'

'We're Number 20—20 Station Street—'

'Telephone number, ducky.' I flinched at the insolence of the drawl, the implication of extreme boredom in the tone. I couldn't for the life of me see why he was bothering, or indeed had bothered almost within minutes of my arrival at the party. 'My!' he'd said, when Fiona's father had done the introductions. Even before I'd taken my coat off. 'Here, let me help you,' My lining was torn, with help the sleeve could easily turn inside out. 'I'm better off doing it myself, I think.' But he'd stood there waiting, watching me, with half-closed eyes sliding up and over my body. I knew that he'd ruin my evening, but there was something about him you couldn't shake off. Like Fiona had been with the waitress.

We danced a lot, he held me terribly tight. That part of it was best in fact—it was the talking that got me down. 'Cigarette, sweetie?' 'No, thank you very much, I don't.' 'You don't, dontcha! What do you do then, eh?' And he leaned forward and deliberately pinched me on my botty. What answer was there to give?

I sat there smarting at his mimicry of my accent, giving no answer at all. If I could have managed it I wouldn't have spoken anyway, not in my normal voice, all evening. It must run in families, I thought, this failure to stay yourself. After several hours I could hear myself making a deliberate effort to ape the intonations of everyone around me. They seemed mainly to fall into two categories. The short and sharp, and the long-drawn-out. The first required an ack-ack style delivery, the clipping off of word endings and between the staccato bursts, quite long, abruptly started pauses. While the long-drawn-out was simply that—achieved by running each word right into the next, essentially low-pitched rather than high. Like his voice, my constant companion's, now. But I hadn't

done my homework, hadn't sat down long enough to study it, simply because before it hadn't seemed necessary. Fiona had waved across the room. 'Everything all right?'
'Lovely,' I'd lied, lifting my glass of champagne.

'But at least you got a man.' Pat sounded despondent. 'Who wanted to see you home. I seemed to be stuck with Mark all night, but he was so depressed over his trouble I had to be with him if only to see he didn't get too sloshed—'

'He's nice, isn't he? When's he going to have to marry the girl? If she's five months gone it'll be showing already.'

'Bitch. That's all they go in for nursing for, you know, most of them—to nab a nice young medical student. My mum was thinking of it for me. I wouldn't have minded either, but I didn't get a good enough School Certificate. You have to be a bit brainier than me to be a nurse. No, it wasn't a memorable evening. Wasn't the food appalling? Mum does a much better spread than that. You haven't been to our house, have you? I never get on that well in those sort of do's. She's a shocking snob, isn't she? Fiona. The whole family in fact. My dad used to know them when they started. Yes, he fitted their upstairs lavatory. An ordinary house they lived in then, my auntie lived up the road. She said they'd never speak to anybody. Terrible social climbers. And as mean as hell as well. They kept him waiting a whole year, quibbling about the lavatory bill. Fiona's like that too. Haven't you noticed?' She laughed. 'They must have shat themselves to see you getting off with who you did. He'd be the ideal in their eyes as a son-in-law. Isn't it funny that they don't put Fiona into those new contact lenses—those glasses of hers put the kibosh on things a bit, I think. Don't you? My mum would have me out of them in a trice, I know. But that's the difference—She spends on important things—they'd probably see it as extravagance! Anyway, enough of that. What happened? Did he kiss you? Yes? And what else? Anything?'

Fiona had asked that, too, the very next morning. But the call had come at a busy time, just as the pubs were emptying and lots of men were coming in for peppermints for facing their wives at home. Our telephone was just inside the shop, put there, despite the inconvenience, to make sure that the shop was never left empty and the telephone never left unanswered. It rarely, if ever, rang for me. My father didn't encourage either my mother or myself to give the number freely. 'How did you get my number?' I said to her in surprise.

'From Piers of course. He was raving about you. Hasn't he rung you yet? No? Oh he will, I'm sure of that. He's super, isn't he? Frightfully well-to-do—has his own aeroplane, can you imagine! In Scotland, to survey the scenery I believe. Much of which he owns, of course. Or will do when dear daddy dies. I'm dying to hear all—oh don't go!'

'I've got to. Really.'

'When shall I see you then to get the gory details? Would you like to come up to tea today? Mummy'll be here, but we can go out for a walk—'

'That's better, yes, the walk I mean. Why not meet down at the Pier?'

'Why not? Which one? I have to confess I've hardly been on the Palace Pier—except once, when taken by a rather common nanny. I'm sure mummy must have given her the sack, I know there was a frightful fuss—'

My father had started shouting. I managed to get in 'West Pier then, at five o'clock!' before he forcibly removed the receiver from my hand and replaced it with a heavy jar of Trebor Extra Strong.

There wasn't that much to tell about Piers. There might have been, but by then I was much too miserable. My answers now were almost monosyllabic and as well I was worried to death about where to tell him he should drop me. It couldn't possibly be outside our shop, that was for sure. I couldn't have stood the comment. I could hear it already. 'How frightfully smart. A shop girl.' On the other hand, if I were to pretend to live in Fiona's area it meant a hell of a hike home. So I settled for the seafront, which was relatively nearer. Then having done that, having given him directions, I started agonising over Station Street. Would he remember I'd called it that? Hadn't he only written down the telephone number? 'I have to go in,' I said. He'd switched the engine off, lowering his head to peer up with what seemed approval at the Regency terrace I'd chosen. He'd slipped his hand straight up my skirt, right past my stocking top, clear over the suspender, bang on to the knicker itself. The bit between the legs. I curled with embarrassment. I knew it was wet. Not wet, but without doubt damp. Damp, from having sat so long in

190

his overheated car. Already damp, in fact, from simply dancing with him close. And damper too from having been excused before we'd left and unable to adequately dry my pubic hairs on the cheaper brand of toilet paper they used in Fiona's house.

'You're damp!' I didn't think he'd let it pass. Were there no limits to which he'd stoop to make me feel embarrassed? 'Am I?' My voice was barely there. He forced the gusset to one side pulling with it a painful displacement of hair. 'Ouch!' I said and tried to push his hand away. 'Ouch! Ouch! Ouch! Just what are you ouching about, my sweet?' And he pushed his fingers even further and more brutally. 'Eh? This?' The tears were coming in my eyes, just from the sheer discomfort. 'It's hurting.'

He pulled his hand away as roughly as he'd put it in and brought his fingers to his face. 'Mm. Mmmmm. Mmmmmm! What fragrance! The best of Billingsgate!— Here, how do you like yourself?' And before I was able to say anything at all, he'd forced his fingers in my open mouth, unfastened the car door, pushed me out, shouted 'Sweet dreams!' and driven off into the night.

'I don't like him, Piers, you know, not at all, Fiona. And he doesn't like me either, not really. He's playing a game, that's all.'

'Shall we have a Kunzle cake each? I can't resist them, can you? They cost a shilling though, that's the only thing ...'

'Have one,' I said. 'I'll pay. Oh listen to this, it's one of my favourites. *My Foolish Heart*. Did you see the film? Susan Hayward. She had a wonderful figure in it. Very high here—' I touched my sweater. 'She'd pulled her straps up extra tight. When I got home, I did exactly the same to mine. Don't they sell them low in the shops? And people go round with them like that as well. Someone should say—'

'I'm wearing a new one, first time on. Do you see any difference in the profile?' She turned to sit sideways in her seat. The Palm Court Orchestra swooped to a crescendo, drowning the hum of conversation from surrounding tables. I made as if to measure, with my arm outstretched and one eye closed, my thumb upturned as we'd been taught to do in drawing. 'Bit bigger, I think. And far more pointed. Nice. Where'd it come from then?'

191

'Harrods. Mummy got it when she was up. It's padded. Feel.'

'What without you trying on? How on earth did she know it would fit? I'd never do that.'

'Greatly Reduced. She couldn't resist. Less than half price, so she said. A fifty per cent saving and more! Anyway, with me and what I've got, the fit is not important. Mind you, I've got much more than Pat. I wouldn't care to see her stripped, would you?'

'Oh, I don't know, she's got dreadfully good legs.'

'Straight, you mean?'

'Well more than that ...'

'I'd rather have your figure. That bosom you've got is bloody good. That's what Piers said. He said that's what he noticed first, your terribly high round titties!'

'He couldn't have. I had my coat on when he saw me first—'

She clucked impatiently. 'Well, anyway, I suppose he meant that when you took it off. It looked good, the dress, I must say. It showed enough, even daddy said afterwards, what a fine-looking girl you were. He said your father seemed a grand chap, with rather a sense of humour, is that right?'

'No,' I said. 'It isn't. But anyway now, about Piers ...'

When I got home he'd phoned.

I'd never known my father so excited except once many years before, when he'd recognised George Formby in the street. 'George Formby, I presume!' And he'd placed himself squarely in the poor man's path, doubled in a deep curtsey, doffing his trilby and offering his hand! Squirming.

'He's an Hon, this boy, and double-barrelled to boot!' He propelled himself along the counter pinging each toffee jar with a blunt pencil, as one might use a tuning fork to test the quality of crystal. 'You've done it this time, girl! Me and your mother could be out of this little lot and living in the lap of luxury before we know it, if you play your cards right! Now this is what you do, you see to it he doesn't go too far. Eat his oats before autumn, as it were! No point running for a bus once you've boarded it—any man would say the same. Stick to your standards, my girl, no shilly-shallying, you understand! These young rakes, a chap like that, the world at his feet and so much wealth to grease his elbows, will expect to just play fast and loose with everyone. Well, not with a daughter of mine! No sir! And I would say as much should the occasion arise. Though I think it won't with you, you know. I gave him to understand on the telephone that your father and family were forces to be reckoned with. You may have been brought up in business, but no one can call you shop-soiled.' He stopped short at that and peered at me, suddenly anxious. But through my numbness and growing despair I managed to shake my head and still his worst fear. He beamed. 'Wholesome. And educated. I wouldn't be surprised if the silly girls that he's been used to can only just about tell the difference between a samba and a serviette. That's all they teach in these finishing schools—the superficial niceties of life. At least you know which artist lost his ear. You must show him your paintings—you never know, he might even buy one!'

'I'm not going.'

'Oh yes. You're going my girl. She's going, isn't she, mam? What, after I've arranged it all, my girl—I'll say you're bloody going. You take this chance—how many more of these do you think will come your way?'

I took change from the till and went out to telephone. 'Fiona? I'm seeing him again. Piers. Yes. My father arranged it all behind my back for the day after tomorrow, Sunday. He's meeting me at Lancing Station some time in the morning—I shall be with him all day.'

There was a silence at the other end. 'You lucky thing,' she said.

'I don't want to go—'

'Oh you do, you'll have a lovely time. I bet he tries to seduce you.'

'Yes.'

'I'd give my life to be right there myself!'

'Oh I'd love you to be. Much nicer than being on my own.'

I knew it was wrong when I boarded the train, my black. It had turned out to be a brilliant day, billowing with air and sun and early spring. The sort of light that called for white.

He'd greeted me with some distaste. 'Why, duckie, you look like a spider! We're going up on the Downs, not into some dark bordello in the Boulevard St Germain! You

193

surely possess something slightly more suitable.'

'I'm sorry.' I sucked the inside of my lower lip between my teeth, a childish habit to stop me crying. I saw his eyes fall to my shoes, frail and fragile, almost non-existent ballet pumps.

'Why in hell have you come in your bedroom slippers?'

I hung my head. The train went back on the hour. I could stay of course; I could sit all day in the station Ladies and pretend to my father that I'd had a fabulous time.

The curtness cut through the sun, a nearby bush of premature blossom shivered when he spoke. 'Coming?' And he turned on his heel and strode towards his waiting car. 'Here. I'm sure I have some Wellingtons in the boot. They're mine, but you can wear them.'

I stared at them stupidly. 'What, without socks?'

'Wot, wiv out socks?' His upper lip curved high over his teeth, almost nearly to his nose. Perhaps he should be wearing the Wellingtons to deliver a crisper kick? 'Sweetie, unless you have a set of extremities out of all proportion to the rest of you, I think we both accept that my Wellingtons will be too large. A pair of socks is neither here nor there. Nothing will balance the difference!'

'Socks would mean I won't get blisters.' I spoke stubbornly, staring no higher than his lapels. Tweed lapels in shades of lovat blue. Pat would know which make it was and probably which mill had woven it. They did that over in her annexe—wefts and warps. She'd explained it all to me one day how she'd cleverly copied a woven herringbone and turned it into a fabric design which could be stamped on oilcloth. But I'd been doubtful, until she'd elaborated further. 'It's a gimmick you see. It means that you could have it for bathroom curtains. Or kitchen tables covered in the stuff.' 'Oh, eating off tweed, a tweed tablecloth, I get it! Very good!'

'Blisters! Blisters! Bloody blisters! What are blisters to me!' He was shouting at me now.

'They're nothing to you if they're not yours. But they're something to me if they're mine.' I couldn't believe I'd said it. Been so unbelievably inarticulate. Me, who'd always come top in English. Especially English Grammar and elusive Sentence Construction. Whichever voice I said it in, I knew what to say. Normally I knew. No one could have accused me of lacking in vocabulary, not when I had a father with the gift of the gab like mine. My eyes stayed glued on the same spot, no higher or lower. Neither of us spoke. In the distance the Downs lay rounded as a pregnant girl. Was that why we were going there, for us to do it in the open? 'Anyway,' I said, defiance rising in the silence. 'I'm not that keen on ten-mile hikes—'

'No, duckie. And nor was Jesus Christ. He seemed incapable of organising his feet as well. But at least you haven't his furniture to carry on your shoulders. And nor am I "thet kin" for that matter either on marathon marches. My plans *à propos* the Downs are merely to exchange the time of day with archaeological pals of mine who are involved in some sort of dig.'

I swallowed, everything including my pride. I could see the stupidity of ballet shoes at digs. 'Well, I'll wear the Wellies if it isn't far—'

But he was waiting now with the car door open, my side, which showed some manners. 'Suit yourself,' he shrugged. 'I simply now have lost interest!' Which didn't show manners at all. His moods seemed to come and go at will; I couldn't make head or tail. We drove, his hand upon the wheel, the other one round my neck, its fingers fondling round my ear. I found it very off-putting until he turned his head to smile at me.

'What ho my beauty! And what have you been up to? Since we met?'

I enunciated as carefully as I could, taking care to avoid the tricky vowels. The Woolworth's imitation of Julie Andrews. 'I had a nice tea with Fiona.'

'Did you now, and how was that?'

'Oh, that was very nice.' I coughed. 'Thank you.' I added.

'It was nice, nice, nice, nice, nice.' He turned it into a chorus. 'They did it twice, twice, twice, twice, twice.' I started sweating.

I refused to go further and meet his friends; I could see even at a distance that they might prove the final straw. I could see from the clear canary of the women's Jaeger cardigans and the quality of the cavalry twill on all the men. And in addition, due to the excellence of the atmospheric conditions, I could hear their voices well enough in advance to know they'd paralyse mine, possibly for good and all. It wasn't a risk I was willing to take, not with teaching as my chosen career. I'd sat down on the lower slopes. He couldn't believe his eyes, not when he turned around to view the distance of the twenty yards between us. It had been twenty yards for more than a mile, his Wellies were playing havoc with my heels. And not only with my heels, but underneath my flowing dirndl skirt as well, cutting viciously into the back of my knees. At the thought of walking this way back to the car again I would have gladly stretched my length and died. Could my father have sued for the cost of the coffin? Or for the use of one of theirs with a crest on, because their son had been in on the kill?

'Okay. Okay, kiddie. Bye for now. I shan't be long. Why not take the instruments of torture off and get a little air to your tootsies ...' And then his voice began to mingle in with theirs, each braying in a slightly different key. 'Henrietta!' 'Why Piers, old chap!' 'Well, blow me down, I don't believe my eyes!' 'How's things then, Hugh?' I shut my eyes and went to sleep.

'Why did he want you to take a bath?'

'Because of my blisters, he said.'

Fiona sighed. 'He's divinely decadent. Do go on. What a day you do seem to have had!'

'Yes, it was horrible. The most horrible day I've ever had. Tell me, Fiona, quite honestly, how do you find my accent?'

She opened her eyes as wide as they'd go and slowly removed her spectacles. 'I can't see it,' she said.

'What, my accent? You're not meant to, not see it. No, do be serious—'

'The point. I can't see the point of the question.'

'Well, what I mean is that I don't sound like you, for instance. I don't even sound like Pat—'

'Heaven preserve that you should. It's frightfully artificial, isn't it? Really suburban. I mean, have you ever listened to the way she says "Really"—it's absolutely ghastly. I'm sometimes embarrassed for her in company— but she does have that super cousin, of course.'

'He's getting married—did you know? He's got to, she's pregnant. A nurse.'

'Oh Christ, really? I shall have to cross him off our list of eligible men. Anyway, to get back to eligible men, what happened then?'

We were walking along the undercliff route to Rottingdean, she in a second-hand sheepskin, another of

196

her mother's bargains, and me draped in moth-eaten fur, reaching right the way down to my feet. There'd been a violent change in weather since the excruciating Sunday.

'What I found so unforgivable was the way he made fun of my accent, that's what I mean.'

'Did he?'

'It put me off. My father was furious when I told him.'

'I should think he was. It's rather rude, apart from anything else.'

'Yes, he was furious. He said that Piers was perfectly right and I shouldn't have taken umbrage. He offered me elocution lessons!'

She stopped in her tracks. 'Elocution lessons? That's crackers! Piers offered you elocution lessons—but that's one of the things he liked about you. The fact that your voice was different, otherwise, he'd have spent my party with one of us—'she blinked—'oh, I didn't mean that, but you know—'

'My dad.' I said it wearily. 'He's the one who suggested it. But it isn't just the making fun—the rest was awful as well.'

'Wakey wakey! Time for off. How were your forty winks?'

I opened my eyes, Piers blotted the view: the sun, the sky, the whole of the Downs. I steeled myself, waiting for the worst, but in fact he seemed now in fine fettle. He'd been with his own kind again and life was obviously more agreeable to him. 'How are the toots?'

'Terrible.'

'Take heart, fair damsel, all is not lost. It's perfectly possible, my sweet, for me to fetch the car and pick you up from here. Stay put—I shall run all the way.'

'Why,' I asked, 'did we have to walk in the first place?'

'Good for you, duckie! That's why. A fellow always has to have the say—lay down the law, all that sort of thing. It's probably put you in your place, I'd say. Shown you who's the master.' He glanced at me, a curious, almost tender, certainly sensual look about the eyes. 'Sorry about the feet—I shall have to kiss them better.' And after he didn't speak again until we reached our destination when I saw quite clearly, as he was getting out of the car, that something had caused him to swell.

There was no one at home. The house was empty; I sensed it as soon as we got there, an imposing building set

197

in its own estate, of course. And arrived at by a curving drive flanked with herbaceous borders and overhung with the heavy branches of ancient evergreens.

'You'll be partaking of the Sunday roast I shouldn't be surprised with Mater and Pater et al. You know how to cope with the cutlery, girl. Start from the outside and then work in, you shouldn't go wrong sticking to that. And remember, when in doubt drop your hankie and let everyone get on with it first, then do as they do.' 'Oh dad, don't keep on.' 'What's up? You're not getting nervy? You'll be all right, just take everything in its stride.'

'It's wonderfully peaceful here,' I said, standing beside the car. 'Not a soul in sight.' No sound at all! Weren't places like this meant to have lots of dogs and things bounding and barking and wagging their tails? Steady Rover! Steady! Steady! Yes, old chap, I've missed you too, y'know. And old retainers tweaking their forelocks, with wives behind them wiping hands on their pinnies? Why, Master Piers! If it isn't you, I'll be bound!

'My folks are away. The house is virtually shut up except for me—when I choose to use it.' He turned his head and the key in the door—and winked. I gave a sickly answering smile. What for? Use it for what? 'Allow me, madam, to carry you over the threshold.'

I would have liked time to make a show of reluctance, to have said—look here, I'm not coming in. Not on the maid's day off. My dad will want to know what veg we had with dinner, and whether your father carved the joint or not. And he'll want to know what we had for pudding, and was there a choice of tea instead of coffee. And I'm not very good at making up, he's better and always remembers exactly what you've said, which means he can trip you later on when he knows you'll forget — But I wasn't given the chance. Piers moved so quickly, quite literally sweeping me off my feet so fast that a Wellington boot fell off my leg to the floor. He kicked it out of the way and, carrying me still, he crossed the sort of hallway that you see on stage in heavy costume dramas. I felt for quite a flattered moment much like Scarlett O'Hara, except that instead of him sweeping me up the staircase, he dropped me on the bottom step.

'Whew, duckie, have you put on weight since last we met? I need a gin and tonic, what about you? Or should you be on a diet?'

'Nothing for me, thank you.' He'd touched a sore point. I was indeed perpetually on a diet.

'Don't be silly, duckie—I'm hardly likely to be drinking on my own! The thought strikes, however—how about some champers? How indeed! Hold still my sweet, don't move.'

I did move though, just to rearrange my skirts which had fallen round my middle. And to take off my remaining Wellington boot. My feet were filthy, though I'd washed them before I'd left home and cut the toe nails too, in case. I tried to cover them by sitting so to speak side-saddle, still there on the bottom step.

'What the hell are you doing crouching there, you funny little creature? Here, cheers!' He held a glass of bubbles in each hand and offered one to me; it meant me standing up. 'How awfully short you are, robbed of your layer of rubber—don't leave it lying around, someone could break their neck,' he said and kicked the Wellington boot.

We drank the bottle between us, I think we did. At any rate next time I looked it was empty and by then we were up in his bedroom.

'You're to have a bath, you little heathen!' I resented the implications, both of them, and coloured up a dull brick red. 'Best thing in the world for blisters. Wait on, and I'll put some salts in the water.'

'Oh yes, I love a lovely smell. What sort do you have? I'm not mad on pine. It's what we have at home—'

'No, duckie. Epsom Salts. Excellent for surface abrasions of the skin—'

'Oh dear! Will it make me need to go? It's not a corridor train ...'

He obviously didn't know what I was talking about, but it didn't matter because, when he'd left the bathroom after pouring in the salts to return to his adjoining bedroom for a minute, I quickly managed to lock the door. It left me on my side and him on his. I took no notice of the pounding fists, but kept my clothes on and merely soaked my feet instead, by sitting on the edge of the bath. I didn't need one, I knew that, by sniffing beneath each arm and bending my head to sniff as well under my billowing skirt. Quite all right. Billingsgate indeed! But I couldn't resist his perfumes—they occupied an entire shelf, the largest bottles I'd ever seen. And half of them not even opened. And I couldn't resist his talc as well and woofed it just

199

where I'd been sniffing. When eventually I emerged I found him lying on the bed, a freshly opened bottle by his side, a half-full glass still in his hand and on his body—nothing at all.

'What sort of dick did he have?' Pat moulded her hands in the air as if enclosing a very large marrow. 'Oh I see,' she said at the expression on my face, and held up her little finger.

'Well, to tell you the truth, I tried not to look. And even when he forced it in my face, I shut my eyes—' I shut my eyes now, remembering. 'He hit me with it though—'

'Where? On the body?'

'No, right across the face. The impact made him shoot off in my ear. And I'd only washed my hair the night before, it was terribly hard to get out—'

'You should have left it there to dry, and then you could have brushed it out. Mark tells me all about these things. He says the feminine equivalent of spunk can ruin a suit, if not treated right away. But men's stuff works the other way around. That's why very young boys and dirty old men have slightly chalky areas round their flies because they haven't brushed with enough attention. It's all a matter of grooming.'

'Well anyway I'd only got my comb on me and the teeth are set too far apart. You need a nit comb for a job like that.'

'He was cross then, that you wouldn't give it?'

'He seemed to be. Terribly cross. He called me a tart for being a virgin!'

'We're all tarts then!'

'Apparently. It's a strange conclusion to come to, isn't it?'

'I think he must have got it wrong—he really meant prick teaser.'

'I wasn't teasing though, but I didn't terribly want to, you know. With him. Afterwards he could barely be bothered to drive me to the station, but when we got there, he said Cheers and he'd see me next week!'

'Oh, I'm sure you'll hear from him again!'

'I don't want to. I hope to God my dad doesn't answer the phone!'

He did though, answer it. And more than that, he made another date, giving—I couldn't believe it—our address for Piers to call. 'It's a good sign that, girl. This coming to pick you up. It means he wants to meet your family. Get acquainted with your mother and me.'

'I needn't be in. He can get acquainted, he can get acquainted all evening with you on his own. I can go to the pictures by myself.'

'Now stop all that, you understand. He must see something in you or he wouldn't have called again—'

'Oh, he sees something in me all right—'

'Don't try to be bitchy, my girl. The fact that he tried to force his attentions was entirely your own fault. You should never have entered that empty house in the first place. It was asking for trouble—'

'How was I supposed to get home, dad? Stuck out there in God knows where?'

'You might have merely stood your ground, politely and in the nicest possible way. That, you see, that course of behaviour, would have earned his respect. He wouldn't then have dreamed of doing anything untoward. As it is, however, you haven't obviously burned all your boats. Now think of us, there's a good girl.'

I could tell when Piers had arrived by the shuffling of my father's feet; he was scraping them like a horse, jog trotting on the spot from sheer nerves and pleasure.

'Here she comes, my little beauty.' But dad's eyes were not on me, so that when I neatly side-stepped the approaching outstretched arm, he lost his balance and fell heavily against a newly delivered batch of Barker & Dobsons, which in turn displaced the entire display of Craven A Cork Tip.

Piers didn't blink. His lounge lizard eyes remained as usual remote and uninvolved.

I didn't care. I'd gone past caring. I'd come out in my second best and hadn't even bothered to wash my hair. With what had happened last time, there didn't seem much point.

'Martinis at my favourite pub—the Grand Hotel?'

'Great!' I felt his glance.

'You feeling yourself, duckie?' Feeling myself? No, not at this moment, no. I have my hands upon my lap, not venturing between it. Not slowly sliding down inside, and touching my slit till it tingles. Later perhaps, when I'm in my bed. I shall pull my pyjamas down or my nightie up.

But not at this moment, no, I'm not. Is that what you want to know?

'Yes. Completely myself. Why?'

'No reason. Unfortunate about your father. Could have been a nasty fall! But he seems a cheerful enough chappie. Nothing could throw him too much, I should say. I pride myself as a judge of character and he's an optimist if ever I saw one! Right, my old china?'

'Right! Yes, he's an optimist all right!'

'Perhaps it was your fall, dad, that put him off. He might have considered clumsiness to be hereditary. After all, you can't have heirs to great fortunes, and all that, moving around like mental defectives, knocking things over when they're called upon to open country bazaars. On the other hand he probably thought you'd had a drink—' My father groaned. He'd been groaning for the past fortnight. The pain was purely internal, it had come from the cruelty of circumstance and the obvious cessation of further telephone conversations with Piers. He hadn't called, simply because I'd said that he was not to, I felt that we weren't suited, was how I put it.

'Suited! Suited! Suited! Suited! Of course we're not bloody suited, but that's the beauty of it, don't you see, duckie? Good God, my forebears would no more dream of being seen in public with a person such as yourself than, well, than almost anything. Now, doesn't that stir the soul to think that democracy is such today that you and I can sit here drinking in the Grand Hotel as if for all the world we were equals?'

'No. It doesn't stir me very much. I might have more fun with a parrot, if I needed everything repeating. Or a bunch of radishes for that matter—'

'Radishes? Radishes? Radishes? Radishes?'

'Yes,' I explained patiently. 'Very bad for indigestion!'

My father patted me brokenly on the back. 'You did your best, my girl. I'm sorry if your old dad let you down. Not too good an evening that, one way and another. A whole carton of Craven A gone west from falling into the fridge. I didn't notice. I didn't find it till the morning. Frozen solid, of course. And stuck to the block of vanilla ice. Was able to salvage that, fortunately though.'

'Never mind, dad, it'll teach you not to play Cupid. You do it too clumsily.'

But it had pulled us much closer together, Fiona and I, the incident of Piers. We met now every weekend, on Saturday mornings if she was here, to go over what she'd got up to. My examinations, my finals, in the painting school, were approaching. and every minute counted away from my work—which meant that socially I had little to report. Her own progress in the world of art had dwindled down to nothing. Her father said she must think of doing something constructive, either that or seriously consider getting married.

'Who to though, Fiona?'

'Oh, anyone with the right income and an appropriate background would do for daddy.'

'Well, why don't you then?'

'It doesn't just seem to be happening.'

'No, not when you go out looking for it, but I expect it will one day. Why not think of taking a job?'

'What sort of job?'

'Oh, I don't know. What jobs are there?'

'Plenty of secretarial—but you have to do shorthand and typing really for that.'

'Why don't you then, learn? Take a course. I would if I was you—then, when I've finished next year, doing my Fifth and passing the Finals—we'd be able to leave here altogether. Go to London, both qualified, me to teach and you working in an office and marrying the Chairman's son!' That's how it came about—the original plan—but then, of course, Derek happened.

'I'm engaged!' I'd said. 'This boy has asked me to marry him!' I stood just inside my parents' bedroom addressing their sleeping bodies. 'Yes,' I said. 'His name is Derek and we've fallen in love. Oh, and by the way, dad'—I backed out on to the landing—'I forgot to say—he's Jewish.'

'Daddy's the same about Jews. That's something they have in common. It's ghastly, isn't it! Here, have a cigarette, it helps to calm the nerves. I'm frightful these days, I can't seem to give it up. I go to these awful do's, get drunk and then start smoking. Smoke non-stop. Just for something to do whilst I'm racking my brains for something to say. They're so unutterably tedious, mummy and daddy's crowd.'

'Poor old Fiona—what about the young Hussar?'

'Humphrey?'

'Isn't he around?'

'Yes, he is. He stayed with us last weekend.'

'Well?'

'Well, it's not like you and Derek. I'm not in love, and nor is he. Oh, I meant to ask—how can I tell him about his halitosis?'

I stopped to send a pebble skimming over the sea. 'It's like a millpond today. Look how calm. Are you good at bouncing them?' I bent down. 'The flatter the stone the better. Here's one, hold on. You try.' I watched as she crouched slightly, then clapped as her pebble travelled the shining surface of the water creating ever-widening circles where it touched. 'Six! That's superb.' I said. 'I shan't beat that.' I aimed my stone, it sank at once. 'What did I say! You win! Now, Humphrey's halitosis! Has he had his tonsils out? You could start off by asking that. I don't know what you do if he says yes, unless you suggest the surgeon may have left a bit behind. That happens sometimes, doesn't it? They leave a sliver of skin—causes a murderous stench I believe!'

'That's what he has—it's terribly tricky. I can't stand it when we're kissing!'

'Have you tried turning up with a peg on?'

'What do you mean—a peg?'

'A clothes peg. On your nose. When you go out to meet him. He might get the message then.'

She sighed. 'I doubt it. He's dreadfully dim.'

I thought carefully. I understood the problem. My mother had put me to have music lessons at one time, but I hadn't physically been able to continue because of the piano teacher's pong. Bread-and-butter breath was what she'd had, and the curious mustiness of over-milky tea. 'This child's nausea isn't natural,' our family doctor had said. 'I think the world of music is going to have to reconcile itself to the grievous loss of her talents! Either that or find instruction elsewhere. To force her to continue with Miss Philbert would be not only foolish and uncommonly cruel but might well lay the foundations for a distressing medical condition known in layman's language as psychosomatic stomach! The symptoms are clearly here already.'

'Oh dear!' I said. 'Honestly, Fiona, you deserve a medal. I'm afraid I couldn't stand it myself. I'd be bound to be bilious. That's one of my things. I have a horror of halitosis. Couldn't you just come straight out with it and say "I'm sorry, sweetheart, but the way things stand, your rather bad breath is coming between us."? Couldn't you?'

She shook her head. 'No, I shall probably soldier on. Apart from that you see, he isn't all that bad—I mean, he fits the bill from daddy's point of view.'

'What a shame. I'm sure it's simply a minor matter, something with his sinuses or an ingrowing epiglottis—can't he have an enema? Or better still, what do they call it? Yes, a colonic irrigation? That's meant to clear the pipes you know, right the way up to the neck! Get your father to suggest it, man to man.'

'Oh, I don't for a minute think I could get daddy to start discussing enemas! I doubt if he'd deign to mention diarrhoea! He's incredibly fastidious, my father! They seem to be, don't they, men—more than women.'

'Not in our house. No!'

'I'll be buggered before I'll have that circumcised sod as a son-in-law! I'll swing for him first, so help me! I'll start on his balls with scissors!'

'Is it because I'm Jewish do you think? Perhaps that's what he has against me?'

'No, honestly, Derek. Really!'

'Mam, mind the shop for an hour or two while I walk this girl amongst the tribe along the esplanade. I'll shove the bloody chosen race right up her throat to give her some idea of what her in-laws are likely to be! And see if an unadulterated diet of astrakhan collars, fur coats, fallen arches and Manny and Izzy and Ikey can't do the trick!'

But it was all a wasted effort. Derek's family got in first. 'A gentile girl, you say! Your mother is wearing black today—we mourn your death, my son!' That's what his father had written back at Derek's news of our engagement. And what's more he'd cancelled his allowance, withdrawn all possible financial support until the boy had come to his senses.

'But you said they weren't orthodox, Derek.'

'They're not,' he'd answered flatly. The money hurt. The pinch of poverty.

'Would it help if you sent my photo? I can look quite Jewish myself.'

But he'd shaken his head in sorrow. 'They'd know,' he'd said. 'By the nose.'

It was his buttocks that drew me to him first, the way they came straight from the waist and then tilted up and out before they turned into his thighs. Like a small and sexy black boy's, with a very straight backbone above and arms that hung slightly away from the main body of the thing. Like the sleeves of a coat in a cupboard. I noticed them, his buttocks, within a week of his arrival, walking behind them up the stairs to a class we shared on Calligraphy. It surprised me, that, being drawn by a bum, and I'd run on ahead to purposely get a good look at the rest of him. He saw me looking, so he said. And had himself, even as early as that, been making surreptitious enquiries as to my availability. But I'd forged a name for having my nose to the grindstone and for being hard to get, and so, he'd given up without trying. 'Hardly the spirit of endeavour,' he'd agreed much later. 'But there again, if you've already got a field full of cattle, why bother chasing one cow!' I'd made him pay for that—but in the end, we both lost.

'It's perhaps because you're nervous, you're tensing it up inside!'

'I'm not, honestly, Derek. Not nervous a bit. Go on, I promise I shan't shout this time. Just push harder, it's bound to go in somewhere!' And all the while I kept thinking what a terrible waste it was, this stud, the sexiest thing in the whole school, searching the length and breadth of my privates for a suitable place to put it! My husband to be! The love of my life! Obviously blind down below! 'Shall I have a look for you?' I'd offered. 'If you pass me my handbag mirror and I hold it just so—'

He'd said to try and show a little sensitivity please, that the fault lay with me and not him. It became a marathon effort for each of us until in the end we gave up. But the trouble was that by then he'd well and truly whet my appetite. I really couldn't wait to have another go, exactly as he'd predicted—with anyone!

'I don't really mind, Fiona, about you spotting him at the bus stop, but it might have been better to have told me instead of Pat. You know how she is—it's all round Brighton by now—'

'Well, everyone knew what a two-timer Derek was, but I was so so shocked when I saw him after you'd said he'd gone, I had to tell someone. Can we meet for tea?'

It was months since we'd done that, Fiona and I, simply because of me being so tied up with Derek. Pat was the one I'd been seeing much more of, from doing our finals together. But now I was alone again and available to everyone.

'He said we were sexually incompatible, you see. Some couples are, apparently. It's to do with the right fit, like having the wrong glove. Nobody's fault.'

'Perhaps it's just as well. He was frightfully good-looking and sexy I know, but he would always have been carrying on behind your back. In any case, you'd have had to take on his religion.'

'Have plastic surgery and a hook put in my nose? My father wouldn't have stood for that for a start.'

'He must be pleased.'

'Over the moon! Especially pleased this week with me—my window-dressing won first prize in the Fry's Chocolate Counter and Shop Front Display! Five pounds! That will go on my fare to London for the interview on that job.'

'Will they let you know on the spot?'

'Apparently, yes. Wish me luck!'

The District Inspector at County Hall was tall and extremely *distingué*. Middle-aged. A lady's man with lots of concertina creases across his lap. A sedentary post apparently, with a wife not too hot on the iron.

I'd just travelled up with a whole load of them— commuters coming to London—and would probably be travelling back with them, no doubt, much later on at tea-time. I was amazed at how alert they'd seemed for such an early hour, but then my father was the only man I'd had to go by in the mornings, and he didn't come alive, could hardly be called even human, till well past ten, with five cups of tea and fifteen Woodbines in him. They'd all had trouser creases too, splayed like crows' feet, ladies' laughter lines, over the top of each leg. So that the eye, starting from the outside edges, could run from one side of the carriage all the way to the other, window to window, covering the contours and counting up the cocks, I worked it out that, including those who passed along the central corridor, pressed occasionally almost in my eager face by the motion of the train—there wasn't a single erection from Brighton station all the way to Victoria. Derek would have said that was unusual. Most men, so he claimed, grew excited by a general jogging. I'd had to content myself instead with sussing out which side their sausages sat. And whether their sets were nestling nice like a hen on eggs or if, in running to catch the train, they'd inadvertently rearranged themselves in some more awkward order. Before Derek, of course, none of this might have entered my mind. But now my interest was bordering on obsession. The District Inspector dressed on the left—was that the norm or not? I couldn't remember now. I know when Derek had told me first, I'd gone home and furtively studied my father. But as far as I could tell, he seemed hung straight down the middle. Either that or it was empty, living in vacant possession!

Yes, he dressed on the left, the District Inspector, and had wonderfully fine filbert nails. A sign of breeding, so Fiona said. He offered me them in a swoop, bending forward over the width of the desk between us, his flies well in evidence against the edge. I took four and allowed his thumb to wander where it would. It rested rather limply on my knuckles until we both withdrew our hands and sank into our opposite seats.

On the desk lay many applications for the post that I was after. I'd been warned it wouldn't be easy. We'd all been discouraged from applying for a teaching job in London, the competition was too keen. Everyone aimed for these jobs. They'd all given up in our year except me, but I had more reason to hope. My reports, I felt, might justify my optimism. And apparently they did. The District Inspector was speaking. I barely liked to look up, from modesty.

'It's frankly years since I read an assessment like this ... will undoubtedly prove an invaluable member of staff ... A highly talented and original artist ... a sensitive, imaginative and resourceful teacher ...' He had a narrower mouth than I would normally have liked in a man and was rather too long in the jaw, with a definite suggestion of an Adam's apple immediately above his tie. But his complexion pleased me, its spotlessness, the age so far removed from acned youth. Even Derek just in his twenties had still been prone to passing boils and unexpected pimples. The District Inspector's skin was dry, its surface lightly scored with criss-cross lines— exactly like an etching. He would have made, for that matter, an excellent subject to etch. In the manner of Rembrandt—all shadow and scratch.

Something in me was moistening up, I could feel it twitch in my knickers. Oh Christ, I thought, it can't be starting up again. But it was, without a doubt, trundling up into my finger-tips, sizzling along under my skin, nothing necessarily to do with anything at all, except an uncontrollable sense of excitement, a washing over. A feeling of being very much alive as opposed to being half-dead. It kept coming, more and more, these days. Up and out of nowhere, suddenly, like the sun—as if I'd started to *shine*. Had he noticed, the District Inspector? Was my warmth making itself felt, filtering across his files? Firing into his fine filbert nails? Something had caused him to stop! Had even occasioned him now to stand and step around his desk towards me, his arm again outstretched. But this time in congratulation, so it seemed! I prepared to stand myself, and would have swooned against his stomach but mercifully dropped my gloves instead. Those interview gloves my mother had urged me to wear to make a good impression. Picking them up I passed his concertina zone so close I could have kissed it. The second went. He shook my hand. After five years of being a student, I was suddenly now employed!

'They should say something on the wireless perhaps. Put it in a special news bulletin. Warning all Londoners that we're coming. About to descend!'

'On the men!'

'I know,' I said. 'Honestly, Pat, can you believe it, I was only there for the day! The District Inspector for a start, I could have had him. Then the bus conductor on the way to the Tate. That Norwegian dentist at the National Gallery. A Serbo-Croat who chased me down the Strand—I spent an hour in Peter Robinson's trying on dressing-gowns to get rid of him! And at the end of it all there was this press photographer who picked me up coming back on the train. He stared at me all the way to Burgess Hill and didn't start talking till then. Bit of a waste really, but he dropped me home at least. He kept his car at the station. That was a help because by then my feet were killing me.

But it shows though, doesn't it, what can be done up there!
I wish Fiona were here—it would cheer her up a bit.'

'Mm.'

I was sorry I'd said it then, brought Fiona into the
conversation. The difficulties of sharing a flat with the
two of them were now becoming more apparent. But at
least that wouldn't take place for a while; Fiona wouldn't
be joining us until her shorthand and typing course was
finished, in something like three months. 'That will be
better really, Fiona, for all the Christmas parties. We'll
have got in with lots of people, by then, Pat and me—'

'That's what I can't bear though, the thought of you two
living it up without me. Or even just the thought of you
with Pat—I shall be so jealous! Don't look like that. I
shall! I've never been that keen on her in any case. Why do
we have to have her?'

'Don't be silly. I can't afford not to share. We have to
have her,' I sighed, 'because you've been dilly-dallying
around for so long thinking secretarial work was beneath
you, that you've only just got around to taking the course.
If you remember, I told you to get on with it as long ago as
last year.'

She started pouting. 'Yes, well it still looked as if
Humphrey might pop the question then. And in any case
since then it didn't look as if we'd get to London, what
with you and Derek—can I take a chocolate from this tin of
Mackintosh's?'

She'd arrived at a happy lull in the shop, knowing it was
my night for minding. Every Monday my parents went to
the pictures, whatever was on, it didn't matter. And then
straight over to the Seven Stars for a pint or two of
Merrydown. It was her first visit, in fact, to the shop. She
claimed to find it entracing. 'How County one feels
behind the counter! The owner of all one surveys! Oh, do
let me serve someone, please! This next person coming
in ...'

My toes curled over in my shoes. 'Best not, Fiona.
They're a funny bunch, our regulars. A strange face can
throw them sideways. They like to know where they
stand.' And I'd put her to sit on a stool by the biscuits
cutting Kit-Kat bars into bits.

'What am I doing this for?' she'd said, stripping off the
silver paper.

'The mice have been at the box, that's why. We just snip

off the teethmarks like that and sell what we salvage much cheaper.'

'Wouldn't it be simpler to keep a cat?'

'We can't have cats, we've tried. It meant my mother spending every day swabbing down bottles from where my father was sneezing on them. He develops dreadful hay fever with furry things in the room. Even caterpillars—he found one once, a pet of mine, that I'd nearly nursed through to a chrysalis, and he was so cross, he dropped it in his cup of tea and stirred it round with a spoon. Strangely enough it didn't drown, what killed it I think was the heat. Yes, take a Mackintosh—I'll tell you which one to try. That, there, the triangle in the veridian wrapper. Milk. Marvellous. Customers used to complain, you know, that our Mackintosh's never had milk chocolates. And they didn't either because I'd eaten them, that's why I was so fat. Do you remember that, how fat I was four years ago? I do!'

'I'd like to lose a bit. I'd like to lose a bit on my legs.'

'Oh would you?' I lied. 'There's no need!' There was nothing in fact to do except lie about Fiona's legs. The ankles were so tragically out of proportion, nearly as wide as her knees, some said—Pat mostly, whose own legs were so indescribably elegant.

She stretched them before her despairingly. Oh dear, oh dear. 'Now tell the truth. What would you do if they were yours?'

I cleared my throat. 'Well,' I went carefully. 'I would probably burn my skirts and stick to trousers.' It was out now, at least!

'Daddy would never wear them!'

'What?'

'Not on me. He says they're not lady-like. Mummy bought slacks for the summer in Fortnum's Winter Sale and he sent her all the way back to change them for a suitable skirt—'

'They won't change things in sales though.'

'No. She was so upset at the thought of wasting that much money and so concerned by what daddy would say if she came home with the slacks again that she just swapped them herself without saying. And came away with a skirt which actually cost twice as much as she'd paid for the slacks! She didn't tell daddy of course. He'd have gone berserk—'

211

'He would have if she'd been caught. They make it their business in these places to prosecute regardless. That's one of the things, isn't it, about the menopause—secret shoplifting. They make scapegoats of the ones they catch just to put off the others. Pat's got an auntie who's always at it. I'm not sure it isn't Mark's mother. Someone quite close in the family. He's married now, isn't he, Mark?'

'With a baby. They're awfully unhappy. I'd love to be married with a baby, wouldn't you?'

'That's what Pat said to me the other day. In fact, I said I wouldn't—'

'But then you've just been engaged. We haven't, you see, that's the difference.'

'I don't think the being engaged is what did it, but the being in bed might have done. It would be nice before we moved in all together, if the two of you could even up a bit. What about when you go to Scotland? Any chance of a bit up there?'

'There never has been before.'

'I think it's really an attitude of mind. If I said to you our life together depended on it, I'm certain you could lose it.'

'Oh, I think I've lost it already, the actual skin bit, I'm sure. On a leather saddle in a riding stable. Most girls do on a horse, or a bicycle seat for that matter. I've looked as well. I can see the little hole!'

I was impressed, why hadn't I? Who would have thought it of Fiona? Perhaps she'd show me where I should look.

It was Pat who'd managed to find us a flat. A dismal affair in a basement, with one window looking out on a wall a foot away from your face. And it was Pat's mother who paid in advance the whole of the first three months' rent. When Fiona saw it first she point blank refused to live there. I didn't argue with her, there was no reason since she wouldn't be sharing till Christmas. 'We can find somewhere else by then,' I'd soothed. 'This will do Pat and me in the meantime.' I personally found it marvellous. 'Do you want to see it first? Before we finally decide?' Pat had said. 'Nope!' 'Aren't you amazing! I would never dream of moving into somewhere that I hadn't seen first—' 'It's in the centre, isn't it? And in London. That's enough for me. Anything as long as it's not at home!'

Pat had not managed to get a teaching job in central

212

London. Somewhere in Essex was what she'd found, which meant that she'd have to start travelling each morning at something like half-past six with three changes on the train and a bus the other end. I thought she was crackers.

'You're crackers. How in hell's name can you afford the fares, for a start?'

'Mum's paying my fares. She says it's worth it not to have me at home!'

'Really?'

'No, not really. She's just paying them because she knows I've been longing for London. Anyway, she claims to be considering it an investment.'

'How's that?'

'Because of Roly Balls. He's at Guy's with Mark, but it's his last year. If I don't catch him now, I never will!'

'I've never heard of Roly Balls before. Is that his real name?'

'Roland. He's fabulous. Fat. I like them fat. Something nice and soft to squeeze. Like you.'

'Thanks!'

'Meant as a compliment, of course.'

I watched her munching up a Mars bar, having just polished off one already. A large saucepan full of spaghetti sat bubbling on the ancient gas stove. We'd only been in the flat several hours and in all that time she'd been eating non-stop. 'Do you usually eat as much as this? Or is it just the excitement?'

Her jaws stayed open in surprise. 'Eating? Oh, I love eating! I could eat all day, couldn't you?'

'Don't you ever find you get fat?'

'Fat? I wish I could. I'd love to be fat, wouldn't you?'

'I have been. Don't you remember?'

'You're always saying that, but I don't. Here, are you having some of this spaghetti? No? Not any? I'll eat it all myself, I'm warning you! Oh, come on—you can't survive on boiled eggs!'

It was Sunday, the day before we started work. I was looking forward to it myself, but by nine that night Pat had made herself sick with nerves. I held her head while she vomited and turned my face away not wishing to catch a glimpse of her regurgitations. 'You shouldn't pump food into your stomach at such a rate, you know. It's a natural reaction, not just nerves. In any case, I don't think

213

I am going to be able to stand it, seeing you eat like that. It'll lead me into bad habits again, and I shall lose this new found figure.'

Pat's alarm went off at six o'clock, efficiently waking me with it. She switched the light on—one barely shaded central bulb hanging from the ceiling, shining straight down into my eyes. It was late summer, the start of the autumn term, and had been a particularly mild season. Even so the room was freezing, icy cold with overtones of damp and a fearful condensation dribbling down the walls. 'This basement in accord with recently passed bye-laws, has been relined throughout. And freshly decorated to render it fit for habitation,' the landlord had assured us on arrival. 'Yes,' I'd replied. 'You can tell it's just been done.' The cement was still sweating.

Pat, in her pyjamas, stood shivering violently beside her single bed staring at the floor on which she'd placed, the previous evening, alternatives to wear. I sat up in my bed; we both sneezed together. 'Bless you.' 'You too.' 'Christ, it's cold! Can't you plug the heater in?' 'Have you got money for the meter?' 'Not change, no.' 'Nor me.'

I stared at her, fascinated by her naked fragility, unable to look away. She looked so touchingly thin, it made me want to blink. Or take her into my bed and cover her from the cold. She was very brown all over, browner than you'd expect from just meeting her face to face, except for two milky horizontal strips above and beneath her middle. I watched whilst she drew a defensive arm across the flatness of her chest. 'Bloody awful aren't they! No boobs as such to speak of!'

I continued to stare. 'They're sweet,' I said. 'Like a child's!' And they were, I couldn't even remember the time when mine must have looked like that. Ten years ago or more. And as well I was struck by the profusion of her pubic hair; there was almost as much between her legs as I, with my tangled tulip cut, had on my head. 'Do you shave every day, Pat?' For I was noticing now how neat and nice she was beneath her arms.

'Every other. Why, do you?'

'No, only when I see it sprouting over-long. Actually though, in wintertime, I let it grow. For warmth.'

She'd put a pair of knickers on, surprisingly large, white cotton. Aertex. With loose wide legs like a boy scout's shorts.

214

'They're big enough, Pat!'

'My brother's. A family joke.'

'Does he wear yours?'

'However did you guess? He's like that though you know, a bit. I'm sure of it, I keep saying so to mum, but she turns a blind eye. He lives there with her, left school when my dad died, to help mum run the business. The apple of her eye, of course, he can't stand me. Well, we can't stand each other—he always was a terrible cissy. He's only got one friend, Maurice, an old man in his forties. They go to concerts together, or out around the country in the car! But it doesn't bother me too much, he takes mum and the business off my back.'

'You're going to be late if you don't watch out. How long will it take for your face?' I'd been amazed the night before to see her taking it off; at the end of ten minutes she'd looked almost a different person—eyeless and pinched and pale. Fiona would be pleased. 'What a particularly plain person poor Pat appears to be underneath!' I could hear it already.

'My face? Oh I shall leave doing my face for the train! Each eye takes twenty minutes at least!'

'Does it? But you'll have to do one on one train and the other on the other! What will people think as they pass you on the platform? I'd never ...'

She slicked herself now into a lacy black uplift brassière, like a kid trying to ape its mother, each side gaped loose and empty. 'Oh, very seductive,' I said. 'Especially with the aertex!'

'I'm going to be late. I'm starting to flap. Quick, tell me what to wear.'

I got her out by half-past six, then fell asleep myself, right through the second setting of her alarm so that today, of all days, on my very first, I turned up late for work.

It was an eventful journey, our basement lay on that bend of road where Old Brompton turns into Earls Court. And it was from that station, the Earls Court one, that I'd taken my tube, slap bang in the middle of the rush hour without even time to clean my teeth and render my breath inoffensive. Standing room only. Six stations to go till I reached Westminster where I'd catch a bus on to Elephant and Castle.

It seemed to start as soon as I stepped in and by South Kensington I knew it couldn't be my imagination, that what my journey had lacked from Brighton was being made up for this morning. 'The way to tell if a man is past his prime is by whether he wakes in the morning with an erection or not!' That's what Derek had said. I hadn't known that, I'd thought that everyone woke like that from wanting to have a widdle. I mean to say that I'd thought that's what it was full of. But he'd said no, I wasn't to confuse the two. Sometimes, so he claimed, he'd had to put a book on his boko to aim it down at the pan in order to piss. And then he'd had to wank after in order to fit in his trousers. I'd taken it as gospel, though I could never imagine my father having to follow the same procedure. Was that why our outside lavatory had always looked so dribbly, from the inaccuracy of his portion's aim, due to the lack of a book? Was that in fact why men liked taking literature to the latrine? Would a rolled newspaper carry sufficient weight?

There weren't many wankers in my carriage, they'd been saving it for sardining up to me. One was so large indeed that by Westminster it was almost in my pocket. No one looked at me at all: from their faces, the calmness of their eyes and the immobility of their mouths, no one would have guessed how vigorous were their lower portions. I held my face up like a flower, studying the coloured map of the London Underground. I smiled at it and once or twice I even shut my eyes, so enjoying myself was I. I'd started throbbing of course, that now familiar surging on the first furtive fingering feel. My mouth had dried, my teeth grew tight, my jaw fell slack and loose. I saw for one swift instant my strange face staring back at me, reflected in the glass-panelled door, as heads had swayed suddenly to one side and caused a sudden gap. We thundered through the interminable black tunnels, now underground, and underhand and under everything. I tried to hold a glance—with anyone, but no one would. They turned their eyes deliberately away as if I was the one who over-stepped the barriers of formality. It had happened before in the cinema; people, strangers tickling my tips and nobbling my knees and generally trying to get chummy—then rushing out before lights up, not even exchanging a name. But anyway, it made no odds, travelling to work this way. Was this how it was going to be every single day? I looked round happily at the shy and stony faces. No one to fancy, not really, not a single one, not like Derek. All more like the District Inspector, nice family men I'd have said. And different women with disappointed mouths and brassière straps all hanging on the slack. Fiona had sent a card this morning, a letter would have been better. 'Lots to tell.' That's all it said, with an upturned mouth like a melon slice. A very good sign that we'd pre-planned to show she was possibly getting it. Pat was all who needed some now—it didn't matter how little. Just so we started the same. And in the meantime, as to me, I had my journey to work—would the going home be as good though? Derek had made no general statement on genitalia at late afternoon.

My Headmistress's name was Mrs Pritchard. She was big and juicy and nice like an extra large portion of apple pie, with the bitter surprise of a clove. I could sense it, the bone at the centre of her sunny butter as soon as she shook me by the hand.

'You're young,' she said, 'and inexperienced. Not normally what I would welcome in a school of this size, but'—my blood ran chill at her iron smile—'we've been led to expect extraordinary achievements from you.' She smiled again, this time as soft as a cushion. 'Whatever sort of spell did you cast on our District Inspector? I've known him many years, but I've never before seen the dear man in quite such a dither!' To my deep annoyance, I began to blush. She found it charming, of course, and at the same time chose to see it as an acceptance on my part of some sort of guilt and thus a complicity with herself. She wagged her finger. 'It's all girls together here, I'm sorry to say! Unless you count Cunzle, our caretaker.' She leaned forward and lowered her voice. 'I wouldn't myself count Cunzle!'

'Kunzle like the cake?' Perhaps it was true about Fiona's meanness—I'd ended up paying for three Kunzles, and she hadn't offered anything. Mrs Pritchard flung a spontaneous outstretched palm against her Spirella'd stomach — the surging slap ricocheted around the room and finally got gagged by her gurgle. 'With a C, but similar enough to remind of one's weakness I am afraid! Now, my dear, to get down to business—I'll tell you what I've given you ...'

What she'd given me, and what I didn't like, was a form, a class of my own. One to take care of and chivvy. One to be on time for in order to do their morning register and count up all their dinner money. One to house in the hallowed sanctuary of my art room, so that they would be forever at my elbow whining about the whereabouts of their Wellington boots and playground plimsolls. And what she'd given me as well were oddment classes here and there like Basic Arithmetic, Remedial Reading and Junior Netball. 'No. Not netball. I haven't played that since grammar school. I barely remember the rules.'

But she'd smiled the smile of a stick insect this time, ready to spring through the leaves. 'Miss Megaphone will refresh your memory. Our capable Senior Sports Mistress.' Hardly that capable or she'd be coping with Junior Netball herself.

'Even so, I'd rather not, Mrs Pritchard. This is a secondary modern school I know, attended by girls who haven't managed to pass their Eleven Plus. It would seem to me terribly unfair that for Games, of all subjects, they should be taught by somebody who finds no enjoyment in it herself. These things, as you know, are so easily transmitted. It would distress me very much to think of somebody unenthusiastic attempting to teach Art, my subject—'

'Yes, well, I hardly suppose, my dear, that for you to stand in a playground with a whistle round your neck and a ball in your hand simply frowning a little, is going to do that much harm to our girls. There'll be nothing more for the moment. Could you kindly tell your colleague, Miss Einstein, to come in on your way out?'

Pat was already in by the time I got home, painting the kitchen floor with purple lino paint, but leaving a narrow strip along which to walk whilst the rest was drying. The place looked transformed. I stood at the doorway not daring to enter. 'What a palace, when did you do all this?'

'They let us off early, because of it being the first day. I've just been shopping—everything came from Woolworth's. What do you think? I thought I'd cover the length of this wall with some of my fabrics. I brought them up as teaching aids, but you should see them! Practically all cretins—including the bloody staff. I don't know how long I can stick it. I think my Headmistress is a Mongol!'

'You're lucky,' I said. 'Mine's not! Golda Meir—sharp

as a tack, tastes like a strawberry! Dreadful building, all dust and dried lice! You know the sort of smell. Mixed bag in the staff-room. Hardly a surfeit of equipment in the stockroom. School dinners as appalling as you'd expect. But, I had a good day's teaching though—'

She looked up. 'What already?'

'Yes, I spent the whole time telling them off. Every single class that came in, I just stood there in front of them laying down the law as to what or not they might expect to get away with. I needed to as well, Christ, you should see them—as tough as old boots. Like street-walkers, the ones you'd get in Soho, some of the sixth formers—frightening, honestly. And huge great things as well. They'd hit you as soon as look at you. But by the end I had them like mice. I'm going to do that with each lot that come to me, just to show who's boss, otherwise everything will be up the wall. I believe in that, ruling with a rod of iron—one of the other teachers was crying by the end of the day. Sitting in the staff-room crying her eyes out. She's in the next room to me—I could hear her lot through the wall, bedlam, poor bugger. She was new as well. There are two of us new—what about you?'

'Oh, my lot have been there since the Boer War, I should think. I'm far the youngest.'

'What was the journey like anyway?'

'Oh dreadfully dreary. Almost deserted actually, because everybody else was travelling in the other direction. I felt like a leper. Good for doing my face though. And I got there on time.'

'I didn't. I was late.'

She stood up to survey the wet and shining surface of the floor. 'It's a good colour, this. Or do you think red might have been better? Well, if we get tired of it, I can always do it over.'

'Can you?' I said. 'It's funny, that. I'd never have thought of painting the floor. I'd probably just have left it with that awful pattern on the lino. It doesn't worry me that much what a place looks like. But you'll make a wonderful wife—the homely touch!'

'Well that's no change, your being late. You're always late. We all know that.'

I laughed. What a nice life, coming home like this. Carrying on so cosily. No father to shout. No shop to have to serve in. No customers irritably tapping the counter with their coins. 'Well, I have to go easy with this Head. She caught me coming in—and what's more she's given me my own form, which means I've got to do all that register thing and take them into Assembly. Unless I can train them up to do it themselves. Perhaps if I make a real balls-up of it, she'll take them away. That's probably my best plan. And the same with Remedial Reading and bloody Junior Netball—'

'Has she given you that? All those things?'

'I'll get rid of it all somehow. Yes. 1D, that's my form. D for duffers! The bottom stream. Poor little sods. Have you got a class, by the way?'

She shook her head. 'No. And not a bad building either. Quite new I think. A bit like a public lavatory. Cold-looking. Clean. By the way, are we going to have some sort of rota here for the cleaning?'

'Cleaning?' Cleaning hadn't occurred to me before. And nor had things like cooking or who should buy the soap. 'I leave it to you,' I said. 'You work it all out and I'll do whatever you say. We'll get on best you being boss. These menial things don't interest me.'

She raised her brows sarcastically. '*La vie bohème*—I get it!'

'I'm afraid I'm awfully untidy, you must tell me if I get terrible. Start nagging me, I shan't mind.'

'Oh no, I'm not doing that. I do a lot of throwing away though, I may as well warn you now. I've had a bit of a clear-out already. Perhaps you'd better look in the dustbin; there were lots of bits and pieces I've cleared. Nothing very important, I don't think ...'

I walked along the corridor away from the kitchen, past the bathroom and into what could loosely be called our bedsitter. In one sense the term was quite accurate since there were only the beds there to sit on. The beds, the dressing-table, mirrored, and a corner cupboard for both our clothes. 'I can see you've cleared up, Pat,' I shouted back at her. 'Thanks for making my bed.' I looked around the room, missing my own familiar mess. Where the hell had she put everything? I cleared my throat and returned to the kitchen; she'd finished the floor and was cleaning the kettle, her paintbrush already neatly standing in a container of turpentine. 'Oh, are you good with brushes? I shall have to give you all mine. I'm awful at cleaning them after. Every single one is quite stiff. It's like painting with a palette knife. I just use them for laying the pigment on the canvas, that's all. No niceties of stroke.'

She paused. 'I've thrown them away, I'm afraid. They're in the dustbin. I didn't think you used them in that state! Sorry! Shall I get them back?'

I looked at her, appalled. My brushes! She'd gone and thrown away my brushes! In the Painting Department a person's brushes were their soul! Sacrosanct! Their prized possession! Nobody touched another's brushes. But Pat had thrown mine away! The sheer vandalism rendered me speechless. I walked out wordlessly in the direction of the dustbins to retrieve the discarded tools of my trade. They lay reproachfully beneath two over-ripe tomatoes, a torn Ryvita wrapper, an old *Picture Post*, a banana skin and a whole gaggle of stuff amongst which I noticed my favourite lipstick and the now crumpled letter from the District Inspector informing me officially of my employment. I came back with both hands full.

'What are you doing?' Pat looked genuinely astonished.

'I'm rescuing my belongings!' I answered stiffly. 'This, Pat'—I held it up—'is my favourite lipstick!'

'But it's all used up. There's nothing left!' She looked perplexed and puzzled. 'I opened it. If there'd been any there, of course I wouldn't have thrown it away.'

'That's beside the point. There may be other reasons why I might wish to keep it. Like needing to take it to the shop when I get round to replacing it. To match it up, I mean. You didn't jot down the make or the shade I shouldn't think, did you? And in any case'—I took the top off and began to unscrew—'there is some left, just here, look, right at the bottom. I manage all right with a matchstick—' She curled her own immaculately coloured upper lip disdainfully and began looking disagreeable, but my adrenalin was now too high to stop. 'And'—I flourished the District Inspector's letter in her face—'this. I was keeping this.'

'Keeping it? What for?'

'Keeping it to keep.'

'I see.' Her voice took on a note of flat finality. 'Keeping it to keep! Is that what you are then—a hoarder?'

'No, not a hoarder. But you have to keep some things. As mementos. Nice reminders. Like small landmarks in your life. You have to do that surely. Like this letter. I'm not going to get this letter again, am I? Not telling me about my first job, I'm not. That's what makes it special. And come to that even the lipstick. I shan't necessarily throw it away even when I buy a replacement, an identical replacement. The first will remind me, you see, this one here will of different times and things. Kisses, you know. Evenings out. Everything like that—'

'A hoarder. You're a hoarder all right. A bloody magpie. Not whilst you're living with me though! Right? We'll make a pact now that when I'm clearing up, I can throw away whatever I think, if it's lying around the place. If you want to hoard, you hoard in your drawers, or your part of the cupboard, not on communal territory, okay?'

I turned on my heel, my arms awash with my bits and pieces, and made an attempt at dignity. 'That suits me fine. Oh, and before I forget. It surely is unprofessional to throw out the *Picture Post*?'

'Why on earth should we want those, once we've seen them?'

'Pat!' I managed to make my voice as reproving as possible. 'Our teaching aids, remember!'

It was our first unpleasantness and, dreading unpleasantness as I did, I made the first move towards a truce. 'Any plans *à propos* your Roly then?'

'Plans?' She repeated coldly.

'Yes, plans. Have you a plan of action for the capture of Monsieur Balls? Are you considering asking him round or inviting him out or anything? Or will you be leaving it all to him?' I was on the right tack, I'd known I was before I started. She'd already begun to melt. My God, but this sharing stunt was less easy than I'd envisaged. We needed a suitable social life if she wasn't to get on my nerves. I'd have enough to tell old Fiona anyway.

'Well. What do you think? I was hoping that Mark might manage something, but of course now he's married, he's no longer as available as he used to be. What I'd like is to have a party. Perhaps at the end of the week, if we can jolly the look of the place a bit. That's why I'm doing all this, trying to tart it up.'

I looked at her doubtfully. Did we know enough people yet? 'But who could we ask, do you think? Wouldn't it be better to wait a bit until we know a few more?' I was unfamiliar with the art of party-giving, never having given one before. It was a mystique to me,

222

though one which I was most eager to become acquainted
with.

'Oh, giving a party is the best way of getting to know
people. You tell everyone you ask to bring someone and a
bottle, and automatically, your circle widens. That's what
I've always found works best. What about you? You must
know at least one person in London, surely. However
slender the thread? What about the ones that Fiona knows?
She was always coming up to London, wasn't she? Or
was it all eyewash, do you think? When is she back in
any case, from Scotland? If she's back in time she could
come.'

'Yes, she could. No, I don't know anyone, isn't it
extraordinary! Oh, except Derek's cousin. I know him.
Michael, he's a solicitor. Or will be when he finishes. He's
frightful though, you wouldn't like him. Smarmy. He
lives in Battersea. I've got his number here somewhere.
Derek stayed with him when he came to London.'

'Well, there you are, you see. Why not give him a ring?
Go on.'

'What? Right now?'

'Yes, why not?'

'And say what?'

'Say hello. That's the way, I promise you—'

He was in, the dreaded Michael, as it happened, but only
just, it seemed. 'You've caught me with my coat on! How
awfully nice to hear you. So sorry about the dooming of
your love affair. Had a card from Derek, strangely enough.
Posted on board. Have you heard from him? No. Ah well.
Perhaps a clean break is for the best. I say, look here, have
you eaten? What about having a bite with me? Yes, do
bring your friend, by all means! Is she as glamorous as
your good self? I have to meet an old school friend for a
drink first, but if he's free, I'll ask him to join us. He has a
hell of an eye for a pretty girl, I must warn the pair of
you—'

'That's it then, Pat! We've bloody done it! Let's dosh
ourselves up! We're going out to dinner!'

Michael's club was in Swallow Street, just off Piccadilly. We went there on the tube. A rather different ride
to the one I'd had this morning. Pat, strangely, had
claimed to find my revelations mildly revolting. 'Really?'
I'd said. 'But why?' The fact of the furtive fingers. The
impersonal pushing of the penises. 'Wouldn't it be penii,

223

in the plural?' I decided to ask Michael. He was well up on Latin being a legal person. I wondered if his old school friend was a legal person too. My father was very fond of lawyers. Legal beavers, so he claimed, were the most prestigious of the professions. 'You come back with a barrister, my girl, and you'll have gladdened your old dad's heart. Don't go squandering yourself now, on any old Tom, Dick or Harry. You could get anything if you put your mind to it. You've had a lucky escape with the yid, now see to yourself and aim for the stars!'

I'd met Michael before, of course. Twice—the first time in those early idyllic days with Derek. And then later on when things between us were going badly off the boil. Both times had been in Brighton, but I knew about this club of his already. The Studio Club it was called, Derek belonged and had managed to wangle Michael a membership, not being strictly to do with the Arts. 'You should join as well. They have women. Painters, writers even actresses—'

'This is the club that Derek said I should join. It doesn't cost that much, Pat. It's exactly for people like us. On our own.' I was over-excited. We were going out. All my doing. Our first date! I squeezed her arm as we came up the steps of Piccadilly station and got caught in the roar of the town. 'Oh, look around!' I gawped. 'What do you think! Isn't it wonderful!' I went like that in cities, warmed to the hum and the heart. The width of the pavements and the height of the poles. The telegraph wires and the traffic lights, and the shimmering shine of shop windows. The magic of the metropolis.

But Pat appeared unmoved, even faintly irritable. The people of Piccadilly milled around us. 'Oh don't they get on your nerves—all pushing! Honestly! Did you see that woman then? Right on my toe—and she didn't even say sorry!'

'Oh come on. I'll say it for her—sorry!' I wanted it to be perfect, our first night out. Why on earth did she need such cajoling? I did a little skip as we passed Swan & Edgar's and laughing linked my arm in hers. She looked at me. 'Calm down.' I clamped my teeth together and silently counted ten. 'Oh, come on Pat! Cheer up! Calm down indeed—what's wrong?'

I wasn't interested to hear, in fact. At even the slight suggestion of her shrug, I could feel my spirits evaporate.

She was opposite to Fiona, that's what I now began to tell myself. Our sharing had been a mistake.

'Will we like them? That's what's wrong. I don't want to waste time with two drips—'

I stopped walking. 'What?'

'Well, we'd be better off washing our hair and tidying up and having an early night than—'

'Pat'—I spoke so severely, as if addressing my girls at school, that for a second she looked quite startled. 'Pat,' I repeated. 'We're never going to be better off having an early night. Not at our age. Got it?'

She hung back reluctantly. 'I'm having second thoughts. I don't feel up to going in. I don't fall on my feet with strangers—not like you, you know—'

'Fall on my feet? Who, me? I don't fall on my feet.' I was quite genuinely amazed. It was happening more and more these days it seemed to me. People making absurd assumptions. Attributing me with quite extraordinary qualities. Placing me an alienating distance from themselves—accepting their own inferiority. When I would have preferred the camaraderie of being equals. 'No, it's not my feet. If anything, it's probably more my mind. I like to keep it open. That's why I never shut doors or drawers, or anything, even my handbag if I can help it—' We'd reached Swallow Street. I started searching for the entrance to the Studio Club. 'And when I eventually get going, I hope to apply that very same principle to my legs. Keeping them open I mean, if you'll excuse the coarseness.'

The Studio Club had a peeling painted door, which had at one time been Thames Green. A favourite shade from the Festival of Britain. Pat viewed it approvingly. 'We could do ours that, you know. Our front door in the flat. Thames Green. And the inside of the toilet.' I turned the handle. She kept saying toilet. Fiona would have condemned it non-U, but was there a nice way of warning Pat? No.

'Anyway, you never know, you may well meet your future tonight.'

'The school friend, you mean?' There was actually now a break in her voice! Not of nervousness, surely? Never!

'That's where you go wrong you see—pinning your hopes on an actual person. Like Roly Balls, for instance. Worshipping from afar. I'd never do that. If you want somebody, you wangle it that you get them. But otherwise, just living in hopes at a distance, you're bound to be disappointed. What I mean is that your future could present itself at any turn of the corner. It doesn't need formal introductions before you start speaking to people, surely. I'd forget about the school friend for a start—he's bound to be bloody awful. Blind dates almost always are.'

He wasn't though, not bloody awful. In fact he was quite the opposite! And Pat obviously thought so, I could tell from the way she blinked. It smacked of success, the whole evening, from the second we stepped through the door. A heady mixture rose to greet us of perfume and garlic and wine, mingling with music—modern jazz—and the tantalising subdued snatch of low talk. We walked self-consciously down the stairs, aware of the waiting eyes beneath. A man with a beard barred our way. He looked like Augustus John but turned out to be the Club Secretary. 'Ladies?' I explained that we'd come as guests, just as Michael appeared from the Gents. He kissed us both before he signed us in and then introduced the school friend, Douglas.

He wasn't at all my sort of chap—too much of the Anglo-Saxon. Too fair and smooth and well-turned-out, like a walking shop-window dummy. The sort you'd come across in Austin Reed's Regent Street window—we'd only just passed them this evening. The look of the young executive, complete with executive glasses. Douglas. 'As in the Isle of Man.' Pat laughed delightedly. Exactly her level of humour. He turned and smiled at her appreciatively, deliberately lingering on her tidy lips and nattily manicured nails. I saw him approve her arrow-straight seams as she turned to take off her coat. I reminded myself to have a word with her over her aertex underwear. It would be heartbreaking to ruin what could be a promising relationship for the sake of her brother's bloomers.

Michael was smiling at me admiringly; I forced myself to smile back. I'd forgotten how awful he was. And what was worse—how short. Had something happened since we'd met? Had someone sliced off his ankles? He slipped his arm ostensibly around my waist, it ended encircling my buttocks. And it was in this bizarre fashion that we entered the bar of the Club. 'What will you have?' He looked up at me. I quickly slipped on to a stool to render us more on a

226

level. People were dancing—merely feet away from us—between the bar and the trio who played far beyond. My heart sank, it meant, of course, that we'd be doing the same. Me and Michael. 'A very large gin for a start!' Drunk, I could dance with a dwarf!

The two of them, Michael and Douglas, had had quite a few already. We needed ours large to catch up, but by the time our table was ready, both Pat and I were aglow. 'Which way to the Ladies' Room?' I whispered quietly to Michael. 'The Little Girls?' he shouted back, and stood up to point with his finger. Several men at the bar crowded round to clap me on my way.

'Are you coming, Pat?' I wanted to know, suss out the state of the nation. 'No, I'm all right,' she started. I pulled a face. 'Oh, yes. Wait, I'm coming!'

'What do you think then?' I said as soon as we got there.

'Phew!' she went. 'What do you?'

'He's it, I think, Pat. You've done it!'

'Do you think so? Yes! So do I!'

The thing was, where though? I was more worried about that than her. Douglas still lived with his mother, who was widowed—the same as Pat's. I watched them over dinner, they certainly suited each other. When they got up to dance I turned to Michael. 'They seem to have hit it off—your school friend and my flat mate. We should congratulate ourselves! Does he have many other girl-friends? I mean, where would he entertain them?'

He wasn't so bad, old Michael. He understood right away. 'Oh I say. Yes, I'm sorry I can't be of assistance. The only girls I've ever met of Douglas' have always had pads of their own. One assumes the worst would take place back there. How large is your flat, by the way?'

'Not large enough, I'm afraid.'

'On the other hand, would you like to sleep with me tonight? Strictly as friends, of course?'

'How sweet of you Michael—some other time. But not tonight I think.'

I shut my eyes very tight, though there wasn't any need in the dark. And pushed a finger in my one good ear to blot out the sound of her groans. My deafness would seem now to be standing me in good stead. A mastoid operation in early childhood. My only physical disability the resulting deafness. But when at last I let my good ear go, I could tell

227

that they'd fallen asleep from the absolute steady silence. I opened my eyes again, still whirling from what I'd been drinking. We were all whirling by the time we'd left the club. And possibly because of that, the lightness of the occasion and the lateness of the hour, it had seemed quite perfectly natural that Douglas should accompany us down. And of course there seemed no reason why he shouldn't come in, once in the basement.

I'd left them kissing in the kitchen, and gone to clean my teeth. Thankful only that Michael had finally seen reason and relinquished all hopes for my favours. And from cleaning my teeth and running my new blue flannel around my face, I'd fallen quite giddily into bed, and left the light on for Pat. When I woke up it was off. But they were both in her bed. It shouldn't have shocked, but it did. Her doing it there the first time! It seemed to me, like throwing away my brushes, to smack of such insensitivity! I wouldn't have done it, not even drunk. I'd have wanted to have a word with the one that you give it to first. Perhaps that's what had put poor Derek off. The attachment I'd shown then to talking. If I'd kept my mouth shut, he might have made more progress opening up my other end.

What did her groans mean? I wondered. I lay there now, flat on my back, my good ear, like a piece of fine electrical equipment, picking up the lightweight cadences of their combined sleeping breaths. And the relentless ticking of her alarm. Had she remembered to set it? I strained to see in the dark. It seemed right, those luminous lines, as far as I could tell. That was one alarm call I should sleep through. To let them get dressed on their own and spare us all the embarrassment, mutual, of a morning confrontation.

That wasn't actually how it happened. They both woke me up with some coffee and watched me drinking it starry-eyed, on the edge of her bed together. They held hands and kissed a lot, oblivious of my presence. Pat had been to bed with all her make-up on, her eyes looked bleak and black with smudged and stale mascara. And on her mouth remained a faintly carmine tinge—I didn't think I'd ever seen her look so bloody beautiful.

All their clothing lay littered over the floor, they'd obviously undressed in a hurry. Stripped in haste. Peeled off at a speed. Hardly able to wait. To fall upon each other like two lustful ravenous beasts! My sleep-drugged sluggishness jolted at the thought. I felt appalling now. I was awake but half-dead, with a diesel drill doing its damnedest in my head. I cowered over my cup of coffee, barely able to bring myself to meet their eyes. But it was obvious that I was the only one of us embarrassed in any way by the intimacy of the situation. I cleared my throat, I felt clogged internally. 'I've got a hellish hangover, haven't you two? Shut your eyes while I slip out of bed—I was so far gone last night I couldn't even find my nightie.'

Pat looked blank and utterly beguiling. Wide-eyed but not quite with us, like someone in a dream. Was she still drunk? Douglas leaned over and teasingly tried to flick my bedclothes to one side. I snatched them back beginning to be alarmed, but he just gave a good-natured frown.

'Oh, don't be a spoil-sport, old thing! Let's take a peep at the beautiful bod!' He was wearing one of Pat's dressing-gowns. A floral Acrilan affair. Man-made fibre, covered in crimson carnations. American. Sent from San Francisco by another of Pat's aunts, who'd been the first of the GI brides. Wash'n'Drip Dry. Faced by the multitude of many such enviable gifts that Pat received, I might well have wished that my mother too had had sisters. Or my father, come to that. It barely met across his front, hardly covered up his nipples. He had a particularly smooth and hard and hairless chest, I noticed, and a mannish nice long neck, muscled somewhat like a giraffe's. And now without his glasses and his Board of Director's suiting, he looked less spruce and taut, more appealing altogether. I didn't let my eyes fall lower down. I didn't dare. In any case it would have seemed like poaching on poor Pat's territory. I coughed. He was sitting discreetly cross-legged, no chance of a glimpse of anything. It was only if he stood, that I'd be privileged.

Pat spoke at long last. 'It's all right! We're all pals together. Let him see, go on!' And as if to illustrate the all-encompassing extent of our togetherness, she deliberately tugged her own sheet to one side and stretched without self-consciousness towards the ceiling. She yawned as we both watched the sinewy lines of her becoming taut then slackening gracefully away. Her hair hung tangled and uncombed around the suntanned shoulders; the entire shape seemed mysteriously more seductive than I had previously judged before. She settled back, the sheet fell even further so that now I could see her navel and the subtle swell of one hip. Her tiny nipples were now erect, had come to a life of their own. Even the colour seemed different—a delicate terracotta where before they had merely been brown.

I swallowed. No one spoke but now they were looking at me—expectantly I thought, as if waiting for what I was about to do. Douglas made the first move, he slowly stood up, allowing the American bride's Drip Dry to fall away and reveal his own personal properties. The clock said ten past six. I would have had to admit that I enjoyed the sight of his offering, despite the reluctance I felt. I'd always liked looking at Derek's, unhealthily much, so he said. He'd taken a bath, that very first time, and had casually called me in. 'Soap it!' he'd said. And had offered the two together—first the Palmolive and then his penis. He'd shown me how to run the bar around the rim, with a hand beneath the balls. I'd enjoyed it all, the feel of it stiffening up—like a lighthouse surrounded by surf—that's how it looked by the end, I said. And I'd swilled all the bubbles away with his super de luxe bath sponge and water straight from the tap. Much too hot! He'd squealed like a stuck pig, struck a new note in the musical register for a full five minutes or so. As a matter of fact I'd felt quite scared believing I'd done permanent damage.

Douglas' looked rather similar, as far as I could tell in the light. 'It's a fair size,' I said conversationally. 'Did it hurt you?' I turned towards Pat. I'd got over my initial embarrassment. Why not involve oneself after all? Since Pat didn't appear to mind—but I felt worried even so on her behalf. 'Keep an eye on the time, Pat,' I warned.

But she lay back with even greater abandon, slanting her eyes provocatively from one of us to the other. 'Perhaps'— she spoke very slowly—'I shan't go in today. Not turn up to work at all!'

'Pat! What? You're still drunk!'

She shrugged. I looked at her amazed. Could one single sexual experience have wrought such a positive change? Had deflowering divulged an unexpected streak of Patty-Devil? Not go in? What gross irresponsibility! I gasped at the very recklessness, barely aware of what Douglas was doing now. He'd disrobed, let Man-Made drop on the floor and stood with his cock at a sly wild salute. It waved there bravely though unsteadily, due to a lack of support, towards the upstairs tenants. A circumcised sod, so I saw, to quote my articulate father. A carefully clipped poodle, a

230

well-pruned privet, a sharpened propelling pencil. He propelled it down now with both hands.

I swallowed again. An explicable supply of saliva was pouring into my mouth. Drowning my front teeth and the tip of my tongue, and drumming out into the back of my tingling ears. All my orifices in fact were receiving emergency oil of sorts from somewhere! Every pore was opening up, extending itself in welcome. 'I need to go,' I said. 'I think.' Something was happening under the sheets, some strange and unbearable pressure, high up in what I took to be my bladder, but at the same time further through than there, was the certain sensation of oozing. This can't be correct without contact, prior to all the palaver, without the excitement of stroking—to be so seduced—on sight! I crossed my legs and squeezed together tightly with my upper thighs. But it seemed if anything to make the matter worse, the unspecific centre of the surging pleasure was becoming more sharp and intense. 'Oh dear,' I said it quietly and to myself. And without giving a second thought I slid a hand in down over my own now hard (and normally so soft) nipples, pausing a second to pass over them another time, so natural did it seem and nice. Down I went over velvety skin until I came to rest in the entrance of my open crinkly nest of hair. My clitoris felt swollen, wonderfully wobbly and stiff. I pressed it hard, and surreptitiously began to rub, holding the bedclothes well up with my other hand.

Douglas raised his elbows away from his body, wriggling his wrists in the air. 'Look, no hands!' And tensing himself, started thwacking away on his stomach. A performing penis, like a seal. What a house pet to have in your pants! How much murkier, marshier, messier women's parts were! Like school atlases, the hillier bits brought out in lighter shades, and the rest all dank and dark and uncharted. Layered like ripe pickled onions and prone to the same sort of smell.

Pat had brightened up a bit and had even begun to clap. 'Oh,' I winked at her. 'Congratulations yourself, by the way. You look better now you've lost it!' She smiled and so did Douglas. 'Your turn now,' he said, and in one quick movement, had tossed all my sheets to one side. 'Caught you!' He tapped my manipulating fingers. 'Here, let me. There's no need for that with me around, kiddie!' I shuddered dangerously inside to feel his hand touching the swell of my stomach. 'It's full,' I said. 'I'm afraid I shall have to be excused.'

'All piss!'

'That's true—'

'All piss and ignorance! Gives the best fuck in the world. A full bladder!'

That's not what Derek had said. Go now if you want to, before we start, for God's sake! Now are you certain you don't feel the need? 'The pressure, you see,' Douglas spoke with enthusiasm. 'Tremendously exciting! Cliff-hanging stuff, so it seems! I promise you. Had a girl not so long ago—we all had her if I remember rightly—the whole of the rugger club. Her speciality was pissing on a chap. Really hot stuff on it she was. A rather chilling experience in the front seat of a parked car come winter, I can tell you! And positively anti-social in the rear of the coach for that matter! Yes, she was a sort of mascot for a time. Can't think what happened—proved too expensive probably. The dry-cleaning bills, y'know. Flannel pants need particular pressing and so do club blazers, come to that. Also I believe the coach company registered a formal complaint—the upholstery becoming discoloured and sustaining an unpleasant smell.'

I listened closely. Could it be true, what he was saying? Surely not! 'Liar!'

'No. Scout's Honour. S'true, old thing! On the absolute point of orgasm. She'd release all inner tensions! The whole lot let rip!'

'A form of enuresis? Incontinence under sexual stress!' I was fascinated by what he was saying. Who would have guessed it to look at him! Michael had said he was good with girls. What a mine of marvellous information—I glanced at Pat to see how she was taking it. She was leaning forward, seemingly not listening, but staring intently at me. My insides lurched.

'I'd best go,' I moved. 'I'm almost sure I shan't hold out—I like to empty the reservoir first thing in the morning before I can face the day. Sorry, Douglas—'

'I'd go on the side of the bath if your legs don't reach up to the sink. Just run the tap, that's all—saves time.' Pat turned to Douglas. 'That's the worst thing about this flat, the bog being out by the dustbins. You have to go right out to the outside corridor. I cock a leg over the sink. You're

232

lucky, you boys, I learnt it from my brother.' Yes, I'd seen her do it the very first day. 'You don't mind, do you? Old habits die hard.' Her wide-legged knickers had helped, of course. She'd drawn the gusset to one side, lifted her left knee over the porcelain and aimed at the ancient plughole. Muscles like a man! I wondered now, with everything more open, as it were, whether there'd be the control.

I stirred myself, not too ashamed to stand and show my body. In fact quite proud these days. 'Christ, you're beautiful!' Derek had said. 'You honestly bloody are!'

'Am I?' I'd still been anxious then. 'Not too fat?' I'd said. That would always be my worry. It had been my worry from the time my father had noticed me starting some shape. 'Have you been at the strawberry sherbets? You're putting some weight on, my girl! I've a good mind to move these Maltesers out of temptation's way as well. Don't think I don't know when you've been dipping in—'

'Fat, my foot! Hourglass! Pocket Venus.' Derek had given me confidence.

'Isn't she gorgeous, Douglas?' Now Pat was being generous! Douglas was sweating on his upper lip. 'I could tell what was there in her clothes.'

I held my shoulders back and tried my best at sucking my stomach in as well as I could in the circumstances. 'I'll be back in a sec, where're my shoes?' I'd slipped them on and gained another several inches, but I still didn't quite make the sink! It was 6.24 exactly, I'd looked at the clock to make sure before bombarding the ancient enamel over the edge of the bath, cold tap full on, top pelt. 'Are you sure,' I shouted above the din and deluge, 'you're definitely not going to school, Pat?' She didn't answer until I returned.

'I'd rather stay here and watch you.'

'Watch what though? Won't you mind?' I felt the need to know. I thought it only nice to ask. I would have minded with Derek. If he'd have invited another. Oh, all men would like it with two girls. That's one of the most normal fantasies! Is it, Derek? Really? More than alone, being in love? But he hadn't answered. Sometimes being in love could make it less successful.

Douglas pulled me very close; in my high heels, I reached almost to his ear. 'Oh come on, I'll be gone tomorrow, kiddie.'

I reared back. 'Gone?'

But Pat answered cheerfully. 'Off to Malta to start a new

233

job! So it makes no odds either way. We may just as well both benefit. Go on, get a move on, you too. It's terribly exciting—'

She seemed at home now, Pat. As at home as I had ever seen her. This wasn't the first time she'd done it—she'd never have been so relaxed. Or eager either, come to that, to be merely an excited spectator. Didn't *two* girls mean having both? But Pat it seemed would remain an observer. 'Have you done this sort of thing before, Patsy?' I managed to ask as Douglas prepared to kiss me. Her mouth curled up each end. 'Millions of times with old Mark. He always let me in on things. The taboos were too great for him to have me—'

Douglas knew his way around all right. 'Stand still,' he said. And led me towards the wall. 'I want to feel just what it is I'm getting!' 6.37 I saw, I'd worked out to leave by 8.10. My conscience could never have allowed any careering off on my part. Part of my attitude to life was to try to cram everything in.

He started with my earlobes and travelled round my neck, tickling with his finger-tips and touching with his tongue. It made me shiver, the skill which he employed, although I felt so much less sexy now. Perhaps then what he'd said was true, the fullness of the bladder had triggered off that very special tension. Because right now, despite the nearness of his bulging dick—which after all is what you're meant to like—I'd begun to *separate* inside. I still felt swollen, as it were, and my nipples were still erect. I felt the need to quicken his desire. I loved the *thought* of Pat as an onlooker—in fact I purposely posed myself in what I knew to be provocative angles. I thrust and trembled and sighed and shut my eyes and smiled. I pushed myself against Douglas and I smouldered in Pat's direction, even licking my lips in quite uncharacteristic lewdness as if to arouse her licentiousness. But all the time I was aware of an alienation—and I was waiting for when he'd go in. 6.57 went the hands of the clock, three minutes more made it 7.00. He was still stroking—one hand concentrating on my upper zones, the other on my lower. Pat was beginning to wriggle. He'd placed an index finger between my lower lips and had begun a delicate movement, encompassing with each further subtle swoop a greater expanse of that inner skin. The rubbing of Aladdin's lamp, a magical affair, intended as in the tale to

234

open up the pleasures of Heaven and Life's unparalleled pleasures. But I knew where he was aiming for and had got my needles ready. They were knitting and knotting despite myself. 'Shall we try the bed, madam?' I allowed him to steer me in that direction, willing myself to unlock. He smiled at me. Sweet. And Pat smiled as well, like a sister, a loving well-wisher. I longed not to let them down.

It was 7.15 exactly by the time we'd got into position. Missionary style for starters, that's what Douglas had said. I'd never known another way. 'Yes, that's how I did it before—him on top.' Douglas had laughed. 'Glad to hear someone has broken the ice already!' I kept my mouth shut, my misgivings were mounting—broken—cracked it, maybe! Or possibly merely scratched it, like something diamond sharp on glass. Fiona had done that in our shop, drawn on the window with what she claimed to be a diamond. A glinting splinter of a thing hanging in an antique ornament from her ear. 'Oh don't,' I'd said. 'My dad will go crackers—he cleans those himself, you know.' She'd laughed and gone on doing it. How were things going with her up there, in Scotland, now, I wondered. Was she at this very moment, at 7.17 precisely, practising Missionary too? They were noted, the Scots, for adopting religious positions, stances, rather extreme. Calvinists. Something cold and austere, which wouldn't suit Fiona at all.

'Shall I put some music on? Would that help us all?' Pat was speaking; I could hear her voice but Douglas was blotting the view. Blotting out everything in fact, the central bulb, the beading on the ceiling, the thought of the long day ahead. The underside of him looked very red, poised as it was above me, like meat roasting on a spit—the blood had run down to the bottom. My legs were wide and welcoming; my breasts, in this position, lolled gently on each upper arm, their centres brisk and businesslike compared to the abandoned surrounds. Douglas snortled excitedly, a bead of something damp dropped from the centre of his face. I fervently prayed it wasn't his nose. His shoulders were raised higher than the rest of him, supported on my pillow by his hands, each side of me. He kept glancing down, towards his lower regions—to see how things were going I supposed. Was his missile to remain unguided then by hand? Would it know the way by instinct, like a homing pigeon? I shut my eyes and counted

235

up to ten. When I opened them nothing happened.

'Should we give it a lead? Show the carrot to the donkey, Douglas?'

'Right! Here we go,' he said. 'Prepare for action.' And leaning back and holding it with one hand, he lunged towards what all of us hoped was a hole!

Boomerangs take well up to half an hour before returning back to base. Douglas' took ten seconds. And an animal bellow of alarm. And a blow to his bollocks that must have sent his senses reeling, such that he might have reasonably believed his job in Malta to be put in jeopardy from the need for hospitalisation. 'Jesus Christ! What do you have in there—a concrete jungle or a jigsaw puzzle constructed from plaster and iron filings?'

Pat was peering anxiously over his shoulder as I lifted my head and looked down. All seemed as it should be at my end—no fighter's fist, no set of knuckles, no demon jack-in-the-box had emerged to deal his poor dong such a blow on the nose. I tentatively walked my thumb and index finger down to feel the tensile strength in that stretch of skin. It lay like a neat piece of plaiting, perfectly intertwined—no Entry sign hung anywhere. Oh hell on earth! No! Not again! I took the stoic sensible line, a nice no-nonsense approach. 'What's up, then Douglas? Won't it go in?'

'Why not? Why won't it?' Pat bleated.

'She's dry,' Douglas turned to me. 'You're dry,' he said. 'That's why.'

Dry? What, dry like certain Southern States or Sunday pubs in Wales? Or like your feet in well-shod shoes or under an oak in the rain? No. More like the dryness fear brings—as dry as a moth in a flame. As dry as my mouth in fact was now—where in hell was all that saliva? And all that oozing stickiness from before? 'Oh, I'm sorry I'm dry. I don't know why, I was ever so wet a while ago.' Even at 7.15. 'Have you got a bit of spit to spare?' I found I was asking Pat. 'Spit?'

Douglas turned 'Board of Directors'; he snapped his fingers efficiently, mopped his brow and settled on his haunches, his game erection resting on my thigh. 'Quick,' he said, 'before this bugger disappears—some Vaseline is called for!'

Pat's eyes swivelled wildly around the room. 'Vaseline! Um, Vaseline! Will Valderma do?'

Douglas started tutting and seized his weapon at source, high at the point of its growth from his trunk. 'Ye Gods!' The mutter turned into a scream—I marvelled at how he'd managed to make that sound through such steadily clenched teeth. We seemed to have some minor emergency on our hands.

'Let's try again,' I said. 'I've got fifteen minutes left, before I get up and dress.'

He sank as if in deep despair. 'Do you mind going out of the room, Pat my dear?' he pleaded. 'Perhaps that's what is putting her off.'

'No, it's not, please. I like her here. I'm always like this I'm afraid. I've been told it's because I'm all tensed up and tight—just spit on it now, you'll see ...'

He worked solidly for the entire fifteen minutes—by the last five I was praying that he'd stop. Now I was sore as well as dry, and near to tears too. He'd gone, long gone, completely limp and lay back at last, exhausted. Pat was white and woebegone, her earlier radiance had disappeared—she looked like a social worker, whose case had come to grief. I tried to comfort them both as best I could.

'Never mind. Now can we have another coffee? I've got to get off to school. You two can stay and start again after a little sleep ...'

My day consisted of double periods. One lasted till mid-morning play, the next one saw through the morning till the school bell announced dinner. Another took up part of the afternoon which left a single lesson time to spare. My spare this afternoon was actually free as opposed to being occupied with Remedial Reading or dreaded Junior Netball.

I'd forged my fragile way to Earls Court Station, having carefully kissed Douglas farewell. I'd held my face well forward, not wishing to arouse him all over again. They were both in bed, he and Pat, by the time I'd left the flat. I'd heard them laughing before I'd reached the landing—but I'd trusted not over me. What the trouble was I couldn't imagine because as soon as my journey began, I felt as excited as anything. When I got back I'd ask Pat if mine was a medical case—Mark would know, we'd ring him. I had no one else to ask.

1D were already in their seats up in my room when I arrived. I'd been a trifle tardy yet again it seemed. Good

God, it meant that I'd be leaving more like eight o'clock, instead of ten past at this rate. Form teachers were meant to be in there first, with the register open, all ready to call their names. 'Someone open the window, please. Who's Window Monitor this month? Pearl Buttons? Righto, Pearl! Not present? Well, you then. Do it. Thank you!' Eleven-year-olds, but rising twelve. The heady age of almost there. An ill-assorted set, their skins still childishly transparent on the whole, except where adolescent acne was already taking hold. They already regarded me with respect; several inevitably sucking up, attempting to forge their places as my favourites. I ignored them and their sycophancies. Everyone says, Miss, you're the prettiest teacher—you should hear what they say in the play-ground—are you married—no, Miss ain't married—she ain't got no wedding ring on. Had I been like that with a teacher? Done such arse-licking until I'd turned her stomach? Probably, or then again, perhaps not. My head ached too much to remember. What had I said I'd do today—bollock them into submission—I still had ten new classes of children to come. Our school went up to a sixth form, and in each year except that sixth, we had four forms. But today, in this state of health, I wouldn't be up to anything, let alone setting myself up as a stalwart disciplinarian.

I stood, feeling lost, at my stock cupboard, before leading 1D to Assembly. My first Assembly as well as theirs—since yesterday morning had simply been signing in. Christ! What would I do for first lesson? 2A, my curriculum said. It would be the bloody bright ones, well, brighter—on this day of all. The idea came in Assembly with eyes shut and hands clasped in prayer. 'Our Father Which Art in Heaven, Hallowed Be—'

'2A? Now sit quietly. That's right. Good girls. Now this morning whilst I sit here trying to memorise your faces, you will use your time making patterns. Hands up, who likes making patterns? Yes, on squared paper like this—with no chance of it going wrong—all right, class? I shall mark them, of course, on the regularity of your shapes. You could do circles all the way down the page, in the coloured pencils that I'll be giving you. Yes, simple circles or even zig-zag lines—or come to that, you could outline the squares and fill them in alternately. Now, who can I rely on to give this graph paper, which is what it's called as I expect you know, this graph paper, one to each person? And if you finish it before the end of lesson, you come to me for a second and do it, the same if you like, but in a different colour.' And in that way, I managed to struggle through the day, sitting before the nation's youth—setting them infants' work. The District Inspector would have eaten his shit!

In all the fuss and frustration, I'd forgotten to tell Pat that I wouldn't be back, not until later tonight. It was Tuesday today, my evening for St Martin's School of Art, where Bernard Bolt, who'd taught me down in Brighton, held his evening class.

'Come,' he'd said, 'to cheer me up, they're an awful bunch of bloody amateurs. In any case, it'll help to keep your hand in—we've got a real live model. I know what you students are like, even the artiest of you—you leave and that's the end of it. Especially when you go into those ordinary schools, death and destruction. I'm surprised that you've succumbed to such a suburban impulse as having a nine-to-five job. You should have held out, you've got the ability. Spent your days painting and got a job at night, any old job, just to keep going. You don't begin to know half of it, you kids, about dedication, do you? When I was your age, I was starving in a Paris attic, but covering canvases as if my soul depended on it. Look at you, you—'

'I'll come! Okay, I'll come!' I said, just to shut him up. But he was right, of course, I knew that he was right. What bourgeois streak indeed was it to single out such a life—banked on one side by authoritarian headmistresses, and living on the other hand with pure suburbia like Pat, and even more, Fiona, when she'd be joining us. My father's influence, of course, whose else? And my own need to be like the others. Even going to Art School for a start, had set me aside enough. Had alienated half the people I'd been brought up with.

I made myself a cup of tea before I left the staff-room, still feeling under the weather, but on the road to recovery. Everyone else had gone except the other new teacher, Miss Einstein. I smiled at her. 'How's it been today?' She was the one who'd been crying yesterday. I looked at her sympathetically, comprehending completely why children would play her up. We must have been surely about

239

the same sort of age, but she was middle-aged already, somehow old before her time. The drooping shoulders did it, to hide the drooping breasts—they hung heavily over her belt, indivisible with her belly. There appeared to be no waist. Nothing there that dieting couldn't cure, of course. And nothing in the wide expanse of countenance that couldn't have been improved with cosmetics and the cunning artifice of somebody like Pat.

She creased her forehead and made a wan moue shape with her mouth. 'They petrify me!'

'Oh, you'll get used to them—'

She winced and wrapped her arms around herself as if in abstract protection. 'No, I'll never get used to them. They'll annihilate me first. I shan't ever understand how I managed to pass my teaching practice—I thought *they* were pretty awful. It was a pure fluke, that!' Her voice was lightweight, like a little girl's, at certain words even babyish. She must have been an only child, like me. But treated as one at home or else the youngest, perhaps. The accent was amazing, top of the class in elocution, careful in the extreme—which meant she probably had a background much like mine as well. But with more determination to disguise it.

'Well, at least today I didn't hear them,' I said. 'You are next door to me, after all.' Not that I'd been very much of this world or capable much of hearing anything at all. But things seemed better now; I sipped my tea. She leant forward confidingly. 'I let them just read round the class, a paragraph at a time out loud. Could hardly be called the art of instruction, I'm afraid. But I just wasn't up to it today.'

'I shouldn't worry,' I spoke cheerfully. 'Nor was I.'

'Oh?' Her expression lifted slightly. 'Are you having troubles with discipline too?'

'Just with drinking. I had a heavy night last night— terrible hangover today!'

She looked impressed. 'I wouldn't think of drinking mid-week. Not when I'd started a new job.'

'No, nor would I normally.' Was that true? Why wouldn't I, after all? This was my life, wasn't it? Other people did all sorts of things mid-week, new job or not. I'd turned in an inferior job of work today, of which I wasn't proud—but at least I had turned up! Didn't industry sustain a loss of gigantic proportions through people's

240

misuse of their pastime? 'Yes, we were getting up to all sorts of awful things, my flat mate and me this morning! Up with the larks—up to larks with the larks—sorry, rather weak! That's the way it is today. Actually, she didn't go in at all, and she's in a new job as well. Teaching. Her first term. In Essex, it's a bit of a traipse, she has to get up at six every morning anyway.'

Miss Einstein shuddered. 'Oh, I only come from Stepney, but that seems bad enough. How nice to be sharing a flat—' Now from looking wan she'd turned to looking wistful. I thought what havoc that swine Piers would have played with her 'naice'. 'Where is the flat you're sharing?' She managed to inflect the question with a strange and sweet formality, the paragon of politeness, as if in fact what she was saying was 'Would you care for a cucumber sandwich?' Had she turned from me, a child in her class, to write upon the blackboard now—I would have aimed an inky pellet at her arse. And pointed my tongue to make fun. The quality of her refinement provoked an alarming aggression.

I travelled to St Martin's on the tube from Elephant and Castle, changing trains at Charing Cross to take the Northern Line and finish up at Tottenham Court Road. It seemed incredibly seedy there on that corner of Upper Oxford Street, with aimless unemployables leaning against the railings of the entrance to the station. And a general feeling of the flotsam and jetsam of the world. I hurried ahead down Charing Cross Road, in an effort to leave it behind. Our shop existed in streets which had that same feeling, and come to that, even the school where I'd now come to teach. Our flat, for that matter, was hardly impressive in its ambience—would there ever be a time when I might hope for surroundings which were a little more salubrious? It didn't depress me these days as much as it had once, probably because of having been to Art School—I'd learned in fact to look for other things besides the obvious poverty. But even so, those satisfactions—a certain light, a startling shade, the multitude of tones in just one colour such as grey, which could catch you unawares—these satisfactions were such a private matter. I didn't expect that other people might share my special sight.

It hit me right away when I went in, even stopping as I

did to visit the cloakroom first. The intoxications of pigment, sized and hand-primed canvas, hardboard, and the vinegar mix of turpentine and linseed oil, all rushed to my nostrils and reminded me of the world that I'd been missing all these weeks. I breathed it gratefully, I drank it up, I buried myself in it and mentally swooned like some rubber fetishist who's stumbled upon a mackintosh shop! I smiled at myself in the mirror and into the eyes of two regular St Martin's students with me. They both gazed coolly back but I didn't mind, it made no difference. In my time I had done the same. It gives a tremendous state of exclusivity—the being a full-time student. There isn't any need to accept the courtship of the commoner. Those ordinary people, the ones out in the world involved in merely mundane matters like the earning of a living. And art students above all, I'd even thought when I was one, carry their edge of superciliousness to an even greater degree. As if they really had been blessed with second sight and an inner understanding of the universe.

I went upstairs to pay my absurdly minimal term's fee and in addition sign myself on as one of Bernard's students. He happened to come into the office just as I'd finished and his face creased and crumpled with pleasure.

'Well, I'll be buggered! You actually made it!' He chuckled and gave me an affectionate hug. 'Hey, what are you doing in here? Not actually filling in a form? And passing over spondulax? Here, give all that to me—' His voice dropped conspiratorially. 'You silly child! There isn't any need for that—you sit in when you want. I thought I'd made that perfectly clear— you're to come to boost my morale. It's not a question of money! We let the parasites pay for you and I, the artistic likes of us! I'll tell you something—we've got a rum bunch this term. Come up and I'll introduce you. They could do with having a young professional to copy. We'll get you a good front seat. What are you doing today, drawing or painting? Not a bad model—a mangy little thing, like a Munch—all white and wispy—'

What a sweet chap, the old fellow was. Someone from another age. Fired by the flame, bitten by the bug, a devotee to Bohemia—but cuckolded by the Great Creative Urge. I'd seen his paintings, I knew his work, I'd curled my lip at the blatant lack of lifting inspiration. But he did all right, the old boy. He exhibited every year and had as

242

much a name as his contemporaries in various stultified Art Societies. I wasn't sure if he didn't even have letters like R.S.P.P.—Royal Society of Portrait Painters or some such artistic irrelevance.

We'd reached the room in which he held his classes, it was already full. Bernard frowned. 'The buggers can't wait to cast their images on canvas—to waste by the hundredweight their Winsor & Newton water colours, oils, gouaches, charcoal, pencils, paper—Christ!' He groaned. 'Oh, would that Providence smiled her fickle smile on me and spared me this ordeal—'

'Now then, Bernard.' I wagged my finger and pulled a mock prim mouth. 'You know as well as me that this is a very nice number! No sooner than they'll have started and you'll be over to the pub. Unless you've changed, that is. There'll be precious little teaching that's going to tire you out!'

'Now, now!' He tweaked my chin. 'It's not like that up here, you know. Not like trying to talk to your normal snooty student who hasn't the time of day to hear you anyway—poncing off the poor old Welfare State, trying to live the life of Toulouse-Lautrec with legs. No fear, these amateurs are quite frankly a paralysing pain up the arse! You've never seen such enthusiasm. Watch them. To a man, like dogs on heat, I promise you!'

I looked around for a drawing board and a wooden donkey on which to sit. I'd bring my paints with me next week, but this first one I'd spend on drawing. Then, having booked my place already in the front line around the model's dais, I stood up and allowed dear old Bernard to effect a few introductions.

'Oh, it's wonderful,' I said, 'to hear you again! Honestly, Fiona, it is! How did it go up there, and when did you get back? Come on, spill the beans! I can't wait!'

I heard her laugh at the other end. 'We've only just got in. Ten minutes ago or so! But I shall have to be quick because daddy's meaning to be on the phone and I'm meant to be in bed. I've got masses to tell but it needs saying face to face for the full effect! Anyway, what I'm suggesting is that I come up to London this weekend—'

'And stay here? In the flat, you mean? There are only two beds but Pat's going home—I know that this weekend. So you could have hers—'

'Well, I tell you why—there's a frightfully smart party I've been invited to and I wangled you in as well. For Saturday night—that should give us plenty of chance to talk. It's tremendous stuff, honestly! You won't believe!'

The telephone had been ringing as I walked through the door. Pat was obviously out, there weren't any lights on anywhere. Unless she was sleeping already. I replaced the telephone and tip-toed down the passage to open our bedroom door. No. Nothing. No one there. Everything nice and tidy, including my bed I saw. She'd made them both again. The place was cold and uncomfortably quiet, it needed a human voice. I shivered and switched the little wireless on, and twiddled the knobs for some music. Songs for late-night lovers—nice for some, I said it aloud but entirely without any rancour. I'd enjoyed myself this evening. Going to see Bernard had turned out not a bad idea. 'All set? Off to the pub?' He'd collected quite a crowd. 'No, not me thanks. Not tonight.' But they wouldn't take no for an answer.

He'd introduced me before the evening's work commenced. In fact had taken the trouble to introduce all the newcomers to his corps of faithful regulars. It was more like a club than an evening class. Someone had said so too—his name was Nicholas O'Dell, an Irish architect who'd just come down from Edinburgh. He'd been in London a week. I found him very friendly, with a thin, long, wiry body like a worm. Around twenty-seven, his hair the colour of sandy clay, and his eyes pale green like grapes.

'That's a bloody good drawing!' He'd come up behind me at half time.

'Oh, I was just thinking how bad—'

'It's obvious you're no amateur.'

'That's probably exactly what I don't like about it—a cheap set of easy tricks. I haven't had a pencil, or a brush for that matter, in my hand for over a month. I always find I strive for effect when that's happened, to prove I haven't lost my touch.' I looked beyond him and nodded towards the easels at the back. 'Are you one of those?'

'Yup! I'm having a shot at oils—I've always had a yen towards them—but I'm making a hell of a mess. It's sliding all over the place. You could probably give me a few useful tips.'

I smiled at such an obvious ploy. He didn't appeal to me

244

in any way but I sympathised over the work problem. 'Oils are a killer, I can still remember that from when I started. But I always found water colours even worse. You have to really know what you're doing with them. No second chance, no going over ...'

Other people now joined in, amateurs all, but every one with an opinion. All united by the binding bond of genuine enthusiasm. Knowledge. An intimate understanding of the chemical changes, the fugitive qualities, the effects of ageing and atmosphere, the out-and-out nature of the practical means employed in their self-expression was of total irrelevance here. Personal experience was the only prerequisite. Opinions based on that alone. Like my father on the subject of politics. 'In my opinion and what I've always found—' That was how he had come to fascism and a deep admiration of Oswald Mosley, indeed. From a personal experience, so he claimed, which dated back to the thirties. 'I'd managed to get this job cleaning cars in a garage—oh, don't look like that, my girl, there were graduates queueing up like the rest of us for anything in those days. Bloody true, there were! Buggers from Oxford and Cambridge glad to get milkman's jobs—' The isolated, though unfortunate, incident, had occurred in a London garage, when a Bentley accidentally ran over his big toe whilst he was happening to be polishing a windscreen. The quite arbitrary fact that the cigar-smoking driver appeared to be recognisably Jewish seemed somehow of special significance. It had triggered off the irrational and almost obsessive hatred of what he so often delighted in referring to as the Chosen Race. His emotional support of Oswald Mosley had led him to almost becoming an actual party member. But my mother had put her foot down. The only time she ever had in my own recollection. She said she'd leave him and take me with her if she had to see another single blackshirt goose-stepping up our garden path. It was humiliating to be Heil Hitlered with neighbours looking on. And extremely embarrassing to be seen stuffing fascist pamphlets down her pinafore pocket. He was to stop this nonsense once and for all. She wouldn't have it! Understood? And so, on the surface, he'd stopped. He surveyed the world and solved its problems, political and otherwise, from the comfortable platform of our shop counter. My mother still maintained, and I occasionally backed her up in it, that she wouldn't like to count the number of customers that he'd alienated and subsequently lost us with his views. A whole philosophy based on self-important ignorance and prejudice.

Bernard waved to me above his students', his amateur students', heads. He winked. But I didn't return the deprecating gesture or actually, come to that, I couldn't quite share his contempt. It seemed to me to be quite marvellous that all these people felt the urge so strongly as to give up one whole evening, and obviously spend as much as they were spending on such grand equipment. One man, now working feverishly right through the break, filling in the background without the model there—he'd actually bought himself a proper, perfectly pleated artist's smock and was wearing a beret on his head to complete the pathetic picture. But, underneath, his pressed and perfectly tailored trouser-cuffs told a different story. We'd never worn artist's smocks at art school, the most I managed were my mother's old pinnies, or my father's discarded shirts, tied round the back of the waist by their sleeves. In addition to the artist's smock, this evening painter held in the crook of his arm at the fine appropriate angle—as artists are always depicted—an extremely expensive painters' palette with each colour in the spectrum squeezed round its edge like droppings in the bottom of a bird cage. But even so there was in his intensity something quite impressive. Bernard would try it on, I knew, pin-pointing this poor little sod—but I'd refuse to join him in his cruelty. We all returned to work. An hour had flown. I'd scaled the heights of satisfaction and descended to despair as I failed to match my image with my hand. Ten minutes before the end I'd torn my drawing up—the work of over two hours. But then in almost minutes I'd managed to capture in a set of lightning lines, almost exactly what I was after anyway. The evening had been saved—I had salvaged something.

Nicholas O'Dell had not been quite so successful. 'What do you think?' He'd called me over. 'What is your expert opinion?'

'Well, now . . .' I studied his messy canvas and held my head to one side as if absorbed in critical thought.

'Go on. You can be as beastly as you like, but give an honest opinion.'

'The basics are there . . .' I didn't care to crush his boyish

246

eagerness.

'Are they? Well, that's a start.' He stood so close that I could smell his slightly sweaty underarms, it wasn't my favourite scent by any means. That's what I'd liked about Derek, how extremely careful he'd been regarding his bodily odours. After-shave everywhere despite the fact of course he didn't. Shave.

'Yes, what I mean is this—' and I gave the keen young architect a full five minutes of considered, though very kind, criticism. Turning at the end of it, feeling suddenly tired, I collided with the owner of the artist's smock. 'Who was that chap in the artist's smock?' I said to Bernard later.

'Oh him, yes he's been with me quite a time, over a year I think. Strange chap. Some sort of an industrialist. Plenty of cash I imagine. Polish prick. I'd thought of trying to flog him something of mine—got no family, just himself. Has a chauffeur who comes to collect him.'

'What's his work like? I didn't manage to see it.'

Bernard held his nose between two fingers as if faced with a putrid stench. 'Just like all the rest of them or, if anything, worse.' We were sitting round a table in the pub, Nicholas O'Dell was on my right. Bernard removed his fingers from his nose and cupped his mouth with his hand. 'What,' he spoke in a loud stage whisper, 'do you think of that young pup—a pushover for you, wouldn't you say?' And he threw his head back against the mirrored wall behind him and gave a bellowing laugh.

He was a pushover, Nicholas, I knew that all right. But nothing about him interested me. 'What's the industrialist's name?' Bernard had stopped spluttering and now exaggeratedly dropped his jaw. 'You don't mean to say that that old fart could stand a chance! Mind you,' he suddenly became sober. 'The money might not be half bad. You could give up that lousy teaching job and concentrate on your work, you idle bitch. Have you thought of capitalising on your obvious physical advantages? Not that any girl worth her onions would put up with an oldster like that in bed! Christ, if I thought for a minute that you would, I'd be trying it on myself! It's allowable now, you know, you're no longer my student— ethically and all that, I mean.' And he lifted my hand, and turned it over to plant a kiss on my palm. I hugged him—he'd always been a favourite, the best one of our teachers, but as to anything further, I knew him too well for that. Too familiar for familiarities.

The flat felt so chilly, and so irredeemably unfriendly with no one there but me, that as I was undressing for bed I changed my mind and decided to have a bath. Back to the womb of warmth and comfort. The bottom of the bath was pock-marked with peeling enamel. I swept quite sizeable pieces into the plug hole, pushing them down with my finger-tips, before letting the water run. Our bath was much like this at home, stained with brilliant orange rust, streaked like an evening sky. If I could have chosen, I would have liked above all else a really sumptuous bath. Black with the proper shower attachment overhead, instead of bits of rubber hose that you had to squash on to the taps. This one didn't even have one of those. I went to the kitchen and brought back a saucepan for swilling shampoo from my hair. Then I got in.

I could have cried from the welcome the water gave me. You were far better off in water than walking around in the air. You opened out, you spread yourself, you surrendered, as it were. You felt in fact the opposite of how I'd felt—was it only this morning—with Douglas. I slipped for a minute completely beneath the surface, outstretched like a floating Ophelia. I felt my hair change character as it got wet. It dripped and clung to my eyebrows and over my ears, and opening my eyes, I saw that hair, much lower down, that nicely bushy shape turn darker still and even curlier, as if it had been permed. I crossed my legs at the ankles and carefully studied my navel. If I pushed hard with my thumb I felt a dull pain start inside and if I rubbed around it with the bar of soap, a tiny waterfall of bubbles poured down into its well. Lying at my present elongated angle, my breasts appeared to be as perfect as was possible. I looked at them dispassionately thinking how strange it was that two such perfectly ordinary pieces of flesh could excite such desire in men. My nipple gradually stiffened as I licked it with my tongue. The other one lay lonely and unattended, still flaccid on the other side. I lifted my hand and rolled the gristly little peak between my thumb and finger—within minutes both now stood proud and erect. I got up dripping wet to take a look in the mirror. I had to admit it made a pretty sight. If someone were to walk in here right now and plunge themselves into my pussy—I thought. I picked up the soap and rubbed it all over my pubic hair—it went white and

248

whiskery with lather. I sat down again, this time with my
knees as wide apart as they would go. What would happen
if I pushed hard in there with a bar of soap? Might it get
lost altogether? Could I close up? Conceal it inside? I
rubbed it the whole length, starting from the clitoris end
until I reached my bum. The trouble was you could be
walking along with bubbles floating out of your bum
like those metal rings that children dip in little pots
of soap solution. People, passers-by, might well approach
'Excuse me miss, you seem to be making bubbles down
below ...' Yes, strangely enough I do, I'd have to say,
it's simply a piece of soap that slipped inside in the bath.
No doubt it will melt away in time— hardly a cause for
concern.

A gnawing tenseness spread slowly around the area. I
varied my movements now using the soap as my weapon
and turning the tap gently to get an even warmer stream of
water between my legs. What a way to end the day. Who
needs other people? I sucked the insides of my lips and
uttered several soft aahs. Then as the delicious feelings
gradually escalated I quickly turned over on to my
stomach and pressed my crutch hard down on the old
enamel. There wasn't sufficient contact though the
thrilling tension remained. So feeling that some peak of
pleasure loomed suddenly in sight, I slid my arm under my
body and straddling myself on my knuckles, worked
feverishly through to the end.

I was asleep when Pat came in, and would have liked to
have remained so, I'd taken such ages to get off. I'd
somehow embarked on long-term planning of my classes,
what I'd give them all to do tomorrow, and how I'd start to
organise an after-school-hours special Art Club—to
which girls with extraordinary ability could come. I didn't
doubt that I should find at least a handful in that school.
With clever coaxing and encouragement, probably even
more. What Bernard hadn't been able to understand was
that I actually enjoyed teaching, siphoning my own ideas
through other minds. Tomorrow I would make up for my
appalling indolence today. I fell asleep bathed in the
smiles of Mrs Pritchard and lifted to the heights by the
congratulations of the District Inspector.

She'd put the light full on and was whirling around the
room. 'Wheee, wheee!' She went. 'Wheee, wheee!' I buried
my head in my pillow and brought my blankets higher

than my eyes, but it wouldn't wash, she wanted an audience. It was half-past two in the morning! I gave in and rubbing my eyes, sat up. 'I got him, kid, wow! Yes! I got him all right—no trouble!'

'Got? What? Who? When?' She dazzled me more than the light.

'Me. I got him. Had him. Ate him up. A piece of cake. No kidding!' Her radiance and the sparsity of hard fact set off a seeping irritation.

'Great,' I said and prepared myself to lie down. I yawned. 'Tell me it all tomorrow ...' It did the trick, she fell beside me on the bed and wrapped her arms around me. I smelt her perfume, Miss Dior mingling with Silvikrin shampoo. We'd have to go halves on a shower attachment. You could get the best ones from Boots.

'Roly. That's who, you fathead. I've just had him—old Roly Balls!' And she sat back to watch the information sinking in.

'Christ, but that's quick off the mark—no sooner the first than the second. What happened to dear old Douglas?'

She tossed the glorious mane impatiently. 'Oh, we stayed in bed till twelve o'clock or so, then had a drink in the pub. Then I kissed him goodbye on the pavement. I'm sure I shan't see him again. But I thanked him for such an admirable service—'

'But where did you bump into Roly Balls?'

'Oh, well, I telephoned Mark, of course, and just wangled it on from there. Actually, I waited a while for you, it would have been better if you'd been there. Mark stuck with us and got to be a bit of a gooseberry, but'—she slid a lacquered nail along her lower lip—'it came out all right in the end!'

Now I was wide awake. 'Pass me my coat, I'm freezing. Can you make us a cup of tea—and put the heater on? I'm buying a hot water bottle tomorrow. I'm certain these beds are damp.'

At ten past three I persuaded her that we should get some sleep. 'It's all right for you,' I said, 'you've been resting all afternoon, whilst I've been slaving away at school. Did you ring, by the way, and let them know at yours? I take it you'll be going in tomorrow.'

'With a doctor's certificate too.'

'That's clever, where from?'

'Roly, of course! On Guy's Hospital headed notepaper! It's useful that, isn't it? The Out Patients Department— there'll never be any check.' But he hadn't seen her home. She'd had to get her own taxi. It didn't sound right to me, smacked a bit too much of Derek. 'You're okay on your own, aren't you? I can't be bothered to get out of bed—run quick and you'll catch the last bus—'

The light was out, but neither of us was asleep. I lay on my side to shut out the sound of her tossing, my weak ear to the wind. From very far away it seemed I heard her final words, and the subtly different note now the first hysteria had seemed to pass. 'The funny thing is, you know, kid'—she paused as if not willing to actually put her thoughts into something as concrete as words—'that of the two of them, I think that Douglas was much better. I mean he really made me feel so extra special afterwards. Why do you think that was?' I gave a grunt as answer. 'Though of course,' she continued, as if now speaking only to herself, 'to have got Roly after all this time of worshipping from afar. But I had to give him my number. He didn't ask for it afterwards. Bastard!' This time I didn't even bother to grunt. Not even in agreement.

I managed, of all things and for the first time, to find a seat on the tube. And I managed—more important—to be almost the first one in. Mrs Pritchard preceded me, but only just, by the length of her Lilley & Skinner brogues. We smiled winningly at each other and she nodded her Marcel wave in matronly approval of my punctuality. 'Nothing to beat an early start—' 'Every time,' I found myself agreeing, a shade too eagerly for comfort. And trailed off 'as you say'. But I'd had a very early training in the art of cliché; it was quite the normal method of communication in our shop. Words arrived unbeckoned, out of nowhere, simply to fill the discomfort created by a silence. 'What a day!' 'Yes, what indeed!' 'This driving rain—' 'Wicked weather—' She sailed above me up the concrete stairs from the senior playground, supported by a smudgy suede-gloved hand, the colour of coffee gateaux. It worried me, the way she slid it up the iron balustrade—the rust could easily ruin it. Perhaps one should suggest she run her other glove coming down, when she was leaving to go home. To even up each palm.

251

We reached the ground floor staff-room having left the problem behind. 'Well,' she laid a friendly, though patronising, rusty glove upon my shoulder. 'This I fear is where you and I part company! Have a good day, my dear! Fight the good fight.' I lifted my chin to the challenge. 'And forge ahead.' Something related to suspicion flickered across her face. But then it had gone. My guilelessness must have reassured. She patted me again. 'Quite so. Quite so.' And moved determinedly towards the room of her high office.

The brief encounter had exhausted me, I collapsed into the lower staff-room and peeled the orange I'd bought at Earls Court Station yesterday and now discovered, as spongy as a rubber ball, at the bottom of my bag. It filled the air and emptiness around me with a joyous pungent juice. I ate each segment slowly, one by one, waiting for the surge of instant energy. Pat had claimed that's what her breakfast did for her. I'd lain, barely awake this morning, watching her munch two Mars bars as she dressed. And three-quarters of a Kit-Kat as she combed her hair. 'You don't deserve a skin like yours—or a set of teeth—with all that sugar, Pat,' I'd said. She tossed it off. 'Oh, it doesn't have time to do the damage. I burn it too quickly in nervous energy—'bye.' And she'd gone.

Winnie Einstein, for various reasons, was the only member of staff so far that I'd got to grips with at all. This lower staff-room unofficially housed the fuddier duddies who'd been at this same school almost straight from college. Certainly long before the days of Mrs Pritchard. They formed a tight conservative clique, a holier than thou attitude and a horrifying disregard for the principles of teaching. The upper staff-room, on the other hand, apart from lying adjacent to my own art room and therefore adjacent to Winnie Einstein, that staff-room, sparser and more spartan altogether, lacking the lumpy armchairs of the lower—all booked proprietorially in order of seniority anyway—that room was where I felt more welcome. One of the regulars came in now. Miss Bowen, Plymouth Brethren, who looked like something from Dickens. She also, unfortunately, shared the same floor as Winnie and myself, teaching by the book and a rigorous system of discipline backed up by the cane, teaching Religious Instruction throughout the school and Junior Maths to the Fifth. That was quite in order. I understood that there

252

were girls in the Fifth who still couldn't spell their own names. This side short of educationally subnormal. Another reason to check your change in different shops like Woolworth's where most of them worked on Saturdays and would work there all week as soon as they managed to leave.

Miss Bowen lifted her equine nose and began violently flaring her nostrils. She pursed her imperceptible lips—I'd read that somewhere, something Laurence Olivier claimed—that your lips disappear as you get older. His had. Hers now were non-existent. The red corpuscles had packed it in. Had given up the ghost and refused to gather any more in any orderly line along her facial orifice. Her pale and creased and dusty skin stretched, quite unbroken, from one ear-lobe to the other, interrupted only by a set of rabbit teeth and the twin exits of her bony proboscis. It was raining outside, but she opened the window nevertheless and frowned disapprovingly down at my orange peel. She put her hand high up to a liberty-bodiced ribcage and spoke reedily in a thin, whining voice full of the gaseous fumes of which she was about to complain.

'I suffer so dreadfully from dyspepsia that I have to beware of even the very air I breathe. I apologise if I seem to over-react, but I haven't had an orange and certainly none other of the citrus fruits for something like fifteen years. The acidity, you see.' She had hung her coat in the adjoining cloakroom and now rearranged her hair. 'It's usually my habit to get here first,' she gave a thin smile, 'and have this staff-room to myself. I like to settle my stomach and organise the day. I find the quiet start invaluable.'

'I'm just off,' I said. And fled upstairs.

The day went well. Being so early, I also managed to organise myself, appointing a whole eager team of dinner money monitors, register markers, and, even should I be so late as to miss the whole of Assembly ever, I appointed a team of ten who should herd all of 1D into Assembly with the minimum of fuss. This I felt was essential if my life looked like continuing on its present course of burning at both ends.

Winnie Einstein was late; I could hear the hullaballoo from the sanctuary of my well-ordered calm. 1D sat waiting for Assembly Bell, their grubby nail-bitten fists folded at my suggestion on their uniformed fronts. Across the corridor I could hear the hysterical persistent whine of Miss Bowen who'd be more than pleased I knew to pinpoint the inadequacies of either Winnie Einstein or myself. 'Not a word now, 1D, I warn you—I'm just going to see to 1C.' And putting a squinting scrap called Sylvia Sound in charge, in the fleeting thought that her surname denoted the required dependence of character, I crossed the corridor to 1C.

The pandemonium died down slowly, starting from those nearest to the door. I stood there, proud and beautiful, magnificently menacing, pointing to no one in particular with my lifted arm. It always worked a treat, that one—I'd tried it before in teaching practice. It set up the ripples of a chilling nervousness, each child glancing straight from me to somewhere over its shoulder at the nearest neighbour in an effort to deflect attention. The next trick was the opening of my mouth, together with a lowering, dramatic lowering of the brow—as if to launch on a bellow to blow each eardrum up in smithereens. It worked. And it was working now. Small girls rearranged themselves from top to bottom, slipped into entirely different shapes. Wiped clean all signs of life from every single feature and stared almost in a state of unconscious terror at my face. Now I could speak.

'Now I can speak,' I whispered. And carefully stepped across the silence as they strained to hear what I'd say next. But instead I swiftly called Winnie Einstein's register and took her dinner money in record seconds before the pealing for Assembly and the coinciding sight of Winnie herself appeared sweating and almost tearful at the entrance of the room. She looked at me with much the same expression as the dog wears in those illustrations for *His Master's Voice* except she managed to keep her tongue still in her mouth instead of lolling, as she might have let it, down to the fold of her chin. I wished she hadn't looked like that—I couldn't help it, it made me want to kick her.

But the work itself, the teaching part, the geeing-up of the children, and the carving out of vulnerable and soul-lifting slivers of imaginative creation, that went as I would have wished. Me or any District Inspector worth his salt. Only one child I managed to miss, to by-pass altogether, to not touch at all. 'I think'—she'd sat there doing nothing long after the others, enthralled by my description of a

254

forest scene in storm, had lost themselves in swirling washes of midnight blue and clouds the colour of cheese, and fearsome Hammer Film trees—'I think,' she'd said to me conspiratorially, 'I'll paint my bunny.' And even then I didn't get it right. 'Well,' I'd said at the end of the lesson, 'it's a very good bunny too.' But she'd looked at me quite mutinously then, her mouth turned down in disappointment at my crass insensitivity. 'It's not my bunny—it's my grandad!' 'But you said, dear, that you were going to do your bunny—' She turned her back and answered short and to the point: 'I changed my mind though, miss.'

By the end of the day I had 119 storms pegged up and pinned and laying flat around my room to dry. And one old gent resembling someone's rabbit.

Winnie Einstein came into the room as I was finally clearing up. 'Good Lord,' she said breathily. 'My word, but you've been busy.'

'Haven't you?' I felt completely knackered, but it would pass, I knew, that feeling, so much of it was backed by satisfaction with oneself.

'I can't thank you enough for what you did this morning—honestly I can't.'

'That's okay. I only hope you'll do the same for me. I was early this morning, but I'm an appalling time-keeper normally. I don't care though. I like poor old 1D, but it gets on my nerves all this register lark, etc. I haven't done dinner duty yet—or playground duty if it comes to that. When are you? This week? And by the way, do old boots like Miss Bowen do those things as well?'

She shrugged. 'It doesn't worry me too much. To be quite frank, I'd as soon do the duties as teach—'

'Why on earth are you doing it then? Why not take another job? Work in an office or something?'

She sighed. 'It's not a decision I remember taking on my own, to be quite truthful. My mother was the keen one—well, it means you've joined the professional classes, doesn't it! That's all-important to her. And to be quite honest, even this is a disappointment. All my brothers and sisters did much, much better than me, straight through to universities, three at Oxford. All academics still—professorships and all that sort of thing. But I failed my first year at University College and ended up at a training college, barely scraping through. I knew I'd fail, you know, and I so dreaded it that I sat with nothing on all night in my mother's back yard with snow on the ground as she slept—so that I'd be so ill in the morning that I wouldn't be able to go and even sit the exams. But do you know'—her voice took on its baby lisping lilt—'I didn't even catch a tiny cold! Can you imagine that?'

Yes, I thought, I can, Winnie, with the sort of luck you have! She hung around until I'd finished then followed me to the staff-room.

'Oh Christ.' I sank into a chair. 'Can you get the kettle on missus?' and I smiled at her to reassure against the irritability in my voice. I'd sounded like my father. 'I sound just like my dad!'

'Oh really?' I wished she'd keep her doggie palliness in some control instead of letting it out on such a loose familiar leash. Now she was pausing in some slow pose of concentrated memory, the kettle, that lift-me-up and life-giver—held limply in her hand. Instead of where it should have been by now, already on the boil. 'Yes,' she continued. 'My father used to rule our roost with a Victorian air of attempted authority—when mummy let him, of course. I honestly think—it's the considered opinion of the entire family—that he chose to opt out of life because of her. She's the hardest taskmaster of all. Absolutely matriarchal.'

I stared at the kettle. My throat, right through to somewhere round my navel, was dusty dry with black-board chalk and too much talk. Each child today had had the benefit of my further education. I'd have to coax my larynx back to life within the next five minutes or else. I interrupted brutally: 'Are you getting the kettle on or not?' And instantly regretted it. The blink came first and then a complicated crocheting of muscles round her mouth, which seemed in turn to radically change the angle of her chin. It jutted, that's all that could be said, like a constipated crocodile, and turned myopically away, making it now impossible to tell just what her mood might be. But I'd become a master-hand at moods. Merely from living with my father and simply from having to accommodate such swift, not even superficial, alterations in the lie of the land of Derek's changeable reactions. Cajoling was the sort of stock-in-trade I practised with my finger-tips. 'Here,' I spoke so warmly that I might have struck a match and lit the fuse between us. 'Winnie. I can't think what I'm thinking of. There is no possible reason why you should put the kettle on for me. Here, you sit down and let me make the tea.' She didn't turn at once, but only in the time it took to swallow and breathe again on a more regular basis. In actual fact it didn't matter much to me if she never turned again because by then I'd taken the cursed kettle from the limping hand and lit the gas and slammed the two together with the appropriate noise and cheerful vigour that one of Winnie Einstein's sensitivity might reasonably expect from someone like me. I had no wish to now confuse her further. She'd marked me down already in a register of her own—as I had already marked her.

We drank our tea together in quite companionable silence. I used the time to wonder what I'd do tonight and what, as well, to do tomorrow with my classes. And then I found before I'd even come to any decision on those two questions, my mind had leapt ahead to Saturday night and what I'd wear for Fiona's party. Winnie was talking. 'Oh, I'm sorry,' I said. 'I was thinking.'

'That's what I was asking. What were you thinking?'

'Oh. Things.' Which would I choose to tell her? What topic would excite her most? 'Well, to be more specific, I was actually wondering what to wear to a party I'm going to this weekend—'

An official of the Electricity Board somewhere had flicked a switch behind her eyes at the precise point of the word 'party'. 'Oh!' She shone. 'A party.' The kiddie lisp was taking over. 'I love parties. I've always loved parties. As a child I couldn't wait to pull the cracker and wear the hat and shake the jelly. You should see the way I shake a jelly.' And laying her teacup on the table, and before I'd had a chance to swallow what tea there was already in my mouth, she'd stood up and was demonstrating in an elephantine movement her personal method of jelly-shaking. I burnt my tongue quite badly as scalding liquid hit me. I judged it fair to say that jiggling her jelly in this grotesque samba tango could wrench both mammary glands clean from her central trunk. But for an instant, as I stood, further nightmares seemed about to happen as she mistook my movement as a wish to join her in her wantonness. I hastily waved the approaching revolving nipples away. 'Time for off—' And at my words she stopped as suddenly as she'd started, the disappointed child. My God, but that highly qualified and academic, intellectual, all-ambitious family of hers—those bright impressive brothers, those scintillating witty sisters, that matriarchal mother, and the dead dejected daddy—what indulgences they must have lavished on this littlest child of all. I looked at her and thanked someone, somewhere, for my own abrasive father. And what it had made of me, such that of the two of us standing there so similar in age, I was the one who patronised with my pity. And struggled somewhere not so far from the surface to control the sadism she so effortlessly aroused in me. It seemed that I had got the better deal.

Pat, it was becoming obvious, was able through some miraculous speed of light to actually arrive home before me. How, I'd said to her, I'd never understand. Was she bunking off the last two lessons, or what? What need was there to hang about, once the day was done? That's what she'd answered when I'd asked. And in any case, so she'd continued, what had I found to do out at Elephant and Castle that could possibly take until now?

'Oh, don't go on. You sound just like a nagging wife! I had to hang the paintings up, and clear my room and after that I had a cup of tea with Winnie Einstein. She did a little dance for me—a kind of cabaret.' I laughed, preparing to elaborate further.

'I've made your bed again,' she said, a trifle sourly before I had a chance.

'Oh did you? That was decent. You don't have to though, you know.'

'I don't have to. No, I don't! But how do you think it feels coming in at the end of a day faced with the sort of mess that this flat is in—'

Oh, hell! Whatever could have happened! 'What's happened, Pat? Is anything the matter?' Something was up, judging by her martyred mouth and the general air of injury.

'Fiona phoned!'

What was I feeling guilty about in that. She phoned. So? 'When?'

'Just now. She said she'd phone again.'

'Oh.' I raised my voice deliberately to strike a chatty level. 'Did you talk to her? At any length I mean? She's thinking of coming up on Saturday—'

'Yes. So she said.' She tossed a titian lock which curled around her chin and turning violently to face me squarely, she almost spat at me. 'Yes, so she said! And what she said as well was that she's sleeping in my fucking bed! But I'll leave it to you to tell her she bloody isn't! So there! I'm buggered if I'm paying half the rent for that stuck-up turd to filthy my bed linen—and in any case for that matter'—her voice became nearer to normality—'it won't have any sheets. I'll be taking those home for mum to do in the laundry. Along with all my washing.'

I got in as quickly as I could, it seemed the easiest entry. 'Oh, will you? What a good idea. I don't know what I'll do with mine, though I've seen there's a launderette near my school. I could take them in in the morning and collect them at the end of the day—that's if one of the women who work there will see to it all for me.' I'd engaged her attention momentarily and lifted the lid from the siphon. 'Otherwise, I suppose I could do it in my spare lessons, in that free time—' She stuck her lower lip stubbornly along the line of her upper. 'What about a cigarette?' I said. But she shook her head without speaking. God! Was she going to sulk? That would make two of them in one day! But no, she'd decided to speak. And she'd decided as well to take a cigarette. I lit it for her and she inhaled, extracting the maximum amount for dramatic effect— I hadn't thought before how like Bette Davis she was. 'You look just like Bette Davis, doing that, the half closing of the eyes. Or perhaps more Rita Hayworth. As she was in *Gilda*. You ought to think of getting a long cigarette holder. It would suit you. Honestly!' I'd scratched the surface of her vanity at least—the alley cat leanness melted into something more Siamese, but even so she wasn't prepared to relent altogether.

'No! I'm just not having it, that bitch sleeping in my bed! You should have heard the way she spoke to me just now! I mean to say, you'd think that pater knowing his precious daughter was planning to live in London—you'd think, since he's in the know—that he would have found a flat for her or us, after all—' She looked very pretty, aggrieved, in a truculent kind of way. Her lips were painted a primrose yellow sort of pink—a peachy, creamy shade I hadn't seen before. I pointed.

'New? Very nice.'

She nodded. 'Yes, new. Now, what you ought to say to her on the telephone is. "Yes, that she can stay, but she'll have to bring her bed"—'

259

'Her bed! Oh, come on Pat! Her bed? How can she bring her bed? What up on the train? Don't be daft—'

'Not necessarily up on the train. Look, I've thought it all out! I'm not daft, and neither are you! This isn't going to be the only time that she'll be coming up and expecting to stay here, is it? And what is going to happen, for instance, when I shall be here too? Where the hell will she sleep then? It's only by chance I'm going home this weekend—it being mum's birthday, I mean. No, what you've got to say is that she must provide a bed. And more than that—' Her voice had now become persuasive, even coaxing. Cunning. 'Yes, really more than that—a—wait for it—double bed! It's obvious from last night, no not last night, the night before, with Douglas—it's obvious that we need one for when we entertain!' I looked at her. She had the business sense my father lacked. Had probably inherited it from her plumber dad. Anyone, anybody, given the right approach to life and money, could make a success of any chosen field. Of course what we needed was a double bed! A comfortable working surface. The space on which to relax. The extra degree of privacy. Privacy. Privacy where?

'I have to admit to you, Pat, that it sounds like a master plan. But where had you thought of putting it, that's if she comes up with the goods? Not in here—'

'No! Ye Gods, you painters—no sense of space—no inkling of design or the artistic appreciation of the possibilities in your environment! The kitchen. Of course! That's where we'd put the double bed, in the kitchen. We ask for a bed-settee. To sit on in the day. And use at random any time, as a breeding ground for passion—turned into a double bed!'

'That's cute. In the kitchen. Of course. But will she wear it? Will she turn up trumps? I mean to say, you said yourself that Fiona is tight-fisted.'

'It won't actually cost her that much. Two quid to be exact!'

'Two quid! What do you mean two quid?'

She stubbed her cigarette out triumphantly in the kitchen sink. The sizzle accompanied her smile. 'I've bought it already, second-hand. They're delivering it tonight!'

It wasn't bad, I had to say, considering the price. It had about it a curiously affectionate air—as one who'd once

260

been loved but now looked rather bashed about. Like a
teddy bear who'd had to put up with too much hugging.
'Oh yes, Patty—I can see all manner of naughtinesses
taking place on this! Oh, what was Roly's bed like, by the
way?'

'We won't go into that,' she said darkly.

'Why not?' I could see she really wanted to say.

'Perhaps it was my fault—I shouldn't have looked—'

'Looked? Looked where? What at?' That was something
she did share with Fiona, a wildly inquisitive nose. An
almost manic need to know. Not something I went in for
myself—for fear of finding something too unpleasant or
disturbing, so I reasoned. In many situations, ignorance
remained a preferable state.

'Stains.'

I was pouring boiling water on some Bovril in a beaker.
'Beg pardon, Pat? You saw some stains, you say?'

'On the sheets! There was no mistaking them.'

I thought a minute. She must be meaning mucus.
'Maybe he butters bread in bed . . .' But I knew what mucus
meant. I'd seen it more than once, and not mine, either. On
Derek's sheets, in Derek's bed. I might have pointed, many
times, and made an issue of it. 'That mucus there. It's
not one that I recognise—not one I've seen before—' A
person's mucus is a source of pleasure to oneself, that
springs in part from instant recognition. Another's
mucus, on the other hand, raises a fearful feeling of
depression. I knew how poor Pat felt. Though it could
have been worse. In Derek's bed, I'd found an alien
snotball one afternoon underneath the pillow. On my
side. In the sun.

'Yes, stains, and what was worse, some stockings and a
brassière hanging in the bathroom.'

'Does he go in for dressing up? Many medical students
do . . .'

She looked miserable. 'These belonged to someone
small. About the size of me—he'd never have fitted into
them. You know how huge he is—' She was being
unreasonable. Of course they belonged to another
girl—there was no reason for him to be celibate. In any
case she herself, Pat, had hours before been with Douglas.
What did she expect?

'Some Bovril? I burned my tongue at school today, I
couldn't cope with anything more solid.'

She shook her head. 'I've had a snack already. What will we do tonight? Roly won't ring, I know it.' I knew it too and was trying to work out how to warn her not to bank on him anyway when the ring of the telephone interrupted before I'd even got there. She ran. She bounded like an arrow from the bow to answer it as if by saying he wouldn't ring, she'd altered the course of fate and made him do so. It was for me. Not bad, well, better than nothing anyway.

'He's nice,' I said. 'An architect. His name is Nicholas O'Dell. Bit niffy under the armholes—'

'Oh, very nice indeed!'

Wine, and bits and bobs to eat, come as soon as you can. What now? Why not! Just give him a chance to change his shirt, he'd said. So we hung around for an hour, just to make doubly sure.

It was straight through on the District Line to Notting Hill Gate, where he lived, sharing a pad with two others, two pals he'd been students with. Get out at the station and walk down Holland Park Avenue—it's the turning on the right before Holland Park, and we're the second house. Right at the top I'm afraid.

'It's a bit of a traipse, this, isn't it!' Pat was wearing her highest heels, though I had advised against it.

'They're only ordinary—well, Nicholas is—you don't want to overdress.'

'They're architects, aren't they?'

'Yes, but Pat, we'll be seeing them just at home. It's not a party or anything special, after all. Only a get-together—all being new in London. Their flat won't probably be as flash as this—' I'd only said that to please her.

'Do you honestly think it's flash, our flat?'

'Well, it is, when you get inside. With all you've done, I mean. Painting the kitchen floor and hanging up your patterns. The approach of course leaves a lot to be desired. But I'm used to a sordid exterior, it doesn't distress me too much.' I was lying. From the pavement, through the greasy green front door, along the depressing corridor before even descending our basement stairs to reach our own flat door, I was already finding to be indescribably dingy and bleak. Even to the point of neither looking left nor right at entry time or exit, but instead keeping a clear picture in my mind of what within seconds I should expect to see. Leaving, the bursting blinding cloud-strewn sky above Old Brompton Road. And arriving, the warm oasis

262

of our warren. 'We're a bit like rabbits. You and I in our burrow. And will be even more so when we put Fiona's bed into action. Who do you think, Patty, will be misbehaving on it first? You or me?' Though come to that, why not Fiona?

We'd arrived already at the corner of our turning. She suddenly stopped and faced me, faintly embarrassed as she spoke. 'Yes, that was what I was meaning to ask—what do you reckon was the trouble with Douglas?'

'With Douglas? Why? He was very good, wasn't he? You said last night he was better than Roly Balls.'

'With you, I meant,' she floundered. 'You know, not getting in.'

I'd known exactly what she meant. But what was there to say. Except the truth, of course. 'I think I tense myself too much. Just at the last minute. I try to loosen up, you know—I think that's what it is. The more they push, the worse it gets. What do you think, anyway?'

'I can't understand the complication. He slipped in me like a spoon in jelly, but I tell you what he said after you'd gone, he said you—'

'Hold on now, here we are!' And we were as well, at Nicholas' number, and more than that was Nicholas hanging high above us and waving from the top-most window.

'The key,' he said, and threw it down. I welcomed the interruption. Who wished to know, in any case what Douglas had bloody said!

The evening was uneven. Pat hated them all on sight, and what was worse, they hated her. She didn't speak, or hardly, for an hour. Which in the end turned out to be exactly right since she'd used up the time with imbibing a sizeable quantity of disgustingly sweet white wine. I'd taken a mouthful on arrival and had tactfully asked to be switched to the sourer vinegar red. Did architects not then earn so much? Not with the L.C.C. Oh, Civil Servants then, like us, I'd said. If you're working in County Hall. We get paid, or I do anyway—Pat was glaring sulkily over the street—I get paid from County Hall as well. That's where I went for my interview. I thought of the District Inspector and the texture of his skin and the way his filbert nails lay so gracefully in their fleshy beds. What finger-tips he had. His hand in mine. Nicholas and his two flat mates fawned upon me, their faces open and uncomplicated. There wasn't a line, a wrinkle or a crease, not anywhere on those facial canvases. The emptiness didn't endear.

The other two appeared to be marginally younger than Nicholas, the difference that National Service can make. He'd done his first before he'd started studying. But all three of them were really Peter Pans, believing their boyishness to be endearing to a girl like me. I could have told them right away that they were batting on a very wrong wicket. But Pat, on the other hand, had always seemed quite partial to that waggy, puppy-dog quality. I couldn't think quite what was up with her tonight— unless her haughtiness was just a cover up for far more complicated feelings. She might have been impressed, it now occurred to me, by the stylish simplicity of the surroundings. The house was very grand. The exterior, smoothly plastered to disguise the bricks, had been painted Persil white. And the heavy wooden carved front door had been brought back to natural gnarled finish by judicious use of a blow torch, and a sealing coat of varnish. Inside was painted white as well, all the way up the stairs with natural haircord carpet on each landing and neatly fitted over every step. I'd thought of our crass Axminster at home. A vitriolic puce and damson jam. Out from the Co-op and nailed to our stairs before I'd a chance to say aye nor nay. 'What do you think then, girl?' My father had stood, with hammer still in hand. 'Eh? What do you think—as the colour expert? Your old dad's not done too badly, has he?' He bent. 'Not a bad pile to it. Almost as deep as a finger-nail, see! Should stand a spot of good wear, I'd say. Yes, what's the general opinion then—it's listed as Primavera, but I myself would call it more autumnal hues.'

Yes, Pat had grown silent swaying up the stairs, now I came to think of it. And when we'd reached their tasteful Ivory door right at the top, her mouth had already shaped itself into a sulky bow. Perhaps she thought I might be blaming her in some vague abstract sense for not finding us a place like theirs. I looked around. They'd painted the ceiling throughout the place a harsh and shrewish acid green, and covered the floor on which we sat in a similarly coloured carpet. But not the sort of carpet that I'd really seen before. This one was like a highly superior home-made woolly one, with separate strands, thick and tufty

264

like an elegant overgrown lawn. I touched it. 'It's like grass, this carpet. Lovely,' I said.

Pat, at the sound of my voice, drained her glass again and teetered towards us from the window. She looked down at the sea of green and, delicately, with one pointed high-heeled shoe, parted the fronds around one foot. 'Scandinavian—bought from Heals. I know the firm— fucking expensive!'

We all looked at her, it was almost the first time she'd opened her mouth since arriving. From where we sat there on the floor, she looked to me—magnificent. Drunk. And randy, so I thought. I wondered which one she'd choose. Jim was who I'd put my money on. He seemed the most conventional of the three. The one who looked as though he had the cleanest vest and knickers. And socks and shiniest shoes. And tidiest drawer. The one I'd bet who cleaned his teeth and possibly even combed his hair before he went to bed. The other one, called Gerry, Gerry short for Gerald—I didn't think would go for any girl. Pat's brother might have stood a better chance, but I wouldn't have liked to put it into words. I wasn't ever that much good at divining deviations.

The atmosphere was warming up. Gerry put some music on, modern jazz—much the same as the Studio Club. Gerry Mulligan. 'We heard some music like this the other night at a place called the Studio Club—in Swallow Street. Do you know it?' I turned to Nicholas. Pat stood above us swaying in a deliberate sort of way deciding who to settle on. The matter was taken out of her hands as Gerry, turning from a pile of records, neatly contained in a pristine record rack, decisively encircled her with a long loose arm as thin as her own, and rhythmically started to dance. I might have guessed that he would be the first to see her charms. Over in Pat's department, in Fabrics and certainly Fashion Design, there'd been a fair amount of stylish effeminate boys. At times it seemed to me she'd been surrounded by them—buzzing along the streets of Brighton. Bizarre and beautiful. Waspish, witty—all fragile, slender, supremely chic compared to the plebeian rest of us. We didn't have those sort of people in Painting. And I don't think they had them in Illustration and certainly not in Sculpture. She had exactly what it took to get on well with them, I thought. She understood much more than me about life's artificialities. I looked at them together and listened to Nicholas' question.

'The Studio Club? We've heard of that, the Studio Club. Hey, haven't we, Jim?' Jim rolled his heavy body over from laying on his stomach; he now lay on his back like me, both hands behind his head, supporting it whilst, like me again, he gazed at Gerry and Pat.

'They look good together, don't they?' I said. 'Beautiful in the same way.' Perhaps it hadn't occurred to them that Gerry might be like that. Or then again I may have been wrong. Nicholas joined Jim in shy embarrassed laughter. Their reaction irritated—it was as if I might have been casting aspersions on their manhood by my oblique reference.

We left at midnight at my insistence which strongly countered their own, and by then too, surprisingly or not—Pat's. 'You can stay then if you like—' But no, she wouldn't, she'd come with me. They all would, in fact! They'd see us home on the tube. But I was tired of them by then. And even a little tired of Pat. I wanted the evening to come to an end and get back to my bed. It had been ordinary, that really was the only word to use. They'd been, the three of them, too much what I'd been used to for the past five years. If this was all that London had to offer I might as well have stayed at home—even with the Axminster on the stairs.

Fiona was meant to arrive on Friday. On Friday evening after tea was what she'd said on the telephone. But in the morning, she caught me just as I was leaving to say she couldn't make it. I didn't try to hide the disappointment in my voice. 'You cow!'

'I honestly, honestly can't help it, darling!' She'd never called me darling, not directly, not before. It stopped me short. 'You see, pet,' she continued. 'One of mummy's dearest friends has let her down over dinner, and to keep the numbers correct, I have to go instead. Something ghastly at the Grand—there's just no way around it!'

'But I've bought bread especially, and cream. And coffee instead of tea.'

'We'll eat it tomorrow. I won't have breakfast till I get to you! We'll have toast and coffee. I'll get back in bed as soon as I arrive. You won't even have to meet me off the train. I'll jump in a taxi and be there before you wake up!'

I was still cross when I caught the tube and stood heavily

all the way to Westminster on the toecap of a certain swollen gentleman to my left. Without saying sorry once.

But when I saw her, I'd recovered. It wasn't my way to stay cross for long. Sulking seemed to me a wicked way of wasting time. I'd said as much to Pat *à propos* our evening at Nicholas'. She appeared to be astonished even at the suggestion! Had claimed in fact, her silence at the start sprang quite genuinely from chronic shyness. That and the fact that she'd started her period unexpectedly at their front door.

'Couldn't you tell?' she'd said accusingly, as if I'd had X-ray eyes. 'That's why I was standing up all night, in case it all came through.'

'Wouldn't standing make it worse—on the principle of pouring? You'd have been better laying on your side like a bottle of vintage port.'

'I couldn't afford the risk, not on their ultra-smart seating! Though I was all right as it happened. I took the precaution, in their toilet, of stuffing my bloomers with Bronco.'

I was right about who she'd chosen. Jim was the one, as I'd thought. 'The only thing that irks though, is that he likes you.' She'd peevishly pressed her lips together.

'Me?'

'They both do. That Nicholas is mad on you. I as usual was left with the pooftah! Not that I mind that one, Gerry. He's a bloody good dancer, isn't he?'

I thought of them swaying so rhythmically together. Two slender bodies, so sexless and sublime. 'Perhaps he'd do for your brother, Pat.'

But she'd wrinkled her nose. 'Oh no! My brother wouldn't do for him. Much too provincial. Not pretty enough anyway! He's not like me, my brother. He's more knitted Fair Isle, if you know what I mean. And actual carpet slippers! Like an old auntie in spite of being so young. It's a different scene altogether from ours. You'd find it hard to believe we're related even.' And she'd shuddered. 'Oh, Christ! I'll be with the drip of course, tonight. I'm going to Brighton straight from school—so I shan't be seeing you till Sunday.'

The flat felt funny without her as soon as she'd slammed the door. I lay in bed listening to her footsteps pattering up our stairs until she reached the ground floor immediately overhead. Straining my good ear, I could even hear the muffled sounds of the early-morning streets outside as she'd opened the heavy front door. But after the dull thud of its closing there was now no sound at all. You could die down here, I thought. I could pass out—whoof—and no one would know, not for the whole weekend. Not till Sunday when Pat came back and found my body. If Fiona weren't coming that was.

She'd rung, Fiona, at that precise moment. Exactly as I'd mentally said her name. Extraordinary, as I'd told her later. And arising from that minor revelation was something even more—we'd both agreed. It turned out that even down to the split second when dear old Douglas' defeated erection had boomeranged back on his bollocks, she, Fiona, was similarly engaged in sexual frolics all the way up in Scotland. And each of us wondering whether the other of us was!

'It's telepathy!' she said. 'We're linked by metaphysical threads. Like twins out of the womb—'

'I saw a film called *Freaks* with Siamese twins in, in the college cinema club. And one of those was being poked,' I said.

'With the other one looking on?'

'Well, no. In actual fact she turned her head the other way and did a bit of knitting. They were joined at the hip, I think. I can't remember now but I know they both had legs and arms belonging to themselves.'

'She'd have been getting a bit excited then herself. Or not?'

'They didn't make that clear. Though she did shut her eyes when the chap shot off and I think that she did drop a stitch.'

I'd had an early night the previous evening, on my own. Really early. Seven-thirty it was when I got into bed. Though it had crossed my mind to go out to the cinema. Michael, of all people, had rung to have a chat and enquire what I was up to. 'What a shame,' I'd said 'I'm just rushing out this instant. No time to even swap good-days. Can you ring me another time, Michael?' And I'd slowly walked into the kitchen to make a cup of tea. The trouble was, a terrible lethargy had settled. It was more than disappointment that Fiona hadn't arrived, though that in itself was indeed contributing to my sense of anti-climax. It's this flat, I thought, that's it. It's giving me the willies! The walled-in claustrophobic feeling, being basement—with no windows. But more than that—the bloody quiet was what I wasn't used to. That's what comes from living above a business. On the premises of the shop. All nicely cocooned out back and down below and up above. Everything throbbing around the central nerve of the counter and the till. We had been offered a business once with alternative living accommodation, but my father had claimed my mother would pine away within the week without the boost of a busy shop bell, without the weight of spent loose change, or the shuffling impatience that spells full shop. So he'd turned it down before she'd say yes—in case. And I had to admit that at this very minute, I agreed with him. I'd have honestly given anything to be behind our counter now—rearranging Wrigley's Gums, tidying Cadbury's chocolates. Refilling rapidly emptying jars. Requesting firmly 'Who's next please?' and 'Come on, kids, decide! Or I'll serve someone else instead!' Instead of languishing in this Earls Court cell.

'What a senseless bloody time to ring!' my father shouted down the phone. 'The shop is full, as you'd expect! What's up then? Are you ill? We thought you must be—not having heard. Can't you send us at least a card?' I could almost smell through the mouthpiece the poignant mix of confectionary and tobacco, could even tell exactly which wrapped hard-boiled sweets my mother was weighing out from the slithering cellophane kiss on the scales. Pascals, but possibly now perhaps their Buttered Brazils, not Fruit Drops after all.

'Sorry, dad,' I said, swallowing very hard on my suddenly tender tonsils. 'I'll drop a line and'—I finished in a rush—'perhaps come home next weekend!' I knew he held the line uncertainly at the other end. Torn between desire to continue taking money and keeping customers happy, torn between those and a natural feeling of wanting to find out more. 'Oh, yes!' I added as bonus, 'I thought you'd be pleased, dad. I went out with a barrister this week! Well, trainee barrister anyway—'

'You'll never believe this, Fiona, but last night being on my own in this place—I actually was *so* homesick of all things—that I got on the phone to my father!' We sat in our nighties in the new double bed in the kitchen. Each wearing a cardigan, with the gas oven turned up for warmth. She'd brought the double sheets from home but

269

had forgotten to bring a pillow. I said later on we'd go and buy her one.

'Whiteleys, that's the place for pillows. So mummy's always saying. Household goods and electrical appliances—unbeatable bargains! You can make a sixty per cent saving on big bath towels and small tea cloths. She bought a shop-soiled toaster there not so long ago for under a pound, you know—'

I'd made no mention of the fact that Pat expected two pounds for buying the bed-settee on her behalf. I didn't think I could stand the strain of seeing her having to part company with her money. Not out of the blue, not without having been warned. But she'd brought me a little present from Scotland. Some barley sugar. 'Oh, Fiona! How sweet!' An inferior make which even my father had refused to stock, for not being value for money.

'It's not one you sell in the shop, is it?' she'd asked anxiously.

'No.' I'd answered truthfully. 'It isn't.'

But she must have doubted me because, before I could stop her, she'd impulsively unpinned a hideous shiny thistle brooch from her suit lapel and pressed it in my hand. 'There,' she said, 'I think I'd like you to have it. I'd actually bought it for our old char. I was only wearing it until I see her this week. Now it's yours.'

But the news she'd brought of her goings-on were more of a tonic than any gifts. 'Shall we get in bed with our coffee and toast before I get settled and start?'

It was patently clear she was no longer pure from the second she stepped through the door. 'Fiona,' I'd said, excited by the rawness of the eyes behind her shiny specs. 'Stand in the light for me to see you better. There's no need to ask?'

'No.' She glowed. 'There isn't.'

I had to admit to a pang or two when at last she started to tell me. Four lovers in a fortnight wasn't bad for a beginner!

'But who were they? Where from?' I asked.

'Oh, I didn't bother with names! I just had them one afternoon out fishing. One by one in the bushes. On a Friday. After an alcoholic lunch brought down by the gillies. But it's spoilt me a bit—you can see.'

I couldn't see, not at all—she looked positively radiant to me. 'What do you mean, spoilt? Leaving your L-plates

270

up in the hills?'

'The having had so many all at once.'

I nodded understandingly. 'And the doing it outdoors. That gives an appetite—the open air.'

'I suppose,' she sighed and gave a beatific smile, 'one might embrace the whole experience as rather a nice form of mass rape.'

'A superior sort of gang bang—were any of them actual workers? I mean, the Lady Chatterley syndrome? Or were you all, as it were, social equals?'

'Interesting, that, though not so easy to answer! They hardly spoke you see. Just got on with the job and as I didn't dare to open my eyes for fear of embarrassing them away, I could only tell by the texture of the tweed. And there isn't much difference in that, or the fishiness of hands that have just held rods.'

'Was one your father, do you suppose?'

'Daddy? Oh, dear, no! Daddy'd gone by then, old thing. He only was there a week. I stayed on by myself at Nathaniel's house. That's what I'm getting to next!'

I couldn't wait to hear about Nathaniel. I, without even meeting him, was already one of his fans. I'd seen every film he'd been in—which was more than Fiona could claim. He always played the sort of roguish country squire part. Or twinkling irascible Army colonels. Or some amused and knighted member of the medical hierarchy. A well-born establishment figure—the kind my father could have bowed and scraped to. But off-centre and anarchic enough to appeal to me. I crossed invisible fingers and silently prayed that Fiona might be generous enough to effect an introduction. There wasn't a chance. No hope in hell.

'It's not even that I fancy him for myself, you know what I mean. He's much too old for starters. But no one could say he wasn't a catch—a household name! And being one of daddy's dearest friends that gives it an extra *frisson*! You don't mind, darling, do you?'

I minded like mad, but managed with an immense amount of muscle control around the outer corners of my mouth to courageously conceal the fact.

'You see,' she continued unawares, 'I'd so loathe it if he fell for you, and it's ten to one he would. He's such a dirty old devil, you can't imagine, and terribly keen on tit! Oh dear—' She drew me close and pressed the hard steel of her

271

spectacle frame against my cheek. 'Even as I'm saying it, I sound so dreadfully dog-in-the-manger. And I know you'd be just the opposite in my position, which makes it that much worse.'

Oh, yes. There was no doubt that I'd be opposite! What? With one of my father's dearest friends? You bet my nubile bum I would! I tried to think who'd qualify. An affair with which of them would carry, as Fiona so succinctly put it—that spot of extra *frisson*? What about old Wheelchair Willie, Ted Grunt's invalid uncle? My dad was fond of him, all right, if only for demolishing at darts. He'd come in for a lot of local criticism over that, not allowing Willie to win. An unfair contest, many claimed, with the board being too high for any invalid to aim. Let alone one like old Willie, who was not only hamstrung by the wheelchair's arms but in addition partially paralysed in both palms. Though active enough in other extremities. Nineteen National Health nurses already, he'd been through, who'd refused to attend him again. Even the women from Meals-on-Wheels were now, too, unwilling to drop off his parsnips and pudding.

He'd had me sitting on his lap some several years ago, on the boisterous occasion of his birthday. A knowing female neighbour has asked me afterwards how it had felt. 'Much like the Chinese joke,' I'd told her, 'Confucius he say "girl who sit on jockey's knee get hot tip".' And it had indeed surprised me with its snaky strength, so much so I'd feared for the contours of my loosely woven woollen skirt, and had sprung up in some alarm. I'd only recently ruined another garment in that similar fashion—from hanging it carelessly in the cupboard. On a peg which had stretched the soft material in such a way that, when I put it on, I appeared from certain angles to be sustaining a small but pointed hunch high up on my shoulders.

Yes, Wheelchair Willie would most certainly have been the most able and willing of all my father's friends to start a torrid affair with me. And I, without any doubts, could never have shown the selfishness that Fiona was now—about passing him on, so to speak. It wouldn't have crossed my mind at all to keep the undeniable *cachet* of a chair-bound lover to myself. Though on the other hand she probably wouldn't have wanted him anyway, since he was almost as old as Nathaniel. 'What was the difference, then,' I said, 'with Nathaniel? Being that much older?'

'Oh, don't be silly.' She sipped her coffee and sucked a glistening gush of Cooper's Chunky from toast to tongue. 'You know.'

'How do I?'

'Well, just guess. To do with the goolies, there's a clue!'

'The goolies,' I said, 'I imagine would, like the rest of the body in any person of advancing years—the goolies would have appeared more *gathered*, if that's the word. More knitted-up, more knotted, gnarled and wrinkled.'

'Wrong!'

'More loose and less elastic?'

'Right!'

'What, all the time, you mean? No air in the balloon at any point? No sage and onion, thyme and parsley stuffing in the turkey? But surely sometimes, Fiona.'

She'd finished her toast and started to lick the sticky tip of one thumb. 'Well,' she sighed, 'that's just the thing you see. I had to work so bloody hard to achieve such minimal results. It seemed to me to be a ghastly waste of time—and all the talking got me down.' She raised her spectacles from her nose, and, dropping them to her nostrils, looked at me steadily as if she were schoolmarm and me the attentive scholar. 'You never heard such talking! A lecture a second, really! Telling me what to do and how to touch—though not so much by the end. He said I was such an appalling pupil. Not near enough concentration.'

I looked at her and seethed. What gross unfairness, what wild injustice that I, who liked nothing better than to talk in bed, especially on sexually educational lines, was now to be denied this chance, simply because of her selfishness. It would serve her right if I gave Wheelchair Willie the A.O.K. in her direction. Tilted his wheels towards her well-kept house. Even pushed him myself all the way there, to present himself to her father. 'I'm here as prospective suitor, sir. Here to try rogering your daughter. I've heard that she's not such a big one for chat—well, the efficiency of my dick, sir, doesn't depend on discussion!'

'Though on the other hand, of course,' Fiona was cheerfully saying, 'I have to hand it out to Nathaniel. If he hadn't gone on quite so much, I would never have had them in the bushes. He'd whet my appetite. Made me

273

curious. And knowing you were back here expecting me and England, or rather Scotland, to do its duty—well that put the tin hat on it, if you like? Hey!' She sat up and blinked, suddenly excited. 'I wonder what we'll catch tonight.'

I felt my envious resentment ebbing, just to see the smile she shone my way. She could do that. 'Though one thing is certain, angel, eh? We couldn't possibly'—she glanced around and shuddered—'bring anybody civilised back here!'

I'd worked out what to wear already, that is till Fiona looked at it. Then I had second thoughts. 'No, come on!' she'd said. 'Don't joke! What are you really wearing?'

'It's what I wore to your twenty-first.' I'd attempted a brave defence.

'Exactly!'

She'd delivered the brutal kick as crisply as someone else that I'd once known, but I couldn't remember who for the minute.

'Which reminds me, now you mention my twenty-first—guess who's going to be there?'

'Where?'

'There. Tonight. At the centre of all the gaiety.'

'Who?' But I knew who, just as I now recalled the all too familiar crispness of the conversational kick. 'Piers?'

She laughed. 'Right in one! He was up there too, you know, by the way. Up there, up in Scotland. Nathaniel claims to have known him man and boy, since he was six, so he said. I told him Piers had a thing about you—that's when I got the first warning signal. I believe they've formed mutual attachments in the past. Both keen on the same piece of stuff, despite the difference in years.'

Now I felt well and truly flattered to think of them having discussed me! He was at least aware of my existence in the world then, Nathaniel. Might even have mentioned me to Piers. That spoilt it then, remembering back, to think what Piers could have said. 'Oh yes, that one. A person of the people. A pretty thing, but—well, you know! Had a pleasant enough father, who as far as I could tell, suffered from multiple sclerosis. Always falling down, poor sod! Ever so slightly awkward, being a shopkeeper. Seemed bent on smashing up stock—' I felt suddenly, undeniably depressed, all sense of joyous anticipation

274

seeping, draining rapidly away. As if somebody had pulled the plug out when I wasn't looking. I not only now had nothing to wear, but on top of that I'd have to put up with the scorn and ridicule of Piers and the like. Fiona could go alone.

'Are you certain, Fiona, that Piers will be there?'

'Oh quite.' She said cheerfully. '*Sans* all possible *doute*! He's the cousin you see—of the host.'

They paid in retrospect, the L.C.C., to keep teachers like me short and strained until our first pay. A full month's salary went automatically, when the month was up, into an account which they'd opened for me in the Midland Bank nearest to school. That applied to everyone. It amazed me, the organisation. The standard of efficiency required to move an operation such as that, with no loose ends out anywhere. My father banked our takings every Tuesday. Also in the Midland as it happened. I used to carry it to the bank in a big suspicious suitcase, which anybody would have been right in assuming to contain an awful lot of money. Money for the mortgage, so my father always stressed, in case I got ideas. Money to pay all manner of mundane matters to do with mere existence. And then anything left over ploughed immediately back into the business. I loathed that phrase—the ploughing back—with its biblical connotations. Linked so inextricably with the Reaping and Just Rewards. When all it meant, in actual fact, was him putting a face on with inconsequential commercial travellers. Ordering with authority! From the Representatives. The Reps, as he chose to call them. Not a breed to be revered I would have thought. But no, he found them extremely pleasant fellows. Full of the little courtesies of life. With company cars and cigarette cases. And shiny lighters of their own instead of matches made by Bryant & May or shabby boxes of Swan Vestas. It amazed me how very alike they looked, all with obligatory moustaches and haircuts which showed their ears. Until I worked it out that of course they were all meant to be Clark Gable. And once I'd stumbled on that fact I began seeing Clark Gables everywhere. On building sites and buses. Bartending and behind the wheels of lorries. All men of coming-on, middling age who would have had Clark Gable as the matinée idol when they were adolescents. The seediest fell far short of the ones who Repped our shop, and presented rather more an ageing Ronald Colman look about the gills. But one or two, more rakishly inclined, aimed even higher than Clark. As far as Errol Flynn, no less. With dimpled cheeks and dipping trilby brims. Those were the ones that I took to least of all. And my father tacitly approved my sour stand-offishness. 'Nice enough chaps, these reps, my girl, but you're right to think to do better! Little or no education between the whole bloody pack of them! Smarm and charm, and a bit of a head for figures. Brylcreem Boys! No better, no worse. Though I'd be lost without them. And that's a fact—fair do's!' But mashers, which was really what those rakier reps were—I could tell from their line of chat—mashers had never been my line in any case. Except Derek of course, had he been born in different circumstances, he might have been termed a masher. It would probably stand to reason that any female worth her salt would get caught in the grips of one sooner or later. At some stage in her life. I reflected now that probably it was just as well that I'd experienced it sooner—with the rest of my days to devote ahead to higher ambitions and better beds. And cocks which fitted more comfortably.

'Pat's lost it by the way. With a bloke she brought back called Douglas.'

But Fiona wasn't listening any longer. As if at the mere mention of Pat's name she'd switched off altogether. I didn't mind. It had struck me in mid-sentence that I'd be silly to continue. Certainly to go on to tell it all, including not only the implied intimacy of a threesome which she'd have obviously resented, but also to go into the complicating fiasco of my own failure at informal fornication. She didn't seem to have suffered such frustrations in that field. In fact the more I thought of it, the fourth of her fucks must have been pretty squidgy indeed. Like batting on a buttered bun. My dehydrated lower zones could well have made a welcome change in that steamy sub-tropical, cunt-clime of hers.

'Tell me,' her voice broke through abruptly. 'What is the state of your bank balance?'

The question startled me. I hadn't one as yet. How could I have without a salary so far?

'I've just been thinking that it mightn't be a bad idea for you to buy a frock—something, you know—' She tugged her nightie down and off her little rounded shoulders. 'Strapless.' I felt a sense of panic, knowing that I was about to be manipulated into spending money I didn't possess. 'I'll lend you some. I'll let you into a little secret— Nathaniel gave me twenty-five pounds! For a handbag I said I'd seen in Bond Street. Made out of lizard-skin. Look, here it is—I'll let you feel—two tenners and a five.' She pressed the crackling paper on my palms and sat back on her heels. Smiling, her arms wrapped right around her waist, hugging herself and her secret. 'You mustn't ever say! You'll promise you never would. Mummy and daddy would do their nut. Accepting money from men. But'—she leaned forward—'I'll tell you something—that has almost been the best part, this money. More than the sex I mean! The feeling, oh I can't explain—the feeling—sort of *kept*, I think.'

I looked at the twenty-five pounds on my lap and thought of the things it could buy. What on earth would I have done with it myself? I couldn't for the life of me imagine. I'd probably have sent some to my dad. 'Dear dad, here's this for you to spend on what you like. I've sold a painting! Yes, I have! So perhaps the years of training weren't in vain! I'm keeping some for myself—ploughing the profits back into the business, as you so rightly say! It will stand me in good stead, as in order to expand, I shall need new brushes and fresh supplies of paint and well-primed canvases ...' Yes, that's what I'd have done without a doubt. Some showing off as if, say, I'd earned it with my talent instead of ... 'Do you look on it as untaxed earnings, then? Do you, Fiona? Tell me?'

She chuckled softly and dropped her chin to look at the rest of her body. 'Well now—earnings you say! You know I never thought of it as that, but now you've put the notion in my mind ...'

I laughed. 'I didn't mean it seriously of course—'

She interrupted. 'Well! Why not? Look,' and in one wilfully childish gesture she pulled her nightie and cardigan up and over her head and threw them back on the bed. 'Look,' she repeated. 'How much would you say I was worth?'

It was a dear little body. The titties tiny but tip-tilted like a child's *retroussé* nose. Set in the surrounding flesh like two firm yet trembling jellies. With curiously vulnerable nipples, more in the mould of rosy unburst boils. Lacking a head. She touched them both, holding each daintily between thumb and finger. I'd seen a

277

painting once like that of two sisters. Early Italian? Tate?
Or National Gallery? Twins, if I remembered right—
holding each other's nipples. But they'd had something
there to hold. Two sharp protruding points, not just a
swatch of arbitrary tissue such as Fiona was offering me
now. 'Look. Look at these!' she said. 'What do you think?
Aren't they a washout! So weak and lacking in spunk!'

'Gristle.'

'Gristle?'

'Yes, that's what it is. Do you remember that very young
model we had? Maureen? Monica? What was her name?
When we were doing Intermediate Life Drawing. She had
nipples like that, I know, because we came in for heavy
criticism over leaving breasts blank at the end. Not enough
delineation. A shabby and superficial use of shading.
When all the time there was nothing there, unless you
made it up. Which then would have become a Work of
Imagination. Quite a separate subject! Bernard Bart put it
down to extreme youth. But she was about sixteen.
Perhaps in your case, Fiona, it's been lack of sexual
experience. Didn't Nathaniel voice some sort of opinion?'

I had such strong proprietary feelings now myself about
Nathaniel—was harbouring quite excessive hopes in his
direction, that even to think of him touching those
undeniably enticing mounds of hers (despite their
botched-up aureoles) made me prematurely old with envy.
I felt as I had done, oh, long ago, in school when Rita
Eaten had won the raffle instead of me. A mahogany letter
rack, faced with Moroccan leather. That was the prize, I
remember. It would have done a treat for my father's
birthday present. But Rita had not been at school the
morning they'd called the draw, so I'd been sent up instead
of her to receive the prize in her place. Everyone clapped,
of course. But it wasn't the same. Playing understudy.

'Nathaniel? Yes, he did. He actually did put the problem
into words. If I recall rightly it was something to do with
snobbery. Mine, he said. My snobbery. My nipples were
something to do with that. I'm not sure now just how the
two were linked.'

'Inverted,' I explained.

She let go of one breast. I watched it bounce down and
then rise up again, not quite certain how long to take in
shivering to a standstill. 'That's it.' She pointed in the air.
For all the world as if an aeroplane had ripped the word

278

'inverted' through the backcloth of the sky. 'Inverted! He said as well that what was wanted was a child. To properly suck them into shape. Can you imagine me coming back from Scotland and saying to mummy, "Mummy dear, I do so hope you won't be cross. I'm going to have a baby. Why? No real reason except to harden my tit ends up. Nathaniel has said it's the way".'

'You could go as a wet nurse to the poor. In places like the Gorbals—or out to British Guiana.'

She stared at me. 'What, not have a baby at all you mean? Just keep dipping them into milk, to give the taste?'

'Well, not quite that. You'd probably have to have your own, I think. No, what I mean is having had it, you could go on to become a wet nurse. The supply of milk does continue where there's a demand. The body rarely lets you down in that respect. And then you'd be assured of stupendous nipples for life! Like the steeples of Sacré Cœur!'

She frowned. 'Not much of a social life of course—continually milking!'

'Possibly not the one you might envisage now, but Fiona—'

'Touch them,' she said. 'Yourself.'

I didn't want to, felt no inclination, none at all. But if she'd said to me to kindly eat her ear wax, I would probably have done so. And begged to be given the recipe afterwards. 'What these?' They gave me instant goose pimples to touch. Somebody could have put a patent on the extraordinary texture. Couldn't Pat's lot be taught a weft and warp to produce a similar surface? Spun from spider web threads and the under-arm fur of new-born baby mice.

She shut her eyes. A smile stretching slowly from side to side. 'Oh God,' she groaned. 'It actually really gets me going. You know what I mean, down here.' And she lodged a hand sideways between her legs, slanting backwards so the back of it, behind the wrist, rested heavily on her clitoris. The unashamed abandonment appalled me. Of course I understood that middle-class girls of Fiona's sort, brought up largely in boarding schools, were bound to be less self-conscious. Or even girls of Pat's ilk, where to walk from the bathroom in your bra and knickers in the bosom of your family, especially with no father on the scene, would be thought to be quite normal. But this

279

obvious—*hedonism*! Is that what going away to school was all about? Did whole dormitories full of ripe, pubescent girls behave in this embarrassing way? My father would have demanded an enquiry.

'Is that enough?' I squirmed, trying like mad to match her smile and keep the conversation light and gay. I wanted to mention Whiteleys and whether they stayed open on Saturdays after the normal half-day. I still hadn't sorted out shop hours. Our half-day in Brighton had always been on Wednesday, but up here all regions seemed to suit themselves.

'That'—now she was speaking again, thank Christ—'is one of Nathaniel's greatest likes of course. Having two girls together. He has asked me how about it. I thought of you at the time.'

The gas, I was grateful to see, was giving up the ghost—flickering lower and lower in the oven. The meter was running out of money. I stopped. 'Loose change?' And started climbing off the bed. Stiffly, as if someone had punched me in the middle and emptied a tin of warm golden syrup in my open stomach. It oozed, or something did. It spun itself a tacky web amongst my tangled lips. It horrified me to notice that my whole body too appeared geared for action, so to speak. The entire circumference of my chest as pouting as an impudent pigeon's. Each starched and prominent nozzle pulling away in opposite directions from the feeble restraint of my fastened cardigan. I quickly folded my arms, a schoolgirl habit based on gossiping neighbours, washer-woman-style. To hide the tell-tale signs from my sensual companion. But she was gone, eyes shut, on a secret smiling journey of her own, legs now thrown wide, one hand well in. Plaiting and tapping furiously as if she were top toast of the typing pool—and abusing the office equipment. Would I ever learn, I wondered, adjusting the spectacles on her nose, to become so sublimely lacking in shame?

'This frock's a flop.'

'Not if you think of the saving!'

'It's silly, Fiona, to ever buy anything at sale price. It's bound to be dud. My dad has always maintained that. They bring them in by the lorry load. Very few are genuine reductions! In any case they couldn't ever have asked full price for this. It's scarcely more than a skirt. Are you sure you found it in Gowns?'

'Gowns Strapless, certainly! That's the fetching part—the fact of it being cut low.' Her voice had acquired an accusatory tone. 'You said you liked it in the shop. What's wrong then, now you've got it home?'

'It must be the merciless light, or this mirror. I don't know which. I look monstrous!'

But Fiona wouldn't have it that I did. Elizabeth Taylor in *A Place in the Sun*, that's who I looked like, she said. I could understand the lines on which she worked, but something somewhere was wrong. The dress had either just one flouncy petticoat too many or else it had several too few. And the top was designed with someone of more modest measurements than mine in mind. I tipped over such material that there was to a quite scandalous degree. 'My cup runneth over, Fiona! I'm sure they could have me on indecency.'

'They? Who?'

'People,' I said miserably. 'In the street.'

'But it's a party frock—you silly fool. You'll feel different amongst all the others! It's just, I'm sure, that you're not used to showing such a sumptuous amount of flesh, that's all. Christ, what! At four pounds, seventeen and sixpence, for what is actually *haute couture*, I'd go dressed in a flag, the Union Jack! I'd be so pleased at the bargain. Doesn't it thrill you to think that those other girls will have paid an absolute fortune for what they'll be wearing tonight and you'll have gone in next to nothing?' Then she laughed and added, cruelly I thought, 'Quite literally, I mean.'

Was I stupid to trust her, I secretly asked myself, as if I had alternatives. Derek had always warned me over my blind acceptance of what other people said. 'Because you yourself have never worked on devious lines, that doesn't mean to say the rest of us share your Christian attitudes to honour, love and loyalties. Nor is there any reason why we should. Have you ever considered *that* before?' I hadn't. There was much actually that Derek fed me, or would have force-fed me, had I allowed it—that even in theory I thought shamelessly puerile and frankly pathetic. On a par with and as profound as the philosophy of our shop counter. If each had allowed themselves the self-indulgence, my father and my ex-fiancé might have had quite fine mutual debates. Not over-taxing to either.

Perhaps, after all, I had been doing Fiona an injustice to entertain any doubts at all, because certainly when she eventually produced her own intended party wear, it looked not unlike my own. And had, according to her, cost even less! She'd inked it herself as it hung in the store. Surreptitiously with her own small fountain pen brought specially for the purpose. 'Parker 51. They're far the best. The flow is so much faster.' So that the management had been forced into a further drop in price. 'But if you ever try it yourself, be very careful,' she'd warned. 'Apply the ink—but wisely, where it won't show in the wearing—somwhere round the hem. Or waist, where it can be hidden by a belt. Otherwise you'll find the thing is unwearable. And don't be put off by assistants who might try to go one better and claim the ink to be the reason why the dress is in the sale in the first place. You can always call for the manager if you're feeling confident enough. It's never not worked for me so far. I'm thinking of starting on furniture—for when we get our own flat. But you must be careful, as I said. It's a wonder I haven't been caught. I take such appalling risks.'

I knew she took appalling risks after ten minutes with her in Whiteleys. 'Oh Fiona, don't! Oh please,' I'd whispered pleadingly. 'Half of these shoppers are plain-clothes police. I'm sure of it. See that one there. She's been trailing us since we came in. I noticed her—' Her hand hovered over a bright blonde hairnet that quite obviously neither of us needed. I couldn't for the life of me see the sense of half she was taking. Was it due to her short sightedness or what? Though certainly I understood that kleptomaniacs never do lift articles that they may need themselves; that's not the impetus at all. But I'd be in a tricky position since she would keep dropping the stuff into the shopping bag I held. They'd have us both as accomplices. I shifted it now to the other arm, attempting to keep it out of her reach, and my usual bodily position much less accessible in case she took to my pockets. My whole future could be put in jeopardy just for the sake of—what? Two tins of Elastoplast. A tiny pale green satin pin-cushion, sewn in the shape of a pear. The spare part of a fruit-juice squeezer. And a bag of upholstery buttons. It didn't appear to be worth it whichever way I looked.

But afterwards, she'd shrugged when I asked why on

earth she did it. 'Is it a recent thing? Or not? When did you start? And why?' But I could get no sense from her at all. Nothing except an emotional outburst as answer—in which she turned the tables so neatly that I was the one who felt guilty by the end.

'I thought at least you'd find it fun. Join the spirit of the thing like a real friend. Honestly. It's like going out with a Girl Guide!'

'I'm sorry Fiona,' I mumbled. 'But I found it so scary, that's all—the almost being caught. A razor's breadth away!'

'But that's the excitement. The whole point. The kick—all the adrenalin pumping! I find it terribly arousing. No, really! I could get off with anyone after. It's the same sort of feeling as sex.'

I knew which I'd choose of the two.

Fiona said we should go in a taxi, something I still wouldn't dream of taking. On principle, quite apart from the cost. I felt more myself on public transport—and of course, had myself felt more. I still hadn't got around to telling her all about that. Though such abortive titillation would probably not impress her overmuch, having neither to do with consummated lust nor the accumulation of unexpected wealth. Though, thinking about it, she, with her enthusiasm, might well have found in rush hour a chance to refine her art to the point where she would be equally practised in lifting cocks and wallets.

People who took taxis were, in my father's book at any rate, hedonistic, self-indulgent lounge lizards. The extravagant sort of spendthrift. Faintly shady cards who wore crêpe-soled brothel-creepers instead of straightforward lace-up shoes. Like Derek. Exactly like Derek, who'd chosen, alas, to take a taxi instead of walk the four miles back one night after he'd missed his last bus. My father had paid. I'd watched him counting out each coin with over-deliberate care into Derek's open palm and prayed that he'd change his mind. Not take the bloody money, none of it. But no—'Oh thank you very much. That's awfully kind!' My father's nostrils had flared with malevolent satisfaction. Another stick with which to beat. 'The bloody tribe! The lazy, luxury-loving lout! Typical, that is, girl! You give a yid a chance to park his arse or else

283

to use Shank's Pony!'

Sharing Fiona's taxi meant I now owed her, so she said, five pounds one shilling and sixpence. But I wasn't to worry, she wouldn't be charging interest rates, not quite yet at least! I got to the tip of my tongue the price of the bed-settee and a tin of Nescafé. And one lavatory roll. And bread and butter and the use of electric light—but no further than the tip. I couldn't have stood the chance, not taken the risk of a scalding rejoinder at that point, not now we were almost there. I had too many other things to think about, like not creasing my precious sawn-off party frock and not snagging my new silk stockings. I sat, most of my buttocks bare, against the cold seat of the taxi, only my flimsy panties between the leather and crotch. White, when what I usually wore was black. With a cheap white suspender belt to match. Cotton, covered with broderie anglaise. Mock. No brassière on at all. No need for one; in any case I didn't own a strapless one yet. The dress itself provided all in stiffened under-support. Strangely now, I did feel deliciously desirable, as Fiona had said I would. 'Here, have a splash of this perfume, my darling—' her humour was all restored. And she dabbed it behind my ears and on both throbbing wrists. Then deep down in my décolletage. 'And what about between the legs? You never know—a handsome stranger my lose his way and end up in the forest!' We'd both laughed very long and very loud. Holding our necks like giraffes, our heads high in the air. I'd never felt as close to her before, balancing so precariously on the frontier of the evening.

'You know what you should do, Fiona—' I felt emboldened by the intimacy. 'Now you have the knack of extracting money from men—'

'What a neat turn of phrase.'

'You should get someone like Nathaniel to come up with some contact lenses.' (And a sculptural plastic surgeon to carve a slive off each ankle?)

'He wouldn't do it.' She spoke abruptly. 'I know. I've asked already. He says my spectacles are sweet. He insists they're part of me. And daddy would say as much as well. They seem almost to be in league.'

'And what do you think yourself then?'

'Oh, I'd give anything to have them off.'

'Well, it's settled then. Save up. You've squandered a fiver on lending to me for my frock. I'll pay you back, but that's not the point. It's an attitude of mind. What will it cost? It won't take you that long, not with large amounts like the twenty-five from Nathaniel—and anything else you might manage to coin. It will give you an aim. Don't you see?'

But I'd lost her interest again. A positive aim apparently was not what she was after. I couldn't quite see why myself. To aim for something—to take yourself to task and set yourself a goal was what it all came down to in the end—even if what it was was barely worth the having.

The house was huge, more like a small hotel with pillars pretending to be Doric columns, almost out on the pavement. The taxi had somehow approached it from Sloane Street. 'It's obnoxiously smart. Lowndes Square!'

I lost her, head and tail, Fiona, when she started to talk like that. Why obnoxious? Why an adjective of that nature? Obnoxious meaning offensive? Objectionable? Sinister? Unpalatable? Uncomfortable? Onerous? She can't have had much of an English mistress in that smart school of hers. Not like mine. Old Turnstile. Her own *Roget's Thesaurus* she'd given me when I'd left. Falling apart in Penguin, with the price still in pencil inside.

Fiona pressed the bell so fiercely I farted. 'I farted! Oh Christ! What now?'

'Whoosh your skirts and I'll whoosh mine. With luck we'll disburse it before the butler opens the bloody door!'

But out of nowhere a dinner-jacketed fellow guest appeared, darting in from the pavement to our side of the pillars. 'Pooh!' he exclaimed. 'I say! Wouldn't you think they'd clear the dustbins before the blasted weekend?'

I trembled with shame and social terror, but Fiona saved the day. 'You blasted would!' she agreed in her best fox-hunting voice, and made an extravagant movement towards the basement area with her arms. 'The offensive receptacles are in that direction, I would deduce—best if we face off this way.'

He adjusted his tie and collar. 'Percy's the name, Frentham-Withers. Puts one in mind of old Venice ...'

I hadn't really ever witnessed Fiona all out. Not no holds barred as she appeared to be tonight. It was a staggering display. I wondered that everyone she spoke to didn't shrivel and curl away. Except that they too were emoting fit to kill. Of course she must have been like that or more or less the same on her twenty-first party, but my time and attention had been monopolised there by Piers—or it didn't jar then quite as much. It sent me straight into a dull decline, much like Pat had been up at Nicholas'. I thought of that—but this scene was more daunting surely than the simple chic of their place. I'd never been so overpowered by such sumptuous surroundings—as if the people themselves weren't half enough to tear my tongue from its roots! They weren't unfriendly though. Not as clipped and cut off, by convention towards breaking obligatory ice, as affairs I'd been to of my father's. 'Don't leave your bag in the bedroom,' Fiona had said once inside, and then she'd winked. 'In case there are people here like me!' 'Oh yes,' I'd answered. 'Of course.' She'd flitted off into the adjoining bathroom. 'Just spending a penny. Don't go—' Go? As if I would go on my own! I'd looked around at the heavy mirrors on every wall. Framed like ancient oil paintings, every one. In walnut, old mahogany and oak. Carved with cupids and entwined flowers. A chiselled cornucopia. Containing, as I turned to each in turn, the silvered shine of my own exquisitely bevelled reflection. My father had taught me to look for the bevel, the sign of a very fine mirror. Just as Fiona had since taught me all about cards—how to run over the print with your finger, to tell if it's stamped or engraved. 'Does it really make that much difference then?' 'Just the difference between two different worlds!'

Our host appeared to be a boy of twelve, but no—seventeen, Fiona said. I don't know why she hadn't said as much before. I'd taken for granted somehow that the person giving the do would at least have been grown-up. Not that it made much difference; the age group seemed to span a massive area. 'Is that his grannie then?' I whispered.

'Yes, I believe it is,' Fiona'd answered me to my surprise. And then, 'Oh you should talk to her. She's an absolute riot I've heard. Really worked her way up out of nothing. Cockney, or so I believe.' She didn't look directly at me as she spoke, but somewhere to the left of my right ear. I glanced discreetly over my shoulder hoping to register just whose eye it was she meant to catch. But there was no one there who faced in our direction. Perhaps she wished to tell the time from the turquoise Louis Quinze clock.

'It's half-past nine,' I said. 'Shouldn't we say hello to the host?'

She jerked her attention back to me and gashed her teeth in a smile. 'Oh, what a good idea!' she gushed. 'Though we possibly might wait for Piers before we go about introducing ourselves.'

What did she mean? Didn't she know him then? Had we come here in fact uninvited? 'Good God Fiona! Are we gate-crashers?' I looked around uneasily, saying it. And her shiftiness increased my suspicion. What a nerve she had—I felt a surge of admiration for her even so. And in myself a thread of defiance. 'Well, while we're here then, we'd better make the most of it!' I looked round boldly, but she squeezed my arm.

'You've got it wrong, silly. We are invited. Of course we are. But I didn't want to tell you before in case you wouldn't come. Piers invited us. At least he said that I could come—on condition that I brought you ...'

On condition! I stared at her. What me? Was I her card of entry? When all the time I'd been feeling so much on sufferance—like something the cat had brought in. The poor relation. A member of staff who'd managed to slip upstairs. It took me seconds to actually grasp the significance of what she'd revealed. I looked down at the crystal contents of my hands, and then further down to where I saw the deep pile of the rug on which I stood was playing havoc with my best suede shoes. Not as bad as if I'd worn my polished leather, of course. They picked up the pile like mad. I'd have come away with those in a furry tidemark all round the sole, like the salt mark left when you walk too near the sea. Nothing could get that off a pair of shoes. Not once the bugger had set. No possible shoe polish on earth could shift the stain. 'I don't mind,' I said. 'Not a bit, now we're—'

But she cut in suddenly before I had a chance to finish. 'Well, look who's here—talk of the devil, it's—' I knew without looking round exactly which devil it was, even before she'd so breathily said his name. 'Piers!' And now for the first time she seemed to be relaxed. So that's what her put-on pose had been! Nerves! Well, fancy that! Piers tried to sweep me off my feet. Quite literally, from behind, with his two hands around my stiffening waist so that my elbow shot high into the air taking my glass with it. I held it fast despite the unexpected flight, but the laws of gravity

287

controlled the liquid content. He dropped me as suddenly as he had that day beneath the ancestral stairs—and uttered an animal yap of discomfort. I turned to see that he was drenched, with a lump of melting ice caught up in his white carnationed lapel. He turned on his heel and left, followed by lighthearted hoots of laughter, and the unconvincing entreaties of his cousin, the host. But from then on, so it seemed in retrospect, everything changed for the better.

'I shouldn't worry about him, not at all. That's always been Piers' stumbling block—the fact that he lacks all humour. Especially when directed towards himself.'

'But I honestly didn't do it on purpose!' I could see that he didn't believe me.

'H'm, he said you were a pretty spirited sort of girl—'

'Who, Piers?'

'And I fully agree! Quite super!'

I'd spent the last six dances with this young host and had long since lost sight of Fiona. For all I knew she may well have been had by the butler and seventy per cent of the guests—or even possibly gone home. Though I'd ruled that out as unlikely. His name was Ernest, Ernest Smythe. 'Pronounced Smith? Or Smythe?' I'd asked for fear of giving offence. I'd read it first before either of us had put it into words. On the card he'd given me. Engraved with, what was more, a *deckle* edge. Another delight of my dad's. The deckle edge. Like bevelled. 'Oh, what a delightful deckle edge, young sir!' he might have exclaimed. 'Well, I'll be damned! A deckle you say? I didn't know that before!' 'Did you hear that, my girl? That which the young sir has said? He'd never heard of a deckle before, and doubtless knows nothing of bevel. It proves the point and goes to show that quite often the proletariat is more acquainted with the ins and outs of protocol and style than even the aristocracy!'

It was hard to believe Ernest Smythe was only seventeen. Was he really so young? Or so old? And how amazing that he too, like Nathaniel (I fluttered somewhere round my ribs as I even thought his name) knew already of my existence. But I had no curiosity now about what Piers might have said. It was enough that I was here and appearing so confidently to hold my own. The interest had started suddenly, right from when Piers had left. Ernest had approached and introduced himself immediately, and then had gone further to make both Fiona and myself feel more at ease now that our entrée had vanished. 'This is my father. Father?' And he'd given I thought, a curious smile. 'May I leave these young ladies in your care, for just a short while, as I mingle—' The father coughed and put a snowy handkerchief to his mouth. I watched him skilfully transfer a gob of loose catarrh and caught the fetid whiff of violet cachou on his breath. That's something I quite approved of, in fact. Making the effort. A civilised touch, to conceal the anti-social aspects of his phlegm. I smiled at him. The grannie Fiona had spoken of before could not possibly be his mother, I could tell. There didn't seem to be that many years between them both. She must have been on the maternal side. The mother of his much younger wife. I smiled again, wanting to make him feel a youngster such as myself could still find time to make old gentlemen understand that what they had to say might possibly still be of interest. Despite the generation gap.

Later, very much later on in time, I used to try to think back to that first impression. The one we both made on each other. If his interest had been kindled at that introduction of his son's, it didn't, I'm almost certain, appear to show in any way. His eyes remained remote and hooded behind his wrinkled eyelids. He nodded courteously enough and asked me to repeat my name. But other than that there was nothing. I remember how impressed I was by his extraordinary pallor, the skin so clear, it seemed almost transparent, lacking essential corpuscles. He was bald, completely bald, and there seemed no difference to the texture of his scalp. No demarcation between that area and his forehead. He was much taller than his son would ever be, even allowing for further growth. He was in fact the tallest person in the room. Was that the reason that he dominated? His voice surprised me when he spoke. With its lightweight quality and gentleness—yes, gentleness. He used it as an instrument, not just of speech, but in a further sense. To stroke. That's what it was.

Almost a week had passed before I heard his voice again. A long enough space of time to have forgotten its special quality. The telephone was the perfect weapon—it lent an extra persuasiveness, an even slightly sinister edge to the soft suede tones. It hadn't occurred to me at all, at any time,

289

that he might choose to ring. But when he did, it seemed entirely natural that he should.

'Where are you off to?' Pat had passed me in the passage, home late because she'd been shopping.

'Oh, I'm out to dinner tonight,' I said. 'In a bit of a rush—'

'Who with?'

'I'll tell you later. Too complicated now!'

It had been like that in fact all week, ever since Fiona had gone, Pat and I hadn't been in once together. Life was becoming a social whirl for each of us in various ways. I'd have to start keeping a diary to preserve all the details for Fiona. I'd meant to say I wouldn't be here this weekend since I'd promised to go down to Brighton. My father had rung as well as sending a letter to say they were expecting me. But I wanted to go in any case, to go over the party with Fiona. She'd left so early on the Sunday, and had been so incapably drunk the night before that so far we hadn't had a chance.

'Dolphin Square, you'll take a taxi, my dear, of course. I'll reimburse you—Nelson House.'

'Where is it, abouts? Near Earls Court?'

'The taxi will know, don't you worry.'

Why hadn't I needed persuading? Was it normal to go out with fathers? Ernest had been phoning all week, but who could take seventeen-year-olds seriously? I'd thought at first that that's why his father was ringing, something to do with his son. But no, apparently not. What the hell was I going to call him? Colonel Smythe? Or, more intimate, Reggie?

The dinner was, so he said, in the nature of an introduction. Something he'd thought of today. Two very old friends of his had already been invited; he thought I might care to meet them. Not purely in a social sense, you understand, my dear. He is very involved in television and since you yourself are an artist ... I couldn't see any connection at all between the two, unless he meant the man might like his portrait done. Or supposed I might care to paint scenery! People interpreted artist to mean so many varied things, from seaside cards to restoration of renaissance works. I'd suffered before from similar confusions. But even so, sitting in the back seat of the taxi, my eyes now anxiously on the clock, I had to acknowledge a mounting feeling of excitement. What cultured company might I expect to share tonight? What pearls of wisdom would assail my eager ears? I sensed adventure, something fresh afoot. A whole new chapter of my life about to start. How superb to be gaining experience!

'Nelson House, you said, Miss?' The taxi driver swung his head around at precisely the moment I'd chosen to adjust my suspender. 'And very nice too!' he added.

'Mm, er, oh yes, Nelson House—whatever that may mean. I don't know Dolphin Square myself.'

'Oh, well,' he said conversationally, 'there's lots of Houses in Dolphin Square, all named after admirals I think. There's Nelson, Beatty, oh who else? The whole bloody lot I believe. And plenty of dirty goings on in all of them, you bet! What's a nice girl like you doing there? Off to see a sugar daddy, eh?'

I went hot, then cold, all over. He didn't seem to be joking. Thank God my father was safely sixty miles or more away, he'd have booted me right up the bum! And sliced off the bonce of my sugar daddy! Bald or otherwise. And followed it up with his bollocks. I should have to be very careful of my step if I cared to keep out of trouble.

Dolphin Square turned out to be a rather luxurious block of flats, situated on the embankment. The driver dropped me off at Nelson House; I didn't care to meet his eye as I counted out the fare. And chose to ignore his parting shot, obviously intended as rather suggestive advice to do with being good or careful.

The hallway was deserted, thickly carpeted and discreetly lit. With anonymous looking doorways placed at regular intervals along a set of seemingly never-ending corridors. I was to go, so he'd said, directly to the lift, and take it to the floor marked seven. Then I was to turn left and place myself quite squarely before the second door that I came to. I did as I'd been told and saw before me the minute and shining microscopic eye. No other door had one. Why then had he? To warn off undesirables? Or not to answer if the moment was too intimate? More likely that. I'd been in bed with Derek when another girl had come to call. She'd nearly kicked the door down, screaming she knew he was there. And what's more with another woman. Another woman! Me, another woman? When I was meant to be the only one? But Derek had stubbornly sworn he didn't know just who the hell she was. 'You mean to say,' I'd said with heavy irony, 'that the previous occupant of this place could well have been named Derek too?' 'Quite possibly so,' he'd actually had the nerve to answer!

I'd rung the bell and gazed ahead, chin up at a flattering angle, knowing of the scrutiny at the other side—but nothing happened. The silence was unnerving. It reminded me of the cell-like quality back where I lived in Earls Court. It would be difficult to know, if given money, exactly where it was I'd choose to live. Had I the chance. It wouldn't be here. Not in a grave like this. How nervous I felt, what nonsense! I pushed on the bell again, and still nothing happened. But then I noticed that the door itself was fractionally open. Was I meant to enter then? To stroll in like an unsuspecting fly straight into the soft-spoken spider's web? The door swung easily at my touch—it was exactly like a scene from Arabian Nights, so utterly unlike the passage I'd just left that I just simply gasped.

It was another world. Like entering a different sort of space, a separate climate altogether. Of touch and feel and smell. I knew instinctively that it was wrong to stay, but the spell was already too potent. I cleared my throat and took another step. The trembling heroine of a horror film? Could Colonel Smythe be cousin to Count Dracula? I never relished bite marks on my neck, especially not with going to Brighton tomorrow. My father's eyes were like a hawk for all that kind of thing. Was I foolish and asking for trouble? But trouble of what nature anyway? All that I'd come for was dinner. And assuming even that the kitchen utensils were dirty, all I'd end up with would be, at most, a spot of food poisoning and a dash of violent diarrhoea.

'Ah, you've arrived, my dear. Good evening.' The voice set off such shudderings down my spine I almost slipped a disc. She's surprisingly young and otherwise healthy—they would have said at Casualties—to sustain such vertebral abrasion! Has she arrived from some volcanic zone? No? She maintains it was merely a greeting!

'Oh, hello. Yes, I'm here!' I said needlessly.

We stood necessarily close in the restricted space of the doorway. He leaned over and shut the door fast behind me. I smelled again that cloying scent of cachou on his breath. Was that his kick then—violets? Did he live on a diet of those? I couldn't wait to see what colour his tongue must be. Much the same as the tongue of a Chow, I thought. Theirs were always a dull purplish pink. Hanging out—quite unlike most other dogs—all the time, as if perpetually on the scrounge. Or perhaps it was a pale rose blue, the shade of a young sow's snout.

'Your cloak?' He meant my coat, of course, but cloak was more romantic. I smiled to show I understood the subtleties wrought by words. He touched my shoulder inadvertently—it didn't seem on purpose—as I shrugged the garment off. And brushed from there along the entire length of one underarm until he'd reached my wrist. I had my back to him, but even so the featherweight slithering touch on my bare skin was as unexpectedly intimate as if we'd kissed. He turned me round to face him, seeming to sense my confusion. 'You mustn't be shy of me,' he soothed. I strained to catch his words.

'All right, I won't,' I whispered back.

'Let me show you around now,' he said.

It amazed me in fact that when he did precisely that, there wasn't all that much to see. Not in terms of actual square footage. The whole place would probably, when I thought of it, have fitted three times in our flat. It's what he'd done with it that made the difference. Each wall, each odd and unexpected surface like table tops and tiny built-in cupboards, were covered in crystal mirror. Some split in tiny two-inch squares like multiple mosaics. Some smoked mysteriously in glowing greys and others reaching from the ceiling to the carpeted floor, majestically framed in glittering gilt and intricate carved ivory. Or hard flat ebony, black to match the velvet-pelmeted curtains at the windows. And black to match the thick fur covering the floors. The only deliberate colour now it seemed to me occurred on the ceiling where one gigantic painting of a nude occupied the entire area. It hurt my neck to look at it. He saw me straining back and permitted himself a smile. 'What you're trying to do is sacrilege. Of course there is only one way to view that work of art. And that is flat on your back.' I hadn't somehow been conscious of the bed at first. Not with so much else to absorb my eyes. And being black as well and similarly clothed in the same fur as the floor, it was conceivable that anyone might confuse the two. 'Lie down,' he led me to it. 'And then look up. But,' he paused, then added gently, 'do take your shoes off first.'

I squirmed inside with embarrassment, knowing I had a hole. Furious that in my hasty flight from home I hadn't bothered to change my stockings. 'What limited life this hosiery has! But hardly the span of a butterfly—' Could I get away with such pretentiousness? Possibly not I thought. I slipped my shoes off with one hand and surreptitiously pulled the hideous hole right over my biggest toe, trying to grip the slack down with the others. Until the whole foot looked deformed. Then I lay down on the bed with both feet hanging out of sight over the bottom edge.

He smiled. 'You're far too low,' he purred. 'Look here—come up much higher.' He patted the many cushions at the top. There was no going against him. No way in which I could enforce my will or try to hide a thing. He *wormed*. Without exertion. I knew it even then, floundering foolishly about the trivial fact of the hole in my toe. As if our future hung in the balance of those broken silk threads. 'Whatever's wrong, my dear?' I hadn't and wouldn't budge from where I lay. 'I only wish you to place yourself in a more advantageous position. Nothing more sinister if that's what you're assuming! How could it be with dinner guests arriving at any second?'

'My stocking's got a hole in it. I don't want you to see!' I felt better as soon as I'd said it, despite the uneasy delivery. Funny how I'd forgotten how childishness felt. And what a stupendous relief owning up brought with it—always out of all proportion to the offence! I thought he'd laugh. That's what my father always used to do, start laughing as soon as he'd won. 'You tell the truth, and every time it's best, my girl. Own Up could be our family motto.' A crest above the Crunchie Bars, for customers to see.

But no. 'How touching and sweet you are.' He put his hand down on my knee and traced the through route to my extradited extremities. The monkey grip of my tense toes loosened. 'Yes there,' I said. 'Can you feel it?' He said nothing, not a word, instead I watched in growing horror as he bent his head as though to actually—kiss it! Oh Christ Almighty, could there be a stink of something there as well? When the hell did I last wash those stockings? And my constant fight against athletes' foot (caught in Derek's bed, I might add). Would he know without looking under?

But I was saved now by the bell it seemed. Trilling at his sealed front door. My fellow guests? This evening's fate? He rose and tenderly helped me to my feet, holding one hand to steady me, as I put my shoes on with the other.

'Come,' he whispered in one ear. 'Your little hole shall be our secret. I will remember it always—as the first gift you will have given me—' I took it he did mean my stocking. Though, strangely enough, each word he spoke was said in such a weighted and important way I gained the impression of weakness in myself, a sly disintegration. An awful readiness, an eagerness indeed to present myself for sacrificial slaughter. As if by even listening only to his sentences I was somehow mutely committed and on the brink of accepting whatever it was he wished to—to what, though? 'That's just it,' I'd have to confess to Fiona. 'At that point in the proceedings, I didn't even know myself!'

But later on I did. Much later on. After the others had gone and long after I should have gone myself. But by then of course ...

I wondered about telling Winnie, feeling the need to spill beans. She'd presented me with the perfect opening. 'Are you ill—or on top of the world?'

'Beg pardon, Winnie?'

She'd cocked her auntie-ish head on to one side, and pursed her lips and narrowed what could be seen of her piggy little eyes. I thought how well she'd play in Gilbert and Sullivans. The Mikado. Himself. Or else the maiden aunt of Minnie Ha Ha. If such a person existed. 'You look so—' She screwed her face up even tighter. But this time I chose, out of a sense of respect, to look the other way. It wouldn't be fair to compare the countenance of a colleague to a bleached and wrinkled dog turd. Those ones which sit on pavements turning white. 'You look so—funny, somehow, I don't know. As if you are still asleep.'

I was asleep in actual fact, still numbed and slumbering. I couldn't even pinpoint it myself. Could it be the effects of the sleeping pill? The first one I'd ever had! I hadn't wanted it, not at all. 'No thank you. I never take pills, not even aspirins, as a matter of fact. I just don't trust them, that's all.' But I'd taken it. Despite the lateness of the hour, or rather despite the earliness. 'But there are only four more hours to go before I shall have to get up. I mean to say I'll have to go back to the flat to change. And to pack all the things I'll take home. I've got to take that case to school with me. I'll be going straight to Brighton from there—'

But he'd placed his finger-tips to my lips and calmed me down with kisses. All over.

'What were you doing anyway, last night? Something rather special?' Winnie and I were queueing up together to be served the abysmal school dinner. Specials for staff, which just meant they were that much bigger. 'Potatoes, miss?' 'No, not for me. And not for you either, Winnie.' I frowned at her eager plate, deciding against full confession.

'Quite special. Out to dinner. With a television person and his wife. She used to be a dancer. One of the TV Toppers—' The kitchen-hand had caught my words, had stopped in mid-helping of a pile of swedes. 'Ooh, TV Topper, miss, you say? They're really good. What legs!'

Winnie sighed. 'My goodness, what a giddy life you're leading. Going out with such glamorous people.'

We walked out of the kitchen towards the lower staff-room where we ate our dinner along with the other old fogies. I'd said to Winnie we ought to think about breaking unspoken rules and eat on our own upstairs. The food itself was enough to upset the system apart from having to put up with colic-making conversation too. There wasn't any real reason come to that why we shouldn't bring our own. 'A bit of cheese and a packet of Ryvita. Or an orange and two boiled eggs. Much better than this muck, now, Winnie—'

'Perhaps we'll start on it next week. The hot food's such a comfort in the traumas of this teaching, don't you find?'

I didn't share the deep distress she was suffering with the girls. In fact in less than a fortnight now, or exactly a fortnight next Monday, my classes were going quite splendidly. Despite Mrs Pritchard's first doubts. 'Good heavens above'—she'd entered my room unexpectedly— 'And whatever is going on here?'

'Collage,' I'd explained, though barely bothering to turn. She'd looked bewildered. 'It's better,' I'd said as kindly as I could, but with a certain coolness, 'to come and look when they've finished, Mrs Pritchard.'

'What confidence! You mean to say she just turned round and left?' Winnie could hardly believe it.

'But, Winnie, what you don't understand, is that we've just come out of training. You can't expect someone who's been in teaching since lord knows when to be up to the latest tricks. Especially not a Head, that is, who's preoccupied as well with administration. She knows that as well as me. If anyone's on the defensive it's surely going to be her. That's my view of it anyway.' It struck me forcibly as I spoke what a difference I felt at work. Here in this educational establishment I knew what I was talking about. My confidence sprang from knowledge and the limited experience gained from teaching practice. I had no fears, no doubts of losing a pupil's attention, simply because I cunningly constructed each lesson to lure that attention. They liked my classes. I taxed their hands as much as their heads and helped them form a definite link between the two. Winnie's was, so she thought, a much more difficult job. She made them sit quite quietly to absorb the knowledge. She fought to force-feed them with facts. My job was of my making.

But, last night how different I'd been.

The dancing wife had barely deigned to shake my hand. Her husband was only too eager. It didn't aid the evening. He'd asked me as discreetly as he could to give him my telephone number. 'What for?' I'd asked in dumb naïveté. 'I'm not trained at all for television.' His eyes had slid towards our host, who was attending to his wife. That didn't please me either, very much. Why wasn't he here, sitting with me? The television man was scribbling something on a cigarette pack. 'Call me.' He said it curiously. Managing almost to make it a menacing command. And then, 'Why haven't I met you before? Has Reggie been keeping you secret?' He lowered his voice. 'The old devil likes to do that with the best!'

I hated him. I loathed what he was saying, as if there'd been others before. What was it then, some sort of syndicate? Where girls got passed around like goods. Chucked out of the circuit when soiled? I stood up. 'Which way,' I asked, 'is the bathroom?'

The man stared up. 'You mean to say that you don't know?'

'How could I? I haven't been in this place before.'

Colonel Smythe had arisen now too and courteously came forward. 'Can I help in any way my dear? Is there something I can do?'

'Your young friend here, this lovely kid, claims to have lost her bearings—' The television man insinuated cynicism. His glossy wife winked over her shoulder and then glanced back coldly at me. 'The ladies' room,' she said in an Anna Neagle voice, 'is in the same place as the gents'!' And she jerked her thumb as direction like a hitch-hiker on the road. The false refinement of her voice fought with her words and action. I liked people who were more in keeping, without all this social confusion. 'Oh, and don't steal the jewels set into the taps! Remember the two-way mirror!'

They all three laughed. It couldn't be true! One of them had been in there already, and the rest of us hadn't been told to look. Unless I was to be the scapegoat. The unsuspecting victim of the evening. The sacrificial lamb then, after all. With the lavatory seat as the altar! What viciousness! What very funny jokes. 'I won't go in there after all. I'll possibly go home instead.' My second show of childishness within the hour. It felt an hour to me. Wasn't time meant to hang heavy when you weren't enjoying yourself? I'd obviously been there longer than an hour. How much more I had to learn about social ease and graces. About passing pleasant hours with people who had nothing in common. My father may have blustered his way and probably enjoyed it. But his aggressive charms were not my own. I wasn't invited for those.

I looked at my watch. Already past midnight. 'Oh, I've got to be going. It's late!'

The dancing wife had looked at her loathsome husband. And from him she'd looked at our host. 'Oh no,' she'd shrilled. 'I'm quite sure Reggie wouldn't like that. If anyone's going, it's us. Isn't it darling?' Her husband jumped awkwardly to his feet, his jowls jiggling in the process. I wondered how low his balls must be—right to the back of his knees, fighting for space with his buttocks. Why ever should the Golden Girl have married him? His wealth and position, I presumed. Fairly obviously not his fidelity.

I remained standing whilst they all three demurred and then the two of them eventually departed. The man had had the nerve to open my handbag now, I noticed, and slip his scribblings inside. I could, of course, have made a conscious and quite public show of passing the particle back, but something in me stopped, held back from doing it. Why should I be put in this position of dumb acceptance, like an animal? Like a horse accepting a saddle, knowing it would mean a ride. I wouldn't have ridden anywhere with him. Except home, of course, as of this minute. Back to my flat with his missus and him as a lift. They didn't offer one. Just went! I began to fret about my taxi fare, now we were alone. Would he forget, Colonel Smythe, to pay it? Reimburse me as he'd promised. I blushed to realise he'd read my thoughts. Had my eyes actually signalled avarice? Printed coarsely across each pupil—or just half the word in each? He fumbled in a waistcoat pocket and brought out a five-pound note. Then followed it with another!

My mouth must have dropped, my jaw swung lantern-like against my neck. I felt its bony frontier. He took my hand and smoothed the first note in its centre, then closed my fingers tight. 'This is your taxi fare, my darling! And this'—he took my other hand now and repeated the procedure—'this is to cover your future fares.'

'Then what did he do though? I can't believe it! A tenner before you'd begun? Is he a betting man by any chance, old Colonel Smythe?' Fiona's orchard was very cold. I wished we could go inside. I shivered and hunched my shoulders round my ears, deciding best how I could say it.

I'd tried to work it out the whole way on the train, but all I did was meander through the moments. Re-living liquid memories of that night, like someone mooning, moodily in love.

'Perhaps that's what it is, then! You're in love!' She'd meant it, Fiona, jokingly, of course. And I'd encouraged her in the sheer unlikelihood of the notion.

'In love? Oh yes, I'm sure. With Colonel Reggie Smythe? Of course I am!' But even as I'd made fun of the fact, I experienced deep disloyalty, a sense of some betrayal to someone who didn't deserve it. Perhaps I shouldn't try to put it into words at all. Why should I even tell her? Tell anyone at all. I supposed because of the money—I couldn't keep that to myself. Not from Fiona. I couldn't resist trying to impress her. A spot of showing off which she'd appreciate. That part of it was easy. That part of it was fun—the paying her back my debt. Whatever it was I owed. Almost six pounds, she'd said it was by the end. How in hell it came to that, no one could ever know! But what did it matter now. Now with my extra income. I had four pounds left for myself—or for genuinely taking taxis! Back to Nelson House on Sunday!

He'd shown me the bathroom when the Terrible Two

had left. It was even more opulent than I'd have imagined. There were indeed fine jewels, quite genuine, set into all the taps—the golden taps, surmounting a golden bath. And a golden handbasin as well. And yes, a golden bog. I wondered what colour it went when flushed with a girl's menstrual flow. A rare exotic sight, no doubt, like a goblet containing rare wine. How difficult to clean, this place must be! Which scouring powder? Which? It was uncanny how he seemed to read my thoughts. 'I clean this place myself, you know. Oh yes, I much prefer it, rather than have possibly unsympathetic people here.'

I hadn't myself exactly found this evening's guests totally *au fait* with his style, but of course I didn't say so. Not then, at any rate. Instead I asked about his wife and where she fitted in. I'd asked already once before about her. After we'd been introduced at his young son's party. He'd vaguely waved his hand as if the matter held but little interest. 'My wife? She must be in the South of France by now, I believe. She's motoring through from Rome. With friends.' And so I hadn't pursued the matter any more. Ernest had told me anyway that they didn't live together, that his father kept a close relationship with the family by dropping in each day. But had for many years maintained his own existence. 'Frightfully friendly, you understand. All completely civilised.' I wondered how my father would feel if my mum took to motoring through Europe. She'd have to start some driving lessons first, of course. Enrol with B.S.M. And I think that he'd have probably put his foot down over that, let alone possible further junketings. A woman across the street had once had it off with a B.S.M. instructor. We used to see his car parked up the road, with the L-plates in the back window.

I shouldn't have asked about his wife, I knew it before he'd answered. The ghost of a frown had flitted across his face, the first time I'd seen him look irritable. The two were obviously clearly kept apart, this life of his—and her. He had no wish to mix them, even by mentioning her name. I quickly asked another question. 'Tell me—is the mirror two-way?' And I opened my eyes ingenuously to make up for my insensitivity. The moment passed, his forehead cleared and his eyes creased up in a twinkle. His dentist was exceptionally good, or else they were all dentures.

'No,' he chuckled roguishly—much in the manner of

300

Nathaniel, I was reminded. The impression gave me a thrill. And so now was the proximity, sending signals all over my body. I looked at him, demanding silently that he return the gaze. He did. We faced each other quite squarely. A head-on collision, m'lord. No chance of side-stepping, no opportunity to swerve. On centre all the way. He took my hands in both of his and brought them to my chin, then tilting down from his great height, he lowered his lips. And kissed me.

His mouth felt dry and dusty, like crinkled tissue paper. A touch of velvet on my own. Each firmly shut, like boxes holding treasures. Withholding trembling times and a vulnerable closeness. So far so good. So very good. He, in his wisdom, broke away, as I was wanting more. I would have liked to stay just as we were, the paunchiness of his stomach so solidly wedged against my own. Something safe to lean against, something substantial in life. Oh yes, I would have stood there like that through the entire night. Two statues frozen up like snowmen.

I watched him turning towards the golden bath and saw him twist the tap—the one with the ruby on top. It caught the light, the crimson stone. Red for danger. And red for stop, of course. And dark, rich roses, meaning love. The back of his neck looked like a reconnaissance chart, each thread-like line looped finely to another, in contrast to the skull-like smoothness of his scalp. I didn't mind his baldness, not a bit, it made him appear more eccentric. It gave him the look of a nursery book Humpty Dumpty. I could guess that his arms and legs were probably quite thin in comparison to his body. 'This love of yours for the grotesque—preoccupation with peculiarities—is far from healthy, I feel! Normality is not to be sneezed at.' Whoever had said that to me? Any number of people might have. Hidebound ones. I thought of Nicholas' friend Jim, and I thought of Pat's Douglas. Both fine, upstanding, Anglo-Saxon specimens instead of ...

'I'm running you a bath.' I must have looked dazed and stupid, in contrast to how I was feeling. 'Before I put you into bed.' No question of asking me first. The second man to put me in a bath. Did I suffer from serious B.O.? I hoped that he'd go out, to let me undress on my own. Not hover around assessing all my underwear like nosy assistants in shops. 'I'll leave you now, to undress on your own.' Oh God, could he read every thought in my head?

The steam was clouding up the mirrors; I surveyed my nudity through what looked like a fine sea mist. And then I stepped into the water. The surface of the golden bath felt much like normal enamel. Perhaps it was, but sprayed this way. How devilishly clever! How cunning! Hey, dad, how about spraying this bath of ours gold? And the lav. And the larder. And the lino. And my larynx—what about my larynx? The girl with the golden larynx—I could go as a Carroll Lewis discovery. I saw from staring straight ahead at the mirrored wall before me that the door, the bathroom door, was slowly opening. I slid beneath the surface of the water, as if its scented transparency might hide my bountiful curves. It seemed so much, much more erotic me lying here quite naked—and he completely clothed. So formally, as well, was what it was, with pin-striped trousers, and dense black coat and waistcoat complete with watch. Rigged out like a city gent, but without the finishing bowler.

I smiled at him; I felt quite at my ease, and wished to tantalise and tease, knowing I looked quite good. The heat of the water had turned my body pink, toasted it up to a tender degree, softened the surface to taste. I felt the sweat form on my face and lifted one hand to wipe it, at the same time licking my upper lip. He didn't move. He didn't say a word. Just stood there looking down at me. Stunned, I supposed with my beauty! 'I'm stunned, I suppose, with your beauty!' Oh Jesus Christ! It was going beyond a joke! I looked at him and at the strange expression on his face, for all the world as if it had been frozen. Carved from granite, very grave and ancient with regret.

And then—a terrible sob leapt, strangling, from his throat. Alarm sprang through my body at the sound. I sat up suddenly in fear. What was wrong? Was he ill? 'What's the matter?' But he didn't answer, not a word, not one syllable of sense. Only a low groaning moan like an animal in pain, with rolling eyes and an agonised anguish on his face. Oh hell, was he having a seizure? Could it be a case of a coronary? Ye Gods, and me without my clothes on or a knowledge of first aid!

He fell to his knees, hitting his head on the side of the bath—hardly a reeling blow, but enough, it seemed, for him to feel the need to bury his face in his arms. I tried to still my mounting sense of panic and, slurping water everywhere, rose unsteadily to my feet. A rippling wave

302

washed over his right ear; he seemed to be impervious, appeared now to almost be unconscious. No sound at all! I carefully stepped over the side and out of the bath. But before both feet were safely on the ground, he'd lunged himself towards me. I fell. I slipped and sprawled all over him. Now both of us were crying. Me just from sheer shock and fright. And he, it seemed, from—love!

He loved me! He'd lost his heart! And his mind had lost all reason! He wasn't sick, except in soul and spirit—he ached, had ached, for me from the minute that we'd met! He wished me now to tread on him, to treat him like a worm. Defile, destroy and defecate! To do whatever I wished. He wasn't fit to touch my feet, he wanted me to—It somehow didn't sink in at all—I couldn't quite grasp the switch. I couldn't fit the two together, this trembling jelly and the distant courteous stranger that I'd seen before. I shrank away from him. But where I went, he followed. Fell squirming around the floor, tugging the towel I tried to wrap around me. Oh dear. 'Don't do that, please,' I said. 'You've not to. Stop!' But nothing, it seemed, got to him. He had quite possibly gone mad, but given time might recover.

'I can't be long now, Fiona. I promised my father, you see. In any case, it's bloody cold out here. Any chance of a cup of tea?'

'But you haven't told me anything at all. Not down to the nitty gritty.'

I sighed. 'It's difficult, that's all. I'm dreadfully confused, I think.'

'But what about Ernest? You said that he's been phoning you—are you going to see him again? And what does his father say about that? And when will you go there again?'

'That's what I mean, there's just too much to think about. Perhaps we can meet tomorrow.' I couldn't bring myself to tell her all. I didn't want her judgement. In any case I needed time to examine it more myself. To try to work out just why I had found it exciting, and whether I ought to go on.

My father had met me off the train. 'It's dead on time today! A fraction of a second short maybe, but nothing worth a complaint.'

'I'm sorry, dad, to disappoint, I know you like a word—'

He'd hugged me in embarrassment and to hide his smiling pleasure. It moved me, more than I would have been normally moved, to do with the state I was in. I felt his ear upon my cheek and smelt his shampooed hair. What little hair there was, of course—a running family joke. 'Mm, you've washed your hair then, dad.'

He took my case. 'What, brought home all your washing, girl?'

'Well actually, yes I have. No drying, you see, in the basement. They can blow out in our back yard.'

We took the bus back to the shop, the evening was growing dark and the street lights glowed. The bus was full of people going home just like ourselves. My father got into a chat with an old chap sitting beside him. 'What do you think then?' he said. 'Of the news?' 'What news?' 'All of it.' 'Which?' 'Well any—take, for instance—'

I turned away and looked out of the window. It all was exactly the same.

I'd refused to do as Reggie had asked, couldn't quite bring myself to kick him. We'd never had a dog at home, and certainly never had cats—because of my father's allergy— and so the feeling of a *thing* around my knees felt very unfamiliar. I felt the need to air the leaping laugh that started in my stomach, from nerves, from nervousness, I now supposed. I couldn't cope, was what it was. And besides, it felt so ticklish, all his little lickings. He'd started slowly with my toes and gradually worked upwards. And then he'd guided me, like a big St Bernard, from the bathroom to the bed—actually on all fours, bumping clumsily into furniture on the way. I didn't like to look at him. Is this how people were? Is that what happened then as they got older—a return to the animal kingdom? Was my father at this very moment playing mongrels on heat, with my mother?

The fur on the bed was nice; the feel of it against my naked flesh. Neither of us spoke at all. He whimpered, salivating by my side, then relentlessly moved downwards. A dumb and awkward animal, whose daintiness now surprised. I squeezed my fists together as he started, hoping I wouldn't giggle. His big and shiny head bent in between my thighs. His tongue licked left, then right, leaving a dampening trail behind it on each leg until it gently came to rest. To rest. To nest. To nestle, flopping,

304

face well forward in my family treasure.

I stared straight up ahead and gave a silent greeting to the nude. What period then would she have been? Early, oh Christ, just when? A mishmash bloody awful piece of work. A fake. An obvious twicer. To me at any rate, with my insight and knowledge. A *Sleeping Venus* in the Giorgione manner with Titian tints but tits more Botticelli and a much more modern-looking face, in the mould of Manet's *Olympia*. I wondered if Reggie knew these things and how much he'd had to pay. The girl lay stretched in an idyllic landscape which might have been done by Raphael. It wasn't by any means or imagination my kind of thing at all. I favoured a franker kind of art, which started as late as Lautrec who, in his turn, was now superseded by my engrossed devotion to and preoccupation with the work of the German Hans Bellmer. Those were the nudes that fired my mind. Perverse and erotically surreal, not some weak pastiche of classical stuff. We didn't really have that much in common, I reflected, on looking around. The attraction of opposites? The mating of spring and—winter? Well autumn, at any rate.

He was still fully dressed, doing his chairman's duties. Putting his client completely at her ease. Relaxing me now. Relentlessly. I would have liked to wriggle right away. It felt so disembodied done like this. Lonely, with no one to talk to. His mouth was full; he couldn't speak in any case. He'd managed to prop his nose upon my pubic mound like a pottery pig on the mantelpiece. I thought of that and gave a smile up to old *Sleeping Venus*, but as I did, a piercing stabbing thread of something close to pleasure sneaked up from down below. It all felt very wet and dribbly because, of course, it was. It felt in fact not far removed from how it felt on trains with people touching me. It felt, oh, somehow awfully ripe and ready for the plucking. The old familiar tightening, the military formation of the muscles—that clenched and drawn discomfort wasn't there at all! I began to pay attention to the game.

The whole of Brighton felt freezing—depressingly, chillingly cold. My father refused to have the only heater in the shop. 'A hazard,' he claimed. 'Not merely safety, but in terms of stock, you understand. Heat dries out the tobacco and would melt all the chocolate and cause the boiled sweets to bleed and stick together—'

'Boiled sweets don't bleed,' I objected.

'They sweat,' he said quite firmly. 'Oh yes! They decidedly do. They're meant to be kept at a certain temperature, in conditions just-so for confectionery—'

'In conditions unfit for humans! Have you seen the state of mam's chilblains? No wonder trade is falling off. It's like walking straight into a fridge. And what about those silly gloves you're wearing? With all the finger-tips chopped off! People don't want their sweets weighed out like that, with old bits of wool in with them—'

I'd left his huffy, high-hunched shoulders and gone up to my room. They'd left it all exactly as it was; it made me want to cry. What poverty. What paucity. What shabbiness. What shame? No, not exactly shame, but just a suddenly seeing it as it was. Instead of as I'd remembered. My mother had had my quilted counterpane cleaned. It danced a riotous honeysuckle haze before my eyes. Beyond it pinned at intervals on the wall were my reproduction Degas'. What the hell had they to do with my current leanings? How long in fact, had they been there—since my second year in grammar school when my keenness was starting to sharpen. And my talents beginning to show.

Reggie had said I had talents last night. So far untapped, so he claimed. I couldn't fault him on that point—all I'd done was lie there. But lie there liking it in fact. 'Am I giving you pleasure?' he'd said. I'd nodded and shut my eyes, then opened them shining, to show or give a show of bliss. As I'd seen actresses do on screen. How different was my situation here in his bed compared to the one with Derek. Or Douglas, if it came to that. How easy, how unreal. He'd risen and carefully wiped his mouth with the nearest thing available. A corner of the tablecloth, no less, which still sat on the uncleared table. I hoped he'd send it to the laundry now—the act seemed to me unhygienic. It now occurred of course as well that he would be clearing the table and washing up no doubt, since there was no one else to do it. A *pied à terre*, but with plenty to do with the hands. I'd have to put down my own foot over that. I wouldn't be used as a skivvy. There wasn't any cause for worry. I lay, a princess, on my perch while he played pauper and serf.

Afterwards, he'd excused himself and undressed in the bathroom. So that was it, there only were three rooms and the tiny space of the hall. The kitchen lay behind my head, and I faced towards the bathroom. I hadn't seen him nude, not once. Would I ever be given the pleasure? He'd returned to me in his pyjamas and, on reflection, I suppose I was pleased. But it made him more grandfatherly. How old was he, I was dying to ask.

'You know how old I am, Princess?'

I swallowed the surging saliva. 'I hadn't given it much thought.'

'Well. I am ...' He paused. 'I am three score and ten—come tomorrow!'

I did my mental arithmetic, my mind going wild at the sum. Cream crackers and cottage cheese! Three score and ten—that was *seventy*! 'Many happy returns for tomorrow. Oh dear, I shan't be in town. Shall I send you a telegram, Reggie?'

He knelt at the edge of the bed. 'Oh my darling child, say that again—'

'Shall I send you a telegram—'

'Reggie, say Reggie again. It's like honey. It's nectar to me in your voice.'

I wondered just exactly what he meant by that. Wasn't my accent too much like his mother-in-law's? Ernest's grannie, who was such a card? 'Reggie,' I said it once again. And gingerly touched him on the cheek. I liked the way it was between us both, me being his big baby, but at the same time me controlling things. Me giving the directives. How subtle and seemingly swift the change had been. How hard to try to register those first impressions at the party.

'Tell me, Princess'—he kissed my hand, and placed it under his arm. I felt him warm both on my palm and on the other side. My blood ran much more swiftly so it seemed than his, but he provided solid river banks. 'Has my young son been pestering you of late? Don't be frightened to tell me the truth—that is in fact the way I found your number. I watched him dialling, you see.'

'And remembered the combination, just like that? How clever. I couldn't do that—' Imagine it though. *Seventy*. My dad could be his son. He probably would have liked to have been, especially if it made him seventeen. But how many years did that make it between us? 'What since the party, you mean? Has he rung me a lot since then? Yes, sometimes twice a day, I think. He imagines himself in love.' What gross imbalance there lay between the two. How old was he then, Reggie, when Ernest was born? Seventy, or sixty-nine to be quite fair since we were still in today—that much minus seventeen. Which made it—fifty-two? Or possibly fifty-one if Ernest were almost eighteen, which wasn't bad. Not bad at all. 'How old were you when you married?'

'It's unimportant, darling thing. There's only you and I.'

'And Ernest—'

'Ah, Ernest. What will you do about Ernest? Do you think that you'll see him again?'

'The trouble is, he's much too young. Too young to interest me—'

'I'd like you to.'

I stared.

'I'd like you to, Princess. But of course, you must make your own decisions.'

There didn't seem much point in coming home to Brighton, not after the first few hours. The school, of course, was centrally heated. And so had been Reggie's place. Home seemed as bleak as the basement in terms of warmth to me. And my preoccupation was with Nelson House and the beautiful taps in the bathroom, and the fabulous fur of the bed. He'd gently peeled it back like a banana skin and slipped me underneath his sheets. And then he'd slithered in as well and passed me the small sleeping pill. He hadn't taken one himself. 'I prefer to not sleep,' he'd explained. 'I like to read and think of many things. I want to lie and look at you, my new and precious love.' It probably was as well to take the pill, that's what I thought later. I never could sleep with any light on in the room, not even a little candle. And certainly not with someone staring over at me each time they turned a page. But he'd done more than all those things; I could tell that he had by the morning. The table was completely cleared of last night's festivities, in fact was laid for breakfast. Just for me. Smoked salmon and an avocado pear. 'What, for breakfast? Meat and veg—or rather fish and—?' I'd spoken out of sheer surprise at the oddness of the offering. In coming days, at later dates, I used to laugh at that, me thinking it was odd at all. I can't remember—and did he also offer me champagne before I went off to work? I

308

hadn't had an avocado, not before. And didn't know how to eat it. And when I did, I hadn't liked it much. 'An acquired taste, for a princess. Like caviar and champagne.' He'd called the car, one on his account apparently. 'What, I don't have to pay him at all?' I'd let it take me to the flat in order to pick up my case. And change, of course, into my teaching clothes. And I'd let it wait to take me to Westminster, then I'd caught the bus on to school. All worked out with calm and consummate ease! Was that what age was all about? Or was it merely money?

Fiona saw me off at the station at the end of the awful weekend. It hadn't been a success. 'You're strange,' she'd grumbled. 'Not, I don't know, not you at all. Is it something to do with Ernest's father?'

But it wasn't only my abstracted air. It turned out she'd gone off with Piers, from the party at Ernest's place last week. I didn't mind. 'Good gracious me, why should I? Do you like him then, Fiona?' It seemed she always had, or so she claimed. But it apparently was hopeless. He'd never found her physically attractive, which made it so much more frustrating—the fact of his fancying me. I didn't know quite what to say. They'd gone to a club and got drunk, to return to Ernest's party for me. 'Where was he though then—when we left?'

'Well, he'd seen you dancing with Ernest, and that was the final straw. He was so cheesed off and pissed that he sloped off on his own.'

I was sorry now I'd said about Reggie to her. 'I shan't see him again, of course,' I said quickly. The train was arriving to whisk me away back to London. 'Reggie, I mean. Ernest's father.' I didn't want her telling Piers. I bought her a platform ticket. It wasn't nice leaving like this, with men and boys and life's experience seeming to come between us. 'By the way, changing subjects, how is Nathaniel?'

'I haven't heard. I haven't heard a bloody word! Isn't it just the limit. I've dropped a line though, giving him your number—' My heart did actually miss a beat. 'Yes, I've got to be careful down here. You know, with mummy and daddy. And even with ringing him up. I can't do it on our home account, I know that they'd somehow trace it. You don't mind, do you, I've done that? I can keep you informed of my plans. He comes down to London now and then. And he does know all about you.'

I crossed my legs when I sat down and stared out of the window. A stranger, a man, of course, had helped me place my case. High up above my head he stretched; I looked with languid interest. How long ago was it when I had travelled up obsessed with the contours of cocks? When now I was so much more occupied with my own. Not cock, of course, I smiled at the chill wintry evening. No, cunt. My cunt. My criss-cross layered route that still as yet had not received the benefit. But even so, was starting to chirp and warble on its own and might soon start to burst into song.

Pat was lying in bed with Roly Balls when I got back. In the old bed-settee in the kitchen. Drinking wine and looking remarkably happy. I hadn't asked her how all that was going. What she'd been up to with whom. Perhaps she'd managed to tame the Gay Lothario. Or was this a mere one-off? I looked at him; we hadn't met before. He winked above her head. I chose to ignore the intended disloyalty. Poor old Patty. A bit like me, with Derek. Everyone had known, oh long before me, and even then I hadn't believed. She obviously did love him to distraction. 'Hello! Have a glass of wine with us. How did the weekend go?'

'A bit of a flop in many ways. I don't really know why I went.' I took my coat off and sat down. 'What a wonderfully cosy scene.' Pat wriggled up to Roly and put her arm around his shoulder. He didn't acknowledge that she was even there, not by a single glance or even a flutter of an eyelash. What a curiously cold fish for a doctor. I wouldn't care to see him with a scalpel in his hand. He must run riot through the nurses of Guy's Hospital. What contrast there was between him and my own current bedfellow. 'Oh, by the way'—I spoke as casually as I could. 'Any telephone calls for me?'

'Masses! We took the bloody phone off the hook to get a bit of peace to be quite honest.'

'Oh dear. Is it off the hook now?' Reggie had said he'd ring about this time. And there was always the chance of Nathaniel. I'd been thinking of that, of what I'd do if ever he got on the phone. Did I wish to be disloyal to Fiona back in Brighton by trying for Nathaniel myself? It didn't seem so vital any more, but then I couldn't guarantee just

310

how I'd feel with his voice, that voice, at the end of the line. 'Any messages then? I mean to say, did you write down any names?' Pat was busy trying to kiss the back of Roly's neck. I watched him shrug her away. It didn't work, she hung on like a limpet. Oh dear!

The list was what I knew before I read it, but Reggie's name wasn't there. And nor was Nathaniel's. It was Michael, and Ernest, and Nicholas. And Piers. Oh Christ! I replaced the idle receiver. It started to ring right away. Reggie. My pulses jumped with pleasure. He was waiting, he whispered in my ear. No other words were necessary. I dressed as if now off to school, thinking ahead to the morning. My single bed looked bleak and lonely, as indeed did Pat's. Her bed-settee had been her best idea so far. They could stay snug in there till tommorrow.

But Roly apparently had other plans. When I went to the kitchen to say goodbye, he was up and already dressed. Pat lay looking woebegone and lost in the bed without him. I thought her perilously close to tears. 'Which way are you going then?' he asked. 'May I share a taxi with you?'

I looked at him uncertainly, keenly aware of an awkwardness. 'Oh,' I tried to keep the coldness from my voice. 'I'm not sure I'm in your direction.'

'Oh, which direction would you think was mine?'

'Well, I'm going down to the Embankment. Towards the Tate, that sort of way—'

'What luck! Exactly mine.' His triumph. He'd trapped me neatly. I sweated underneath my clothes, knowing how Pat felt. I'd watched Derek once responding too readily to another girl. And she flagrantly flirting with him. The bond was such across the room between them both I felt quite sick, quite bilious with my jealousy. An ugly coarse emotion, which twisted all my features. I didn't look at her, at Pat lying there. We both knew what his game was surely! The unfairness was I didn't want him. Not want or like him in any way. Too young for a start now, for me!

I wondered fleetingly how they would react if they knew who it was I was going to. He probably couldn't conceive that I might actually prefer to sleep with a geriatric, instead of a stud such as him. The thought reminded me of Reggie's lips and what they'd coaxed from my clitty. I turned away towards the door, to leave them to say their goodbyes. 'I've got to be going, it's getting late.' To my further disgust he followed closely on my heels, without even a kiss blown to Pat.

'Roly—' The pain and disappointment wavered in her voice.

' 'Bye, Patty,' I said. 'I'll see you.' I went with the minimum drama, trying to keep everything light. Perhaps that's where she was going wrong, trying to pin down the bastard. I'd probably made the same mistake. How much nicer men were like Reggie. 'That was rather brutal, Roly.' We stood outside the street. He hailed a passing taxi which didn't bother to stop.

'Bastard!'

'Exactly what I thought myself.'

'What?'

'You are,' I said, 'a bastard.' He looked up towards the sky and laughed.

'You cheeky little thing!'

I dug my hands deep in my pockets and looked at him disapprovingly. 'Nobody should treat people as you obviously do—and least of all people, Pat.' He frowned. I looked away and up the road. 'There's one,' I said. 'Let's run!'

He tried to hold my hand first. Then he tried to kiss me. I kicked him hard and pinched his neck until he gave a bellow. The taxi slowed, the driver turning round and opening the glass divider. 'Beg pardon, guv?' The interruption cooled him and seemed to curb his ardour.

'You've got a nerve, a bloody nerve,' I said. 'As if, even if I'd fallen head over heels for you, I'd ever do that to Pat!'

'Do what?'

'Do this!' I waved my hand between the two of us. 'Do just what you've been doing. Or trying to at any rate. All that!'

He rubbed his neck and frowned. 'My Christ, you're a little bitch.'

I didn't bother to answer. He probably thought Patty a bore. And would have thought me one too I expect, if I had thrown myself at his feet. A boy, that's what he was, a greedy boy. When what I was used to was men. 'You can drop me here at the corner.' I leaned forward to the driver and jumped out as soon as it stopped without turning round at all. Roly must have lowered the window when I left. I heard him shout. 'I don't give up so easily, you know!' But by then I'd approached Nelson House.

It was exactly as it had been on my previous visit, no one in sight, not a soul. And the lift as sinister and silent as before. The only difference was that this time Reggie's door was shut. He opened it immediately, almost as if he'd been standing behind it waiting. I fell inside, or felt as if I fell, so pleased was I to be back. Back amongst all that luxury, surrounded by sumptuous surroundings, bathed in the warmth and the glow. My senses swooned. Much more in fact than on the first occasion, knowing, I supposed, what further pleasures lay in store. Reggie stood looking at me, then crumpled to the now familiar position—on his knees. I stroked his pale bald head, it was really like patting a pet. He buried his face in my skirt and shook, almost trembling with delight and joy. We were together again. My sweet lover. 'I've missed you so much. So unbearably. I can't tell you, I can't begin to explain how long a single day can be without you here. My Princess. My love. You're my life—'

I stood reflected many times, an infinity of me's. Young and ripe. Desirable. He, melting at my feet. Yes, Princess wasn't bad, I supposed— a bloody sight better than Bitch!

A fiver, he'd pressed in my hand, next morning, for taking a taxi. I didn't ask what happened to the car account. I supposed it was out of discretion. This way no one could link me up with him; calling a cab in the street, I might have been anybody. It suited me much better. I made on it, in fact, by taking the bus and pocketing all of the fiver. It meant leaving a little earlier, though still ended up making me late.

'You honestly push your luck with your unpunctuality!' What a whine Winnie had when she wanted. I'd run up several flights of stairs and fought for the breath to reply. 'Mrs Pritchard apparently has noticed. You ought to go easy,' she warned. 'Thanks, Winnie. I will look out. Phew, those stairs really wind you, you know.'

'I don't,' she smoothed a hideous half a mile or so of serge over an elephantine haunch. 'I've never run up in my life. Not here or anywhere. It's not good for the heart!' Not if you're wildly overweight, not if you've stuffed a pint pot in a peanut, no.

'It might be good for the figure. It could count as curve control, Winnie.'

She grinned. I wished she wouldn't. 'I am actually on a diet. A new one I started on Saturday. Bananas.'

'What?'

'Bananas. Only that. The Banana Diet it's called.'

'It would be, I suppose. Fairly obvious.'

'Faintly embarrassing side-effects, like passing an awful lot of wind.'

'Passing? Breaking surely, isn't it? Or would the end make a difference?'

'What end?'

'That's what I mean, which end? Nose or knicker?'

'Well, burping I suppose, more than anything.'

'I'd give it up. I'd let it go. It doesn't sound much of a diet. Oh, by the way—what are you doing with all the skins? Aren't they meant to be good for the complexion? Rubbing them on. Or is it avocados? It's avocados I think. I had an avocado for breakfast this morning, you know.' The need to confide overtook me. I wondered what Winnie would think. I knew she'd disapprove of the money. I felt that instinctively somehow. It struck me now that Pat probably would as well, they'd both misunderstand my motives. They'd think as Fiona certainly thought, that old men meant only money. I didn't expect a single one of them to understand that with Reggie it really was love.

I thought I'd spend the evening in with Pat, assuming that she would be in. She wasn't when I got back home. Had she been and gone already? I put the kettle on; by the time it had boiled she was back. Back from the shop opposite, the small delicatessen with the sexy assistant. Male. We'd talked of him already. I'd thought how bold she'd been to ask which lavatory cleaner he thought best. They'd entered into a long discussion about which brand reached furthest round the bend. 'Harpic,' she said he'd said. I knew it was Harpic anyway.

'You're shameless. Honestly you are. You'll be buying your Tampax there next.'

'They don't sell them. I wouldn't mind. I've never minded asking men for sanitary towels in the chemists.'

'Oh, if I see it's a man and not a woman assistant I walk to another shop.' She thought me over-sensitive. And she was probably right.

All was not well; I could tell by her face. 'Hello, Patty. How's things?'

'A bit depressing, you know.'

I decided to play it light again. 'No, what?'

314

'You saw.' She turned a gloomy face towards me at the gas stove.

'What, Roly? Yes, that looked all right. You seemed quite pleased with our old bed-settee.' I walked across and sat on it, holding my cup of tea. 'I haven't had a chance to try it out myself—' A spring or some subversive lump of stuffing bulged somewhere beneath my bum. I eased myself away. 'It's bumpy, Pat. Did that get in the way? Or is an uneven surface more exciting?'

She poured herself a cup of tea and sank down beside me, sighing tragically. 'Don't joke. I'm just not in the mood.' The telephone interrupted what I knew was going to be a deluge of her grief. I wouldn't have minded comforting her. I felt so happy, so magnanimous and all-embracing in my present mood I could have run the agony column of the world. 'Dear Sad and Lonely—Why not stick your finger up your nose, then bring it down and lick it. It gives a very nice and salty taste—you'll find that you'll soon be smiling—' She put her tea down carefully on the floor in an attempt at false decorum, then sent it flying with her foot as she rushed to answer the phone. I genuinely hoped it was for her.

And it was in a way—for us both. Nicholas and Jim were wondering what we were up to. They'd been asked to the Studio Club and recalled that we'd been there already. Would we like to join them for a spot to eat? 'Hold on.' Pat had passed the phone to me; I covered it with my hand. 'What do you think, Patty?' She shrugged. 'Well answer, missus. They're waiting to know!' She bent to examine her nails, her shoulders slumped in deep depression, unable to make a decision. Going out was preferable, I could see, to staying in with her waiting, cross-fingered, for Roly the Bastard, to ring. He wouldn't. And if he did I had a feeling he would ask for me! 'Nick, just had a word with old Patty here—we both think we're dying to come.' Pat walked out of the room. I watched her bony pelvis swing from left to right. A pre-pubescent body. But with a woman's head. Would Reggie, could Reggie ever envisage love with her? I smiled. I didn't think that Reggie could, would, had ever or should ever love anyone other than me. It was inconceivable. Out of the question. He was mine. Yes, of course. All for me. 'Okay, Nick. Got it. See you in an hour.'

How long ago was it that we'd taken this route before? 'It's only two weeks, you know. Two weeks to the day in fact that we last went to the Studio Club. What do you think of that?' I nudged her. 'Pat?'

'What do you think?' she said ignoring what I'd just said. We sat on the Piccadilly Line passing the Green Park platform. The carriage was almost empty, so that each of us were faced with our reflections. Her face appeared, pale and tragic. A shadow really of her former self. 'What do you think?' she repeated. 'Of Roly?'

I studied the map of London's Underground system, as if giving thought to her question. 'Well, he's bloody attractive, I will say. And seems very addicted to you. Doesn't he?' That way I felt, that way of wording it would give her, and her pride a fair chance.

'I don't think he is, you see. That addicted, I mean. Do you?'

'Oh don't you, Pat?' I'd carefully battled back. The train was slowing into Piccadilly. Situation unresolved.

We somehow got there before them, but only by seconds. Nicholas and Jim followed us cheerfully down the stairs. It was nice. I'd forgotten the smell. And the music. And the feeling of everyone being so much and much the same. Someone had painted, since we'd been there last, the entire reception area a particularly piercing pink. Which served as a striking background to the current exhibition of lino prints and lithogaphs. A students' show. From Camberwell School of Art. Organised by one of the members who happened to teach in Graphics. Pat thought them very good. I found them rather puerile, but her show of interest heartened me even so. We examined them, each in turn, after we'd shed our coats. Nicholas fell naturally in with me, and Pat accompanied Jim. How easy and nice it was with them. Not one of us on the defensive. Not one of us wanting to push too much, merely to make an impression. Pat spoke well and we listened. I fervently prayed she'd catch Jim. The club had served her well before, and in this light he looked not unlike dear old Douglas. His shirt was pink, his bow tie was bright yellow. The combination pleased her. Of course last time they'd met she'd had her periods, I remembered. And looked a bit peaky and grey. Tonight the fine tragedienne role she played gave a chic edge to her prettiness. Like chocolate—the pull of bitter black compared to milk. I hoped he'd note the difference. We had a drink and then sat down to dinner, after joining the friends who'd invited them. And after all of us being

316

signed in. They were nice as well, the other two. An architect, bearded, black-haired who looked rather feminine and fey, with a waistline not unlike Pat's and a nervously high-pitched laugh. His wife was shaped from solider stuff, from commoner clay. The combination was attractive. He set her off. The squareness of her face, the boyishness of her hairstyle, the severity of her suit. She wore a white silk shirt and a scarf tied like a tie. I thought her quite impressive. A journalist, they said, who worked on a woman's magazine. Well more than a woman's magazine, in fact—something like *Ideal Home* or *House and Garden*, whichever was meant to be the better of the two. To do with design—which made us quite a visual set of people. She was talking about a Finnish chair she'd seen and Pat had claimed Italians designed much better. They disagreed and Jim joined in as well, quoting the level of environmental awareness in the Scandinavian countries.

My mind drifted back to Reggie. A nagging worry surfaced again—not really worrying, but just a doubt, a question mark so far. Why was it I was so involved? What was his curious hold? I'd told him that I wouldn't come tonight. I'd told him that I'd spend it back with Pat. He understood, had asked, had rather begged, that when I thought of retiring finally for the night, that I should ring him first. I would of course, when I got back. Whatever time, he'd said. He didn't sleep, so I could always get in touch, all night. Perhaps that's what it was I liked. The knowing that he was always there, without being too demanding. That wasn't my worry. I hadn't seen his cock.

A superb pianist was going to play tonight, a Welshman called Dill Jones. A legendary figure in the world of modern jazz. The architect, Johnny, and Joyce, his wife, were becoming increasingly excited. Nicholas asked me to dance in the pause between dinner and coffee. He danced well; I idly supposed that he did everything well, or moderately so. What a very nice husband he'd make. I would have dearly liked to find him more attractive. But I knew from the feel of his hand as we danced that his flesh wouldn't mix well with mine. It sweated. It sweated cold, not in a—Latin way. Not flowing somehow. It didn't feel like mine. He held me tremblingly, his other hand too high up behind my back. I liked to be held dancing much lower down, in the small of the back in fact, and closer too. So that the erogenous lover zones were pressed hard up

317

against each other. That way you could tell how your partner felt. I think he had an erection. It swung now and then on my thigh, which meant it must be pointing down, instead of up. Like boys. Derek had claimed that after the age of twenty or so, you'd be hard put to find them right up. Erections, that is up against the stomach, pointing towards their nose. He'd shown me, offering to measure to exact angle and degree. Nick's was hanging at 40°. I wondered what Reggie's would be. °? A surge of love came with the thought. A tenderness. A tear. 'What a hell of a girl you are!' Nick suddenly squeezed with his clammy paw. But my legs were aching, I felt a dragging in my back just where his hand should be. As well I felt a thudding high behind my eyes of distant approaching headache. My periods were on the way.

'Oh shit, my periods have started!' Pat sat in the next lav to me. We, of course, were the only ones there.

'Oh hold on,' she shouted back. 'They've got a machine. I'll chuck you one over. Just a mo.' I sat there waiting, reflecting how well things were going. It was in this very same spot, of course, that we'd decided on strategy last time. I caught the oblong cardboard container and unfurled the comforting contents. Two safety pins fell on the floor, I picked them up and put them in my handbag for future use. A wonderful object, the safety pin. So neat, so nicely designed. So, above all, streamlined and efficient. Functional. Though old-fashioned. They'd be hard put, this team of young architects, to aspire to design such as that.

'They've asked us back,' Pat said. 'We'll go, won't we? What do you think?'

I thought. If I went too, of course, then at the end I'd leave. But if I didn't go, there was the possibility she'd stay. 'I'd go if I was you, Pat. But perhaps I won't. I promised I'd talk to Reggie tonight at some point or other.'

'Oh, come. I shall be disappointed not to go. He seems quite keen tonight. Jim.'

'I know, isn't it nice the way it's working out? But I don't fancy Nick, you see, that's the trouble. It'll go best with just you and Jim.' She wanted to be persuaded, I could see. In any case I was right.

'I'm terribly sorry, Nick! You do understand, don't you though? I'm up at dawn in the morning on a special project at school, to do with a thrice-life-sized mural

318

featuring amphibians—monster lizards, newts, toads, frogs, crocodiles, alligators—'

'I say, how very impressive. I'd really love to see that when it's finished. What lucky kids to have you as their teacher!'

'I shall invite you to see it when it's finished. We can have a special viewing.'

'I shall hold you to that, remember!'

Oh hell! I'd have to do it now. Would the District Inspector approve?

I went home by myself on the tube. I didn't mind. I made them see I didn't. Johnny and Joyce had a tiny car, an open one which just about held the five. I waved them away down Regent Street and walked back to Piccadilly. Men murmured, passing, all the way. My own fault at that time of night. And men murmured at the other end, along the Earls Court Road. I prayed that they wouldn't follow. It would have been the easiest thing in the world for someone to force their way through our front door. I slotted the key in quickly and thankfully sneaked inside. Alone. The light in the hall wasn't working, which meant groping my way in the dark, down the stairs to our own front door. A dangerous hazardous path. Anyone could have been waiting for me at the bottom. The thought sent my heart to my throat. But no one was there. The flat was empty and, as usual, as cold as the grave.

Reggie was waiting. I rang him. He understood. Oh, how he always understood! It felt like talking to a father—not my father, of course! 'Time of the month,' was what I'd actually said, with no hesitation at all. He hadn't answered right away. 'Reggie?'

'Princess.' The single word flowed over me, securing me in his devotion. We talked, just talked for nearly half an hour, or more.

'I must reimburse you, my darling, for the tedious telephone bill.' The bill? I hadn't thought about the bill! What, tuppence or tuppence halfpenny? I laughed out loud. How sweet. How very considerate! He'd probably pass me two pounds for that! His syrupy voice continued. 'I don't want you at any time to have to think twice about ringing me, about visiting me, about communicating with me in any way—merely through lack of money.' I shut my eyes and leaned against the wall, cradling the mouthpiece in my palm. Oh dear, oh dear, how wonderful

319

this was. The basement had grown beautiful. Quiet, but with a perfect kind of peace. My period pain subsided to a rather pleasant sort of ache. An ache which merely made me more aware of what my body was. A woman's!

Seven seconds or so, but certainly not more between me tenderly replacing the receiver and the instrument shrilling again. I knew that certainly, about the time, because I'd checked my watch. Ten past one. In the morning of course. Who on earth would it be at this time? Reggie. 'Hello,' I said softly. 'Is this a second goodnight?'

'HELLO!!' The voice came booming through the room. An ultra-charming bellow. I choked. I couldn't speak at all. 'HELLO! HELLO!' It came again, belonging of course—to—Nathaniel! He told me exactly who I was and what a cunt to have kept him waiting! Four hours in fact! From nine till now, he'd been ringing me every half-hour. I swallowed at the end of the dreadful diatribe and said I was frightfully sorry. I'd been out. 'You've been in, you little liar! And engaged there precisely twenty-seven minutes! What the hell could anyone have to say at this blinding time of night, that could take so bloody long?'

He was wanting of course to find out it Fiona was up. 'She's not here. Not at all. She's at home. She only comes up occasionally—'

'Who?'

'Fiona!'

'What's Fiona to do with this?' His voice had altered in its tone. Still fierce. Still angry. But now with some fun in it. It offered me a lifebelt thread of courage. Ye Gods, but he was frightening! Would I ever feel at ease? 'Eh? What's Fiona to do with this? I perfectly know the set-up, she's in Brighton with mummy and daddy. And you're in London here all on your own. I'm coming over. Now. All right? No need for a special welcome!'

He'd crashed the telephone down before I had a chance to answer. A dreadful panic rendered me incapable. For several whole minutes it was simply impossible for me to take a step—in any single direction. The beds were made. They didn't look too bad. The room was tidy too. Pat had cleaned the bath, I knew. And cleared any muck to the dustbin. But God Almighty! Entertaining film-stars! At what was now going on for two o'clock! What would there be for us to talk about? Would I offer him tea, or what?

I went to clean my teeth, and run an old comb through

my hair. And whilst I was at it there at the sink, I wiped both the taps with some Vim. She wasn't very good at doing taps, Pat. Much better at sweeping floors, and dusting horizontal surfaces, and tidying up as she went. But shiny, tinselly things like taps, and silvery objects like kettles, she never bothered with at all. I could see myself in them by the end. I could never quite do that in Reggie's. The gold was not a good receiver of the features on my face. Hell! Why did I feel quite this guilty? Betraying two of them, that's what it was. Both Reggie and Fiona, as well. Not, I thought defiantly, that there'd been any choice in the matter, my end. She shouldn't, I pursued it savagely, she shouldn't have bloody well given him the number and obviously—the address—in the first place! Or, come to that, told about me. But my heart was lunging around like a bat. I'd had a bat fly once into my hair, round at the back of my neck. In the gloaming when it must have thought I was a thicket. My father had made it an occasion to bollock me for not making the best of myself. 'A daily comb and a good cut and that wouldn't have happened, my girl. Had nature intended you to look like an overgrown bramble, you'd have berries growing out of your ears. And a lot of bird shit on your brow—' But the sensation still hadn't left me. Two terrified, entangled creatures. Each struggling to extricate, to free itself from the other. They'd had to cut it off, my hair, to free the frightened bat. The first time I'd ever had it short. Some people did that to each other. Derek, I supposed, more mute, but in a similar state of panic, with me.

My panic still had not subsided. Where, for instance, was he phoning from? Nathaniel! I sat down on the old settee and said his name again, this time out loud. 'Nathaniel!' Old me and Nathaniel! 'Wheee, heee!' The errant spring twanged with my childish jump of joy. He'd said that he was stranded! How was he stranded, here in London? A man with money like that? Couldn't anyone book into a big hotel at any time of the night? They weren't full up, they couldn't be. Not this far away from Christmas. Perhaps you had to have a case with you, some formal trivia like that. To show you wouldn't run off, not paying the bill. Though I'd read quite recently about a Hollywood star who had admitted to precisely that trick. For her and her children, when they were hard-up, taking their cases and leaving them. After staying at wherever

321

hotel it was for months on end without paying. Judy Garland, wasn't it? I'd thought it awfully clever at the time. He meant to stay here for the rest of the night. Christ Almighty! And I had my periods! I'd wear my nightie, I'd be all right. And I'd wear my knickers as well. Of course. Just as I usually did. He must know women had periods. What did those others do? I could warn him of course when he came through the door.

When he came through the door, I warned him. It just jumped out before I could stop. Right upstairs, with him on the doorstep! With his case on the pavement behind! I blurted it, knowing at last what blurting meant. A stiff tongue and a set of rubber teeth, and lips as cold as snow drifts. But the words still clear as a skylark's song. I sang it over Earls Court. He stepped back, obviously enchanted. I had enslaved him with the frankness of my message! Not one iota, no, so afterwards he claimed! Merely reinforced the rumours that he'd heard. From Piers, of course, who else? And Fiona? In some rare disloyalty. Well, perhaps not rare. I ruthlessly strove at some reality. No one could help it, sometimes. Not even me. 'What did she say? No, exactly. Did she mean that I—?' But all that searching came much later on. And by then I didn't care.

His luggage was exquisite, it really was. It shone in the light like a chestnut. My father had yearned for shoes like that. They sold them at Russell & Bromley. Punched with tiny little holes to make a patterned surface, the stitching showing all around the uppers. Shoes fit for toffs and no one else, he felt they'd suit him a treat. I'd thought of buying him a pair in two weeks' time when I had my first salary. 'It's the time of the month. I'm terribly sorry. You can't come in, I don't think—'

'Fucking Jesus, you've flooded the basement! What's it look like—the biblical ocean? A replica of the Red Sea?' I stared at him helplessly and stood aside as he swept into the passage, slamming the heavy front door behind him, with no consideration at all. The lights, of course, weren't working and with the street one now blotted out, we stood in total darkness. 'A hell hole!' he thundered. 'Pray God!'

I was petrified by the noise of him and overwhelmed by his presence. He was wearing, I saw before he'd shut the door, a massive coat like a cape. Or a cloak such as highwaymen might sport, and a deerstalker hat on his head. He was very tall. What, six feet two? Taller in fact

322

than Reggie? He seemed to be much bigger in every way. His arms I felt, his thighs, his neck I imagined resembled hefty branches of a well-built tree. An oak. And Reggie a conifer, his hairless head a smooth and shining cone. Nathaniel was hairy; I couldn't as yet see his scalp but his beard covered most of his face. No sooner had it ended on his cheeks, it seemed his eyebrows had already begun. But in between this furry continent the salient features shone. Even in that shadowed light I'd recognised—I'd recognised—my master?

Cain and Abel. I put my mind to other things like that, to these comparisons, as I led him down to me the now familiar stairs. He would have fallen had I not. And I was going first. The Education Authority of London's County Council had not been known to give employment to a caterpillar. A crushed though needy teacher. 'She doesn't look, oh I don't know, quite normal—would you say? Hardly a figure of authority. The face appears quite, dare one say it, flattened! With a curious impression of coconut matting—' He tripped quite heavily as it happened on luckily the last step but one, but I'd managed to neatly step aside. The light shone out of our basement door and from it I witnessed his flight. The chestnut case fell crookedly to the floor as he went hellbent, in an effort at some balance, towards the basement dustbins. I didn't say a word. But the incident slightly unhinged him, I could tell. He'd made himself look a little ridiculous, and it surprised me that he'd mind so much. It somehow seemed out of keeping. A curious inkling of his vanity arose in me and that gave me a feeling of confidence. Well, not of *confidence* exactly. I still felt wormlike, cowering and what was worse, cruelly, cowardly young! I think now, looking back, that he intended that. It was part of the camouflage, a necessary strategy, the playing-out of roles. And I accepted mine then right away. Quite blindly in my ignorance.

He came inside, and put his case down in the kitchen, then ambled down our passage. I followed at a distance, studying the cut of his clothes. What would my father have considered him? An out-and-out bounder, or not? His clothes were unconventional, completely the reverse of Reggie's. He looked, what—Prosperous Bohemia crossbred with Country Gent? With a spotted cotton hankie round his throat *à la* Working Man. The working man on a building site, or a playwright's idea of a costermonger.

323

He was of course a Theatrical Person, and was playing well, all sorts of roles. He turned and for the first time smiled. I honestly thought I might faint. There was such power and charm and geniality there. There was such underlying SEX! A huge and cuddly polar bear, with the cunning and guile of a wolf. 'Tell me, child,' he boomed. 'How many bunny rabbits live in this hole? Are there others as well as yourself?'

Even in my half-dead, dopey, head in the clouds confusion, a warning sizzled inside. I didn't want him wanting anyone else but me! I couldn't risk even Pat. The sensation wasn't pleasant, and why at this especial stage? When nothing yet had happened even—excepting, of course, he was here. And I had dreamed and longed for just that much to happen. For me to be in touching distance. He advanced. He came towards me. I started to shake, I couldn't help it. I hadn't spoken more than half a dozen words as yet. Would he find me incurably stupid? A deaf mute like, who was it played the part? That actress in *Johnny Belinda*. Big eyes and not much botty on her? She copped it in the stables. I could, it seemed quite on the cards, be likewise in the kitchen!

I made him let me wear my nightie and my knickers. He laughed and said he didn't mind as long as I did everything I was told! I thought of Fiona as I opened out the old settee, whilst worrying would it support him, support us both. He brought out a bottle of brandy, which saved me having to make tea.

It wasn't a very romantic light, not even a shade on the bulb. I stood on a chair and tried to tie an old red petticoat of mine around it, one I now used as a paint rag. 'Is it Christmas? Some fiendish festivity? Or a feeble attempt at a Maypole?'

'I'm trying to tone the lighting down a bit—' I floundered from my chair. My arms were aching holding them up high. The bulb had swung and hit me on the head. I felt a fool, as he well meant me to.

'Why not switch it off? A simple procedure. Watch.' And he'd plunged us both into darkness, barely relieved by the furthest light in the hall. It worked fine, once my eyes had grown accustomed to the gloom. His was a shape you couldn't miss. Especially when he was naked. He'd thrown his clothes haphazardly to the floor. Reggie always hung his up carefully. We obviously, Nathaniel and I, had more in common, basically. His bare flesh glowed, he lowered it groaning on to the bed. The springs screamed out in protest. I apologised for them.

'We bought it secondhand, the bed-settee. It's not very comfy. I'm sorry—'

Bur he pulled me down beside him. 'Brandy?' he said.

'Oh, thanks!' It burned its way into my chest, a fierce and fiery trail. I burped immediately, but managed to keep it back, swallowing hard instead. My stomach gurgled in return. I crossed my fingers in the dark. Praying he couldn't hear. He heaved around to settle himself more comfortably. 'That's better—now child, let's chat.'

He wanted it all, the ins and outs, from the start of my whole life story. With full details of sexual encounters. 'And then? And then? Go on! Go on!' I didn't say about Reggie. Had I ever been in bed with Fiona? That was one of his very first questions.

'Yes, this one. The one we're in right now. But having breakfast, that's all.' But saying it had brought it back—the wantonness that I'd witnessed. The delicate fur that she'd disturbed so frantically with her fingers. I couldn't say that to him though. No! Or how she'd offered her nipples. That texture though was unforgettable. I ran my thumbs over my finger-tips, lightly. Just as I'd done on her. 'I've touched her though—' I'd said it to him suddenly. The words had just slipped out.

'You've touched, Fiona? Where and how?'

'Like this!' And I touched his nipples. I hadn't done it ever, not before, touched a man on his titties. It surprised me in fact how similar they were to mine. His hardened up right away. I stopped.

He offered me another drink. 'You're a virgin then, I gather?'

'Am I?'

'We'll have to wait and see—unless you'll allow me now.' I didn't want him saying that. He could tell he'd gone too far. 'Come here, you silly little child. We've got plenty of times ahead ...'

Did he mean to see me then again? Given the chance. Without Fiona. We'd drunk, or rather, he had swigged, about half of the bottle of brandy before getting down to business, as he chose to call it. 'I challenge you!' Is what he said? 'Here! Have my set of tools!' And he'd drawn himself higher in the bed and arranged me much lower beneath him and between the boulders of his knees. They lay on either side like rocky Scottish moors. I knelt, a nervous animal, between the two, but comforted by his overwhelming kindness. He'd clearly see to my condition. Could obviously find a nice solution to it all. I had to wait just for the right circumstances, but till then of course, I'd try to do as I was told. And endeavour to raise an erection.

I thought of Fiona, what she'd said—how thankless a task hers had been. But that was not my own approach. Was it something to do with my teaching? Dedicated to the life, the one of total self-sacrifice. How opposite to my Sweet Princess role with Reggie. Though perfectly possible for me to encompass both. Each end of the scale, I thought. Adaptable. That's me.

He left at some ungodly hour, long before Pat came back. She found me sleeping in the kitchen. 'Hey, who's been here? Have you been entertaining?'

I tossed up whether to tell her, and decided I'd better not. 'No, actually I haven't. I'm only sleeping here because it's warmer . . .' I could see that she didn't believe me, but if I told her the truth, I knew she wouldn't be able to keep it to herself. And certainly not from Fiona.

Her night, she said, had been heaven! Roly could spin his own balls! That was good at any rate. We breakfasted together, both sitting on the bed. 'I'm seeing him again tonight, yes, I'm coming to the class.'

'What, Bernard Bolt's?'

'Is that all right? Do you think he'll have me in it?'

'Is Jim joining as well then?'

'We thought we would together.'

'That'll be nice. We'll go to the pub after.'

The tube was packed, even more than usual, due to a fault on the line. I hung upon a strap in front of a line of seated men. No one offered a seat. They never did, I'd come to expect that they wouldn't. They stared at me and at my outstretched shape, but I ignored them all. Lost in my thoughts of the night. There was a poster on the platform at South Kensington, with a blown-up drawing of Nathaniel, publicising a film of his now currently on release. I could go and see that tomorrow. And nudge my next-door neighbour. 'See him! That star! We've slept together! Oh yes, in my back kitchen. On a very old bed-settee. Two pounds ten or thereabouts. A bargain.

Secondhand.'

Fiona was right, he was bloody hard work. The brandy perhaps caused paralysis. It wouldn't have made much odds that I had my periods or not, I somehow felt. But even so he'd taken me through it step by step. 'That's it, start there, just at the tip. Christ Almighty! Let go! Not like that!' My grip was like a navvy's, so he claimed. A navvy's fist holding a hammer! But when I tried the other way it was more like a dropped stitch in knitting. 'No! Much too loose!' He wasn't circumcised, unlike Derek, and I had a job with the slack. I could have said to him, 'Look here, this loose material is getting in the way! Can't you think of having a tuck in it?' He made me do it with both hands, one holding down the yardage at the base and the other tip tickling at the top. It was incredibly tiring, the only place to rest my wrist was on his crinkly bollocks. 'Ouch!'

'Oh, I'm sorry!' I said. 'Am I wrinkling them!'

'You girls,' he thundered at one point, 'make appalling mistresses! Both you and Fiona—what's the matter? How can you be so ham-fisted?' I didn't answer. The comparison seemed so unfair. She was short-sighted after all, with a preference for gang bangs. She'd failed her exams where I had passed. And passed with flying colours. I bent my head and miserably applied myself to his prick. I tried to think of it as something else. A completely different object like, well, like uncooked pastry, plasticine, a piece of pottery clay. It didn't work, of course, since they were so much stiffer. Until I felt like hitting it into shape. 'Right,' he said. 'Well go on then, suck on it!'

One of the seated passengers got out at St James's Park. I sank down gratefully, although it was only one stop. I could have bitten through it at one point. And swallowed it like an oyster. Making medical history? Would he have died from the fright? Or from critical loss of blood. 'This chappie here has had his thingie bitten off! Poor bastard! See, here are the teethmarks. Clean through, resulting in seizure. Write "Coronary" on the death certificate—rather more circumspect!'

He'd risen, however, at an amazing speed, once he'd decided to rise. And had shot his load without me even knowing much about it. I had to take his word that it had happened. Straight down my throat, so he claimed. I sucked my tongue, trying to detect a different taste. Custard cream? Sour milk? Something cheesier. I felt like

327

shouting hip hooray, had he not shouted for me. A bawling yodelling, fit to wake the dead and empty all the cemeteries.

'Oh, shush,' I begged. 'You must be quieter'—once I'd emptied my mouth. The satiated sliver slid out of my lips like a leaking of lukewarm water. 'You'll get me thrown out of this flat, like that. We're not meant to entertain men.'

He'd put a large and hairy hand underneath each of my armpits and pulled me up towards his face and kissed me hard on the lips. It was the first time, in fact, that he'd kissed me, despite all our different intimacies. I kissed him back, liking it very much. I would have much preferred to start from there instead of to finish like this. In fact, I now felt quite aroused myself, ready for fun and games. But he was tired and wanted to go to sleep. He snored as loudly as he laughed. I got up to shut the door and bumped my knee against the bed trying to get back into it. 'What in hell are you up to, woman?' He'd woken up immediately. 'For Christ's sake, it's like Paddington Station. Get in, and go to sleep!' But when I did, he wrapped his bear-like arms around me, and cradled me like a baby. 'You're adorable, little one,' he whispered. 'And I love you to distraction.' Just that, and the way he said it, made me stay awake all night.

Bernard Bolt wasn't there right away, so we started the class without him. I volunteered to pose the model, since nobody else seemed professional. 'Standing? Or sitting? Which would you like?' We ended with having her lying, curled round on the dais, in a faintly foetal position. One of the older of the old ladies claimed it to be too difficult, so I helped her to start in Bernard's absence. And from there went to help various others. Pat was late as well. Perhaps she had changed her mind. It was a shame because both Nicholas and Jim, as well, were there. And so was the Polish industrialist. I smiled at him. He courteously clipped his heels and formally bent at the waist. How Continental. He introduced himself—William, pronounced Vilhelm—and asked my advice on his canvas. I ran a practised eye along its surface. Oh, no doubt, yes, the best money could buy. 'You ought to really work on cheaper stuff than this—it's a waste, paying this at your stage.' I looked at him straightforwardly. He began to blush. With

anger? But I continued. 'I'll tell you why. It's because the
results are misleading. This very good canvas is going to
make your amateur efforts look better, which in turn—'

'Sweet madam'—his voice was icy cold—'this advice is
quite beside the point. Not at all that which I wish to hear.
Better that you should—'

'Oh, excuse me,' I interrupted him as brutally as he'd
interrupted me. It took him by surprise. Bloody nerve.
Who the hell did he think he was? In any case, Bernard had
come. I gave a devastating smile and confidently walked
away.

Nathaniel had asked to see my work. When he'd woken
up. 'Show it to me. Now,' he'd demanded as he was
dressing.

'Oh no, another time—'

But he wouldn't take no. He'd insisted. 'You're good,'
he said. 'You're bloody good in fact! How much for this
drawing here?' He'd chosen the nude I'd done the week
before in this very room with Bernard. The question had
caught me quite off guard. I wasn't yet used to selling!
Twenty-five pounds! He'd rolled it up and taken it under
his arm! Twenty-five pounds! The same as Fiona! But
honestly made—not like hers!

Bernard was slightly drunk, I could smell it on his
breath. Brandy. It brought back Nathaniel. 'You're late
Bernard, where have you been? Propped up in the pub?'

'Celebrating,' he slurred. 'A splendid commission. A
portrait. Means flying to Mozambique!'

'Mozambique! My God, sounds mad!'

'Five hundred quid, no less!'

He bought us a round in the pub and we cheerfully
drank his good health. 'I tell you what, I was thinking, you
know—that I'll need someone to stand in for me on this
evening job. I'll be off in a couple of weeks. It may as well
go to you as anyone else. Would you like it, eh! Yes or no?'

'Who, me?'

'Why not? You know the ropes. It's a simple enough
task. In any case you'd probably make a better job of it
than me. My heart's no longer in it.'

I bought the following round as a celebration of my
own. A lecturer no less! My dad would be thrilled to bits.

Pat had missed most of the class—an unexpected staff
meeting. I would have found it difficult to guide her
drawing constructively. 'Shocking, isn't it! I've never been

329

keen on nudes. But never mind. It's the occasion that really counts.' She and Jim sat hand in hand like a pair of well-blessed lovers. He stroked her hair and kissed her fingers, and held her drink up to her lips. Like a mother and child. He took care of her. She blossomed with the attention. Poor Roly Balls, not that he'd probably care.

I looked around me happily. Bernard was quarrelling loudly over the merits of Henry Moore. Nick stood at my elbow, eager to catch my every word. A friendly group with everything in common. But my mind was elsewhere. Drifting between Nathaniel and, yes, Reggie. Two days since I'd last seen him. Forty-eight hours without playing Princess. I'd telephone when I got home.

The line was engaged, which surprised me. Pat had brought Jim home with her. They sat entwined together in the kitchen. I felt very much in the way. I could go to Reggie, of course. With my nightie. And my knickers and sanitary towels. I thought of the beautiful golden bath and the silky fur on the bed. Pat, I supposed, would be dossing down on the bed-settee. Why suffer in solitary gloom? I picked up a pair of shoes which I'd carelessly left by the window. One of them was sprouting mould. A certain sign of damp. I coughed. A cold? The second time I tried the telephone was clear. 'It's me,' I said.

'My darling.'

'I phoned you a minute ago—'

'I was talking to Ernest as it happens.'

'How is he?'

'Enquiring of you.'

'Of me? How would he know that you've seen me?' I was shocked.

'It would appear Princess, that someone's been indiscreet ...'

Fiona. It was Fiona of course. Who must have told Piers. Who in turn must have got on to Ernest. How paltry. How inbred and petty-minded.

'Shall I come over?'

'Oh, Princess,' he bubbled with pleasure.

'So long!' I shouted in at Pat, but received no answering sign. I banged the door behind me in the passage, to emphasise my departure. Several taxis, empty, cruised along the street. It was good, this stretch of London, for getting taxis so quickly. Now that I was taking to the habit. I still had Nathaniel's twenty-five-pound cheque in

330

my handbag. Sitting in the back of the cab I took it out for the thrill of seeing the famous signature. How tempted I'd been to show Pat. What a thrill! What a boast it could be. To Fiona above all, of course. But impossible. Frustrating that, having to hug this glorious secret to myself. Perhaps Winnie would have to be my confidante and friend. A deserted Dolphin Square, and eerily empty Nelson House, as usual. When did other people go in and out? Were they all night-livers like Reggie? Did sly seductions and Bacchanalian rompings take place behind each of those doors?

Reggie was wearing a pair of clean pyjamas when he opened the door. Nicely ironed and smelling of starch, of all things. From being packed next to shirts I supposed. They didn't put starch in pyjamas. Especially not pure silk. He fussed and flurried around me, taking my coat and making sure of my seat. 'Have you eaten? Some champagne?' I surrendered to the luxury. And assumed my royal mantle. He wanted to know exactly what I'd been doing, down to the last minute, since we'd last been together. I thought about it. 'Well,' I might have said. 'I've had a mouthful of famous dick for a start! And a splash of rare spunk up my tonsils. And a fistful of scrotum to boot—'

'I've done nothing of any importance at all—except, oh yes, I've got a new job.'

He listened carefully to the details of Bernard Bolt and his offer. 'I'm not sure you should take it. It's not the job for my Princess.'

I stared at him. 'Why not? I think it's marvellous. I'm flattered as a matter of fact.'

'I'd rather you spent that time with me. I could pay you at twice the rate.'

'Pay me? What, pay me like a prostitute?' I watched him flinch. 'Don't be so coarse, please, Reggie!' He sank to his knees at my feet. I studied him rather disdainfully. 'Get up!' I said it coldly, with contempt, for various complicated reasons that I didn't fully understand myself. He squirmed, but made no effort to get up. I prodded him with one foot. 'Get up! Or I'll kick you.'

'Kick me,' he said. 'I deserve it.'

Winnie and I went out to lunch. Out to the pub up the road. We both felt outrageously naughty. 'No reason not to, of course, Winnie.'

She'd taken some persuading. 'What if the children should see us? What if the girls smell our breath?'

'What, beer? A lager? Don't be daft. What difference would it make? Come on, let's both be devils. Live a little while we can.'

Once inside with a hot shepherd's pie, I showed her Nathaniel's cheque. She couldn't believe her eyes when I pointed out his name. 'No! Really! Honestly? I say. Imagine that—you and him.' I couldn't have had a more impressed reaction if I'd written the script myself.

'It is exciting, isn't it?'

'When will you see him again?'

'Oh,' I hedged. 'When he gets back I expect.' I hadn't bargained for that one. Would he ring me ever again? I didn't like to think that far ahead. 'He'll be gone for a month, so he said—'

'Will he write?'

'What, to me? I shouldn't think so. These things are not so cut and dried as that, Winnie.' Her questions irritated. She seemed to be missing the point.

'Let me look at the cheque again,' she said. 'Oh, I say, yes. It is awfully exciting?' Better.

I sighed. 'I suppose I ought to put it in. Into the bank I mean. But I don't like to let it go. You know what I mean—'

She nodded. 'I do, indeed.'

Should I tell her all about Reggie? There seemed no reason now why not. She'd hardly spill the beans to anyone important. Her mother or possibly one of her sisters or even to one of her brothers. 'I'm working with this rather charming colleague, who sleeps with this sweet geriatric. And when his gummy mouth's not on her muff, she jerks off this famous old film-star! Oh yes, we talk about it freely in the staff-room!' She shivered when I went into the details. 'What's wrong? Are you cold?'

'Just excited!'

I looked at her with interest. 'What, aroused?'

A daft expression settled on her face. 'A little,' she said demurely.

'You've got shepherd's pie on your chin. Can you wipe it? It's getting on my nerves.' I wondered what a man might do with Winnie. Of course she felt, she had her feelings, just like us. Like Pat and Fiona, and me. But it hadn't occurred to me till now. 'Have you never done it, ever?'

'Oh yes!'

'What, you have? Or you haven't?'

'Oh, I have. With an Indian waiter from the Old Bombay up the road. Under the counter—'

'What, just like that? You amaze me, Winnie. Where was your mother?' I was deeply impressed by the danger. 'What if she'd discovered you?'

'It was all over before she'd even pulled the chain. He was fearfully quick. And clean. He wiped himself with tissue when he'd finished—'

'What did he do with the tissue though? Did he eat it to destroy the evidence? What a fascination with detail you do have, Winnie.' She smiled, she seemed to be enjoying it. Well, I was enjoying it too. It never failed to surprise, Life, when you scratched beneath the surface.

'That wasn't the only time, of course. I've done it as well with an African—'

'You're very ethnic in your choice of partners—'

'Ooboogu.'

'Beg pardon?'

'Ooboogu. Yes, that was his name. A fellow student, but a family man, with something like six children—'

'Quite a tribe.'

'Exactly. I didn't want to become entangled.'

'It's a chequered career then, Winnie. Not quite inexperienced, I'd say.'

She drained her glass. 'I'd like some more.'

I rose. 'My round.'

'No. Sex.'

I couldn't stop thinking about it or her or that, throughout the rest of the day. A shame. A waste. What could I do to help? No one I knew seemed to fit the bill. 'You should join my painting class,' I said, when I saw her in the staff-room.

'I don't paint though, or draw, or do anything like that. You have to be able to do it.'

'No you don't. Don't be daft. They're all amateurs. No one can tell the difference, honestly. Only me. You won't be going in under false pretences. And it's nice. You meet people. Lots of men.'

'On which night? Oh, a Tuesday. I can't come. My night for helping mummy in the shop—'

333

'Bugger mummy. And sod the shop. It's you we're worrying about.'

Nathaniel arrived back much earlier than the month. Two weeks to be exact. The weather conditions had been unfavourable for filming. I knew of his arrival before he'd phoned me in fact. Fiona had been pleased to inform me that he was staying the night with her parents. With her of course, as well. With plenty of chance of a spot of slap-and-tickle and how's-your-father on the back stairs, or locked up in roomy closets. I stiffened when she told me and tried silently to control the irrational reaction. 'That'll be nice,' I said. 'When's he coming then?'

'Tomorrow.'

I could have said to her to please give him my love, that I couldn't wait to see him. I could have tipped the wink, passed on a piece of practical advice on the extraction of his seed. You'll find, I could have said, that if you wrap your tongue round your teeth, it lessens the hazard with stray pubic hairs. I'd gone through agonies of prickling discomfort once with Derek, when one of his hairs attached itself to the roof of my mouth, then slipped to the back of my throat. Nothing would budge it, not even ice-cream.

'Tomorrow tea-time. He's taking us out to dinner. East Street I expect. The oyster bar, English's.'

'Oh yes,' I said bleakly. 'I know.'

'My favourite. What do you think I should wear?'

'Let me think now—' A cabbage? An empty old bottle? A cushion, two ounces of marge? 'I like your pink, I think.' That makes you look very plain.

'Perfect. How clever you are. And sweet. I wonder how much he'll give me. I shall have to box clever of course.'

'Of course. I expect you'll manage it somehow.' When I put down the phone I felt sick.

It was quite unreasonable, of course, and I hadn't given him that much thought to tell the honest truth. Life with Reggie seemed so cocooned and comfortable. A regular routine, a fine adjustment of power and comfort and professional satisfaction.

The District Inspector had been to see me. He'd called in quite unexpectedly, in the middle of the afternoon. The room was in an uproar of intense creative activity, each single pupil deeply absorbed in what they were doing.

334

Perfect conditions. Impressive. I hadn't seen him enter, one of the girls had told me. 'Miss—' she'd nudged me, pointing shyly. 'A man—' He'd smiled and nodded. I'd risen from the floor. We'd embarked on a complicated process involving wire and *papier mâché* formed and moulded into magnificent flying birds. I'd planned to hang these three-dimensional lightweight sculptures from the ceiling. A few were already finished and swung gaudily above our heads. We shook hands. 'You seem busy. I approve,' he said, 'of your efforts. Explain them to me. What it is you're doing—' I launched into the complications of the craft. 'Whose idea? Oh, your own? Mm, well done!'

Mrs Pritchard had come up in the middle of things and smilingly looked on with a mixture of pride and suspicion. 'I don't pretend to understand the ins and outs of any of this—' she waved an arm encompassing the scene. 'But then, I'm just an old traditionalist, I suppose. Schooled in the art of perspective.' The District Inspector smiled politely. I didn't say a thing. We waited, he and I, for her to go.

'Show me some other projects.'

'Will you excuse us, Mrs Pritchard?' She took the hint and went. I walked the District Inspector into my tiny stock-room and began to show him some work. His eyes, though interested in what he saw, rested on me with a warm amused detachment. Could I have had him? Probably. If I'd wanted to, but I didn't.

'I'm organising an exhibition called Art in Schools—'

'A straightforward, self-explanatory title—'

He laughed. 'Quite explicit. In keeping with the confines of County Hall. In any event, I plan to stage it around Christmas time. I would like your participation.'

'Oh, that would be nice.' I spoke enthusiastically. 'How would I be involved?'

'Well, these are early days of course. Nothing as yet past paper stage. However, I see you as having a section to yourself—'

'My own stand?' I'm very good at getting stands. You should see me working the Earls Court route. A real old pro at it now. And would you wish to use me as an exhibit too? Sitting bare-bosomed up on a dais with my drawers around my ankles?

'Yes, your own stand. And for several afternoons at least,

335

a practical demonstration.' Voyeurism! Within the limits of the L.C.C. Clerks queueing up for a gander. Secretaries staring, shy and sly. A riproaring misuse of the Rates. Could there be questions in the House?

I smiled. 'Oh, I'd like that a lot.'

Before he'd left, I'd told him about the life-sized mural.

'Featuring fearful amphibians? Yes, interesting. The curious colourings. Raw Umber right through to the Cadmiums. But would it be finished in time? I'd like to use it very much.'

'I could start on it almost immediately. It will mean, of course, working after school. The caretaker is not too keen on that, I know. I've had trouble already with the Art Club.'

'I'll see to it, I promise. We can't have exciting educational enthusiasm on a level such as yours hampered in any way by petty-minded bureaucracy!'

'Exactly, I agree!' We shook each other warmly by the hand, assuming conventional fomality. And then he went.

'He fancied you, miss, didn't he?'

'Don't be cheeky. Get on with your work.' That was the way to maintain discipline. Erecting a barrier between you.

I'd put Nathaniel's cheque eventually into my bank; it boosted my first salary no end. 'What do I do with this, please? How do I pay it in?' I'd asked the woman in the Midland Bank, and I'd passed her the cheque to see. Her eyes widened at the signature, and she shot me a suspicious frown. 'I'm a painter,' I explained unnecessarily. 'He bought one of my works.'

'Oh, very nice too,' she smiled, relieved. Yes, I had nothing on at the time. Not a stitch. I could have caught my death, of course, but he'd demanded a special showing. Rather early in the day. I never knew the light of dawn to be so northerly and cold. I'd choose a studio facing south, if ever I had the choice. 'You need a paying-in slip, there's one on the counter, there.' She showed me helpfully, as comfy and warm as an old tea cosy. Unmarried, I saw by her finger. Had never been even engaged, not even the faintest tinge of white on the fine, even pink of her hand. Women had to watch that little give-away sign if they ever took off their rings, pretending for various reasons, like new jobs or illicit relationships. Camp Coffee worked as well as anything else. A nice, neat strip of it rubbed in some cotton wool.

'Have you seen his latest film? He's playing a randy Archbishop.' She glowed. The bank was empty but for us. 'Is he really as naughty to meet? I'd love an autograph—if you could get me one. I could show off to all my girlfriends—'

I drew myself up magnanimously and exuded, as one in the know. 'I don't see why not. You must give me your name and I'll ask him.'

' "To Daphne—with love" ?'—that would do.' When I left she was still simpering.

I thought about her, walking back along the Walworth Road. How could she live contentedly without the company of men? I passed the Men's Outfitters and stopped to study three chopped-off torsos wearing varieties of underpants. A baggy aertex pair. Some neat Y-fronts. And one patterned like Bermuda shorts. Two young housepainters, wearing spattered overalls, streaks of vivid emulsion, large patches of shiny gloss, stopped and nudged each other. 'What's your preference, love, then, eh?'

'Something substantial,' I answered pleasantly. And walked on, my shoulders well back. Dignity incarnate. The awful thing, of course, it wasn't true. What I liked best was Reggie. Without a cock at all, or so it seemed. He worried sometimes over that, that I might feel dissatisfied and drift away. He didn't understand.

And nor did Pat. I hadn't brought myself to spill the beans. She was in love with Jim now, so she swore. And he, thank God, was head over heels for her. They spent each single evening now together, and this weekend, she was taking him home to meet her mum.

'Will you get married?' I'd asked. It seemed to have happened so quickly.

'We've talked of it. Do you know what—his dad's a Master Builder.'

'No! Really? You possibly could amalgamate. I mean, your families, in business.'

'It's nice.'

'It's nice, I quite agree. You must have lots in common. Backgrounds matter a lot. Being similar, I mean.'

Perhaps that's why Winnie and I seemed to have so much in common. Both brought up behind shop counters. Charged by the thrill of the till. My father had rung up. 'Oh hello, dad!' I was on my way out to Reggie's. 'This is late, for you to be ringing—'

'Business is bad. We're still open. I'm waiting for pubs to start emptying. Should do a spot with Extra Strongs. Last night someone pissed up the window. Really far gone, he was. And puked all over the pavement. I had to wake your mother up to swish it down with water.'

'Oh dear.' I shut my eyes and smelt my wrists. Reggie had bought me some perfume.

'What's wrong?'

'What's wrong?'

'I heard you sniff—'

'Oh, did you? Only smelling my scent, that was all.' A silence fell.

I heard the tick of Pat's clock. Not much in use these days. She spent most of her nights now at Jim's. 'You don't mind, do you? It's just that much more comfortable than the old bed-settee in the kitchen—'

'Not at all.' I could have said I didn't spend much time there, here, I meant, now any longer myself. Nowhere could compare with Reggie's place for comfort after all.

'How's mam then, dad?'

'Oh, much the same. How are you, my girl, eh?' We'd reached a standstill. He was sorry that he'd phoned. 'Coming down? At any time?'

'Oh yes, of course. I'll let you know.'

'You do that then—'

'Okay, dad. I will.'

Poor sod. The miserable old bugger. I should go down and buy him his shoes. Or send him the money to buy them himself. Which way would he appreciate most? I thought of him when I got to Reggie's. Just as I thought of Nathaniel. He would have been deeply shocked, of course, had he known about either of them. He'd probably have been very pleased if I'd fallen in love like Pat. Though possibly not with an ordinary son of a working-class Master Builder. His delight in lineage would have been dealt a blow. So I really had nothing to report in the way of a Social Romance. No reason yet to get into Moss Bros. and dress up like a penguin.

'I spoke to my father tonight.'

Reggie sat cradling my shoes. 'Did you darling? What a lucky man—'

'Why lucky? He sounded quite sad.'

'I meant, Princess, that any man who has the honour of conversing with you, is automatically placed in a highly favoured position.'

'Don't be so silly, Reggie. You make yourself sound ridiculous!'

He bowed his head and kissed my feet. 'It's you—'

'How is it me?' I kept a sharp edge in my voice. It was part of the game, as we played it.

'It's you. I feel so nervous in your presence—'

'Fill up my glass. And be quiet.' I went back to reading my book.

It had occurred to me of course that in my present regime I might easily well miss Nathaniel. And so when Fiona had said he was passing through Sussex, I assumed that he'd then pass through London. And I arranged to stay in those few nights. The trouble with Reggie, of course, was that he never took me out. Since be barely went out himself. A trip to Lowndes Square seemed about his limit. 'But what about films and things? And exhibitions and other people's dinners? And parties?' He had no interest any longer in any of these. I was now what he lived for. But he didn't make a fuss, not even when I said I couldn't come. And the leash being loose proved much stronger.

Nathaniel rang early in the morning, before I'd left for school. The day after he'd been down at Fiona's. 'Where are you ringing from?' The morning seemed suffused with blinding light. I answered the phone in bare feet.

He spoke in a lowered voice, the sort of one he should have used that night here with me. 'Oh, where am I ringing from? Fiona's.' She'd have knifed us both had she known. 'I didn't want to miss you, little one. I'll be in London later. So keep this evening free.'

'What time?'

'I'll ring you. Better still, I'll call. I'll have my car by then. Just be there—'

'Yes, but Nathaniel—' He'd gone before I'd managed to ask would he make it early or late. And where we'd be going. And what should I wear. But I walked to the station on air. His poster was still up I saw, passing through St James's. I looked around and smiled at the weariness around me. How grey they seemed. How grumpy. How ground-down and how grim. I stretched my neck. Young and straight and strong. And when I reached Westminster, I flung myself joyously from the train leaving six solid stands in my wake.

Winnie was thrilled when I told her. 'Perhaps it's love. Perhaps he's fallen for you! Is he married by the way, you've never said?' Trust her.

'Separated, I believe. But honestly, you know, that's not important, Winnie!'

'I like to know though, where in fact I stand. I said as much to Ooboogu Alarmi from the start—'

'Alarmi? What a lovely name. And apt I suppose in the circumstances. But you and I are different kettles of fish, you see, Winnie.'

'Yes. I see that.' She sighed rather wistfully.

'I'm not that keen on getting set up for the future. I like to live it now. Whatever *it* is—'

I got home rather late, but it couldn't have made much difference. He'd never have rung before 6.30. Surely not, that wasn't evening. Pat was out; I ran the bath. Just as Roly Balls phoned. 'Hello sweetheart,' he said. 'I was hoping that you'd answer. Where's Pat?'

'Pat? She's out. She usually is these days. A hectic social life!' That should do him in, I thought malevolently. But no.

'Oh good! Well that's great! How about it?'

'Go to hell!' When I got back the bath was full, up over the overflow. I heard it pouring down outside into the basement drain. One of the things that we'd been warned about. Oh blast bloody Roly Balls!

I was ready by half-past seven, dressed in my very best. The topless creation that I'd bought with Fiona. I poured perfume down each arm and picked up the phone to check TIM. Pat's clock was several minutes slow. I started curdling with excitement wondering just where we would go. The silence was unbearable. I went out to sit on the lavatory and wait there for my famous date.

'What the hell are you wearing, child? The torn half of a Christmas cracker? Probably cost you a fucking fortune! Some money-making manufacturer scrimping on his material—should be hung, drawn and quartered—like hairdressers! All of 'em!'

'You're late,' I said, 'and don't shout!'

I'd been waiting for almost four hours and was not in the mood for his rhetoric. The back of my dress was badly

340

creased from sitting carelessly whilst falling asleep with
my feet in the oven. He'd woken me with his finger pressed
continuously on the front door bell. Now we stood there
on the step together. He'd been drinking. He swayed and
in steadying himself managed to land with the force of one
elbow against the entire panel of bells. I could hear them
pealing fiercely throughout the pitch black building.

'Oh God! Now look what you've gone and done!'

He righted himself and stood up artificially as if to brisk
attention. Then just as suddenly de-stiffened and subsided
again into self-indulgent chucklings. 'C'mon—I'm here
to take you out. Fetch your shawl, we're about to get
going.' And he turned with a swirl and got into his car.

By the time I'd run down to the basement for my coat
and to turn off the lights, he'd started honking his horn
loudly enough to invite the risk of arrest.

'Are you fit to drive?' I got in doubtfully. He turned to
look at me with great difficulty; the small interior of the
vehicle enclosed him like a glove. The street lamps slanted
sideways in on us, emphasising his bulk and etching the
bearded impressive splendour of his face. Larger than
life—that's how he looked. I prickled with pride to be with
him.

'Hello.' He stroked my hair. 'And how are you, little
one, girlie, eh?' My bones dissolved to biscuit. He put a
heavy hand upon my knee and slid up to the tip of the
mountain. He patted, an affectionate gesture. 'All clear?
Up here? The painters gone?'

I nodded, a child, responsive, speechless. How feeble,
how completely spineless. I gazed at him coyly, like a fan,
instead of an equal companion. Shouldn't I actually
demand an apology? For his lateness, his lack of
politeness, some evidence of normal decency expected of
normal people. But he wasn't normal, not like Patty's
beaux. And the choice after all was mine, to be with him
rather than them.

'Peckish? A little foody-ponks and a drop of some
drinky-poo?' A degree in philosophy, Fiona had said, at a
startlingly early age. A brilliant scholar who hadn't
chosen to turn to acting till well past forty, or so. I
wondered whether to lisp back in return, to affect Winnie
Einstein's delivery. Best not. Best shut my mouth and keep
my peace, especially on his delay. Any questioning or
pedestrian demands from me might well be construed as

341

nagging. Not a pastime for lovely young women of the world, out with well-known actors. I blinked and batted my lashes, and settled back in the venal embrace of his bucket seat and prepared to enjoy my evening. In twenty minutes' time it was tomorrow. But let that mundane fact merely take care of itself—who knew what the morning might bring?

It brought, apart from other things, a confrontation, *the* confrontation with Mrs Pritchard over my lateness, of course. She'd caught me sneaking in through Senior Girls, red-handed, right in the act. Her upper lip drew coldly to her lower as she peeled back the cuff of her shirt to examine the watch on her wrist. 'Over half an hour. This really is unforgivable! However, here is hardly the time or the place for lengthy recriminations. This situation, the repeated occurrence of your unpunctuality, must obviously now be resolved. I regard it very seriously. I take it your class has had to call its own register, collect its own dinner money, and in addition, conduct itself into Assembly? Quite! Be so good as to call into my office at the end of afternoon school. I trust that you won't be late for that—'

The skin of my forehead had been fitted by skilled craftsmen, more accustomed to working with drums. The crisp staccato of her delivery bounced like juggling balls against its brandied surface. I'd have to find a milder drink than that if I hoped to hold this job and Nathaniel. I ached in every orifice—each pore, each nail, both eyeballs, every hair, pulsated with deep felt pain. But I swam still, gloriously light-headed. Exuberant and buoyant. The dehydrated crew of one small craft amidst a sea of trouble. That thought, that little piece of poetry, spun through my mind as she spoke. It made me smile, a foolish act. She stepped aside to let me pass. 'Oh, thank you, Mrs Pritchard.' I could have sworn she was testing my breath. But I had got there just one jump ahead and blasted her with Extra Strong before running confidently up the stairs to my room.

Winnie was horrified. 'How awful! How can you possibly be so calm? I couldn't, I'd have a breakdown. I'm dreading she'll get me in there, on discipline, as it is. Some nights I hardly sleep—'

'Don't be daft. How can she get you "on discipline",

with the shortage of teachers today? Any more than me on my lateness, what! When I'm spending so much extra time here after school, to enhance the reputation of this place and do the honours for the District Inspector! With any luck she'll take my class away—but that's what I've been working towards ever since I started ...'

Winnie heaved a deep and trembling breath. Her blouse shuddered with internal combustion. Her belt strained on its over-worked buckle. I changed the subject. 'How's the calorie count?' And stopped listening till after she'd told me.

'What's your opinion?'

'Sorry. About?' She'd startled me with her question.

'Sideways. Do I seem slimmer?' She'd taken in a baffling amount of breath and posed in profile like a photograph of Mr Universe. I took my time in answering, studying the sucked-in stomach, and the gigantic proportions of the distended ribcage. Her cheeks grew very red, her little eyes bulged larger with each second. I watched a set of veins start pulsing in one temple. She could quite well explode. In months to come, long after this room had been redecorated, we might still come across stray pieces. I say, would this be Winnie Einstein's lobe? It looks to me like the left. See here, it carries fragments of a small gold ring. A family gift for her twenty-first.

She'd come to the end. I'd out-tested her strength. 'You wouldn't do well under water, Winnie. Sub-standard lungs, I should say. Is it smoking do you think?' She'd sat down quick, puffing and woofing like a stranded whale, eyeing me sadly but unreproachingly.

'You don't see a change then?' she said.

'I think you've lost. Around the middle? Am I right?' I could see no difference.

Fiona had been caught. I couldn't believe it. With a ball of wool and a fish slice, slap bang on the ground floor of Brighton's biggest department store. They were suing to set an example. Nathaniel had been there when it happened. 'What, with her, in the shop you mean? Actually there, by her side?' I felt the pang of jealousy, seeing the two of them strolling together, drawing admiring glances of recognition from other passing customers—'Good Lord! You know who that is, don't you now—that actor—what's his name? We saw him in that thing the other day—you didn't like it much—'

'No, no! You silly girl. I was there when the cops rang up. Preparing to leave as it happened—out on my way up to you. Hence the unpardonable delay, of course, in case you hadn't noticed—'

'Over four hours, I expected you about seven . . .'

He buried his boffly chin into the side of my neck leaving a clutch of fluffy rice grains rolling down to my cleavage. He waved a fork, a glistening prawn fell to the floor; a passing waiter scooped it up even before it landed. We'd finished the wine, the first of it. 'More wine,' Nathaniel thundered. It came.

'Will they put her in prison? Or what will they do? Fine her? A cautionary word?' I couldn't wait to hear the worst. Poor girl, but it served her right. It wasn't as if she hadn't been warned, by me as a friend, any rate. I couldn't help feeling what a piece of luck it was that I hadn't been with her too, with my shopping bag as the dumping ground. And my undoubtedly guilty countenance to give us both away.

'Let's drink to Fiona,' he raised his glass. 'To little Fionapoo, come on now—both of us together.' He clinked my drink.

'Fionapoo,' I echoed, hoping they couldn't hear me on the adjacent table.

We'd been approached on and off all through the meal, by acquaintances and strangers. He hadn't introduced me once. I'd sat there like the unemployed, waiting to be noticed, trying to look pleasant and pretty. But in the end I'd given up and merely carried on eating regardless. 'Hello, old fellow! Fancy, you! I'm your greatest admirer, you know!' The Fiona saga came in in dribs and drabs. A bombshell delivered as shrapnel.

'Probation, no doubt! With a fine I expect—and lots of the worst publicity!'

'In the papers? Oh dear—'

'Daddy won't be pleased. Though in all truth'—Nathaniel laughed and tugged his beard—'it might do the old devil a spot of good—pricking the demon pomposity. Poor little Fiona. By the time I left she was in quite a state. They'd apparently found all manner of things in her room—remarkable objects, bearing no relation to anything at all—'

'I can imagine,' I said, remembering. The terrible thing

344

was, of course, the most frustrating aspect of it all was that ostensibly I didn't know of this development in Fiona's Brighton life. Nathaniel was on the inside, had happened to be there. Would Fiona ring and tell me? Or would I, like the rest of the world, have to read it in the local papers. 'Local girl caught Lifting. Daughter of Respected Resident. Found with a Fish Slice and Wool.'

'Your drawing has been much admired, you'll probably be pleased to hear!' Nathaniel beamed at me. 'If Fiona had persevered at Art, she wouldn't be in this pickle now I expect.'

'Do you think so? I don't agree. It wasn't a case of perseverance. She would never have been any good—'

'Bollocks!'

I plodded on bravely. 'Well, they said at our art school—'

'All rubbish—'

'Can I finish? May I please make a point?' I turned to him primly.

'Not if you're going to talk twaddle. Don't quote me some art teacher's shit!'

I shut my mouth. He'd touched on something. I felt my guts draining away. Is that how Reggie felt when I spoke sharply then to him? Weakened and wonderfully—what? Dismissed and harshly disciplined, dying to get back in favour. To be held in a *louche* lap of love. I stared at my plate, moving my jaws mechanically, trying like mad to concentrate on something else—on Fiona's plight, on the chance of old Pat with a bun in the oven, on Winnie with big Ooboogu—anything to halt and freeze the ducts behind my eyes.

'Girlie?' The kindly concern is what did it. A huge tear ran right down my cheek and splashed into my *Crevettes Sautées à la Crème*. 'I'm not certain,' I'd said, 'that that's what I want. I've never been that keen on shellfish.' He'd ordered it anyway. 'It's got brandy in, be a good child and eat it all up!'

'I'm sorry.' I bent my head. 'Don't look at me. I'm silly.'

He pushed his plate away and carefully placed his glass at the furthest end of the table, and doing the same to mine as well, he turned and in full view of everyone, folded both arms around me. Then he kissed me hard on the mouth. There wasn't anything I'd have refused him after that.

She'd rung me, Fiona, in the morning, just before I'd set

off for school. Minutes after Nathaniel had left, in fact. I jumped guiltily and tried to sound natural. 'How nice. How're things? This is early!'

She'd been crying. All night, so she claimed, and half of all yesterday too. I'd never be able to guess, not from the whole wide world what had happened! It was just too stupid, too ridiculous to believe! I wondered whether she'd mention the fish slice and the fateful ball of wool. I'd be able to ask her what colour. Pale fawn? Something frightful like that. Duck-egg blue? Sugar pink? Blackbird brown? 'I've been pinched!' She used a tragic key.

'Have you? Whereabouts?'

'In the basement—'

'On your bum!'

'Well lower ground floor to be exact. Pinched for pinching—'

'Oh, Good Lord! Oh Jesus God! How awful!' I gave it all I'd got.

'My parents are—'

'I can imagine!'

'They searched my room, well, mummy did. Behind my back as well. She found the whole caboodle, from months and months ago. I should have brought it all to you.' To me? My God! Why take this out on me? I didn't need the stuff!

'You should have thrown it all away—'

'What made it worse was that they found all sorts of things of their own—ashtrays from daddy's office, and boxes of paper clips—apart from that lavatory paper from the Grand Hotel, with Grand Hotel printed along it—'

'You're crackers to ever take brand goods of any kind, Fiona love.'

'And different things from mummy's friends. A fearful row about that—all the labels I'd cut from their coats. A whole collection, from Hartnell to Harrods—'

'What in hell would you do with those?'

Her voice descended to the depths of misery. 'Nothing. Except rummage through them. Now and then.'

'Oh Fiona.' She needed help surely. If only to sharpen her choice.

'Your father should have got you contact lenses. Those glasses have misted your vision.'

'The dreadful thing is . . .' Now she'd started to sob. I felt numb with guilt for multifarious reasons. It was obvious

I'd have to be late! A risk of a bollocking from Mrs Pritchard. I'd have to plead crisis in my immediate circle. The fatal disgrace of a friend. Yes, a casual thief! Specialising in miscellaneous objects of all description. The Curse of the Magpie, it seems! 'Yes, the dreadful thing is,' she choked, 'that if I'm put on probation, and even if I'm not, the question of me coming to live in London can be forgotten now!'

Our plans up the spout. The future kyboshed. No twosome tap-dancing the town. 'Well. Never mind. That doesn't matter now. It's you we're to worry about. Will it be in the paper, do you think?'

'They seem to think so, yes.'

'Well, take your glasses off when they come for the photo. Outside the Court, after the hearing, I mean. You never know what could come from that—film offers, anything.' It presented her with other aspects after all. I detected a new and optimistic note by the time we said goodbye.

He was filming, Nathaniel, all day today, playing a roguish old anarchist. A role he felt well-suited to. 'Complete and absolute crap, of course—the whole saga from start to finish!' And he'd thrown back his head and gulped his brandy in one go, then broken his wind in my face.

I thought about what he'd said. I was sure it was absolute crap. Come to think of it, I couldn't remember anything he'd done that wouldn't be included in that same category. Nothing at all, not a single film. And he'd never been on a stage. What a waste, when with his brains and mind and magisterial presence and even just his—gustiness—he could have been a great Shakespearean actor if he wished. Falstaff. Sound and Fury. Anyone.

'Why do you do it?'

'What d'ya say? Did you speak to me? Dare to address?' And he'd taken a bloom from the bunch on the table and plunged it down into my bosom. The water dripped from the wet stem straight through the thin material. Water could stain, I wasn't pleased.

'Yes, why do you waste time on crap?'

'CRAP! C-R-A-P!' He spelled it out in a roar, emphasising each letter with a blow on the table, his fist bunched up like a hammer.

The Head Waiter hurried forward, horrified. Behaviour such as this, criticisms of this kind could be catching. Other people I could see on surrounding tables were indeed already looking suspiciously at their loaded forks. 'The food is not to Sir's liking?'

Nathaniel looked at him in astonishment. "S'delicious!' And to my horror now broke into song. "S'delicious, 's'delightful, 's'delovely!' The whole room lit up. 'Who?' He turned to me.

'Who?' I repeated.

'Who.' He spoke like a querulous child. I wished to God I knew who bloody who was. 'Who?'

'Mmm?' How difficult the old could be.

'You give up then, girlie? You don't know who?'

'I don't.' I said wearily. 'No.'

'Cole Porter.'

'Oh yes, of course.'

Yes, he was filming at Elstree. Or Shepperton. Some quite famous place in the country. He'd left me early to go and get changed. 'Changed? Changed, but where? Here in London?' We'd spent a bad night on the creaking settee. He didn't mind as much as me, but that was because he easily occupied the majority of space. I'd existed along his left arm. A mishmash of muscle and bone constituted a pretty poor mattress, as Slumberland may have discovered. My father insisted on 'interior sprung' as opposed to everything else. No make, just that. He'd have point blank refused to even sit upon our bed-settee, let alone sleep for seven or eight hours. 'The spine requires especial cossetting. No human in his right mind can hope to stretch out on something the consistency of a city street and then hope to hold himself like a man. On two feet I mean, instead of four. You get my meaning, girl.' It hadn't occurred to me that Nathaniel possessed a *pied à terre*, but obviously he did, if clothes existed such that he could get changed.

I'd lain back watching him prepare to depart. Fiona had rung just after. 'Why couldn't we have slept somewhere else then, rather than here Nathaniel?' I'd asked as disarmingly as I knew how.

He'd started coughing, a major event at that time of the morning. Thank God I'd thought to shut the window, sound rising the way it did. He hammed it up, slapping his chest and throwing the leonine head first left then right, then finally forward and back to hang on his shoulder-blades. I addressed his well-fleshed Adam's Apple. I didn't see as many of those these days, it struck me, as I used to. We children used to pick out people's Adam's Apple; the really protruding ones, and persecute their owners quite unmercifully. Perhaps now everyone had more to eat. That's probably what it was.

'This basement can't be good for chronic chest conditions, such as yours Nathaniel—'

He gave a curdling whoop of First Grade Phlegm and Cream of Catarrh, a joyous, juicy timbre. Then spat out in the sink. I turned away. Good God Almighty, spare me this! I prayed he'd run the tap. 'Can't we,' I wavered, 'if we meet again (never take nothing for granted, girl) sleep in another place?'

He spoke, when he'd found his vocal chords again. They lay, it seemed, deep in his stomach. And until the upper sediment had been removed, no word could escape from his person. I waited. 'Tonight then, girlie?'

'Yes.'

'I'll ring.'

'Okay, but—'

'No but, you bitch.' His croak grew faint. 'You'll hear me when you hear me.' Not, I thought mutinously, if it means waiting another four hours.

So all was uncertain for this evening anyway. Winnie offered to wait for the outcome of The Confrontation. 'Don't bother,' I said. 'No, bugger it. I can give you the news tomorrow.' And I'd set my special group of after-school pupils on the technical task of suggesting scales, and fins and fronds and lumps and bumps, all characteristics common to amphibious creatures. First to be captured in charcoal. Whilst I went for audience myself.

I dismissed it from my mind as I shut the door behind me. My strategy had worked. There was nothing more to be said. Her coolness, Mrs Pritchard's, flew far above my head. I'd educated my brain to vacate the premises of my body whenever it was being used as a punching bag in punishment. I whistled as I went back to my room, loudly, to make sure she heard.

I was the last to leave, as usual. The caretaker twirled his keys, his tea was getting cold. 'Have I time to telephone?'

'Where?'

'To a friend.'

'Not from here. No, most definitely not. It would be more than the worth of my job to allow staff to use Head's own telephone. I'm surprised, Miss, you should be suggesting—'

'Goodnight.' My father would have said the same. Abiding by the rules. That's what they're for—to stick to, given as guidelines, girl. But I took a different view. It could be said, it could be claimed that rules were there to be broken. There to provide alternatives to imaginative persons.

Reggie lay heavily on my mind. I'd neglected him, I knew. The thought of him alone and old, cocooned in luxury, cut off but in a sense—incarcerated, brought me quite close to tears. Many things brought me to tears these days. Many men, I corrected myself. Reggie. Nathaniel. My father too, perhaps him most of all. Did Pat pitch herself to high emotional states like this, with Jim? Would her mother manage to steer the *sortie* this weekend into talk of mortgages and such? And if she did, would tearstorms start to manufacture themselves behind Pat's neatly mascaraed eyes? Even Fiona's tears were formed on a factual basis—her contre-temps with existing laws, antediluvian some might say, relating to property at large. But mine ...

I'd meant to ring Pat, in fact, in case Nathaniel had called whilst I'd been here at school fostering teenage talent. Had she blown through the basement, as she was sometimes prone to do around this time of day, early evening? There was a phone booth by the bus stop on the Walworth Road. I went to enter it, but was slapped back by the acrid fumes of adolescent urine and some foul stench, like breath, which blew out from the very phone itself. I decided to wait. It was just as well, a bus, my bus, was rounding the bend. With luck I'd be back home, surely by seven at the latest.

She'd left a note. Two telephone calls. Piers. Reggie. And more. The more said 'Am in the corner pub with Nathaniel, join us.' I'd thought she'd signed her name in red. Purely illusion, of course. But both my eyeballs flooded blood, my body had come straight to the boil! How dare she! He! Both of them! Be in the corner pub! Without me, on their own together. Fiona I might have understood, she'd met him first after all, but—! Why couldn't he just have sat outside in his car? Or in here on the bed-settee? Waiting for me. Alone. I ground my teeth and kept my tongue well back for fear of biting it in desperation over their disloyalty. Like a mad dog. A mad dog on heat, I could have said!

It took me seconds to dump my things and deodorise my arm-pits. I sprayed like a slut, straight on to ten hours' sweat—the accumulation of a stressful day. I didn't care. I looked a fright. Hell hath no fury, neither doth it give the time to doeth the face and hair. I was out of the flat and in the pub in under five minutes flat. I started chattering right away, my teeth, my double molars, from tension, as I saw his arm draped round her slender shoulders.

She was looking beautifully demure, the cunning bitch, down at her Rosebud fingernails, High Gloss to match her mouth. She'd drawn an especially feline chin on today, a clever trick of shading using Leichner's Theatrical Range. Strange that her draughtsmanship was so concise in cosmetic areas and so extremely sub-standard otherwise. She'd even managed a realistic dimple, à la Ava Gardner in one cheek. I had to admit she looked ravishing. Her hair had grown even in this last month and hung like Tallulah Bankhead's. Not an idol of our day, of course, but one had to acknowledge the mane. I searched for some discrepancy—the one faint hope, the flatness of her chest. But even here the outlook seemed improved. She must have cottoned on to Fiona's trick and taken up Sorbo rubber. They had them now, the newest thing from the U.S.A. 'Totally Natural to the Touch!' I felt certain that Nathaniel had been feeling. They welcomed me with genuine pleasure, which heightened my own sense of chagrin. How could all be as innocent as it appeared? I hadn't told her about Roly. I'd put on a face re his overtures. Nathaniel waved me to sit down beside him and slipped that spare arm easily around me, just as his other—on her. Pat smiled happily, I played the ventriloquist's dummy and managed a stiffened version of the same.

'Been here long?' I cleared my throat. A dozen frogs of fearful tension were strangling my epiglottis. They squatted, oozing bile along my major arteries. Like traffic lights, all green.

'Since opening time!'

'You haven't!' The blood rushed from my toes and

knuckles straight to the tips of my ears. I could feel them humming near my cheeks, hanging bright and alive, with a seeming life of their own, no part of me. Like the kidneys of a new-slaughtered sheep. My nose went like that sometimes—the sign of acute indigestion. Inherited from my father, so he claimed. 'Our circulation, girl—not quite like other people's. A sensitivity of the large intestine linked up with our mucus membrane. Stress. At all costs avoid it if you can. Especially with food and drink in the offing.'

They were in the offing now, imminently so. A packet of crisps in one hand and a gin and tonic in the other. Pat had had three of them already, so she said now, standing up.

'Sit down,' Nathaniel growled. And grabbed her skirt playfully. Pain skidded along my skin. He liked her. Hell!

But she tossed her locks, though looking at him still through Subtle Mink flirtatious lids and Fabulash perimeters. 'Got to go—'

'Her boyfriend's waiting—Jim—an architect—awfully good-looking—' I explained over-quick, unnecessarily. Nathaniel was winking. Up at her, not sideways towards me. I bent, pretending to rummage in my bag, my Adam's Apple the size of a Grannie Smith. Had it been a Bramley, they could have made a pie, big enough to feed the whole of Dr Barnardo's.

'She's gorgeous, simply divine! That little flat mate of yours!' Nathaniel turned to me enthusiastically, having followed the last of Pat's clocked seams right the way through the door. She might have been a bone, the first that Fido had seen after a fortnight on bread and water.

'Divine,' I agreed dejectedly. The evening, tomorrow, this year and next. The whole of the rest of my life was being lightly crucified by his comments. This must have been how Fiona felt, imagining Nathaniel with me. That didn't help though, not at all. That wholly extraneous knowledge.

'What's up? Hey, girlie. Look at me!'

The Spirit of Dunkirk! A sense of humour then at least. After all, there was always Reggie. What shade exactly would my father choose—for those long-looked-forward-to shoes? I'd go, goddammit, down this very weekend and buy them in Russell & Bromley. 'A bit of a change of scene then, dad, from Dolcis or the Co-op Men's Footwear!' 'The working man wears his dignity in his soul, my girl, not on

352

his s-o-l-e!'

'Nothing's up Nathaniel, that gin and tonic can't see to. Another, I think if you're ordering.'

'Better! That's very much better! For a moment there I felt an unpleasant wind from the wearisome little green goddess. We don't allow that totally destructive lady in our presence—' He pinched my chin (that, lacking the lush Leichner touch). 'There's enough to go round for everyone.' I knew that. Yes of course I did, with somebody like Nathaniel. But I wanted to be the special few, which in my book included—well, allowed for—just me and at most his mother.

'Yes, look at me before I made the break and learn from my example ...'

'... Bugger the bacon slicer—you know what he said was the matter?' A shrill and piercing scream sliced through the thronging playground. I looked at Winnie. 'Oh, don't get alarmed. Doris Wellington going too far. Shall I sort it? You just get everyone in line, it's time to go in in a minute. I'll see you later on.' I caught her arm and pretending to plead, to make her feel more important, lowered my voice. 'You'll quite like the intimate details. Ring up mummy and say you'll be late. One evening doesn't matter here or there with bacon, that's the beauty—it doesn't go off.' I hadn't convinced, I could see. I would have to be more provocative, raise a much riper carrot. 'Vaginismus!'

She looked startled. 'What?'

'That's what Nathaniel said I had!'

'He didn't! Whatever does it mean?'

I turned to walk away. 'Tell you later.' I spoke mysteriously over my raised right shoulder pad. 'After school. Tonight. Eh, okay?' Now I was confident that she'd come. I felt the need to tell someone.

'You're not odd, there's a name for it girlie—Vaginismus. The medical title. The vagina goes into a spasm—'

'It's doing it now Nathaniel,' I wailed. 'Could you force it open, do you think? With your fountain pen—or finger, even?'

'Christ! Would you ask a fucking dancer to put his foot into a vice? I need my fingers, every one. They're part of my stock in trade—' And to illustrate his point he picked up a

cigar and put it theatrically to his mouth, his fingers
raised, the little one crooked, the way Fiona said you
weren't supposed to drink tea. He tickled the tip of my
clitoris. 'Snap dragon,' he chuckled. 'Quite apt!'

I warmed to him at least for that, to speak so figuratively
using a flower. He might have said a mousetrap. Or a set of
rusty dentures. But being more mature, he understood.

'It hasn't always gone like that—I think it's the parts
that bring panic, Nathaniel.'

He raised his head and placed the cigar on the bedside
table. Veneered in the manner of walnut. Walnut Whirls
with a nut inside. One of our biggest sellers. When I had
still been eating sweets I could polish six off in one sitting.
Decapitating them like Gulliver would a Lilliputian
snowpeak. I like it here, Cadogan Court. Pleasantries with
the Hall Porter. 'Good evening, Sir, and Madam too of
course. A certain chilliness I fear.' I'd walked to the lift
with dignity, as if I was Nathaniel's daughter. I might
have been, the way we'd entered, laughing, relaxed,
unself-conscious. When had the demon needles begun to
knit? How had the sealing wax come? He'd plunged his
hand inside my skirt, the minute we'd got in the lift,
popping the waistband button. Grazing the skin of my
stomach with a badly clipped nail. We'd had a tussle
around Floor 3, approaching his own, which was 5.

'Hold on, what if someone's waiting for this lift! I don't
want to get out undressed!' But nothing it seemed would
detract him. 'All right then, I'll undo your flies! What
about your shy chump chop shocking Cadogan Court?'

When the lift finally arrived we'd embarked on the
friendliest of fights. 'Get on, you fucking whore!' he
thundered, 'and leave a man's prick with its privacy.'

'The same applies to pussies—'

'I shall piss on it—here in the corridor—'

'No, Nathaniel, now you're going too far!'

But he had, in the fire bucket. Straight into the sand,
seeming to go on forever. With me in agony and shame,
cross-fingered that no one should come.

The decor was thirties style. Early Fred Astaire. If
Nathaniel had been Fred and I'd have been Ginger, we'd
have danced to the bed together. We didn't. Not at all. Oh
no. Nathaniel liked it on the floor.

He knew the Elephant and Castle well, that's why he
drove me to school. And in any case he claimed it to be

354

actually on his way to Shepperton. In fact there was the faintest possibility that he'd be passing on his way back. Would I care for a lift? Should he pick me up?

'No, don't. Please,' I'd begged. 'It's not worth it. I'll be back in the flat at some point.' Was he saying he wanted to see me? Three nights in a row? Surely not! My bruised and bleeding ego had needed time to mend. At least an hour from that first gin with Pat, until at last I'd got my feelings under control. He hadn't mentioned her again. Perhaps that's how he was, a man like Nathaniel. The attention wandering, like an insect caught by colours. A bee, a butterfly on scent and sight, but returning to base. Base being me.

The sexual side of things at Cadogan Court had frankly been a fiasco, just as the night before in those terms, had been non-existent.

'Yes, Brewer's Droop, you see, Winnie. And a state of semi-consciousness, brought on by the drink as well. So all he did on the bed-settee was have a bloody good sleep. They must have heard him snoring as far as South Ken. I had to sleep on his arm—'

'Yes, but last night—all this vagiswhatsits stuff—I want to hear about that!'

I pulled my coat on, purple cloth—'Christ, child! What's this made from—cellulose? You need a fur, some skin in weather such as this—we'll have to see about it.' That's what he'd said this morning.

Winnie and I were in the staff-room—preparing to go and have tea. 'I've spoken to mummy—she was awfully put out. I had to lie, tell her we had a staff meeting!' Winnie looked woebegone and worried. 'I hope she won't check with Pritchard.'

'She won't check. You're not a child. Good Lord, what mischief might you find from Elephant and Castle through to Stepney?' I pinched her arm comfortingly. 'Blimey, you're surely let off the leash long enough to have a cup of tea.' She shrugged unhappily. I studied her. 'You know what, old Winnie, old girl—we should go, you and I, up West one day. And buy ourselves some new clothes. Our money's come in now after all.' A frown was forming, hovering above her eyes. With drastic tactics, I could divert it before it landed. 'Now that you're losing this weight I mean—everything's hanging off you!'

'Oh well! Now that you come to mention it, I could drop

a size I should think ...' She beamed, we were in there all
alone, and she lifted her arms in the air, sashaying round
the room. In seconds she'd start snapping her fingers and
yodelling a Spanish *olé*.

'*Olé*! Ah cha cha cha!'

'That's wrong,' I said sourly, before I could stop. What
right, after all, had one human being to dampen the high
spirits of another?

'Cha cha cha! *O mia cara*!'

I buttoned my coat and gave up.

Lyons, Westminster, was where I said we should have
tea. Welsh Rarebit, Winnie had decided she was having,
and had already launched into a lengthy description of her
preferred consistency of melted cheese, before we'd left the
staff-room. She followed, I went first, out through the
senior playground, so it was me who saw the Aston Martin
first. I stopped. But she continued, banging her hefty bust
into the back of me and snagging my stocking with her
well-worn attache. 'Oh shit!' I said. Nathaniel broke into a
deep bout of chuckling.

'Charming! The welcome one receives, this side of the
River Thames!' He got out of the car, doffing his
Deerstalker towards us.

'My stocking,' I explained. 'Not you. How sweet—
Nathaniel, this is Winnie.' The street, the school and all
around was mercifully empty. He must have waited ages,
or else just chanced his luck. 'How did you know I was still
here? The girls and all the other teachers have been gone
for hours.'

He gave an uncannily accurate approximation of the
caretaker's normal expression. Winnie and I burst out
laughing. 'I asked, no, I enquired of the old retainer.'

I glanced at Winnie. She'd turned an extraordinary
raspberry red, with two shining buttons as eyes—somewhere in that mass of mute adoring flesh. Her mouth
flicked up each side like a satiated beast, almost as if she
slavered at the sight of Nathaniel standing so near.

He noticed, and now turned to her, always the
professional charmer. His voice took on a deeper tone.
'Ah, Winnie! What a pleasure this is!' I stood well back, in
case she fell. She'd ruined one stocking already. He took
her hand. She wriggled and simpered, not speaking. They
didn't move, it seemed to me for what must have been
several seconds but appeared to be more like hours. The

356

whole scene was so incongruous in the particular setting. Winnie, like someone's maiden aunt, though so young and so fresh and unlined. And Nathaniel, the bluff old buccaneer, dressed as it were from a film set. A swift presentiment of unpleasantness, as light as a falling leaf, touched me, then departed. The spell had ended, Nathaniel opened the door and we all three of us squeezed into his car together.

He'd see her home, that's what he'd said, right at the end of the evening. And he'd dropped me first at Earls Court, back at the flat, in order to call back later. 'I'd rather sleep at Cadogan Court, if we're spending the night together.' I'd made that clear.

'Don't fucking fuss!' He'd waved an impatient arm.

'But I'd like to go back to the flat at some point to change my clothes, that's all Nathaniel—'

'Sure, sure, child, shush! Christ!'

Winnie's eyes were larger than they'd ever been in living memory. He'd driven us straight to Chelsea, to a pub behind the embankment. I'd suffered pangs at the sight of the river. A few stretches further on Reggie lay waiting whilst I played the Gay Deceiver. Or would have done, given the chance. When we'd got into the car Winnie, for some asinine reason, had chosen to sit on my lap. I'd had to plead mercy at Millbank. And buckled right down on the kerb when we got out of the car to change over. 'They've gone to sleep I think,' I gasped. 'My legs, I'm sorry Nathaniel—'

He'd roared from the wheel. 'Where the fuck has she gone—back where she belongs—in the gutter!' The small car shook with his laughter. Winnie joined in from sheer nerves. She couldn't believe it still, I knew, that he actually was here in the flesh. She kept cavorting, tugging down her roll-on, tilting her mammary shelf, applying herself assiduously to his every word. She looked to me quite hideous. But apparently not to him. That's possibly what appalled me even more than the pain of Pat. Were all women equal in his eyes? Each there to be made available. Might my mother had stood a chance as well? And her blind old auntie Mavis?

'What will you have then, Winnie, m'lass? But first let me, or rather, allow me, to divest you of this, your outer layer!' He stood behind her in the warm interior of the low-lit pub and helped to remove her coat by undoing the

357

buttons for her. The garment sprang apart with ease, but his hands remained where they were, firmly fixed on her solid front. She squirmed. They shook. And thudded through his fingers. He held on tighter than before. 'I never thought to find such bountiful tits,' he beamed. 'Over a handful, each one!'

I thought I'd be sick all over the bar, vomit straight into my neighbour's vermouth. I say, barman, my drink has turned solid! The zest of a lemon, old chappie, not this—the whole of the bloody old grove! I headed for the Ladies. 'Powder your nose? Winnie?' I threw back over one furious shoulder. She made no answer, none at all. Nathaniel had his head buried like a vampire in her neck. She stood, eyes shut, the angle of her face quite horizontal with the ceiling, its expression—bliss personified!

Two other pubs—before we came to rest, with Winnie sparkling like—like Andrews Liver Salts. It was the last time I'd help her on discipline or advise her on social improvement. Nathaniel flourished between the two of us, delegating favours quite equally. Our final watering hole—since all we'd done was drink—turned out to be a tiny but crowded theatrical club. At least I had plenty to look at.

Winnie continued to amaze. I began to see what might have beguiled Ooboogu and the wand that she'd waved on the witless Indian waiter. Music played. She stood, inviting Nathaniel to dance! I sat and watched savagely, my first time as a soured wall-flower, as Winnie repeated the staff-room performance of wantonly shaking her jelly. A small crowd gathered to cheer. Of course they were all theatricals. She gave it all she'd got, encouraged by their attentions. I studied my drink. Dry white, he'd ordered for us all. A menu lay on the table—were we ever going to eat? I signalled a passing waiter and standing, shouted over to Nathaniel and Winnie on the floor.

Nathaniel was in the process, I couldn't believe it, of removing his jacket and shirt. People were cheering 'Trousers down!' But Winnie was next in line. He lunged at her, his powerful body wet with sweat, and ripped her blouse wide open. Buttons popped all over the place. The blouse fell back, over her shoulders and slithered down her arms to the floor. She stood there like the proud prow of a ship, radiant and regal in her hefty, blancmange-pink brassière. The crowd went wild as a madcap pervert, bent

358

on mischief, darted forward and undid it from behind. She dimpled, squirming 'Dearie me! Oh don't! You naughty boy!' The lisp was becoming more pronounced with every word. Nathaniel beamed, his belly belching over the workman's belt which held his trousers up. 'Whoa there, my beauty!' Winnie pranced in imitation of a horse. A thoroughbred but built on heavier shire lines. The last supports, cup D, strong cotton, were cast gaily to all four winds. She waved her Berlei like a flag. The people gasped. Her breasts were unbelievable.

I could have left, and might have done, from simple feline pique. I doubt they would have noticed. In fact, I'd even started searching in my bag to see how much I had in the way of money, and whether or not it would have run to taking a taxi over to Reggie's—

'Hello! It is you, isn't it?'

I looked up. Joyce, of Joyce and Johnny. Nick's friends from the Studio Club. She was wearing a pinstriped suit, with a collar and tie, as before. But her hair was even shorter. She looked like Peter Pan. 'You look nice,' I said. She shrugged, self-deprecatingly but with impressive confidence.

'What on earth are you doing here?' Her voice was intriguingly low. Perhaps that's what it was about her—an actressy kind of quality.

I pointed to the centre of the floor. 'I'm with the cabaret—'

'What, Nathaniel?' She seemed surprised.

I nodded. 'Well I was ...'

'He's a bastard like that,' she laughed. 'But never mind, come and have a drink with us.'

Johnny wasn't there. 'He's round with Gerry.' Gerry? Oh Gerald, the young exquisite. Flat-mate of Nick and Jim. Joyce's 'us' was completely women. Each talking of auditions, past and present or taking place tomorrow. All actresses. 'I used to go through all this shit,' Joyce whispered to me. 'Before I joined the world of journalism—it's soul-destroying stuff, as you can see.'

I looked around; they didn't seem that much different to the faces in our staff-room, the lower staff-room at least. Or come to that, the countenances of my fellow travellers on the morning tube. More make-up, that was all. As Pat might look in fifteen years or so. But Joyce was different. I glanced discreetly, when I could, at the firm lines of her face. She caught me once, but paid no special attention that might have made me self-conscious. I felt like a shy first former with everyone's favourite prefect. 'Oh, by the way, before I forget—we're having a party,' she said. 'Johnny and I were drawing up a list last night. We hope very much you can come. It's in our place, the new one, the house that we've just bought. To celebrate the move.'

I'd heard all about the move already, and about the marvellous house. A simple terraced one, off Fulham Road, but ripped apart inside and redesigned by them both. Pat had claimed it 'unbelievable'. The height of modernity. Praise indeed from her.

Winnie now clothed again, dripping with sweat and delight, had been sent over to reclaim my company by Nathaniel. 'I'll come,' I promised Joyce. 'In a fortnight? Yes, that'll be fine!' And I turned to Winnie. 'I wonder you noticed I wasn't there!' As coldly as I could.

I'd had a bath and dressed again, waiting for Nathaniel to return. Forty-five minutes he claimed, it would take to drive Winnie back to Stepney. The time was now half-past two. I'd been waiting for over an hour. He'd invited us both back to Cadogan Court. 'A threesome,' he'd growled. 'How about it?' Winnie had simpered, patently unsure of what to say. But I had point-blank refused. I knew who'd be worst off between the three of us. Me, as a fine sandwich filling, bordered by these loaves of bread. I had no wish to be enveloped, smothered, suffocated by Winnie's billowing breasts. Hadn't even Fiona's non-tips turned my stomach? Nathaniel was not pleased with me, or with my prim reaction. Winnie had grimaced sympathetically behind his back as if both she and I were still in league. But I couldn't forgive her disloyalty. How could anyone not see he was mine? They'd laughed as they were leaving. 'See you later,' I'd said to Nathaniel. He'd thrummed up the car as an answer.

Half-past three. Going on four o'clock. I thought of summer holidays I'd had. And how it felt to read I'd got Matric. 'Well done, my girl! She's done splendid, hasn't she, mam? For that you shall have a watch!' His own. It hung too loose around my wrist, getting wet each time I did the washing-up, and banging against the bottles whenever I served in the shop, until it became a vicious bone of contention between us—and he'd taken it back, for

360

some peace. I'd give a ring tomorrow, to tell them both I'd be down. Four-thirty! Was the phone not working? Had Nathaniel crashed his car? Not got through. He surely would have rung. I picked it up and dialled O. 'Hello, could you test this line? I'm expecting a call and have reason to believe I'm possibly out of order.' No chance at all. 'Thank you, that's good. It's obviously working,' I said with pretended relief. I looked at my shoes, still brown I saw—when would the bleeding show through? But I sat up, I didn't care; like Florence Nightingale I'd see the ordeal through till dawn. He was a bastard, yes I knew! A monstrous bloated bugger. Screwing the daylights out of dopey Winnie Einstein in the comfort of Cadogan Court. This very moment, at this precise second poised above her like a raunching, randy—Five! Five exactly when it rang. To the tee. On the dot, smack on, with a shrill. My nerves were primed for shock, however. I'd rehearsed my reaction for hours. I picked it up.

'You fart-faced, unfaithful fucker!' I said. 'If you think you can come for me now, you can stick that flaccid thing you call a prick right the way up your own arsehole!' And I put it back down with a bang. It rang again.

'The trouble is you see'—I was shouting now and spitting all over the receiver—'you're a sackful of shit in any case—no use in bed to man or beast—let alone to the female sex—but just because you're a jaundiced, old film-star hack whom no respectable repertory company, even, would employ, you think you can fucking pick and choose! Now sod off! You understand!'

Once more—the third time running! I picked it up, and this time simply listened, saying nothing. 'Hello, love. Ted here. Ted Grunt, y'know, greengrocer. Sorry to have to keep ringing. There's been a bit of bad luck. I mean—' He paused. 'Bad news, my love. There's been a fire, y'see. And. Well. Your mam and dad. I'm sorry to say. They're both dead.'

Fiona paid for the tickets, the most expensive seats, so that we wouldn't have to queue. *Sabrina Fair* is what we were seeing. Humphrey Bogart and William Holden. But Audrey Hepburn was the real reason. Pat had said she was having her hair all cut off in the same style. Today in fact, in preparation for her wedding. 'Mind you,' Fiona said, following the usherette, 'when you come in to all your

361

money, I'll expect you to pay for everything, whenever we go out—'

'No change, you mean, in our relationship then, Fiona?'

She'd squeezed my arm affectionately and laughed. 'No, but seriously, I do deem it an honour to be out with an heiress.'

I could have wished she wouldn't talk like that. I might have said 'Christ, can't you shut your greedy mouth? My poor old parents are barely in their coffins—' But I chose to say nothing at all.

They were barely in their coffins. The firemen had claimed it a difficult task to salvage much in the way of remains. The blaze had taken hold and become sweepingly uncontrollable in what seemed seconds, so would-be rescuers reported. And I believed it to be true, knowing my father's insistence on sleeping with his stock. The bed itself was bordered on each side with cartons, cardboard and highly inflammable, of cigarettes and wrapped and packet confectionery. And being basement, their bedroom would have been first to go. Both police and insurance believed the cause of the fire to have been the paraffin heater and I would have agreed with that as well. The one was all we'd had, carried from room to room at my father's command. Always a hazard, I'd said so hundreds of times.

The film had started, Audrey's doe eyes swamped the screen. Fiona nudged. 'Nice make-up, eh?'

'Yes. Pat's already doing it. Tickling the end of her eyes up. And wearing two lots of false lashes.'

'Two lots?'

'Yes. Theatrical ones, one on top of the other to make them that much thicker. Didn't you notice them at the funeral?'

'No. I thought that was her mascara. It was running. Right down to her mouth. Not meaning to be bitchy.'

'Oh,' I said mechanically. 'I thought it very kind of her to cry. And you. Well everybody really.'

She squeezed my hand. 'Out of sympathy. We're all upset when you are.'

I stared across the sea of hats ahead. Was it only ten days since it happened? And not just that, but all the other things as well. I'd travelled in a state of shock, down from Victoria at dawn. And had travelled so, it seemed, from that time right up until the funeral, when they'd both been buried. A twin burial, exactly like a wedding. Riding

362

tandem. Playing doubles. Not going it alone. I'd thought it best that, being my decision, to satisfy their wishes to the end. A Cemetery Affair in Consecrated Ground was my father's idea of a Do. With lots of mourners. Ted Grunt and half the Darts Team vying with all of the pub for the honour of being pall-bearers. Though whilst alive he'd spoken often of the Special Significance of Cremation. The purging by fire of the spirit. This way he'd had it both ways.

Fiona didn't like *Sabrina Fair*. We walked along the sea front afterwards towards her father's office. The Channel churned to our left, a gusty wind destroyed the curls we'd only just combed in the cloakroom. I'd been staying at Fiona's house since her father had so kindly taken all under control. I didn't think my father had a lawyer. A bank, but nothing more. They were, it seemed, the trustees of his entire estate. But Fiona's father was acting for me now. Six months or so, before the insurance would pay out the bulk, but until then it seemed that money was no problem. I couldn't quite, still, believe it. The implications were too wide and too significant to understand in one! I needn't, for instance, teach again. Not unless I wished to! I could pack up my job this minute, just like that! I didn't have to enter ever again that evil, dank, dark Earls Court basement if I wished! Rush-hour, buses, tubes, travelling anything but First could well be a thing of the past! My painting could take precedence now and if need be for ever—it didn't matter if they sold or not, no longer my means of support! Oh no, it certainly needed thinking about, there wasn't a short cut to that.

I would have liked to have advice, other than strictly professional. Nathaniel, for instance, his wordly anarchistic judgement. And Reggie. But both those avenues were closed. I'd decided that in these last days.

It was Piers who'd spilt the beans on Reggie. On Fiona's instigation. I'd told her of our deepening intimacy in a way to divert the talk away from Nathaniel. 'What? That old lecher, Reggie? You can't mean it! No, never him!' And when Piers had arrived from his parents' home to pay polite respects to me on my sad bereavement, she'd urged him to vicious enlightenment. 'Of course, duckie! Didn't you know! What, old Reggie? A lovely old pervert! Been practising masochism for many years! Has elevated it to the higher realms of art. Sordid in spots and has to take

363

care—since a scandal—what—oh, six years ago? Drove a girlie to play it a little too hard—cut his cock off, some actually say! Why? Don't say he was trying to make you his Princess? Reggie's Princesses if gathered all together wouldn't fit in the Royal Enclosure—' I probably cried more readily over that than over my Sudden Losses.

No, she wasn't that keen on *Sabrina Fair*, Fiona. She'd found Miss Hepburn's choice of lover ridiculously unrealistic. 'Who in their right mind, given the alternatives, would have Humphrey Bogart instead of William Holden? Answer me that now, who?'

The wind cut through my new black coat. 'Who? Lauren Bacall for one.'

'Oh well that, that's a different thing—she's his wife. I'm not talking about fact, only fiction.'

We turned the corner. 'How do you mean?'

She chose to take me literally and launched into a lengthy explanation. But I'd stopped listening long before it ended. I found I did a lot of that these days. What was it called—withdrawing into one's own brown study? Especially with Fiona. I barely admitted it to myself, but in honesty she bored me. Thank God we'd never shared a flat. I thought about Bernard's letter. Dear old Bernard Bolt, he was the one I'd turned to in the end. His reply had arrived this morning. Mozambique for Christmas! Well, why not? 'The colours here are fucking unbelievable! They'll blow your eyeballs out! You've come into a spot of dough, you say! So every cloud's got a silver lining—concentrate on your proper calling—get a bloody paint brush in that idle hand of yours. See how you like it at Christmas (80° in the shade!) And after then, well, who knows ...'

Fiona nudged me. 'Hey!'

I turned to her. 'Do you know what? I think I'm actually feeling so much better now, that I'll go back to London tomorrow.'

Pat was in the flat with Jim, busy painting the kitchen. All white. They kissed me, both of them together and made me a cup of tea. 'How's things?' I said.

A lot had happened since I'd seen them both here, or even since Pat and I had been together on our own. She was pregnant, which was why they planned to get married. 'Not that we wouldn't otherwise,' she'd whispered big-eyed at the funeral. Jim didn't look like someone with a shot gun at his head. 'Mum knows. She doesn't mind a bit. She's mad about him anyway.'

The all-white made the kitchen look much bigger, and much lighter too. Something had changed. They were putting the finishing touches. 'It's different here, isn't it?' I looked around. Pat beamed and slid a smudgy hand round Jim. 'Spotlights!' she said. 'By Jim.'

'They're great.'

'But come and see the other room.' She led the way towards the door.

'No, wait . . .' I couldn't think what else was different. 'I know! The bed-settee! It's gone!'

They laughed and looked at each other. 'He couldn't bear it,' Pat explained. 'He claimed it was highly unsanitary! Jam-packed with vermin and unmentionable secretions! We burnt it, out there in the basement—' She stopped abruptly, but I didn't mind. There were bound to be these cross-references.

'Secretions, you say? I'm sure!' I raised what I hoped was a quizzical brow. They both laughed in obvious relief.

'Oh yes. The thing we meant to ask you too'—Pat paused obviously shy—'do you mind awfully if we put you in the kitchen on your own? We're about to bring your single bed through from the passage. We'd thought of living on here for a while, after the wedding, you know. Until we get sorted with mortgages and such, and getting a place of our own.'

It was no surprise to me. I'd thought of it myself, how suitable the basement would be for them both. But not with me as well. Oh no! I wasn't that green. And anyway, I'd honestly be bloody glad to see the back of it. To get a studio on my own, or something. All perfectly feasible now. 'Christ, be my guests. Of course not, don't be daft! No, honestly, what I'm after is a great big studio room or something, if you know of one—my circumstances have altered you understand!' I made my voice as pompous as possible, saying it. It was still, my sudden wealth, a source of self-consciousness, especially to me.

They did know of one, exactly right! No! Yes—the perfect answer! A beautiful place, if it was still to let, at the top of Joyce's and Johnny's! Where they were holding the party. You know, the one tonight!

Something jolted in my mind, some clearly forgotten fact. 'Tonight?'

Jim spoke. 'Yes. Isn't that why you've come back, we assumed—'

'No, Jim. I'd honestly f—'

'You're coming though. Isn't she, Jim, with us?' Pat spoke firmly.

'Of course she is.' Jim turned to me. 'We'll be off in a couple of hours. We'll have a drink first over the road. I'll ring Nick now, he can join us.'

I surrendered weakly to their bland enthusiasm, letting their sun soak through me. I felt a twinge. 'What, dancing on our graves so soon, my girl?' Not dancing, dad—tip-toeing, truly, simply that.

I wore my black. When all of this was over I'd give my whole wardrobe to the Salvation Army, down to the last dark depressing stitch. And buy some more, a cloudburst full of colour—cerise and shocking pink. Viridian green and all the blues. A tingling tangerine—I'd blaze my way to Mozambique! Put nature itself to shame!

Pat wore white. Regardless. 'Will you be wearing white for the wedding, Patty? Even though it's just in the Registry?'

'Of course,' she answered confidently. 'No one can tell. On the outside. That there's two of us in here.'

Quite true. Well, come to that, no one could tell whether all the brides who opted to wear white were bloody virgins or not. I kissed her cheek and squeezed her bony shoulder. 'You look lovely,' I said.

'So do you.'

I did, I knew. Sorrow, I'd say, did actually seem to suit me. It lent a fine mysterious charm, such that I could have caught anyone. Anything. Though these last two weeks, ten days, eleven or whatever it was, all that had bled into the background. Not uppermost in my mind as it had been before. Except at night, alone in my bed, eyes wide open in Fiona's mother's guest room. Oh yes, I'd touched myself in there all right, from the sheer need for some comfort. An animal urge, quite primitive, like a beast of the field. But without fruition. Each joyless, self-exploratory session. It was time I was touched by another.

We weren't the first to arrive by any means. Guests overflowed down the stairs. Nick relieved us of our coats. He hadn't come round, we'd met him there instead. 'Would love to, of course, but can't, have to help Joyce with the glasses,' he'd said cheerily on the telephone. It

366

was nice to hear his voice again, just that had the feel of friendship. He greeted me now with a bony bear hug. 'Good to see you, kid. Pecker up!' His ginger beard tickled my chin. I caught a whiff from his armpits. Perhaps we all should club together and give him deodorant for Christmas. Or not. It didn't matter that much anyway, the unfortunate pong.

'Good to see you Nick, too,' I squeezed him hard. 'Thank you for all your sympathy.' They'd sent a telegram and flowers, the minute they'd had the news. A bloody sight more than Nathaniel had done. Or Winnie. Or Reggie. Or Ernest. A nice letter from Mrs Pritchard though, and the District Inspector! I'd finish the term for sure, and complete everything for the County Hall exhibition.

We went upstairs, greeted by various people on the way, colleagues of Nick's and Jim's. Until at last we reached the top and arrived at the heart of the party.

It was quite difficult to tell in the superb but lowered light, how large the room might be. It occupied, anyway, the entire square footage of the house. Had clearly been built on a flattened roof, its ceiling, as it were, completely of glass. I felt uncannily at home from the minute I stepped foot there. 'It's marvellous! It's mad! My God. I love it.' That's all I could say.

Jim laughed. 'Hold on—let's ask Johnny or Joyce. Cross fingers anyway that it's not gone already—'

'Oh dear, please do find out.' He slipped away, and Pat followed. Nick had gone for a drink. I stood alone. And looked around. That's when I first saw him.

They found me underneath the coats, that's where I'd crawled to, they said. Asleep, and smiling, Pat claimed, who'd stumbled on me first. 'You missed it all! The entire thing. Where did you get to?'

I shrugged and looked around. 'Is it over? No, obviously not—these coats are still here, so there must be people—' A hardy nucleus remained, the sort who always do, to see it through till dawn. 'I'll wash my face and come on up. I promise. I'm wide awake now!'

Pat had lingered back. 'Are you all right? Really?'

'Yes I am.'

'I saw you,' she said, 'going off. He looked great! What did you get up to? And more to the point, where?'

'Hello,' he'd said. 'And what are you?'
   'An orphan.' It was the first time I'd said it.
   'An orphan, eh? That's sad.'
   'It is a bit.'
   'Let's dance.'

'You have no objection, I take it? To misbehaving in broom cupboards?'
   'None at all.' I'd dropped my skirt.
   'That's good.' He'd undone his trousers.

'A remarkable ride!'
   'Yes, smooth as silk.'
   And I laughed all the way up the stairs.

FULL UP

To Sarah
The Shiniest Star

I was branded on both buttocks with the sure indentation of a whole row of gas taps, each outlined in a faint film of grease.

'You've impressed me,' I said.

He smiled, knowing he had. Who would have thought that this Savile Row suiting, its lines so smooth and self-disciplined, contained such a wild and impertinent weapon. What wisdom, what vigour—what width!

When he unplugged me, the noise was like a soft cork coming out of a bottle. 'Care for a Cuban?' he produced from his waistcoat a moulded, fine leather cigar case. Why not, yes, why not smoke his cigar—celebrate Castro together.

We stood, still half-dressed, companionably smoking—my skirts hitched high on my small shoulder straps, my filmy pants snagged on one shoe. His immaculate trousers, less immaculate now, hung at half-mast from their mooring. 'The occasion, surely,' he said it first, though I had meant to for the last few moments, 'calls for champagne.'

'On the house,' I was able to answer.

We shuffled together towards the large fridge, standard catering model, reserved strictly for drinks. 'Well stocked with champagne, Moët Chandon, I'm afraid, not Dom Perignon. And not even Vintage.' I said all that to hide my shame, to sidetrack his attention away from the hideous contents that some indolent slob had chosen to stow in the fridge. A battered blancmange, its turreted peaks bruised like a child's badly made sandcastle. The flaky remains of some badly burnt rissoles mixed up with some stale mashed potato. A glutinous glob of spilt greying gravy hung like an icicled finger, almost touching the crazily stacked champagne bottles. 'Stacked by a cretin,' I added, 'as you can see.'

He turned with new interest at my words. 'Really! A mental defective? You employ handicapped persons as part of your staff? That's certainly rare in a restaurant—a high risk I believe. The danger, I mean, from hot flying fat and the degree of high temperature generally. They're like

371

children, you see, the same curiosity and the same unawareness of danger. It's as if that warning device were turned off, its mechanism underdeveloped. And, of course, this being so, the resulting breakages and inevitable losses in food fuck up the fine Samaritan urge to afford work opportunities to these unfortunates: altruism defeated by sheer economics. Nevertheless, I commend you on your humanity. No wonder this small restaurant of yours exudes such irrepressible warmth. It must have taken a very long time—'

'Two days. We've been open two days.'

A sense of surprise shivered through me, or was it my bum getting cold? Two days, was that all? Had it taken two days to disrupt my whole life to this point?

'Though, of course, we'd thought of it—Vincent and I, my partner, I don't think you met—we thought of it long before this. I say "long", though it was actually last week—'

'Wouldn't it be nice to have one's own restaurant, and not have to fuss over food. Just go there with the kids, and Auntie of course, then come home without paying—Vince, are you listening?'

I watched Vincent combing his hair carefully over his scalp. It was blowy outside and he'd walked from Sloane Square, holding his hair in place with his left hand and having to skulk through the side streets because of it, instead of cutting a fine figure on the King's Road.

'I'm surprised you don't go in for a wig, Vince. They do wonderful ones these days. You can't tell the difference, they don't come off in bed—' A Gentleman Caller of mine, a dear love, wore a Crown Topper. Should I spill the beans and say which? Or would that be dreadfully disloyal of me? Yes, it would. Vincent shuddered. 'A toupée, oh, it's not that bad yet! Is it, darling?'

'No, of course not,' I lied. 'Only joking.'

I looked around. A layer of dusty fluff stirred slowly under the sofa, imprisoned beneath the Heal's black leather which I'd bought as a sign of mourning when The Old Man had died. I'd bought lots of black things that year, I remembered. Black lipstick, which I'd have to give up, it made my teeth look too yellow. Black plates which the children disliked. Black pillows and sheets which showed all too clearly afterwards if I'd not slept alone. And

372

I'd taken a black boy as a lover. Just the once, a sweet student who'd come searching for digs. He'd enrolled at the Commonwealth Institute that morning, and was already missing his mother. Above the sofa, the Francis Bacon hung skew-whiff against the wall. It had been hanging that way for over a week.

'Isn't is glorious,' I said to Vincent, 'not to have someone cleaning. Coming in and clearing up, restoring terrible order — though no doubt,' I sighed, 'it will soon get me down. The kids took it upon themselves to do the shopping list last week; it was completely indecipherable. All chewing gum and chocolate bickies.' Vincent turned from the mirror, his follicles now facing immaculately one way. With order restored and his vulnerable scalp thus thatched and hidden from sight, he was able to give me his full attention. 'You'll have to put an ad in the *Chelsea Post*, or on one of the Sloane Square shop boards. That reminds me, I saw a tart's card in the pet shop window, advertising her pussy. "PUSSY FOR SALE", there was no mistaking—rather ingenious I thought.'

'Pussy for sale.' I repeaed his words. 'Yes, that's good. You know, I've always thought that I wouldn't mind that, with my own little clientele. It could be quite cosy, if you gave cups of tea and took time off for chats in between. I think where lots of girls go wrong, and don't enjoy job satisfaction, is in not making the service personal enough—'

'That's why you'd be so bad on the game, it's not meant to be personal in that sense. No involvement emotionally — you wouldn't survive for a week. Though it might make sense, my darling, I must say, if instead of being open-house here continually supplying every Tom, Dick and Harry not including your Gentlemen Callers—if there were some way to convert your generous spirit into terms of hard cash in the hand.'

Hard cash in the hand was an obsession with Vincent, who'd been on and off the dole since his first days in Rep. His two bitterest disappointments, professionally, were that he'd failed to play the film roles, firstly, as the homosexual friend of Rita Tushingham in *A Taste of Honey*, and, secondly, as the homosexual friend of Julie Christie in *Darling*. Our relationship, his and mine, was played out with these parts still in mind. As if a third similar role might present itself and he'd be able to audition well-prepared. Which was why one was left with the feeling of having been rehearsed. Even badly rehearsed, the hysteria pitched a little too high.

'I'm starving!' he exclaimed now, one hand on his stomach. Like Hamlet denouncing his sanity. Then, 'What have you got?' 'That's just what I've said, Vince, I've got nothing. It all seems to have gone! Where and how, God only knows, but different people keep popping in and the kids bring back half the school—you're right, it is like open-house. I'd be better off with a restaurant.'

Vincent had taken the few steps to the kitchen and proudly returned with some cheese. A soft triangular piece of Dairylea processed squashed beyond recognition but still safely edible in its silver paper. 'I found this,' he said tearing it off. He shut his eyes as he ate and composed a fine profile, his chin high like Ivor Novello. Or that other famous profile actor, John Barrymore. Senior or Junior? No, wasn't that the Fairbanks, Father and Son? Vincent would know right away. I watched him poised in pure delight, sucking down Dairylea. Could almost see the yellow denseness sliding through his throat, as thick and as creamy as catarrh. And probably as comforting.

'How divine!' he murmured. Divine? Dairylea? Not as nice as the Brie I'd bought yesterday, or the Boursin Fine Herbes, for that matter I thought. What bugger had eaten both those then? Vincent opened his eyes. 'A brainwave! Of course!' What, the processing process at Kraft? Vincent's theatricality could get on one's nerves if he weren't such a friend, fond and true. 'It's only just sunk in—the restaurant. A restaurant! Our restaurant! Why not —run between us—partners, my pet! Oh, yes, what a brilliant idea!'

I looked at my watch, the kids were due back, and Auntie. 'We'll be eating out tonight, Vince—you'll come, do, my treat. It's seven now—'

Vincent was clearly over-excited. He clasped his slim frame with both arms, until his fingers almost met at the back. He managed to look quite epileptic, the body so warped and the face so intent. I'd noticed before — this physical buckling of Vincent's body when his mind seemed caught in a spin. The limbs reflected the mental tension.

'Yes, it's seven o'clock now.' I spoke extra normally in an effort to calm him. 'They should all be back here by now. Auntie's taken them out, over to Battersea Funfair. Perhaps I should cruise over the bridge in the car, in case they can't find a taxi. It's pretty bad on Saturday nights. And Bogey's too small to walk back by himself, which means the girls will keep taking turns giving piggy-backs. It's very dangerous that, in prepubescence, giving piggybacks, so I've read. Almost been medically proved already as the root of prolapsed wombs in menopause—'

Vincent shuddered. I'd broken the spell of his intensity. 'How riveting, darling. I didn't know that.'

I laughed. A pleasant evening lay ahead, all eating out together. The only question was: out where? Which restaurant? With our own, we'd have no need to wonder.

We sat around a comfortable table for four, all six of us, especially laid in the window of 235, a bistro-type restaurant on the King's Road. The sort that might suit Vincent and me. I'd chosen it in fact for that very purpose, intending a surreptitious study. A glance on the quiet at their organization, at their service and mainly their menu. Vincent, as yet, was not much concerned with the practical running details. He seemed not quite convinced of my participating, not even when I pointed out that the two were linked. The ability, or the will—and the wish.

'Oh, but I can see it all so well, can't you! Together, you as Earth Mother, Mummy to all—and me as the gracious Mine Host! Ooh!' He shrilled and drew his breath. 'Ooh, dearie me, I say!'

Auntie blinked, and smiled at me. 'What's Vincent saying?'

'Yes, what is he, Mum? What is he talking about?' Tallulah, my oldest, blinked at me too. Blindly behind her glasses. Zsa-Zsa, her sister, was pouting; as usual looking uncommonly like a young camel. Everyone had warned us, The Old Man and I, that we invited disaster with such a choice of name. So exotic, so hard to live up to. But I had no doubts that my ugly ducklings would emerge much later as swans—as I had, by one means and another. Bogey my two-year-old beauty, was less handicapped it seemed by his name. Everyone wrongly assumed him to be named after Humphrey Bogart; in actual fact Bogey merely referred to a slight blockage of one nostril. An irregularity at birth causing an abundance of snotballs. I might have wondered if his condition were hereditary, but there was no way of checking on this since I'd never known who might be his father. It's true that for the one whole winter following his birth I did pay additional attention to those Gentlemen Callers of mine with uncommonly severe sinus trouble, and signs of sustained coughs and colds. But since that season was particularly harsh, and all seemed to fall in the grip of the weather with more or less similar suffering, I relinquished my fruitless quest.

A waiter came to take our order, as I was about to explain our restaurant idea. He was young, with hair like Christ, wearing a Habitat apron: navy blue with wide butcher-boy stripes. Vincent simpered, 'I like your pinny.' The boy tossed his mane and ignored us.

'There now, she's taken offence! I must mind my p's and q's! Naughty Vince—smack his pandy and ask for more.' Vincent rapped himself over his knuckles. The children dissolved into wild paroxysms of mirth. The waiter walked away. Vincent pursed his mouth exaggeratedly and stared deliberately at the boy's backside. 'Oh my, with a neat little botty like hers, you'd think she'd try to be nicer.'

Bogey sneezed and showered the surface of the table with mud-toned mucus. Vincent winced and held a delicate hand to his eyes. 'Darling,' he said to me. 'The little chap's condition would appear to be worsening. Oh dear,' he peered in horror through his fingers. 'Someone please mop him before I vomit.'

Nobody had a hankie. Auntie leant forward obligingly. 'Shall I use this clean serviette then, on little boyo's nose? Or am I to leave it on my lap? It don't do much good down there.'

Bogey put out a tongue to catch the flow and smacked his small lips in delight. It was just as well, I sometimes thought, he enjoyed himself so much. Come famine and flood, this son of mine would probably survive us all, a cycle of self sufficiency.

Vincent's handkerchief was from Turnbull & Asser and was tied silkily around his neck. 'Sorry, I'm sure, but no, it's not for sacrifice. I'd have to burn it afterwards. Here, have my napkin.' And he threw it in Bogey's face, who, thinking it was a game, promptly threw it back glistening on one side. It landed on Vincent's hand. 'Ye gods,' he screamed. 'How disgusting!', and jumped violently to his feet knocking, in so doing, his chair back into the legs of a

376

passing waitress. She dropped the carafe that she was carrying. The contents splashed Vincent right up to his crotch, all over his new Oxford Bags. The first time on. I looked at him and then at them. He burst into violent tears.

The Honourable Hannibal Knutt was waiting by the time we finally got back. We walked home. The children ran ahead, while I followed slowly behind with Auntie on my arm. Battersea Funfair had done her bunions in. She'd insisted on coming out in her bedroom slippers, but was now complaining of the pavement's chill striking right clean through the soles. 'That's why people wear shoes, Auntie,' I patiently tried to explain. She didn't like shoes, but favoured wellington boots instead, as being much more comfortable. But those were for winter and we were now in spring. Her slippers were usually from Woolworth's, mauve whenever possible, mock satin, quilted. They looked hideously out of place, even in the streets of Chelsea, at the bottom of her dark lisle stockings (to hide her elastic supports, worn for varicose veins). But Vincent found them very camp. 'Oh yes! The height of chic!'

He gave a despairing groan. 'Oh Christ—look. Look who's there. He'll wake up half the street.' Nutty had sighted us as soon as we rounded the corner. He was outside my house sitting in the middle of a heap of scrap metal, honking his horn as a welcome. Vincent spun round. 'I can't stand it, darling, not today. Nutty would be the last straw. That car of his is a positive disgrace, it's a wonder your neighbours don't register a formal complaint. Or apply for a reduction of their rates. What is it meant to be, anyway?'

'It started life as a Land Rover. Very suitable for scouring his estates. It's a country car—' I could smell the manure from where I was. 'I quite like it myself. It's quite relaxing. You don't have to worry about the kids. Spoiling the upholstery, I mean. I much prefer it to a smart saloon. I find they give claustrophobia.'

Nutty suffered from claustrophobia. Which was why all his cars were open. The one he'd given me was open too, a Morgan Sports, bright yellow to match my front door. And soon, in fact, to match the entire frontage of the house. 'The painters are coming tomorrow—they'll be painting the brickwork bright yellow.' The children could hardly wait. Vincent held his hands to his shoulders in horror, palms facing outwards, fingers lightly curled. I thought how much cleaner his nails were than mine. But mine were painted Biba Black so no one ever knew. 'Yolk yellow?' he said sarcastically. 'Canary? Cowslip? Or urine?'

Auntie suddenly fell on one ankle, snagging my Ossie Clark sleeve. 'Dew, dew. There's clumsy I am. Oh, there now—see what I've done. Your lovely frock, all ruined.'

'It's all right, Auntie,' I soothed. 'It's ever so old, this one—'

Vincent arched an eyebrow. 'One *week* old! I know Ossie's latest things.' He stopped in the street at an extra-loud hoot from Nutty. 'I can't come on, I simply can't. He's so ghastly. No, honestly—but before I depart, my darling, do, please do, consider our restaurant. Its not as daft an idea as you think—'

'Isn't it?' I said. 'P'raps not.'

Nutty's normal eye bulged, bull-like, at the thought. His other swivelled wildly, like a bright ball bearing released from a magnetic base. The children loved that eye of his. Tallulah was banking on it rolling right out of its socket one day and bouncing down over his bones. They looked at it now and all laughed—Bogey, the loudest of all, clapping his pudgy little hands together in delight. Auntie shooed them out of the room. 'Say good night now to your mam.'

Nutty smiled benignly at the scene. 'A credit to you, the team. Only wish, m'dear, they belonged to me. Any thoughts in that direction?'

'No, Nutty. Not about that. What do you think of the restaurant idea?'

He glanced at his watch. 'Which one? Well, it's up to you. I've eaten myself, but I'm eager to oblige. How about Greek or Chinese?'

I gave an exaggerated sigh of utmost exasperation. Of course he didn't notice. 'No, Nutty. I'm not talking about eating now. I mean the restaurant *idea*. Having my own. I mentioned it just now. Three minutes ago, remember?'

You had to be brutal with poor old Nuts. Though he'd managed to scrape into Eton, they'd only kept him there because of family connections. Or as an example of vacuity due to determined inbreeding.

378

His eye began to bulge again, and his left leg started to shake. 'Sit down, Nutty, you'll spill your drink. Well, what do you think of the notion?' I stood before him smiling kindly. He was still, without doubt, a handsome man, though gone to seed now somewhat, mentally. Bats in the belfry and given to bluster. 'Oh I say! What fun! And who shall finance this splendid endeavour? Might I be allowed in as a partner?'

Lionel Striving was coming for lunch, I changed the sheets in readiness. His masculinity was so abrasive, you could almost graze yourself on it. Sometimes after we'd been together, I'd feel the need of a bath, and a big swill round with lanolin. Bogey's Johnson's Baby Lotion. Why did I keep seeing him then? Because I couldn't say no. And in any case despite his bull-like loving, his cock was incredibly short. I'd nearly laughed the first time I saw it and would have asked what had happened, but I thought it cruel to make anybody mind about mere lack of inches down there and I wanted him to know, to understand someone warm like me, that there were some women in the world to whom that sort of thing was not important. I put his lunch on a tray and carried it up to the bedroom. Cornflakes, and the top of the milk straight from the fridge, nice and cold. He arrived on the dot, as per usual. I accepted his brief-case and brolly and passed him his usual hanger—a birthday present from me.

We kissed with cheeks, he spoke at once. He liked to speak, non-stop. In that way I quite enjoyed our meetings, it meant I could lie back and listen. Or not, or think of other things against the sweet companionship of another human voice. 'Feel this,' he said, and drew my fingers to his flies. 'I've had this huge erection all the way from Eaton Square. It leapt into life at the traffic lights. Simply from thinking of you.' I could feel nothing. 'Quite an embarrassment, paying off the fare. Had to hold my brief-case in a pertinent position in case the chap should see—'

'How sexy,' I murmured, still searching.

'Yes. Shows something, eh? About the state of me. Stallion stuff, I'd say. It's either that or love. Come on then, let's put it to good use. Knickers down, knees up! You riveting, randy whore!'

He lay heavily on top of me, rubbing himself up and down. Good old-fashioned missionary style. 'The only

379

way for me. The fair sex down under, in their place, all proper.' I'd tried to introduce a string of variations. 'Look here,' he'd said. 'This isn't some sort of novelty act. We're not touring the Halls, you know. The fact that missionary is the most used way of doing it, from here to Timbuctoo, is simply because it's been tried and tested and found to be simply the best.' I didn't agree, and in any case, it wasn't true, what he said about Timbuctoo. I'd read somewhere they did it there like dogs, with the woman's face shoved hard in a bush.

A layer of sweat was forming between us, his rib cage pressed hard on my nipples. I thought of the plans for our restaurant. When this was over and Lionel had eaten his cornflakes, I'd walk up the road to the Estate Agents. Giddy and Giddy & Son. Would the son be Giddy too? Lionel erupted and roared. I took it he must have come off by the crashing crescendo and shouting. My twatty was starting to ache. My pubic mound, the bone down there, was feeling extremely sore. It usually did, with Lionel. The fact of his foreshortened dick, no doubt, caused our frames to come that much closer.

He'd flopped, spread-eagled on my body. Panting and winded with his tongue lying pink and glistening on his lower lip. I wished he'd move, but knew better than to suggest it. My skin was starting to prickle and itch. 'Excuse me,' I said carefully. 'But I think I've got to scratch—'

He didn't answer. I tried to lift his head as gently as I could. 'Lionel?' Nothing. 'Lionel?' He took no notice. 'Lionel. Your milk is getting warm.'

'Oh hell, is it?' he lifted himself at last. 'Mmm. I needed that. I really did.' He tweaked my cheek and stretched. 'How are you feeling? In the pink? We certainly do make music, eh!'

'A very pretty tune.' I smiled at him. He stood and flexed his muscles. 'Look at that. Look. Feel. Go on, just have a feel. Not bad for forty-odd would you say?'

'Not bad at all, Lionel. Must be the cornflakes.' It occurred to me that if there was such a thing as purple flakes, he could combine his favourite food and his favourite colour. It was quite fortunate that cornflakes were his favourite, a fact we stumbled on at our first meeting—which led directly to the luncheon invitation which was now a regular weekly event.

He peeled the silver foil from the mouth of the bottle, and tilted the contents carefully, making certain that the creamy top should stay intact. The top was half the enticement of the feast. He caught me watching him and, unconsciously almost, straightened his shoulders and sucked in his stomach.

'Another birthday soon,' I said. Ours fell within days of each other.

'I know. I shan't be here.'

'Oh dear. Why not? Where will you be?'

'New York, I think, on that date. Or possibly Washington, one of the two.'

'That's a shame. I was going to combine it with opening a restaurant. Celebrate the two together.'

He stopped, mid spoon. I watched a soggy flake fall on the sheet.

'You what?'

'You heard.'

'I know. But let's get this straight. You say you're opening a restaurant? And you'd like to do so on my birthday? How sweet. But I shan't be here.'

I let him go on thinking it. 'Well, in that case, I'd best open it on mine—'

'Now, wait a minute. Hold on there. What's made you think of a restaurant?'

'To get something decent to eat. For me,' I said. 'And the family. Quite simple really. I don't know why I didn't think of it before. Though I didn't think of it this time, if it comes to that. Vincent did. We're doing it together.'

'You're not! That great big poof and you!'

'That's right. The two of us.'

'You're mad. You're daft. You're crackers!'

'Oh yes. That's nice.'

'You are. Who'll run it then? Who'll do the work? Who'll organise it all?'

'Who'll cook?'

'What?'

'I said, who's going to do the cooking. You must have a cook in a restaurant. Mustn't you?'

'Well yes, darling, I suppose you must. I quite honestly hadn't thought of that. Had you?'

'No Vince. I've only just thought of it now. Who do we know?'

'Who's keen on cooking?'

'And who's good at it too, I suppose.'

'Rufus Justice. What about him? You always talk of his dinners. Those parties of his. He does all the food, for as many guests as a restaurant.'

'That's different though. It takes him weeks—'

'Too slow you think—'

'Yes. Much. In any case, he's got a job. A barrister, remember? That keeps him pretty occupied. He wouldn't have time, shouldn't think. He'd like it though, I'm sure.'

'Well why not ask him? He'd do it for you. You know he would.'

'I know. It wouldn't be fair though, would it. To ask him to swap Chambers for our kitchen. Though he has said I can count on his support.'

'You've told him then, already?'

'Oh yes. I've told them all.'

'Oh, what did Brad say? And Ulysses Stuffy Uphill?'

'Oh, sweet they were, the both of them. Of course several may be wanting special measures—'

'Their drinks you mean? There'll be none of that. No swigging our profits away. No special anything for anyone. They're all going to have to pay. Oh yes dear. That's understood. Everyone darling, all the same. We must make that a rule.'

'What, even the children?'

'Well, p'raps not them.'

'And surely not poor old Auntie?'

'Well, that's what I mean, you see. The list could start getting endless—really, darling. I'm not exaggerating. We have to draw the line.'

'We'll draw it after Auntie. And you and me of course. And whoever'll be helping out. Who will be helping out?'

'With what?'

'Well, with waiting on tables. And washing up. And taking tips and things.'

'Bags me, the taking tips. I am qualified, after all. The greatest tip-taker in Notting Hill Gate. By the way, how are things regarding premises?'

'Oh yes, I meant to say. They called me up from Giddy's. There is a place not far away that's just come on the market. Hold on a sec, I've got it written down. Yes, here. In Holbein Place—'

382

'Where's that?'

'Let's look it up in the A to Z. H, h, h. Holbein. Got it. Ooh, nice, around the corner from the Royal Court. See, here, it leads off from Sloane Square. That's good, I'd say. Let's look at it.'

'What, now?'

'Why not.'

We'd taken it on sight. 'Oh darling, isn't it *us*!' Vincent was over-excited. 'Just look at this dear little hatch which goes up and down from the kitchen—'

'Dumb Waiter—'

Vincent looked shock. 'Oh dear, is he?'

'The hatch,' I said. 'That's what it's called. A Dumb Waiter.'

He smiled in obvious relief. 'Really? How simply divine. You're knowledgeable I must say. A mine of information.' He leant forward and whispered to me. 'Isn't it ghastly—the smell of the grease. Don't let's stay too long. It will start to seep into our clothes.'

'We'll open the windows when we have it. Or install some sort of air conditioning.'

I agreed with him, it was pretty ghastly. Much like the present owner. We'd shaken hands, but his had slipped from mine like a fish straight out of the sea, coated in a stinking film of oil from where he'd been cooking a fry-up. It amazed me to see how full the place was with people actually eating. My stomach heaved at the sight of the stuff, not helped by the skin condition of the so-called chef, who seemed to be suffering from a particularly scaly form of eczema. He'd have to go for certain. And so would the washer-up, the surface of whose person was similarly affected. It was obviously contagious. They both smiled at me. And at Vincent. 'God Almighty!' he'd murmured and clutched on to my arm, backing discreetly away. 'Mutt and Jeff,' I'd murmured back, but tried to give an answering smile and put up a good show on both our behalfs.

'The kitchen staff?' The owner accompanied us out of the kitchen. 'Do they, um, I mean—' I floundered, but Vincent continued. 'I think my partner is wishing to know if the kitchen staff come, as it were, with the place. Since we have staff of our own, you understand.'

The owner shrugged. 'It's up to you. You're lucky to

find anyone these days. These two have been with me a week. That's how it is—they come and go in the catering trade. You've probably found that yourself though.'

We nodded, each disinclined to reveal our amateur status. 'I'm leaving for precisely that reason—it's a bloody dog's life, I tell you. I'm taking up tailoring with my son, he's teaching me how to do it. Nothing could have persuaded him to come into business with me. Bloody shrewd too. There's more profit in a pair of pants than bacon and eggs, believe me!'

'We may not be serving bacon and eggs. Ours may be more haute cuisine,' Vincent said loftily. I stared at him, impressed by his confidence. I hadn't thought what we'd be serving. Just food was as far as I'd got. The owner made a face at 'haute cuisine'. 'That's a fool's game for a start. Even assuming you can find the bloody chef. They tried that lark, the previous people here. And left in the end with not so much as a how's-your-father.'

'How's your father?'

'He's fine, and how's yours?' The owner laughed. 'Don't mind me. I'm known for my sense of humour, though I've nearly lost it in here—' I looked around at the clientele, a strangely mixed bag as far as I could tell. Halfway between a workman's café and a straight suburban teashop. Several little old ladies sat on their own, pecking away like genteel birds. The price must obviously please their pockets, living on restricted incomes. The owner caught me looking and nodded in their direction. 'Pain up the arse, that lot. Try to get away without paying, half of them. Do you know what one of them did the other week? Brought a dead fly in her handbag and stuck it there, right in her salad! I saw the old bitch do it, with my own bloody eyes, God'strewth! I waited out of curiosity to see what she would do. Of course she ate it all up, didn't she first—then called me to look at the fly! "Very nice too," I said to her, "would you care to eat it for afters, madam? I'll call down to Cook for some custard." '

Vincent shuddered. 'What repartee.'

'It's my sense of humour, I told you. Yes, they come in here,' he looked around. 'All walks of life, I tell you. After a week, you lose all faith in the human race. Just animals, they are, you'll see—'

'How long,' I asked politely, 'have you been here, then, Mr —er?'

'Bummer.'

'Beg pardon?'

'Yes. Bummer. Bummer's the name. Sydney Bummer. Let's say Syd though, it's Syd to my friends, which of course is what I hope we'll be. If you see your way clear to buying the business, you can study the books—they're all here.'

'Books?' Vincent echoed vaguely.

'They tell all about the turnover,' I said. I'd heard about books before. They were something you showed to accountants, though there was no reason why we need be bothered.

'I'm throwing the goodwill in for nothing—'

'How sweet of you, really, too kind. Isn't it darling?' Vincent smiled and turned to me. I nodded.

The owner beamed. 'I thought it might be an incentive, to speed up the deal, so to speak. If you were wanting to, you know, you could take the place over tomorrow—'

'Tomorrow! Hear that?' Vincent turned, eyes shining, to me. 'Mr Bummer said tomorrow!'

'I heard him, Vince,' I said.

'Tomorrow's too soon. Next week would be more like.'

'Oh no—throw caution to the winds! Live dangerously, darling!'

'No, Vince,' I said. 'Be serious. I'm not having Scabs in the kitchen, nor his sidekick, not stirring my gravy—'

'I quite agree, a ghastly crew. They can go, though, at a moment's notice, that's what Sydney Bummer said. We don't have to open tomorrow, not business as usual, not that. But I see no reason, darling, none at all, not to start clearing the place and redecorating. The sooner the better, I'd say.'

I had to break off at 12 o'clock to meet up in bed with Brad.

'Can't you ring him and put him off?' Vincent said. 'And help me finish this ceiling?' He'd wrenched his neck at the start of the job and had been in a bad mood ever since. It was my idea that we should paint the restaurant ourselves. Not simply because of the saving, but as much because I liked to see the look of things change beneath my brush. A labour of love is how I saw it. Vincent had been all for bringing in professionals. 'Oh no,' I'd said. 'They'd never get it done. Look how long those are taking to paint my front, not to mention the to-ing and fro-ing. Auntie claims that one of them had bladder trouble. He's in and out of the lav all the time.'

'Wanking probably dear.'

'Over Auntie? I very much doubt it.'

'Or you.'

'Or even you, Vincent.'

'Everything's possible. I shall look with more interest, which is he?'

'The sandy one.'

Vincent screamed and curled his lip. 'Ooh no! Not him! Oh well, we'd best forget it.'

I'd cadged a can of colour from them. 'It'll be lovely, this yellow, for us, Vincent. Be like walking into an egg. Rather appropriate for a restaurant—'

'Should we paint the outside White Eggshell?'

'Nice idea, but no, better red. Red and yellow.'

'Well, you're the expert. I'll leave all the colour to you, darling.'

'Don't sound so dubious. You have to be bold. It'll be beautiful, honest, I promise. A home from home. That's the point, isn't it?'

'I suppose so,' he said grudgingly.

It was a larger job than I'd imagined and even I was beginning to be daunted. This was our second day. 'Take a break then, Vince. Have a drink, go on, the pubs are open. I shan't be that long anyway.'

A drip of emulsion fell on his upturned face. 'Oh shit. I'm fed up with this! Right then, that's it. I'll go for a drink, and I'll time how long you will have been gone—'

'Yes, I don't mind. Why should you do more than me. Give me an hour, that's all. I could put him off, but I can't. He's so gorgeous—you know how it is—'

'Oh, all right. How long then?'

'An hour. I've just said.'

'I've only got an hour, I'm afraid, today Brad.'

'Come on sweetheart then. Let's get started. Don't waste it.'

'What's it to be?'

'As starters?'

'Mmm.' I watched him getting undressed. The youngest of all my Gentlemen, with legs that went up to his ear

386

lobes and a body like Michelangelo's David. Good at any
age, of course, but better at twenty-two. 'Hung like a
horse,' I'd said to Vince. 'I could tell by the bulge in his
jeans, dear!' Not that size had meant that much to me, or
did now, for that matter—it was just that having had
Brad—

'Sixty-nine?' He flashed perfect teeth.

'Why not?'

He guided his upright equipment within inches of my
nose. I sniffed at it. 'Mm. Smell of rubber. Have you been
elsewhere, sir?' 'What thoughts!' he scolded. 'Suspicious
girl! What, me with another?' I laughed. His gross
infidelities were a running joke between us, as indeed were
mine. A friendship lacking possessiveness, which was why
it has lasted so long. Nineteen, he'd been. Driving a
minicab, in those days, one of his many jobs.

I opened my mouth as wide as I could. I had to, to get his
dick in, and nearly gagged as it hit my throat. I began
breathing through my nose. Poor Bogey would have a job
with sixty-nine in future years, I thought, unless they
managed to unblock him.

Auntie came knocking at the door. 'You in there, love?
Would you like some nice tea? I got the kettle on the
boil—'

'Not now, Auntie! Perhaps a bit later.'

'That's it then, love. Mind to come after then, is it.' I
heard her humming down the stairs. Perpetually cheeful.
Brad was her favourite of my Gentlemen Callers. 'There's
good-looking, he is—like a film star.'

He'd removed his cock at her knocking. ''Nother way?
Eh, sweetheart? Say which.'

'Well, what's the time? Oh dear, not long. Side by side?
Me on top? I don't mind.'

We did it both ways and finished, laughing, on the dot.
No time for tea with Auntie. 'I'll stay, you go,' he said. 'It'll
give her a thrill, poor old girl.'

'You're sweet,' I said. 'Same time, next week?'

'Sure thing. Be good.'

I was still smiling when I got back to Vincent. 'It's easy
to see you've been screwed.'

'Of course,' I answered. 'That's the point of poking—
that people should see. Cause and effect—'

'Get this in your hand, you horny bitch.' He passed me a
brush. 'And try cause and effect on this ceiling.'

387

Vincent knocked off at six o'clock. 'I'm knackered! In any case, darling, I do have a date—'

'Oh, do you? Anyone I know?' I doubted that it would be. Vincent's preference tended towards rough trade, rather than people one might meet socially.

'Well,' he said vaguely. There was a silence, neither of us spoke.

'You must be careful, Vince,' I said at last. 'Remember poor old Pokestrong—' Arnold Pokestrong had been found, six months or so before, in more than mysterious circumstances. An Inspector Nark from Scotland Yard had called on me soon after. 'A routine visit, Miss, that's all. We're visiting all Mr Pokestrong's friends. I take it you were a friend of the deceased? We found your name in his address book.'

'Oh yes. A friend, of course. I was always very fond of old Arnold. Though I hadn't seen as much of him lately—'

'You wouldn't have cared for the sight I had of him then, Miss. Not being a friend I can assure you. Even I as a total stranger was, how can I say, deeply shocked—'

'Oh dear, don't tell me.'

'I wouldn't dream of it. The state he was in. You know of course, you're familiar with the case I take it, that a revolver held that closely to the head would cause it—the head I mean—to be blown to smithereens. Which was exactly what happened to your friend, Mr Pokestrong. Can you credit it, can you envisage the scene! We found one of his eyeballs lodged high up in the curtain pelmet, and the other underneath the settee! Both surprisingly intact, one even complete with lid—'

Vincent sniffed. 'My trade's not that rough, darling. In any case, poor old Arnold invited disaster. And I'm far from being a masochist. Though,' he straightened his back with a groan and massaged the side of his neck, 'no one would believe it looking at me today. I leave you to it, sweetie.'

I didn't mind him leaving me. In fact I even preferred it. I'd brought the portable gramophone with me and my newest Barbra Streisand record, 'The Way We Were'. Not one of Vincent's favourites. Now I could play it all night.

'I'll stay on and see it through now. Finish the whole bloody thing, after I've seen to the kids, that is.'

I rang them, Tallulah answered. 'Yes?' she shouted into the phone. I could hear Bogey sneeze in the background.

'It's me.'

'Oh, hi there Mumsy! Zsa-Zsa's just burning the toast!' Almost everything Tallulah ever said went with an exclamation mark. A sense of drama.

'Is Auntie there, chicken?'

'Yes, somewhere. I think she's taking a bath.'

'What, now? It's a funny time to take a bath—'

Tallulah started to giggle. 'She tripped on a pot of paint! It spilt all down the garden path! And splashed all up Auntie's leg! Right the way up to her knickers!'

It wouldn't have needed to go very far. Auntie's knickers began at her knees with good old-fashioned modesty and the reinforcement of sturdy elastic.

'Is she all right though?'

Tallulah was not noted for kindness. She continued to giggle. 'Oh yes. Except that her botty's all yellow! We saw it, she showed us. She did! The path looks ever so pretty. Like the one in *The Wizard of Oz*!'

'Oh yes,' I said. 'The Yellow Brick Road. Follow the Yellow Brick Road.' I sang it.

She squealed at the other end of the phone. 'Oh Mummy! Don't! Your voice is so horrible!'

'Thank you,' I said. 'See you in a minute. I'll bring home something nice to eat.'

'Oh goody! I'll have Kit-Kats—two of them! and don't forget Bogey's bananas. He's eaten all the ones that were here!'

'What, seven since yesterday?'

'Yes! And he's pooping a lot!'

'That's not the bananas then. They'd have the opposite effect. He must have been eating something else as well—'

'Zsa-Zsa can't find her new plasticine!'

'That sound much more like it then. Well it's better out than in.'

I stopped off at Safeway's on the way back and shopped somewhat haphazardly, but in the end the queue was so dauntingly long that I left my wire trolley where it was with everything still in it. I could take the kids out to eat, and Auntie and her nice clean botty. To The Great American Disaster, that was their favourite these days, though not necessarily Auntie's. Or mine for that matter, I thought. Not relaxed enough for me. Too frenzied, and not enough elbow room. Not that there'd be that much elbow room in our place. An intimate setting.

Zsa-Zsa opened the door. 'Nutty's inside,' she announced. That would save a tenner or so. 'Might I make this meal my treat, m'dear?' 'Thank you, Nutty, how nice.'

He greeted me as usual with exaggerated formality, his cock eye on the move. The children gathered round to watch it bounce. 'Hullo Nutty. How are you?' I bent to pick Bogey up, hoping to show the question needed no answer. The bore who bored for England, someone had brutally said of Nutty. Bogey's nose was on the run, he buried it in my neck. 'Oh Bogey baby, just hold on. Quick someone, pass a hanky.' Tallulah threw over a dishcloth. Zsa-Zsa uncrumpled an envelope. I sighed. 'Oh Christ! For goodness' sake!' Auntie came into the room.

'Auntie,' I implored. 'Bogey's nose. Have you got a paper hanky?' She picked up the bottom of her pinafore. 'There's my pinny for little boyo's nose.' I gave up.

Nutty had come in a taxi. His old heap had eventually given up the ghost. 'Been a stout old fellow, the Land Rover. Tried and trusted for many years. Coughed his last though now. Couldn't get it to budge, not an inch.'

'It will be joining the others then eh, Nutty?'

''Fraid so.' Nutty had a cemetery of deceased cars on his estate, given over now to the chickens. The children loved it, collecting eggs amongst gear levers and steering wheels.

'What will you do, get a new one?'

''Nother Land Rover, no doubt, know of one not far from me. By the way, old girl, that same chappie is selling a vintage Rolls. Thirty-two or thereabouts, been in his garage since forty-five. Interested?'

'What? Who, me?'

'It's your birthday, isn't it, next week?'

I laughed. 'Oh don't be daft, Nutty! What would I do with a Rolls!' I stared at his one good eye, the other spun feverishly round. Auntie smiled at him innocently. 'Rolls-Royce is it, then? There's posh. I'd like to ride round in that, indeed I would.'

Nutty bowed. 'Then, Madam,' he said, 'you shall.'

Rufus Justice rang as we were leaving for The Great American Disaster. I could barely hear him above the general clatter. Bogey had broken Tallulah's straw hat, a fragile affair dating back to the previous century and only just bought in a jumble sale. She'd delivered a blow to the back of his head which caused him to lose his balance. He lay now bubbling at my feet whilst Zsa-Zsa, springing to his defence, had tugged the sleeve of Tallulah's frock so hard that it had ripped right out of its socket. Tallulah screamed with outrage. And Auntie joined in for good measure.

'Is everything all right your end?' Rufus Justice sounded anxious.

'Oh yes. The same as usual.' I managed to make myself heard. 'Not a frightfully good time, not just at this moment though, Rufus. Why not ring me later at this number?' And I gave him the number of our restaurant.

He rang just as I'd finished the ceiling, I stood with the brush in my hand. 'Hold on, Rufus, I'd better put this brush in water—it'll dry hard otherwise.'

'What brush? What is going on? And where am I ringing you anyway?' He hadn't believed me, Rufus, not about running a restaurant. 'But why? What's the reasoning, dear? I've known you long enough to understand how attracted you are to hare-brained schemes, but a restaurant is frankly ridiculous. You have no understanding of food. It's an art which has somehow by-passed you. Unfortunate but, even so, true. Have I managed to make myself understood?'

'Oh perfectly. An admirable presentation of your case.' That was the trouble with Rufus, he conducted all conversation as if he were still in court. 'It hasn't influenced my decision though, not in any way, Rufus. I'm sorry.'

'I'm sorry too,' he sighed heavily. 'I'm far too fond of you to wish to see you make a spectacle of yourself and a scapegoat of those of us who will undoubtedly be required to grace your emporium.'

'Oh Rufus, I shan't mind if you don't eat there. I hadn't expected it, quite frankly. Your standards I'm sure would be far too exacting for amateurs like Vincent and me.'

'What brush? Well Rufus, a paint brush—I'm here painting up our restaurant of course. That's the number I've given you—'

I heard him groan. 'Oh God, you've not gone ahead?'

'Despite your good advice. 'Fraid so, Rufus, never mind we'll communicate after hours.'

'Now is after hours isn't it?' he managed a note of pure misery. 'I'd rather hoped we'd get together at some point or other this evening.'

I looked around, there was still a lot to do. The restaurant occupied two floors, ground and below stairs, where the kitchen was. And, come to that, the lavatory. The only lavatory in fact, intended as unisex, and only able to be reached by walking through the kitchen. Hardly hygienic, that. And hardly convenient either. What if a queue should happen to form between boiling fat and the frying pan?

I'd brought in a fresh stock of yellow emulsion, and had covered almost everything in sight, but only on the ground floor. Now I was half way down the stairs. I'd never really done stairs before, not all the banister bits, which were taking amazingly long.

'Well Rufus, I'm only half way down the stairs—though you could come and give me a hand. Vincent was here until earlier, but now he's pursuing his private life.'

He grunted. 'And by so doing, is displaying remarkable sense. What on earth possesses you to venture into the tedious province of painting and decorating! Surely to God you could afford to give that task to some small firm or other?'

'Labour of love,' I said briefly. 'I don't for a minute expect you to understand.'

He sighed and remained quite silent. Oh dear, now he'd sulk for days.

At four o'clock the telephone rang. Auntie was still waiting up. 'The kettle's boiling dry back here, and I'm getting a little bit sleepy, love.' I managed to persuade her to give up the vigil by promising a prompt return. And in any case, by that time I could barely lift my brush. One wall remained—and the outside lav, which I couldn't have faced tonight. The cistern dripped rusted moisture on to the head of whoever performed at the bowl. We'd be in trouble over toilet facilities, according to Rufus. In big trouble with sanitary inspectors and health authorities. He could see it coming. Such trouble indeed that it might result in the closure and condemnation of the entire property in its present state. I chose not to believe him, but he was adamant, quoting certain bye-laws, recently reinforced, appertaining to this very problem.

I thought about it now, driving in my open Morgan through the empty streets of Chelsea. Up a deserted King's Road, past the Town Hall on my left and Chelsea Registry on my right. A party was ending in Carlisle Square, two girls puking up on the pavement. My puking days were long since passed; I'd learned now to encompass drink. Though not drink and pot put together. 'Smoke this'—Brad had offered me his joint only the other day and after only three puffs I'd passed my breakfast all over his brand new suede boots.

The light was still on in the hallway and on the top landing too, but that was always left on all night for the children to go to their lavatory. I supposed we could replace ours in the restaurant of course, put in a new bowl and cistern, to render it slightly more appetizing. Though unisex it would have to remain, simply through sheer lack of space. People didn't have separate loos for men and women in their homes, I thought, why should we?

I went upstairs to check on the kids. Bogey had kicked off his blanket; the girls slept beneath duvets, but the condition of Bogey's breathing had suggested that a duvet for him might be dangerous. He sneezed in his sleep as I bent to kiss him and he woke up with a satisfied chuckle. Next door another child cried out, still dreaming, but when I went in there was no sound at all, only regular steady breathing. Auntie was fast asleep as well, her false teeth soaking in Steradent and her head covered completely in curlers. She was wearing a warm winceyette from British Home Stores and a Fair Isle cardigan for extra warmth, despite the central heating. She'd knitted it herself; it had taken her six years during which time she'd gained so much weight that now it no longer fitted, but suited a treat for sleeping in. I left her door ajar as I had found it. She liked to see to the children at night, in case I was entertaining. This arrangement suited everyone. I went to bed myself, too tired to take off whatever make-up may still have been on my face, and fell asleep with yellow emulsion in my hair and a streak of it all down one cheek.

In the morning I drove the girls to school, and dropped Bogey at his nursery. 'When can we come and see our restaurant?' Tallulah squinted at me. I leant forward to polish a spot of scrambled egg from her spectacles. Those eyes of hers needed attention, extra attention I thought. Though the optician had claimed that eventually the eye would right itself. The one was looking now past my shoulder, as the other fixed on my nose. Zsa-Zsa gave a hideous grin and displayed her unfortunate gums. Of course she could have those cut back later on. A twinge of

393

discomfort pulsed somewhere in me at the thought of the knife and the chisel.

'What's that, pet?' I said with extra sympathy to Zsa-Zsa to make up for planning her pain.

'I'm telling them all at school,' she grinned even wider, 'that the ones I like can come and have free food. And the ones that I don't won't get nothing!'

'Anything.' Tallulah corrected. 'Not nothing.'

'Nothing.' Zsa-Zsa looked mutinous.

Tallulah contined. 'When? You haven't said. When can we come and see? Tonight?'

'Oh yes! Tonight, can we, Mum?'

'And bring some friends if we like?'

We'd reached their school; they climbed over the side and jumped safely on to the pavement, both of them shouting at once. Bogey gurgled by my side licking his wet upper lip. I wiped it with the handkerchief I'd pinned on to the shoulder of his dungarees. Why hadn't we thought of that before?

'Tonight? Well yes, perhaps you can all come and see the place then. Have to be careful, though, of the paint. It's still pretty wet, I expect. So best to bring no friends, I think. Just us, until it's ready.'

Vincent arrived at the restaurant with a big black eye and a very bad hangover, and slumped himself into a seat.

'Watch out,' I said. 'Still wet! Ye Gods—what's up with your eye? Did you end up fighting for your honour?'

'Oh darling, no jokes. Not this morning. As you can see I'm not in the mood. Jesus, any chance of a cup of coffee? Or a cold beer or something? My throat's like the bottom of a baby's pram—all piss and biscuits, I tell you!'

I sympathised and popped over to the off-licence for his beer whilst waiting for the kettle to boil. That's something we'd have to reapply for, the existing licence to serve alcoholic beverages. According to Rufus it wasn't as simple as it sounded. 'You'll have to present yourself in a court of law and prove that you're both sober citizens, for a start, my dear!' Nobody, in a court of law or out of it would have accepted Vincent as such this morning, I reflected when I brought his coffee. He'd aged overnight.

'You look about eighty this morning, Vince!'

'And you're going bald,' he said bitchily. I laughed.

'Poor old Vin! Well then, what happened?'

'He hit me.'

'What with—'

'Well darling, not his handbag.'

'Oh dear, did you put butter on it?'

'Butter?'

'Yes, butter. The best thing for bruising—'

'What, *Last Tango* butter you mean!' We both laughed then; he was feeling better. I decided against pursuing things. Vincent was never one for indulging in details.

'What do you think then'—I waved my arms around—'of the decor?'

He followed my actions with his eyes. 'It's a curious effect—all the yellow. It mostly makes me feel sick. One can only pray it won't effect the same response from others.' I could see what he meant in fact. Now, here in the light of the day with shadows cast and weak sunlight slanting over everything, there was a certain biliousness about it.

'Perhaps it's you,' I said accusingly. 'The sight of yourself has put you off. It's putting me off to be quite frank. Can't you turn your back or something, just for today.'

He hunched a huffy shoulder, and pursed his mouth to a prune. We neither of us spoke, but the silence, though lasting almost till lunch time, was of a friendly nature. I couldn't remember a time, not a single one, when relations with Vincent were other than cordial, in fact. I spoke first, that was usually the way of things, to protect his pride.

'I hope things won't get on top of us, Vince.'

'Things, darling?'

'Yes, you know, make us nervy and irritable. With each other I mean, running this.'

He laid his brush down on the draining board and yawned, then winced with the pain. 'Oh dear, I ache in every orifice—'

'Every?' I raised my eye brows suggestively. He'd never actually made that clear to me, Vincent, who did what and to whom with him. I would like to have known in fact, very much. I felt he might have several tips for me as to comfort. It was difficult to tell with Vincent which way would be to his liking. The preference for rough trade indicated that he felt himself feminine, in which case he'd presumably have it up his bum, playing the passive partner. Though on the other hand he sometimes came on so strong with me, and bossy to boot, that I suspected he

395

was in fact butch. It would have been nice to ask outright, though the fabric of our friendship resisted such familiarity.

'You're a coarse old cow,' he said now. 'Shall we push off for something to eat?'

Shepherd's Pie was what we decided on, up at the Queen's Elm pub, which enabled me to call in at Old Church Street and pay off the painters there.

'Oh darling,' Vincent was whining now, desperate for a hair of the dog. 'Don't you think if they've finished painting your front you could send them down to finish off the restaurant? There's still the outside all to do. I simply couldn't face it darling, honestly!'

I'd forgotten about the outside. Christ, yes, there was that to do! But I was disinclined to look as if I was giving in that easily. We played those games, cat and mouse.

'Well, I don't know—' I drew the words out reluctantly, although I'd made up my mind.

'Dearest heart, my darling child—' he put on his pleading face.

'All right, you've talked me into it. Though they may not be free, of course.'

'They'll be free if you pay them enough,' Vince said. A good point that, regarding paying. So far I'd forked out everything and with things standing as they were—with Vincent almost insolvent as actors of questionable talent usually are—it looked as though this would continue to be the case. Not that it mattered to me. The money was there to be spent.

Auntie came up to the pub. She liked a nice drink, midday, and enjoyed sleeping it off afterwards. In bed with her telly on, fully dressed, but with her hefty corsets undone. Gossard these days, instead of Spirella. In two pieces, instead of the one. So that somewhere in the region of her heart there hung a pouch of flesh, as soft and white as pastry. Bogey was extra fond of kneading it, pushing his tiny fingers in until he lost them there, all ten. Oh yes, she served her purpose well, in every way acting as substitute Granny. As indeed she had been a substitute mother to me for so many years in childhood.

'Dubonnet and Pernod, please for me.' Auntie's latest alcoholic enthusiasm.

Vincent was ordering. 'Christ,' he said, 'I'm sorry,

Auntie, I can't say it! You'll have to ask, I don't trust my stomach!'

'I shall,' she answered him happily.

We sat by the window, just behind the door, watching people come in. Vincent went white when his drink hit his stomach. 'Oh hold on to me, darling, do.' I put my arm around his shoulder, and he leant his head against mine.

'There's a black eye he's got! Where did he get it from?'

'From Sainsbury's, Auntie,' he answered.

Zoë Knickerbocker arrived half-way through, hot on the heels of Ulysses Uphill; Stuffy we called him—though not to his face. He was one of my Gentlemen Callers—a fact of which Zoë was unaware. I didn't mind—Christ, I had enough to spare after all. And as far as I could tell she hadn't any, apart from the blotto bastards who occasionally fell out of the Queen's Elm into the nearest free bed. She kept hers double in case. Fingers crossed and knees wide for anything that came her way. Three abortions, I'd seen her through. One indeed, I'd even been called upon to pay for, though I obviously wasn't the father. She'd promised faithfully to pay me back, but I didn't expect to see a farthing, knowing farthings no longer existed. Instead I'd sent her to be fitted with a coil, like mine. Though lately I'd taken to reconsidering my coil after I bumped into somebody who's had herself satisfactorily sterilised. 'Why not?' she'd shrugged, stirring the spoon in her coffee, 'after all, let's face it, at our age, we're not looking to have any more.' 'What sex, or babies?' I'd asked respectfully. She was sixty, but still having periods. Not a medical phenomenon, though worthy for inclusion in the *Lancet*, I would have thought. Or at least as an item on the Woman's Page in the local paper.

'Oh, babies of course, my dear. You won't see me giving up sex! Hell, no. Sex goes on till you reach the coffin! And for some—' she leant forward confidingly, exuding a drift of Caleche '—and for some I've heard of—the coffin is where it continues.'

She'd caught my interest, I'd never known a necrophiliac.

Two holes, she'd claimed, they'd punched in her stomach to sterilise her. One to pinch up the tubes, and the other for the torch to see what they were doing. 'Were you

conscious throughout, then?' I said. Suddenly squeamish
for no reason at all, except feeling I might make a fool of
myself if they did all that to me, by shouting out when the
scalpel hit my stomach. Though of course they'd
obviously use a local anaesthetic, or so one would hope.
And it would give a good chance of a read. I'd been
meaning to get on with the latest *Guinness Book of
Records* for some months. Studying that, a book that size,
meant my eyes mightn't wander round to see what they
were doing down below. I'd ask my gynaecologist what he
thought. He'd never been that keen on my coil, but refused
to give me the Pill, simply because of some varicose veins
that developed whilst carrying Bogey. And the last time I'd
gone to have a nice, new, clean one put in because the old
one was looking so battered, he'd taken it upon himself to
scrape around my womb. He'd claimed several small
strong barnacles, as if he'd been deep-sea diving in a
Mediterranean lagoon. 'Not a bad trip then,' I'd said
crisply, when at last I'd surfaced to consciousness. That
was the trouble with inner workings, like taking a car to
the garage. The medical profession prospered on mystique.
Women weren't in a position to query, but were forced
back into the foetal position, gaping at both ends. I'd
gaped when he'd given me the bill. And I did more than
gape, I ground my teeth in discomfort and at the
humiliation of having to walk round for a full week
afterwards, looking like Donald Duck: my spine at the
angle of a diving board, bum out, knees bent like Max
Wall doing his professor's walk. Like a very bad period
pain. What had he scraped my inner linings with, a razor
blade! And all this pain because of the fear of procreation.

'I'm thinking of having my fallopian tubes cauterised,
Zoë. Why don't you?'

Zoë smoothed her hair, and tugged her sweater tight.
'Why, do you think it would suit me?' she turned,
addressing the table.

Auntie smiled and nodded, 'Nice'. She'd switched over
to port and pints to go with her peanuts. 'Three Ps, see,'
she'd explained. Like Philosophy, Psychology and
Politics.

Vincent's attention had been wandering. 'What! Suit
you? Oh yes, without question, Zoë darling!'

'But isn't it painful?' Zoë placed her hands protectively
over her nipples. A solitary drinker sitting nearby dropped

cigarette ash into his Scotch. 'I'm frightfully sensitive
there,' she continued. 'But I do suffer badly from sinus.'
We all stared at her, was she drunk or what?

'What the hell are you talking about?' The real object of
Vincent's attention had swayed his way out of the pub. I
was surprised that someone quite as gay as that, so overtly
lashed and lip-sticked, had been allowed into the place.
And it was interesting as well that Vincent had found him
so riveting. Still, his judgement, so normally scathing of
'drag', might be swayed by the loss of his eyesight. The
black eye now was closing up. He focused on Zoë with the
other. She turned his attention to me. 'Fallopian tubes!
Her suggestion not mine—'

Vincent frowned 'Well! Oh, I lose patience! Sort it out
for yourselves. I shall go and relieve myself downstairs—'

He returned with Ulysses Uphill. 'Look what I found in
the bog!' Zoë spun round, 'So that's where you'd got to, is
it. I thought you'd deserted us all.' She spoke accusingly,
almost demanding his presence. A mistake. That wasn't
the way through to Stuffy, I knew. He needed a great deal
of air.

We smiled at each other, he and I. 'How's the Thesis
going, then, Ulysses?'

He nodded and pulled out a pipe from the pocket of his
Harris tweed jacket. 'It's going, it's going,' he mumbled. 'I
shall soon bring some more for a Reading,' he ended
vaguely, filling his pipe.

The smell of tobacco was pleasant. Zoë scowled and
looked from me to him, then back again at both of us. 'A
Reading,' she said sharply, 'what Reading? Will I be
invited?'

Ulysses pulled on his pipe and stared over Old Church
Street, ignoring her. His silence spoke louder than words.

Vincent was feeling more himself, despite the dramatic
eye. The present silence, started off by Ulysses, hadn't
seeped through to him. Auntie started on another bag of
peanuts. 'Nuts?' she waved in front of Vincent's nose. 'Oh,
thanks Auntie. Do for my afters!'

We'd all finished our Shepherd's Pie. All except Zoë.
Ulysses wasn't eating, he wasn't much for food. Vincent
turned and looked at him. 'Still taking care of your figure,
Ulysses—my what I'd do for your waist line!' Vincent was
just as thin in fact, but his was the outcome of rigorous
slimming. Another of his continuing obsessions. 'It went,

no, truthfully it did—my body. Around about twenty-seven! The whole lot, I swear, from ankles to earlobes just absolutely sort of *caved* in! Difficult to explain—but all the tautness, darling—you remember taut! There's nothing quite like teenage taut! You know what I mean, it went!'

Oh yes, I remembered 'teenage taut', when my budding breasts were as firm as my buttocks. Hard to believe, but true! I could have sat on them, if someone had turned me upside down and wished to address my knees. But 'teenage taut' develops into something else with women, equally nice, only different. With men like Vincent though, in his emotional line of business, when outline could be said to be all—age obviously meant a turn for the worse. He spoke now, cutting abruptly across that very thought. 'What do you think then, Ulysses, about our restaurant plans?'

Zoë still held the scowl she'd assumed over the subject of the Reading. And Ulysses continued to ignore her. The reading of his Thesis was something between him and me. A private procedure. A privilege which he bestowed on me. One in fact which I wished he wouldn't. My leanings were not in any way towards Medieval Literary Anarchy In Verse, but I understood that it might well be, his Thesis when finished, an extremely valuable work. To scholars.

He took off his glasses and polished them, steel-rimmed National Health, the sort that John Lennon once wore. But Stuffy, in his, looked more like Stanley Spencer, with the same sort of haircut and fringe. Actually fashioned, so he led me to believe, with a pudding basin placed on his head, the hair beneath being shaved off with his razor. Like a medieval warrior in fact, well in keeping with his Thesis. He polished the glasses with Auntie's unused paper napkin (she liked to save napkins for Bogey's nose). I watched them moving methodically round, much in the manner he used for my nipples. One of the most arousing of my Gentlemen Callers on those—though you wouldn't have guessed it from looking at him. Except that Zoë for instance, who did have a nose for these things, she must have sensed it somehow—his low-keyed, though humming, sensuality. He looked so attainable, that was the trouble. Not being obviously attractive, physically. Well, not like Brad, let's say. But appearances in these matters can be hugely misleading—something Zoë had yet to learn. Nobody spoke; we waited for Ulysses. And that was another of his things. The ability to make you wait, although on reflection, what he actually said—when he chose to say it—was never that pertinent anyway. But Zoë couldn't be bothered to wait—'Restaurant! What restaurant is this? You've said nothing to me about restaurants.'

Ulysses blinked. Auntie shut her eyes and smiled—I'd have to take her home soon. Zoë turned her face to me, and then spun round to Vincent. The light caught her nose, just where she'd had it bobbed, high up on the bridge of the bone. We'd all told her she was crackers, last year when she'd had it done. It had changed a haughty, noble nose into a small pig's snout. In summer time, it caused no end of trouble, keeping it out of the rays of the sun. A complicated business involving a transparent plastic shield tied round her head with elastic. Her friends refused to lie on the beach with her like that, let alone walk along the street. But I didn't mind, not brought up with Auntie's excesses. Ridicule didn't affect me any more. It was true, now I came to think of it, we hadn't as yet told Zoë about our restaurant. I'd been too busy breaking the news and testing the temperature with my various Gentlemen Callers to concern myself with anyone else. Apart from the immediate family. It seemed to me that those two separate groups would be the most affected—the principal beneficiaries in this changing life style of mine. And in any case Zoë had only just returned from wherever it was she'd been. Researcher cum glorified secretary on a series for television, I think it was this time. Person to Person. Or Heart to Heart. Just like John Freeman's Face to Face. What exactly Researching involved was vague, but it meant that she wasn't completely broke. And now that the job was finished, she was on the look-out for another. I tried to remember if she'd ever cooked for me, actually offered me food that she'd prepared herself in the various rooms she'd lived in. But nothing came to mind at all, no memory except of mildewed bread and crusted cheese much as I might have offered myself before the kids had forced me into a more bountiful order. We still needed a cook, for sure. And not *only* a cook for that matter. I glanced at her surreptitiously. What about waitress? Or would her now unfortunate profile tend to put patrons off. Someone should have put a ruler to her nose, the original one that is, and then given instructions exactly how much to take off. The proportions in a person's face ought not to be tampered with lightly. In Zoë's case, I considered the excessive millimetre of that inch removed to be as serious indeed as rape.

What was the lighting like in our restaurant? Lighting made all the difference. If we had the sort which started at a standing person's chin, Zoë might be in the clear. And I believed in fact that's what we did have. Each table was lit individually with an evil and unflattering light which struck those seated straight between the eyes. Not only blinding them momentarily, when they bent to examine the menu, but also pinpointing pimples, open pores and pendulous pouches beneath eyes, noses and chins. We ought perhaps to see it. It wasn't the sort of lighting that even I, with less than average vanity, would care to subject myself to.

Auntie slumped on to my shoulder. She seemed to be falling asleep. 'I'll have to go, I think,' I said, 'and put old Auntie to bed.'

Ulysses stopped polishing and put his glasses back on. 'I'll give you a hand with the old girl—'

'Oh, that's sweet, Ulysses. How kind.' His hand brushed against mine under Auntie's arm. 'I'll leave you then, Vincent, to enlighten Zoë all about the restaurant. Perhaps we could think of recruiting her in some capacity or other?'

Auntie's eating and drinking habits were beginning to make themselves felt. I'd have to wean her away from port and peanuts, I reflected, as I heaved her up the stairs. Something more sensible like Slimline tonic and a spirit perhaps, something like vodka might help to correct the balance. We paused on the first landing; one more flight of stairs. 'Oh thank you, Ulysses,' I said. 'I think I can manage from now on. I'll just pop her in the loo. I'm sure she wants to go.'

That wasn't as simple as it sounded. I struggled with her back suspenders as she stood waiting, docile, for the signal that she could start. The corset was new and the mechanics seemed particularly stiff. 'Hold on, Auntie,' I said anxiously. 'Don't go ahead until I say when!' I peeled it all back just in time. She flopped, a radiant smile upon her face. 'That's better,' she said, 'thank you, love.'

I left her back suspenders dangling down, the stockings supported by those in front. She pulled her bloomers up herself and wavered towards the door. 'I can manage now, on my own, I think. You go and see to Stuffy—'

I saw him waiting down in the hall. Had he heard her calling him Stuffy? She'd never quite grasped the Ulysses part. That was our fault, Vincent's and mine, for always referring to him as Stuffy in her presence. He probably wouldn't have minded that much, though humour was hardly his bag. She clung like a child to the banisters and eventually arrived at her room. 'Have a nice snooze, Auntie—see you later.'

'And you too, love.' She gave a sly wink.

Vincent allowed us half an hour and wisely left Zoë behind. 'She's still up there, in the Queen's Elm if you want to chat. She's terribly keen on the restaurant. Were you thinking of her as a waitress?'

Stuffy had left me still floating. I could in fact have just done with a little snooze myself, like Auntie upstairs. But Vincent was all for action. 'You've sent the painters then I see,' he said.

'Yes, with full instructions, but I'd better go down, just to supervise and make sure they've got the right place—'

'They're not that daft, surely, darling.'

'Oh I don't know. I wouldn't say that. I've told them bright red for all the outside. And the lavvy, oh yes, I've said that.'

'What, red! It'll look more of an abortion than it does already, painted red—'

It did. They'd done it already by the time we got down there, brilliant pillar-box red, like a spectacular street accident. Very shiny. 'Gloss?' I was appalled. 'Why use gloss? Why not emulsion? Gloss takes so long to dry.'

They were using it, gloss, on the outside too. And had chosen of their own accord to pick out various wooden features inside the restaurant for some reason. 'Seemed to look better,' they announced with pride. 'More finished, if you know what we mean.'

'That will put the Opening off for up to a week, waiting for this lot to dry!' Vincent wailed.

'No it won't,' I comforted, 'contemporary paints dry much quicker—it's to do with the chemical balance. They've gone into it scientifically. Ultra Fast Dry—or Polyurethene, that sort of thing, you've seen it on the telly.' The painters looked bewildered. That wasn't what they'd been using, but I couldn't have stood a scene with

403

either them or Vincent. The session with Stuffy had left me lacking the necessary edge. We crossed the road, Vincent and I, to gauge the effect from the other side.

'It stands out, Vince, you have to say that.' I felt a squiggle of pride. 'Owners of all we survey!' We'd made that arrangement between us, though I had supplied the money for what remained of the lease. A snip, they'd said at Giddy & Giddy, with five more years to go. But Vincent was the one who'd be running it. Seeing to the food and such-like, throwing out undesirables, engaging staff ... Which made us, in my view, perfectly equal partners. The biggest part of my day, though admittedly not non-stop, was after all committed first and foremost to the children. I looked at my watch.

'I'll have to be getting along, they'll all be back from school pretty soon. Why not come with me? Let's leave this lot here, they can hardly do further damage and we've got loads of things still to discuss.'

Sydney Bummer had left a message to ring him. Auntie was wide awake and full of beans, like a baby, all fresh from her nap. 'We had a bit of a chat, me and Mr Bummer. He was saying what a nasty old job it was—running that restaurant. Yes, yours. I wouldn't have it though. I said he was wrong. "Well we'll see, Gran," he said. I told him no, I was Auntie—' She was full of it.

I dialled Sydney Bummer's number. It was purely a friendly call from him, just to see how we were doing. I passed the telephone to Vince.

'Oh, great!' he enthused, 'almost opening! A chef? Well no, not yet, but almost. That's just what we're going into. Oh, thank you. That's just what we're going into. Oh, thank you. That's very helpful, yes. Hirastaff, Soho. I see. And Catering Employment, I've got it. Both in the phone book, right-o. Thank you so much Mr Bu—, sorry, Sydney—you're being a tremendous help—'

'Ask,' I mouthed to Vincent, 'how the tailoring is going.'

'Oh yes,' he said into the telephone, 'my partner here is enquiring, Sydney, as to how the tailoring is going.' I could hear the laugh from the other end: 'Tailoring, sailoring! Oh, I'm doing none of that, not yet, no! I've told my boy, I've got to have a rest, a little break after the bloody restaurant game! You'll see! I'll check in a month, O.K.?'

'More like a year,' Vince said primly.

We looked through the Yellow Pages together. Vincent took Classified (Central) and I took Classified (South West).

'Catering. Quality Caterers. Private Catering Service.' I read out. 'There's one here called Winterhalter Gastronom Ltd. And another called Huseyin Yakup!'

'Yakup! Yak-up! Instant returns! Hardly English, I don't think, darling. What about this one? These are Catering Contractors—High Table—'

'Sounds like the Last Supper. Is that what they serve, d'you suppose—'

'Another one here, Prêt-à-Manger. Or Ye Mecca. Or Harold Passmore. Passmore, we'd like a second helping please—'

'I've got one. The Whynot Outdoor. Or the Kookarama Caterers; I expect they supply poached parrots, that's what it sounds like to me.'

'You're thinking of La Cucuracha, darling.'

I sat back, exhausted. We'd been searching for something suitable for over an hour. 'I don't know why we don't take Sydney Bummer's advice and get on to those two he said. After all, he must have tried everyone in his time. And he didn't get Scabs from there, not either of those places. He said Scabs just walked in off the street. Perhaps he didn't have scabs then, they might have come up in the steam.' I was feeling very discouraged. Rufus had refused point blank on the phone to have anything whatsoever to do with the cooking. I hadn't in my heart expected that he would, not ever, so his attitude came as no surprise. It was just that he was by far the most knowledgeable of my Gentlemen Callers on food. Then, having refused, he asked me, as I told Vince afterwards, what sort of food we were serving—

'Well, edible, I hope you replied.'

'No, he meant what nationality! I know, I was as astonished as you are now! He said what was the restaurant going to be—French, Italian or straightforward British. British meaning, so he explained, a place like The Hungry Horse. You know, Yorkshire Pud, and Steak and Kidney. And Treacle Tart and Roly Poly and Spotted Dick for afters—'

Vincent shuddered: 'Christ, consider the number of calories!'

'I had to say I didn't know—'

'Well, sweetie, we're not having pasta, that's for sure!' Vincent smoothed his hand-span waist and stamped an elegantly shod foot. 'It'll have to be French of those three.'

'If we can get the chef though, Vince—'

'I'm sure it's quite simple, you'll see.'

Catering Employment was right out of chefs; plenty of washers-up. Renta Staff wanted some French chefs themselves; all they could offer were cooks. Two in fact they had, just put on their books today, who'd double up with other kitchen duties too. All-rounders, both of them, brothers-in-law, who preferred to work as a team. 'Perfect!' I mouthed at Vincent, I could hear the man's voice quite distinctly. Vince put his hand on the mouthpiece for a moment.

'Not French, you didn't hear that part—'

'So what, not French?'

He raised an eyebrow 'No. Greek Cypriot,' he whispered. 'What sort of food do Greek Cypriots cook?'

Socrates Parthenou and Aristotle Papadopoulos arrived the following morning. They laughed as soon as I let them in, each short and dark and swarthy. 'You boss? Yes, missus?' They looked from me to each other, grinning from ear to ear and nudging delightedly. 'She boss lady!' And then they broke into their native tongue. Was it Greek? Or Cypriot? Or both? I wasn't au fait, I hadn't an ear for much beyond Paris or Rome. They might have been speaking Swahili or uttering oaths in Egyptian for all that I'd have known. I stood there awkwardly with them, trying to play the Grand Dame, praying that Vince would come soon. He'd know what sort of things to ask them. 'Shall I show you the kitchen?' I said politely, after I'd twice cleared my throat. They nudged each other again at the question and burst into a wild bout of laughter. Possibly nerves. A new job and all that. I smiled and offered my hand. 'But first of course, you must tell me which is which of you—'

'How on earth do we tell them apart, darling?' Vincent was struggling to cope. I felt more confident myself, having watched them working together, assessing the kitchen equipment. They seemed more efficient than one might have guessed.

'The shorter one is Soc and the thinner one is Ari.'

'Soc and Ari! You're joking! You must be!'

'Soc and Ari. They're brothers-in-law. Soc's married to Ari's sister. He's got seven and three-quarter children. The three-quarter is due in June. They live not too far from you, Vince, somewhere off Ladbroke Grove. You could come to work together, think of that!'

'Why?'

'Well it's nice, the thought of a team.'

Soc slithered around the kitchen door, smiling from ear to ear. They'd laughed out loud when I'd introduced Vincent, looking him up and down, obviously finding the end result hilarious. His Persil-white pants were terribly tight, he'd just had them back from the laundry. And he'd chosen to wear them with a very white shrunken sweat shirt. The two together pin-pointed the blackness of his bruised eye. 'He boss,' I said firmly to Soc and Ari, attempting to restore some order and soothe away the mortified expression on poor old Vincent's face. The announcement caused further hysteria. 'He boss? No! He no boss! You boss lady!'

'We both boss.' Vincent announced loudly. I looked at him. It sounded like a calypso. He boss. She boss. We both boss, man! He obviously had the same thought, we caught each other's eyes. I couldn't help it, I burst out laughing too and thank God Vincent joined in. It helped at least to break the ice between the four of us.

They were very impressed with the decor. "S'good, no? S'nice, is the colour of the sun in our country!'

'Oh, in our country too.' I was leaning over backwards. A fraction more and I could justifiably be accused of being partonizing. All we needed were procelain teacups, with the little finger held at a genteel angle.

Ari, the slim one, ventured a tentative finger towards a scarlet shelf. The painters had run amok after we'd left them that day, using up the rest of their paint, so that now alternate tables blazed pillar box red above the rest, as shiny as polished pimentoes.

'Is sticky, no? Look, is wet I think still!' Ari leant forward to wipe his finger tip on Vincent's pristine trousers, taking them to be his painter's dungarees. Vincent leapt back in alarm with a strangled noise in his throat. He'd purchased those pants in St Tropez; they held many happy memories. 'Watch out,' I warned. But just too late, he'd backed straight into a table. 'Don't speak—' he ground through tightly clenched teeth. 'Don't say a word, that's all!'

But it wasn't as bad as we feared in fact, more staccato, like a morse code in red ballpoint. And only on one buttock too. Soc rubbed at it lightly with the turps I'd run to buy. Vincent stood by in his briefs. *Eminence*, white as well, but the paint hadn't quite seeped through. 'Lucky that, Vince. It might have looked as if you'd started menstruating. Having red on your knickers!'

An unfortunate start to the day, it might be said, but in the end it made no difference. It had given an air of activity and established some sort of relationship between Soc and Ari and ourselves. The beginnings of a staff at least. And the most important of the staff to boot. 'You cook?' I'd asked the question diffidently, gesturing over the gas stoves which ran down the length of one wall. They'd both nodded over-vigorously. 'He cook!' 'No he!' 'Yes me!' I was satisfied one of them could, at least. And which one made very little difference.

'They seem extraordinarily familiar with the utensils at any rate, Vince,' I said to him when we were upstairs. We could hear the sound of Soc and Ari laughing as it drifted up the Dumb Waiter. The Dumb Waiter was giving us trouble, the pulleys were splattered with paint, and the whole thing was sticking half-way.

'We could cut a hole in the side of it, and serve half-way up the stairs—'

'What, bring the tables down you mean! One on each step I suppose!'

Vincent was getting irritable. The turps had left a stain. Nothing that Extra Strength Daz won't see to, I kept trying to tell him. But he had lesser faith than me in the latest miracles of science.

An acrid smell of steaming fat seemed to be surfacing from somewhere. Subtle at first, like someone passing wind. I'd thought it was Vince and would normally have joked and drawn attention to it, but due to his irritability had refrained. Now it was unmistakable. 'Oh! Ugh! What's that?' I exclaimed. We both inhaled together. 'Open the door, quick!' he said. 'Those two are stewing plimsoll soup or boiling boot blancmange!'

Soc had discovered a whiskery saucepan of solid grease, which he felt might well be useable. 'Is nice! Is good, yes?

Have flavour I think. Plenty old and many meats—' He'd bent to sniff it. 'No, is wrong. Is fish, not meat. I taste.' I turned away and watched Vincent pale a little by my side as Soc enthusiastically plunged a thumb around the rim of the saucepan. It was hot but it seemed to make no difference to the leathery surface of his skin. Acclimatisation to conditions, like Arctic explorers and such. A childish joy suffused his face, he gave a little hop. 'Is fat for chip!' He smacked his chops. 'For chips,' I echoed. Vincent put a trembling hand against his stomach. I turned to address him, to tell him of Socrates Parthenou's culinary discovery. But the fumes got there before me. We watched whilst Vincent's slightly pink, turp-stained posterior fled in the dirction of our unisex privy.

I managed to persuade Soc to relinquish his find; it followed fast in Vincent's wake and mingled with his own offering to Sloane Estate Sewers. Soc poured it down with a flourish. 'Vamoosh!' he cried looking at me. 'Vamoosh,' I echoed, with feeling. It was touch and go as to whether I'd make my own contribution too. I swallowed hard and smiled as he pulled the chain. Danger averted.

Ari was going over the contents of the cutlery drawer with Vincent. There was, so he claimed, 'mucha missing'—chef's essentials, such as sharpened knives. Ari slid his index finger across his Adam's apple to indicate just how sharp. And skewers which should have been there, were now not present any longer. And all manner of general cooking utensils like cork-screws, a lemon squeezer, a fish slice, the kitchen scissors, palette knives, perforated spoons and a two-pronged fork—for instance.

Soc returned from the outhouse, having chosen to sit at the plumbing. Obviously, by the state of his trousers which he held unselfconsciously at half mast, 'Is no paper!' It took me several seconds to grasp the significance of the statement. Many of my Gentlemen Callers enjoyed a read when they went. But Soc was referring, I could see by the general pointing action, to something a little more basic. It was as well I'd been married myself. I gave him a page of the *Guardian*. The Arts page. He took his time in taking it, caught by a moody, photographic study of Sheila Hancock. 'Is Melina Mercouri!' he scowled and spat on it. A political animal then. And healthy internally too. Not everyone I knew would risk wandering that way before wiping. I remembered that there was no soap out

there and passed him the Fairy Liquid. And no towel
either come to that. What an enormous shopping list was
accumulating!

Vincent had started making notes of all that seemed to
be missing. Not only from the cutlery drawer. Whole
mincers and blenders, a pressure cooker and both electric
kettles! 'Both?' I said. 'Well that's not right. We used one
ourselves—when—on Monday.'

'Ah,' Vincent said darkly, 'before the painters came—'

'Oh, don't be daft, I don't think they'd have taken
things.'

'Why not? They are all who've been here. Unless you've
been leaving the door wide open for people to walk in off
the road.'

I hadn't, as he well knew. We'd both kept it tightly shut,
simply to keep all previous clientele out. RE-OPENING
SHORTLY. SHUT FOR DECORATIONS—we'd had to
hang those notices in the window. Not that it made much
difference. 'When?' was everyone's question. When
indeed!

Sydney Bummer's inventory could well have been
inaccurate; I might have reminded Vincent that neither of
us had checked it. I'd found it confusing, sorting out pedal
garbage bins from piping bags and nozzles. And Vince had
been impatient: 'Oh let's just get on with it and open,
instead of all this gawping, checking and cross-checking
on ghastly little lists. It's too depressing isn't it—as if we
were both bloody bank clerks!' I had to admit I agreed.

I looked over his shoulder now, at his notes. 'Should I
got out with Soc or Ari. Take one of them with me at any
rate, they know more than you or me, over to Mence
Smith's or—better still—around the corner. You know
who's there?'

'Who?' Vince sounded cross. Not in the mood for
guessing.

'Elizabeth David, of course. Her shop, she sells all sorts
of wonderful things for the kitchen. *Bain-maries* and so
on—'

'What the hell are bloody *bain-maries*?'

'Double saucepans, one fits in the other. So's sauces
don't get all that skin on them. The bottom saucepan's full
of boiling water. That's the principle of it anyway. *Bain-
marie* just sounds more exotic.'

'More expensive too, old darling. Perhaps you and I

410

should forage first. It's time that these two had a break. Hey, how do you think it works with them?' Vince lowered his voice to a whisper. 'Are they counting this day as employment?'

The thought had occurred to me as well. They were putting in all they'd got. What reason, except to be paid? And what would they do now at midday? How long would they take for their lunch?

They answered without being asked. Each held up their wrists simultaneously and pointed towards open mouths. There was no food at all in the place. Not anything in fact, except water flowing from the tap and a bag of Tetley tea bags that I had brought from home. Soc seized a thick glass-handled tankard from its hook: 'We go pub!' He held the tankard to his lolling tongue and rolled his eyes to the ceiling, like a dog at the end of a walk. 'Got big thirst! Soc and Ari go for Guinness!' So say Tarzan. He speak. To his Jane.

Ari whooped with excitement and jigged a few steps. Soc fell in heavily with the rhythm, the tankard still clutched in his hand. We left them together, Vince and I, singing, engulfed in wild laughter. And walked soberly round to 46, Bourne Street to suss out Elizabeth David.

We left a pile of purchases too heavy to carry ourselves, arranging to pick them up later with the car. 'Are you, sure darling, these are all right? You know what you're doing, you think?'

'Everyone needs a *Bocal*, Vince. It's a straightforward preserving jar. And we need a *Bassine à friture* as well, it's just a deep fryer, that's all. And a *Cercle à flan*, a *Chassenoyau*, a *Chinois*, *Cocotte* and *Couperet*. And Ari has underlined on your list at least one *Couteau à découper*—'

Vincent exploded. 'What do you mean "everyone needs a *Bocal*"! The only thing we'll be preserving is our sanity! And as for a *Chinois*, *Cocotte* and a *Couperet*—'

I took the chance to interrupt during that speechless second. I was quite enjoying myself, airing my French. 'Yes, and in addition to the *Couteau à découper*, Ari also underlined the *Couteau à désosser*—'

Vincent was dangerously quiet. I took his arm and squeezed it.

'—carving knife, and boning knife, specifically in that

411

order. But I'll stop now, Vince. You can relax.' I could see I was starting to jar—or *Bocal* as we say in French.

But something else, it seemed, was on his mind. Not just my purchases, but more the manner in which they'd been purchased. He felt that now we were in the trade ourselves, we surely ought to be buying Wholesale. Direct from Wholesalers in fact, instead of over the counter like the rest of the general public, 'Ordinary Retail' as he called it. That hadn't occurred to me, but now he'd mentioned it I saw it might make sense.

'Not just equipment you mean to say—but actual food as well?'

'Of course my pet, otherwise where's the profit?'

'Where indeed?' I echoed. But what would it entail? Tracking down warehouses? Where though? Around Wapping, Whitechapel, Wembley, Wimbledon, Waterloo?

'It's difficult to know where to start though, Vince—'

'What do you mean, start?' Tetchy. Testy. No wonder life found him in his thirties and still single. Many would-be partners must have been put off by this tone of his. I decided to overlook it.

'Looking for Wholesale, Vince.'

He tutted, impatiently on edge, and we hadn't opened yet. 'You speak of it, Wholesale, as if it's an abstract quality of life! Like Pride—'

'Or Prejudice?' I offered to help him out. He ignored it. 'Wholesale doesn't exist in Timbuctoo you know. Look I'll illustrate what I mean. We're going to be needing vegetables, right?'

I nodded eagerly, 'Oh I agree. For the meals you mean. I think so don't you? It's usual, isn't it, in restaurants—Meat and Two Veg. on the menu. Unless you think otherwise of course. I mean we could just be serving Chop Suey, or Fish and Chips, or Ham 'n'eggs. Or Tea 'n' Toast—'

'Please. Now you're being silly.'

I was. Yes. Shot through with this gaiety. 'Anyway, go on. Vegetables, yes we'll be needing them, so?'

'Follow me. And just listen. This is what Wholesale buying is all about.' We were almost back to our restaurant, just one more corner to round, on which, as it happened, was situated our nearest greengrocer's. A sizeable ship, a thriving business, to judge by the varied selection. As good as you'd find anywhere in fact, which

412

said much for the neighbourhood tastes. Though not as good perhaps as Kirkwood's used to be, when it thrived on the King's Road near me. It was from Kirkwood's that I'd tasted my very first avocado. 'Four pears please,' I'd said there one day, years ago now of course. 'What, William, Comice or avocado, miss?' 'Whichever's ripest,' I'd floundered. And so started a taste and enthusiasm. But Kirkwood's had long since, several years at any rate, been bought out by the boutique belt, its footage encompassed into the current Antique Market there.

This greengrocer was even keener on display than Kirkwood's used to be, with oranges, apples, bananas, melons and grapes all arranged in a rococo abundance of colour. I was quite keen on the imaginative setting out of stuffs. In that way Mence Smith's was my favourite, but that's because they always used the pavement space as well. And were helped immeasurably these days by the advances in shades of plastic. Even the primary range of straightforward blues and reds and yellows had latterly become much more intense. So that ordinary objects like buckets and brooms and dustpans assumed a special magic. The spirit of the Mardi Gras.

A shirt-sleeved assistant came forward. Vince simpered and picked up a plum. The assistant gazed stonily back at him. 'Yes guv?' Strange that, what animosity Vince's charm aroused. But it never put him off at all. 'The chap in charge?' he delivered it like Laurence Olivier. 'Yussir!' A new voice joined in from the back; behind us in fact stood the owner, a cigarette packet in his hand. 'My poison!' he announced cheerily, a cigarette already in his mouth. He took it out and waved it in the air. 'I'm of service, what's it to be?'

The transaction took all of twenty minutes, and two quick Scotches round at the pub. It was agreed that Twiddles, Tom Twiddle himself, should supply us with all our vegetables. He'd encompass our order in his own each morning at Covent Garden. Wholesale, with just a bit on the side for him. Almost Wholesale.

'Well done, Vince! How terribly clever!' We stayed on in the pub for another. He smiled, relaxed for the first time it seemed to me since I'd met up with him this morning. 'That's all right, darling. By the end of the day, we'll have tied up the meat the same way, and fish as well, and dairy produce—milk and eggs and butter. Bread—'

413

'And wine,' I finished for him. He turned, malevolently? no surely not, and said, 'Wine. Well, we'll leave wine to you.'

Nutty would know where to go for wine. 'Play your cards right, and he'll pay for it, darling.'

'No, Vincent. That's not the way we should run things. And in any case, if Nutty feels he can get a financial foothold, he'll be round here all the time. Driving us all mad.'

We waited at the side of the kerb to cross the road. Vincent, suddenly excited, sighted an approaching milk float, an Express Dairy one. He stepped recklessly off the pavement, and hailed it with a flourish. I could see the driver was in two minds whether to stop or not. My partner drowned in the top of the milk, before we'd even opened! The vehicle slowed down; the driver, a wizened, weather-beaten man with a nose like W. C. Fields, remained in his seat without moving. Vincent gushed, and swayed to the offside of the float. 'Do you deliver in this street?' He indicated our restaurant frontage up the road with a further flourish. The driver stared at him sourly. 'No, I don't, I'm just taking a short cut on my way back to the Battersea Depot.' Vincent stared at him nonplussed. 'But that simply doesn't make sense. What are you doing this side of the Bridge?' The driver started up his engine. 'Mind your own bleeding business.' Vincent just managed to leap aside in time. 'Charming!' he shouted. 'You turd!'

Soc and Ari were sitting, waiting benignly for our return. Up in the window, with their noses and kitchen aprons pressed hard against the pane for the amusement of passing people. One or two glanced curiously over their shoulder. There was, three doors away, a very small Voluntary Contribution Centre to Aid the Mentally Handicapped. Soc and Ari and their antics appeared to emphasise the poignant need for such a charity.

'They hardly engender confidence, those two.' Vincent sounded anxious.

'Oh, I don't know. I find them quite cheeky chappies. Cheerful little sods, that's what you want in the kitchen.'

'We'll probably have to ban them then, from contact with the customers—'

I didn't answer; he glanced at me. 'Oh Christ, I'd forgotten the toilet!'

414

'It'll be all right on the day, Vince. Honestly, love, just don't worry.' And actually when we entered it afresh after the gap of several hours, I began to feel reassured. Apart from Soc and Ari, the place did seem to possess a certain gaiety. A clumsy gaiety, true, wrought by the amateur application of the paint; but probably due to the glistening red, it had the air of a children's playroom. An atmosphere, already. I left them there and took my car round to Elizabeth David to collect my culinary booty. They, all three of them, rushed enthusiastically, even Vincent, to bring it in on my return.

'Is nice, no, yes? I like! I use!' Soc had unwrapped the meat cleaver. 'Is chop, chop, chopper! I chop off the head of Ari—' He swung it perilously close, not only to the head of Ari, but to the head of Vincent, and also the head of myself. I'd only just seen the latest Sam Peckinpah film *Bring Me The Head Of Alfredo Garcia*. I must remember to tell Vincent after, how a head looked when lacking a body.

Soc was reluctant to part with his find, he tucked it well under one arm. Silly, it was certainly sharp enough to split a hair. Perhaps what he was doing was shaving. Underarm. It would have to have a good wash if that was indeed what he planned.

Ari, meanwhile, had discovered the *couteau à découper*, and had already cut open his thumb. I'd watched it happen, helplessly unable to stop him in time. They'd warned, at Elizabeth David, how sharp the carving knife was. But Ari had run his thumb along the blade, from the handle to the furthermost tip. Blood dripped from his bitten nail, giving the torn serrated edge a strangely surrealist quality. We stared at it, all of us, dumbly. I moved first and turned on the tap. Oh God, did this mean everything on the menu might turn out red? None of my Gentlemen Callers much liked ketchup. Or eating shredded Elastoplast.

The telephone rang as I managed to stem the gaudy flow; we all of us watched it dwindling under the cold tap, until the merest hint of crimson combined with the icy water and then gave up completely. The cut itself was long and deep; I privately thought it could do with a stitch, but couldn't face the palaver. Ari gazed at it, a Hamlet air of tragedy to his stance. Soc could hardly stop laughing. I wrapped a Kleenex Man Size tissue round the wound,

folding it carefully first to hide one of Bogey's bogeys, and
sent Vincent off for Elastoplast. When he came back with
it I was talking on the telephone, with Soc and Ari
standing either side of me, mesmerised, as if believing that
Alexander Graham Bell might have only just invented it.
Either that, or something in the lilt of Auntie's always-
loud voice at the other end was striking some spiritual
strain in each of them. Perfectly possible. She had that
effect on the children. Soothing. She wasn't soothing me
though now. 'They've just rung up from Boyo's nursery.
Waiting for someone to fetch him. Shall I go in my
bedroom slippers? I'm all ready, love, if you are too busy. I
can catch a bus along the Fulham Road. Won't take a
minute. I'll ask them to put Bogey out on the pavement.
The girl said they want to shut up and go home
themselves. He's a good little boy, he won't move. He'll sit
there tidy on the kerb. They can give him a little sweetie to
keep him going—'

'No Auntie,' I said with some urgency. 'I'll go for him
now, right away.' She could be forgiven, Auntie, for
suffering from kerb confusion. Much of my own
childhood, and certainly all of hers, had been spent on the
curve of a kerb along with other children up and down the
street. What she couldn't quite grasp was that the safety
factor of kerbs in tight Welsh communities couldn't be
compared with those of the Finborough Road, where
Bogey's nursery school was situated. A direct route
thundering with juggernauts and articulated lorries
hell bent towards the motorways and arterial links of
London.

I put the phone down, breaking the spell on Soc and Ari.
They looked at each other sheepishly. 'Sorry Vince, I have
to go. Poor Bogey's being abandoned—I'd forgotten
completely about him—'

Vincent passed the tin of Elastoplast over to Soc and Ari.
Neither managed to open it. 'Is shut!' Ari said in surprise.
'Is not possible to open,' Soc added, agreeing. I could hear
the sigh start up in Vincent's stomach. 'Here's a coin,' I
said quickly. 'They're always hard to open, those tins.' I
had seen Soc look at the chopper. That would have opened
it all right, in one fell swoop. Split in two, straight down
the middle, spoiling at least several plasters.

My words had just sunk in to Vincent. 'You're going!'
He looked wildly around him, lost at the thought of being

left alone with Soc and Ari. No need to be, they'd all three be quite safe.

'But what shall I do while you're gone?' Vincent's voice rose in panic. 'While you're gone?' I hadn't in fact intended returning!

'Oh well,' I said uncertainly. 'There's lots to do, I'm sure. Like make a list of what there is to do,' I ended lamely.

He saw me up to the door and into the car. We both watched from our side of the road a traffic warden smartly slipping a parking ticket underneath my windscreen wiper. 'Fine,' I said mechanically.

'Is fine?' Soc had followed us up and now was standing behind me, squinting up at the sky. He nodded. 'Yes, is fine. Was raining a little. But now, is fine.'

'God preserve me and my sanity, darling. These two will finish me,' Vince murmured in my ear. Soc laughed delightedly and pointed at our heads so close together. 'Boss man, he love Boss Lady! Is good. Is fine, like the sky!' Looking in my rear mirror as I left, I could see Vincent still on the pavement gazing beseechingly after me, with Soc prancing monkey fashion by his side.

Bogey was sitting in a plastic bucket with another one upside down on his head, behind the door, asleep. It took the girl in charge and me almost five minutes to find him. She thought she'd seen him in the garden last under the gooseberry bush, where Auntie was always telling him he'd first been found. When she wasn't pointing out storks in story books, that is, and trying to explain some sort of link up with our chimneys.

He'd sneezed, that's what gave us the clue. And then he'd sneezed again. When I lifted him out, he was still asleep and snuggled himself up in my arms. The girl smiled in relief at the thought of going. 'I'd have stayed, I'm sorry I had to phone—but I've got a date with a dentist—' she explained apologetically. 'Oh, not too painful I trust,' I said. She looked surprised. 'I trust not either. We've only just got engaged.'

Bogey woke up when I lowered him gently into the car, and crowed with joy at my face. I tickled him softly under his chin. He dissolved into giggling hysteria and widdled all over the seat, slapping his little plump hands delightedly into the spreading puddle. 'Oh Bogey, now look what you've done!' All my fault; tickling small children, I should have learnt by now, ought only to be done immediately after visitations. He sat in it smiling happily and I left him there in the warmth. I worked it out that by the time we'd driven home, he might just start to feel uncomfortable.

We turned into the top of Old Church Street; there was just time to drop Bogey off, sponge down the seat, swill his botty, change his clothes, and whizz back for Tallulah and Zsa-Zsa. Not that I did that every day. We had a rota of mothers who collected in their cars. And another rota which applied to delivery in the mornings. But I had blotted my copybook some time past on the morning delivery. The headmistress had complained of my lateness and unreliability to a fellow parent, one noted for her fanatically correct qualities in these two very areas. It occurred to me now that with the running of the restaurant and the need that Vincent seemed to be displaying over my physical presence, it might be advisable to belong again to the delivery and collecting arrangements. I slowed down and signalled to turn right and park outside our house. Not something I would normally do for any length of time these days. Not in springtime, nor in autumn either, with the open Morgan. The chestnut tree extended from the front garden, casting branches entirely over, not only the pavement, but almost half the road itself. Its buds secreted a strangely sticky substance directly on to the seats of the car. It had taken me several seasons to realise that it was the tree and not someone with a perversely childish sense of humour wiping toffee papers overnight.

I waited some moments before being able to steer over and park. Bogey began wriggling by my side. I looked at him. We smiled happily at each other. Were Tallulah and Zsa-Zsa ever quite as equable as him? Or did the youngest child in a family benefit from all the experience of bringing up the first few. The road was clear, but not the space immediately before the house. An unfamiliar car occupied what I had come to claim as mine. My Residents Only Spot. A large, unwieldy vehicle, with haunches as big as a bridge from behind. But beautiful. Brilliant yellow, exactly the same as my Morgan. And now exactly the same as the entire frontage of the house. The realization slowly dawned as I pushed my gear into neutral, hugging the side of the kerb. I switched the engine off and simply sat there staring. A 1932 Vintage Rolls, Hollywood style. Sunset Boulevard. That's what Nutty had said. My God, and now here it was. A present from him to me. I opened my door and got out. Bogey lifted dripping fists, and faintly steaming sleeves in my direction. I picked him up and placed him on the pavement, then holding one of his tiny hands, walked round to the front of the Rolls. Oh yes, there was no mistaking it was mine. Auntie, complete with curlers, a floral pinafore covering her frock, sat proudly in the front seat obviously awaiting the owner's arrival. Me! Nutty was nowhere to be seen, he'd simply left it and gone.

'Shy, poor thing, I expect it was—a beautiful present then, isn't it—oh, hello Bogey boyo. Come up and sit on Auntie's lap.' Auntie was in her element.

'I shouldn't, if I were you, Auntie. He's sopping wet. Spoil your pinny.'

But she took no notice at all, just swung one heavy leg aside, catching Bogey on the shoulders with both hands and lifting him, dripping, through the door of the Rolls. For some reason she had chosen to sit at the wheel. In the complicated process of leaning out, her elbow caught on what looked like a klaxon horn. Is that how they signalled in thirty-two? Whatever it was she'd started off it now refused to stop. A raucous, piercing sound ripped through the peace of Old Church Street. It sounded like a non-stop cross between a stuck pig and a raped giraffe. Bogey began squealing in joyful sympathy and, as far as I could see, was surreptitiously leaking again all down Auntie's leg. What the hell had they been feeding him all day? Piped lemonade by the look of things. Passing traffic began slowing up, with smiling drivers and passengers. Windows were opening up along the street. Neighbours were watching, some waving. Auntie looked around happily. 'There's nice it is, this noise.'

I grabbed the horn tightly by the bulb. The sound of it ceased immediately. 'Dew, dew, you've stopped it now, you have. Leave it, there's a good girl—everyone likes it, look.' Auntie was seldom cross, but did suffer from disappointment on a simple scale. Both she and Bogey looked at me reproachfully. I removed my hand. The mechanical screeching started again. God Almighty, what had Nutty given us now! Auntie's elbow had obviously triggered something off; put a spanner, so to speak, in the works of the vintage Rolls. 'Give me Bogey Auntie,' I said, driven by desperation. 'And do what you did just now, again—just lean like you did on the horn. Perhaps that will shut the thing up, since that's what started it off—'

She did as she was told, obedient as a child. It worked until she went to pull away, when it started up again. 'It seems to need the weight on it, love. Do you want me to sit on here?'

Bogey's bottom was icy cold, Auntie's leg would be soon. She suffered already from stabbing arthritis. 'I'll sit there and see to it, Auntie. You take Bogey in and change him. And dry off your leg at the same time. I'll try and turn this bloody noise off. Tallulah and Zsa-Zsa will get home somehow, when they see that I haven't turned up.'

They did precisely that, arriving about twenty minutes later, dropped off at the top of the road. I could see them dawdling all the way down, deep in conversation. Probably about periods, the latest favourite theme. An Indian girl in Zsa-Zsa's class had started hers already. 'What, at nine?' I'd said in some surprise. 'Are you sure, Zsa-Zsa? Perhaps's she's just saying—' But she'd pressed her elongated upper lip hard down on her generous lower, and had shaken her head in a positive way. 'We've all seen her bleeding,' she announced darkly. The image of the bright and virgin blood flowing between the dark child's limbs had been at the time strangely moving. I thought of it now, seeing my girls. And the thought led me straight back to Ari and his split thumb. Hell, they'd all flown straight from my mind, Soc and Ari; and Vincent, awaiting my return.

I twisted viciously on the complicated wiring of the horn having managed at last to locate what looked like the source of something pertinent. The dashboard was incredibly involved, with many knobs, push buttons and protruding screws that I couldn't make head or tail of. Typical of Nutty to have chosen this very time to disappear, having first placed poor Auntie at the controls. He could well be gone for a week, from some misplaced stab at self-effacement. Gifts, so he felt, should be given without fuss. And certainly without the expectation of thanks and gratitude.

The girls drew parallel to me now, with whoops of

420

surprise at the sight. 'Is this ours?' Tallulah kicked the nearest tyre.

'Don't do that. Don't do anything, please,' I begged.

Zsa-Zsa looked in. 'Why not, Ma? Why not to do anything?'

My index finger was caught up in a fine link of wire. The other hand still firmly clenched the horn. The two, I prayed, led straight to each other in some way. 'Shush,' I said closing my eyes. 'I'm trying to stop this bloody horn from blowing. Now wish, both of you, now, together!' I opened my eyes to see that they'd both shut theirs, and were holding their fingers crossed for wishing. Slowly I eased the pressure of one hand, whilst increasing the pull on the other. I held my breath, it seemed to be working at last. Then, gingerly, I removed my grasp completely from both. 'Silence reigns. Whew!' I gasped. 'Thank you girls!'

They beamed at me. I kissed them both. 'Was it us? Did we do it, Mummy? Did we help?'

'Help? I'll say you helped. Do you know how long I've been stuck here? Half an hour, with my hand on the horn—'

They looked at each other and burst out laughing, then chorused together to me: 'As the actress said to the bishop, you mean! Can we have a ride round in the car? Oh please, Mums! Can't you drive us all down to the restaurant? You said you would—you've been promising—you know you have! Is Vincent there? Let's go and see him now—'

'A quick visit then, before tea. Go and call Auntie and Bogey. I'll wait here, working out what's what and how to start this thing—'

I only prayed that nothing untoward would happen, no crashing spectacularly on the King's Road, not knowing the ins and outs of Nutty's insurance arrangements.

The girls arranged themselves in the back behind the dividing glass panel. Electrically operated, as they soon discovered. Auntie sat next to me in the front with Bogey, now dry, on her knee. She'd put her chapel hat on for the occasion. A dusty straw affair with quite unsuitable Union Jack streamers hanging on one shoulder. The glances of amazement from the amused and chic coterie on the King's Road had as much to do with her chapeau as the car, I felt. She thrived, as usual, on the attention. And by the time we'd passed the Chelsea Odeon, now closed for alterations, she had taken it into her head to wave her hand

421

in gracious affectation, much in the manner of the Queen
Mother herself. Had she worn her Woolworth pearls and
her other bonnet, a turquoise toque from C & A, the
passing pedestrians might well have mistaken her for that
Royal person. A clutch of American tourists clicked
excitedly on the corner of Radnor Walk, and one with a
whirring cine camera crossed over to our side recording us
in a running position all the way down to the opening of
Royal Avenue. Auntie was ecstatic. And so were the girls
in the back. The first time, to their knowledge, they were
on film! They wound down the window and hung out like
two unattractive flags. The American, whilst continuing
to focus, shouted out 'Say, kids—so what are you called?'
And it was only when they readily shouted in return
'Tallulah and Zsa-Zsa!' that he fell back and stopped
filming, feeling for the first time that he may have been
taken for a ride by two plain and plainly precocious Limey
brats.

We majestically rounded the sweep of Sloane Square,
where Bogey cooed at the pigeons after Auntie, relaxing
her hand-flapping turn, had lifted his small wrist to wave.
Several of the pearl-grey birds fluttered past our expansive
windscreen, an indication of just how slowly we were
going. It didn't get up much speed, a magnificent vehicle
like this. I'd ridden in them before. Many times, with
Tallulah's father. They weren't built with excessive
motion in mind. They moved instead at a grander pace.
Not like my Morgan Sports. I didn't much care myself for
this degree of dignity, but it suited Auntie a treat.

It suited Vincent too. And it certainly suited Soc and Ari.
They greeted us as we drew up outside the restaurant like
the reception committee of a tribal community in the
outback of Equatorial Africa, who'd never seen a wheel in
their entire existence let alone four of them supporting
such a streamlined chunk of machinery. Vincent couldn't
get over it. 'Oh darling, it's simply divine—' Soc and Ari
echoed the same refrain, but in their own way. 'Is bloody
swell! Boss Lady very rich!' They both looked at Auntie
with a mixture of rare regard and awe, and down at Bogey
as if he were Little Lord Fauntleroy. Then they stood
uncharacteristically silent for a moment, rolling the
bottom edge of their kitchen aprons nervously in their
fingers. I introduced them all round. 'This is Socrates
Parthenou, and this is Aristotle Papadopoulos, they are

brother-in-law—' Both the girls burst out laughing. Soc and Ari joined in with relief. 'Is Soc and Ari. Him and me,' Soc explained to Auntie. Ari nodded vigorously and placing a comradely arm around Soc's shoulders, he gave him a smacking kiss on the side of his cheek. Bogey clapped delightedly and blew kisses out to all of us.

'This is it then' I said to everyone.

'Is this it?' Auntie looked dazed.

'Is it,' Soc and Ari chorused, convulsing the girls even further. Vincent turned impatiently. 'Christ, let's get inside then, shall we. We're all out here like a garden party—'

'Be careful,' I warned, 'of the paint, kids. And Auntie, watch out how you go.' Auntie walked before us all, with her skirts pulled tight to her legs, showing the outline of her back suspenders and the bottom line of her bloomers. Both Soc and Ari had the decency to look away. Of course, where they came from, the women in Auntie's age bracket were held in particularly high regard.

'Do you like it, Tallulah and Zsa-Zsa?'

'Is nice, no, little misses? Is bright. Is nice and bright, yes? Is bright like the sun in our country.' Soc and Ari were anxious to please.

'Aren't they like monkeys?' Zsa-Zsa whispered. 'Look at their legs, they're all bent.'

Tallulah pinched her. 'Don't be so rude.' Zsa-Zsa grimaced back, looking for one split second uncannily like Ari. Pray God the wind wouldn't change.

'If the wind should change, you'll stay like that my little lovely.' You could always rely on Auntie.

'What do you think then, Auntie dear?' Vincent stood, hands on hips.

'Yes,' she said. 'Nice and slim.'

'No, Auntie,' I hastened to explain. 'I think Vincent means what do you think of the restaurant.' She looked around. 'Is this it?'

'Well, yes, and downstairs. That's the kitchen, down there.' I pointed down the Dumb Waiter.

'Is that how you get there, in that?' She looked bewildered.

'No auntie. That's the Dumb Waiter—'

'Poor thing,' she looked sad. 'There's a pity.'

Tallulah was nudging Zsa-Zsa. 'There's someone who can't speak down there—'

423

'Where?' Zsa-Zsa was rather keen on the infirmities of others. 'Let's go and have a look. Can we go?' She turned to me. 'Is he deaf as well as dumb?'

Vincent snapped his foot and, groaning, put a petulant wrist against his eyes. 'You're all insane—'

Bogey sneezed six times in rapid succession, showering Soc and Ari. Vincent screamed, 'How disgusting!' as Soc and Ari shook themselves dry, like terriers coming out of the sea.

Tallulah tugged me by the sleeve. 'I want to spend a penny. Where's the place, Mum?'

'Oh, downstairs. Through the kitchen. We're all coming down, I'll show you.'

Soc and Ari led the way. The banister rail was still sticky.

'Sticky. Is sticky. Yes is, is sticky.' Three stickies before they'd even reached step six.

'It's sticky, this paint, isn't it love?' Four stickies.

'It is sticky, yes Auntie. Mind.' Five.

There seemed to be a transformation in the kitchen. A lot of blood about. I quickly looked at Ari's thumb. Had his fountain of blood been reflowing? But no, the pale pink of his Elastoplast shone clear as a baby's scalp. 'What's all this?' I turned to Vince. 'This blood? Not, surely, human?'

Soc and Ari started to grin and open their eyes very wide. They looked at each other and then back at me. 'Is body, Boss Lady! We kill! We take the chopper and we go choppity, choppity, chop! Chop! Chop, chop!'

'Chop?' Auntie's voice sounded faint.

'Tlop. Tlop, tlop, tlop.' Bogey crooned to himself contentedly.

I saw Zsa-Zsa's mouth about to open. 'Don't,' I said. 'There's a good girl. Your Uncle Vince might lose his marbles. That's true, isn't it Vincent?' He was looking very neurotic. And edgy.

'I've come to a decision. While you were gone. We're—' he cleared his throat. 'I mean to say that what I think—well—we've been hanging around long enough. Let's open the restaurant tomorrow!'

The butcher had been, that's what had galvanised things. And one fridge, the smaller one, was full of meat—hence the gore. But from there in fact, everything else had

424

plopped into place. The greengrocery and fruit would be coming via Twiddles at the crack of dawn. Vincent had rung the local depot of Express Dairy, who'd start delivering tomorrow. And after all of that had been arranged so efficiently in my brief absence, there did seem no valid reason in the world why we shouldn't declare serious intention and open. After all, that was the whole point of the operation. Or had been originally. For the first time a sliver of doubt threaded through me. We hadn't thought much about menus. 'What'll we serve? People to eat, I mean. Food.'

Soc and Ari fully agreed. 'Is nice. Food. In a restaurant. Boss Lady know her onions.' They each of them nodded solemnly.

I looked around at us all. 'What would you like to see on the menu? We should all really just say our favourites and ask Soc and Ari if that's what they can do—'

Vince coughed and cleared his throat. 'Might it not be better done the other way around, darling? One hardly imagines the repertoire to be extensive.'

'Blancmange. Vanilla. In the shape of a rabbit. That's my favourite of all in the world. I'm fonder of afters than befores. I always have been. I like a nice rice pudding. And I like treacle tart and custard. And gooseberry fool and double cream. And Christmas pudding I like. Oh, and sherry trifle with ice cream. And spotted dick with treacle, and chocolate cake with currants—'

'Currants, Auntie?' Zsa-Zsa asked with interest. The question startled Auntie, lost in her childish reverie.

'Currants, love? Yes, I'll have some. I've always been keen on currants.'

A crash came from the direction of the outside lav, and then a stifled cry from Tallulah. She emerged to the sound of the gurgling cistern, the lavatory chain in her hand and a gout of scarlet paint all down one side.

'It came away when I pulled it and I fell against the door. Look,' I could hear the break of imminent tears in the tone of her voice. 'I'm covered in paint.'

'Never mind. It'll all come off. Don't worry, it couldn't be helped. It's a hell hole, that lav. That's another thing, Vince—don't we have to start getting permissions?'

'It is possible, perfectly possible, to operate proceedings whilst awaiting these various documents. It's a question of

Applications to relevant Bodies. Your licence, for instance, to serve alcohol, can be provisional until you and Vincent, as joint proprietors, are authorised. You will, of course, both be required to attend a Court of Law and—'

Rufus' voice droned through my tomato-red telephone. That was one of the very good things about telephones. You could yawn without giving offence. Brad, burrowing down below between my legs, under my orange duvet, bit tenderly on my clitty. That stopped the yawn.

'Oh—ouch!'

'What's that?' said Rufus, surprised to be interrupted. Brad chuckled wickedly into my pubic hair and eased his thumb into my bum.

'Sorry Rufus. Yes, you were saying—the Sanitary Inspection? The placing of what, did you say?'

Brad pulled the duvet down leaving my body bare and, grinning up at me, slowly removed the intrusive thumb and sniffed at it appreciatively. 'Shit,' he mouthed at me silently and blew me a loving kiss. I ruffled his hair with my free hand, and slid one finger over his large hard shoulder, in under the muscled arm. Then I brought it up and smelt it. 'Sweat,' I smiled back at him, mouthing it silently too. He lifted his hand and pointed to the telephone, indicating that he wished me now to cut the crap and get on with it and him. I nodded, and spoke into the mouthpiece. 'Oh dear,' I put a sudden note of urgency into my voice. 'Oh dear, Rufus. I'm sorry, I have to go. I shall see you tomorrow, at the Opening. Come early, about six o'clock. I'm asking loads of people to drinks, first. And then if they'd like to stay on and eat, they can. But it'll be like a normal restaurant—I mean to say, they'll have to pay. Even you—do you think that's too awful?'

I'd thought it was rather awful, asking, actually asking close friends to pay. But Vincent insisted, and I could see his point of view. Best to start as you mean to go on. And after all, they'd be getting drinks free, at least for an hour and a half.

'That's about right, darling, an hour and a half of solid boozing—get them so sozzled and in need of another, they'll gladly pay for the rest.'

'What, food do you mean Vince?'

'No, not just food, don't be foolish—but drinks, I mean, as well. Straightforward drinks, like a bar.'

That was one of the things that Rufus was referring to,

426

the fact that we weren't like a bar, and were strictly not allowed to serve alcohol without food. Our licence didn't run to it. He'd blown me a raspberry, right in my face, Vince, when I'd pointed that out to him.

Brad had popped in unexpectedly, not a habit much to my liking. But this evening, this eve of our Grand Adventure, I was prepared to forgive. He'd dropped a fare around the corner. Someone I knew in fact, a rather neurotic divorcee, who lived in Elm Park Gardens.

'I'm surprised she didn't ask you in—'

'She did.' He'd grinned.

'Well?'

'No!'

'Why not?'

He'd slipped his hand inside my blouse and squeezed a still soft nipple. 'Saving it all for you, honey.'

'Honey yourself.' I'd kissed him. Rufus had rung after the fuck, the first one, that is. We were just now up for our third and Rufus had rung again, having checked on Statutory Regulations appertaining to Restaurant Acts since 1967. Only trying to help, of course. But I'd have to speed things up a bit with Brad, there were still lots of phone calls to make. Lots of people to invite.

'No, I don't think that's too awful at all.' Rufus sounded most loving. Brad pushed a swelling penis hard on the palm of my hand and curled my fingertips around the smooth and circumcised glans. Rufus' voice dropped to a low and lustful pitch. I had better stop him now, before he started to declare himself. Brad believed him to be my trusted lawyer. Which he was, of course. As well.

'Right, I shall see you tomorrow then Rufus. Got to go. Thanks a lot for the phone call.' I could imagine the hurt expression on his face.

'That guy really bugs me, whoever he is. Talking to you in my time.' Brad frowned sulkily and clenched a powerful fist. 'He'll get a mouthful of this, next time. Fucking knuckle sandwich, got it!'

'I have indeed, or so it would seem,' I said, squeezing hard. 'Phew, you're cocky!' I steered it now towards my sticky nest. 'There you are, nice buttered bun—'

'Right, here it is. I'm ramming it in. Jesus Christ, don't let go, I'm slipping. Oo, it gives a funny feeling, kid. Like skating, like losing your balance. I'm mad on your body, you know that? I'm mad on the second and third. All this

427

spunk—you drain me dry, you really do. But I can't get enough. You know after the last time, my balls were so loose, so empty, I mean—they hung right to the back of my knees. I had difficulty driving, I can tell you. Adjusting the set, so to speak.'

'Oh, sorry about that, Brad. You might be better off with someone your own age, you know. Someone with less of an appetite than me.'

'I love you, you randy old cunt.'

We left it that he would be calling in at the opening Do, fitting around his cab fares. A temporary job this latest, a mini-cab firm, back to where I'd first met him.

'How much,' I'd said, 'do I owe you?' We'd come to the end of the journey. His driving had been atrocious. He'd stared at me, more at my mouth than anywhere else. I'd always responded to that. A trick of Cary Grant's originally, though Brad would barely know that. 'How much?'

He'd glanced towards my house. 'I'll swap.'

'You'll swap?' I'd said. I liked the way the light caught on his skin, catching the pale, fine golden hairs across his wrist. I guessed his chest to be quite smooth, with no hairs on at all except a halo around each youthful nipple.

He'd winked at me. 'I'll swap,' he'd said again. 'The fare for your telephone number.'

'You cheeky thing!'

'That's me!' And he'd winked again.

After he'd gone, I got on to Vince. 'How's the list going?' I said.

He sighed. 'Oh I don't know,' from the other end of the phone. 'I shan't be asking that many. I expect you, darling, to do most of that. The ones I know, in any case, don't have the money. There wouldn't be that much point. We don't want to get caught napping with a crowd of out-of-work actors. We're running this thing for profit.'

I thought of his black eye. 'What, none of your friends, Vin? Or intimate acquaintances?'

'No, what's the point.' I thought he sounded depressed.

'We'll meet up in the morning. I'll arrange for the kids to be dropped at school. They'll be all right. We'll go to the restaurant together, shall we?' I usually could cajole him out of his intermittent despair.

'No, I'll see to being there in the morning. You go and

get all the booze. There's still all that to be seen to. Who did you arrange to get it from in the end?'

'Oh all around, just different people. They seemed to think Soho was best. Nutty said somewhere in St James', of course, but it seemed to be so expensive. I've told him he can supply the champagne for the Opening. That appeared to keep him happy. Apart from that, I'm just getting ordinary things like Red and White, and different spirits like gin, and Scotch and vodka. That's right, isn't it? Oh, and brandy I thought—'

'Crème de menthe, darling. Don't forget crème de menthe!'

'What?'

'Yes. For me.'

'For you?'

'Well,' he sounded impatient. 'After all, if we're going to get launched on this ludicrous venture, we may as well see to ourselves.' I was shocked. I hadn't thought that he was feeling just like me.

'Oh Vince. I quite agree.'

'Well good then, that's settled, isn't it. Crème de menthe for me. And what's going to be your comfort?' My heart sank, I'd half hoped we were going to pull out.

'I'm thinking,' I said.

'I know, darling. What you drink at Mario and Franco's, the stuff they set light to, you know.'

'Zambucca. Yes, that's an idea. With the coffee beans floating on top. Yes, that's what I like. I'll have that.' Strangely enough, the thought cheered me, just as the crème de menthe had cheered Vincent. By the end of the conversation we both were quite looking forward to the morrow and all that the morrow might bring. And by the time we said good night to each other, it was with a sense of suppressed excitement. But I had lots of phone calls still to make and many more people on my list of invitations to make it all go with a swing.

I was the first customer into the Soho wine store. Delmonico's, that's where I'd gone to, parking outside in Old Compton Street. Bang on the double yellow. There was no other way, they didn't deliver. Not the same day, anyway. But the advantage of Delmonico's at this late stage of the game, until we found another way to do it, was that they did sell at wholesale prices if you paid cash on the nail. I put myself in the hands of the assistant, a sexy Italian man of somewhere around my own age. 'Signora?' Marcello Mastroanni lines around the eyes. And a lower lip a bit like Rossano Brazzi's, as he'd been in *Summer In Venice*, or was it *Holiday In Venice*? *Venetian Holiday*? Oh hell, *A Venetian Summer*? I gave up, attempting instead a spot of Sophia Loren smouldering. He got the message at once. A queue was forming behind me, but we didn't allow it to interfere. Jesus, you never got this in Safeways. Not this tingling you wouldn't say where.

'I'm afraid my order's very big. I'm going to need a lot.'

He held my gaze and murmured his approval, then pounded one foot on the floor like a horse on heat. Though in fact it was merely a signal for extra assistants from below to attend to the growing crowd of customers.

'I give you, signora, my fulla attention. You say to me now whata you want.'

Not always easy to put into words. 'Now, where shall I start?' I said busily. After all, first things first. Poor Vince was back there in a sea of fresh veg whilst I was allowing my fancy—

The whole procedure took under an hour, and several assistants to carry all the cases of intoxicating liquid to the car. I'd somehow managed to miss a ticket. 'You lucky, signora!' they said shaking their heads. 'You crazy to parka that there!'

My one was the last to leave me, checking that all was all right, and that nothing could possibly fall from the open car.

I could barely see over in the rearview mirror, I should have to drive on the side ones. 'You cana see?' he murmured anxiously. How sweet, the Latin solicitude. 'You coma again, signora?' I nodded, unsmiling. High passion. Sultry, like—oh well, La Lolo. She'd do to be going on with.

'Ah, molto bella!' He spoke so appreciatively, I almost let myself smile, which would have spoilt the whole effect in one fell swoop. 'Bon giorno. You aska for me, Giorgio, when nexta you coma—?' I batted at him heavily with outrageously half-lidded eyes and, with the merest indication of a mature and knowing pout, I let him understand I'd understood.

430

The restaurant was in an uproar when I reached there. Vincent was near to tears. Soc had just dropped a dozen eggs all the way down the stairs and, in doing so, had slipped and broken his fall on the kitchen door, wrenching it from its sockets. It hung now precariously on one hinge, supported cross-like on the back of Ari, playing the part of Christ trudging up to Calvary. Two Sanitary Inspectors were studying our Arrangements, and looking extremely severe. A very young police constable was drinking a cup of coffee, his open notebook on one knee and a biro behind his ear. I looked at the biro with interest. I wouldn't have put mine there, for fear of it marking my cheek, unlike an inoffensive lead pencil. His cheek, I saw now, was in fact marked. Why hadn't he put the top back on?

'I've been here since the crack of dawn!' Vincent said accusingly; his lower lip trembled dangerously. 'No point at all. On my own for hours. No deliveries came—Tom Twiddle died in the night—'

'He didn't! Tom Twiddle? I don't believe—'

''Fraid so.'

It was the young constable who'd spoken. I looked at him with surprise. Not only young, police these days, but confident as well.

'Oh, did you know him? Mr Twiddle?' I asked politely. The Sanitary Inspectors had returned to the Outside Arrangements, and were pulling the chain again.

'Did I know the deceased? Indeed I did. He was married to my cousin's auntie. Not exactly a blood relative—but family even so.'

'Did he supply you with vegetables?' I continued to make a show of interest. This constable was obviously local and might be of great help to us a propos alcohol after hours. I knew myself from long experience that the popularity of many establishments existed solely on this service. And that if we were to adhere, Vince and I, too closely to the licensing laws, our clientele might fall away like flies.

'Not me personally, no. I'm not much a one for a full-scale meal, not since my mother went—'

'Oh dear.' I made a suitably sympathetic face. Death seemed to streak through their family. 'You're on your own then—'

'No. I'm with Dad. Mum went off with the window

cleaner. They've settled in Australia.'

A curdled gurgle came from Ari, still wedged underneath the door. He looked so natural in that position, like an ornament on the mantelpiece—one of those plaster ones of long thin girls with salukis—that no one had thought to relieve him. The whole of it in fact, it now occurred to me, might have been from a Joe Orton play, or something by Stoppard. *After Magritte.* Vincent had started to shake, it was clearly time I took control.

'Soc,' I said pleasantly. 'Could you possibly help Ari?'

Soc looked at me and then at Ari in amazement. 'How I help? He have the door to the kitchen on his back. He look like a silly snail.'

'That's as maybe, Soc, but you see it won't be possible to let him stay like that. Not with opening this evening.'

The light dawned, and the penny dropped. Soc knew what had to be done. His brother-in-law must be removed from his present recumbent position. He pushed him hard with both hands, away from himself in a rapid propelling motion straight towards the two emerging Sanitary Inspectors. They watched in astonishment as the kitchen door crashed against the opposite wall, narrowly missing one fridge and a crate of full milk bottles. Vincent burst out crying. At that moment, Auntie arrived.

It was amazing what a difference Auntie always made, bringing her own brand of abstract calm, reducing total chaos to the norm. Soc and Ari were the first to feel the effect, being almost as childlike as she. And next, of course, was Vincent. He always felt better when Auntie was there, always more in the ascendancy with someone to condescend to. Even the three strangers in our midst, though I dealt with the Sanitary Inspectors and the charming young constable.

After the three of them had gone we opened another bottle of champagne, which made, by then, our fourth. Nutty had had three dozen delivered, though he hadn't shown up in person. His telegram had indicated that we might expect him this evening. Soc and Ari were already drunk, sitting each side of Auntie, nestling in like two small birds against the mother hen. She'd tilted her hat at a tipsy angle. 'There's a lovely time we're having!'

'We still haven't got any vegetables then?' It was the first time I'd dared to broach it, but Vincent was now appearing to be more relaxed. He waved his glass in answer. 'Vegetables! Pomegranates, peas, potatoes, parsley, parsnips, pears.' It sounded like spot the odd one out, that you get in children's comics. Two, I'd spotted. Pomegranates and pears.

'Shall I hop out and get some then? Twiddle's, I take it, are shut. As a mark of respect to poor Tom. Not a bad way to go, in your bed—'

Vincent sniffed. 'Depends who you're with, I suppose.'

'Yes, but it has a certain dignity, I mean.'

'As I said, it depends who you're with.'

Twiddle's was shut, with blinds drawn down almost to the bottom of the windows. Almost, but not quite. Just space enough to display a dozen or so bunches of black grapes, which someone had thoughtfully placed there as a tasteful sign of mourning. Would the constable wear a black arm band? Or didn't the Metropolitan Police Force condone such affectations on their uniforms. The public could, after all, construe a stripe of that sort as an extra degree in rank. I looked at my watch. It was Wednesday. 'Early closing,' I said. 'Don't forget.'

Vincent yawned. 'So what,' he said. 'There won't be much eating this evening. People, I'm sure you'll find darling, will be far more interested in drinking—' He yawned again, and stretched his elegant legs. Soc and Ari, watching him closely, immediately did the same. As best they could, with their limited physical frames. They reminded me, in their poses now, of the gonks that the girls used to have. A weakness, the gonks, of Zsa-Zsa's in particular. One hundred and seventeen and a half, she'd managed to collect by the end. The half being the head and shoulders of one that Tallulah had spitefully scissored in two during a quarrel. For a year or more, the amputated lower limbs had rested in the S bend of the lower lavatory, causing a mysterious blockage, such that the cistern would continue flushing for a quarter of an hour. The plumber, who eventually discovered it, had handed me the little legs with quite a suspicious look as if I had dismembered some small foetus of my own, and chosen this as the means of disposal. He was Irish and obviously Catholic. That reminded me.

'Quite hopeful, I thought, the findings of the Sanitary

Inspectors. We seem to have just scraped through, Vince. But we have to supply soap and towels, isn't that what they seemed to be saying?'

They'd said a whole lot more, of course, but the champagne had sweetened the outcome. They'd fallen for Extra Brut. We'd made them promise to come back with their wives and have a meal on the house. Vince had proffered that invitation; in fact I felt he'd made a mistake. He seemed to be making more than one mistake this morning. And what's more now didn't mind. Which was all to the good. Vince, when minding, was very tiring. I preferred to carry the can, to that. I looked to left and right. Jesus God, what was it—'He stood alone when all around had fallen'. That's how I was standing now. But I didn't mind, it was all so amazingly pleasant. And I had a good feeling about tonight. Like a benign producer, who knows he's backing a winner.

'I'll go out then, I think, and get some food. Pity about the Express Dairy, Vince. Didn't they say on the phone?' The Express Dairy had failed to deliver. They needed to have it in writing. Vincent had bought the crate of milk bottles and the doomed eggs, a dozen of which, of course, Soc had done in and now had to be replaced. Yes, Vincent had bought those from the Welsh Dairy up the road. Hardly wholesale, of course.

'Cream. And cheese. Oh, and butter Vince. You didn't think of those—'

'Don't forget Dairylea, for us. Oh, and single cream, not double. Bigger profit margin, I'm sure.'

Would the profit margin ever appear? On paper, there, where we could see it? In any case did it matter that much? We were hardly Heavy Industry. Not likely to affect the National Deficit in any direction. Either way.

I found myself in the Welsh Dairy too. Bowen's. She came from Bridgend. I'd have to bring Auntie in to meet her.

'My auntie, I'll have to bring her in to meet you, her mother's brother used to be a gardener in the Blind School in Bridgend.'

The woman's eyes brightened immediately. 'Oh, who would he be then?' She called her husband. 'Dai, there's a person here whose auntie's mother's brother was a gardener in the Blind School in Bridgend!'

Dai came from Cardiff himself. Clearly the ins and outs

of hired help several generations before in an establishment for those without sight was not about to arouse his interest. I could see he considered Bridgend to be one of the arseholes of South Wales. Auntie wouldn't take to him at all.

'Oh I'm not sure you might have known him. I didn't know him myself. Rather unfortunately, in one sense, he went totally blind himself. A direct result of the gardening. Severe sunstroke, they said. One blazing afternoon in August. He fell flat on his face in the fuchsias.'

Mrs Bowen clucked sympathetically. 'The right spot then to do it.'

'Yes, he just stayed on inside.'

On my way out I remembered bread. 'Is this all you've got left?' I said. I'd thought of buying proper bread. Long French loaves, the crusty sort to lend a spot of class. Chop them into little chunks that people could tear with their fingers. The Bowens only had Hovis left, two sliced and one uncut. It would do for toast, of course, with the corners off, with pâté. But perhaps we weren't putting pâté on the menu. I'd have to buy some menus. Christ, what a cock-up already!

'Tell me,' I leant forward attempting to enrol Mrs Bowen as as ally in this hideous mistake of ours. 'Tell me, do you know of anywhere close where I could get French bread at this hour—'

'What's wrong with British?' she frowned. 'These grains, this wholewheat here, they use in Hovis, comes from Carmarthen they say. There's a granary not far from the Great West Road run by Elwyn Hughes. Your auntie might know him—Glamorgan boy—'

'Thank you,' I said and escaped.

The Food Hall in Harrods saw to my needs. I paid a quid to a boy to help me take it all out to the car. The bill gave me awful goosepimples. But at least we were now prepared to do business. The pâté had cost me the earth. Much more than I could remember any of my Gentlemen paying when we'd been out to dinner. Never mind, tonight we could reckon on running at a loss. Tomorrow we'd be starting in earnest.

And I was lucky too with the menu cards. Fluorescent pink from a sweet little place near South Ken. Designed by a student from the Royal College. The size of the *Evening*

Standard, with nothing on them at all.

'Are you sure they're menus?' I asked the young man serving.

'Not sure at all, but they might be.'

'It's the colour that's caught my eye.'

'That's what caught mine as well—that and the student, of course. I'd have them dear, if I was you. He'll be delighted to know they've sold.'

I pictured them sitting on our scarlet tables, and warring away with our yellow walls. 'I can't resist, it's a silly buy—but I'll have them anyway.'

Auntie was fast asleep when I got back, stretched out on one of the tables, with her handkerchief across her face and her legs hanging over the side. One slipper had fallen to the floor. I picked it up and fitted it gently to her foot. She woke up with a start.

'Oh, there you are. You're back then. Did you manage to get what you'd gone for?'

'Yes. I did. I got everything, I was lucky. Half day closing, but not at Harrods.' I smiled at her. 'Have a good sleep? You'll need that with the high jinks later on.'

Her face lit up like that of a young girl anticipating her first dance. A fine dew of perspiration lay upon her upper lip and in the crease beneath her chin. She mopped at it now with her hanky.

'Where is everyone?' I looked around, no sign of Soc or Ari. No sign of Vincent either, come to that. They surely hadn't buggered off, with all we had to do!

Auntie blinked. 'They've buggered off.' It sometimes amused her to swear. I laughed.

'Oh, have they then! That's nice. And where have they buggered off to?'

Auntie laughed too at my 'buggered off'. 'Home, they said. To change for tonight. To change for the party, they said—'

'What, Soc and Ari, change? Are you sure? Changing into what?' She must have got it wrong, Auntie. She quite often did, after all. What the hell was their game, Soc and Ari? What on earth would they be coming back as? Maitres d'hôtel or the like? Or dolled up in national costume? Little skirts and skull caps on their heads?

'They've gone,' Auntie said. 'For their whites, which Soc's wife has been busy washing. I think they've gone to help her iron the hats. Those big chef's ones, you know.

They've got a lot of tucks in them, and seaming. Very hard to do. I offered, but no, there's nice they are. They said they'd do it themselves. She's not been well you see, she's expecting—'

'Yes, Auntie, I know. Did they say what time they'd be back?'

'Well, they left here a bit after Vincent. Time for him to get to the top of the road—'

'You mean Vincent doesn't know they've gone?'

Auntie looked anxious. 'Oh no, he doesn't. He left them in charge. I promised that I wouldn't say. I didn't do wrong, did I?'

'No, of course not. Everything's lovely. I've got all the food anyway. Enough to do everything cold if we like. That would certainly cut down on cooking.'

'Cold, love? Not very cosy, cold. Can't you manage to heat something up for people? A nice hot gravy?'

'On salad?'

'Oh, it's salad, is it? You count me out.' Auntie pulled a babyish face of dislike. 'Old lettuce leaves and sliced cucumber, ughavee! Cold comfort!'

'A nice vinaigrette, made by Vincent. That's one thing I know he can do—'

Auntie pulled an even longer face. 'A lot of old grease poured all over.' She managed to make it sound like diesel oil. 'Better to serve beetroot sandwiches. There's no one who doesn't like those.' To be followed by banana sandwiches as dessert?

'Oh, by the way, where has Vincent gone? Home to change as well?'

That I would more readily believe to be true. Vincent sometimes changed as many as four or five times in a day, especially when things weren't going well. He actually believed in some superstitious way that what you wore could alter or affect events around you. Auntie confirmed this to be the case.

'I must be thinking of that as well,' she said. 'What frock and hat to wear. My new two-piece from Tesco's, the one I got last week.'

Auntie was terribly keen on Tesco's and took a weekly trip by bus and tube over to Brixton, which boasted the biggest Tesco's in Central London. She claimed their Acrylic range, in fact all their Man Made Fibres, could knock spots off Fortnum & Mason's, which she'd found to be dreadfully disappointing. She didn't care for the colours for a start, and too much of it at Fortnum's was fashioned from old-style stuff like Pure Silk & All Wool and 100 Per Cent Cotton. Auntie was all for progress. Her new two-piece was a violent lime, about the colour of bile. Vincent had shaded his eyes when he'd seen it, and begged her to switch it off.

'With your turquoise toque?'

Auntie considered it carefully. 'I had thought my pink sequin beret—' *My* pink sequin beret, she meant. My Biba one with the matching bolero. She unfortunately, or otherwise, couldn't get into the bolero. She had tried, but it barely went past her elbows. 'I can't get it to budge,' she'd complained, still struggling. 'Don't try then, Auntie, that's best. Otherwise it'll only tear.' A shower of glinting sequins had drifted like snow past her knees, coming to rest on the top of her Surplus bootees. 'There's pretty,' she'd said. 'I could think to stick them on with glue, in a bit of a pattern, look.' But the beret had not the same problem over fit. She and it had become inseparable.

'Well, you'd match up with the menus anyway. Exactly the same colour, see.' I showed her the fluorescent pink and she clapped her hands like a child.

'Oh, there's lovely, yes, indeed, we'll match up with those a treat. Oh, that's it then. Shall I wear these bedroom slippers with it? These mauve ones, or get some new? Peter Jones have got some pretty primrose, quilted satin in the window. With fluff all around the ankle. A little bit pricey though, that's the trouble. I don't really like paying much—'

'Oh go on, Auntie, treat yourself. You know that you can afford it.' I knew she could. It wasn't the money, it wasn't the price that kept Auntie out of smart stores. She felt much more at home in the chain ones, that was all. More at ease, with fewer glances from astonished assistants and fellow customers. She kept most of her worldly wealth with her at almost all times. She had it hidden in an old envelope at the bottom of her big Mock Croc handbag. A very nice line put out by Marks & Spencer's, but only available in limited outlets. She'd got hers from the Newport branch when she'd gone there for a friend's nephew's wedding. We'd had words, she and I, more than once, over this. But Auntie, when she wished to, could become extremely stubborn. She didn't believe in the validity of banks. Nothing could persuade her that putting money where you couldn't see it was in any way safer than having it here in your hand. Her mother before her had felt the same. She'd put all of hers in a pillow case, and slept on it every night. And when she'd died they divided it up. Auntie still had her share. And stored it in similar fashion after I insisted that she take it out of her handbag. She'd compromised. The bulk of it in her bedding, and a working capital beside her in her bag. Only I knew that it was in there, but how much I could barely guess. Two hundred, two hundred and fifty? Somewhere around that sum.

'I'll come with you Auntie, now if you like. We can walk from here up to Sloane Square. Peter Jones is half day Saturday.'

Auntie shook her head. 'No, love, I think I've decided. The primrose might just be too much. Introducing that extra colour. Best to stick with what I've got. The Tesco two-piece—what about you?'

I had to admit I hadn't given it that much thought. And in any case the issue was complicated by not knowing quite what my function was going to be. Was I expected to waitress? And who would be manning the till? Or seeing to drinks then, come to that?

The telephone rang. 'The Brick Bistro?'

'What's that? Oh, yes!' It was the first time that someone had said it. We hadn't in fact thought much of the name. We were meaning to make up another, Vincent and me. But between us, in our dilatory fashion, we'd neglected to inform the painters. And they, in our absence, had simply repainted the existing sign. It stood in bold raised letters, above the door and windows, picked out by them in yellow. But with the bottom of the B in Brick missing, so that it actually read The Prick Bistro.

'I understand,' the voice continued, 'that you've been closed for redecoration—is it also true there's been a change of ownership?'

'It is,' I said importantly. 'But I'm sure you'll find the welcome just as warm.'

'Mm,' the voice assumed a slightly unpleasant edge. 'Well to be absolutely frank, the Brick was never noted for the warmth of welcome. I'm ringing to enquire if the prices are the same. I happened to drive past the other evening, and the décor appeared to me to be, hmm, rather more, what shall we say—more trendy. One rather hopes that nothing quite as revolutionary has occurred in the kitchen. I happen to have patronised the old Brick for quite some time—it seemed to be value for money—'

'Oh,' I interrupted eagerly. 'That is exactly what we hope to continue, of course, why not come and try us.'

It was becoming important to convince this man. Our very first customer possibly. I should have liked Vincent to be on a telephone extension and reiterate what I said. There was a silence at the other end. Perhaps I'd come on too strong.

'We're actually opening up tonight, with a celebratory party. Why don't you come, Mr—? I didn't quite catch your name—'

'That's because I didn't give it. I shall think about your invitation. Not much of a party man myself. What I'll probably do is let you get into some running order and pay you a visit next week.'

How sour some people sounded. Was this how it would be? Or did I have the right to refuse entry to the unpleasant? I'd have to ask Vincent about that one. There was no real reason to accept every Tom, Dick and Harry. Not if you didn't like them.

Auntie and I couldn't leave now, of course, I realised that. Who would let in Soc and Ari? I dialled Vincent's number and let it ring for a full five minutes. There was no answer at all. At this rate I'd be opening on my own—well, with Auntie at my side. Though, come to that, it wouldn't matter much. Just like giving a party, but not on home ground. I set about unpacking all my purchases. Auntie attempted to help, bumbling about the kitchen and bumping into me each time I turned round. My menus lay unwritten on, blazing beautifully on their own. It seemed a shame to have to sully them. Perhaps we could ask people just to take pot luck. Was it really necessary to offer a choice? After all, when you went to dinner in a person's home, you had to eat what they gave you. And we'd only have mostly friends having meals here anyway.

Someone was knocking upstairs. Soc and Ari? Vince had his key. Auntie went up to answer the door, and came down with Zoë Knickerbocker. She was wearing black sheer stockings with a seam up the back and a tight black short-sleeved dress.

'I've got my pinny. I bought it in Barker's. A proper

waitress apron. Well, more French Maid in a Feydeau farce. And suspenders as well—do you like it?'

Auntie and I both stared at her in amazement as she bent over to show us her bum. Did she think they'd be eating down there on the floor out of dog bowls, or what? She stood up and took a deep breath to show off her breasts to advantage. The pinny was very pretty in fact, frilly and bibbed and made out of nylon organza. Auntie felt the fabric between a critical thumb and finger.

'Artificial,' she said approvingly.

'Oh yes,' Zoë answered. 'Drip dry.'

She seemed so at home I couldn't quite bring myself to ask what she was doing here. We hadn't discussed it as yet, Vincent and I, quite what to do about Zoë. He must have asked her behind my back. It made no odds, we could certainly do with her help.

'Ulysses said you were opening and could probably do with some help. He's coming later, isn't he? To the party I mean—'

'Stuffy? Oh, good old Stuffy. That was nice of him. I was meaning to ask you if you wanted a filling-in job, Zoë.'

'Tell me,' she pirouetted on her platform soles like a ballet dancer whose pumps have strayed into cement. 'Where shall I start? And what would you like me to do? Where's the music in here, anyway? You've got to have sounds for some atmosphere.'

Black Soul was what Zoë said we must have. Records by people like Barry White. And Isaac Hayes. 'You've heard of him, he did Shaft.'

Auntie had pricked her ears up at Shaft. Shaft was her favourite film music. 'We've got Tamla Motown at home. Lovely records done by Diana Ross and different negro boy singers—what's the set of them?' Auntie turned to me. 'Related to each other, brothers, isn't it? Or cousins. You know, there's a little one. Always laughing—'

'Jackson Five.' Tallulah and Zsa-Zsa had been terribly in love with Michael Jackson last year.

Zoë wrinkled what was left of her nose in a look of deep disgust. 'The Jackson Five! Diana Ross! Oh no. Tamla Motown's old hat—Curtis Mayfield and all those cats, they're the ones you want now.'

Zoë prided herself on knowing the latest 'in', and because of that, she earned Auntie's regard.

'By the way, what I meant to ask was, what sort of food

are you serving? French? Italian? What are the cooks? What nationality are they?'

A manic scampering was starting upstairs, a staccato drumbeat on the front door, and a sound of high-pitched excitable squealing, obviously aimed through the letter box. Zoë looked startled and abruptly stopped questioning me. Auntie laughed and sighed with relief.

'They're back, the boyos are back—'

I managed to leave an hour for getting myself ready, after I'd seen to Tallulah and Zsa-Zsa and Bogey. They would be coming, for just a short while. I'd got Vincent at least to agree—but grudgingly.

'It's not a party at your place—it's not the same as home. We have to start remembering, darling, that these premises are actually open to the public. They'll be our eventual patrons. It's hardly conductive for passers-by to peer in and catch a glimpse of what seems the start of a kindergarten—'

But I'd fled before he'd managed to get really into full swing. There was a side to Vincent that was frightfully suburban. It wouldn't have put me off, not at all, to see a lot of children in a restaurant. And certainly not if they were obviously the children of the owner. In fact quite the opposite surely. Wouldn't it show simple faith in the food? After all you wouldn't wish to poison your own family. There were for certain, to my knowledge, at least two restaurants, Italian ones in expensive Beauchamp Place, to which the patrons were proud to go and be hailed by the proprietor's relatives.

But I had to admit that he looked magnificent, Vincent, though still disagreeing with him. He'd arrived, all done up, just before I'd left intending to leave Soc and Ari in doubtful control with Zoë. He'd caught me in the nick of time, as I was settling Auntie in my passenger seat. She was agitated and upset, in an agony of indecision over the primrose satin slippers in Peter Jones. I'd solved it by saying I'd buy them. A small present for all that she'd done. A piddling price for me to pay by any standards, hers or mine, for all that I owed her in fact. But Auntie was proud and misguidedly puritanical about the acceptance of all gifts. As if they were bribes and enticements, which may bring her to deeds she might later regret. I actually felt the same way, though in recent years had been learning to come to terms with it. To accept a little more graciously, understanding what joy giving could give to the giver.

Vincent would have caught my eye and attention even if I hadn't known him.

'My Christ, you look incredible Vince! A Cossack! All cream, how original!'

Not half as original as it seemed apparently, simply a copy of an outfit of Ricci Burns—the hairdresser of Mick and Bianca Jagger. Vince had seen a photo of him wearing it in somewhere like the *Daily Express*, and had had it run up by a boy who made costumes for the Ballet Rambert. Each sleeve umbrella'd down below his knees. He'd have to be careful, stirring even simple stuff like coffee. Let alone the possible complications of soups and suchlike. He'd have to be careful standing, come to that, it also occurred to me. The paint, as I feared, was still tacky to the touch in places.

I bore this in mind, changing now and choosing what to wear myself. One thing, there was plenty of selection. An abundance of old clothes of everything, going right back. To before my mother had been killed. I unfolded the frock I'd been wearing that day, blue cotton with white cuffs and collar. Too small now for even Tallulah or Zsa-Zsa to wear, but still in prime condition. My Best, it had been, I'd only worn it twice before. Each time to Sunday School. But it was Wednesday then, that day they'd put it on—because my mother was coming to see me. There was the hint of darker things than that as well. Snatches of half-conversations. An air of troubled tears and tension mounting up as the day of her visit loomed nearer. Quite ordinary things like having my bath, or being tucked into my bed, or on that very Wednesday morning whilst eating my breakfast—I had the feeling that it might well be the last time I'd be doing it, in that house. It dawned on me eventually that my mother might take me away.

She didn't come. She'd died. She'd gone to Heaven, that's what they said. She'd been killed on her way down. They'd made me say a prayer for her to God, kneeling beside me in the dark. Asking His Everlasting Understanding and Forgiveness for my mother's Waywardness and lapse of Faith. I did obediently as I was told and prayed for my mother's Salvation. I didn't mind at all that she hadn't come. I had no wish to leave where I was living. I liked it there with everyone, and Auntie.

I looked at myself in the mirror, and thought 'How incredibly plain'. As easily plain as poor Zsa-Zsa in this light, taking the features one by one, unassisted by the aid of cosmetics. Nobody knew of course, except myself, how extremely plain I actually was. But they hadn't had to learn to live with the inadequacies of my basic equipment. They only saw what was presented to them—a concoction of subtlety and skill, a combination of many other women like myself who'd made use of their odd looks, almost ugliness. I was big of course, which helped a lot, built on the lines of Earth Mother. Generously endowed everywhere, but still perfectly in proportion with a fine length of leg to balance it all up. I looked at my body critically now, turning sideways to suck in my stomach. Still firm, the flesh. Still there, the breasts and buttocks, not falling yet, surprisingly. I pulled my arms back and jutted my front—as proud as the prow of a ship. Oh yes, a body built for men. To ensnare and enfold. Seductive, but still comfortable. As if Sophia Loren had been put in the mincer with someone like the Queen Mother.

I rubbed my damp hair with a towel, nothing much more was required. It clung uncharacteristically in tight curly tendrils around my skull. The result of my recent perm. Friends had been horrified before I'd had it done, my strong straight hair hanging like shiny metal to my shoulders had seemed such an integral part of my appearance—like Joan Bakewell and hers. And the change of colour from almost black to hennaed red hadn't gone down too well with them either. But I knew best, much better than anyone else on the ways to extend my appeal.

I pinned the drying hair behind my ears and prepared to start work on my face. Auntie chose that precise moment to knock on the door and barge in. 'I can't decide between the two—what do you think?' she said. We stood there looking at each other. Me, tall and nude, still suntanned from last summer. She, short and floury white, corseted from her midriff down, two hefty brassieres in her hand. One peppermint green, the other a ripe rich peach. Her breasts hung down like carrier-bags, the nipples on a level with her navel. Or where her navel must be, nestling secretly behind the corsetiere's armour. We neither of us felt any self-consciousness. I was as familiar with each dear fold of her body as she certainly was with mine. The fact that at some time, in infancy and the ensuing years, her

444

shape had been much like any other, and that only in adulthood and now in old age had it become like this through sheer neglect—that's what struck me as tragic. That this piece of machinery through misuse had not afforded her more pleasure of the sort that I so enjoyed. That to have been through life and die a virgin like Auntie, seemed such a waste.

'That's pretty.' I pointed to the peppermint green.

'Marks and Spencer's. New Line of the Month, it came in on Monday. Women fighting before they sold out!'

I envisaged a sea of sweating, wild-eyed Auntie figures triumphantly waving peppermint-green underwear high above their heads in the direction of the till. Like a lingerie forest, no less, with my own Auntie the indomitable leader.

'What's the trouble then, why don't you wear it?'

Auntie held it close to her skin. 'My blouse though, you see, is see-through. You can see it, you see, showing through. See?'

'I do see. But I don't think that matters, does it? The green will go nicely with your lime-green suit. You'll be wearing that, won't you? With the blouse?'

It was worth putting everything into words with Auntie, I found. She might well, if she'd taken it into her mind, have just gone out in blouse and bloomers. Like a child of the streets back home.

Her face puckered. 'I'm not sure now at all. I was thinking to wear my Crimplene. The floral I got at the Co-op. The dustercoat.'

'Yes. With what skirt?' I tried not to sound too doubtful.

'Well, a safety-pin? Pinned down the front? No need for a skirt then you see?' Auntie's voice wavered unhappily, knowing that wasn't the answer. She patiently needed me to make the decision for her.

'Oh, I should stick with the original plan. The lime-green's lovely, Auntie. With the see-through blouse and the nice new bra, and the beautiful bedroom slippers—you'll be belle of the ball, believe me!'

I'd convinced her. She turned, humming happily.

Twenty minutes it took to do my face, to transform it from a badly empty canvas of barely formed major features to a vibrant pool of beauty. Who was it who taught me the tricks of the trade? Sweet Stephen, my husband, as long ago as that. So that even before I was out of my teens I was

445

practising the intricacies of full theatrical make-up. It amused him, it amused us both when he went out dressed as a girl. 'My friend and I,' he used to say, in a high false voice at a chosen cosmetic counter—'my friend and I would like a spray of Chanel No 5, before we decide to buy.' And I'd be standing there beside him, barely able to control my convulsions.

I left the doing of my mouth till last, to match up with what I would wear, and turned my attention towards my wardrobe. It ran the whole length of one wall, an open-plan fixture custom-made for my clothes. I chose the shoes first, as a start. My highest heels, which brought me now well over the six-foot mark. Like all my other so-called faults, my height I'd decided to emphasise instead of disguise. Like, for instance, having Auntie here to live with me as instant explanation of my origins instead of pretending they were what they weren't. But these decisions, like going ahead and giving birth to Bogey, were ones only I could make. I couldn't have taken them, or made up my mind so definitely if I hadn't been in this blissfully single state.

'Wow! Wowee! Hey, Mums you look ever so nice—' Tallulah and Zsa-Zsa chorused approvingly. They'd been taught to express appreciation instead of holding back in misplaced politeness. Bogey looked up and joined in, dripping delightedly, one thumb stuck in his mouth. 'Thumb.' I frowned tapping it lightly. 'Tum,' he repeated happily, leaving it where it was. Zsa-Zsa removed it firmly from his face. 'Naughty!' He looked at her openly in surprise, then started giggling again. 'Naughty Bogey! Naughty boy!' Zsa-Zsa greatly enjoyed the role of disciplinarian.

'All ready to go then, are we? Coats on. Come on now. Where's Auntie?'

We waited whilst Tallulah ran up to get Auntie from her room. I adjusted a curl in the mirror. I'd chosen to wear my Zandra Rhodes, a toss-up between that or the Thea Porter, both equally sumptuous and startling as gowns but the Zandra Rhodes won marginally on points for being a one-shouldered affair. It plunged diagonally from directly beneath my leaf ear-lobe to barely above my right breast. There was no question of wearing a brassiere, nor of concealing each prominent nipple. The fine material tantalised them into life. I presented a pretty explosive

446

image. Too much? Should I be more subdued? What, and look like everyone else? I adjusted the silvery lily in my hair. One of Zandra Rhode's signatures, the lily. A recurring motif which ran through many of her designs. Who'd bought me this dress? Was it Nutty? Or one of the others. It was sometimes hard to keep track of. I thought of poor old Nutty now, and of his desperate devotion. A Sir, he'd be, when his brother died. If I chose I could end up a Lady. And if I gave old Nutty a son and heir, I could claim to have mothered a Lord. That might have appealed immensely at one time to me. But not any more. I'd gone past it, something that Nutty, still entrenched in social mores, would never understand.

Auntie was taking her time, it seemed. I despatched Zsa-Zsa now after Tallulah. Bogey leaned against my knee. I resisted the impulse to pick him up. He could have played havoc with my hair. How strange it must seem to be as small as Bogey, on nodding terms with only shoes and legs. It would be nice for all of us if we could stay that small. Like kittens who seem less lovable when they grown into cats. Someone should patent a shrinking powder to cut everyone back to size.

Now Zsa-Zsa had seemed to have disappeared. What the hell were they up to up there? Bogey crooned contentedly down below. I propped him like a piece of pottery against the wall. 'Stay there, little boy,' I said seriously. He watched, waving, whilst I made my way carefully up the stairs, negotiating one step at a time in my precarious heels and swirling hem.

'Auntie!' I shouted. 'Tallulah! Zsa-Zsa! Where have you all got to? The time is getting on. We really ought to be going.'

'Auntie's broken her bloody zip. It got stuck half-way—' Tallulah's voice floated down. 'We're putting her into something else. We're being as quick as we can. Poor Auntie's upset, we won't be long—' I descended the stairs again. One more up there would hinder rather than help. The phone rang as I reached the hallway.

It was Vincent. 'Where are you?'

'I'm here.'

'Well that's obvious.' He sounded impatient. 'Aren't you coming? There are people arriving. And I don't know what to do.'

'Play host,' I said, trying to calm him down. It didn't

bode well for the future that, his constantly rearing panic.
No wonder he didn't do well getting parts, producers must
find his fusspotting a bit of a pain in the arse.

'That's all very well. Play host, you say! It's you they're
all coming to see—'

'Give them a drink. We'll all be along in a minute.
Auntie's broken her zip.' And I put down the receiver
quickly before he had a chance to reply. There was in me a
certain quality that appealed to hysterics. A curious calm,
a kind of haven that drew neurotics with a rare magentic
force.

Auntie appeared at the head of the stairs wearing what
looked like a nightie. Which it was, as it turned out.
Brushed nylon and highly inflammable. If someone
should decide to stub their cigarette out on her, she'd burst
into flames without question. Charred Auntie. 'Will this
be all right?' she quavered.

'It's lovely.' Too late for a change. 'What a good idea.
Who thought of it?'

'Tallulah.' Her sight must be worsening.

We arrived in the Rolls just as Nutty drew up in a jaded
Land Rover. The contrast between the two vehicles
seemed particularly poignant. It was the first time I'd seen
him to say thank you face to face. He squirmed in deep
embarrassment, eye-bouncing and turning bright purple.
Passers-by paused in curiosity at the scene we must have
presented. Me like a Grecian goddess. Auntie attired as if
for the boudoir, right down to her bedroom slippers.
Tallulah exceptionally squint-eyed with excitement. Zsa-
Zsa all teeth, tickling Bogey. Quite safe, he'd only just
emptied his bladder. All of us gazing at this stammering,
strange-looking person, babbling as one possessed.
Nutty's dad had died in the loony-bin, as, some said, his
brother would too. And it's true that Nutty himself
sustained a loose-screw somewhere. I'd thought so in those
early days when he'd prevailed upon me to play games. I'd
grown frightened, genuinely in fear when faced with that
look of insanity, alone with him there in his house. And it
was because of that, the feeling that the line was too fine
between life and death, my sanity and his madness, that I'd
since refused to participate. Though that in itself was still
playing the game, still pandering to his deep masochism.
He claimed it was impossible now to even see me without
getting an erection. The fact that each time he'd tell me of

this, knowing that I'd answer sternly that I wasn't interested, heightened the erotic tension. I wasn't by nature sadistic, he'd forced me to assume the role. My eyes dropped to his private zone. His member indeed did seem swollen. It bulged behind his cavalry twill, pointing towards the pavement. I hoped Auntie hadn't noticed. Not that she'd know what it was. How sad to never have held a cock in the hand. To stroke, to suck, or to stiffen. Though what she hadn't had she didn't miss of course. I'd see to it that my girls didn't suffer a similar fate, though they'd probably see to it themselves, without help from me—the way they were going. All three of my children and their friends exhibited the normal preoccupation with each other's parts, to judge from the number of Hospital Games they played behind locked bedroom doors. Bogey was pigeon-holed as patient. Hovered over, stripped and shivering with pleasure, beneath the hungry curiosity of half a dozen small and serious schoolgirls with Kleenex Tissues tied round their heads like nurses. I sometimes wondered whether this assuming the centre of such a sexual stage so soon might not damage my son in later life. Would he feel drawn to public display of his person? Strip off, strolling along Oxford Street. Or, more decorously, take to exposing himself on the top seat of double-deckers?

That's where, after all, I had got my first glimpse of Man's Wonderful Trouser Worm. Aged about ten, the same as Tallulah, wedged between it and the window. Very well fed, was my first reaction, if not to say positively plump. Gorged and without doubt moving in my direction! As pale as an uncooked pork chop, with a slit-like eye in the centre of its head. It wasn't shyness, certainly, that prevented our closer acquaintance, but simply the fact that I had to get off. I've always been able to recall its appearance, though not that of its owner.

Now Nutty, from nerves, plunged his hand in his pocket, as if trying to conceal his discomfort, when in fact the jerky action he'd engaged upon only drew our attention even more to that area around his old-fashioned, buttoned flies. His fingers moved feverishly behind the material—was he wanking himself or what! Out here! In the street! A stone's-throw from Sloane Square! How unseemly. And how out of character.

But a final wrench, in full view of spellbound family, soon revealed the source of his struggle. It wasn't his

449

manly masthead after all, that appeared to be ripped from its roots, but instead the passionless source of the swelling was withdrawn from the confines of his clothing—a long, shiny leather jewel case. He thrust it awkwardly under my arm. 'Ha, happy b-b-birthday!' he stammered. 'For, for you. For ne-next week.'

Pearls. The sort I didn't like. Discreet and perfect. And real. Impossible to wear without worrying. Ones that would have to exist, living most of life unloved and locked up in a vault. Insurance, of course, for the future. Collateral. For all that that word meant. They lay on their bed of crimson velvet, glowing, yellow as ancient teeth in a set of very old gums. Depressing me. I looked at them stonily, saying nothing. Nutty anxiously registered my distaste.

'Do you like them?' He shuddered in agony.

I debated for seconds. Well, why not. 'No. I don't. To be perfectly truthful, I find their obvious costliness offensive. And besides which,' I put on my scolding voice, 'you should never give anyone pearls as a present. "Give pearls. Give sorrow." That's what they say. An old superstition, Nutty. I'm surprised at your insensitivity—'

Despair and delight danced all over his face. In disgrace. He had brought the wrong present. With luck I'd ignore him the entire evening, which ensured his enjoyment already. I watched his surreptitious fingers sneak into his trouser pocket. This time there could be no doubt at all as to what it was they were doing there.

There was hardly anyone in the restaurant after all. I couldn't think what Vincent had been fussing about. Nor could he, now that we'd managed to get there.

'I just panic if you're not around. That's all. Don't be cross, darling.' He looked at me beseechingly, needing my full approval. Funny that, when Nutty needed the opposite.

'Cross?' I answered confidently. 'I'm not cross. There's too much to be pleased at.' I looked around. It was small, our little place. Enough to seat twenty-eight people at most, with a bit of a squeeze, that is. But the proportions, the enclosing quality, only served to make it more intimate. Like walking into a womb. It suited me well. In the winter it would look even better, with the lights and the warmth and the welcome. Better even than it did tonight, when one might have wished to dim the harshness of the clear spring evening outside. Or to reduce the definite fug that was building up in here. There was an air-conditioner, I knew. It was simply a case of locating it, which would have been easier had I not mistakenly painted it out in my purge, in an effort to unify everything. We could go into all that tomorrow though. Tonight wasn't really for serious.

Zoë appeared now from down below, followed by Soc and Ari. She looked tousled, elated, her lipstick all smudged. One bra strap was obviously loosened. Should I tell her, or not? It took a trained eye like mine to suss out that she dipped sou' sou' westerly. Others would probably not notice. But it would help if she'd clean up her mouth. People would assume we had strawberries on the menu. She smiled dazzlingly in our direction, waving madly like Auntie Mame, as if the honours of playing hostess rested exclusively with her.

'I've a feeling Zoë is drunk!' Vincent muttered in my ear. And continued with great intensity, 'She must be. She's kissing Soc and Ari!'

Something had certainly put those two in the mood, because now they were all over Auntie. 'Is nice. Is pretty. Is pretty nice!' Soc ran his hands over her nightie, snagging it here and there on the stiff Spirella beneath. Auntie beat at his predatory fingers with her handbag, but ineffectually as she sometimes playfully smacked Bogey. But Soc would not be put off. He'd found the squashy bit of her unsupported midriff, and bending his head he bit it. Not hard, but more with the nuzzling motion of a horse, starting from under one elbow all the way round to the other. He moved in a crab-like fashion on his crooked legs. Auntie seemed dazed. But delighted. Ari pressed close to the two of them and clapping his kitchen-care hands high in the air, began chanting an incomprehensible chorus. It sounded after several repeats like—'Oh Auntie! Oh Auntie! Can I drink up your Chianti.' So much so that soon Tallulah and Zsa-Zsa and even Bogey in his lisping fashion had joined in and were chanting it too.

The party had got off to a flying start. Two hours later it was still spinning. But giddily now. Food was called for.

It was a stranger who actually asked for it first, who'd wandered in straight off the street. He was to be forgiven for believing the place to be a bona-fide restaurant after all. By that time most people were sitting, if not exactly with meals and knives and forks, and salt and pepper, at least with plenty of glasses. Zoë had homed in on him first of course. The sight of a strange new man. 'Hello sailor!' she afterwards claimed to have said to the first of our true patrons. The greeting could not have been more inappropriate. He was dressed in the garb of a mourner, an official of death with a face to match, who'd been tying up poor Tom Twiddle's funeral.

Zoë's greeting had set off a strange chain reaction. His death-mask had swiftly disintegrated. It split first in vivacious vertical stripes, then criss-crossed into fey horizontals. The results were quite hideous, revealing such teeth as to make Zsa-Zsa's seem like small pearls. But more was to come—his voice, high falsetto, sopranoed a request for the menu. Zoë fell back in surprise at his words. Seconds later she'd collared Vincent, who in turn had come rushing to me. 'There's someone wanting to EAT!' he'd screamed, wild-eyed. 'The public. A person who'll pay!'

He didn't pay, we wouldn't have it. Nobody paid in the end. Except Nutty of course, who paid for it all—to make up for my discarded pearls. He wrote out a cheque for £500 made payable to The Brick Bistro. Vincent insisted on showing it round and dragging poor Nutty with him to receive all the thanks and back-slapping. But when they arrived together at my side, all I gave was a cold withering glance. I would've preferred to be much warmer and as nice as I felt inside, but Nutty had only just bought my displeasure. It wasn't now mine to withhold.

At half-past eleven, a complaint came down from upstairs. Not serious but tetchy, about the noise, from the occupants of one of the flats.

Rufus Justice had arrived very late. None of the others had come. Not Brad. Not Lionel, who'd said he'd pop in on his way to the airport this evening. And not even Stuffy, which seemed the most strange. Only Rufus, and Nutty of course. It didn't matter, it made no difference, in fact it was very much better. It hadn't occurred to me what might happen if they'd all turned up there together.

As it was, now, Rufus was looking at Nutty with more than a hint of suspicion. He'd been present at the cheque charade and had drawled, 'Chap seems frightfully generous—or is he simply showing off,' raising a cynical eyebrow.

None of my Gentleman Callers could claim that I'd led them to believe that I was theirs alone. I reserved all rights, as it were. But I could see that the reality might be hard to accept if presented too rudely—like a dog's nose, rubbed in its own dirt. In any case, looking facts squarely in the face, Rufus himself was married. True, no one had ever met his wife though she was a minor celebrity. An opera singer who had in the past appeared at Glyndebourne but now pursued her career on the continent. They'd lived apart for many years, but, he claimed, preferred to remain married. If only as a preventive measure against either getting trapped in matrimony again. I'd known him now for almost five years, ever since The Old Man had died. Rufus was one of the executors of his Will, fighting hard for my Claims. It wasn't altogether clear to me just what my Claims and Rights amounted to. Those of a Common Law Wife, legally recognised in law. Especially a Common Law Wife with Issue. The Old Man's filial relatives, those distant family connections flung in all corners of the world, had fought it tooth and nail. But there could be no doubt that Tallulah and Zsa-Zsa were quite obviously The Old Man's kith and kin. You only had to look at them to see in Tallulah his cast of eye, and in Zsa-Zsa the equine gums. We could only cross fingers, he and I together, that having obviously inherited his looks they would not take after me mentally. Instead of the other way round. But as far as I could tell so far, the supposition appeared to be fact—like a famous quip of George Bernard Shaw to the actress. Which one? Was it Ellen Terry?

It had taken a celebratory sherry at the end of that long legal tussle to open my eyes as to how Rufus felt. In his Chambers, near Lincoln's Inn Fields. We'd toasted each other, clinking glasses. Mine slumped and spilt all down my dress.

'Oh God!' I'd groaned. 'Now look what I've done!' I was due at the Hampstead Theatre Club in a little under an hour.

He'd unzipped me before the first drip hit the floor. Taking charge, full control, as he liked to. And had sponged down the silk in seconds. 'This will dry with a press.' And before my astonished eyes, he'd taken a small travelling iron from the top drawer of his filing cabinet. The one labelled A-Appliances.

'Appliances,' I'd read out loud. 'All domestic?'

'Not all.' He'd smiled. 'A toaster—'

'Of course. An electric kettle? A shaver? And a—' I thought hard. 'Um, oh yes, a hairdrier.'

'No, wrong. Not a hairdrier. But everything else. It pays to be organised when leading a bachelor existence like mine.' He'd laid a towel inside my dress, between the two layers of material. 'We'll give it five minutes to absorb excess moisture. Then iron. Take no time at all.' He'd turned and looked at me from head to toe. 'Are you cold? Would you care for my coat?'

The time was high summer, his question was silly. The temperature soared in the seventies. I stood there, pleasantly cool for the first time that day, wearing simply my light bra and pants. Both white, thank God, clean on today. But, 'Oh, thank you' I said, out of modesty. He'd proved himself to be a very good friend. No other thought entered my mind. I harboured no hopes for anything further than that. He was personable and highly impressive in Court, but I couldn't imagine there to be a sensual side to his nature.

He removed his coat and held it towards me. 'Let me help you.' It meant turning my back to slip each wrist into the waiting armholes. As I did so, his hands slid on my shoulders. We stood, from necessity, very close. His front firmly up against me, whilst I faced in the other direction. I made as if to move away, to button the coat together, but he tightened the pressure from behind. I could feel his hot breath on my neck.

'I can feel his hot breath on my neck,' I thought. It seemed to quicken. And mine did too. I glanced down, my chest was growing goose-pimples. Two huge ones pointing out of my seamless bra. Now Rufus had found them, his breath had deepened into something else, a steady gasp. It seemed the only sound in the whole of Lincoln's Inn, and it set off a curdling excitement. The River Thames ran through my drawers. My secretions could be used as office adhesive. My eyelids drooped. Through the open window, I could see the roofs of High Holborn. I hoped that they couldn't see me, standing now in the Inns of Court with a member jammed into my knickers. God knows when he'd managed to get it out.

Had it burst its own boundaries? Would I turn to witness a gaping hole in Rufus's immaculate suiting—and the floor strewn with stray bits of serge?

But it was out, no doubt about that. Hot-foot on the path to my pussy, keeping to the left of the gusset. I remained where I was, but awkward now, with his aubergine easing inside. There seemed no question of a frontal confrontation. We each preferred to pretend that it wasn't happening. My knickers slipped to above my knees. I bent as if to retrieve them. One breast fell out, the other flowed over. My movement, my forward movement afforded Rufus his opportunity. Insertion. Where each of us wished it.

We fell into a rhythm, my nose on my knees. I hoped that he wouldn't take long. The law of gravity began taking its toll—three tears fell, black with mascara.

The gurgling started in somebody's throat—was it mine, just prior to fainting? No, Rufus's. Gradually becoming a roar, and receding as rapidly as it started.

A rat-a-tat-tat! At the outer office! The return of an Articled Clerk. And the hurried need for each of us to get dressed, and my dress still not ironed. But the bond had been formed, the die had been cast.

It surprised me, the sensual side he displayed. He had an obsession with all forms of underwear. Almost each week he'd present me with something, some satiny, lacy, filmy scrap. He'd brought one along this evening. Had cornered me somewhere between the till and top of the kitchen stairs. 'Here.' He said it with heavy emphasis, a meaningful look in the eyes.

I took the tissued envelope in my hand. It was hard to believe it held anything, it felt as light as a leaf. 'Oh Rufus, how sweet. Not another pair. I can't wait. Shall I open it now?' We always went through that procedure, played the same charade. It excited him, the sight of sexy lingerie in the light of day. And in public. It never ceased to amaze me, his inventive approach as to where to present his offerings. A turquoise petticoat in Trafalgar Square. A satin waist-slip in the Strand. Directoire bloomers by Buckingham Palace. A no-bra bra near a bus queue at the top of Tottenham Court Road. A pair of french knickers at Finchley Road tube—the supply and the settings were endless.

'How naughty!' I said, unwrapping the latest. 'My goodness which way do they go?' The elasticised lace lay looped in my fingers attached to two wisps of sheer nylon. Black and a brilliant violet, looking as if they'd fit Bogey's tiniest teddy bear.

A fine line of sweat formed on Rufus's face, on his upper lip and his forehead. I could tell that his hands must be clammy too by the way he wrung them together. I glanced around; Nutty was glowering on the far side of the room, trapped by a crowded table. I'd sent the children home already, under Auntie's auspices. Vincent was waving his sleeves vivaciously, displaying his actor's training. Six months in Scarborough Rep, he claimed, to teach him all that he needed. Zoë was sucking a stick of celery, legs crossed, leaning on the front door—as if to suggest that whoever might pass, wish to enter or else to go out, would first be required to penetrate her. She looked quite engagingly pretty, flanked in the shadows by Soc and Ari. The lighting was kind to her nose. They'd had a good time here tonight, our resident chefs, Soc and Ari. Accepted as guests along with everyone else. No cooking of course, simply serving my purchases. Tomorrow they'd have to start working.

'They go that way,' Rufus was speaking.

'What, which!' Rufus pressed close with one thigh. He'd startled me; I'd lost the thread, momentarily. With his pressure my attention returned. I must subconsciously have been anticipating his next suggestion. Deducing the lie of the land. Calculating how clear was the coast. How deserted it might be below. Rufus clearly was wishing to consummate the confection that lay in my hand. He usually did. Intimacy occurred as promptly as was physically possible, after the passing over of presents. It had led in the past to hair-raising situations—a finger-width this side of scandal. Once on the tube-train I could barely believe it! Me in a button-through dress, jam-packed in the rush hour against his smooth front. Jostled to climax by the crowds, and the courtesy of London Underground. That was the time of the french knickers at Finchley Road. The fact of their wide-leggedness had at least aided Rufus's entry. Something he must have considered when suggesting I change into them in the Ladies.

'Free Traders,' he said now.

'Oh really, which three!' I looked round the restaurant with interest, wondering who had caused him to change the subject. Was there someone here I didn't know?

'That's what they're called, these little scanties. No gusset—for easy entry. Free Traders. Popular with prostitutes.' His knee now was starting to tremble.

'I see,' I said, looking down.

'Your legs go in here.' Rugus spread out his hands and slipped them beneath the fine cobwebs. 'This here, well, that's where your pussy—' He cleared his throat. 'What about it then—give it a try?'

I led the way down the banistered stairs to the dark recesses of the kitchen. Someone had left a gas ring on. It burned like a cool blue halo, lending an almost religious light, quite catholic in its quality, to the romantic setting.

'What are you wearing? Which ones have you got on down there?' Rufus bent and felt under my skirts. He knew my underwear, eyes shut, just from touch. 'Oh those,' he said, stroking the crotch. I stood with my legs wide apart, towering high up above him, whilst he groped around in the flowing folds of my Haute Couture. His hands ran around the bare flesh of my legs, sliding over my thighs to my buttocks, then easing up to the hip-bones on either side where the top of my pants smoothly ended. Hipsters from Holland. From Amsterdam, brought back from a flying visit when Rufus had been sent to submit a study on a particular point of pornography. His experienced finger-tips eased them down, brushing lightly over my labia. 'Lovely. Mm, lovely,' he murmured, lingering in there with one thumb. One of the first things about Rufus that had struck me with force was how beautifully he clipped his nails. Like the lawns of a well-kept country estate. Or a poodle, up for the Cup at Crufts. No cuticles, no rough skin to scratch where one might least expect it. I relaxed at the butterfly touch and stepped out of my pants as he asked me:

'Lift your dress, yes, go on. I want to see.'

It was easier said than done. The magnificence of my Zandra Rhodes lay in how much there was of it. I looped and gathered up as much as I possibly could, holding it high up above my waist, exposing the rest to his gaze.

'That's it. Leg up. And now the other. How do they feel—the Free Traders?'

'Tight,' I said briefly. They were cutting in. Cheap

second-rate elastic. I'd be left with a dreadful, bright red indentation. Branded. By street-walker scanties. I looked down. The bright violet, dark puce in this light, stretched tautly over my stomach, beginning beneath my deep navel. It split, divided at the junction of pubic hair. I could feel it join up in the small of my back. Which meant my extremities were available to all the world, just as if down there I wore nothing.

Rufus was now, rather recklessly, removing the whole of his trousers. He often did that. He liked to rub legs—that's how he chose to explain it. But I wouldn't have thought this quite the time, or the place. Our tableau was occupying the direct route to the outside lav. We'd be probably better off there.

I patted his pecker, and held its head, and spoke as one might to a pet. 'Let's go in the lav—'

'In the lav! Oh good lord! Not that sordid God-forsaken sty!'

'Safer.' I led him away.

The two of us fitted in quite well. Just the right sort of squeeze. And I was able, by sitting on the lavatory seat, to lay back and loop my skirts on the chain. Rufus straddled over me, one hand for support on the lavatory roll, the other on top of the cistern.

We decided to leave the washing-up till the next day; the whole place was a scene of wild disorder. Ash and spilled drinks and fag ends stubbed out in pockets of pâté, and the atmosphere heavy with party fever. The normal end to that sort of evening. Soc and Ari seemed incapable of coping. When would they prove worth their hire?

'We'll see to this in the morning, Vince.' He'd obviously gone past the stage of caring. I took matters firmly in hand. My batteries after all had just been re-charged by Rufus. I could feel the brittle Free Traders biting my cheeks as a reminder. And I could feel as well his oozing spunk. I could have done at that point with a gusset. These open endings were all very well, but they didn't give much sense of security. I bade goodnight to departing guests, with both legs squeezed tightly together. That way at least his semen might swim in a direct route from my snatch straight into my shoes, instead of staining my Zandra Rhodes. It cost a hell of a lot to dry-clean.

Nutty was almost the last to leave. He lingered long after the others, looking imploring and wretched. 'What's the matter with you?' I snapped at him sharply. For once I felt quite as I spoke. It had been a long day, and would be again tomorrow. The realisation was gradually beginning to dawn on me, to sink in, just what we had started. The daily grind of being in business, like starring in a long-running show. Except that this one hadn't yet got the necessary organisation to run on efficient lines. But we'd get it right. In the end.

Soc and Ari sat slumped, half unconscious, Zoë had long since departed, muttering something about finding Stuffy. She must have been upset that he hadn't turned up. Vince swayed, frail and splendid in his finery—the evening had yielded nothing in the way of new relationships for him. But then it never did. His encounters were less straightforward than that. Would he go on the toot now or not? He seemed tense. We smiled at each other.

'Shall I drop you? Shall I see you home?'

But he shook his head. 'No thank you, darling. I don't know yet what I'll be up to—'

'How will those two get home do you think?' I pointed at Soc and Ari. I'd told them they ought to be going, what seemed now like hours ago. In order to catch their last tube or bus. It was obvious that Vince wouldn't share a taxi, although they lived in the same direction.

'May I be of help?' Nutty coughed and moved nervously forward. 'I'd be pleased to be used as a chauffeur, my dear—' Perfect. Demeaning. I yawned and turned to switch the lights off.

'O.K. Nutty. You can drive them.'

It wasn't until I was home and warm, stretched out in solitary splendour on my Slumberland mattress, that I realised my knickers were missing. The ones that I'd stepped out of for Rufus. I remembered I'd seen them clearly on the floor, by the light of the blue gas ring. But there was no doubt about it in my mind, they'd gone by the time we returned from the lav. Whoever'd taken them had certainly seen us.

Syndey Bummer, our predecessor in The Brick Bistro, had stayed open all day. Starting, in fact, by serving breakfasts. Neither Vince nor I were much good in the morning, though we might manage something midday. But in the actual effort of opening midday lunch had oddly not been discussed.

My telephone rang at half-past seven, before I'd even aroused the children. It was Vince, being bossy. He'd had a good night, fallen on his feet with an Irish chippy from Willesden.

'What about lunch? Will we do it?' he breezed. All action. The top of the morning.

I blinked several times to focus my sights. The room smelt strongly of sleep. A not unpleasant mix of my bodily perfumes. The Old Man had always been keen on my smells. Like warm milk and cut grass and clean hair, he claimed. And so had Stephen, though I had liked his more than mine, his silky poreless body. So small beside my own. Perhaps that's what pleased me most about Vincent, he reminded me physically of Stephen.

'Lunch?' I'd actually forgotten the restaurant! 'Oh, the restaurant! You mean doing lunch today there.'

'I'm at Covent Garden. With the friend of my friend. A fruiterer and vegetable porter. He can get all the wholesale we'd possibly need. He knows everyone in the business. You should see him.' Vince dropped his voice. 'His shoulders—' His voice trailed off. 'And his friend supplies wet fish as well.'

'That's useful. Wet fish. What about smoked? Smoked trout, I mean. Or smoked mackerel?'

It was coming back to me now, all the things I'd ever eaten in other people's restaurants. The trouble was, should we make ours posh? Or rather more run of the mill, as in the days of Sydney Bummer.

'Yes, all of that. Smoked smokies, the lot. Shall I put in an order, do you think?' Vincent sounded over-excited. From one extreme to the other. 'Open up an account with these blokes?' I thought of Nutty's £500 cheque. Good for floating.

'Yes, why not.'

Auntie accompanied me to the restaurant, when I'd dropped the three children at school. She'd slept the night in what she'd been wearing, her brushed nylon—minus all that went underneath. They lay, a neat pile, at the bottom of her bed. Covered decorously by her cardi.

I took her up a nice cup of tea, milky, four lumps as she liked it. With the tea-bag still at the bottom sending darkening swirls towards the surface. 'Nice cup of tea, there's nice.' She smiled, struggling to sit up in bed. A curler had somehow got caught in her pillowcase. It rose with her, attached to her scalp like a billowing growth. A goitre such as you sometimes see sitting on old ladies' lapels.

'Hold on, Auntie!' I bent to undo her.

'Thank you, love. There's a good girl you are.' I smiled; she said it with such feeling, such satisfied well-meaning warmth. As warm as toast, that's what she was. It made you feel good to be near it.

She thought that she'd wear her slippers again, though one had got splashed with champagne. 'A champagne slipper, like Cinderella! No Prince though, there's the pity.' But her eyes had remained as bright as ever, she'd never really expected one.

'All set, Auntie? I'd like to get off. Got your hat and your gloves? Got your handbag?' No need ever to ask that, of course. The Mock Croc, Marks and Spencer's bag had accompanied us last night, snagging the brave brushed nylon as badly as Soc and Ari. She was wearing outdated ski pants today with the elastic going under the instep, to keep them straight, unwrinkled, looking as if they'd been ironed on. Her suspenders showed clearly beneath, and a bulge of spare flesh round the top of each leg where the edge of her panti-girdle ended.

'Do these look all right?' She felt sure they did.

'Do you really need the panti-girdle, Auntie? It might look better without—' I regretted it as soon as the words left my mouth.

'Go without!' It was as if I'd suggested she walk out naked. Go starkers all the way to Sloane Square. She shook her head, blinking hard, beside herself. 'No, I couldn't do that. Not go without.' It occurred to me what a comfort the corsets must be to all women who were like Auntie. Caught in the clasp, the continuing embrace of their own constricting confines. So that even if an approaching male were to want to, he couldn't not without considerable inconvenience to either party. And a lot of side-play with hooks and eyes, and zips and lacings and so on.

I calmed her down and at last we set off. 'We're doing lunches, Auntie. Dinner, I mean. We're doing dinners now, in the middle of the day.'

Auntie was still a little ruffled. 'When else would you do

461

dinners then, tell me.' Despite her eagerness for progress and all things modern, she stayed stubbornly with the language she knew.

'We're trying them anyway, midday meals, but if it gets too much, we may well have to stop. We'll see how we get on today.'

We opened the door to a curious calm, the sort that precedes the storm. Soc and Ari, and Vincent, must all be in the kitchen. Upstairs there was no one at all.

It had all been cleared though, beautifully—I had to say that. There was no sign of last night's festivities. And someone had dressed all the tables with flowers. Daffodils to go with the walls.

'There's nice.' Auntie blinked and bent down to sniff. 'Not much smell though, never is with daffies. Fresias, they're what you want for a lovely smell. They fill the room, they do.' She burrowed her nose deep into the blossoms, then lifted it buttered with pollen.

'Stay still,' I said. 'Your nose needs dusting.' That close I could clearly see the face-powder on her skin, applied like flour on pastry. Puffed on too liberally and then just left to settle, like sand, in her finely etched wrinkles. Not that she had many of those, her cheeks were as smooth as a baby's. Smoother and pinker, plumper and altogether prettier than my own highboned facial structure.

There was the unmistakable sound of singing down below, accompanied by a transistor. Two voices joining in to Pete Murray's signature tune. Two of them, Vince and another's.

Auntie looked startled. 'Who's that then?'

It wasn't difficult. I knew the timbre of Vince's voice quite well. He'd under-studied once in the Eastbourne production of *Oklahoma!* and had even auditioned, unsuccessfully, for *Hair*, wearing a borrowed wig.

'It's Vince, Auntie, obviously.'

'But I mean the other. There's someone with him I think.'

I felt a jolt of misgiving. Vince did do that sometimes, get carried away with enthusiasm. Who the hell had he found now? Though, whoever it was, he had a nice way with flowers, and clearing-up. I led the way down the spotless stairs: each one had been swept and swabbed. 'Hello,' I shouted. It was best to give warning, in case they might be making use of the architectural features as Rufus and I had

462

done last night. Soaring in song together, in tune with the BBC. 'Hello!' I shouted again to make sure. 'It's us. It's Auntie, and me!'

There was a scuffle on the other side of the door. Were they re-arranging their clothing? 'Look, Auntie, this paint is completely dry.' I ran my hand round the banisters. lingering purposely. The door didn't open. There was silence now. The transistor had been turned right down. 'Why are we waiting then? Go on, go in there—' Auntie was getting excited.

I knocked just once, and was about to knock a second time when the door flew back in a flourish combined with a fresh burst of music. Quite apt as it happened. Shirley Bassey hammering out the opening of 'Hey Big Spender'. She shouted it straight at Auntie and me, the minute we walked in the door.

Vincent stood, wreathed, in smiles, radiant as a bride with the band of gold fresh on her finger. His arms were flung out each side of his body indicating just where we should look. He was alone, that perhaps was the biggest surprise, though the room took a lot of beating. It was indeed a hive of activity. Hobs bubbling. Pans boiling. Things steaming. Stuff simmering. As if the engine room of an ocean liner had assumed a life of its own, pumping, gurgling, geared into animal action yet maintaining ferocious efficiency. Aware, like a row of prancing marionettes, that above was the hand of control and discipline. It couldn't be all Vincent's doing. And certainly not Soc's and Ari's. Whoever it was had that magical touch of coaxing life from the inanimate. Vincent this time might have stumbled on our salvation. The embodiment emerged from the lav at that split second, as my eye accustomed itself to the uplifting scene.

''Lo Missus!' The voice came from the North. Confident, curt and, though friendly, with a hard edge to it bordering on caution. Vincent turned theatrically, spinning on the balls of his feet and extending his fingers in introduction. 'Dick! I don't think you know him!'

I didn't know Dick. 'No, I don't think I do. Hello Dick.' I held out my hand. He ignored it, but nodded his head instead. 'This is Auntie,' I added.

''Lo Auntie!' He pronounced it Anty, like ants in your panty. She smiled back at him. 'Oh, hello Dick. My father's name was Dick, short for Richard. Though everyone called him Dai. I don't know why because that was his brother's name—and they used to call him, well, sometimes Billy. And other times Will or William, but we all knew who they meant—' Auntie's voice trailed away. Vince laid a kindly hand on her arm. 'Dick's our new cook. He's a wizard with food. What do you think of the kitchen?' He was looking at me when he said it, almost pleadingly, I thought. There was no need, no need at all for apologies. From what I could see of the activities of Dick, it was all I could have wished.

Dick turned his back and picked up a spoon, applying himself to a saucepan. 'I've got to get on. No time for this gassing. There's loads of things to be done. Who's peeling these sodding spuds for a start?'

Auntie stepped forward eagerly. 'I like to do peeling,' she offered.

'Right, roll up your sleeves then, Auntie, and get going on this lot.'

I admired his air of decisiveness, I could see why he'd impressed Vincent. It was quite hard to tell which way he was. My guess would have been he'd have either—man, woman, boy, girl, even the cat or canary if it happened to suit him and helped towards what he was after.

He was after a rather large share of the profits. Vincent thought he was worth it. 'But what about Soc and Ari?' I said. Vincent shrugged and consulted his wrist-watch. 'Where are they?'

True. Where were they indeed? Without Dick we wouldn't be open for lunch and probably not even for dinner.

Vincent and I went upstairs to the restaurant.

'Where did you meet him? Last night? But I thought you'd fallen on your feet with the chippy from Willesden—'

'One thing led to another. A whole lot of them lodge in this one rooming house. We had a bit of a ding-dong, that's how I met Dick. We're lucky, he's just between jobs.'

'Where was he before?' Not that we needed References. Soc and Ari had not had any. With good reason—they didn't deserve them.

'Joe Lyons, I think. Brixton Hill. But before that, the Gay Bistro in Barnet. And a fish and chip shop over at Shepherds Bush, and even at one point a stint at the Savoy.'

'Quite varied then,' I said with interest. He was young to have moved round so much. Mid-twenties, though possibly not even as old as that. People who worked in the catering trade, with long hours sweating in kitchens, seemed to age as fast as footballers. The strain of it showed in the face. It showed in Dick's. Deep lines ran down from his nose to his mouth, bordering concave cheeks. He was terribly thin, not like Vincent, not affected slimness like that. But stringy and muscled, quite small-boned. With an impression of restless energy, even, perversely, of strength. There was probably nothing he couldn't lift with ease. Even me. Though I was twice his height. The leanness was alley-cat as opposed to lounge-lizard. One more reason for Vincent to like him.

'What shall we do with Soc and Ari? Supposing they turn up of course, and there's no reason to think otherwise, Vince—'

He shrugged, an unlovely habit. 'Sack them I suppose.'

'Oh, no! I couldn't do that.'

'Why not? They're nothing to us. And we've never been that over-confident in them, have we.' Vincent had never held loyalty high on his list, though he felt it towards Auntie and me. But we, I suppose, were more like family. One he'd chosen himself to adopt. He leant forward and kissed my cheek. 'Don't be soft.'

But I wouldn't give in quite that easily. 'Soc's wife is expecting in no time at all—can't they take a second place to Dick? We'll pay them the same as they're going to get now. It's just that he'll be in charge.'

Vincent looked doubtful. 'It's a very small kitchen. I don't know if Dick will agree.'

'It is a very small kitchen for the three of them. But they, all three, are very small people. And what you're suggesting, Vincent, is rather small too, if you don't mind my saying. I think that it's terribly mean.'

He stared at me, slightly taken aback. Then he sniffed. 'Well, we are partners. If you feel so strongly, all right they stay on. But they'll have to prove that they're worth it.'

'So will Dick though, Vince.'

'Well darling, at least he can cook.'

'I can see that he can—but the proof of the pudding is the eating!'

Zoe was not coming in today, but she would be in this evening. When I'd rung her up, she was still in bed.

'Stuffy's here,' she said.

'Oh! Is he really!' I could barely contain the surprise in my voice. 'Oh! Give him my love,' I said lamely. What on earth was Stuffy doing with her? Had he slept the night there? With Zoë?

'I don't know about that.'

'Don't know about what, Zoë?' I thought she sounded aggrieved.

'Giving your love—' She abruptly replaced the receiver. I sighed. It spelt trouble. We might well lose a waitress.

I saw Soc peering in through the window, then Ari, squeezed over his shoulder. The sight warmed my soul, they looked so familiar. They spotted me and started to shout. I hoped that Dick wouldn't be too hard on these two terrible little turds. I'd grown fond of them both despite their inadequacies, and I knew that the kids had. And Auntie.

We opened up at 12 o'clock sharp, and by half-past had done eleven lunches. All was chaos downstairs in the kitchen. The Dumb Waiter was refusing to work, which meant that every single dish was being passed up the stairs on a rota. Like a line of firemen passing buckets of water. Through from Dick, at the start of the chain in the kitchen, up to me who was serving the tables. Auntie was proving the weakest link, stationed half-way up the stairs. And Soc, it seemed, was barely better—screaming each time that Dick's plates were too hot, he'd dropped the first three on his feet. And so he stood now in a pool of stewed steak, with carrots stuck to his crepe soles and creamed potatoes cooling on his socks—which made him completely immobile.

Vincent trembled at the top of the stairs in the grip of terrible stage fright, as if our disinterested clientele were distinguished drama critics. He was barely able to pass on each order, shouting it down the empty Dumb Waiter to Dick. No wonder he didn't get work. His diction was such that the back of the stalls could quite rightly demand reimbursement.

'What's wrong, Vince?'

'Don't know. Just jittery.' He ran his tongue over his teeth. A case of dry mouth.

'Have a drink. That might help.'

'Oh, I daren't, darling. Not in this state. How'—he looked round the restaurant fearfully like a criminal out on the run—'how do you think they're liking it?'

I followed his eyes. 'They seem fine.' He was losing his cool for no reason, with this particular lot. They ate without appetite, almost mechanically, and would have done so whatever they'd been served. Which was just as well from what I could see of the quality of our cuisine. I studied a plate of Sausage and Mash, and another of Shepherd's Pie. Auntie was flustering up the stairs with Fish Fingers; I suspected she'd secretly stolen one from the state of her teeth when she smiled. 'Two Tinned Pears and Custard coming in a minute. And one Vanilla Ice with Jam,' she announced with an air of importance. Dick had decided on the menu. Auntie was all approval, as Tallulah and Zsa-Zsa and Bogey would be. All those under ten, or toothless.

But I'd held my counsel and kept all doubts to myself. It was hardly the time to start rocking the boat. Dick's approach to food was at least basic. And no one had so far sent anything back. Perhaps, with some subtle persuasion on my part, more sophisticated dishes might be introduced for the evenings. We hadn't discussed it together at all, Vince and I, me out of delicacy. Apart from his nerves, it was obvious that he'd defend Dick to the death. But I couldn't for the life of me see how our wines would wash down with this form of tuck. A vision of Rufus presented itself, delicately probing with his connoisseur's prong through a pile of Dick's overdone cabbage. Both Vince and I, though unable to cook ourselves, had done enough dining-out to distinguish the rough from the smooth. Perhaps on the other hand we might manage to make our notably mundane menu a positive mark of the place. Serve champagne with Dick's pork chipolatas. And port with our tinned pears and custard. It could be considered a kind of jape for the jaded palate—a return to childhood treats. I must make a note, a special request for trifle, and banana blancmange. And greengage jelly, that glorious bright green. And paper party serviettes with painted balloons on the borders.

'The bill, Miss!'

'Certainly, Madam.' I smiled at the woman before me. Her husband scowled sourly at Auntie's ski pants and then towards Vincent's half profile.

'You've spoilt this place. It used to be decent!' He said it with savage delivery.

467

'Oh, I'm so sorry, Sir,' I answered him smoothly. 'Was the meal not quite to your liking?'

His wife chose to answer the question for him. 'Our peas were cold!'

'How were your Qs?' I asked lightly.

'Beg pardon?' They were openly hostile.

'Your bill.' I handed it to them. They left without leaving a tip.

Vincent had watched, standing well away.

'They won't be back,' he fretted.

'No, thank God. I don't think they will.'

'What was wrong?' He was biting his nails.

'What was wrong, Vince? Well, they just don't like us. That's okay. You can't win them all.'

'Cheeky things! Cheeky things, that's what they were!' Auntie looked het-up and indignant. 'They didn't deserve Dick's lovely dinner. I had a good mind to say, I did, myself!'

'Oh Auntie, don't ever, please don't. If this goes on we shan't have a business. No one will come anymore.' Vincent genuinely seemed to believe what he was saying. I looked at his worried face.

'Oh, don't be daft,' I said reassuringly. 'It's up to us how it all goes.' I lowered my voice and glanced around at the remainder of our grim patrons. What a gloomy contrast to the dazzling décor. 'Ghastly decorations!' 'Gives one quite a headache!' 'I agree, puts one right off one's food!' I'd been hearing all that since 12 o'clock. 'These aren't the sort we want in here in any case, Vincent. We're inheriting these from Sydney Bummer—this trade will pretty soon fall off.'

'That's what I'm afraid of.'

'And be replaced.'

'By what though?'

'By friends, Vince, of course, who else?'

He didn't reply. I knew why not. He was thinking the same thing as me. Dick's culinary range didn't match up to that. Just as we, and the Brick's gleaming face-lift, appeared not to suit its past patrons.

We ground to a halt at half-past two, by which time we'd served twenty-seven lunches. And survived the strains of the fierce fight which developed between Dick and Ari. Soc claimed to have had both hands badly burned, though close examination failed to show any signs. 'Him do it. Is

468

Dick. Yes, Boss Lady, he a fiend. Dick the Devil. He vicious. He—he—!' The diatribe ended with violent spitting in the direction of Dick.

Dick coolly looked on, one eyebrow raised, 'Piss off, you Cypriot runt.'

An expression of pain and deep, injured pride on a national scale passed over Soc's twisted features. He turned to Ari and poured out an incomprehensible torrent in their native tongue. To which Ari reacted by grinding together his broken front teeth and kicking Dick hard on both shins.

'Christ almighty. You cunt.' Dick slammed a saucepan, fortunately empty, on the nearside of Ari's skull. The unexpected blow knocked him clean off his feet. Dick took the opportunity to further the fall with a few swift boots up the backside. Soc was shuddering, wild-eyed, against the knife and fork drawer hugging a clutch of wooden spoons against his heart like a crucifix. And moaning a continuous low-pitched growl like a zoo-reared lion in labour.

It was Auntie who managed to intervene and restore an uneasy order from chaos.

And it was only because of Auntie's continued presence in the troubled kitchen that we finally closed in dubious calm. Not one of us dared to enquire of Dick what he'd planned for this evening's dinner. With the way that things were between Ari and him, not to mention the still-smouldering Soc, who kept licking his hands like a beast with a wound—we'd be lucky if Dick deigned to show up.

My bright pink menus lay pure and pristine, still unwritten upon. Vincent had chosen to chalk up the midday choice on a piece of old board—Dick's suggestion. It might have done all right for lunch, despite disgusted reactions from already irritable regulars, but I didn't feel it would do for dinner.

'We ought to know well in advance what's on, for writing out all the menus. One on each table, don't you think, Vince?'

'Oh, I'd leave that all up to Dick,' Vince said fearfully.

'What, the actual writing?'

'Well, he's done all that. He must've done, with his experience.'

'Can he spell, do you suppose? Does he know there are

two 'n's in dinner?' I knew perfectly well how Vince would answer: 'Don't be bitchy.' But I felt both that and frustrated. Something had got out of hand. The reins had been snatched from our fingers. The evening threatened ahead. I viewed it with a sense of foreboding, leaving Soc and Ari to clear up. Dick had got changed the minute he'd done the last orders.

'Where's he going?' I'd whispered to Vince.

Vince had winced and started perspiring again. 'Why do you keep asking me all these things? I don't know—'

I'd kept my silence. I could've been childish and replied: 'Well, he is your friend!' But instead I said, 'Perhaps that's what they do, chefs, go off in the afternoon. Shall I ask him?'

Vincent rolled his eyes to the ceiling. 'Oh God, no! For Christ's sake, no, don't do that. He's sure to be back. We haven't paid him yet. Just treat it as perfectly normal.'

Dick emerged from the lavatory, where he'd got changed—our only place for privacy—as Rufus and I well knew. He buckled the belt on his skin-tight jeans, almost as tight as Brad wore them, with a similar display of what was inside. I could hear Vincent's intake of breath. Despite myself and this lunch-time's troubles, due to Dick's aggression, I had to admit his attraction.

'This toilet here is a bit of a come-down. Full of crap!' He frowned in disgust, tucking his tee-shirt into his jeans, a black one with very short sleeves which barely covered his pectoral muscles. Like the ones Marlon Brando once wore. We stood like an audience looking at him, ashamed at our faulty facilities. Full of crap! Who'd done that? Who'd sullied our sanitary arrangements?

I stepped forward. 'I'll clean it,' I said. 'But who's been? Was it one of the customers?' I didn't think so, no one had asked me the way. But then they'd all been here before and must've known what to expect. Not many, not those forearmed with knowledge, would brave coursing through our kitchen.

Dick slicked a comb through his long side-burns and over his smooth straight hair. I knew the style, from way back in the fifties.

'It's not a clean-up that's called for, it isn't that, Missus! It requires some re-decoration. A more modern toilet and handsink put in. I've got a mate who could do it for nothing.'

470

'Nothing?' Vince echoed before he could stop.

Dick spun round. 'Well, not nothing! You geezers expect sodding blood from a stone! A fair rate for the job's what I mean—'

Vincent quivered, beginning to blush. His reaction reminded me of Nutty, when I gave him the hard word. Did we appear, with our exchanges, as unpleasant as this to onlookers? But even so, I stood saying nothing. I could hear Auntie's stomach behind me, gurgling with emptiness—we'd none of us eaten. Not that I felt like it now.

'Right. I'm off then. I'll see you—' Dick flung over one shoulder, stopping briefly to light the cigarette that he'd already rolled. I watched him cup his bony fingers round the flame, as taut and tense as an animal trap. Like a cage. He slid a sly shiny eye in our direction, winked swiftly, 'S'long!' And was gone.

'Auntie's flagging, I'm taking her home.' Auntie sat at the top of the stairs. Things seemed better since Dick's departure. Vince had become more himself. Even Soc and Ari, scuttling between pot-scouring and swilling out cloths and swabbing down the kitchen floor, seemed to be humming in some sort of harmony. It was as if the troops were now on time-off. But it was as well to remember the necessity for a commander-in-chief. We'd probably learn to work as a team, with our leader, before very long. And it was in that mood that I'd taken Auntie away, dropping Vince at Sloane Square Tube Station. We were meeting later, it was all arranged. In the meantime, Vincent went off home for a rest. 'Sleep at our place, if you want a lie-down,' I'd invited. 'Rather not, darling. I feel I need absolute peace, your place is like Paddington Station—the children and all that. You know what I mean. And the off-chance of Gentlemen Callers—' He waved his limp wrists wanly in the air. Looking drained out and defeated. I squeezed his arm, and kissed his cheek. 'You know best, Vince. I'll see you. About six.'

The telephone was ringing as I opened the door. 'Just a sec, Auntie. Stay there while I answer it.' She'd fallen asleep, chin slumped on her chest, half-way along the Kings Road. I'd taken a short-cut off to the right through the quieter side streets so that the noise of the traffic wouldn't waken her. She swayed where she was, just inside the front door, still sleepy and dazed from the drive. I

471

would put her straight to bed of course and see that she didn't come to the restaurant tonight. We sometimes overlooked her age and the effects of that limiting factor.

It was Brad on the phone. 'Can you hold on?' I said.

'No, I can't. It's a call-box. No change.'

By the time I'd got back out to see to Auntie, she'd already gone up to her bed. 'Auntie?' I knocked softly in case she was sleeping, and peeped round the door to make sure. She was. She lay spread-eagled on her coverlet, a quilted relic of her girlhood, now frayed and thinning at the edges, but still sweetly beckoning with blushing carnations. I covered her lightly with one of her coats, she usually complained of the cold when she woke. She'd undone the side-fastening of the fitted ski-pants, it revealed her elasticised stomach. I stared for a second at the fascination of stretch and shrinkage as each breath was released from her body. At the end of each of her legs her slippers hung down, a snug fit. They'd been a good buy, if not exactly suitable for wear in our restaurant kitchen. I could see a slight film of grease on each sole, and dicoloration on one upper. Bedroom slippers were intended for boudoirs. I took them off, easing each in turn, and placed them next to her handbag. Then I left the room and went down the stairs to await the arrival of Brad.

'Sweetheart, you stink! Jesus, open the window!' Brad was recoiling in horror and I'd barely got in the car.

'Care for a run, kid?' he'd said on the phone. 'I'm off out to Roehampton, delivering documents from the British Museum to some barmy old trout, Professor something. I don't have to be back on the dot, I thought we could doddle, you know—'

'Doddle? I see, Brad!' I'd laughed at the word. It was one we recoursed to quite often, dating from our very early days when getting together had been difficult. 'I'd love a doddle, a real one. Best bring a blanket I suppose. Where are you thinking of, down by the river?'

'Same spot, kid. In view of the lock. Deserted at this time. It's not that good weather.'

I'd noticed a certain amount of oiliness as I'd pulled the comb through my hair. An unfamiliar sensation these days since the drying effects of my perm. But I wasn't concerned as the curls slid about, the end result was quite flattering. The whole head of hair resembled a ragged chrysanthemum, glossy and bronzed, certainly striking. It didn't occur to me that I might smell.

Brad hissed a long breath between his straight even teeth, a Hollywood set, all his own. 'Pooh, what a pong! Where've you been, in the frying pan?'

'Is it that bad?'

'It bloody well is!'

I bent my head down and opened my jacket, then plunged my nose into my blouse. I sniffed. Was there an odour? It was so hard to tell, oneself. But I certainly knew what Brad meant. On mornings after I'd eaten out in certain restaurants you could smell right away which they'd been, from the lingering whiff on whatever I'd worn. And even sometimes on my hair. Insufficient air-conditioning. Faulty ventilation. A coagulation of the atmospheric conditions collecting in people's clothing. If this continued I could clog all my pores and slide from my sheets on the sheen on my scalp.

'Just as well then,' I said.

Brad was getting up speed, pressing his spruce, plimsolled foot on the pedal. Thick rubber-soled 'Red Flash', he wore, the same as Wimbledon champions. It used to be Running Track, blue and white, shoes. But not any more. They were out.

I looked with interest at the footwear of all my admirers. The contrast pinpointed their characters. Rufus for instance had always worn suede, punched with holes and tied up with neat laces. A Bourneville brown, except in Court when they were leather, in black, and lacking the punch holes. Even in summer there was no deviation, no concession was made to the weather. Whereas Nutty for instance made a big thing of peering at the barometer each morning and would attire his extremities accordingly. The fact that he invariably chose to wear wellingtons whatever the state of the sky said more about his sexual leanings than his degree of sartorial interest. Lionel Striving wore boots, with elasticised sides, in the same range of shades. From a khaki-kind of an olive-green right through to a subtle toad. But in the summer, he favoured shoes. Sharp, plaited-leather, Italian style. The sort worn by successful gigolos. With his head for business and his esteem for high finance he might have done well with the Mafia. Ulysses, Stuffy, like Stanley Spencer, wore sandals

473

all the year round. Open-tied like Christ, Our Lord. But with warm socks when winter came round. Auntie was knitting old Stuffy some socks, navy blue but with Fair Isle toes. She'd reasoned, quite rightly, that unless they were there no one would notice the work.

'Yes, it's just as well,' I repeated to Brad, 'that we're going to be out in the open!'

He kept his eyes firmly fixed on the road, skilfully overtaking, then reverting to the left-hand lane which would take us through to Kew and eventually to Roehampton. 'I'm not sure I'll fancy it even then!'

I laughed. 'Well, I will have enjoyed the ride.'

He turned his head to look at me. 'I shall have to spray this interior. Shout when you see a shop, sweetheart, for some Fresh Aire or something like that. I'm planning to pick up more fares later on—I wouldn't survive the shame. What sort of stuff are you cooking in there? It could finish us, this sort of stench!'

I didn't laugh now. I knew he meant it. How fastidious he was, and how clean. Like a cat. He'd been shocked by the state of my place and my personal hygiene come to that. I hadn't given my personal hygiene much thought until I'd met Brad. Stephen had been as obsessive, it's true, about bathing and constantly changing. But not The Old Man, his mind had been occupied with higher things— 'The Philosophical Significance of Paradox'—and other associated themes. Mundane matters such as bodily fragrance were dismissed and tolerated along with animal functions. In his final four months we'd had a hell of a fight, the daily nurse and myself, to even achieve the necessary bed-baths now and again. He preferred his sores, so he said.

'I could dip in the river, Brad. How about that? When we stop off I'll buy some shampoo!' It was April, cold enough, in the water anyway, to freeze the brass balls off a monkey. Madness. I hadn't meant it.

'Yes, that might do it!' He didn't smile and, spotting a shop, drew into the side of the road. My fault of course. I should have known better. Bradley was slightly short on humour, especially the sort laced with heavy irony. It quite often sailed over his head.

But when I was in, it wasn't all that bad. Not a soul to be seen for miles. I undressed by myself behind a bush whilst Brad kept cave round the front.

'There's no need, Brad,' I said. 'There's no one around. And if there is I've got my bra and pants on—'

'Take them off I want to see you naked.' I crouched, goose-pimpling, in the breeze despite the weak shaft of sunshine. It could as easily start to shower at any minute. 'April Showers Bring Forth May Flowers.' I'd recited that in one school concert and spoilt the whole of our class's show by not being able to produce my spring posy. It had somehow got stuck up the sleeve of my cardi. Which meant that I mucked up the punchline.

I debated whether or not to relieve myself, hidden on all fours in the bracken. Probably best to save up the warmth, I should need it much more in the water. Passing my own, as we called it. Supplying the hot tap—Tallulah and Zsa-Zsa showed particular affection for the process in our local swimming pool, but more often in icy seas.

'Are you ready?' Brad was sounding impatient. I'd forgotten that after all this sluicing he was expecting a poke of sorts. When I smelt that much sweeter of course. I picked up my shampoo and ran to the bank. 'Here I go!'— and splashed in like a dog, starting to swim right way. He stood there staring after me, now grinning in open approval.

'How is it?' he shouted.

'It's lovely,' I lied. 'Really warm! Why don't you come in and see for yourself.'

I looked down, whilst keeping on the move. The first shock of the icy contact had subsided to a general numbness, but by swimming as vigorously as possible I felt the return of my limbs. The water just here was surprisingly clear and appeared to be teeming with fish, almost as if I'd stumbled straight into a shoal. I switched from breast-stroke to crawl to keep my legs closer together. What if one of these piscine particles chose to swim into my person? Silently easing its scales inside, flapping its fins up my uterus and trailing its tail on the lips of my labia. I suddenly felt very alien and vulnerable, swimming alone.

'Come in,' I pleaded. 'And keep me company—' I needn't have, Brad was already half-stripped. I trod water, watching the rest of his torso emerge. He must've been, physically, the most perfect specimen a woman could find. A tanned, muscled triangular mould, with a long neck and member to match. Even off-duty, limp as it was now, it swung seemingly half-way to his knees. Christ Almighty, could I take all that? Full marks for Accommodation. Perhaps I should think of putting the sign up in my bedroom window, and when my Gentlemen called switch to Full. The thought of the bedroom reminded me of Auntie, which in turn brought the children to mind. I should have to be getting back quite soon to feed them, at least to see them before getting off to the restaurant.

'Buck-up, Brad! I'm getting lonely—' He was carefully folding his clothes!

I turned and swam in the other direction. 'Race you!' I shouted over one shoulder. 'To the other side, right?' The splash as he dived in was answer enough. I concentrated hard on each stroke.

There were cows in the field opposite, strange that, somehow being so close to London. They stood rooted solidly to one spot, like lumps of chocolate mousse splattered with whorls of white cream. Several were lying on the grass—supposed to be a sign of rain, that parking of arses, making sure of a dry spot to sit. They weren't that daft then, cows. I harboured a fondness for the gentle beasts, myself. They put me in a mind of Auntie, that same bovine quality she had.

The other side still seemed far away; I glanced over my shoulder to see how far Brad had progressed. It was quite an even race between us, I wasn't often beaten by men at swimming. The powerful width of my shoulders, and the length of my arms and legs coupled with my natural ease at athletics made me a formidable competitor.

He was nowhere to be seen! I turned, and stopped swimming altogether, treading water again on the spot. 'Hey, Brad!' I broke off as his hands brushed my feet— 'You bastard—let go.' My 'go' ended in a gurgle as the river entered my mouth. He was pulling me down under to join him and I only just managed to snatch br‍ ath

He looked like a blurred impressionist painting. One of a God under water, or of an angel flying through space— streamlined, with a shimmering edge. And amazingly pale and amorphous, his usual symmetry destroyed by the weight of the water above. Did I look like that too? A slow stream of bubbles escaped from my mouth. For a smoker his lungs were remarkably sound. So were mine, but I wouldn't have liked to stay down much longer. His arms encircled my waist, he slid, wrists crossed, both hands on my buttocks so that one little finger was snugly fitted between them. And then he tightened his hold. We had, from necessity, to keep moving our legs in order to remain where we were. But somehow with a skill born from mutual needs and an intimate knowledge of each other's bodies, we met at our pubic zones. His erection took longer than usual to rise. He must have been running short of breath, like balloons before they blow up. I very much hoped that he wasn't planning an under-water eruption. We both could explode if he chose to shoot-off down there with the shoals and the slime. A tiny team of teenage tadpoles wriggled their tales past my toes and beyond, a gossiping group of minnows made gestures over Brad's shoulder. I'd somehow managed to sit on his lap, each leg either side of his hips. His cock was inside me, like a cork in a bottle. Had he trapped half the river up there? I had a brief vision of Roehampton Water flooding the width of my womb, crammed with the vast minutiae of sub-aqueous life. 'This woman is giving birth to two carp—twins by the look of them, Doctor!'

I waved my legs in a regular rhythm, as if I was on a bicycle, my hands tightly crossed round Brad's neck, employing my elbows as paddles as well in case we should drift to the surface. Behind me and underneath my upper thighs I could feel his knees doing the same. They rose and banged my slippery bum with monotonous regularity.

But now, at last, my lungs were giving out, I couldn't remain any longer. I brought my face around closely to Brad's and rolled my eyes to indicate desperation. He was pretty near the end. I could tell by the veins distending along each temple and the stretched-tight look of his neck. I removed one hand and pointed above. Would he come out—of me, not the river? Apparently not, his plan was to stay. We rose to the surface as one. Like two stuck dogs before water's been flung.

'Whew, whe-e-e-e!' We said it together, heads back, both gulping in air. Was it free, this stuff? One of life's necessities, the only one—under water. Delicious relief eased through my body, my head had begun to thump and inside my ears a pounding had started, like an amateur on his first drum.

'I love you!' Brad said. He meant he loved Life. We both

understood what we meant. I hugged him.

'I know. Isn't it glorious?' I said. 'Let's get out and go under a tree.'

'You make it sound like the toilet,' he said.

'You've reminded me. I wonder if I can.'

'Can what? Eh, sweetheart? What?'

We struggled to stay joined together, united by his strip of gristle and the plaiting of our pubic hairs. It wasn't easy, not as simple in fact as down under. We appeared to be caught in a criss-crossing current, maybe matching the mood of the moment.

'Pass water. In the water I mean. I wonder if I can with you in me. I doubt it, but let's see now, I'm trying.' I shut my eyes in an effort to concentrate, and willed my bladder to burst its boundaries. Nothing happened. Nothing at all. I tried to relax. 'Will you talk to me, Brad—tell me something, any old thing. To take my mind off, perhaps that'll work and release the tension—'

'Aren't you attempting the impossible? I think we've got too much going here.' His words petered off in a gasp.

It was pretty gruelling, we'd be better standing. The thing was becoming a farce. I kissed his neck. 'Let's go to the side.'

'I shall lose my hard-on.'

'Don't look so tragic. I'll hold it, and swim back one-handed.'

It didn't take long, and when we could stand I guided my handful inside, barely softer than when we had stopped. He wrapped himself completely around my body. One leg over mine, his hand in the small of my back, the other playing with one nipple. We kissed and kissed. It started to rain, very gently at first then more freely. Like in a film, symbolical. Except if it had been a film the camera would be trained in another direction by now and not on our ecstatic bodies.

'I'm coming.'

'So am I.'

'No, I'm not. But I'm something.' I was. It was hard to know which though, or what. I was gripped in my entrails with an agonised sweetness, dissolving deliciously now. 'Oh, ooh, I'm doing it!' I gasped and let myself go.

'Doing what?' Brad managed to ask between moans.

'Can't you feel it?' We were waist high in water.

'I'm coming—' Brad's voice dropped to a whisper, full of vibrating intensity.

'I'm pissing—' I struggled to finish. 'But now I'm coming as well, just like you—'

Auntie was in tears by the time I got back. She was standing, crying silently at the kitchen sink, chopping a sprig of spring onions.

'It's best, Auntie, when you're doing onions to run them under the tap, then the joice doesn't get in your eyes. I read that tip in a *News of the World* that someone had left on the train,' I said, trying to be helpful. But she barely acknowledged my presence.

'Auntie?' I said anxiously, it wasn't like her at all. 'Are you all right?' The children were due back home any minute, all being dropped by the new rota that I'd managed to join. In a fortnight's time it would be my turn. For the moment I could relax.

Auntie's shoulders drooped even lower, she gave a shuddering sob. Two transparent tears welled over her lashless lower lids and came tumbling down each of her cheeks. The sight was somehow immensely moving. Something was badly wrong.

'Auntie, what is it?' I walked towards her and put both arms around her neck. Her head fell on my chest like a broken flower. We stood there together just hugging each other, me strong, and she weak as a child. I picked up a tea-cloth and wiped her tears. 'Now then, Auntie, you tell me. What's the matter?'

Her handbag stood on top of the stove, covering the two front rings. It was wide open. Inside, I could see, from where we were, the confusion of Auntie's conglomerated possessions. Her keys, a clean hanky, several carefully folded serviettes for servicing Bogey's nose, a whole range of assorted cosmetics and creams, from Savlon to an old pot of Snowfire.

She gestured towards the bag with one hand, clinging numbly to me with the other. 'My money,' she whispered brokenly. 'It's all gone. All gone, but for fourpence ha'penny.'

'All gone, but for fourpence ha'penny!' I heard myself echoing foolishly. Her words were quite difficult to grasp, their significance failed to sink in. What did it mean, the missing money? I felt myself growing cold.

479

'Now, Auntie.' I shook her very gently. 'Did you drop it, do you think, somewhere?' It didn't seem likely, I knew perfectly well. She kept it sealed up in an envelope, the bulk of the notes, with loose change floating haphazardly amongst all the other things. In this case the loose change was the fourpence ha'penny, hardly worth anyone's time.

Auntie started to sob again, this time not quite so quietly.

'Now, now,' I soothed. 'It's not that bad. How much was there anyway?' She didn't answer. I repeated the question. Auntie still worked in old currency. Her reply would include things like shillings. It did. She cleared her throat, then managed to mumble, 'Four hundred and ninety-eight pounds. And ten shillings. A brand new old ten-shilling note—'

The 'brand new old ten shilling note' snagged my attention, distracting me momentarily from the shock of how much there was missing. Was it illegal to harbour the note? Would it increase its original worth in future years to come, for novelty value or as an antique?

'Good God!' Now it hit me. 'Almost five hundred!' It was madness to carry so much, but pointing that out would do no good. Recriminations wouldn't vouchsafe its return.

'Let's sit down,' I suggested. 'And think where you've been, and when you last opened the envelope. You've looked in your room?' It wouldn't be there. It was never separated from the handbag. And the handbag was rarely, if ever, separated from Auntie. Except, of course, except—I tried to divert my train of thought. It was useless. Except at the restaurant.

'Do you think it's been stolen, Auntie sweet?'

She nodded like someone struck dumb. I could judge her reaction. I knew how she was feeling. Betrayed. Not just the money, but the fact that someone could quite cold-bloodedly have plundered her precious handbag. The act itself was deeply shocking, quite apart from the actual loss.

We sat side by side on the black leather sofa, not speaking, trying to think back. 'I last saw it, I think, no I didn't, not then—or did I—' She couldn't remember.

'Just go easy,' I said, exercising my patience. It was hopeless to know where to begin. 'Right, then, what about

480

yesterday? You had it then, you remember, because it was a toss-up wasn't it, over who should pay for your primrose slippers at Peter Jones.'

'That's right, love, I had it. Right here in my hand.' She looked sadly down at her fingers. They trembled badly like someone in shock, which she was of course. So was I really. I tried to remember all the people who'd been present at our opening last night. It could quite easily have gone in that crowd. After all, who had taken my knickers? But the two, I knew really, were unconnected. The motives were hardly the same.

'Did you put down your handbag, Auntie, at all—at the party last night?' She didn't. Not once, not to eat or to drink. It had hung on her arm all the time.

'That means then,' I chose my words carefully, 'I suppose, that it must have been taken this morning.'

Vincent was walking down Holbein Place going towards the restaurant. I spotted him as soon as I turned the car around the bend leading from Sloane Square. His walk had a certain jauntiness in contrast to how I'd last seen him. You could tell, it was strange, even from this distance, that he was a homosexual. He waved his spine like a wand. Bringing a fairy to mind. The association of ideas. Should we bring in the law? Consult the police? We ought to, about Auntie's theft.

I drove slowly along. A passing car hooted me from behind. I waved it on, the woman driver frowned as she overtook me. For some reason, barely known to myself, I dreaded breaking the news to Vincent. His psyche was fairly frail at the best, how well would he take this fresh shock?

'You think it was Dick.' Vince sat in the car. I'd parked it not far from the restaurant.

'I don't think at all.'

'You bloody well do!' His voice quivered with accusation.

'It might have been me. Only I know it wasn't. It might have been you, come to that.' I spoke with exaggerated reason. It was the only way to keep the situation calm.

'Oh sure!' Vince said sarcastically. Our friendship seemed suddenly sour. Business partners were probably best chosen from people one barely knew, to keep a degree of distance.

'Or Soc and Ari. Or just Soc.'

'Or Ari—'

'Exactly,' I said. 'Oh dear. How very depressing. What should we do, do you think? Call in the Yard, or confront them ourselves?'

No one was likely to voluntarily own-up, and a search was out of the question. I couldn't see Dick accepting a frisk. Though Soc and Ari would undoubtedly enjoy my fingers searching their persons. In any case, it would be to no avail. Dick had vacated the premises, and Soc and Ari had had all afternoon to do whatever they wished with anything they'd taken. If indeed they had taken anything. Would they do that to Auntie, of whom they seemed fond? With money as motive, who knows.

Vincent was silent. He sat looking troubled. The light glinted on one silver hair that I was sure I hadn't seen before. Were our worries turning him grey? I decided I'd better not mention that fact, for fear of a full-scale breakdown.

'What do you think then, Vincent?'

'Do nothing.' He spoke as if to himself. 'Don't tell them. Pretend you don't know.' He turned to me. He was clearly as upset as he looked. 'Just to get through this evening.'

'I see your point, Vince. It'll be a strain, but it's probably best. We can go into it all in the morning, then if for some reason anyone walks out, there's a chance of getting new staff. Tonight is too much the eleventh hour—'

Would it show, I wondered, the shadow of guilt? Would the evening reveal any remorse?

I'd put Auntie to bed with hot milk and two aspirin, with Tallulah in charge of the others. Even Bogey seemed stung by her air of grief. He'd sat on her lap sadly patting her cheek, trying to lift up her lips in a smile. She'd gazed unseeingly at his round little face, not even tending his nose. The girls had reacted quite characteristically with over-dramatic blood curdling cries of what they'd do to whoever had done it.

'Let's go in then, revisit the scene of the crime. Oh, Vince—not with that expression!'

'Which one?' He turned his face towards me.

'That one. Tragic as Hamlet.'

'I've never played Hamlet, that's one thing I haven't—'

'Well, don't start rehearsing it now.'

482

Soc was wearing new shoes, I noticed them straight away. And Ari was sporting a brand new tee-shirt with a picture of Popeye printed all down the front, the outline deformed by the shape of Ari's low-slung stomach—so that Popeye appeared knock-kneed.

'You like, Boss Lady? Is Popeye, see!'

'Popeye! Popeye!' Soc started scoffing. 'Pooh, pooh to Popeye. Is silly person. He go stuffing the spinach—is not true. It no make nice big muscles, the spinach. That Popeye, he got a loose screw!'

Soc raised his finger in a corkscrew action against Ari's nearest temple. And playfully punched Popeye's raised clenched fist. Ari howled his displeasure, Soc's hands were both wringing wet. The sound must have been much the same as those twins, fabled to have been reared by wolves— Romulus and Remus, if I remembered right. The one voice now joined by another, Soc's own, as Ari stamped viciously on his new shoes. They were canvas, a pale baby blue. The sort of shade that show every mark.

'Boys. Boys. Keep calm.' Could we last without Auntie sleepily keeping the peace? 'Where's Dick?' I looked round.

'He no here.' Soc looked sullen. 'But is fine by me. Dick big prick! I no like.'

Ari nodded vigorously in perfect agreement, their own tiff forgotten already.

'Is not nice person, is nasty man, this Dick no good for the restaurant—'

They stood hunched together looking solemn, and shaking their heads to and fro. Like those little dogs, a cross between toy and ornament, that car owners put in their rear windows. The ones with heads on a separate spring so the thing is on the move all the time, mile after mile of canine activity.

'What time are we opening, Vince?'

'Around half-past seven, I think Dick said—' Vince trailed off looking disconsolate.

I looked at my watch, it was ten past six. 'Plenty to do then—'

'Oh, really. Like what?' We were totally lost without Dick, which was plainly ridiculous.

'Well, Vince. Dick only does cooking—what about all the drinks? It's different in the evening to the middle of the day. For a start, have we got any ice?' My mind was beginning to chug into action, it was simply another party. Dispensing, just like a chemist. All that had to be planned were prescriptions. The phone should start ringing with bookings soon. It was strange that it hadn't done so already.

'Has the telephone gone? Have people been ringing?' I turned to Soc who was nearest. He lifted both hands like a Jewish Momma. Oyvé, in a Cypriot accent. 'Is ringing, and ringing and ringing! I no touch. I no like the telephone. No!'

Ari pointed. 'Is dangerous electrics to touch telephone with wet hands! I say to Soc no do it!'

'Couldn't you have answered then, Ari?' Vince's voice held a certain strain, but he was trying very hard to overcome it.

Ari rolled his eyes in alarm. 'No, no, no, not me. I no speak the English. I no understand. I make bad mistakes in the message!' He clearly spoke from experience.

'That's all right—they'll ring again—' As I spoke, as if to prove my point, the telephone started trilling. I curtsied to Vincent and gestured him on. 'Patron, the first of your bookings!'

There was no ice. There was some, but it wasn't enough. Dick arrived as I made the discovery. 'So what, there's no ice! Makes no odds!'

He'd bought a very big bunch of freesias. 'For Auntie, where is the old girl?' The question was posed so innocently it reversed my rising suspicion. Were the flowers some sort of suppliant, or did they stem from genuine fondness? How significant were Soc's and Ari's new purchases—had they suddenly come into money? I decided I'd have to do as Vince said, put the matter right out of my mind. In any case, there were at this point, more immediately pressing problems. The question of ice for a start.

'I know where I can get some. From that ice-cube machine in Sloane Avenue. They've got one there, in front of Moon's Garage. Zoë was saying about it.'

'What's the point? The previous bloke who ran this—'

'Sydney Bummer,' Vincent supplied.

Dick didn't acknowledge the information, and pointedly ignored its source. 'The previous bloke who ran this joint didn't have fancy ice, I'm sure. Nor much in the way

484

of wines.' He nodded dismissively towards Soc and Ari. 'Cypriot shit, I don't doubt. El Bull-Ox, something like that.' The temperature had escalated since his arrival, you could almost touch the tension. The telephone was ringing now non-stop as if we were the only restaurant around.

'How many friends, would you say?' I asked Vincent. He had chosen to sit in the hot seat, with the responsible role of juggling the bookings. Not one I would have undertaken lightly. How could you tell when people would leave? What if they lingered on?

'An hour and a half, I'm allowing them. Is that right?' Vincent had drawn up a plan of the restaurant, with each table numbered from one to ten.

'I don't know, Vince. It seems to be cutting it fine.' I couldn't recall for the life of me how long I spent at a meal. Wherever I've been to, we'd sat there all night. Start to finish, until it closed.

'Make it longer for friends, Vince! And anyone we vaguely know!'

'There aren't that many, actually, darling. Mostly strangers. The friends don't seem to be bothering, the buggers had it all free last night. I knew that was foolish, I said so—'

I left him juggling with his lists, and went in search of ice. Soc and Ari were working with Dick, maintaining a tight-lipped silence, and nudging each other at his every order. It seemed the right moment to go. As I got in my car, Zoë arrived in a taxi. Our quota of staff was complete.

I got back with my bagful of ice-cubes, two hundred and fifty I'd bought—a waste, Dick would say. But it wasn't in me to serve drinks like Scotch, and gin and tonic without the clinking of ice. It seemed so uncivilised, so second-rate. Someone had to maintain some standard.

It wasn't Dick, as Zoë had noticed. 'I don't think much of our menu, dear! Or of the chef, come to that—'

'Oh, don't you? Dick? He's very nice—he's—efficient.'

'He's damnably rude. "Short Snout", he called me. "Hey, Short Snout, come here!" Can you beat it!' She smoothed her hands over her waist-line. 'An extremely coarse little morsel.'

'You look nice, Zoë. Is that a new dress?' I put off picking up a pink menu. They lay in a pile, next to the till, badly crossed-out, with lots of corrections.

'No, not quite new. Second hand, pure silk. Do you like it?'

She looked quite different to how she'd looked last night. Today she was favouring the twenties. Her dress, cut on the cross, was ultra-defining and designed for someone much smaller. Her curves pouted out before and behind, with an arousing display of cleavage.

'This neck wasn't like this originally—I've spent all afternoon on alterations.' She stroked the firm line from her chin to the start of the swelling division. 'Is it too much? Have I gone too far?'

'Not at all. It's provocative,' I said, and added, making sure no one heard: 'It'll take their minds off the food.' She seemed now quite different to how she had been on the telephone earlier today. I wondered whether or not I should tell her all about Auntie's trouble, but decided it wouldn't help matters. I picked up a menu instead.

'Cauliflour Cheese', I started to read at the top, followed by 'Livar and Bacon', My eyes slid down, I was suddenly sweating. 'Pork Pie' was underneath 'Cold'.

'Lovely puddings, dear!' Zoë perched her chin on my shoulder, pretending to talk like a parrot. 'Oh my goodness, I say—"Mince Pies and Hot Custard", I haven't had custard for years. With luck he might whip up a blancmange.'

'That's what I thought of this morning. And jelly—as a sort of snob joke.' I turned a tragic face to Zoë.

'It's not funny,' she answered.

'No, I know.'

'I like your menu. I like it, Dick. Some spelling mistakes that's all.' The heat was immense in the kitchen. Dick turned.

'That's all right then, some spelling mistakes. The bastards can read it, they know what it means. They've come for the grub, that's the main thing, not for a lesson in grammar.'

Vince popped his head round the door. 'We're open! Someone's just come in. Jump to it—we're almost completely booked out! I can hardly believe that it's true.'

They had managed, in the short while that I'd been for ice, to mend the ailing Dumb Waiter. Dick had done it, he'd brought his tools. The whole thing now swung up quite smoothly. It wasn't everyone who could've achieved such a miracle. Certainly not Soc and Ari, or Vince—he had certain virtues then, Dick.

'Are you coming up, to see to the drinks?' Vince was over-excited. I'd been made Barmaid to his Major Domo. Zoë was Resident Waitress.

'I'm coming, just getting my ice.'

My very first order was for two Gins and Tonic, and one Straight Scotch-on-the-Rocks. 'There you are, you see!' I hissed at Vince. 'I couldn't have done that with no ice!' His answer surprised me, even rankled a little. 'Don't start making trouble, with Dick.' But I had no time to dwell on anything. Dick. Vince. Me. Even Auntie was swept from my mind. Twenty minutes, I reckoned later, it had taken to transform our restaurant from rather a restful room of tables to a tower of blathering Babel.

'Two Sausage and Chips for Table Two! And where are the Coffees for Number One! And I still await Three Sardine Salads, half portions to do as Hors d'Oeuvres— you've sent me up Stuffed Tomatoes instead, shall I suggest where you shove them!' Zoë bawled cheerfully down the stairs. Dick's answer could clearly be heard. I turned up the music slightly louder, which made it near maximum volume. I thought my eardrums would burst, explode like two fireworks each side of my head, a mix of fine bone and warm wax.

Vincent was clearly hysterical. He ran like a rat with a bad case of rabies from table to table taking orders that Zoë'd just taken, and delivering all the wrong dishes. 'The bottle of White, the Dry, where is it?' he shouted wildly at me. We were selling a surprisingly great deal of wine, despite the food's unsuitability. And what was more, our Menu was being received quite favourably. Dick had priced it astoundingly low. But we were making it up on the wines. 'The bottle of White, the Dry?' I repeated. 'You've had it Vince, ages ago!'

'I haven't!'

'You have!'

'You liar!'

'Vince,' I protested. 'Look, I'm checking it here. See this chit? That's Dry White, Table Ten.'

His eyes swivelled ceilingward. 'Well, what's for Four?'

'The cheap stuff, the Red. You remember. Here, look— Three for Four—'

'They don't like it. They say they want White, just the

one—there are only two at that table—' I looked over—there were.

'Well, why did you order "Three cheap Red for Four"?'

'I meant to say Five—'

'Vince! How am I to know! I'm not a mind reader—you're mixing me up now. I'll have to re-do all these records! Otherwise it's all to cock when it comes to paying the bill—'

'Bill please, barmaid, for Number One! They say they can't wait for Coffee!' Zoë made sure to scream as loud as she could in the direction of the Dumb Waiter. 'They've timed it, they claim it's taking longer to come than the rest of the meal put together!'

At her words, the Dumb Waiter delivered Four Coffees. 'Too late,' she yelled gloatingly back. 'Returning Four Coffees, a spot more expresso next time!' Tempers were tingling. I glanced around. Everyone seemed to be drunk. Or was it just my imagination? Zoë tottered past with a tray of greasy plates. 'Dirty dishes coming down, Dick, on the Dumb Waiter—would it be asking too much to wash them before serving up?' Theirs was a running verbal battle. 'Come and wash them yourself, you big cunt!' I didn't dare to dwell on how things were down there with poor Soc and Ari. Soc had appeared sweating profusely at the top of the stairs, wiping his face with his apron. 'What are you doing?' Vince had demanded. Soc had puffed out his cheeks. 'I come up for air. Plenty hot! And that Dick—he just hit me. I—'

'Go away! Get down, go–go—' Vince shooed him away like a hen. 'He can't stand here in front of the customers surely—' Vince appealed to me. Soc stood there streaming like a fountain statue. I could see he might well put people off their food; it was as if he was actually steaming, like a horse at the end of a race. Though some restaurants I'd seen did allow their kitchen staff out, if not exactly to mingle amongst the diners, at least out on the street for a smoke.

'You do have the door open down there, don't you Soc?' I said kindly. He looked at me as if bewildered; the question seemed simple enough, had Dick been poaching his brains?

'It's perfectly true, though, you must admit, Vince—our air-conditioning needs some attention.' My own eyes were smarting badly already from the smoke and the sweat and the steam.

'Oh, never mind that, darling, not now—one thing, for Christ's sake, at a time! Now go away Soc, I shan't tell you again.' Vince waved his fine wrists towards the kitchen. Soc shambled away like a dog.

'Poor Soc,' I said.

'Poor Soc! Poor me, my God, what's up now with Seven?'

Someone on Seven required the Ladies; it meant half the table standing up to let her get by. Which in turn required a gread deal of scraping and drawing-in of chairs around Table Six.

'Bloody hell!'

'Beg pardon?'

'You've snagged my tights!'

'Old fellow, you've spilt half my drink!'

The interchange was taking place between two very different groups. Table Six, upon which the drink had been spilt, consisted of four Hooray Henrys, young ones, aged around seventeen or so. With spots on their spots, and high voices still amazingly unbroken. What age were we allowed to serve alcohol, was it sixteen? Or more, perhaps eighteen? We might be breaking the law with this lot, though if we were, we weren't the only ones. They were pretty drunk on arrival. One had had the audacity before they were seated to slip his index finger down Zoë's flamboyant cleavage. Whilst another, I'd seen behind Vincent's back, was attempting a camp imitation. They'd ordered a bottle of Moët Chandon, Non-Vintage. I planned to charge them a fiver for it. They were now already into their third.

The five-some on Table Seven were mixed sexes with a very wide range of ages, and backgrounds, as well, on the surface of things. Three middle-aged balding, stock-size business men who'd exclaimed with delight at our prices. And two very tarty girls in their twenties, disgruntled at not being taken out on the toot to somewhere much smarter than this. One had decided to stick with her Whisky, all the way through the meal. It was she whose unfortunate tights had been snagged. The Scotch had released her aggression. 'New on today, weren't they, Dawn!' She turned to her friend, lip quivering.

'Yeah, new on this evening!' the friend, Dawn, shrilled.

'It's the fault of these fucking tables! They're too close together—there's no bloody room to swing a cat—in't that right, fellas?' she challenged her companions. They didn't want trouble.

'Girls. Girls. All is well. Plenty more hosiery where they came from.' Then to the truculent Table Six. 'So sorry, young chap, about the spilt drink—might one be allowed to replace it?'

The girl accosted me on her return from the Ladies. 'It's fucking ropey, your toilet arrangements! It could ruin your hairdo, a trip through that kitchen—look, mine's falling already. Not to mention the grease on your clothes—' I could hear her exclaiming, expounding the theme later as they were leaving.

'No, Dawn, I definitely don't advise it. Can't you hang on until you get to Harry's hotel? It won't take long in a taxi. Cross your legs and think of the Crucifixion.' I wondered if they were Catholics.

We were glad of their table, of any table, in fact. A small queue had formed just inside the front door, and was severely hampering service. Zoë had already dropped half a Lager and Lime in an old lady's open handbag. I'd seen her do it, the old lady hadn't. She might not discover it until she'd left and gone home. 'But my goodness, my contents are floating. A large bubble appears lodged in my wireless licence, now how did that ever get there!'

Vincent darted hither and thither, a desperate smile on his lips. 'Would you care for your bill, Sir? No? Yes, of course it's no trouble, your tenth cup of Coffee. Just coming—' Each time he passed me, he made a terrible grimace. I made one back out of sympathy. 'The buggers won't go,' he muttered through clenched teeth. I could see that they wouldn't. But why? Were we making the welcome too warm? Was I making my measures too large? Zoë came for a tray of Zambucca. 'Seven Crême de Menthe Frappé for Table Ten,' she sang out. 'And two more Brandies for Five.' Vincent was passing. 'I think she means Four—' I breathed hard. 'Four for Five', Vince?' My voice sounded strained.

'Two for Four.'

Zoë, thankfully, heard. 'Two for Five, as I've said. Fuck off Vincent, old bean. If you don't mind.'

The small queue at the door had suddenly grown.

Vincent tried hard not to notice. 'There's a lot of them there, Vince,' I felt bound to say. 'Never mind, we'll know another time not to over-book.'

'Bitch.'

'Not meaning to be, but let's face it — each small mistake. It has to be out in the open, don't brood. I'm not doing all that much better with the bills!'

His face cheered up ever so slightly, to hear of my own inefficiency. If I'd been in charge, instead of him, or instead of Dick—everyone seemed in charge but me—I wouldn't have put me on the till. Money, the adding up, etcetera, had never been my forte. But thankfully most of these paying customers were considerably less in control than me. And as I was erring on the side of our profit, the Brick Bistro couldn't complain.

They went in a rush, just as they'd arrived. Six tables emptied at the same time. So that now the entire central corridor was blocked with a queue at each end. One waiting impatiently to get to their tables and the other fighting to leave. The word must have spread about our sanitary arrangements. Since Dawn's friend went, no other woman had been. Six or seven had disappeared down the stairs at different times and come back with a look of disgust. Now and then I could hear from the kitchen the sound of a bellow from Soc, and various high screams which sounded like Ari. And ominous scrapings and thuds interspersed with Dick's demonic swearing. But other than that there was not much to choose between the tension above or below stairs.

'You've got those receipts, Miss? I've worked it out—you've overcharged by two pounds. Two pounds and twelve pence, no I tell a lie, two pounds and thirteen! Look here!'

I studied the man instead of his bill. He was sandy all over like a spadeful of beach, with a bristling moustache in each earhole. His process of hair growth was somehow reversed. The centre of his head must be full of strayed filament from the inside-out setting of his follicles. His ears represented small exits. What discomfort the poor man must suffer. How could a person begin to think clearly, with a brain box of tendrils and curls?

'It's all correct.' I spoke precisely. Quite confident that I could cope. This wasn't the first query of the evening. I was becoming practised at pulling the wool where totalling was concerned. 'Look, Sir—Three Prunes and Custard, you had with your Port. And the lady had Peppermint Creams. That's the discrepancy I think you'll find. You hadn't allowed for those four.'

'What four?' His voice was getting louder.

'The Three Prunes and One Peppermint, Sir.'

An ugly flush was suffusing his sandiness, each moustache stood on end in his ears. 'Are you trying to stand there and actually say that you're charging that much for those sweets?'

I smiled at him tolerantly, he was shouting so much he was drowning my latest Stylistics' 'You, You Make Me Feel Brand New!'

'Now then, Sir, by sweets I take it you mean the Peppermint Creams? Rather than what we loosely term in this country to be the "Afters" or the "Second Course", or more accurately, the "Pudding"?'

'You're trying to fox me!' He was losing control; people at the nearby tables were nudging each other. 'What I'm asking is how in hell this bill has become so exorbitantly high! Seventy-five pence for a plateful of Peppermint Creams! I ask you—not even After Eights!' He was looking around, attempting to recruit support from adjacent onlookers. Several people were waiting impatiently now behind him to settle their bills.

'I couldn't get After Eights,' I said. 'The shop had sold out. I'm sorry. Tomorrow perhaps.' He stared at me disbelievingly, as if I were not quite all there.

'I can't believe,' he said eventually, 'that you'd charge, for what most restaurants give away as a matter of course—'

'They're more established than we are, Sir. We can't afford charity yet. The lady ate every single one. They're quite a superior brand—let me see—the full dozen, twelve I believe we gave? That's only sixpence a peppermint. Served on the premises, you see. You're actually getting our seat, our lighting, electricity, decor, ambience—in short you're paying for overheads. Now, do we agree that's quite fair? Quite. Thank you, Sir. Next bill please.'

'That seemed to go smoothly enough, you see, Vince.' I turned to him after I'd skilfully cleared the small queue. Vince looked dazed. He moved now like one in a trance. No mad table hopping. No manic hysteria. He'd played his

492

crescendo already. It was my turn now. More mine and Zoë's. His Head Waiter role had dissolved. He'd ushered the public into our emporium. Zoë and I had to ease them out, making certain they all paid first.

My additions were becoming more wildly erratic hour by hour, as the evening wore on, as in a sense was the general service. But amazingly, most people seemed to accept it all as part of the normal procedure. If asked, we could quite truthfully have stated that our first night was proving successful. 'I've made two pounds in tips, just from Table Ten,' Zoë confided exultantly. 'And I expect to make even more from Four. They're Red Indians, they don't know what day it is—'

Vincent was standing within earshot as she said it. 'Your tips should go straight in a Service Box and be shared amongst everyone, Zoë.'

'Bollocks to that, Vince!' She turned on her heel and narrowly missed colliding with a courteous American couple who were just on the point of departing. The man came towards me first to pay his bill. His blue-rinsed, plump wife hung behind. He smiled behind his rimless specs. 'My, what a cute little place it is you have here! I can't tell you how we have enjoyed it!'

His pleasant wife approached and nodded. 'Your food is so typically English—we're from the Mid-West, it's my first trip, you know. But my husband was stationed in Britain during the War. He said our little meal here tonight took him right back to those wartime years—'

'I can believe it.' I smiled back winningly. 'Whereabouts were you stationed?' I looked at her husband.

He beamed. 'Ilkley Moor—'

'Oh, Ba Tat!'

He looked thrilled and astonished, and so did his wife. 'Ilkley Moor Ba Tat—why we sing that back home!' She turned to her husband. 'Don't we, dear—I know all of the words, don't I!'

'How amazing,' I said. 'As a matter of fact, I'm not sure, but I think our cook Dick comes from Ilkley.'

'No, really!' they chorused together.

'Yes, Dick, he's downstairs.'

'Why, you'd sure like to meet him—wouldn't you, dear?' the woman said to her husband.

'Surely!' he agreed. 'Just to hear the great accent again—'

Vince stood guard in my place at the till, whilst I led the Americans downstairs. 'Whoo, whoo!' I went, to give prior warning. I couldn't be sure what to expect in our kitchen.

They couldn't have heard. Soc was picking his nose over a plate of stewed prunes. And Ari had his flies half undone. Dick was in the middle of scraping someone's left-over custard back into the saucepan on the stove. Was this what our patrons were privileged to glimpse whilst tripping out through to their toiletries? I could see by the light shining under the door that someone was out there this minute. From the sounds there seemed to be trouble with the flush. Introductions were effected against a background of persistent chain-pulling.

Dick scowled as the American offered his hand. 'Pleased to meet yer! My mother got knocked up by a Yank in the war. The bastard scarpered before she had the chance to pin it on him. She tried to abort, but it didn't work—I came along instead!'

Soc and Ari were listening with fearful fascination. Dick's reaction was so unexpected in face of the American urbanity that it took seconds for me to realize exactly what he'd said. The man blinked. His wife smiled. Both were taken aback, but sheer good manners and years of social training saw them through. He showed his teeth, top and bottom, in a good-natured grin.

'Why now, what the heck—I know our boys weren't as well-behaved as they might have been—but those Yorkshire lasses were so darned cute, I suppose one could barely blame them. May I offer my own apologies on behalf of the American Army, son.'

The 'son' was unfortunate, I afterwards thought. It heightened Dick's obvious hostility. It certainly could have been quite on the cards that this dignified man was Dick's father! I made matters worse by unthinkingly enquiring as to whether or not they had children. The woman's sanguine expression had slipped. 'Our Lord saw fit not to bless us with offspring, and my gynaecologist later concurred.' She'd leaned confidingly towards me, as she said it. Soc and Ari strained forward to catch what she was saying, not wishing to be excluded from any of these exchanges. Soc obviously got the wrong end of the stick as

494

he watched the woman pat her stomach. He took the action and her overall plumpness as a sign of a late-stage pregnancy. He patted his own and broke into a grin. 'Yes, lady, I coming a baby too! Soon, my wife she have it. I hope very much for a little girl baby. I have plenty plenty boys!' He raised his eyebrows high in his oily hair and, putting on a look of concern asked with commendable interest: 'You, lady, want little girl? Or want boy?' And he picked up a nearby loaf of bread and began humming 'Rock-a-Bye-Baby' with it cradled along his arm.

This affecting tableau was interrupted by a tearful young girl at the end of her tether. The unfortunate phantom flusher. 'I can't just seem to—' Her high voice broke unsteadily. She completed her sentence by pointing. No one spoke. The American moved forward. 'May I be of assistance?'

'He understands closets,' his wife whispered proudly to me.

The girl gave a whimper as a sign of distress. I walked forward in front of the American; the girl greeted me with relief. 'It's my—' she lowered her voice, and continued, 'my Tampax, you know, the cardboard container—it keeps bobbing about on the surface. It's frightfully embarrassing if a man—'

She was aged about eighteen and had been well brought up. Home Counties, by the cut of her hair. It hung each side of a centre parting, burnished brown, like a conker. She spoke with bit of a lisp.

'Run along,' I said. 'I shouldn't worry. That sort of thing often happens. It'll soon go away as it gradually gets soggy. No reason to get upset.'

She gave a trembling smile of heartfelt gratitude. 'Are you sure?'

'Quite sure.'

'Thanks awfully, you're terribly kind.'

Dick was throwing a rasher of bacon, recently fried, on a thick slice of bread, upon which sat a lightly poached egg. He reached to a shelf and unscrewed a large bottle of Crosse and Blackwell Tomato Ketchup and shook it on top of the bacon. Then, ignoring us all, he opened his mouth and crammed in as much as he could. 'My, my boy—that looks good!' the American said, all geniality.

Dick looked at him with open dislike. 'Would you two Yanks sod off outa this kitchen?'

495

'Well, darling, I suppose you can understand it. His reaction—in defence of his mother—upholding her honour for past humiliations. Unwed and seduced by our Allies. After all—'

'He's a bastard!' Zoë stated, quite accurately. 'And added to which he's a bully. A bloody sadist with a very peculiar sense of humour. He's stopped "Short Snout" for me, now it's "Dung Drawers"! There's no depth to which I'm sure he wouldn't stoop.'

Zoë was dearly drawn to the double negative. 'These poor patrons of ours, I pity them really. He could be peppering them all with powdered glass!' She shuddered. 'You'd never catch me eating here. The food's frankly rubbish. I'm amazed that they've eaten it—aren't you?'

I was amazed, but I'd gone past caring. We could've served Fried Lice and Camel, people would probably have been just as pleased. But the evening quite suddenly was taking its toll. 'Aren't you tired?' I sat down. 'Zoë?'

She shrugged. 'I should be, but strangely enough, no, I'm not. I'm conserving my strength for much later. I'm crossing fingers that Stuffy'll come round. He did last night, but—' she pulled a doleful face. 'He didn't do much. I have to say that.' I didn't answer; she continued without noticing. 'He was here, you know. He was here at the party last night. But it must have been seconds only, because I didn't see him. Nor did you, by what he said to me afterwards.'

An uproar had surfaced now unexpectedly between a couple who sat near the door. 'My God!' Zoë gasped. 'What the hell is she doing? Quick, go and get one of the boys.' Vince was downstairs smoking with Dick. Poor Pot, from what I could smell. Cooking had ceased, we were trying to clear up, but six tables of people remained. All couples, cooing and doveing, except this one now, Table Two. They struggled together in a fight to the death and could well go straight through our window. The woman was hitting her companion with his briefcase, whilst he retaliated fiercely with her handbag.

It was strange, but I hadn't seemed to notice them before, they'd appeared to be so featureless and grey. But now I remembered another fight of this same nature taking place between a similarly undistinguished pair, half way along Park Lane. And the ages, too, had been about the same, mid-fifties or thereabouts.

Neither spoke, neither uttered a sound, not of pain or surprise or outrage. They just lunged, grim and silent, scuffling together as the chairs all around them started falling.

The other tables stared over, appalled. 'Shouldn't we stop them?' I heard someone say. 'Best not, darling. They know what they're doing,' came the guarded reply.

'Have they paid their bill yet?' Vince wanted to know, standing well back in the shadows.

'Oh, for God's sake, Vince!' Zoë exploded. The couple in combat looked like Kung Fu fighters in a momentary pause, preparing to pounce. The woman's grey hair had been piled in a bun, low at the nape of her neck. It now hung like a heavy London fog, drifting in wisps round her shoulders. Her companion's locks had been carefully combed from a very low, left-hand parting over the hill of his balding scalp. The arrangement was sadly disturbed, so that now the top of his head was revealed, as bare as a baby's bottom, whilst on the left, a long strand of hair curved to his cheek in a ringlet.

Vincent's question was more sensible that Zoë'd supposed, but they had paid their bill as it happened.

'Chuck a glass full of water—aim it straight at their gobs. Or better still, a bloody great bucketful. That should see the buggers out!' Dick had suddenly joined us. He stood at the stairs staring over. 'I'll do it. I'd love to.' He shot down for his bucket.

'I bet he would too,' Zoë muttered.

Vince slipped past the pair to open the front door and prepare the pathway for Dick, who planned to flush them out like fleas and had brought up not one, but two buckets.

'Ouch!' I shivered as his torrent of cold water made first contact with the two forms. Their bodies buckled and fell apart.

'What a bastard—he's really enjoying it. Quick, look at his face. Just catch that expression. I wouldn't like him at the end of a whip!' Zoë caught hold of my arm. The combatants, in shock, seemed stuck to the spot. Dick continued; he planned to get rid of them. The remainder of the restaurant patrons were making small movements to prepare for their own departure, as if feeling that unless they went out under their own steam this demon usurper might start on them with the watery whip from his buckets. Three slurps saw the pair to the door and the rest of both pails pushed them on to the pavement. We clustered, Zoë, Vince and I, watching Dick chasing them up the street. They ran like defeated rats—he, ludicrously, still holding tight to her handbag, whilst she wielded his masculine briefcase. As they rounded the corner of Pimlico Road I watched her raise it once more. Soon the frontage of Casa Pupa might be imperilled, but for the moment our windows were safe.

The restaurant was empty. Our patrons had fled. It was quarter past twelve by my watch. 'Clear up tonight? Or finish tomorrow? Lunchtime—are we doing it or not?' It seemed we were. Dick said so. 'A chance to get some coins in the kitty!'

I couldn't help noticing how confidently he hailed his cab, as if to the manner born. Vincent was rushing to catch the last tube, closely pursued by Soc and Ari. They bounced bowlegged, badly, like worn tennis balls, never higher off the ground than the width of their shoes. Soc, of the two, moved more painfully. His new shoes were pinching his feet. The thought of his shoes, Ari's tee-shirt and the cool insouciance of Dick's cab-hailing reminded me of poor Auntie's loss. Which was the culprit amongst our kitchen staff? And would tomorrow bring confrontation?

Stuffy and Nutty were sitting together, singing, in the back of the yellow Rolls-Royce. It spoke much for the vehicle's sound-proofing properties that from the pavement you couldn't hear a squeak. In fact, driving towards it in my Morgan, I wouldn't have known until I was parking behind it, in front of the house—I wouldn't have known that anyone was in it at all. A flaring match had caught my attention. My first thought had been that a wino, or one of those roaming old women with their worldly possessions in one carrier bag, had decided to squat for the night. I couldn't blame them, in their position I probably would've done the same. Why should all these empty cars, clean and warm and dry, occupy so many miles of street when gipsy souls were simply seeking a temporary roof? A whoosh of Fresh-Aire, that's all that was needed the following morning. Fumigation for critical cases.

I walked past, not looking, up to my front door. Nutty wound down one window and stuttered, 'G-good morning, Madam.' I turned round. Stuffy still held the lighted match, it must almost be burning his fingers. 'Good morning,' he echoed, smiling foolishly. 'We've been waiting for you to return.'

They were drinking Champagne straight from the bottle, it bubbled down over their chins. Stuffy had perched it between his corduroyed knees, the green shone in front of his match like stained glass. I was tired. They were drunk and behaving like children.

'I didn't know you knew each other?' I wished they'd both go away. What would happen if I, like Dick, resorted now to two full buckets? I held my watch to the light— well past one o'clock. Further up was a cop on point duty, permanently positioned outside the house of some Judge, Lord Chief Justice Something, noted for the severity of his sentences. A likely victim, a certain target for retribution and revenge. The cop, I could see, was looking this way. I recognised him at once; Tom Twiddle, deceased—his nephew no less. The young policeman who'd called round at our re013rant on the morning his uncle had died. How remarkably small the world was really. 'Don't talk rubbish!' The Old Man would've retorted. 'Don't talk rubbish!' were the very first words I'd heard him say—not to me, but to someone behind me. In the Turner Room at the National Gallery. For years after he told people that he'd picked me up, just like that, in Trafalgar Square. The startled recipient of his scorn, a total stranger to each of us, was extolling the virtues of Turner's Venetian Period. He'd quickly moved on at The Old Man's outburst. I'd remained rooted with shyness. We'd looked at each other, he was hard to ignore—especially since now he was winking. He was wearing a hat, a Homburg, I think. Beneath it his hair was quite white. It rested on the black velvet collar of his thick black cape, under which emerged bright yellow trousers. He made an arresting figure, a cross in his stance between Robert Graves and Augustus John with the long upper lip of a horse.

My shyness increased. I was used to oddness, with Stephen—but his had been secret. And anyway, we two had been so young together, more equal from all points of view. Education; we both had left school at fourteen. Both orphans, though he was from an orphanage. And sexually, we were like brother and sister. At his death I was technically virgin.

The Old Man spoke. 'How lost you look, child. I might care to make you my mistress. Come and have tea, we'll talk about it. I shall take you this evening to the Last Night of the Proms. Malcolm Sargent has a waist-line very much like yours. But I'd like you with a little more meat.'

After the Proms we'd walked in Hyde Park and then through to Kensington Gardens. We'd sat on a bench watching strange men walk past. 'They're all Homos,' he said. 'Homosexuals.' I knew what they were, they were what Stephen had hated, vehemently so. But I looked back at The Old Man innocently.

'Are they? Oh, really?' I'd said.

He'd continued explaining the subject to me, fifteen years ago few would have done so. But I knew all about it already from Stephen. I was more interested in straight-forward sex, that's where my ignorance lay.

'Do you know—' he'd said suddenly, taking my hand, 'why the breath smells after people make love?' I didn't. 'It's because,' he continued, squeezing my fingers and now lifting them to his tongue, 'it's because the seeds of life are dying, even before they've lived.'

I couldn't begin to understand what it was he was saying. But by then he was running his lips very gently all over the palm of my hand, and pressing his tongue to the centre and breathing soft breath on my wrist. My elbow ached from the awkward angle, but I wouldn't have cared if it cracked. Because his other hand was inside my blouse, drawing blood from a sleeping stone.

That night he forcefully de-flowered me in the large front bedroom of Old Church Street, the same one that the girls now slept in. The bloodstain is still on the carpet, he'd encircled it with Quink Blue-Black Fountain Pen Ink. It lies approximately beneath Zsa-Zsa's feet.

'Where are you off to, little one?' He'd fallen asleep as soon as his body had rolled off me. I didn't mind, it had given me a chance to study the room I was in. Auntie's bedroom, back home, the one that we'd shared, had always been terribly cold. We used to rub each other's chilblains since as far back as I could remember. Getting up in the mornings was agony. I dreaded the icy embrace of the lino, and the chill china rim of the Wo-wo.

'Wo-wo? What's a Wo-wo?' Stephen had asked. 'It's a—' I'd found it difficult to find the right word. We'd always called it Wo-wo in our house. Was it perhaps Auntie's invention? 'Well, you probably know it best as—potty.'

'Oh, po! Or a "Gozunda"? Have you ever heard that one? I haven't, I just read it in a comic.' Much of our culture had come from comics, Stephen's and mine—Desperate Dan, and Keyhole Kate and Lord Snooty—all that team. The Old Man had been quite genuinely amazed; for all his voracious appetite for reading, he'd never heard of one of these people. But in his later years his sight so frail that he could barely see the pictures, let alone the words, it had been one of his greatest joys to go through old copies of *Beano* and *Dandy* with Tallulah, when she'd been tiny.

I'd lain that first night, simply looking around. The Old Man always slept with the lights on throughout his life. It sprang from a dread of the dark. But I didn't know that—I just thought how wasteful to be going to bed with them on. Though in a sense it wasn't like light at all. Light, at home, had consisted of candles, until much later on when electricity had come. Though even then, for going to bed we rarely switched on the lights upstairs. Simply to economise. It hung in each room from the centre of the ceiling, on a wire the length of the rulers at school, ending in a clear, low-watt bulb caged in a hideous shade of mock vellum. Pale beige with loops of brown cord. I'd spent years of my life studying its ugliness, whilst Auntie lay snoring beside me.

The Old Man's bedroom was entirely different, not like a bedroom at all. Ours had been empty of all save the bed, a brown wardrobe, and the wash-stand, of course. On top of the wash-stand stood a wide off-white bowl with a jug of cold water to wash with. And a matching container for holding the soap. All displaying the same dying rose.

Stephen and I hadn't had a bedroom, simply a room with a bed. And a small metered gas ring and fire and two chairs of the hue of stale cocoa. Not even a table to eat our food from, or a surface for Stephen to write his songs. But it didn't matter, we ate off the floor. The whole of our life was a picnic.

The Old Man's bedroom was wallpapered with volumes and volumes of words, in the form of books, folios, periodicals, pamphlets, theses, essays and exercise-books full of jottings. There must have been, I lay there counting, at least eleven or twelve lights in the room. None hanging from the ceiling. All Art Nouveau original lamps, The Old Man had carefully explained. And he'd drawn my attention to the succulent colours, to the turquoise, sea-greens and serpent yellows. And to the loving, looping lines and the curves. I'd listened, and looked, enthralled and aroused. I'd never seen light presented like this. Stephen and I had had in the corner of our Kilburn bedsitter a very old standard lamp, as brown as the cocoa-coloured chairs. A print of a billowing ship in full sail glowed dully over its shade. It was the first piece of furniture Stephen had damaged as his drinking grew gradually worse.

And from stroking the sensual lines of his lamps, we stood before each one in turn, The Old Man turned his attention to me. 'Will you take off your clothes.' It wasn't a question. I couldn't say no. He'd laid back, fully dressed with his hat on his head, smoking a pipe—simply watching.

'How incredibly elegant you are for a child. What style to that long, pale young body. But it needs to expand, to mature and to realise what power it will hold over men.' The Old Man had spoken as if to himself. But now he spoke gently to me. 'Come here, my gauche and blushing girl. I'm going to teach you to love.'

And he had. I turned my gaze away from the room, slowly towards his face. His head, mouth half open, lay back on his pillow. The closed lids of his eyes lay like eggs in the shadowy depths of his sockets. The profile resembled that of a Roman Emperor, the sort you see on old coins. And it also looked, for some reason, religious. I felt I was in bed with God. Had he entered, the Spirit of the Holy Ghost? I certainly felt quite spiritual, quite other-worldly and extra-special. My Inner Being had been softly brushed, it was still slightly trembling at the touch. We'd lain side by side at the very beginning, and he'd kissed me from my mouth to my neck. And from my neck he'd gone down further still, till his head was in line with my titties. And then he'd done what I'd thought wasn't possible. He'd put the two of them into his mouth, pressing them so close together each side—cupping them tight with his hands.

I'd shuddered, it was such a thrilling sensation to have him actually—suckling! I wonderingly touched The Old Man's large head. I fondled the nape of his neck where I'd liked him touching me, as he'd done just before. His

502

sucking stopped quite abruptly and his body moved further down, now past my navel. I could feel myself sweating with shame. What was he hoping to look at down there? Except a large landscape of hair! I stared straight ahead. Oh dear, wasn't this rude? Stephen and I had both slept in my nighties, entwined and slithering as our shiny mock satins had slipped and slid against each other. Our actual flesh never met. But The Old Man was going much further than that, entering another area. The introduction of our, not merely outer, but inner flesh was about to take place.

I shut my eyes. He was certainly making a wonderful meal of my—thingy.

He was speaking to me! But I hadn't heard. He repeated what he had said. 'You're intact, little one. Your precious jewel is here for me to possess. See, I introduce my evil snake into your innocent Garden of Eden!'

I watched with astonishment as he fell back on his haunches, like a drawing I'd once seen of Pan, and proceeded to hoist with one hand something I'd not noticed before. Was he wearing that there when he'd got into bed? He'd thrown back the sheets in a flourish when he'd moved from my neck at the start. The bedclothes lay crumpled, hanging half off the bed. Now he pushed them down even further and started nuzzling with his banana— that's what it looked like to me. He was running the tip of it from the top of my slit nearly right the way back to my botty. And each time he did, he spat on his fingers and transferred that same spit to his tip.

I liked it a lot, I had to admit. It was silly, but also exciting. It was naughty, all right. But it wasn't enough. I began slowly moving my body. He was pleased, I could tell by the soft deep sly chuckle. And he'd chosen that exact point to enter.

He'd started to talk to me as soon as his thing eased inside, probably on purpose to take my mind off the pain. And it was very painful too, what he was doing there. I tried my best to widen myself. It was as if I'd had to open my mouth, stretch it in order that someone might fit in a Thermos flask, those were the relative proportions. I gazed at him, my head on my pillow, as if from another planet. He'd taken his own pillow from the top of the bed and placed it beneath my pelvis, explaining how if he hadn't done this, my 'cunt' would be at the wrong angle. He kept

503

saying 'cunt', the word seemed to please him. But my mind was more on the pillow. I was worrying now about whether I'd stain it with the juices that seemed to be flowing. Would he change it, put a clean pillowcase on after all this was over? Or go to sleep with my feminine odours nestling around his nose?

'Your cunt is perfection,' he murmured. 'My angel—'

'Is it?' I'd bitten my tongue to transfer my attention away from the source of the pain. He was penetrating now so deep inside I feared he might fracture my womb. Or worse, rip right through my internal workings and emerge at the top of my head.

'Perfection,' The Old Man murmured again. 'A pulsating pathway of petal-soft skin teasing me slowly to Paradise—'

Me? Who, me? Apparently so, there was no one else in the bed. He was going round in a corkscrew fashion, holding tight to the base of his stem. And from that he quite suddenly changed direction and went in the other way. The switch took a few seconds, though it must have seemed more, to set up a new set of sensations. It was as if my insides were made of suede, and from stroking the surface in a certain way someone had now gone against the grain and created a quite different texture. I could only just about stand it.

'I'm not hurting you, am I, little one?' The Old Man whispered solicitously. I unclamped my jaws and whispered back, 'Not all that much. A bit. But it's nice.'

He'd positioned himself in such a way that his head was framed by one lamp. The light surrounded his head like a halo, suffused by the mane of white hair. I wanted to lie there for ever.

'This is the first and the last time I shall allow you to lie there.' My heart leapt to my throat at his words and then as quickly dropped from the sheer disappointment. What was I doing wrong? Where had Paradise suddenly gone to, and the tease of my petal-soft skin? But the tone of his voice became tender. 'I tell you this as I pillage your innocence and remove you from youth's pedestal. But after tonight we prepare to be partners, each equal in love to the other. You'll be mine for as long as I live—'

Stuffy and Nutty continued singing, both so slurred that the tune was unrecognisable, but it might well have been

504

the Eton Boating Song. The Old School of both of them, I suddenly realised. It was strange to think that Stuffy had been there. He so hated everything it stood for and made such efforts to conceal that fact of his education. And indeed had made such remarkable progress in declassing his accent, it would have taken an expert to know.

I'd joined them temporarily in the back of the car. 'You can't sit in here all night, you two—'

Stuffy put his hand on my knee. 'Can't we come inside? Can't we share your couch, my comrade and I, can't we please?'

'Don't be so silly, Ulysses. Why don't you just go home? Where have you been,' I turned to Nutty, 'to have got into such a state?' I frowned and spoke with extreme severity. Nutty's eye started nervously swivelling. 'I, we—well, you see, w-w, we—'

Stuffy came to the rescue. I'd never seen him more confident. Nor for that matter, more drunk. 'We collided up in Camden Town, I was coming out of Compendium—I'd just bought a book which you will enjoy, but be that as it may, my dear—and from there we've pub-crawled our way across town. Several stiff ones in the French, a swift visit of course to the Colony to pay my respects to Muriel, and a taxi to dear old Sean Treacy, here at the top of the road.'

'The Queen's Elm. That's where you've been. Have you eaten?' They both shook their heads, silent, like two bad boys being told off by their mother. I could see the whole scenario, I could tell what the saga had been. United by joint adoration of me, drowning in mutual sorrow. 'Well,' I said sternly. 'You should have thought earlier, and come to the restaurant to eat, instead of drinking like that on empty stomachs.' Stuffy groaned as I mentioned restaurant and Nutty immediately joined in.

'What's the matter with you two?' I was losing patience, tomorrow had turned into today. 'I'm going to bed.'

'Do you have to, really?' Stuffy suddenly said.

'Yes, I do, I'm afraid, I'm terribly tired—'

'Run this ridiculous restaurant? Do you have to?' Stuffy's expression was terribly serious, making him even more Stanley Spencer-ish. I thought of the hours we'd lain together, his scholar's body so enveloped by mine like a small boat alongside a ship. They sat facing me in the luxurious interior of the faded, old-fashioned Rolls. I'd perched myself on the pull-down seat, the one to the left of the door. It struck me how very similar they seemed, Stuffy and Nutty together. Even down to their ridiculous names—Ulysses and Hannibal—Stuffy and Nutty. A music-hall touring team, clog-dancing and tapping the spoons. They both gazed at me as if I was their life-blood and about to cut off their supply. Nutty's left elbow had started to jerk, it echoed the rhythm of the eye. Up and down, and left and back. The puppeteer must have gone for his tea and left the poor marionette in first gear.

'Actually,' I said, making movements to leave, 'it was really rather nice in our restaurant tonight, though in one respect I must say, remarkable. The occasion was noteworthy for one reason—not a single friend turned up. Not even to give moral support.' I opened the heavy door of the car; they sat there in joint dejection. 'But never mind, there'll be other nights—now I bid you good-morning, gentlemen.'

At just about dawn the telephone rang. I'd been dreaming that the telephone was ringing, so at first I didn't bother to answer it, believing it to be a dream. 'Were you sleeping?' The voice sounded almost next door.

'No, just dreaming.'

'It's been ringing and ringing for ages—'

'That's what I was dreaming. I'm sorry, who's that?'

'It's me.'

It was Lionel Striving, all the way from New York. 'How near you sound.' I was surprised.

'That's the third time you've said that!' How impatient he sounded—as well as sounding so near. I must have been very deeply asleep, my brain felt exceptionally sluggish. I coughed in an effort to clear my head, at the same time clearing my throat.

'Have you got a cold?'

'A cold? No, I haven't, Lionel. Have you?'

'No, not a cold—but I tell you what—'

'What?'

'I've got a bloody big erection. I can see it now. It's sticking right out of my pyjamas, that's why I'm ringing—to tell you!'

I looked at my watch, it was ten past five. Was it worth being woken up at this hour to learn that Lionel was erotically aroused? Which part of his pyjamas might the prick be poking through? I'd place bets on the bottom button-hole.

'Yes, I'm sipping this brandy and reading in bed. These Reports are confoundedly confusing—then out of nowhere your face appears—and you're bending to pick up a sweater, or something that's dropped to the floor. Do you remember, when you did that—when? A week last Tuesday? And you'd taken your tights off already? Do you remember?'

'I do remember.' I was growing sleepy. His voice was becoming excited. 'I'm holding it now, this erection. Because I remember exactly. You were wearing that beautiful dress, bright green. And you were wearing lots of rings, little tiny turquoise ones, and you'd painted all your fingernails to match. And as you bent over—' I stifled a yawn. 'As you bent over. Christ, my bloody prick might burst—I could see the bare backs of those beautiful thighs and all the dark hair of your bush. It really turned me on, do you remember? And I had to have you, I couldn't even wait to take of your dress—uh-uh—' His voice slowed down. 'Uh, uh! I think this is doing it! It is—by Jesus— I'm bloody coming—I'm coming, my darling, can you hear it?' I heard his gasp and strained for more, for the sound of a fountain, an oil-well erupting, a saucepan of milk boiling over. But all I could hear was the wash of the waves and the fish as they snoozed in whatever ocean lay between Lionel and me.

The next day was Saturday. Rather, that day was Saturday, this one—the one I was in. I lay in bed reflecting on that fact. Lionel's call had disturbed me, I couldn't drop off again, not completely. I hung instead on the numbing ledge that exists between sleep and half consciousness. My thoughts droned in depressing circles over what to do about Auntie. Would it perhaps not be better all round if we chose to ignore the theft? I could forage from my various accounts for five hundred pounds and just reimburse her. After all, why not for once let the guilty party off, the thief get away, the culprit escape? The poor bastard was, in a sense, just as much of a victim. It all evened out one way or another. I had plenty, and because I had, so had Auntie. A confrontation would serve no purpose except to create an atmosphere. The more I pondered, the more certain I became that this was the wisest course. In time, whoever it was who'd taken

Auntie's money, might carelessly leave some clue. Inadvertently give themselves away. By then, though, we might not even be interested. Zen and the wisdom of Solomon. The Old Man, I felt, would have approved.

Around seven o'clock I could lie there no longer and got up to make myself coffee. Now might be the right time to test Bogey's bed, to see if he'd managed to stay dry.

He had. Good boy. His lashes fluttered, a small smile flickered over his face. As if even before he'd opened his eyes he could sense I was standing close. I studied his mouth, the bland curve of his lip. Did it resemble Brad's? Or could the chin be said to be nearer to the confident jut, say, of Rufus? And what about the soft grey eyes; when solemn didn't they look most like Stuffy's? But the hair, the mop of tight dark curls—the same as Lionel Striving's, only longer? Poor Nutty, the only one not on the list. And the only one of all my Gentlemen who genuinely did like children, who would have been overjoyed to have assumed the mantle of fatherhood. If I'd granted the honour to anyone.

Bogey woke up and from simple pleasure proceeded to wet the bed. Who of my lovers had the weakest bladder? Perhaps the parentage may be traced to that, wasn't it meant to run in families? Like pigeon-toes, and varicose veins, and warts and going prematurely grey. Though further conjecture was a waste of time—I'd never wished to know who the father was. It was enough that Bogey existed. He'd been granted to me by the group. A group baby. Like bulk buying—there was lashings of love to go round. And I had had no father figure whilst I was growing up, and hadn't seemed to suffer.

Bogey chuckled and wriggled around, increasing the width of absorption. I watched the advancing damp creep to the edge of the tiny bed. 'Naughty boy.' I tried hard to frown. His chuckling stopped. He sat up straight trying to gauge my reaction. 'Naughty,' I said and shook my finger, pointing at the sopping wet sheet. He looked down and laughed, then looked once more at me. I shook my head disapprovingly. His own small one now followed my action, copying it exactly so that we each of us must have resembled mandarins who communicate mainly by nodding.

I didn't smile, my eyes didn't soften, just the right degree of severity. Wasn't that how toilet training was supposed to be? Not too stern, not too much tension otherwise the problems occur in later life, wasn't that when they surfaced? Something to do with retention. The retention of turds, later translatable into the accumulation of possessions. Possessions and property and a general hoarding. I should have to watch it with Bogey. With the girls I'd never given it much thought, but they were never quite so incontinent. Or if they were I perhaps placed their dying father rather higher on my list of priorities.

Bogey was finally getting the message. His expression was heart-breaking to watch. The soft lower lip was starting to tremble, he puckered it up in a pale pink bunch like a tightly packed bouquet of rosebuds. At the top of his face his small forehead was knitting, converging in a criss-cross of scribbling lines above the pale smoky globes of his eyes. Rain clouds were starting to gather in these. As I blinked, he blinked. Tears fell. Just two of them first, then the others followed over the tight little scrunched-up shape of his cheeks. I couldn't bear it. I picked him up. 'There, baby! There, there it's all right!'

He flung his small hands around my neck and buried his head just beneath my left ear. I could feel the sleeve of my negligée, Hollywood Thirties from Portobello, dampening now like his bed. What did it matter? My little boy was cuddling up to his mother. Wasn't that one of the primary functions of Woman? To exude warmth when it was required?

He kissed my ear, I kissed his back. And then I kissed it again. And it was in this way entwined and embracing, exchanging our tokens of love, that Auntie arrived and discovered us.

She'd had a very good night's sleep, a full twelve hours in fact. 'What's the time then?' she asked, as bright as a button. Clearly the unpleasant events of yesterday would not impinge on today. Bogey, happily reinstated in my good books, cooed and stretched out to touch her. 'Hello, Bogey—and how's little boyo today? Oh, an accident, is it, in bed? Never mind, Auntie will change it now—or shall we have tea and toast first?' She turned to me enquiringly.

'The kettle's just boiled, but you go on down, Auntie. I'll just change Bogey, and look at the girls.'

'I've just looked, love. They're still both asleep.' She smiled. In her quilted dressing-gown, bright shiny purple with a waistcord of curdling cerise, she put me in mind of a kind of tea-cosy. Rather risqué, and made in Hong Kong. But the comfortable countenance reassured, her cheeks looked like sweet orchard apples. I was sorely tempted to take a bite.

The thought must have transferred itself to Bogey, because now he was expressing the wish to be held by her and not me. What diplomacy and charm this child possessed. What a way he had of making all of us feel needed. 'Come to Auntie, then, now is it? Ooh, there's a boy you are! You dangle us all, you do!' Auntie took him and, tutting away, proceeded to take off his small, stretchy towelling sleeping-suit. His stomach curved smoothly in an egg-like shape, like a cupid, straight from his chin. And beneath the shell-like structure of his circumcision, the legs fell away, still with baby folds of flesh at the top of his thighs. Before very long, the frame would emerge and he would begin to look more like a child instead of a cuddly doll. It had happened before. I'd seen it with Tallulah and Zsa-Zsa, hard bones replacing the softness. A magical metamorphosis. And soon, of course, the girls themselves would undergo another. The subtle process of bodily change, of transformation into young women. I couldn't remember how mine had occurred. What had come first— under-arm hair? A shy down, anxiously studied, a shadow cast between the legs in the shape of a straggly triangle. And the sensation of sweating, I could recall that, of steaminess and sudden, inexplicable, lickety lubrications. It was as if a dry suburban house had turned into a damp sub-tropical cave.

'I'll wash him, I'll powder his little bots. We'll go and dry your dangle, won't we, Bogey—' I could hear Auntie musing away to herself and Bogey's answering chirrups as I went down the stairs to the kitchen. Had she forgotten completely, or what? Would the theft not be mentioned at all? I considered it carefully. This was all quite in character. Auntie had a built-in protection, whereby all that was deeply unpleasant to hear was deliberately put to one side. Not head in sand exactly, nor head in clouds—but something more child-like between the two. It was an enviable trait, it meant that she was more able to weather the storms of emotional and mental stresses. And in later years, I'd noticed she'd become even more of a safe, calm harbour despite several hazardous passages.

She came into the kitchen now, carrying a fresh, fragrant Bogey. 'There's a lovely day it is outside. Look at the sun, it's shining! Shall I take them out to the Park this morning? For a picnic and then to the Fair?' By Park, Auntie meant Battersea Park, the only park she acknowledged. Like shops and large stores, the less smart the better. She equated Hyde Park, say, with Harrods. And St James's with Fortnum and Mason, and Kensington Gardens was probably Simpson or possibly Debenham and Freebody. But Battersea Park, like Clapham Common and at a pinch perhaps Primrose Hill—they were more in the mass-production mould, the chain stores, the Tescos and Woolworths, and therefore earned her approval. And of course Battersea possessed the bonus of swings and roundabouts, the fairyland of Battersea Fair. It was hard to tell who enjoyed it more, Auntie or the children, their degree of delight was the same. At the mention of Fair, Bogey clapped both his hands. Auntie had placed him in his high-chair, a childish throne which he refused to relinquish, battered by years of harsh monarchy but still surviving through the reigns of Tallulah and Zsa-Zsa. It had been re-painted several times in an effort to restore its appearance, but constant scratchings with small spoons and pushers had reduced the surface to a piebald effect of Pillarbox Red overlaying Leaf Green, which in turn overlaid Lemon Yellow.

Auntie considered it critically now, her hair-curlered head on one side. 'Am I to buy a bit of Fablon from Woolies and give this a nice new covering? Tartan, I thought for a bit of a change, though I might well be lucky and find Leopard-Skin.'

'Are they doing adhesive Leopard-Skin now? In plastic, I mean, by the sheet, Auntie?'

'Well.' Auntie looked vague. 'I don't know that they are, but they could be. I'll ask in the shops.' Her quest of the week, she enjoyed a good quest, a purpose, tracking down treasure.

'It could be quite smart, Leopard-Skin Fablon, for the restaurant I mean, on the tables.'

Auntie nodded. 'Nice and clean.' The reminder, restaurant, hadn't ruffled her sanguine approach to this sunny day. 'Are you going in there this morning? Are you doing the dinner? I can see to the girls and boy—'

I thought hard, I didn't quite know. Did they really

require my presence at lunch-times? Zoë had decided to do it, to turn up in the mornings as well as the night for the welcome additional income. 'I'm saving up, you see, for some sort of decent holiday. Greece I'd thought, or maybe Tangiers, though I have a hankering for San Francisco. One of those cheap charter flights you can get that take off about two in the morning.' I'd warned her not to expect the same tips or even the same team of people. 'No, I know. Vince was saying they're miserable sods—the mid-dayers. But I don't mind. As long as you're paying me I may as well work. It keeps me off the streets—just.'

They could surely manage without me being there, then I'd go in this evening all fresh. Didn't my first and foremost duty and pleasure rest with my family?

I walked out to the garden to study the sky, to see if the sun would remain for the day. It glimmered through, clear and untrammelled by the traffic of gathering cloud formations. Promising hours of delight on the skin, the tinging of pink into biscuit, blushing pale flesh into beige.

'What about Brighton? Be there in two hours, if we wake up the girls and get going.'

'Brighton, oh Brighton!' Auntie beamed. If there was one place she enjoyed, it was Brighton. Even marginally more than Battersea Park and almost as much as her weekly treks over to Tescos at Brixton. 'What, driving do you mean? In the Rolls?'

'On the train, I think. That much quicker.' She tried not to show her disappointment over not going there in the Rolls, a nice chance now missed to bask in the admiration of the populace out on the prom. 'The Rolls is slow, Auntie. It would take us all day. Even going there in the Morgan is twice as long as taking the train. You want to be there as long as possible, don't you, to make it worth while?'

'I do. Yes, indeed. Will the shops be open, not half-day closing in Brighton on Saturday? There's a very good Woolworth's not far from the Clock Tower—we might find the Fablon we want.'

I'd ring Vincent up, I thought, from the station. At a little less ungodly hour. It was still only half past seven or so. He was having a lie-in this morning, sleeping till at least nine o'clock, so he'd planned. Not going to market

512

for food. He and Dick had done all that yesterday. And in any case from what I could judge, our menu didn't require the refinements of fresh vegetables or daily sojourns to Smithfield and Billingsgate. I packed up our swimming costumes, including the one used by Auntie, her favourite, a two-piece covered in sea-horses interspersed with white spray. The bottom half was as big as her knickers, it reached to her knees like Bermuda shorts or a gentleman's Victorian swimsuit. The top had fierce reinforcements, ice-cream cone in shape like a fifties-style sweater girl. It cut Auntie's bosom in two so that in it she boasted four breasts before you even got to her midriff. 'Did you pack my bathing cap?' She wanted to know. Her bathing cap was actually a wig, a waterproof wig, an American Import from Peter Jones, pre-curled and pre-tested, and pretty. Very pretty in fact, the shade Auntie had chosen, a very pale platinum blonde. Curled up in the manner of early Mae West. Auntie wore it sometimes in the bath. She'd bought it in the depths of winter and as yet hadn't tried it out in public; this would be its first spring showing—her Easter bonnet.

Tallulah and Zsa-Zsa were very subdued, they'd stayed up late the night before, involved in a game of Monopoly. Tallulah had ended up owning Park Lane and all the adjoining properties, including the four major stations. But Zsa-Zsa had capital, more in the bank. The resulting friction had ended in blows, a physical fight all the way up the banisters. Tallulah's glasses were broken. She looked now at the world through a strip of clear Sellotape which Auntie had stuck over the cracked lens. Another small task for Monday morning, a further trip to Tallulah's Optician.

Zsa-Zsa had bitten her own lower lip, when a sharp right-hand swing aimed at her chin by Tallulah had trapped the lip in her long upper teeth. The gash almost, but not quite, needed stitches. They'd arrived down at breakfast like two wounded warriors; Bogey had found them most comical. His reaction in fact had so angered Zsa-Zsa that she'd bared her fierce teeth in a frightening snarl and had menacingly approached his high-chair, as if to inflict a similar wound on his quite undeserving person. But Auntie'd forestalled her. 'We're going to Brighton, Brighton Pier! On the beach girls! And paddling—now eat up!' And she'd passed Zsa-Zsa's

Weetabix straight into her hands, with the milk ready poured in the bowl.

There were all excited, though the girls couldn't show it. Zsa-Zsa claimed that it pained her to smile, and Tallulah had trouble selecting her clothes through suffering from multiple vision.

'Oh come on,' I said, 'it can't be that bad,' as she tried to get into her jeans. 'Put your leg here—in here!'

'Where? In there? Is that right?' She lunged one foot into my lap, losing her balance completely, almost tearing the denims in two. In the end she decided to wear a dress. The one she chose was long, to the ground, sprigged with daisies. It came with its own frilly pinafore. In it she looked like Little Bo-Peep. Peeping through a pair of cracked spectacles.

Zsa-Zsa was going in full riding kit, wearing jodhpurs that she'd swopped with a girl at school in exchange for a second-hand Scotch kilt. And the strange thing was that the jodhpurs suited her. There was really no need for the horse, Zsa-Zsa's own small profile was the perfect substitute. The blend of human and beast. We made a strange mix. The girls had dressed Bogey. He came as a carpenter's mate, in a set of minute striped dungarees, but with a tulle poke bonnet on his head. Auntie's touch. 'To protect his head and the back of his neck from the heat of the sun,' she'd explained. We didn't demur, it was scarcely a scorcher, not this early in the season. But Bogey was bedazzled by his poke bonnet, he couldn't get over the bow. And he knew it already; he'd seen it for years being worn by Tallulah's large teddy. The bear was about the same size as himself, a friendly but deaf and dumb buddy. Hugged to death, smothered by love and now hatless into the bargain. The bow of the bonnet had been tied at the side as if on a grand box of chocolates. It flopped from the level of Bogey's ear, obliterating a full half of his face. He peeped over it teasingly like a Gaiety Girl, with the air of an innocent flirt.

Auntie had foraged and managed to find a very old pair of Clark's sandals. The flat sort with a tee-strap sported by Boy Scouts and cross-country hikers. She wore them with her thick lisle stockings and a pair of fluorescent pink ankle socks rolled very low over the ankle in the manner of golfing ladies. She felt the sandals to be more suitable for shingle than her usual bedroom slippers. She wore what appeared to be an Institution dress but was actually an Orderly's overall from a Uniform Specialist shop that she'd chanced on along the Edgware Road.

They'd all of them groaned when I'd appeared in my jeans.

'Is that what you're wearing!' They'd pointed. 'But this is an outing—a special event!' I'd been forced to go back and change, and now emerged as a cricketing umpire, in white from head to toe. As unsuitable for a trip on a grimy train as anything any of them were wearing. They chorused their approval.

We drove in the Rolls to Victoria Station. Two exhausted Champagne bottles lay in the back still, and countless stubbed-out cigarette ends as evidence of last night's carousings between poor old Nutty and Stuffy.

I parked off Buckingham Palace Road, just at the Brighton train platform. 'Stay here, all you lot,' I ordered 'Don't move. Auntie, keep your eyes on them. I'll run round and get the tickets.' The train was in, we'd arrived on the hop, not knowing what time it went.

'If you run quick, Missus, you might catch this. It's due out in under five minutes.' The ticket collector smiled at me with a special degree of sympathy. People often did that when I was out with my lot, as if they were not quite all there, and I was the kindly Voluntary Worker who was taking them out for the day. I ran. The crowds parted, the people sprang back at this pristine fluid white figure fleeing a would-be assailant. I barged in at the top of the ticket queue. 'Do you mind very much—two tickets, three halves to Brighton, oh yes, please—all Day Returns!' Then, 'So sorry!' I gasped to the rest of the queue. 'But my train, it's just leaving you see!' Theirs might just as well have been leaving too, I afterwards thought guiltily.

Telephoning Vincent was out of the question, we just managed by seconds to board the train. We did so despite Auntie's flapping Clarks sandal. She'd stored them so long, some twenty-two years, that in daylight they were deteriorating fast. 'It's the sun, I expect it's melting the rubber, it can have that effect—we've done it in school. In science—' Tallulah expounded. 'No, it's not, not the sun—it's the storage—' Zsa-Zsa rejoindered. Auntie's feet fell apart. Not completely but almost, they joined at the heels, soles and uppers. Each time that she lifted her legs in

515

a step she left half her footwear behind. I bundled the kids in and then hauled her up.

'It's going,' she wailed.

'I know, Auntie. Come on, you must hurry, he's waving his flag—'

'It's gone now, my sole—I can feel it.' The guard slammed the door, barely missing her skirt. She hung on me heavily. 'Oh dear, there's a do. It's dropped off—look, see, from the window.'

I squeezed past her whoofing and phewing figure, and poked my head out of the window. As the train gathered speed and curved out of Victoria, the small shape became smaller and smaller. The shrivelled sole of her old Clarks sandal already collecting dust.

Much of the journey down was spent in to-ing and fro-ing from the buffet. I'd forbidden that Bogey should have anything to drink. The girls supplied him instead with nuts. He was sneezing them out through his nose. Zsa-Zsa held one up. 'Look at this—it's been in and come out, exactly the same!'

'It could be different.' Tallulah looked serious. 'Bogey may carry a collection of nuts up at the top of his nose. Like a camel with water, couldn't he, Mum? And be firing them like little cannon-balls.'

'Don't be silly,' Zsa-Zsa said shortly. 'You say stupid things.'

'I'm stretching my imagination. You're meant to do that, aren't you Mum—'

Auntie was listening with interest. 'Not tell lies though, Tallulah, not fibs, I don't think.'

'Well, Auntie, it's quite hard to tell the difference.'

'It isn't.' Zsa-Zsa had decided to argue.

'Yes it is,' Tallulah joined in.

''S'not, so there!'

''Tis, 'cos I know. And you don't!'

'Do!'

'Don't!'

'Yes!'

'No!'

I put my hands over my ears. Bogey laughed and did the same, first lifting one hand of Auntie's to show that she should too. We sat there like a trio of monkeys. I'd had a small brass trio once. Hear No Evil. See No Evil. And Speak No Evil. Perhaps not exactly in that order, and we

516

weren't the same as them, we were all the Hear No. Tallulah and Zsa-Zsa stopped abruptly.

'Sorry, Mum,' they each said in turn.

'That's all right. Let's be nice though, the rest of the day. It's depressing to hear all that quarrelling.'

They fell silent and started to look out of the window, and before very long were engrossed again in intense and whispered discussion. But this time on far friendlier lines. That's how it went with those two. Auntie was playing happily with Bogey. This Little Piggey Went To Market, with his fingers as well as his toes. She'd removed his small plimsolls and spotted blue socks in order to play the game properly. Her own plump toes curled up and out of the tattered remains of her sandals. Our first task on arrival at Brighton was the purchase of suitable shoes. I knew perfectly well which ones she'd choose. The beach shoes in transparent plastic. The sort they sell specially for shingly shores. As flat as her Clarks and her slippers. A day of delights stretched before us in Brighton. I shut my eyes, and arrived there still sleeping.

The first thing I did was, of course, to ring Vincent. He answered the phone right away.

'Hello, Vince!'

'Oh, it's you.' I thought he sounded disappointed.

'Yes, were you expecting someone else?' I could hear his hesitation. Oh dear, an emotional matter? Another affair of the heart?

'I was expecting, yes, as a matter of fact. Look darling, let me ring you back.'

'Well, Vince, I'm in Brighton—'

'Who with? How bizarre!'

'With the kids, and with Auntie. To take her mind off the money, you know. Just for the day, is that all right? Can you manage?'

I don't know why I was feeling so guilty. He didn't answer for a moment. And then he said as if thinking carefully. 'What a terribly good idea. No confrontation this morning then?'

'No confrontation at all. I think I shan't bother, we won't get it back. It would just cause a lot of embarrassment. I shall give it, the money, to Auntie myself—'

'You're a saint—'

'No I'm not.' I looked out of the telephone kiosk window towards Auntie and the three children. People

517

were turning in an amused fashion to stare at their odd attire. Auntie's socks were so shockingly pink that they seemed to light up the whole station. Her sandal uppers were still strapped to her ankles. I could see a policeman approaching.

'Oh, Vincent—I'd best go I think! There's a copper accosting old Auntie. I'll see you tonight—be about seven I should think. Is that O.K.?'

It was hardly a question, I didn't wait to see if it was O.K. or not, but put the phone down hurriedly just catching his 'Have a good day!' I could see Auntie's bewildered expression in the face of the policeman's first words. Tallulah had taken it upon herself to answer him. She was turning now and pointing in my direction. The policeman followed her fingers with his eyes.

'Can I help you?' I said, approaching. He regarded me with respect, as his gaze flickered over my finery. My whites had survived the grime of British Rail remarkably well. In the dingy gloom of Brighton Station I might have been Isadora Duncan dressed for a day at Deauville.

The policeman now appeared to be tugging his forelock. Or was he merely scratching his forehead? 'All in order, Miss.' He spoke flatly, with old-fashioned formality and a very strong Sussex accent. 'I thought for a moment that this little lot were lost, but I can see that they're clearly in good hands.'

Auntie had recovered her composure and confided. 'We're off to the sea-front for a paddle.' The policeman bent and tweeked Bogey's cheek. 'Will this little lady be paddling?' Bogey's bonnet was sadly skew-whiff so that now the bow sat high up on his ear, and he looked like a beribboned debutante at her first dance. Zsa-Zsa giggled, she'd been put in charge of his collapsible push-chair. It lay still folded at her feet. I picked it up, it unfurled like a brolly, striped nylon, clear red and white. Bogey started jigging and swinging his arms to show that he wanted to sit in. He looked like a baby chimpanzee, like the ones they dress up for television commercials.

The policeman bent from his waist again. 'Let me help the little lady into her chariot.' And he picked the writhing Bogey clean off the ground and manouevred him unsuccessfully into the push-chair. He sat uncomfortably, two little round legs squashed into the hole meant for one.

Zsa-Zsa continued to giggle. Tallulah blinked up at the

518

policeman. 'That's all wrong. He doesn't go that way.'
Bogey stared down at his legs, mystified. It was time to be
moving on. Passers-by were beginning to linger, intrigued
as crowds are by the sight of others engaged in confab with
policeman. A curiosity not untinged with malice, the
hope that someone else is getting it in the neck, being
found out, landing in a whole load of trouble.

Tallulah brutally tugged one of Bogey's small knees,
trying to bend the whole leg back up double. He screamed.
The sound was high and clear like the top note of a
soprano. He held it inordinately long as if he'd embarked
on an aria.

'Bloody hell, some people don't deserve to have
children! Look, the Law has arrived. Damn good thing.
Who are they anway, an odd-looking crew—gipsies d'you
suppose?' The voice seemed immediately behind me. I
swiftly picked up Bogey and replaced him correctly. We
moved, all five of us, away from the scene and majestically
out of the station.

We took a taxi from the station to the nearest shoe shop,
on the way passing a store that sold sports clothes.

'They've got shoes, look there! Those are shoes in the
window, lace-up ones.'

'They're for football, Auntie,' I said.

'They look strong enough,' Auntie persisted.

'Not for walking though, Auntie.'

'Why not, nice long laces.' Once a notion took root,
Auntie could sometimes turn stubborn.

'They've got studs underneath—'

'You could saw them,' she said. We'd arrived now at a
quite normal shoe shop, double-fronted, with plenty to
choose from. The taxi slowed down. 'Will this do? Shall I
stop?'

'Thank you, driver. This seems to be perfect. We're here,
Auntie.' Her whole face lit up. 'Freeman, Hardy and
Willis!' she exclaimed. 'Oh good, I prefer them to Dolcis.'

The buying of the shoes took over an hour and a half by
the time Tallulah and Zsa-Zsa had decided they should
have some as well. Bogey fell asleep in his push-chair, a
boiled sweet bulging out of one cheek. The motherly
assistant had given it to him; he'd enslaved her with one of
his smiles. Auntie had bought the exact shoes which I'd
predicted, the very pair of transparent plastic.

'Now, my dear, that's all settled. You've got your beach

sandals, now how about a pair of nice shoes to go on top of those lovely pink socks? My choice, personally speaking, would be red. I always think pink and red go lovely together, a real treat!' The assistant beamed, she'd taken to Auntie. 'Do you ever wear heels, dear? No? Well now, that seems a shame. They do lengthen the leg, you know, heels. Here, just try on these—the shade's called Carnation. You prefer the Fire Engine Red? Well, isn't that strange, because I do myself! But not everyone understands colour. They think we old souls should be dowdy and grey, them dark browns, all them fawns—I can't stand them. You're like me, dear, you go for the bright. Well, you have to. It keeps you so cheerful.'

Auntie agreed, she kept nodding her head. Whilst she nodded, the assistant slipped on the shoes, then stood up and taking Auntie by the hand, she led her like a child to the mirror. I was quite amazed. These were the first high-heels Auntie had ever had on.

'Gosh, they're great, Auntie!'

'You look taller! Are you having them? Oh do, they look lovely!'

Bogey was still awake at that stage; he regarded the proceedings with rapture. Auntie chose to refer to him for the final judgement. 'What do you think then, Bogey—boyo?' He clapped his hands in approval, as enchanted by bright colour as Auntie herself. She studied the mirror reflection. 'Well, I have to say they feel strange. Will I be able to actually walk?' she asked anxiously. Her feet were slightly pigeon-toed, but the fact of the heels was forcing her now to stand in a different way. To splay the foot at a different angle, outward instead of in. She took a few uncertain steps.

'That's it, dear,' the assistant encouraged. 'You'll get the hang of it, in no time at all. And when you do, you mark my words—you'll throw away all your old flatties. Won't she though?'

By the time we emerged, as Auntie had announced, it was well after opening time. I had managed, by a mulish determination, to resist the sales lady's advances. She would've very much liked to complete the full set by selling to me and to Bogey. But Bogey was by then fast asleep. I'd suggested that it seemed a shame at this point to disturb him.

The other three were all wearing their purchases.

Tallulah's striped baseball boots looked strange with her sprigged gown and pinafore. But possibly not as outlandishly odd as Zsa-Zsa's striped boots did with her jodhpurs. Auntie, entranced by her feminine feet, was very afraid of falling. I suggested she push Bogey's pram for support. She did so, staring spellbound at her shoes. I could see the crash coming, but was unable to swerve Auntie or the push-chair in time.

'Can't you look where you're going!' Auntie'd managed a head-on collision with a large collie dog and its owner. 'So sorry!' I said, hurrying on, holding Auntie's arm with one hand and steering the pram with the other.

Auntie decided she could do with a drink. The children wanted to go on the Palace Pier.

'We can do both then, you can drink on the Pier. In the bar at the end—'

'By the Ghost Train!' the girls clamoured. 'Can we go on the Ghost Train today?' We saw them in, Bogey squeezed tight between them. They had money for more than one trip. 'I'd like to stay on all morning!' I heard Zsa-Zsa confide.

Auntie chose to start with a lager, following my example. Just a half. It wouldn't have done to get too drunk on a day like today.

'What a lovely day indeed we're having.' She smiled and beamed round the bar. We'd sat in the window in order to watch when the children emerged from the Ghost Train. I could see in the distance the coastline of Sussex curve round the cliffs of Rottingdean. And, closer, I could see the seafront of Brighton itself, iced white like a wedding cake spiced with pale fondants. And in the middle I could see the Hotel. The Grand Hotel, the first Grand Hotel that I'd ever slept in. And the first time too that I'd been to Brighton or been away anywhere with The Old Man.

'I shall take you,' he'd said, 'for a dirty week-end. People will know perfectly well what we're up to. I shall take you from Friday, returning Sunday, to Brighton where everyone goes. It's tremendous fun going down on the train and coming back with the same couples. One's able to detect the subtle changes that the week-end has wrought in relationships. I shall teach you how you can tell.'

And he had. He'd pointed them out to me, travelling down and then travelling back. One pair in particular stayed in my mind, the man was so obviously married, and

521

the girl so obviously not. They'd held hands on the Friday, he'd kept kissing her ear, she'd wriggled seductively close to him. But on Sunday they sat separately, not side by side, but stiffly opposite each other. And she'd yawned whenever he started to speak and was consulting her watch all the time.

'What will you do this evening?' he'd asked her bleakly.

'I shall go out, of course,' she answered. 'And what will you do, watch television, with your wife?' she'd cruelly added.

Their week-end had quite obviously not been a success. The Old Man had smiled into my eyes. I'd smiled back with no worries at all about ours. It was the week-end we'd fallen in love.

I hadn't been certain up until then. I'd found the sheer difference between us divisive. Not just of the age, but of outlook as well. All this knowledge and my limiting ignorance. The formidable force of his life's experience humbled me into servility. It was not his intention to cause this effect; before Brighton he was quite unaware that this was the case. Before Brighton I was still inarticulate and shy. Before Brighton I still dreaded my periods.

I'd been with The Old Man for just on three weeks when he'd suggested our week-end in Brighton. I'd taken my Personal Pocket Diary, a self-present from Smith's, to the bathroom. It contained, in its binding, a slim, gold-tipped pencil. The tip to prevent it from being lost. I eased it out, and leafed through the pages. My periods were due That Week-end!

Three days to go, and each day, every hour I tried hard to break the bad news. But as each opportunity presented itself by a silence in our mutual accord, or a moment of vacant emotion, or a chink which could have been filled, I shuddered away, I just couldn't.

If it should start, the curse—how aptly called—as we approach Brighton Promenade, I would divert his attention to the other direction. And slyly slide into the sea. 'The girl has gone! She's not here any more!' I could hear his loud roar of alarm. And he'd trace my path with his keen hawk-like eyes over the trail of fresh blood till he came to the edge of the sea.

It started, it must have, going up in the lift, the opulent lift of the Grand. I'd known because I'd slipped into the Ladies Powder Room to avoid the embarrassment as The

522

Old Man signed us in. 'Mr and Mrs Cecil Clotworthy! That seems a good enough name to choose. Where can we be from—Chipping Norton?' The Old Man had chuckled to himself. And that had been just before the luxurious ascent to our suite. It was all clear then, not a spot to be seen, the slide upwards must have started it off.

Our suite boasted a brilliant sea-view. I crossed the room to the window, drawn as if by a magnet, like all children are by the powerful pull of such a vast amount of water. And not merely static stuff at that, but the relentless and fearful life-force that oceans contain. The Old Man had followed me silently, I could sense the bulk of him near. He came closer and lifted a wing of my hair and slid an insidious tongue in my ear, then stood back.

'These ears are like sea-shells. A cliché,' he said, 'but certainly true in your case. You are a creature of the deep. The sea is female, she claims her victims. You two have much in common. And, too, those accumulative waves resemble the womb in a sense. It's understandable why men in frail and destructible craft are drawn to return again and again knowing that death may await. The meaning is deeper than mere economy.'

I felt myself seizing up at his words. Did he wish for a deeper discussion? I swallowed hard, I didn't know then that he expected no such thing. Nor ever did in fact. Not from me or from anyone else. He thought aloud; it was simply that he pursued his own reasoning logic. During the years I accepted all this, and ceased to worry when sometimes at night I would wake to his voice next door in his study debating aloud with himself.

'Are you cold, child?' The Old Man lifted my hand, it seemed as blue as the sea. That must have been quick, the sudden withdrawal of blood from my outer extremities. The swift results of my seizing up?

'Not cold, no I'm not. It's lovely and warm in this room.' I glanced around shyly. 'It's nice and big.' Then faltered. 'Is that the bathroom?'

The door had no lock, rather bad I thought, that: you'd think money might buy some privacy. The Honeymoon Suite, The Old Man had said. Was this how honeymooners behaved then? Completely abandoned and able to walk in and out as the mood and curiosity caught them? Stephen and I had had no honeymoon, but apart from getting dressed up together, we were both highly circumspect regarding each other's toiletries. I'd never seen him swilling himself, nor he me. Our privates were private. Which made the discovery of his corpse that more shocking. I'd never seen him before in the bath.

I knew what to expect, before I took down my knickers, but the scarlet gout still shocked. I stared down at it dully. Small clouds of pain were starting to ache in the curve of my spine, my legs felt as leaden as water-logged pillows. My lower lip started to quiver. Would we go back? Would we catch the next train, our dirty week-end a fiasco? Would The Old Man start scolding for wasting his time, or simply sustain a cold silence? It was my fault, I knew perfectly well that this clearly was what would of course happen. Now all that was left was confession. I swallowed hard. It was quite difficult, there was a tennis ball stuck in my throat where my Adam's Apple had only just been.

As I stood there, in shock, a further spurt as if from a faulty faucet bubbled brightly through my long pubic hair. It was time, I reflected, for a trim. After all, pubic hair just like privet hedges looked better when pruned up a bit.

'What on earth are you up to?'

The Old Man held me by the shoulders, we were both tall but he was much taller. Blood trickled quite swiftly, like a thin mountain stream, down the inside of both my thighs.

'Glorious gore! Well, thank God for that! Quite a relief—I'd really begun to think that this old boy might quite well have inadvertently impregnated you, child! Next week, when this is over, this sweet menstruation. I shall organise safe contraception, my little one. You must forgive me for not having done so already. But I couldn't be sure until this period had come. Take a bath, I shall call for champagne!'

Auntie had already drunk up her half. 'More lager, love? Shall I get it? Or will you?' Her cheeks were already pink with excitement.

'Not another, I don't think, Auntie. Do you? We'll probably eat before very long, you know. A nice lunch—'

'Oh, some wine—' Auntie brightened, my denial of lager had disappointed.

'Well, why not champagne?' The Old Man's memory still lingered at the back of my mind. Auntie brightened still further.

'Oh, well then, we'll go.' She stood up a little unsteadily, the fault of her footwear and the unfamiliarity of wearing high-heels, rather than the effects of her half. An extremely old fisherman, like the Ancient Mariner, stared with what seemed like approval and gave a strange bird sound high up in his nose before taking a puff on his pipe. As we passed him in walking towards the door, I could have sworn that one hooded eye winked. Not at me, but at Auntie who'd moved on ahead. It was certainly the first time in my living memory that I'd seen Auntie arouse a man's interest.

She wanted, she said, to eat at English's.

'Oysters at English's, it's just taken my fancy. I've never been there, have I, before?' Auntie frowned in the effort to remember. She hadn't, she'd always when offered the choice chosen under the Pier. Or fish and chips straight from the paper. Or Wimpys, or The Golden Egg. Why then this sudden switch of Auntie's? Could her new shoes have made such a difference?

Tallulah and Zsa-Zsa were alone at the Ghost Train.

'Where's Bogey?'

'He's inside.'

'What? Alone?'

'Not alone,' Zsa-Zsa answered baring her teeth. 'With the ghosts.'

'He's perfectly safe.' Tallulah looked serious. 'We tied him, you see, with the bows of his bonnet. He won't fall. Look, here he comes now, the car's coming out!'

I looked with concern at the Ghost Train Exit. The push-to gates were opening out, the front of the heavy vehicle emerged. Bogey sat, strapped and stuffed like young poultry, high up in the second compartment. On seeing us his small round dazed face broke into a smile of pure sunshine. His dimples bore deep into each of his cheeks. His eyes became slits in his happiness, they glinted like splinters of flint. The reproaches I'd formed on my tongue towards Tallulah and Zsa-Zsa's gross cruelty— those reproaches died still unsaid. There probably wasn't anything much that could swerve Bogey's unerring nature. He was born to be pleased and unsullied and safe, in the same mould as Auntie, but smaller.

I rang English's Oyster Bar from the telephone kiosk.

'Best to ring first and book a table. They might not accept us otherwise. As it is, even with booking, they could turn us away at the door.' I thought it wisest to prepare for the worst.

Auntie became highly indignant. 'Not accept us? Well, why not?'

Tallulah was matter-of-fact in her reaction. 'Unsuitably dressed,' she said briefly as if the matter of whether we got in or not was of minimal importance.

We all looked at each other critically. Auntie, perhaps, looked most eccentric. Mine was high glamour, with a theatrical twist. And the children were just fancy-dress and amusing. A snooty head-waiter might tolerate them, permitting his own self-indulgence, but the two girls and myself could see without saying that Auntie presented a problem.

We made our way slowly from the Pier, past Old Steine and through to the corner of East Street. 'Ughavee, Jaegers,' Auntie said crossly.

'Let's look in the window.' An idea had formed in my mind, but it had to be carefully presented. 'Just for a laugh—'

The window featured a flowing cape in a gloriously sharp tangerine; whoever had dressed it had certainly known a thing or two about window-display. And more than that, an eye for colour that even Auntie couldn't fault. 'Well, I never, my goodness. Who would have guessed!' The girls pressed their noses on the glass and misted it up with their breath, in order to write their initials. Bogey leaned from his push-chair to do the same. Auntie was completely entranced, not just by the cape, but also what went with it. My plan might possibly work.

The cape was artfully arranged to reveal enough of the patterned robe underneath, a rococo print based on old wallpaper, a jungle of riotous roses. Pink ones, crimson, scarlet, puce and a particularly singing yellow, which was picked out tonally by the tangerine cape and the choice of small beads round the neck, and as well by the slick matching beret.

'It's nice,' I said, 'Auntie?'

'It is. How much is it? I can't see the price. Is it there?' She peered through the glass. Beneath us the children had managed to fog up the width of the window. 'Don't do that girls; no, Bogey, be a good boy—we're just about to go in here.'

'Are we, love?' Auntie looked very uncertain.

526

'We are.' I dismissed her reluctance.

'But they won't have my size—' Her voice wavered and fell.

'They go up to Size 16, I think even more. Besides these sort of clothes always fit, cloaks and capes—the fit's unimportant. And the same with the dress, see, it's more of a Grecian tunic—'

'I don't look too fat? You're sure now, you'd say?'

'You look gorgeous,' we all chorused in turn. The cape was too long, and so was the gown. Both were meant to end lower mid-calf. But on Auntie they reached down right to her ankles, leaving just room to show her new shoes. The pink socks, though much brighter, picked out the pink rose, and fought fiercely with the brave cape. But it didn't matter, the whole thing was so brilliant, like a walking herbaceous border or a Woolworths seed packet of bright, dashing dahlias. Auntie's face glowed a pretty pink pearl. She still looked eccentric, but reminded me now of marvellous Margaret Rutherford who I'd once seen in Pall Mall, flying along in a similar cloak, covered in amber.

They placed us downstairs in the Oyster Bar, in the Banquet facing the door. So that when people came in they could instantly see us. It was like being on permanent show.

Auntie was thrilled; we studied the menu, as everyone else studied us.

'Do you mind if I smoke?' Auntie asked the next table, lighting up before the man there could answer.

'Not at all, madam, no. Here, allow me to light you.' Auntie's match was refusing to strike. The man arose and flicked his lighter, his eyes flickering warmly to me. I smiled. He smiled back.

'There's nice, ooh, that's kind. The silly old matches must be damp. I'm hopeless with lighters, I have them, then I lose them—'

The man dropped his lighter in her hand and enclosed her fingers around it. 'A small present,' he said smoothly.

'But—' Auntie was astounded.

'No buts, madam. My pleasure, I assure you. And if you should lose this one in your usual fashion, it's hardly a tragedy—the lighter is only a throw-away one, an inadequate offering in exchange for your brightening my view.'

Auntie couldn't get over her gift. 'It's like Christmas today.' She glanced down. 'Shall I tell him that we've got a restaurant as well? Why not write down the address, in case he's passing?'

'What, passing from Brighton? He probably lives here. Not everyone goes up to London.' Tallulah had decided to join with the adults and give us the benefit of her opinion. 'In any case, he'd probably consider Mum's restaurant to be pretty rotten, compared to this I mean.' She glanced round. 'Look at that!' A waiter near by was engrossed in a flambé, pouring Brandy and making it burn. 'Could you do that? Could Soc or Ari? Could Zoë, could Vince, do you think?' Tallulah's tenacity could be very tiring.

'No. Now, decide what you want.' Her questioning reminded me of what I'd forgotten, amazingly enough, yes—the restaurant! I looked at my watch. Half-past one. How were they doing?

'How are they doing, do you think?' Auntie said.

'That's funny, that's just what I was wondering.'

'There's a name for that—Extra Sensory something,' Tallulah started importantly. 'We've done it at school.'

'That's something different, that's not the same thing.' It was Zsa-Zsa's plan now to quarrel.

'It is the same, so there!' Tallulah flared quickly.

'No, it's not.'

'Yes, it is, so shut up. There, take that!' Tallulah lifted her fork like a spear, ready to impale Zsa-Zsa's left thumb. Auntie just managed to move it in time and the fork fell to the floor with a twang.

'Allow me.' The man from the next table bent swiftly to retrieve the fork. His gaze had barely left our small group since he and Auntie had last exchanged words. 'Waiter!' He raised his voice imperiously, subtly stressing their difference in station. If fate had been different, I found myself thinking, the roles might have well been reversed. The hurrying waiter was about the same age. 'Sir?' he said in a tone of respect. The man lifted the fork. 'A fresh one of these.' 'Certainly, sir! I am so sorry! Of course, I shall bring it at once!'

'Christ Almighty, he'd have been lucky here not to get a boot right up his bum!'

'Whose bum? What are you saying?' Zoë swayed in. She was late arriving this evening.

528

Vincent enlightened her. 'We're talking,' he said, 'about the wonderful restaurant she went to, down in Brighton. Dick was saying this guy who was bollocking the waiter would've had a big boot up the bum if he'd spoken like that to one of us!'

'It's not the same though,' I chimed in quickly. 'We're amateurs—'

'I'm not,' Dick said sourly.

They'd all been there already, except Zoë that is, when I'd arrived. They'd all been in there slaving. Midday had been hell. They might not do it again, it was just too miserable for words. Soc and Ari had welcomed me with deep grunts of relief and high squeals of unparalleled pleasure. 'You no go again? Is terrible here, you no here and that Dick he come bossin'! He hit my head with a box of eggs—' Soc couldn't get it out quick enough. 'And then he spill oil and I slip and I fall, see here bad, bad graze on my elbow—'

'You happy, boss lady? Your Auntie, she fine?' Ari interrupted Soc's hysterical saga. I had come dressed in black. He had clearly mistaken it as an indication of mourning and grief.

'She's fine, yes of course. She's at home, she's quite well,' I reassured Ari and glanced at them all. Vince stood with his face to the wall.

No one looked ashamed at the mention of Auntie—after all any one of them could have caused her a coronary.

Vince continued to study what it was he was facing. 'We're full up,' he said. 'Every seat's taken. From eight until twelve—no free tables at all. Look, it's here on this seating arrangement. Their names and everything, how long they should stay, when I'll ask them to go—what do you think?'

There were several familiar names on the chart, including Stuffy and Nutty, I saw. And also a note: 'Rufus rang.'

'When did he ring?' I wanted to know. Dick had taken the call.

'I dunno, what's it matter? He rang that was all. I told him you were off with some geyser—'

'You said what, Dick?' I demanded.

He shrugged. 'Eh, what? You heard!'

'Why say that when it wasn't even true?'

He grinned and turned what had just looked like a sneer

into a smile full of mischievous cunning. 'Well, perhaps not this time but it might have been. We're two of a kind, me and you. It takes one to recognise one, they say! Box clever, you'll get round poor old Rufus—'

I ignored his attempt at intimate charm, though I could see it might well work with others. 'Did he say he'd come in tonight?'

'There's no room if he does, darling.' Vince sailed past as I asked Dick the question. 'Not a single seat left. Really, your lovers will have to learn to organise themselves if they wish to see you. I've put Stuffy and the nauseous Nutty both together as they've requested. But is that wise? I didn't know they even knew each other.'

'Nor did I, not until last night.' Was it only last night that I'd seen them? And was it only this morning that Lionel had made his cock-in-hand call from New York? 'Lionel rang. Lionel Striving, from the States, at about five o'clock this morning. You remember him, Vince—'

'I do indeed, darling. What did he want at five in the morning?'

'A wank I believe, but one in my hearing.'

The menu tonight was the same as before, but with several slight refinements. 'Hot sossage roles' replaced 'Cold Pork Pie'. And 'Corned Beaf Fritters' came instead of 'Cauliflour cheese'.

'What's this here, Dick? I can't make it out—' And I couldn't. The word had been crossed out three times until now there was hardly any space on the crowded, rewritten menu to barely decipher a thing. It looked like a lavatory wall. The sort of graffiti done by under-fives, as badly spelt and confused.

'That? Oh, that's "Bubbole and Scweek",' Dick replied.

'No, Dick—there—what's that word?' I asked. Vince bent forward to take a guess, as Zoë came up to join in too.

'It's "Riddles",' Vince said.

'No, it's not! No, it's—"Noodles",' Zoë declared.

Dick frowned. He was having as much trouble as us. 'It's—it's "Rissoles",' he finally announced.

'Rissoles? Spelt "Rizholes"! You'd have fooled me!' Zoë struck home with a vengeance. 'You're dyslectic, Dick, surely! Completely word blind, I swear it. Your spelling is out of this world—'

'So's your snout!' Dick said cruelly. 'What happened, darlin', did the surgeon slip with his scissors?'

Vincent intervened. 'Oh, don't be so childish, you two. Zoë, get ready. There's still all the tables to lay. And the candles to light.' He turned to me. 'We're using candles instead of these lights—better, darling. The lighting's atrocious in here—it puts ten years on before you've bent over! Last night I felt ancient, I honestly did, and there's nothing like candle-light for flattery.'

'There's complete darkness in your case. That would be an improvement.' Vince looked cut to the quick at Dick's deliberately wounding words. We could have done with old Auntie and her brand of sane wisdom. I stepped in.

'A small drink first, I suggest—to start our second night off with a nice swing!'

Zoë confided afterwards that it was the first thing all day she'd allowed to pass through her lips. 'I'm not only saving, I'm slimming as well. Two pounds I've lost since this morning. I think all that rushing at lunchtime lost one. I hope to lose one more this evening!'

Stuffy had called in on her late last night. 'Completely arse-holed of course! And he fell asleep when his face touched the pillow—but—' Her expression softened at the memory. 'It was great in the middle of the night. Except he kept muttering that I seemed much plumper. I think he thought I was someone else.' A thread of disappointment ran through her last words. But then she brightened and added, 'I don't care though. I don't really honestly mind that much whoever he thought I might be. I shall get him in the end, I'm quite sure—simply by being around.' I looked at her. Was she in love? Was she simply a 'one-man woman' as those stoies I'd read in my teens used to say? Suggesting subtly that this was the best. And yet of course that's what I'd been both with Stephen and The Old Man. But he'd grown sad and concerned, The Old Man, towards the end over my love and loyalty. 'I appreciate your fidelity, child—' Still 'child', though by then I'd borne two. 'But I question the right of any human to demand such sacrifice from another. My body fails me, it is no longer capable of arousing or satisfying your own. And you are at your peak and will be for years. It's the waste that is more appalling, even than my constant frustration.' And he'd turned his tear filled eyes to the sheet to hide his deep and obvious distress. The situation was unfamiliar. He was Knowledge and Strength. I was Ignorance. He'd been teacher and tutor to my student so long that the reversal of roles seemed impossible. And yet it happened. In those last few years, from the time he'd become totally bed-ridden, I emerged as the sexual leader.

'Is it permitted,' I'd enquired of the undertaker, 'to place personal possession in the coffin?'

'Not only permitted, but indeed quite customary,' he had assured me gravely, then adding, 'providing, of course, the possessions in question are in scale and in keeping with the width of the coffin. We cannot accommodate three-piece suites or more than a full set of clothing.' He had allowed himself a thin smile at his jest, more a maiden aunt than a man.

He would not have approved the possessions. I placed them carefully under the pillow, beneath The Old Man's great head. We'd spoken of it before his death. 'I'd like to be buried with these,' he'd one night announced. 'Just like this, just under my pillow. The idea amuses me that in years to come when they dig up my withered remains, scholars and wisemen will be scratching their scalps trying to figure out what these things are. Should one label them, do you suppose, *"Prosthetic with scrotum for simulated ejaculation—price £16.50 inc. V.A.T.?"'* He had stroked the soft beautifully modelled male genitals that I'd helped to strap on his frail body. A narrow tube led from the tip to the hollow scrotum behind, which was now at this moment filled up with warm water for 'Realistically Simulated Ejaculation' to occur. It was The Old Man's favourite toy. Along with my Angel's Delight. 'A New Treat for the Ladies', the pamphlet had read. 'You have had the Vibrator and the Love Eggs—now the two are combined in one erotic package. Complete with tiny motor, batteries and strength-tested lead. This ultra-smooth beautifully moulded pleasure egg is the ultimate delight. The vibrations can be controlled to your own desire.' I'd ordered both, through the post, out of interest. The climactic cock to see if it worked—and the Angel's Delight, for its name. 'Take off your clothes!' The Old Man had commanded. 'Or better still, no, keep them all on. And sit like that with your legs apart. Just slip the egg in past your knickers. I like to see the flex emerging, it's as if you'd devoured a rat—sucked it, straight in, unmercifully between those strong labiae of yours.'

The sight had excited him, so he claimed, as much as

anything since he had loved me. His one regret was that we'd left it so late. How our sex life would have benefited before! I'd smiled at his enthusiasm and had moved in much closer, the Angel's Delight in my vagina. 'Would you care to control my vibrations?' I said, and offered him the small switched-on motor. He twiddled the knob. 'This knob twiddling suits me—it is so reminiscent of your nipple. Would you unbutton your blouse, child, and pass me one breast—we could embark on a fine duo-action!'

I hadn't expected to become so aroused, it seemed years since I had felt quite like this. The Old Man's failing strength and, worse, his failing spirit had occupied all my thoughts and channelled attention away from the sensual needs of my body. And, as well, the two girls were still very young. The last lips on my breast had been Zsa-Zsa's.

He tuned the motor down to low, a small wave invaded my vagina and set off a wash of rippling currents which seemed to extend to my womb. What muscle control I must be achieving! The Old Man gently turned the switch, manoeuvring it up to high, and adjusting the egg by easing the flex to the outermost stretch of my opening— my vulva? Or not? I was always confused on the accurate labelling of myself.

'If you bend over, child, yes like that—you can see, actually see yourself swelling.' I'd shut my eyes, but at The Old Man's words I'd opened them and bent as he'd said.

'Here.' The Old Man had shifted his hand from my nipple. 'See, your clitoris has a life of its own. Look how swollen it is, almost crimson and bruised, engorged like an insect with blood—'

He held it carefully between finger and thumb and rolled it as if rolling a joint, tenderly so as not to spill the precious contents within. I'd seen Brad do the same so many times since, though it seemed to me that Brad's greater reverence was reserved for the weed rather than for me.

The Old Man's hand was trembling now, I'd have to be careful of course. I would certainly have to consult his physician as to how much excitement he could stand. But the look on his face dispelled any doubts regarding these sexual aids. The lift to his spirit, the new life they presented exonerated possible risks.

'It's working!' he quavered. 'I see by your face. You're

transported, my child—I've achieved it. Come closer to me— I shall enter you now with my sturdy new, ready-made weapon!'

I slid the egg out, and switched off its battery. No need to waste it, they cost money.

The ready-made weapon was so like real flesh that it made my own flesh crawl to feel it. I'd fitted the penis as the pamphlet suggested with a sheath of fine Fourex Skin—price 82½p per packet of 3 inc. V.A.T. The sheaths were made of a soft natural membrane, actually obtained from young lambs. If I shut my eyes, I could easily imagine I was being fucked by a whole flock of sheep.

I cuddled The Old Man carefully, kneeling above him, as he'd once kneeled above me—so towering and strong in those days. And I kissed him gently over his face, closing his eyes in their deep sunken sockets with the touch of my lips on his lids. How like a corpse he looked for that second, so much so that I shuddered. The tremor, misunderstood as one of pleasure, inflamed his state of excitement. He gasped as I eased my haunches down, then up, then down again. Oddly enough the terrible tension of the ludicrous situation, aided I had to admit to myself by the bulk up inside me—all these factors aroused me immensely. I'd never loved The Old Man as much as now in his moment of weakness. A sob arose from these mixed emotions, was I sad, was I happy—or what?

'You're right my child—you're ready I know. Your passion has reached its peak.' His bed was prepared with a rubber sheet. In those days I still gave him his bed-bath; it wasn't until later that a trained nurse was essential.

'Shall I help you?' I offered, my hand moving down.

'What, to squeeze my new scrotum? How dare you?' And with the delight of a boy who sets his first train in motion, he squeezed hard and released the water.

It flooded my passage, pervaded my parts, as sweet as a douche. It cleansed away the musty cobwebs of frustrated months when masturbation might have heightened misery, and intercourse was out of the question. I relaxed completely and let myself go. Was I passing some water myself? I couldn't tell, the release was such that I didn't know where it sprang from.

The Prosthetic with Scrotum was showing its age, it looked more worn than The Old Man's smooth corpse. But its battered appearance, the result of much ramming, had endeared it much more to us both. I kissed the old faithful, and lovingly fitted a fresh Fourex Skin on the rubber, then I lifted the pillow with its cold satin shine, and arranged the penis under The Old Man's left ear. The right, I reserved for my Angel's Delight. That still looked as good as brand new. I held the pink egg in the palm of my hand for the last time. Ought I not perhaps to anoint it?

The Old Man's hands lay crossed on his pubes, locked together in permanent prayer. He wouldn't have liked that, he refused to recognise Religion, it fitted so falsely with Logic.

I kissed the cold knuckles, it was like kissing stone. As I bent, I switched on my small motor, and with the other hand I slipped the smooth egg up inside me.

Grief fought with Sensuality, both wiping out Guilt. The Old Man would have been proud. I studied his face, I dwelt on his lips and reflected on how much Wisdom, through words, they had imparted.

'My child, oh, my child—' I said the words for him, as I tightened my thighs in a climax. Then I slowly removed my Angel's Delight and laid it to rest with its Master.

Soc and Ari were engaged in what seemed like discussion actually inside the deep freeze. The lower limbs emerged untidily, and an elbow belonging to each. Dick didn't seem to be anywhere around in the kitchen, unless he was inside the oven.

'What on earth are you doing in there, Soc and Ari?' Soc slid out. 'Am squeezin' him plackheads! Is much simple in the cold, Boss Lady. You have some, you have plackheads? I do, I do for you?' He nodded so genially, I hadn't the heart to confess that I did my own. When I could find them these days, that was. Are blackheads, like the dewy first signs of beauty, reserved exclusively to youth? Apparently not, if Ari was liberally sprinkled. 'Come out Ari, you can't do that in there!' What if Soc were popping these small encrustations straight into our vanilla ice-cream. Did they do currant ice-cream, sultana and such? We might pass it off as nut crunch.

Dick emerged from the lavatory and kicked Soc up the arse. 'One for good luck, you crass turd!' Ari protested on behalf of his brother-in-law who was whimpering now like a wounded beast. It occurred to me that Dick's uncalled-for aggression could be channelled and put to some use. Nutty, for instance, would swoon with pleasure if I employed the same brand of viciousness. But would he react with a man?

Dick was peering into a variety of saucepans, all boiling away on the gas stove. 'Taste this.' He plunged in a long wooden spoon and offered me the pale beige contents. 'What is it?' I said dubiously, the smell was quite nauseous. Dick frowned. 'Never mind that—enough salt?'

'A spot more sugar is called for,' I said carefully. 'It's custard isn't it?'

'Is it fuck! It's soup, bloody soup from a packet—'

'Ah.' I drew the word out, and nodded my head. 'So it is. I see it is now.' I picked up the empty soup packet. Chicken Noodle it appeared to lay claim to be. The Noodles had congealed, that was obvious. They clung together in a glutinous mass, much like home-made sticky-paste concocted by children from plain flour and water.

'They should be shot, the makers of these!' Dick said savagely, and poured the whole lot down the sink. We looked at him speechlessly, Soc, Ari and I. The sheer waste seemed somehow so shocking.

Dick moved over to the Dumb Waiter and bawled up to Vincent, 'Chicken Noodle off' I just caught Soc's muttered 'Is true. Is all off down here.' His first stab at original wit.

I steered my mind away from the sight of the menus and this latest defiling caused by Dick. There were now so many crossings-out that only a squint-eyed person with eyeballs in all directions could hope to decipher the contents. We might be called upon to issue spectacles, special ones like they have for 3D. On the other hand we could forfeit the menus and merely pin up a board which said MUCK. 'Madam, what would you like to drink with your Muck? Moët Chandon? A very fine choice, I myself quite agree, no expense should be spared with the booze you imbibe with this Swill. Pigs practise this same principle—oh yes, their palates apparently are impeccable!'

A stampede of footsteps up above our heads heralded the first of our arrivals. The sound was followed by Vincent's thin scream summoning me up to my position at the bar. The panic was contagious.

'Here arse-hole, hold this—' Dick nudged Soc roughly and passed a full frying-pan sizzling with pork chipolatas. The sudden movement sent the fat literally flying, it slurped straight from the pan to Soc's open-toed sandals followed in seconds by seventeen small sausages and Soc's intimation of agony.

'Pick 'em up!' Dick commanded completely unruffled. 'And run 'em under the tap. Not the cold one, you fool—' I moved to the door, I could imagine the comments, 'Tasty bangers, eh what! A very fine flavour—Athlete's Foot, if I'm not much mistaken!'

Our first arrivals were men, dressed as Boy Scouts, who had forgathered in London for a Conference. They seemed surprised that we weren't aware that this week was International Boy Scout Week, starting tomorrow with a rousing rally along Rotten Row in Hyde Park. And ending in seven days time with a Display of Tree Climbing on Barnes Common.

'Get a load of those knees!' Zoë murmured in passing. They'd all ordered Lemon and Lime, except one who felt safer on Coke.

'Lemon and Lime and what though, Vince?' I kept a tight rein on my patience. If he was going to start mucking me around, confusing orders as he had done last night, we'd have to make other arrangements.

'That's it,' he said bleakly. 'Not much of an order.'

'Charge them extra for non-intoxicants, I would.' Zoë tapped her high heel almost wantonly, and flung her full bosom towards them. The nearest blinked behind his glasses and smiled nervously in my direction. 'Jesus God, look at that one!' Zoë's lip curled contemptuously. 'Do they screw or not, Boy Scouts? Do they take the vow, like priests?'

I gave the matter brief thought as I measured out Lemon. 'Baden-Powell poked, didn't he Vince?' Vince wasn't concentrating, there were two new arrivals. Both women, dressed up as Girl Guides.

'He was married I mean, I don't know about children,' I continued, pouring out carefully.

'There you are then!' Zoë beamed triumphantly, as if she'd just proved her own point. She'd not yet caught sight of the Girl Guides behind her. The place was beginning to look like a fancy dress do, all we needed was a nurse and two vicars and perhaps a miner with a lamp on his head.

'I don't believe it!' She'd seen them. 'Two more bloody perverts. The full moon must be bringing them out. Where are they sitting, Vince?' she hissed in a whisper.

537

'Oh, do put them on the next table to the other team!'

They knew each other, as it all turned out. The Boy Scouts were not too pleased to be greeted. 'I thought this was to be just buddies, us chaps all together this evening,' I heard one of them grumble. 'How did the Girls get wind of where we were. There's a traitor in our midst, that's obvious!'

The Girl Guides both ordered stiff Vodkas and Tonic, large ones with not too much ice. 'I've heard that before, that they're terrible boozers.' Zoë gave a satisfied smirk. 'All Women's Movements are much the same. Alcoholics Anonymous consists almost wholly of women who've become Winos with the Women's Institute. It's that knitting and sewing, it's thirsty work—they switch to spirits as a change from tea!'

The Girl Guides toasted each other loudly and drank the whole lot in one fell swoop. 'Did you see that! What gulpers!' Zoë gasped. 'I shouldn't care to see those two cock-sucking! They'd swallow the lot, balls and all, poor bugger wouldn't know if he was coming or going—'

'Zoë, love—less soliloquising, more service, if you don't mind.' Vincent employed a note of weary sarcasm. He looked worried and grey, not himself. Or rather, quite himself—the himself which was surfacing lately. What was wrong? No doubt an emotional entanglement.

I consulted the chart of who was coming this evening. Nutty and Stuffy were due in an hour. I wondered if Zoë was aware of that. She was taking the order from the two Girl Guides, who were giggling together quite foolishly.

'They're gay,' I said on her return.

'That's what I think—both bloody Leslies.' Zoë winked as she said it. 'Not that you and I mind, surrounded as we are by homosexuals.' She turned to Vincent. 'That's right isn't it Vince! One has to be big in these matters.' And she accompanied her final statement by goosing him with a banana.

'Oh, for God's sake, Zoë! Cut it out, can't you see—there's a whole lot more coming now! And Dick's had a disaster, he says, in the kitchen. Ari's spilt strawberry jam on the Rissoles, and Soc's just burnt half the Corned Beef Fritters!'

'Rufus rang.' I made my mind go a blank, preferring to consider Rufus's call rather than charred Corned Beef

Fritters. But mental escape was patently impossible, the restaurant was, quite suddenly, full.

'Bread! Where's the bread?'

'What?'

'The bread!'

'There's no bread!'

'Fucking hell!'

'Not my fault! We've run out!'

'You bitch!'

'Thank you dear! You bitch, back!'

Zoë and Vincent were having one of their rows, the evening had been one long bickering quarrel. 'Come on you two, go easy.' They glared, one on each side. 'It doesn't matter now about bread. Who wants it, this late?'

'That man over there. He wants it to mop up his gravy. And he's asked as well if we've got marmalade. I think he's expecting some toast.' Zoë looked lined, which she didn't look often, there wasn't enough slack on her face. Not with all they'd taken off when reducing the size of her nose. 'I don't want to upset him. I think he's good for a big tip. I can tell now which bastards are best. He's got a button-hole you see—that's always a safe bet to go by.' Lionel Striving wore buttonholes and was as mean as all-get-out, quite embarrassing when tipping I recalled, on the rare occasion that we'd eaten out. Always asking if I had change of 5p.

Vincent looked disgruntled, he hadn't received a tip at all. 'You're too grand dear, too much major domo.' Zoë had tried to make up earlier on for the remarkable size of her tips. The two Girl Guides, both thoroughly drunk, had left more as a tip than the price of the meal. The Boy Scouts had left barely nothing, but a coloured couple from the Civil Service, celebrating his passing an exam which edged him up two extra increments and meant he now had his name on the door—they had bought Zoë a whole bottle of Daquiri, which she insisted on selling back to me before they'd even reached the door. 'Will you purchase my darkies' Daquiri?' she said. 'I'd much rather have cash in hand.'

I hadn't the heart to refuse her request, though Vincent claimed I'd pandered to her greed. 'Mercenary cow,' he'd muttered.

Nutty and Stuffy came late; seven minutes or so, Vincent accused them.

'I could've let your table go more than a dozen times—'

'What, in seven minutes? Remarkable!' Stuffy gave as good as he got.

Zoë had dropped two Jam with Rice Puddings the minute she'd seen Stuffy enter. I watched one splash the entire back of a vicar, yes one had come in after all, and wondered if I should tell him or not. The jam glistened darkly amongst all the white rice; if it continued to trickle in the way it was doing, he might find it in his pocket when he got home.

Stuffy reacted sheepishly to Zoë's obvious approach. I watched him closely whilst pouring his Campari, discreetly so, and noted that his slight discomfiture in the face of her adoration contained at the same time a degree of self-pride. Not exactly the air of a stallion, his stature and spectacles cancelled that out, but something much more insidious. You could tell he was getting his oats.

Zoë offered both cheeks in affectionate greeting, her hands suddenly free of rice pudding. The floor was awash with the milky substance, but no one appeared to mind, or even to notice come to that. The evening had reached a high note of hysteria, such as happens when for no real reason the crowd gets caught up in contagious pleasure— the smiles spread with accumulative force. I'd experienced it often in theatre audiences, in pop concerts, on picnics and New Year's Eve when each person indulges everyone else with an almost religious fervour, all forgiving and suffused with love. Anyone could have done anything tonight and found a favourable reaction. 'You say you'd like to stab my back? Here, old thing, take my knife—it's much sharper!' 'Do I mind that you spit quite so much when you speak? Not at all, dear—I find the spray rather refreshing!' 'What's that, you've been rogering my wife for three weeks? That's fine—I've been fucking yours for years!'

Nutty took the table intended for two, just to the left of the till, whilst Stuffy did his best to maintain his balance against the force of Zoë's embrace. The chair Nutty chose faced exactly my way with his back, as it were, to the kitchen. An ominous calm ensued from there.

'Everything all right, Vince, I mean in the kitchen?' I'd already declared last orders for drinks, though last night I'd taken terrible risks with our temporary licence and extended it far beyond time.

Dick had appeared at the top of the stairs, staring resentfully around the full tables. Meals, miraculously, were appearing and served barely before they'd been ordered. I had to hand it to him, Dick's decisiveness and direct frontal attack where food and brute force were concerned could have made him a very good man at Auschwitz. He'd have served up the Jews instead of starving them. Cooking by gas of course. In fact, now, all evening regardless of orders, stray dishes appeared in the Dumb Waiter—five Chips, seven Mash, four Boiled Carrots and six Shepherd's Pie left over from lunch time, re-heated and wrinkled on top.

'Who ordered these, this rubbish?' Zoë wanted to know. Vincent looked equally mystified.

'Not my lot, my dear. They must be all yours—'

· 'Shepherd's Pie? I thought that was off. It smells as if it is—what a bloody stinking mess—I'm not taking that to any of my tables!' Zoë flounced away. I came to the rescue. 'Nutty's always keen on Shepherd's Pie. They used to serve it at Eton—the best thing they had. You'll probably find Stuffy likes it too.'

Zoë blew a raspberry, the sound passed unnoticed by people on surrounding tables whose conversations seemed equally peppered with the same blasts of rude anal explosions. Didn't it take longer than that for wind to formulate, or was our food more ferocious than most. Did the true trencherman fart more than others? Or was that the distinction made between glutton and gourmet? The Old Man was drawn to making these distinctions. Food and Sex shared very much in common, that was his continuing claim. And it was from this basis, understanding the essentials, that he cooked so superbly himself. I was rarely, if ever, allowed in the kitchen, just as my role was clearly defined, those years, in our bed. But as his powers decreased and his potency waned, his cooking became non-existent. Until in the end his diet consisted of whatever it was Nurse decreed. A soft, milky diet it was for the most part. Not unlike that which I served to the children, his children—those small versions of him. In fact sometimes, spooning in variations on Farex, it was hard to distinguish his soft gums from Zsa-Zsa's. Both toothless, and pale as pink silk. Both vulnerable machines made to masticate food, but each missing the last vital link of the teeth. Hers were coming. He'd had his already.

541

I ignored Zoë's raspberry. 'Shall I ask?' I offered. 'If they'd like Shepherd's Pie? I don't mind.'

Zoë wrinkled her nose. 'But it's curdled, I promise! Just smell it yourself—I don't care to think where it's been!'

'Don't fuss-pot now, Zoë.' I spoke to her firmly. 'Both Nutty and Stuffy will love it.'

'But it's not what they ordered—' she objected afresh, looking past me at Dick who'd appeared up the stairs. She lowered her voice, but not very much. 'That bastard should be booted straight out of here. He's running this place, if you'd care to ask me. You and Vincent have been reduced to mere pawns—'

'Prawns? I'll have prawns, that is if I heard you correctly?' A heavily built man, sitting close by, tilted his chair towards Zoë. The back wooden legs squeaked in protest, he had already eaten two dinners, straight through from Starters to Pud, proclaiming our food delicious!

I couldn't understand it, the general reaction seemed to be that the food was exceptional! Flavoursome English! Top grade Transport Cafe, low prices with Very Fine Wines!

Of course, most of our clients—patrons? customers?—were middle class, and most keen on a 'find', especially one with low prices. And we were a bargain, I could quite well see that. And I'd purchased the wine wisely and well, such that a connoisseur could have quickly recognised that this wasn't cheap carafe gut-rot. This additional bonus was paying big dividends, far more than if the wine had been inferior. Vincent approvingly noted this fact. 'More Minervois for Table Ten. One bottle—no, they say two! And a Côtes du Roussillon for Table Four, and three more for Six, in a sec.'

I was quite pleased with myself; Vincent originally had accused me of the utmost extravagance regarding the prices I'd paid for the wines. 'They're cheaper than that at the Liquor-Mart, a litre of Valpolicella costs something just over the pound. And Tesco's do Red, White and Pink Charbonnière for much the same, you've gone mad with these wines. It's not as if they're even going to notice the difference—' I remembered the warm eyes of the Italian who'd sold them. Soon I'd have to re-order again. Would he remember me? Probably so, once seen rarely forgotten.

'Any chance of a drink around here?' Dick's dry voice sliced through Zoë's sentence and the man's interruption.

'No prawns, sir,' I apologised and then turned to Dick. 'You're doing well, Dick, tonight! A.1.—plus service, so everyone says—'

'Yes,' Zoë sneered. 'You're even giving us what we're not bloody asking for! What are you trying to do, finish off all the scraps?'

Dick stared at her coldly with open dislike, and deliberately chose not to answer. She persisted however, she refused to give up. 'It's all right for you in the kitchen, not facing the customers—but I'm expected to serve it—'

Dick examined his nails and carefully picked a shred of cold cabbage from the half-moon of one of his thumbs. 'You can stuff it,' he said slowly, 'as far as I'm concerned, all the way up your own arsehole. And serve it from there straight on to the plates—'

Zoë seized her chance. 'I may do that.' Then she added, 'Certainly no one would detect any difference.'

She turned away and returned with the tray of Shepherd's Pie held in her hands. 'Here,' she said, holding it towards me. 'You can serve this, I refuse responsibility. If anyone's going to be poisoning Stuffy, I'm damned if it's going to be me. Better still,' she stared at Dick, 'you do it, you arrogant bastard, and just see how their faces fall in disgust at this puke-making sick you serve up!'

Dick looked laconically at the tray, and then all around the restaurant. 'Which cunt is it meant for, they all look the same?' He flexed both his fists, revealing long muscles up along both his arms. His tee-shirt today was even tighter, it seemed woven in one with his skin. The effect, with the truculent cast of his brow, was more than a little menacing.

I pointed to poor Nutty's table. He was already in a state of nerves, I could tell by the violent eye movements. He'd been trying to catch my glance since he'd arrived, I was aware of it but just that much too busy to bother. He was clearly enthralled by my cruel indifference. Dick's harshness might just tip the balance and shift him right over the edge. We didn't want an exhibition before all the other tables had completely cleared and gone home.

'Oh, do be careful, in your manner of serving, Dick.' I'd agreed to give him a bottle of our very best Claret, in exchange for attending Nutty's table. 'Yes, he has rather a nervous disposition. You go first, and I'll come and introduce you. Both those men are quite close friends of mine.' I couldn't bring myself to look at Nutty, as I introduced him to Dick. It was as if the chemical components of his flesh had changed gear and shifted to something completely different. Not unlike the bubbling substance some years ago in the television serial, *Quatermass*. Could Dick's wavelengths have wrought such a positive change in that second it had taken to introduce him? Without a doubt, these things did happen—hadn't I reacted similarly to Brad? Though our relationship was threaded with humour. Brad's eyes displayed light-hearted mockery, self-mockery too, which was always a winner. They teased, whilst Dick's clearly terrified. They terrified Vince, they antagonised Zoë, they dictated to poor Soc and Ari. What they did to myself was a little more complex, they reminded me of Stephen's final despair and the underlying fury that that had masked.

Was it irresponsible of me to have got them together, would I live to regret the final outcome? They fitted so well, shivering Nutty and Dick—the Rabbit and the Snake. Nutty was so hypnotised so that when Dick addressed him directly, his stammer rendered him speechless.

'Where do you live, Squire?' The 'Squire' held a sneer, a deliberately insulting accusation. It contained centuries of class hatred in one single word. 'What's that, Squire? I didn't quite catch it!' Nutty was struggling, not to utter a whole sentence, but simply to start the first word. 'W-w-w-wi! W-wil, will, will! Will. Will. Will!' I looked away, out of pity. Stuffy chose to polish his spectacles, but I saw that Dick was actually leaning forward to stare more closely at Nutty's poor mouth. Nutty's tongue seemed completely paralysed. 'Will. Will. Will,' Dick repeated with relentless cruelty. 'Shall I have a shot at finishing it for you? Our doctor back home had a shocking stutter—by the time the old sod had asked for your symptoms, you'd started a new fucking illness!'

Nutty's dud eye did a looping somersault, at the fair rate of fifteen knots. I wished that my girls, who so enjoyed Nutty's eye, had been there for the impressive spectacle.

'Yes, Squire,' Dick continued, quite ruthlessly. 'It's the scourge of the privileged classes, they say, this difficulty with verbal delivery. Yet the Conservative Party and this country's Government are crammed full of you stuttering twerps!' He leaned further forward. 'You'd be hard put, I tell you true, Squire, to find a milkman, or a miner, or a munitions worker with a similar affliction to yours! Now tell me why you think that is? Do those silver spoons you're bloody born with get tangled up with your tonsils?' He suddenly smiled. The effect was quite shattering. He looked, all of a sudden, like Puck. Completely beguiling, a beautiful boy. I thought, afterwards, that that must have been the precise moment that Nutty had fallen.

The evening had continued to climb quite steadily to the climax which later took place. The signs were all there, but I just didn't see them. In any case, separately, they didn't mean much. Dick had repeated his original question. 'Well, own up, Squire—where is it you live? Will, you say—Will, Will, Will—I've got it—you live where I do! In Willesden!'

Nutty had managed to shake his poor head, squirming over his cold Shepherd's Pie. In a moment, I knew, Dick would force him to eat it, despite its congealing, chill greasiness.

'Do I take that as "no", that mute nodding of yours?' Dick demanded, enjoying himself. 'Well, Squire—Will, Will, Will, Will!' He stretched back in the chair he'd pulled up for the purpose, and raising both arms in the air he linked them insolently around the back of his head, displaying dark under-arm growth.

It was riveting to see, the tight curling profusion, especially since his arms were so smooth. Men, in the same way, found girls' crotches arousing. Pubic hair peeping around flimsy panties.

I glanced around, we'd been there mere minutes. The restaurant appeared in an uproar. Vincent approached, and now so did Zoë.

'Who's meant to be minding the shop down below?' Vincent tried to make his voice pleasant. He nodded in Nutty's direction; his dislike of him was quite obvious, and had been whenever they'd met. But this evening he'd been given a greater cause. Dick was his friend, despite Dick thinking otherwise.

Zoë was holding a muffled conversation with Stuffy, who'd been ploughing through his Shepherd's Pie, silently, not participating in Dick's and Nutty's appalling exchanges. Even now, at this moment, Nutty was still attempting desperately to say something. Vincent's intimation that Dick should return to his station of duty below, seemed to exacerbate matters for him. The most sought for sentence came out quite clearly, in his most charming and cultivated manner. 'Will you permit me to offer you a drink? I live in Wiltshire—are you ever down that way? If you are, you might care to pay me a visit.' He glanced down at his grey Shepherd's Pie. 'This dish, you know, is my absolute favourite. A nursery treat, I remember. Cook used to make me one of my own—then later, at school—' His voice trailed away, we were all gazing in surprise. I couldn't remember a single occasion when Nutty had managed to say so much, without one single stammer or pause. Dick, from the look on his face, appeared more surprised than the rest of us. But in that same look another one surfaced as if Nutty's small show of strength presented an unlooked-for challenge. His interest, I thought, had been roused. They could be locked in eternal combat, those two, neither ever quite winning.

I'd returned to the bar, two people were waiting to pay their bill at my till. They were arguing fiercely over who should do it. She said she should, it was her treat, they'd agreed that it would be before she'd invited him out. He'd replied that was cold-blooded blackmail. I looked at them both, between totting the bill and handing it in their direction. They both made as if to grab it from me. The woman's grasp was much stronger, her companion retreated, shrugging off his defeat. Were they married? Divorced? Or estranged? They were certainly that, whether married or not to each other. Both wore a wide wedding band, but in this light it was hard to see if they'd been cut from the same strip of gold. The woman smiled at me, but sadly I thought. I returned her smile, mine was quite effortless. 'Is this your restaurant? You're new, it's quite different. We used to come here in the old days.' She glanced towards the door, the man she'd been with had already left. Without her? Or would she find him moodily waiting to start up again, there outside?

The bill was quite small, they hadn't drunk much. Things might have improved if they had. I was pleased for her though, that she hadn't spent much, hadn't wasted too much of her money, on what had plainly been an abortive outing.

'Did that bastard let her foot the bill?' Zoë'd joined me; we watched the woman walking alone, wending her way to the door. 'She was his secretary, you know—I heard it all. Yes, he was her boss—'

'I think at some time or other, he was certainly more than her boss,' I said, sorting loose change. The till seemed to bulge with its contents. Could it be that we might make a profit from this daft venture of ours?

The sight of the notes, all those fivers and oncers, reminded me of dear old Auntie. I suddenly yawned, it had been a long day. I wondered if she was alseep. If I rang her now it would make no difference, she always slept right through the ringing of the telephone. And if she was awake, she might welcome the call, might even pop down for a night-cap.

I telephoned. 'Auntie?' She'd answered at once.

'There's funny, I was just ringing you! My hand, just this moment, was picking it up when it rang. It felt like an electric shock!' She laughed, in a particular way that I knew very well. I wondered what exactly she'd been drinking. I was faintly surprised, it wasn't like Auntie ever to imbibe on her own. She seemed in control, but suffused in the gaiety that spells several stages short of oblivion.

'Would you care to come here, to the restaurant, for coffee?' Coffee would keep her on her feet.

'Coffee?' she echoed. 'Oh, I've just had loads of coffee— Gaelic Coffee. It didn't taste very Welsh.' She giggled. I could tell that she wasn't alone. 'Guess who's here—shall I tell you—Brad is! Yes, he is. Just passing in his cab. I gave him coffee. He supplied the cream and Irish Whiskey—'

'Put him on, Auntie.'

'Can I still come? I'm still dressed up in my finery— Brad's being awful—he says I look lovely. You should hear all the things he's been saying. Oooh, he's terrible really, I keep telling him that—here he is. Shall I ask him to drive me?' Her voice was wavering with happy optimism. She was with someone she liked and trusted. It wasn't the first time they'd spent time together. Brad's habit of dropping in unexpectedly and the fact that we'd never stuck to a schedule, not once in our long relationship, rendered him really to be one of the family. Much more than my other Gentlemen.

'All right, don't put him on. I'll see you both in a minute. Ask Brad if he wants something to eat—' But I could hear his far-away answering shout. 'Only her, tell her, Auntie—I'll eat her!'

547

The tables were gradually thinning out. The calm from the kitchen had commenced. It was at this point approximately that I'd made the query to Vincent as to whether all was well. He hadn't answered, he'd reached that point of exhaustion where he couldn't be concerned. The second I'd replaced the telephone after my call, it had rung immediately for Vincent. I'd answered the phone. The voice had been Irish. The Irish chippy from Willesden? Or had he been Welsh? I couldn't remember. 'It's for you, Vince!' Hearing the voice at the other end of the phone, he'd turned his back to me. He hadn't ever done that before.

Soc and Ari were singing the Greek Cypriot Anthem. Dick sat outside on the step, he was holding a languid conversation with someone ensconced in the lav. There was no mistaking the stuttering, Nutty had reverted once more from his position of dignity to that of a gibbering idiot. Soc and Ari stopped singing. I could detect on their breath the sweet unmistakable scent of Sherry. The cooking Sherry shelf was bare, two bottle tops poked out of the dustbin. 'Boss Lady, you lovely! Your Auntie, she no here?' They stood like two terrible trolls, grinning inanely from ear to ear, their arms linked in brotherly affection. Or rather, brother-in-lawly affection, if there was in fact such a thing.

'Auntie? No, she's not here—but she's coming in a moment.' I wondered briefly if they could be conscience-stricken, or were they as transparently honest as they seemed. I shut my mind firmly off from the subject: if Auntie could do it so could I. 'Yes, boys,' I continued. 'She bought a new dress and a cloak today, down in Brighton. She'll be showing it off right here in a minute. You'll have to tell her it looks nice.'

Soc clasped Ari, as if Ari was Auntie. 'Oh, Auntie—you have the new dress! Is lovely! I like! You beautiful lady, like my mother. I love you, is good!' Then he turned to me and said seriously as if addressing a priest. 'In our country we love very much the women—the mothers, grand-mothers and aunties. We love them as much, we want them you see, as we want our wives and our daughters. Is good, no? Is right?' He nodded several times, and ended, speaking as if to himself, 'Is no wrong yes, is right.' Ari kissed him swiftly, hard, full on the mouth, as if he were stamping an envelope. Or placing the seal on an official

548

document, one that was going to the Nation. I had an insane image of Soc, backed by Ari, lavishing lashings of love on their womenfolk. Claiming Droit de Seigneur from cradle to coffin, age presenting no barriers. Both sweeping the board of the generation gap, their generosity uniting the whole.

Upstairs something was happening, I could tell by the sounds of small cheering. Vincent and Zoë, and Stuffy it seemed, were greeting the arrival of Auntie.

'She's here!' I said.

'She am here—she arrive! Your Auntie, she come! We go, we go say hello—' Soc and Ari scampered up the stairs like two mice up a maypole, their front paws as active as their feet, slicking their hair and wiping their mouths in swift and excitable movements.

Auntie stood in the centre of the stage surveying the scene like a Queen, with all the graciousness of Royalty greeting her Senior Court Dignitaries. In the flickering shadows cast by one candle-light, her new robes assumed extra glamour. The sharp tangerine lines of the beautiful cloak throbbed with a new orange dimension. Her small bright yellow beret had slipped to one side and much more to the back of her head. It looked like a halo, a heavenly light such as you see round the head of Our Lord in luridly illustrated Bible stories. The matching beads that she wore around her neck glistened like freshly picked berries. You felt you could eat them, and eat Auntie too, the effect was so succulent and ripe.

An elderly woman of about Auntie's age, seated nearby all alone, dressed severely in silver and black, was regarding the scene with great interest. Her appearance spoke unmistakably of the restraint that she must have practised in life, in her attitudes and in regard to her relationships. The interest was tempered with faint disapproval and at the same time with unalloyed envy.

'Who's that?' I heard a masculine voice whisper at Auntie's arrival.

'Some actress, I suppose—could it be Sybil Thorndike?' an answering voice whispered back.

Only about three or four tables remained occupied—people lingering with their drinks. I followed as Soc and Ari threaded their way past them, whooping as they went. 'Auntie! Auntie! Is Soc and Ari come to see your nice dress. Boss lady, he ask us—no, she tell, is new! Ah, yes, we see, is divine!' Soc and Ari flung themselves like two fawning dogs on the floor, feeling the hem of Auntie's long gown and kissing the rim of her cloak. Her pink socks twinkled through, her high-heels curved down under her comfortable instep. Soc saw them first. 'She have new shoes!' he shouted as if pronouncing a ship's maiden voyage. 'New shoes—she have!' And he proceeded to slaver, almost licking each toe-cap in turn.

The elderly woman rose in distaste, the scene had become too Bacchanalian for her to bear. Auntie smiled as she passed her. The woman seemed temporarily blinded, but managed a stiff twist of the lip before leaving.

'Hello, Auntie.' I went forward to kiss her. I could smell my perfume on her neck. Shalimar, a scent The Old Man had first bought me in Paris, the time he'd taken me to Balenciaga and dressed me completely in black. I was barely nineteen. The Master himself had approved The Old Man's final selection. He'd sighed with deep pleasure and conversed with The Old Man in his native Spanish language. Afterwards The Old Man had told me what he'd said, that I'd looked, in the black, like a lovely girl-widow. The reverse of a white-clad child-bride. I don't think that he knew that in fact I'd been both, before I'd met The Old Man.

The Old Man had taken me that first day, in my black, to dinner at the Coupole. Picasso had been there, he'd done a drawing of me on a food-stained linen napkin—which The Old Man, by mistake, later in London sent to be washed at the laundry. When it came back the drawing had vanished. The Old Man showed me how not to mind. And on our last night in Paris, we'd dined late at Maxim's. Mistinguette sat two tables away, surrounded by fawning young men. 'You'll be like that when you're seventy.' The Old Man had smiled. 'But your admirers won't be all homosexuals.'

After Maxim's he'd taken me on to a night-club run exclusively by women. I wouldn't have known, I'd thought they were men, immaculately suited and coiffured. After five minutes, one had asked me to dance, first asking The Old Man's permission. He'd given it roguishly and pinched my behind as I was led firmly to the small dance-floor. The youth, it was hard for me to think of her as a girl, had held me tightly against herself. I could feel no swell of breasts, and when at one point she guided my hand to the small of her back, the lean buttocks felt just like a boy's. The record we danced to was 'La Vie en Rose', sung by Edith Piaf, but after that first song I lost concentration. I couldn't have said what it was that they played. I could see The Old Man watching us and at the beginning, each time we'd danced past, he'd winked and I'd grinned gratefully back. But, as the music continued and the sinuous body against mine moulded itself cunningly to me I was aware of a change taking place. The youth clasped my hand more tightly in his, hers—and dropped both our arms to our sides. So that now, not only did the entire front of me touch his, hers, but by subtle pressure on my thigh his, her, own snaked between my two legs. We swayed, barely moving, in one spot on the floor. I couldn't have greeted The Old Man if I'd wished, he belonged to a far distant world. I hoped for his own sake that he couldn't see, because now the youth was kissing me passionately. And I was returning the kiss. And the hand which just a second ago had exerted pressure on my thigh, had sneaked slyly around and in between us it was stroking my pants like a thief. Straight through my glorious Balenciaga, stroking until I could have cried. And would have done, if his, her, lips had let me. There was no room for tears on my face.

'*Ma cherie*.' The voice was hoarse and thrilling, murmuring in my left ear. I could smell the powder on the smooth skin and the impression of scent in the curve of the neck. The effect was unbearably moving, it reminded me so much of Stephen, of his fragrance and fragile strength. But this youth had a purpose, she, he, wanted me badly.

'*Ma cherie*,' the voice murmured. I made no reply. I couldn't speak French anyway.

But now she—strange that, how quite suddenly I regarded her as she! Was it the scent? Or the voice, so low but so feminine? Yes, she was now suggesting very much more. The words were ones that far exceeded my flimsy knowledge of French, but even so the way they were said, from the ardent delivery to the quickened breathing and suggestive movements she made, left me in no doubt as to what might be their meaning.

Th situation distressed me. I didn't dare to look in The Old Man's direction at all. I hadn't looked, not for a full five minutes or more, so that now as I did and saw he wasn't there, stark fear sliced across my emotions.

Stranded in Paris! With no place to go, except into the arms of this exquisite creature—the idea both thrilled and appalled me. This wasn't what I wanted, not without The Old Man to tell me if I should, or I shouldn't. Would it count after all, with her being a girl? Would it be viewed as the same, infidelity?

I felt a new pressure on my elbow. Was this an Excuse-Me Dance? The pressure increased and my dancing partner gradually released her hold. A hopelessness bordering on despair and panic surged through me at the thought of losing her. We stared at each other, unwilling to part. I turned my head towards the unwelcome intruder. The Old Man's hand released its pressure. 'Come children.' He was addressing us both.

We didn't go to where we were staying, not to our hotel at all. Though it wouldn't have mattered what we did there, tonight was our last night in Paris. And they were worldly enough to have accepted anything. Neither did we go to the girl's own place, as I'd hoped. Long after, The Old Man had told me why not. I'd been surprised when he did, that it hadn't caused me more pain, the fact that she lived with a mistress. Mistress? No, that wasn't the word. With her lover, a girl much like me. And I'd been surprised as well to discover, when The Old Man had told me, how old she'd actually been. In her early thirties, according to him. They'd known each other since she'd been my age.

I didn't go further in that discussion, I shrank back, not wishing to know the exact ins and outs of their relationship and whether I'd been the first that he'd watched with her, or not. Because though my feelings may have faded for the girl, I felt fiercely possessive over him. And it was this dangerous jealousy, if that was the word, that spoiled at the start my full enjoyment of our bizarre arrangement as the three of us approached the ambience The Old Man had selected.

It was within walking distance of where we'd just been, but I had no idea of the district at all. Saint-Germain, Les Halles, the Champs Elysée? It made no difference, because I was obsessed whether or not The Old Man was holding her hand, she on one side of him and me on the other. He was holding mine tightly, as he usually did. But he spoke all the way, rapidly to her in his unfailing French—he spoke eighteen languages. She'd answered him lightly and laughed several times. Were they talking of me, both, between them? Were they plotting a lurid and mutual seduction? I clung miserably to his tight hand and wished we were back in our hotel bedroom packing for our morning departure. I wouldn't have minded if I'd been in the middle, sandwiched between them, the succulent filling. But The Old Man stage-managed it all. He strode us along, until we suddenly stopped outside a tiny patisserie. A powdery smell of choux and puff lingered around the entrance which appeared to lead past the shop itself straight through to the bakery behind. And still further behind—Paris like New York was like layered cake, always more underneath—still further behind was a minute garden. We crossed it and reached a locked, shuttered building, which resembled a Bohemian studio. But it couldn't be that because the light wasn't right, which was why working painters used garrets. This one was low and overpowered by all the surrounding buildings. I wondered now who it might belong to, as The Old Man produced the right key from the large bunch of keys that he always had with him in the inner pocket of his cloak.

It was quite dark inside, but not for long. A small torch hung on a hook just inside the door. The Old Man must have known the place well, his hand sneaked instinctively for it. The place couldn't have been wired for electricity. Wide church candles shone waxily in the light of the torch, as The Old Man flashed it around.

'Hold this, child,' he said softly, handing me the torch. 'And shine it as I light all these up.' My senses thrilled that I'd been chosen, and not the girl, to do this small task. But as I watched him move away, leaving swaying pools of light in his wake, I realised that that had been part of the plan: the girl had moved closer beside me. We were already kissing each other.

It was she, and not he, not The Old Man at all who stage-managed proceedings from there. It was she, who even without moving from the original spot where it was I'd been handed the torch, had undressed me. Had removed my black dress. It had slithered, my beautiful Balenciaga, from my shoulders straight to the floor. I'd shivered as her hands had followed its flight and come to rest on my thin flimsy panties.

She'd led me, still wearing them, but now nothing else, through what seemed like a forest of small flames. I couldn't tell, the images blurred. Was that person over there The Old Man?

I was lain upon what felt like very smooth velvet. The girl, for a second, had gone. I shut my eyes, it was so like a dream that I couldn't be sure she'd been there at all. Then I felt her return, as naked as me. She slid her hand into my panties, those same fingers that had searched in that space once before on the dance floor. She withdrew them, the tips were quite drenched.

I fell asleep, and woke all alone. The body, her body had gone. I wasn't afraid, somewhere quite close I could hear the drift of familiar voices—The Old Man and the girl were conversing together in an unmistakably intimate manner. But now I didn't seem to mind. The flickering candle flames reflected my own bodily sensations. They may, quite easily, have darted like that all over my skin for all I knew—the effect now seemed much the same. She had kindled me gently, applied her own light so skilfully to mine that I progressed from the smouldering start to the state of the candles around me. They waved and faltered weakly, like wands appearing to fall in the wind.

And there was wind now, or a chill gust of night air had entered the place. And in seconds several candles were extinguished. I shivered again, but not this time with pleasure as I had when her hands were upon me. And I shut my eyes tightly. The voices weren't there. For the first time I did feel that I was quite alone, and fled from the fear far away, once again, into sleep.

Shalimar, that same scent sat on Auntie's soft neck as happily as it had, all those years ago, on the smooth boyish neck of the girl. My brief embrace must have lasted fractionally longer than normal welcome merited. Auntie withdrew and looked at me anxiously.

'I put on a little dab of your scent, only a bit, love, at the back of my ears. Not wastefully, not even a dab on my wrists—in case Soc and Ari needed a spot of help with all this old washing-up. You don't mind, love? It's just that, somehow, this French perfume seems to go that much better with these clothes. Rather than my old Californian Poppy or the Juice of Dew Violets, you know?'

I laughed and gave her another kiss, one unconnected with memories. How strange that those memories had surfaced tonight.

'Where's Brad, Auntie? Didn't he bring you?'

'Oh yes, Brad! He did bring me, but on the way here he had a call to pick up a fare. And the funny thing was—do you know who the fare was? It came through on that speaking machine—a gentleman they said called Mr Rufus Justice! And do you know where he's to drop him? Yes, here! But I didn't let on, love, that I knew the name. I just sat there. Mum's the word! Brad said to say that he'll pick up this chap and deliver him here, then come in himself for a night-cap.'

The momentary panic must have shown on my face. Vincent, watching me, laughed and, in a voice of mock horror, exclaimed, 'Oh darling, your past is catching up with you!' It was a rare and, because of that, a welcome return to the easier days of our former intimacy. He never, if ever now, relaxed in the same way. Had the arrival of Auntie anything to do with it? He was holding her arm with desperate affection, hanging on, as if for grim life. Or was it grim death? I couldn't remember how the saying quite went. But it didn't much matter, one way or the other. He took her hand. 'You look absolutely divine, darling Auntie! Where have you been? I've missed you so much!'

It was of course the very first time Vincent had seen Auntie since her loss. He wouldn't mention it, I knew, if she didn't mention it first. Perhaps this ardent welcome he gave her was a show of unspoken sympathy. She beamed at him. 'It's new, the whole outfit, it's new—top to bottom!' She pointed a matronly toe. 'New shoes, look, high heels, Vincent. Nearly as high as yours.' She glanced down at Vincent's stacked King's Road lace-ups. 'Well, p'raps not as high, but nearly. And d'you know what, Vincent— there's not a thread of Man-Made, no Acrylic, Synthetics, not nothing in this frock of mine, nor in the cloak, nor the beret! See, look on the labels, ALL WOOL!' She strained around to yank forward her labels, scruffing the back of her own neck. Like a rabid terrier attempting to produce evidence of its own identity.

'All Wool! No, Auntie dear! But why?' Vincent's voice contained genuine horror. Auntie's dress sense up till then had actually tickled his fancy. The fact of Tesco's Brushed Nylon and affiliated fabrics from all her other chain stores, had seemed to him the height of camp chic. All Wool was a different matter.

Soc and Ari sensed the drama, something serious had obviously happened. They took up the chant, wearing woebegone faces. 'Hall Wool! Hall Wool! Why, why? Why, Hall Wool? Why, Auntie, why Hall Wool?'

Auntie looked now as alarmed as they. 'What's the matter?' she said to me. 'What's the matter, Zoë? Was All Wool all wrong—?' Zoë had joined us, she was looking contemptuously at the swooping, gesticulating chorus, performing as if from Cole Porter. Or an amateur performance of Gilbert and Sullivan. 'They're pissed!' she said. 'Auntie, pay no attention. Those two have been on the cooking Sherry.' She nodded towards Soc and Ari. 'And he—' She bent forward after glancing at Vince, 'He is so bloody neurotic, he doesn't need anything to send him over the top! They're crackers, the lot of them. Auntie old love, I don't think I could stand another night of it. Have you met Hitler yet, he's in the kitchen dishing up all the shit? I tell you straight, Auntie, I'm scared still to serve it. I keep seeing this powdered glass!'

'Dear oh dear, it's like that, is it? Never mind Zoë, love. You look very nice, I must say, tonight. Less make-up on than usual?' Auntie meant it kindly, but had touched a sore spot. Zoë's nose shone out like a beacon, unpowdered and filmed in a shroud of chip-fat. Soc's and Ari's looked much the same. But perhaps Zoë's looked worse, her nose pores were much larger from where they'd been stretched with her Op. She herself was the first one to point it out. 'Save's carrying a handbag,' I think I'd said to lighten her obvious gloom. 'You could pocket it all in your pores—' She had, mercifully, managed a small smile.

Her hand now flew up to the centre of her face. 'That's what I mean, you see! There's no bloody time to think of your looks. Though I must say—' Her face quickly softened as she looked behind her towards Stuffy. 'It has worked quite well with Stuffy, cross fingers. There's talk of him taking off for Hamburg—'

'Hamburg?' I echoed. I couldn't imagine Stuffy anywhere other than England.

'The home of the Hapsburgs,' Zoë explained, importantly as if sure of her facts. 'It seems that in his thesis, indications are emerging that the Krauts are responsible for more than just the last two World Wars—in medieval poetry, I mean.'

'Oh dear,' Aunti said sympathetically. 'Poor Stuffy.'

'Oh, not Oh dear, Auntie. It's good!' Zoë glowed. 'Good for me, my German is fluent. *"Guten tag"*—that means "Good day"! And it means as well, that there's a bloody good chance of little me going with Stuffy to Hamburg.' Zoë winked in my direction. 'He's giving me a Reading tonight!'

Soc and Ari had clearly not followed this side conversation of Zoë's. They'd been gazing adoringly up at Auntie. She patted them both on the head. And when her 'Oh Dear' to Zoë was so patently not the right answer, she'd given the boys her full attention. Vincent had withdrawn into a strange worried state, even Auntie it seemed couldn't reach him. 'How's it going, then, boyos?' She addressed them like Bogey. And like Bogey they answered by sniffing her first and slyly poking and prodding. She lifted the wings of her cloak like a bird and enclosed Soc and Ari, one on each side. Their craggy brown faces and dull crooked teeth displayed like discarded dentures, the full set top and bottom, looked at odds in the folds of her magnificent garment. But at the same time strangely at home, as if they'd replaced something else that was missing. Of course—she wasn't carrying Mock Croc!

'Why not sit down, Auntie—and have something to drink?'

'Ooh, something to drink! Soc and Ari, would you like something nice with me?' Auntie gazed fondly down, first to her left and then to her right, as if addressing two small Pekinese. They both nodded, tongues hanging. All three repaired to a corner, the darkest without any light. 'Well, I don't know about that!' Vincent said sourly. 'Kitchen staff fraternising with customers!'

Zoë sailed past, undoing her pinny. 'Have you been in the kitchen, lately? Our Chef is fraternising like mad with old Nutty, no need to spell it out further? Oh, is it all right, I'm shoving off now. Stuffy's going. Sunday tomorrow, we're not open are we? Monday? Well, I don't know, I'll see. In any case I'll let you know, I wouldn't just leave you in the lurch!'

We watched them go, Vincent and I. 'What does she mean, in the lurch?' Vincent looked irritable.

'I think it means, Vincent, that we're going to need a new waitress.'

'And a new chef—'

'New chef? What? Dick's—'

'Chucking it in! Yes, latest development! Dick's going as Nutty's new butler! He told me now, ten minutes ago—'

'Has he told Nutty yet?' I said calmly as best I could to control my amusement. But Vincent didn't react, his mournful face remained exactly the same.

'Dick does as he likes, it doesn't matter what anyone else thinks with him. They go along with everything.'

'Only if they're a certain sort of people, Vince.' I spoke gently now, he seemed so lost.

'Oh I know that someone like you would withstand him. You've never been manipulated though.'

I didn't answer, it wasn't true. I thought above all of The Old Man. Had he manipulated me? Or could his influence be regarded as education?

Vincent stared ahead. The lines around his mouth began knitting together uncontrollably. I could feel one shoulder lightly lean on my own. 'I've done a terrible thing,' he said brokenly. 'So dreadful, I daren't even tell you I've done it. But I have to, or I can't go on living.'

A table was clearing, the last, near the door. I looked at them, and smiled my 'Good Night'. They'd long since paid their bill, we'd been serving them coffee for over an hour it seemed. Vincent's words set up such a terrible chill, I wished the table would stay. But they'd gone now and we stood there together, Vincent and I, with the silence growing between us.

What had he done? Whatever it was, now was not the moment to be told. It would have been, but even as his quivering lips opened and started to speak in low explanation, the sound of doors slamming as from taxis and cars arriving outside our establishment, wrecked the sensitive timing. I dreaded to look, recognising the voices, not just of Brad, and of Rufus—but also of Lionel!

'Lionel Striving! Christ—Vince—!' I knelt down on the floor, cowering beneath my frail till. Vince looked down in surprise.

'Wasn't he in the States—Lionel Striving? You said he was there.'

'Well, he was,' I said desperately. 'But he's not now is he—he's here! So is Brad. So is Rufus. I can hear them—' The door opened.

'I can see them,' Vince managed to mutter. He bent down as if for a bottle.

'Jesus God!' I whispered wretchedly. 'There's bound to be blood! Any chance of some sort of an escape route?'

We both looked despairingly at the open Dumb Waiter, me still on all fours and Vince folded from the waist, his neat buttocks high in the air.

'What the hell are you two doing?' Zoë's voice rang out clearly, facing us as she rose up the stairs. She was wearing her coat, her pinny in her hand about to be stuffed in her handbag. 'There's more buggers just come in—shall I tell them to fuck off—? Bloody hell! Just look at that—' Her voice stopped short, her jaw dropped down. 'They're fighting now!'

The Dumb Waiter was quite large, the width of a window-sill, a deep one. The sort used by children on snug wintery evenings, when, accommodated on cushions, they'd fit themselves in to study slow snowstorms, entranced for hours by the swirling flakes. Warm and secure, and safe. Feeling quite the opposite to how I felt now, suspended half-way to the kitchen. Above, a storm of a different sort was raging far more fiercely, whilst below the startings of another, less furious but with almost equal vehemence, was surfacing between Dick and Nutty. I could have done with a cushion not just for my coccyx, but to hold tight over my head.

Brad's voice was the loudest. 'You'll get this straight up your hooter, mate—overtaking on the inside!' I could see his clenched fist, though my eyes were shut tight. Vincent's thin voice wavered. 'Please, lads—' Lionel Striving was coughing, offensively so; it went with a dismissive sneer. 'Old chap,' he was saying.

'Yes, my man,' added Rufus, calmly. The sort of calm and air of authority to rightly infuriate everyone. 'I was probably, as passenger, the very best person to judge accurately who was to blame—'

'Blame! Bloody blame!' Brad's strong voice rose, stronger. 'This four-eyed fart nearly ripped off my bumper!'

'You exaggerate, you weren't even scratched. In the States, where I've come from—' Lionel's words were now drowned by a crash like an exploding bomb from below in the kitchen. The Dumb Waiter gave a dangerous shudder. I prayed that I shouldn't be sick. A small sticky glass of discarded Chartreuse and the sour ash of someone's cigar tainted what air I was trying to breathe. I hoped Vincent wouldn't forget I was here. If I screamed now I knew no one would hear me. The violence was catching. The uproar below had spread without doubt to above. Everyone shouted.

'You bastard!'

'Ye Gods!'

'Now look here!'

'This aggression, you know, is uncalled for—'

'Chaps like you—'

'All you lot—'

'Yeah—your fuckin' class—'

It was hard to tell Brad's voice from Dick's. Or was it that what they said was the same. Dick's was closer, that was all I knew—mere inches away on the stairs.

I dipped my thumb in the tacky Chartreuse, and licked as I listened, all ears. Two new voices entered now, female. One shrill and one soft. Zoë's first, followed faintly by Auntie's. 'Stuffy's glasses—they're broken! You buggers— take that and that and that. And that!' A regular beat, beat, beat accompanied Zoë's words like the rhythm employed by a drummer. She was wielding her handbag around numerous heads. I could tell by the shrill yelps of pain. A crescendo of voices, joint victims, joined in.

'Hell!'

'The bitch!'

'My eye's bleeding!'

'I'm cut—' 'Serve you right—look at me!' 'Hey, look out boys—she's heaving that table!' Zoë, amazon-like, took on all, avenging Stuffy's poor spectacles. She needn't have bothered, I knew he had more in reserve. Five or six pairs at least, from what I could remember, for deciphering rare manuscripts.

There was a terrible scraping, as of wood upon wood— then a thunderous rumble and roar. A table was going, there was no doubt of that. It fell heavily just short of the window. I guessed this was so by the shimmering tinkle of shattering glass. That small case to the left-hand side of the door which contained decorative objects of Vincent's. Quite unsuitable, I'd warned at the time—they were bound to get smashed in the end. Lots of Babycham Bambis batting their lashes, doing very coy things with their legs. Very kitsch, so he'd claimed—and good for a laugh. Someone was having a laugh now—a high-pitched hyena soaring hysteria which I recognised as belonging to

560

Soc. Ari joined in. They must have both surfaced, believing it to be a big game.

'I chuck now!' chuckled Soc. I heard the sound of his chucking as a plate made contact, closely followed by others from Ari, blended with a bouncing from my side of the stairs. Dick and Nutty were involved in a ball game. They ricocheted from wall to banister, quite often banging shoulders with me. I wondered exactly how many inches of plywood and nails lay between us. Then split seconds of silence, till it started again. Dick, so it seemed, must be down! Because now Soc and Ari must have seized this advantage to repay for all grievances past. I could hear them hissing and squealing and bubbling together, like low beasts bent on revenge.

'See, I take this bowl of rice pudding and I stick down his trousers like so!' Ari could hardly get the words out. Soc gave a whoop of pure joy. 'I piss in his ear—no! Yes. I think I do. I think I piss in this filthy pig's ear. He no good. Hold his head— here I go. Look here Auntie—I make pee-pee in dirty Dick's earhole!'

Where was Nutty? Unconscious? Apparently not, he was speaking in low tones to Auntie. They must have both turned in alarm at Soc's and Ari's intended misdeeds. I could hear Auntie's soft remonstrations. The fact that I could was not simply that now they were clustered so near to the Dumb Waiter, but that quite suddenly there did seem to be over all a calm starting after the storm. But it was a shade too soon to be able to tell whether it was safe for me to emerge. The violence had broken out, that was the strange part, quite independently of me. There was no real way that any of the participants might have linked me with those others involved. The knowledge comforted me. I'd been spared confrontation. It was worth hanging on a bit longer. I drained the Chartreuse, my first drink tonight. I was quite looking forward to another. Brad quite clearly had gone, I'd have known if he hadn't. So had Lionel. Were they fighting it out on the streets, in their vehicles, each racing together crashing through red lights and pedestrian crossings, swerving round corners on kerbs? Zoë's shrill voice was missing, which must mean that Stuffy by now had absented himself.

What of Rufus? Was he there? And if so, did it matter? Might I dare make my presence felt at last?

I scratched like a rat on the side of my cage, trusting

someone might hear me. No reply. None at all. 'Vincent,' I wavered. There was silence! Good God! Had they left me?

I thought about Vincent, to subdue my panic. He had been on the point of confession. What could he have done? What might it be that was almost too appalling to tell? We used to, I remembered, play that game as children—would you harbour a criminal? A murderer? A thief? A spy? A spy who had betrayed his own country! That one, I remembered, was considered the worst, the most heinous crime of them all. It was wartime. And a spy, it was pointed out, caused the death of millions whilst a murderer usually only one. Could that be it? Not a spy, not that—I couldn't imagine Vincent diddling MI5. But he might have murdered, in self-defence, any one of the sadistic louts he went round with. And justifiably so. I decided in my mind I'd stand by him. If he ever let me out.

I lifted my arm to strike the Dumb Waiter and opened my mouth in a wail. All the breath left my body as I sharply shot upwards, zooming too swiftly to the surface.

The restaurant, was this it? A landscape of table-legs and stray dishes of cracked crockery and large spoons. And spare bottles—the sort used as weapons. My till hanging loose leaked a littering of silver as limp notes floated down to the floor. Far away near the door a jewelled collection of Bambi splinters glittered and shone.

Vincent bent anxiously, holding his stomach. 'Oh darling—such goings—on! The place is quite wrecked! And I'm feeling so ill. I think I've developed an ulcer!'

'Tell me, Vince.' I spoke slowly. 'Whatever it is, I'll stand by you. You need to know that. You were saying, before, you had something to tell me—'

His answer so filled me with flooding relief, and I found his delivery so tragically funny as he tearfully confessed, that I unfolded myself from the restricting Dumb Waiter and slowly sank to the floor. Poor Vincent thought that I'd fainted.

I was still on my knees, half laughing, half crying and telling Vincent he wasn't to worry, when Rufus arrived. My head rose at the sound of his voice. 'How do I look?' I whispered to Vincent. But Vincent, now with the weight of worry, great worry, lifted it seemed from his life, was still not controlled enough to answer. I left him there at my feet, radiantly weeping.

'Hullo, Rufus—how lovely to see you!' I glanced down at my clothes—remarkably spruce considering all they'd been through. Crease-resistant, quite certainly. Rufus wasn't alone. I was expecting one of the others to walk in behind him, Brad or Lionel, but not this person.

The impression was of a formal figure, much like Rufus himself, well-suited and smoothly urbane. There was something vaguely familiar there, but I couldn't in this light pin down what it was. Three bulbs had been broken.

'Be careful there, old chap, where you step—hell of a lot of glass!'

Who was he then? Another driver, like Brad—part of the same mini-cab company? They were eccentric, they employed all sorts from Greek gods such as Brad to defrocked priests, and doctors struck off the register. This one looked too successful though. A professional man. An entrepreneur, but one very far from failure. From some reason, as yet unknown to me then, I guessed his name to be—Guy.

'Guy—let me introduce you,' Rufus was saying even as soon as I'd thought it! But something was occurring downstairs in the kitchen. A rustling and shuffling and the sound of low murmurs. Who was down there— I'd completely forgotten! My mind was momentarily distracted.

My limp fingers fell, reminding me, as they contacted hair, that Vincent lay sprawled at my feet. He lifted a happy, tear-drenched face. 'I love you,' he sang, 'you're the tops—'

'Look here, old girl! What the hell's going on in this hole!' Rufus coloured and blustered. 'Bloody Bedlam broke out a short while ago, whilst I was waiting for Guy here. You missed it, old chap! Just as well you got lost—no driver in his right mind could've kept up with the maniac cabby I had! I shall put in a formal complaint to that company! Funny, I've been using them for years, but lately their drivers have been completely irresponsible. This one tonight coolly entered what was clearly a one-way street off Sloane Avenue—just like that! I cautioned him, and do you know what he had the nerve to claim? That it was much the best short-cut! That's where we lost you—it's a wonder you found this place. Frightfully sorry, old fellow!'

Guy Watever-his-name took it all in his stride. He'd been studying me closely throughout. Now suddenly he leaned forward.

'Well I'm damned! If it's not you! The adorable one!'

The light caught one cheek, and I knew why I'd thought 'Guy'. He looked like the actor Guy Rolfe, with the same long lean face, lined from cheekbone to chin like dimples stretched out in two skeins. I'd thought it before when I'd seen him in Brighton presenting his lighter to Auntie. He was the one who'd been brisk with the waiter. He needn't start being brisk here. There was no sound at all now from the kitchen, nor any sign of Auntie. I strained my eyes; in the darkest corner there did seem to be something moving. A large shifting shadow made up of more than one person, more than two, I now saw, as three heads sharpened fleetingly in silhouette, Auntie, bookended by Soc and Ari, melted in one loosely-knit lump. Her voluminous cloak provided a blanket for whatever was occurring beneath. I had a feeling, it made me feel nice, that much stroking was going on in Auntie's cloak. Perhaps Pure Wool led to these things.

Zoë had gone and so had Stuffy, without saying 'Good Night'. I didn't mind, Zoë's face was enough. Her gaiety was almost contagious; to touch her, like a leper, would have been to have caught it. I felt that I wouldn't see them again, either apart or, more likely, together. And now Rufus was speaking of going away! Paying a visit to his wife in Australia!

He told me quickly, whilst Guy—the person called Guy—a past colleague of his at the Bar, whom Rufus now trusted would look after me in his absence—whilst this Guy had returned to his car for cigars. We didn't sell them, not the brand he preferred. Ours were Manikins, hardly the same!

'What do you mean, Rufus—look after me?' The cigar incident, though slight, had ruffled me. As much as the waiter thing in Brighton.

'Legally speaking, in a legal sense. Sorry. Let me say it again. We are amalgamating, he and I. He'll look after your interests in my absence.'

I looked at Rufus. He seemed uncomfortable. There was a familiar bulge in his pocket. 'Is that a gun in your pocket? Or are you just pleased to see me?' A favourite quote from Mae West.

He tugged at the bulge. Was he getting it out! He was. 'A small present. Victorian!' He opened the fine linen, frilled camisole-knickered affair. 'See, quite authentic. Slit from stern to stem. Original Free Traders, one might say. But of course in Victorian times, with a more practical purpose—for pissing through, legs apart, under crinolines. Described in *Walter—My Secret Life*. You remember, I read that bit out. Any chance m'dear?' He grew more agitated as Guy re-entered the door. 'Blasted nuisance, he's dropped in on me tonight. Had it all prepared, you know. Had to cancel a cab that I'd ordered to come here. Guy arrived out of the blue. Ten minutes more and I would have missed him—can't be helped. It's given me the chance to introduce you two. He has restaurants, a whole string of them, in the family. Left by his father—isn't that right, Guy?'

Vince had crept away, he must have crept on all fours. I found a sprinkling of his tears on the floor.

What was happening down below? Was Dick entombed down there with Nutty?

Guy was talking now. 'I seem to have lost your attention!' His tone was so challenging, I chose to ignore it.

Rufus was studying the Menu. He had unfortunately chosen to read one with considerable crossings-out and one with the most bizarre spellings. 'That little son of yours is coming on! Look here, Guy, this child's only two and a half. Amazing, eh, education these days! I know I couldn't have formed capital letters at two. And look, the little chap's managed to state his food preferences—' I didn't enlighten his ignorance. He'd never find out in Australia.

'Might I look at your menu?' What a damnable man this Guy was with his cool, amused air, his expensive cigars and that warmth waiting there in his eyes. Something kindled deep in the bowl of my stomach.

'No. You can't,' I said carelessly. 'We toss them away at the end of each evening. You see, we never have the same thing on twice. That way gives greater variety. No one ever knows what to expect.'

'How original,' he murmured. The dimples deepened as if suppressing a smile. I'd made it sound as if we were producing rare concoctions of culinary art, each dish created, each taste and flavour teased from the ephemeral air. Guy carefully appraised each inch of the decor, and as he did so I saw to my horror that a scarlet gout of that hideous wrecked decor had transferred itself to his suit! Jesus Christ, it had to be him of course!

'You've got paint on yourself.' I got it in first, subtly suggesting that he was at fault.

He glanced down. 'Have I really—how frightfully careless. I apologise for ruining your paintwork. I must have disturbed a surface.' He smiled, all charm. What a clever bugger, what a bastard to be on the wrong side of.

He stood up, he was tall, even taller than me. 'I'd love to look at your kitchen.' He said it ingenuously, like an eager young boy trying to impress his best friend's mother with his manners. It was extremely hard to refuse. Refusal would have appeared not merely churlish, but would have placed him at an advantage, putting me on the defensive. As if I really had something to hide. The loaded silence hung between us. Rufus looked anxiously on, aware of a tension, unhappily knowing he himself was very much outside it.

I was cross with myself and annoyed that the man was undeniably making progress. 'My interest,' he said, as if reading my thoughts, 'is purely professional. I like this small place despite tonight's skirmish, it has an excellent feel. My family's business used to be like this—their very first restaurant, I remember. But then, as happens, they expanded until the whole has now become sadly impersonal. An empire, but lacking what you obviously have here—people who cherish and care.'

I laughed, looking around. It sounded harsh and coarse, rather more than I'd meant.

'Oh, the people here certainly care all right—come Monday we shall be without both a waitress and a chef. I say chef. I actually mean cook—and even cook might be placing too fine a distinction. We use shovels here rather than spoons.'

My honesty must have disarmed him completely, for he threw back his head and laughed loudly. A faint five o'clock shadow, though it was now well past that, darkened the line of his jaw. Those dimples of his must be devilishly difficult, not to say dangerous, to shave. I stopped myself, this wasn't right. I knew the danger signals, the warning signs that spelt deeper involvement. It always started at just that point of noticing physical landmarks. The lie of an earlobe, the light on a lip, a slight imperfection enough to endear, or a gross one—enough to enslave.

Where was Brad? Where was Lionel? I crossed my fingers mentally now, willing them not to arrive. I could have coped, have managed somehow between Brad and Rufus and Lionel. But things were different now with this Guy.

The telephone rang at precisely that moment, as if to answer my prayer. I picked it up. 'Will you excuse me?' I'd turned my back towards Rufus and Guy and prepared to speak in a low voice to Brad. I rehearsed the words before I said them. I was too tired, was what I'd say. On the point of exhaustion and off home in minutes. I'd see him when I next saw him—next week?

A thin high nasal voice spoke my name and asked me to wait. She was putting a Mr Lionel Striving on the line. Thank you, ma'am, my pleasure, I'm sure! I waited in desperation through the pips, which seemed to go on for ever. Then, for no reason at all, they suddenly ceased, the line went completely dead. I turned round. 'It's gone dead,' I foolishly announced for no reason at all. Guy and Rufus were talking together. A cooing and billing, as from contented doves, issued amongst muffled chucklings from the depths of Auntie's dark corner. She'd be pleased to see Guy. She'd said he was lovely. She'd lost the lighter coming back on the train. Had left it, she'd claimed, in the Gentlemen's Toilet. She wouldn't have it that they weren't like that on trains, that the Toilets were neither for Gents nor for Ladies but for both, and for children, even dogs. The phone rang again. I lifted it mechanically, expecting the same harpy. 'Hello, kid! How are you keeping? It's me, Brad—I'm on my way to Bristol, can you believe! I was in your caff—where were you, for Christ's sake? Fuckin' poncey maniacs, trying to kill me! One cunt in particular! And you should have seen the pompous prick who was my fare—but I had to split before I could sort them all out. Sorry kid, I left a bit of a mess. But I had this job to go on to. Just getting on the motorway now—the bloke's paralytic. Too drunk to drive home, got to be in Bristol by the morning. Not a bad old chump—already offered me an enormous whack of money to run his main Massage Parlour! Yes, no kidding! Male-Female Saunas, mixed! Says I'm made to measure for the job—can't get over my beautiful body—'

'Don't boast,' I said. 'None of us can.'

'No, seriously though—' I had been serious, but didn't interrupt any further, not wishing to stem the flow of his sheer youth and vitality. 'I mean to say, he's a nutter but I may give it a whirl. So if you don't hear for a couple of weeks you'll know I'm up there—'

'Pummelling,' I said.

I turned to see first Nutty emerging from downstairs, followed by a dazed, damp, chastened Dick, with Vincent bringing up the rear. The trio looked somehow complete in itself, like a triangle, perfectly met. Each in a way equal, not much on its own, but made by coming together. Dick's cheek was bruised, I could see now quite clearly.

'What happened down there?' I said before I could stop.

Nutty answered. 'Dick fell.' He said it quite simply, but I remembered out of nowhere that, despite Nutty's appearance, he was deceptively strong. Indeed, more than that, he was actually an expert at Judo, even had his Black Belt, I believed. A leap of delight rose in me at the thought of Dick tasting his come-uppance.

'My dear.' Nutty, his swivel-eye steady as a rock, was addressing me, fully in command. 'I thought I'd drive these two fellows down to the country tonight. A spot of fresh air will do them both good, get away from the Smoke for a while. I wondered,' his voice faltered and for an instant he was the old Nutty, 'if you had the keys handy of the Rolls. Be more amusing to take the chaps in that. Dick here, says he's never been in one!'

I looked directly at Dick. I knew his game well. I understood what he was after. If he wanted the Rolls, it was his, I didn't mind. I'd had enough material possessions showered on me to last me a whole lifetime. 'Take it, of course,' I said lightly. 'Look, here are both keys, take the two of them—'

'Oh, no, n-n-n—' Nutty demurred, not completely ready yet to be cast away so brutally. But Dick intervened. 'Thanks, missus.' He stepped forward and took both keys in his hand. 'Case one gets lost, Squire, only sensible.' He'd redressed the balance between them. I wondered, just briefly, where Vincent would fit in. But they needed him there as a buffer, to dilute the violence. I could see it now. He stood there gazing at me. 'Are you sure it's all right, darling? The strain's been so great—I just feel I might die if I don't get away—just for a little while?'

'Do.' I meant it.

'But will you be all right? Will you manage?' Vincent's voice almost broke with emotion. I leant forward and kissed him.

'Haven't I always, Vince? Of course, don't be daft, you go off. I'll let you know, I'll give you a ring. I might not open on Monday.' Or ever again, it occurred to me. That's how it was, to be your own boss, you could do what you liked, when you liked. Or not if you didn't, it was up to you.

The telephone rang, would it ever stop ringing? This time Lionel got through right away. 'God Almighty, you're elusive. I've been trying to reach you for hours—all day! Where the hell have you been? I flew in this morning and came straight to the house—not a sign of life there. I'm only here on a flying visit. Quite literally. I'm ringing from London Airport—they've called my flight—didn't you get my letter? I've got this project, a big one in Pennsylvania—and I've got this cock-rise, just talking to you, already. Three erections I've lost through lack of opportunity! I even came round to that address of your business. By God, but it's rough—do you know what you're at? I couldn't see you, but I didn't dare wait—some bitch heaved a table—split my eyebrow right open. It's lucky I escaped with my sight. No, I beat the hell out of there. I'd already been menaced by a rough-neck cabby who claimed damage whilst driving along—I shall be glad, I can tell you, to get back to the States. At least there you learn to expect violence! The only thing is—my angel, I miss you. God Almighty, this is bursting my breeches! Christ, they're calling my flight again! But my balls are like bullets! Tonight at dinner with this client—I couldn't control it—we were eating oysters—and I kept thinking of your cunt! I'm sure he got wind that something was up when the table-cloth started stirring—dare I wank—no I daren't—and besides there's no time—'

I cut his voice out by the touch of a finger. If I hadn't he could well have missed his flight. And I might find him, if this happened, hot-footing it back. I had other things on my doorstep. To make doubly certain that we were indeed cut-off. I kept my finger for a further second on that vital part of the receiver. And then cancelled out all further calls by leaving the thing off the hook.

'Am I to take it that we are at last alone?' I turned round at the sound of Guy's voice. They had all disappeared. Dick, Vince, Nutty had gone. And, mysteriously, Rufus as well—no fond farewells.

'No, we're not. My Auntie's here, somewhere.'

We gazed down together at Soc and Ari. They sprawled, sleeping peacefully, like two satiated cherubs, mouths open, each side of Auntie. Auntie was sleeping, herself, a wide smile on her face. As if she'd slipped from delight into dreaming. There was no reason why she should ever learn that Vincent had taken her money. Taken it as well for the simplest of reasons, not from personal malice or a sense of resentment, but merely to pay off large mounting debts. His sartorial interests had led him to financial deep waters, unpaid accounts at places like Mr Fish, for his shirts, and at Turnbull and Asser for silk trifles such as hankies. I'd had to laugh, when all the time I'd been afraid he was under pressure for far more menacing reasons.

I could feel Guy beside me: a light spiralling started deep in my stomach. 'It seems a shame to disturb them,' he murmured. His hand brushed my own.

'It does,' I said thickly, my throat had seized up. I passed a small fart in excitement, and prayed that it wouldn't pong. He seemed not to notice, his lips brushed my hair. 'Now would seem a good moment to show me your kitchen—'

We went down. He began to impress me.